THE TAMMY MELLOWS COLLECTION

THE COMPLETE TRILOGY

TINA HOGAN GRANT

TINA HOGAN GRANT

BOOK ONE IN THE TAMMY MELLOW SERIES

RECKLESS
BEGINNINGS

Reckless Beginnings

Edited by Cat Chester of Pink Proof

Cover Design by T.E.Black Designs – http://www.teblackdesigns.com

1st printed in 2018 by Page Publishing

2nd printing 2021 by Tina Hogan Grant Books

Better Endings

Copyright © 2020 By Tina Hogan Grant

Edited by Pink Proof

Cover Design by T.E.Black Designs – http://www.teblackdesigns.com

The Reunions

Copyright © 2021 by Tina Hogan Grant

Edited by Crystal Santoro Editorial Services: https://chrissyseditorialservices.org/

Cover Design by T.E.Black Designs – http://www.teblackdesigns.com

❋ Created with Vellum

To My Mom & Dad

Dad you are missed every day.
Thank you for showing me the joy of books

Mom, you are the strongest woman I have ever known.
I follow in your footsteps with a zest for life and adventurous ways.

RECKLESS BEGINNINGS

BOOK 1

"Readers will be pulled in by the emotional intensity of the story. Tina Hogan Grant has a great sense of storytelling and she succeeds in keeping readers engaged through each page of her gripping story." - *Readers' Favorites*

"I started Reckless Beginnings at 10 pm last night and stayed up all night until I finished it at 8 am this morning, I was unable to stop and I loved it.

It is definitely a book to read, you will not be disappointed." *Amazon Reader*

"I loved this story, it was amazing!! It totally captured me from page 1 .After reading the first few chapters I was addicted and couldn't put the book down. I did nothing for the rest of the day." *Stewart Book Reviews*

"Reckless Beginnings has excellent character development, and Tina Hogan Grant does a fabulous job of showing the heartbreak of being involved with a drug addict. Compelling, heart-rending read. Couldn't put it down." *Michele L. Khoury Author of Busted*

PROLOGUE

Tammy, the youngest of three sisters, remembered the phone call as if it were yesterday, even though it was almost three years ago, back in 1977. She was fourteen at the time and had already gone to bed when the ringing from the phone downstairs stirred her from her rested state.

She immediately knew it was her father, John calling from the United States. No one else phoned in the middle of the night. He had moved there shortly after her parents' divorce, accepting a job promotion he couldn't refuse as a speaker on artificial intelligence, and now lived on the outskirts of Boston. He had always called late on Thursday evenings because of the eight-hour time difference between America and England. But, on that particular night, he called on a Tuesday—which had Tammy concerned.

Her parents had divorced when she was eleven because of her father's extramarital affairs. Tammy would never forget the day her family became divided. Like every morning, she had come downstairs wearing her pajamas. The house was silent except for the faint sound of crying coming from the front living room.

Tammy tiptoed softly toward the slightly open door and peeked in. Her heart ached with what she saw.

It was her mother, Rose; she had heard crying. She was sitting alone on the green couch with her hair in a tangled mess, wearing her pink satin bathrobe and holding a tissue to her eyes.

Fear swept over Tammy. Why was her mother so upset? She wanted to rush in and hold her and tell her everything was going to be okay. But Tammy felt her mother needed to be alone in her thoughts and stepped away from the door without being heard. Not trusting her older twin sisters, Donna and Jenny, to be quiet, Tammy decided to keep what she had seen to herself.

Later that morning, Tammy's questions had been answered. In a more composed state, their mother gathered her three girls into the family room. Still dressed in her bathrobe, her hair uncombed and her eyes swollen from her many tears, she held Tammy and her sisters tight. In a soft, broken voice she told them that she and their father were separating and that he had moved out of the house.

Crushed by the news, Tammy and her sisters clung to their mother, unable to control their tears. She had friends in school that came from broken homes and had listened with pity to their stories of violence and hatred before the divorce. They had told her how they hated spending weekends and holidays with only one parent. Was this how it was going to be for her? Tammy wondered.

Tammy was thankful she never saw violence, but she was devastated that her father was simply gone. No explanation, no goodbye, no hugs of reassurance that everything was going to be okay. She had felt abandoned and unimportant. How could he just leave without saying goodbye? When would she see him again? She had so many unanswered questions. Why did this happen? Why didn't they love each other anymore? Whose fault was it?

Unable to hold it together for her daughters, Rose was an

emotional wreck. The man she had loved for almost two decades was no longer in her life, and she was terrified of being alone.

Left in a garbage bag on the steps of an orphanage when she was six days old, where she remained until she was sixteen, Rose realized John had brought stability and a sense of belonging into her life for the first time.

She had met John in London on a bus on her way to the hotel where she worked as a chambermaid. John was on his way to college where he studied electronic engineering. The attraction had been mutual. He was infatuated with her beauty and her perfectly toned body. Rose was mesmerized by his handsome looks. His strong, defined jawline and his short, thick black hair that swept away from his face. Sitting across from her, he made her laugh and sometimes blush with his cheeky grin and the occasional wink directed solely at her.

John was a man with a brilliant mind. Rose admired him for his superior intelligence and his ambitious work ethics. In his younger years and straight out of college, John worked hard and was recognized for his achievements, becoming highly successful in the field of artificial intelligence. He spent his evenings working on his other passion, writing, with the hopes of being published someday.

His plans hadn't included becoming a father to twin girls at the young age of twenty, and then again to Tammy at the age of twenty-two. Refusing to let fatherhood get in the way of his career, John became the sole provider, traveling a lot and leaving Rose to raise their daughters.

Eventually, his hard work had paid off and he managed to buy the family a beautiful four-bedroom home in the small, quaint northern English town called Tridale, which had lots of charm and history dating back to the Roman era. It was located on the valley floors of the Dales, surrounded by moors and rolling hills laced with heather and bracken.

John had been the backbone of the family. Everyone looked up to him. He provided structure and discipline; he set the ground rules and enforced daily chores for Tammy and her sisters.

The divorce hit each of the girls differently. Tammy missed having the authority figure of her father in the house. Jenny blamed him for abandoning them and became extremely protective and close to their mother. Meanwhile, Donna blamed both parents and began to travel down a road of self-destruction, wearing heavy makeup and skimpy clothes and drinking copious amounts of alcohol. For Rose, it was a constant battle, and she feared Donna was spiraling out of control. No longer able to handle her, Rose discussed Donna's behavior with their father and between them, they decided she might be better off with him.

For the next three years following her parents' divorce, Tammy spent her six-week summer vacations in America with her father and Donna. She and Jenny hated Donna being so far away. They talked once a week on the phone, but it wasn't the same. The sisters' bond had been broken.

Tammy and Donna reconnected each summer, but Jenny couldn't get past the grudge she held towards her father for breaking up the family. And, because she chose to stay in England with her mother during those summers, she began to grow apart from not only her father but also Donna.

Moving Donna to the States hadn't helped. For the next three years, she continued to act in a destructive manner, skipping school most days and spending her time drinking and hanging out with bad company. John suspected she was also using drugs. Unable to control his daughter anymore, he was at his wit's end and didn't know what to do.

Arrested one night for under-age drinking, Donna was escorted home in a patrol car. John expressed his concerns about his daughter's behavior with the officer, and they decided between them it might be better for her if she was placed into a juvenile home until she turned eighteen.

At the time, she was seventeen, which meant she would only be there for a year. John thought it was a good idea—after all, a year wasn't that long—and he pursued it the following day. Without having discussed it with Rose first, he found an all-girls home for troubled teens called *New Beginnings*.

A week later, after Donna was settled, he called Rose and explained to her that their daughter was out of control and needed professional counseling and guidance; something he couldn't give her. With the thought of her daughter being in a home tearing at her heart, Rose protested and objected to his decision, but it did no good. John was comfortable with his solution and the choices he'd made.

Within three weeks of Donna being admitted, John received a phone call from the director, telling him Donna had run away and couldn't be found. John had intentions of visiting her soon, but now that his book had finally been accepted for publication, he had been spending every spare moment trying to reach the deadline and the days had turned into weeks. The director went on to tell him that she had never really settled in. She rarely talked to the other girls and spent many hours sitting alone in isolated corners. She mentioned they had called and left numerous messages regarding Donna's behavior, but he had never returned their calls. John remembered those messages; there were three of them. He had planned on calling back after the deadline.

After apologizing profusely, Susan, the director, informed John that they had never had a child run away before and suspected Donna had left through the kitchen door, where the staff come and go and deliveries were made. She added that they pride themselves in providing an excellent home for all their children and emphasized again that Donna was the first case of a runaway.

John appreciated her sincere apology and had no harsh feelings. The only person he felt anger toward was himself. An unhappy seventeen year old would always find a way to leave if they really wanted to. No one was to blame but himself. He had selfishly ignored his troubled daughter's cry for help.

The lady on the phone told him the authorities had been notified and if they had any news, he would be informed immediately. John thanked her, hung up the phone and even though it wasn't Thursday—his day to call—he knew he had to tell Rose and reluctantly dialed her number.

Tammy had gotten good at eavesdropping on her parents' weekly conversations without being detected. She remembered on this particular Tuesday night how she quietly peeled back her sheets and tiptoed barefoot across her bedroom. Pinning her ear to the door, she heard her mother's voice echoing in the foyer below. Holding her breath, Tammy slowly pulled down on the door handle, praying the door wouldn't squeak when she eased it open. Thankfully, it had not, and Tammy released a sigh of relief. The light from the foyer lit up the landing outside her room, allowing her to find her way to the top of the stairs. Without making a sound, she had taken her usual spot on the last stair, pulled her white nightgown over her knees to keep out the chill, and peered down between the railings.

Her mother was dressed in her usual nighttime attire: a pink bathrobe, matching slippers, and her hair pulled back into a ponytail. Her back faced Tammy. Grateful her mother and father had remained friends after the divorce, their calls were usually pleasant, filled with jokes and laughter, but this phone call was different. Her mother sounded scared. Tammy sensed the fear in her voice. Only hearing one side of the conversation, Tammy had a hard time understanding what they were talking about. She only heard the strange questions her mother was asking.

"What do you mean she's gone, John?"

Who was gone? Tammy wondered.

Her mother became angry. "She can't just disappear, John! Someone must know where she is!"

Glued to the railings, Tammy was dying to know who and what they were talking about.

Then her mother began to cry hysterically while she held the phone tight and screamed into it, "She's still a child, John. She's just seventeen. You should never have put her in that home! She isn't an object you can just discard because she's in your way. She's your daughter!"

Tammy remembered how her heart sank to the floor when she suddenly realized they were talking about Donna. Her sister had run away and was now missing. She wanted to race down the stairs and snatch the phone from her mother's hands and ask her father WHY? Why had he put her in that awful place?

Donna had written a letter to Tammy and Jenny, telling them how much she hated being in the home. How no one wanted her anymore and she was going to run away. Frightened by what she had read, Tammy showed the letter to their mother. As upset as she was by both the letter and the fact that Donna had written to her sisters and not her, Rose never believed Donna would actually run away. "I'm sure she'll be okay. She just needs time to adjust. It's all new to her. We have to trust your father's judgment. He said this would be good for her. I have to believe that. She is a very troubled young girl and needs help," her mother had told her. But she had run away, and now no one knew where she was.

After spending her first summer in the States, Tammy had known she wanted to someday live there. Now since the disappearance of Donna, she wanted it more than ever. She needed to know what had happened to her. Waiting for the authorities to call wasn't enough. She needed answers. Why hadn't Donna contacted any of them? Was she in trouble? Was she hurt? Tammy didn't even want to consider her worst fear. The fear that maybe she was dead

Tammy last saw her father two years ago when she was fifteen. He had managed to squeeze in a short two-day visit to England while on a book tour, but other than that, he had apparently been too busy for her to visit the States during the summer holidays.

At that time, it had been a year since Donna's disappearance and there was still no trace of her. No matter how much Tammy pleaded with her father to allow her to move to America, he had always come up with a different excuse. His latest was: she needed to finish school in England.

They had been sat at a small round table in a quaint English tearoom when he told her about his latest reasoning. Tammy's seat was next to a large picture window that looked out onto a busy street, clustered with many shops, restaurants, pubs, and people eager to spend their money. They were having lunch before he left the next day for his return trip home. His visits were always the same: short and rushed. Staying for just a few days, with never enough time for Tammy to persuade him to let her move to the

States. His work as an author engulfed him entirely, leaving little time for anything else. When he wasn't writing, he was traveling the world promoting his book or doing research for the next one.

Sitting across from him with her back to the window, she had her arms folded high across her chest, expressing her disappointment with pursed lips and sullen frown when she was once again told "no" in a stern voice by her father.

"I just don't understand why I can't go to school in America. It's just the same over there," Tammy argued.

Frustrated, John rolled his eyes at his daughter. "No, it's not the same, Tammy, and I've explained this to you repeatedly. The schools in England are far better than those in the States, and are you aware that students over there do not graduate until they're eighteen? Whereas here in England; it's only sixteen. Do you honestly want to be in school for another two years?"

Tammy thought for a moment. "Not really. But if it means I can live in the States, then I'm willing to make the sacrifice."

Even though John had been living in the States for a few years, he still had a thick British accent, which usually became more pronounced when he was angry. "Enough of this nonsense, Tammy. My mind is made up. You're to complete school over here, then, and only then will we discuss you moving to the States." He scowled at her from across the table and, without saying another word, looked down at his food, picked up his fork, and continued to eat his meat and potato pie in silence.

Tammy was tired and frustrated by his excuses. He used to say it was because she was too young or because he was too busy, and now it was because of school. When he first moved to the States, he had promised her that one day she would be able to move out there with him, but he had always found a reason for it to never happen.

She pleaded with him in an annoying, childish tone. "But I've lived here all my bloody life! I want a change and I want to live with you. I'm so tired of living here. There's absolutely nothing here for me. You know how much I love it over there."

John was beginning to lose his patience with his daughter. They went through this every time he visited. He saw the shock on her face when he raised his voice at her. "You're only fifteen years old, for God's sake! You have your whole life ahead of you. There's plenty of time for you to move to the States. If that's what you truly want in a few years, we'll discuss it then, understood?"

As hard as she pleaded, she knew he had made his decision and it was final. She was to finish her schooling in England. Two more bloody years of being unable to look for any clues or leads as to the whereabouts of her sister. It upset her tremendously. What if she was in danger? A lot could happen in two years. She hated not knowing.

She needed to know something. Anything. She couldn't wait until she was legally an adult. But, at least by then, no one could tell her what she could or couldn't do.

That was the last time Tammy had seen her father. She was now seventeen and living in her own flat in the northern city of Leeds. Donna still hadn't been found. If she were still alive, she'd be twenty years old. Tammy had to believe she was. She couldn't bear the thought that she might be dead.

Her flat was a place of convenience. Somewhere to eat, sleep, and bathe. She had made no efforts to make it feel like a home. The walls were white and bare with no pictures or decorations. She had little furniture; just the basics to get her by: a bed, chairs, couch, table, a TV, and a few bookshelves. She would make her real home in America.

Tammy didn't know how, but some way, she was going to get to the States. She'd lost faith in her father helping her. For the past five years, he had point blank refused her requests. But the pay of a waitress wasn't much and didn't go far. After paying her monthly bills, she had little left over for the so-called *America Fund*.

After completing school, she was anxious to leave home and took a job in the restaurant of a five-star hotel, working mainly nights. The job required no previous experience or special training, and she was hired the same day. Tammy figured she could always look for a better job later, if she was still in the country. But, for now, it was a way to make her own money and begin saving for her move to the States.

While still in England, nothing in her life could be permanent. Even her boyfriend Ian; whom she'd met three months ago at a disco. It was his dancing that caught her attention. He danced exceptionally well and wasn't afraid to dance alone. He was somewhat attractive, but if it weren't for his moves on the dance floor, she'd probably never have noticed him. His hair was dusty brown and cut short. She'd never really liked short hair on a man, but it suited him. He was a little bit taller than her five-eleven frame and skinny for a man of his height. Like most English people, including herself, his skin was pale; almost the color of ivory, and his freckles were plentiful on his arms, the tops of his hands, and all across his nose and cheeks.

He noticed her smiling and swaying her hips to the beat of the music as she watched him from the edge of the dance floor. He returned the smile along with a playful wink. He turned his body toward her, moving it in a suggestive manner as he held out his hand, inviting her to join him, which she did.

That was the beginning of their causal relationship with no strings attached. That night, Tammy took him home to her flat, where they frolicked beneath the sheets until the sun came up. In the three short months they'd know each other, she still knew very little about him apart from the fact that he was a waiter at a tearoom and still lived with his parents. She didn't need to know anything else. It was the perfect relationship; when she needed a little bit of fun, he was just a phone call away, but she chose not to share with him anything about her plans to someday move to America. She had a mission, and nothing or nobody was going to stop her.

It came as no surprise to the family that Jenny was going to marry Stuart. It had been expected since they started dating in grammar school when she was just fifteen. Being the most domesticated of the three girls, Jenny wanted nothing more than to settle down, buy a house, and start a family.

Tammy was pleased to hear that her father would be attending the wedding. Her mother asked that she reserve him a room at the hotel where she worked, which Tammy happily did.

On the day of his anticipated arrival, Tammy paced around the restaurant nervously, still trying to do her job while waiting for the announcement that her father was in the building. She wasn't going to ask him if she could go back to America with him this time. She already knew what the answer would be. His stay would be brief, as usual—three days—enough time to arrive, spend the night, attend the wedding, and leave the next day. Nonetheless, she wasn't going to deny that it would be good to see him and catch up.

It was over six months ago when Tammy last spoke to her father on the phone; that's when she learned she had a new step-mother called Joanne and a two-month-old half-brother called Andrew. She had felt a tinge of jealousy toward her unknown new sibling. She had always enjoyed being the youngest child, using it to her advantage in her earlier years by bribing her older sisters when she busted them doing something they weren't supposed to be doing. She had often used her title as "the baby sister" for never getting accused of any wrongdoings. Her parents always believed she was just too young and innocent, but in most cases, she had to admit she probably was the guilty party. Whether it was for drinking from their father's gin bottle, stealing cigarettes from their parents, or using their mother's makeup, Tammy joyfully watched while her sisters took the blame for such deceitful actions. Even at seventeen, there was still something special about being the youngest child. So, now that she had a half-brother of over sixteen years her junior, her title, in her eyes, had been stolen. Tammy felt cheated.

Polishing silverware, Tammy's mind was consumed with a plethora of family issues when the deep voice of her boss, John-Pierre, the maître d' of the restaurant, called across the room. His loud, thick French accent snapped her out of her thoughts. "Tammy, your father's here. He's waiting for you in the bar."

Jean-Pierre was a typical Frenchman. Aged around mid-fifties, he was pudgy and round with fat rosy cheeks and a full head of jet-black hair. His thick black moustache covered his upper lip and curled up into little circles at the ends. Growing up in Paris, France, he'd worked at some of the finest restaurants before moving to England with his family four years ago to learn the English language.

"And please, make it quick. You're still on the floor for another hour," he added.

"Thanks, Jean-Pierre. I won't be long."

Always feeling nervous around her father and constantly seeking his approval, Tammy stalled to quickly run her fingers through her red hair and smooth out her polyester uniform, which consisted of a dark blue mid-length skirt and a white blouse. She remembered hearing the disappointment in his voice over the phone when she told him she was a waitress.

As Tammy walked toward the bar, she pictured her father sitting alone with a Guinness Stout in one hand and a cigarette in the other while fully concentrating on The Times crossword puzzle. She peered through the double glass doors before entering and spotted him immediately. The image of her father was exactly as she had predicted.

Slowly approaching him, she realized one thing was missing: the cigarette. In silence, she stood behind him for a moment, chuckling to herself that he wasn't aware of her presence. She gave him a gentle tap on the shoulder. "Hi Dad!"

Her father removed his glasses, turned his head in her direction, and gave her a big smile. "Tammy! Good to see you," he said, giving her a hug.

"You too, Dad. It's been a while. I couldn't help noticing that you're not smoking. Crossword puzzles and cigarettes always went together," she said jokingly. "Don't tell me you've packed it in?"

"Actually, yes, I did," he said with a hint of pride. "It's been about four months now. I guess we haven't talked on the phone in a while, huh? But, if I can do it, so can you," he said, nudging her arm.

Tammy was shocked. Never did she imagine her father would quit smoking. "Wow, Dad, that's brilliant! And you smoked a lot too. About two packs a day, right? How'd you do it? Cold turkey?"

"No, cold turkey proved too difficult, so I weaned myself off gradually. It took some time, but now I feel marvelous!" He gave her another nudge to the arm. "You really should give it a go, you know."

"Nah, I'm still young, Dad. I can wait a few more years. Besides, I enjoy them too much!" she said with a laugh before glancing down at her watch. "I'm terribly sorry, Dad, but I have to make this short. I'm still working, but I get off in about an hour. Will that crossword puzzle keep you busy till then? I can meet you back here after I've finished my shift."

"Sure, that's fine. I'm all checked in."

"Great! I'll look forward to it. We certainly have some catching up to do. I hear you've been traveling all over the world promoting your new book?" She checked the time once more. "Anyway, I really do have to get back to work before Jean-Pierre kills me." After a quick hug and a peck on his cheek, Tammy returned to the restaurant thinking how good it was to see her father again after such a long time.

*N*ow older, her anger dissolved, Tammy accepted the fact that it wasn't up to her father to fulfill her dreams of moving to the States. So, after finishing her shift, Tammy spent the rest of the evening with him, catching up on family news. He explained how being a writer had become much more challenging with an eight-month-old baby in the house, and he told her all about her new stepmom and half- brother as Tammy smiled and laughed along at his stories. Tammy then dropped the bombshell question, which is when the conversation took on a more somber mood.

"Any news on Donna, Dad?"

"No, I'm afraid not. When I moved to Lonesridge in Northern California last year, I left my new address and phone number with the children's home and the police."

"I'm really scared that something bad may have happened to her. It's been three years since she disappeared and we haven't heard anything."

"I know, me too, Tammy. The police have nothing to go on. It's like she just vanished. No one has seen her, and no one recognizes her from any of the photos that were circulated. I also gave them your mother's new number when she moved to that house in London to be a nanny, and they have your number and Jenny's, too."

"Yeah, Mom loves working again. Apparently, the family is well off and they treat her like a queen. I guess our old house was just too big for her after we all moved out." Tammy suddenly had a thought. "You know, it just occurred to me that we *all* have new phone numbers since Donna disappeared. What if she's tried calling one of our old numbers? We'd never know it. What a frightening thought. She has no idea where any of us are." Tammy reached for her father's arm. "Dad, she's out there somewhere with no way of calling us to ask for help!"

He patted Tammy's hand. "I hope that's not the case. I have to tell myself every day that she's okay and there's a perfectly good explanation why she hasn't contacted any of us. You might not agree with me, but it's how I keep my sanity when it comes to Donna."

"I understand. I just miss her so much. I try not to have terrible thoughts, but the more time goes by, the harder it gets."

Her father leaned in and gave her a gentle hug. "I know. Let's hope that someday soon, she'll return to us safe." He paused and smiled. "On another note, I spoke to your mother yesterday. She told me she'd be arriving tomorrow."

"Yes, she's taking the train up early in the morning. She's going to stay with Jenny for the weekend and take a late train back on Sunday night. She's looking forward to seeing you, Dad. She was upset when she first heard about you marrying again, but she's okay with it now. It's great how you've remained friends."

"Your mother and I had three wonderful daughters together. I screwed up our marriage, and it's only thanks to your mother that we have any kind of relationship today. It's her you should thank."

It saddened Tammy that Donna would miss her twin sister's wedding. She often wondered how Jenny was coping with her disappearance. She rarely spoke about it. Maybe it was just too hard. Growing up, they looked identical. Both had long, straight brown hair, light blue eyes with short eyelashes, and a fair complexion. If you didn't know that Donna had a slight curl to her smile and was a little skinnier than Jenny, you wouldn't be able to tell them apart. And, like most mothers of twins, Rose always dressed them in the same outfits.

Before saying goodnight to her father, Tammy arranged to meet him in the lobby the next day at noon. It seemed much easier for Tammy than trying to give him directions to her place. From there, they would ride together in her father's rental car to the wedding.

~

Because they were saving to buy a house, Jenny and Stuart had chosen to have a small, simple wedding with family members and a few close friends, followed by a buffet at a local hotel. Jenny looked radiant in her beautiful white gown, carrying a delicate bouquet of white roses and peonies. Tammy felt a twinge of jealousy as she watched Jenny walk down the aisle to her soon-to-be husband, saying her vows, and beginning her new path in life with solid plans for the future. It was far more than she'd ever had.

With the wedding ceremony over, Tammy had a chance to catch up with her mother. It had been a few months since they'd last seen each other. She missed her mother and always cherished their time together. Dressed in a cream-colored, knee-length dress with matching pumps and purse, Tammy's mother still had a slim figure, as always, and looked much younger than her age. Her makeup was light and fresh and her blond hair glistened in the sun. Her eyes sparkled and she looked genuinely happy.

Tammy told her how great she looked and her mother chuckled and confided in her that she had a new boyfriend. Having only seen her mother with her father, and with no inclination that she had dated anyone since the divorce, Tammy was surprised by the news. It was going to take some time to adjust to the idea of her dating somebody else, but she was delighted for her and it brought comfort to Tammy, knowing her mother wasn't alone.

After the reception, Tammy's father mentioned he wanted to have a chat with her and Rose and suggested going to the bar at the hotel where he was staying. Tammy rode with her father while her mother stayed behind to say goodbye to the last of the lingering guests, promising she'd take a taxi to the hotel shortly.

An hour later, they regrouped at a quiet corner table in the hotel bar. After taking a sip of his Guinness, a cheeky grin appeared across John's face, directed solely at Tammy. He leaned back in his chair with his arms folded over his chest. "So, Tammy, what do you think about coming back to the States with me?"

Rendered speechless with her eyes wide open, Tammy froze. Repeating in her head what her father had just said. *Did he just ask me to go to America with him?* Still holding her glass in mid-air, unable to contain her excitement, she screamed, "What! Are you serious?"

Other customers stared in her direction, silently questioning her sudden outburst. In fear of spilling her drink, Tammy placed it on the table before jumping up from her seat and running over to her father to give him the biggest hug he'd ever had. She didn't need to think about her answer. "I would love to!" she squealed. "When do we leave? I'm ready right now!"

John laughed at his daughter's enthusiasm. "Now hold on a second, Tammy," he said, peeling her grip from around his neck. "There are some details we need to discuss first." He looked over at Rose and his smile quickly disappeared. "Like your mother, for instance," he mumbled under his breath.

Rose's eyes had narrowed and darkened immensely, pulling the skin tight across her flushed cheeks, and her lips drew into a thin line as she scowled across the table at her ex-husband. It suddenly occurred to him that he perhaps should have discussed his idea with her before asking Tammy, but it was too late now.

"Rose, are you okay with this?" John asked, a look of guilt painted across his pale face.

Rose sat up straight and rolled her shoulders back. She wanted to make him feel uncomfortable. He was wrong to ask Tammy to move with him at such short notice, especially with no prior mention to her of his ridiculous idea. "Well, it's quite a shock, John. You never mentioned taking Tammy back with you until now. Don't you think that's a little unfair? Why hadn't you talked to me about this earlier instead of surprising me like this? You know I'll never see her again if she moves to the States. Look what happened to Donna. No one has seen or heard from her since she left with you. She could be dead for all we know."

John shook his head impatiently. "Oh, don't talk like that!"

"Well, she could be. We don't know. It's been three years since anyone has heard from her. I'm not losing another daughter, John." Her voice raised a notch with every word. She was almost on the verge of tears.

Tammy walked over to her mother. "Oh, come on, Mom, don't be like this. I'll keep in touch and I'm not going to disappear, I promise," she pleaded as she wrapped her arms around her mother's shoulders.

Rose looked up and met Tammy's eyes. "But when will I see you again? I can't afford to fly to the States every year to come visit you." John quickly raised his arms to calm them both down. "Okay, guys, let's not get ahead of ourselves here. This could just be a trial. She may not even like it in the States and may very well choose to move back to England."

"Not bloody likely," Tammy whispered under her breath.

John paused for a moment. He was walking on eggshells and needed to find a way to please them both. Choosing his next words carefully, looking directly at Rose, he said, "If she likes it, I promise I'll send you a ticket to come visit her. If she doesn't, then I'll buy her a ticket to return home and provide for her until she finds a job. How would that be?"

A silence descended over the table while Rose contemplated John's suggestion. Tammy and her father held their breath with anticipation. Both thought it was a good plan, but it seemed Rose had the final say.

After a few moments, Tammy grew impatient. "Oh, come on, Mom! What do you think? We'll still see each other. Please, Mom, just say yes. You know how much I've wanted this...and for so long. Please say yes. Please!" she begged while squeezing her mother's hand tight.

With a moment of hesitation, Rose gave them her decision. "Okay, Tammy, I guess you can go." She didn't want to see the disappointment on her daughter's face if she'd said no. In the same breath, Rose quickly turned, pointed her index finger at John, and stiffened her voice. "You better take good care of her, John." Raising her voice, she continued to speak. "And don't you dare loose contact with her, like you did with Donna." She turned and looked at Tammy. "And you must promise me, Tammy, that you'll write to me every chance you get."

Rose felt her body tremble as she hugged her youngest child. Was she doing the right thing by allowing yet another daughter to move so far away to another country? Silently, she blamed John. If it wasn't for him moving to America in the first place, she wouldn't be having this conversation or having these fears, and Donna would still be in their lives. With tears in her eyes, Tammy hugged her mother tight and promised to write as often as she could. She couldn't believe she was finally going to America!

CHAPTER 4

After the initial shock had sunk in and her mother had been persuaded that everything was going to be okay, the rest of the evening was spent discussing the move.

Overjoyed and riddled with excitement, Tammy couldn't believe this was finally happening. On the contrary, it warmed Rose's heart to see such a joyous smile on her daughter's face. Even though she was going to miss Tammy deeply, she was truly happy for her. She knew in her heart it was time to stop being selfish and, perhaps more importantly, it was time to let her go.

John told them he would be in England for another week. He was leaving tomorrow to go down south to Surrey to visit his sister, Maddie, and his brother-in-law, Dave. While there, he would purchase Tammy's plane ticket and she could take the train down at the end of the week. They would then leave from Heathrow Airport in London the following Monday.

Tammy soon realized she had a lot to do in just seven days. She had to decide what she wanted to take with her. The airline would only allow her to take one suitcase, which meant she would have to donate the rest of her things to charity or give them to friends at work. She also needed to give notice to her landlord and her manager at work. Sadly, she realized she wouldn't be able to say goodbye to Jenny. She would still be on her honeymoon on the day of her departure. Tammy had no doubt Jenny would be crushed, but what could she do? She was afraid if she didn't go now, her father might never ask her again.

With so much to do in so little time, the week flew by quickly. When Tammy wasn't working, she spent every spare moment going through her belongings, deciding what to keep and what to part with. She had friends from work coming by every day, taking the things she no longer wanted such as clothes, dishes, records, books, and furniture. Where had all this stuff come from? She never realized how much junk she'd accumulated.

Tammy knew she was going to need to set a day aside for the three-hour train ride to Surrey and so gave five days' notice to her landlord and her job. She appreciated their understanding and both expressed how excited they were for her. Everyone at work was truly happy for her. Some even confessed how envious they were and most agreed they needed to get together for a going away party. It wasn't every day someone from work was moving to America, they proclaimed.

By the end of the week, Tammy had managed to get rid of most of her possessions, except for the bed, which she planned on leaving behind. With all her dishes gone, she was now eating only take-out meals—it was as good an excuse as any to live on junk food for a few days. Her one suitcase was packed with clothing, toiletries, a few photographs, and a few of her favorite books.

Tonight was going to be her last night at work. Tomorrow, she would be taking the train down to Surrey to meet up with her father. She couldn't believe how fast the week had gone by and yet, to her surprise; she had managed to check off everything on her list. Tammy was ready for her big move to the States.

There was no turning back now. Deep down, she was extremely nervous and couldn't deny the anxiety bubbling away in her stomach. England had been her only home. She would be leaving behind so much, including her mother, sister, and friends. She would no longer have a home to call her own and would have to find new restaurants and shops to call her favorites. After the move, the only people she will know will be her father and his wife Joanne, whom she had yet to meet. Tammy questioned if they would get along and, at times, even questioned if she was doing the right thing by leaving her whole life behind.

When Tammy arrived at work, Jean-Pierre told her that he had to change the schedule, so she was now going to be closing the restaurant at eleven instead of getting off at nine. Tammy couldn't hide her anger. "Jean-Pierre, how can you do this to me? You know it's my last night," she shrieked while stomping her feet in protest. "I was hoping to go out after work. I won't get another chance!"

"Oh, stop with your whining, Tammy," he snapped in his fancy French drawl. "It couldn't be prevented. Someone called in sick. What was I supposed to do? I know it's your last night and I'm sorry." He placed his hand on her shoulder. "Tell you what. Because I feel so awful about this, why don't you let me buy you a drink at Danny's pub after work?"

Having calmed down after her initial outburst, and having no actual plans, Tammy accepted his invitation.

Ten o'clock couldn't come fast enough. It had been a busy night for the restaurant, and even though it was now closed, it would still take Tammy another hour to shut everything down before her shift was officially over. During her last hour, co-workers approached her to wish her well and say their goodbyes before leaving for the evening. Some even brought tears to her eyes with their heartfelt farewells.

By eleven o'clock, she was the only one left. So much for a leaving party, she thought. The only task remaining was to turn off the lights. But, as Tammy stood by the switch, she hesitated and took one last look around the restaurant as if capturing the memories she would be taking with her. That's when it hit her. It felt so real—she'd never see this place again. Not wanting to cry or become too emotional, she quickly turned off the lights, leaving only darkness behind her, and headed over to Danny's pub to meet Jean-Pierre.

After putting on a sweater over her uniform, Tammy stepped outside into the cold, damp night, only to be greeted by pouring rain. "Well, what a bloody surprise," she mumbled to herself sarcastically. Rain was the one thing she wasn't going to miss about England. Feeling irritated because she no longer owned an umbrella, Tammy pulled her sweater over her head to keep her hair dry and ran across the deserted streets to Danny's pub. As she quickly scurried through the parking lot, she noticed it was full. "Wow, it's busy here tonight," she said while heading toward the entrance. When she reached the door, she saw there was a sign posted on it. Tammy squinted her eyes in the dim light and read the words out loud. "Closed for private party."

"Well, that's just bloody great!" she yelled in disgust and looked up. The sky was turning darker by the second, unleashing torrents of increasingly heavy rain that was pelting the ground under her feet. "Now what am I going to do? This is turning out to be a bloody horrible night!"

Tammy assumed Jean-Pierre had also seen the sign and gone home. Upset that the pub was closed on her last night, Tammy turned around and began walking back to the hotel so she could call a taxi to take her home. It looked like she was going to be spending her last evening alone. Dodging the ever-growing puddles as she hurried across the parking lot, she heard a male voice call her name.

"Tammy! Tammy! Wait!"

She stopped and turned around, still partly hidden underneath her sweater. She squinted her eyes through the darkness and craned her neck forward, trying to recognize who was calling her. She couldn't quite make out who it was. He was wearing a black overcoat and carrying a large black umbrella, which cast shadows over most of his face. As Tammy began to run toward him, the familiar silhouette of Jean-Pierre came into focus.

Puzzled, she ducked under his umbrella and pulled her wet sweater back down over her head. "Jean-Pierre, why are you still here? There's a private party inside. Look," she said, pointing at the sign, "the pub is closed. I thought you'd already gone home. Do you want to go someplace else?"

"It's okay, they are letting the locals in. Come on, let us go inside, mon amie," he replied.

Feeling much better for knowing she wasn't going to be spending her last night alone, Tammy linked arms with Jean-Pierre and threw him a smile. "Let's go. I need that drink you promised me."

Once inside the pub, Tammy was amazed by how busy it was. Loud music was playing and people were dancing, laughing, and singing along to the music. Along one of the walls of the dance floor, she saw a buffet of delicious food. She felt like an intruder. This was a special party for someone, and she wasn't supposed to be here. That was until she noticed the large banner spanning across the room that read, "God help the U.S.A!" in large red, white, and blue letters.

Shocked, she quickly spun around in a circle, trying to focus on the people amid the haze of cigarette smoke and flashing disco lights. It took a moment to sink in, but she soon realized they were the faces of all her co-workers from the restaurant. With a hand over her gaping mouth, Tammy turned back to face Jean-Pierre. "Oh my god! This party is for me? It's a leaving party?" She still couldn't quite believe her eyes.

At that precise moment, everyone turned to face Tammy and yelled, "Surprise!" in unison while raising their glasses in her honor.

Jean-Pierre wrapped his arm around her shoulders and gave her a tight squeeze. Using his other hand, he handed her a glass of champagne from the table next to him. "For you," he said with a huge grin. "It's the drink I owe you."

Wiping the tears that were now rolling down her cheeks, Tammy took the glass of bubbly. "Oh my god, Jean-Pierre. How did you ever pull this off? This is just too weird! I had no idea you were planning this...I'm going to miss you all so, so much."

Jean-Pierre smirked. "Let me tell you, it was not easy. You are a hard one to keep a secret from. Now do you see why I had you close the restaurant? I had to make sure you were the last to arrive. I am sorry if I upset you, mon amie, but as you can see, my intentions were good." He laughed as he hugged her one more time and raised his glass. "Here's to you, Tammy. I wish nothing but the best for you and your new life in the States. We are all going to miss you incredibly. Especially that redhead attitude of yours that always kept us on our toes."

Tammy hugged him back. "Awe, thanks, Jean-Pierre. I'm going to miss you too." They walked arm in arm toward the bar where everyone was gathered. Feeling like a celebrity and overwhelmed with different emotions, she made a point of greeting everyone with a tearful hug.

Tammy spent the rest of the night hugging, laughing, and dancing with friends. Many tears were shed, memories were shared, and promises were made. Everyone seemed to want to know what plans she had for when she landed in the States, but she genuinely had no idea and replied she would figure it out once she got there.

As the night drew to a close, Jean-Pierre held a shot of tequila, took Tammy's hand, and led her to the center of the room. Everyone else grabbed their glasses and followed them. Jean-Pierre waited while the crowd formed a circle around him and Tammy. Feeling a little tipsy, Tammy could feel her emotions beginning to rise again. She squeezed Jean-Pierre's hand harder, feeling the dam of tears in her eyes threatening to burst at any moment.

The crowd stood in silence, waiting for Jean-Pierre to make his speech. He turned to Tammy, giving her a warm, loving smile. "Tammy may all your dreams come true in America. It's not going to be the same here without you. Be good to America and it will be good to you. We will truly miss you and we love you. Bon voyage!" Sweeping his raised glass in an arc toward the circle of friends, he added at the top of his voice, "To Tammy!"

Everyone lifted their glasses and bottles in the air and yelled in reply, "To Tammy!" She embraced Jean-Pierre with force, staying in his arms for a moment as an uproar of applause and cheers filled the pub. Unable to control her tears, she allowed them to fall freely down her freckled cheeks as her lips trembled and her body shook with the burden of her imminent departure.

As the pub began to empty, Tammy said goodbye to the last of her friends and fought to bring her emotions back under control. Jean-Pierre then called for a taxi to take Tammy home. When it arrived, she once again thanked Jean-Pierre for everything. Noticing she was unsteady on her feet, he took her arm and walked her out to the waiting car. As it began to pull away, Tammy turned her head to look through the rear window. Seeing Jean-Pierre still standing by the curb, she gave him one last wave, knowing it would be her last.

Once inside her flat, still feeling a little drunk, Tammy knew she had one more thing to do. Something she had been avoiding all week but knew she could no longer put off. Even though it was almost three o'clock in the morning, the alcohol she had consumed was giving her the courage to finally get it done. Taking slow and careful steps so as not to stumble, she managed to totter over to her bed, sit on the edge and pick up the phone that was lying on the floor. The dial tone meant the phone company had not yet disconnected her services. She wasn't sure if she was relieved or disappointed to hear it. After she dialed the number, it rang three times before a sleepy voice answered. "Hello," it said in a questionable tone.

She took a deep breath. "Hi, Ian, it's Tammy."

Ian instantly woke up. "Tammy! Where've you been? I've not seen you all week. I've called you millions of times, but you've never called me back."

"Yeah, I know. I'm sorry, I've been really busy."

"Is everything okay?" Ian asked.

"I'm so sorry to be calling you at this hour, but there's something I need to tell you."

"Couldn't it have waited till morning?"

"I'm afraid not." There was a moment of silence between them while she hesitated.

"Tammy, you still there?"

"Yes, I'm still here, Ian." She took another deep breath. "It can't wait till morning because I won't be here."

"You won't be here? What do you mean you won't be here? What's going on?"

"Ian, there's no easy way to say this so I'm just going to come out and say it. I'm moving to the States with my dad. I leave tomorrow. I'm meeting him at my aunts in Surrey. I've been wanting to tell you, but I just didn't know how. Please don't be mad at me."

"You're moving to the States? And you're telling me this now, in the middle of the night, just hours before you're fucking leaving!

What about us, Tammy? What about your job and flat? Doesn't anything matter to you? Including me?"

She decided she needed to be honest with him. "Ian, I've known for a week. Since my father asked me. I've already quit my job, and my flat is empty except for one suitcase. This is something I've wanted for a long time so when he asked me, I just couldn't say no. I don't know if he'll ever ask me again and I'm not giving up this chance. I'm sorry, Ian, I don't know what else to say."

"But what about us, Tammy?" Ian asked again.

"I hate to say it, Ian, and I'm truly sorry, but it's over. We've only been dating for a short while and we both knew it wasn't serious. But, for me, moving to the States *is* serious. I'm sorry if I've hurt you in any way, but my mind is made up. This is the reason I haven't told you up until now. I didn't want you to try and talk me out of my decision."

Ian couldn't believe what he was hearing. "But you just left me totally in the dark. I thought I deserved better than this. I wondered why I hadn't seen you all week, or why you hadn't returned my calls. So, that's it, eh? Just like that. Poof! You're gone." He continued to speak; the anger and frustration clear in his voice. "I agree that we were just having some fun, but we were friends, Tammy. Well, at least, I thought we were. So this is how you treat your friends, eh?"

"I said I was sorry. What more do you want me to say?"

"What time are you leaving in the morning? Can I at least see you before you go? I deserve that much, don't I?" He was almost snarling down the phone.

Tammy didn't blame him for being angry. She felt awful, mainly because she'd actually grown quite fond of him. "I'd much rather you didn't. As difficult as this is, I think it's best we just end it tonight." She could feel the tears glazing over her eyes. Not wanting him to hear her cry, she spoke with a sense of urgency. "Ian, I really have to go. I need to get up early. It's been nice knowing you and I had a lot of fun. I'll never forget you. Be safe, Ian, and goodbye."

Before he could answer, she quickly hung up the phone and yanked the phone line out of the wall socket. She feared he might try to call back in an attempt to convince her to stay. She knew he wouldn't show up at her door because, like her, he didn't drive, couldn't afford a taxi, and thankfully no buses ran in the wee hours of the morning.

After a night of painful goodbyes, Tammy's emotions were in turmoil. Feeling alone, insecure, and unsure of her future, she once again questioned the choices she was making in her life. With her head spinning and anxious for tomorrow to arrive, she lay on the bed and curled her body into the fetal position as if to protect herself from the inevitable. In no time at all, perhaps thanks to the alcohol, she drifted off to sleep.

The next morning, an intense throbbing headache woke Tammy up from a deep sleep. She slowly pulled herself into an upright position and pivoted her legs over the edge of the bed. Despite the pounding in her head showing no signs of mercy, she needed to find strength to face the new day. Grasping her temples with both hands, she moaned out loud. "Oh God, why did I have so much to drink last night?"

Still in her now wrinkled uniform, which she no longer needed, Tammy slowly hoisted her limp, aching body to a standing position. With her eyes squinted, she tried to shut out the intensity of the bright daylight streaming through the bare window. With an almighty effort, she just about managed to raise her arm and look at her watch through narrowed, unfocused eyes. She saw it was ten o'clock and gasped. Her train to Surrey was departing in an hour!

"Oh crap! You have to get a move on, Tammy!" she hollered to herself in a rush of panic, drowning out any previous thoughts of hangovers and headaches. With no time to waste, Tammy quickly gathered up her jeans and t-shirt that she had purposely laid out on top of her suitcase the day before and fled the room to take a shower.

By ten thirty, and after a cold shower, she was dressed and feeling somewhat normal again. She picked up her suitcase and handbag and took one last look around her now empty flat. It had been home for almost two years. Now that it really was time to leave it, a weight of sadness pulled at her heart. "Farewell, flat, I'll miss you," she said softly before placing the key on the counter and heading out the door.

The train station was six miles away. Knowing there was no time to wait for a bus, Tammy opted to walk the few streets into town and grab a taxi instead. She arrived at the station with just ten minutes to spare. Thankful her father had purchased the ticket in advance, she scurried over to the ticket booth to pick it up. The elderly man behind the counter informed her that the train was on time and would be leaving from platform nine in five minutes.

With ticket in hand, she ran through the station as quickly as her old suitcase on frail, plastic wheels would allow. She reached the platform and checked in her luggage with the conductor before leaping on board the train to the sound of the final whistle for departure. Breathless but happy to find a window seat available, she plumped herself down in a state of exhaustion just as the train began to pull out of the station. This was it. Her journey to the United States had begun. She was finally on her way.

As the train gained speed, she watched through the window as her hometown faded off into the distance. With mixed emotions, she whispered, "Goodbye, Leeds. I'll come visit you again soon, I promise."

Still suffering from the previous night but delighted to have the double seat all to herself, Tammy lifted the arm to the adjoining seat and arranged her body comfortably by curling her legs up and resting her tired head against the window. She closed her eyes to block out the rays of the mid-morning sun gleaming through the window, and in no time at all, she drifted off into a deep sleep.

Images of her new life in the States painted themselves into her dreams; she was living in the big city—maybe it was New York—and she was driving a big American car. She was with friends and her sister Donna was with them too. She didn't know where they were going, but they all seemed happy. They were living the American Dream.

Stirring from her sleep, Tammy checked her watch, and rechecked when she realized she'd slept for most of the three-hour trip. Finally, the train pulled into the station and she quickly ran a brush through her hair and touched up her lipstick with her favorite color, Ruby Rose, before exiting and stepping onto the platform.

Scanning across the sparse gathering of people waiting at the small, quiet station, it was easy to spot her father waving in the distance by the green wooden benches. She beamed a radiant smile and waved both hands above her head in excitement as he began to walk toward her.

Spanning her shoulders with his arm, her father gave her a tight squeeze and a cheerful grin. "You made it!"

"I did," Tammy said with pride.

John loosened his grip so Tammy could turn to face him. "I wasn't sure if I would. I didn't realize how much there was to do in just a week, but I managed to get it all done...just! And here I am." Still smiling, she continued to tell him more. "Last night, my work threw me a brilliant leaving party. It was a total surprise!" She gasped, remembering her shock of everything from the night before. "I had no clue. I don't know how they pulled it off without me knowing, but they did."

"That's great! They must have liked you a lot to go to all that trouble. Sounds like they gave you a really good send off," John remarked while they stood waiting for her suitcase to be unloaded from the train. "You can tell me all about it when we're in the car. Aunt Maddie and Uncle Dave can't wait to see you."

"And I can't wait to see them! It's been a long time. I haven't seen them in ages...in fact, I don't think I've seen them since you and Mom got divorced."

"Well, looks like your suitcase is ready," her dad replied, pointing to the cartful of unloaded luggage. "Let me grab it for you and we'll make a move."

Smiling from ear to ear, Tammy replied, "Great, thanks. One step closer to America!"

CHAPTER 7

It was only a fifteen-minute drive to her aunt and uncle's house. It looked exactly how she remembered it. They'd lived on the quiet cul-de-sac for more than twenty years. Raising two sons, Peter and Shawn, who now had families of their own, they'd lived the old-fashioned life, with Maddie staying at home to look after the boys while Dave worked to provide for the family. All the houses in the neighborhood were elegant detached family homes with immaculate well-maintained gardens. Her aunt's house, located at the end of the road, still had the white painted siding and black decorative shutters that Tammy remembered so well. The quintessential picket fence, still laced with white roses, brought her right back to her childhood days.

As they slowly pulled into the driveway, Tammy couldn't help but smile as she watched her aunt come rushing out of the front door and skip with joy down the three front steps. Trembling with excitement, she anxiously waited for them to exit the car. Tammy was delighted to see Aunt Maddie still looked the same and didn't appear to have aged much over the years. Still wearing her shoulder-length, sable-brown hair clipped away from her ever-youthful face, it was clear to see time had been good to her.

Aunt Maddie was most famous in Tammy's family for two things: her cooking and for always wearing brightly colored aprons. Today, she didn't disappoint, as she had chosen to wear a luminous pink apron with vertical red stripes. The minute Tammy stepped out of the car, Aunt Maddie squealed with delight and engulfed Tammy in her arms, holding her cheek to cheek while squeezing her tightly.

"My dear Tammy, it's so good to see you!"

"Hi, Auntie Maddie. It's good to see you too," Tammy managed to say, while still being smothered by her aunt's embrace.

Finally releasing her hold, Maddie took a step back while holding Tammy at arm's length. She took a good long look at her, inspecting her from head to toe, and smiled with pride. "Look at you. You're all grown up and so pretty. I just love your beautiful red hair," she said, combing it with her fingers. She turned her head in the direction of John, who was busy unloading Tammy's suitcase from the boot of the car. "She definitely has your Irish blood, John."

"What makes you say that?" John said sarcastically.

Maddie laughed. "Oh, give over, John. Still sarcastic as ever, I see." Pulling Tammy by her hand, she headed back towards the house. "Come on inside and let me fix you both something to eat. You must be starving after that long train ride."

"I'll be right in. You two go ahead," John replied.

Entering the house, Tammy's head was once again flooded with childhood memories. Nothing had changed. It was an open- plan home with no shortage of natural sunlight, thanks to the generous amount of windows. A white-tiled kitchen bar, complete with ornate wooden stools, separated the kitchen from the main living and dining area. Glass French doors from the dining room opened out onto a large brick patio, furnished with a round wooden table and chairs. The outdoor seating area was dressed with red and white floral cushions and shaded by a matching umbrella. Maddie's china collection, consisting of delicate teacups, teapots and plates, was displayed around the dining room on high wooden shelves, adding an essence of English charm to the decor.

In no time at all, Aunt Maddie got busy in the kitchen, doing what she loved best: entertaining and cooking. Tammy took a seat at the counter and engaged in cheerful conversation and laughter while her aunt glided around the kitchen with ease, fixing a hearty-looking lunch.

"I bet you're excited about moving to America. What a fantastic opportunity," Maddie remarked while slicing up some turkey.

"I am, but I'm a bit worried about Mom. I don't think she likes the idea."

"Oh, don't you worry about Rose. I'm sure she'll be just fine. Maybe a little lonely at times, but Jenny will be just a few hours away. Now, where is your dad? These sandwiches are almost ready."

After unloading the car and taking the suitcases upstairs, John joined them in the kitchen. Feeling famished, his eyes almost popped out of his head as he welcomed the oversized turkey sandwich that his sister placed before him.

With lunch devoured and stomachs filled, they took advantage of the pleasantly warm afternoon by relaxing outside on the patio.

Tammy thought back to all the Christmases spent at her aunt's house, when cousins, aunts, uncles and grandparents traveled from all corners of England to come together for the festive activities. It saddened her that many of the families from back then, including her own, were no longer together. All had gone their separate ways. Sadly, annual holiday gatherings were now something of the past.

Her daydream, was interrupted by her father.

"I meant to tell you this earlier, but I've not been able to get a word in edgeways with you and your aunt nattering all afternoon. Your mother is coming down tomorrow by train."

"She is?" Tammy replied excitedly. "Oh, that's fantastic! Auntie, when was the last time you saw my mom? It's been ages, hasn't it?"

"Oh my goodness, I'm not sure. But yes, it has been a rather long time," Maddie said, serving everyone a cup of tea.

"She'll only be here for the day. We'll have to pick her up from the train station in the morning," John stated.

"Oh, I can't wait to see her. It's going to be just like old times," Maddie said, clasping her hands together in joy.

Later that evening, Uncle Dave returned home from his lifetime job as an insurance salesman. Tammy had never known him to do anything else. He hadn't changed much either, except for the few gray strands invading his light hazelnut hair, which he wore short and well trimmed. He was still the tall and lanky uncle with the prominent nose and sharp chin that Tammy remembered.

He set his briefcase on the floor at the bottom of the stairs and walked over to Tammy to give her a big hug. "Tammy, sweetheart, it's so good to see you! Hey, what happened? You're not a little girl anymore."

Tammy chuckled. "Good to see you too, Uncle Dave."

For dinner, Aunt Maddie treated everyone to some of her home- made cooking and filled their plates with roast beef, Yorkshire pudding, mashed potatoes, and gravy. Fresh-baked apple pie and custard followed for dessert. After the delicious meal, John and Dave retired to the den for what would probably turn into an intense game of chess. Both were brilliant chess players and no doubt eager to finally have a game against a challenging opponent. Tammy, tired from her trip and sensing it might be a long game, decided to leave them to it and called it an early night.

Anticipating the arrival of her mother was also weighing heavy on her mind, adding to her fatigue. Saying goodbye to her wasn't going to be easy, and Tammy was worried her mother may dissolve into an emotional wreck during their final farewell. Although she was expecting there to be some tears shed between them, she didn't want it to be any harder than it needed to be.

CHAPTER 8

*H*er mother's train arrived on time at precisely ten o'clock the following morning. Tammy and her father waited anxiously on the platform as they watched the train slowly pull into the station and come to a halt amid a billowing cloud of steam and smoke. Up until now, Tammy had been okay with saying goodbye to her mother, but as she stood waiting for her to exit the train, she could feel her levels of anxiety beginning to increase. First came the sweaty palms, then the butterflies churning through her stomach. Trying to sooth herself, she gently rubbed her belly in a circular motion. It didn't help. Instead, feelings of dizziness and nausea began to creep in, and her heart hammered against her ribcage.

It occurred to her that this wasn't going to be easy, even after living by herself for almost two years; her mother had always been just a train ride away. After tomorrow, she'll be six thousand miles away. No longer would she be able to simply jump on a train whenever she felt the need to visit her mother. Tammy had never realized how much she took her for granted: not until this moment.

Lost in her thoughts, Tammy suddenly spotted her mother stepping off the train and quickly changed her state of mind. "I can do this," she whispered to herself. She held her head an inch or two higher as if to convince herself it was all going to be fine.

She admired her mother from afar, dressed casual and looking good in blue jeans, a purple t-shirt, and black low-heeled pumps. She carried a black purse over her shoulder and a black cardigan hung loosely over her arm. Her mother had always taken pride in the good looks she was gifted with, and enhanced them perfectly with just the right amount of makeup. She never had a hair out of place and her nails were always beautifully manicured.

"There she is, Dad," Tammy said while waving to her mother.

Rose spotted them right away. She smiled and waved back. Tammy took a deep breath and exhaled just as sharply before walking toward her. As they grew closer, Tammy quickened her pace, greeting her mother with open arms and smothering her with a loving embrace. "Hi, Mom, it's so good to see you."

Rose gave her a peck on the cheek. "You too, dear." She turned to her ex- husband and gave him a courteous but friendly hug. "Hello, John," she said, using a dry, flat tone. Clearly sparing no emotion.

"Hello, Rose," John replied, matching her flat tone.

The tension between them was undeniable. Tammy sensed her mother's sadness. Her father chose to be quiet as they walked back to the car, walking two steps behind them while Tammy held her mother's hand and made small talk. Rose made light conversation about the brilliant train ride and the nice weather they were enjoying.

Rose's state of mind improved when she was told they would be having lunch at Maddie's and, as expected, the reunion was bittersweet, continuing where they had left off all those years ago. It seemed time had stood still for the two of them. With so much to say to each other, neither one could speak fast enough.

Tammy's attempts to join in on their witty conversation and

their reminiscing about the good old days had failed miserably. Caught up in the moment of seeing each other again seemed to have made them oblivious to Tammy's presence. She chuckled to herself and opted to take a back seat at one of the barstools, resigned to the fact that it might take the ladies a while to fix lunch.

While the women chatted, Tammy glanced out at the patio and saw her father and uncle had stepped outside, presumably so Uncle Dave could have a cigarette. Aunt Maddie had never smoked and wouldn't allow it in the house. After all the excitement of the morning, the thought of a cigarette appealed to Tammy, so she decided to leave her mother and aunt to their happy reunion and joined the men in the backyard for a smoke before lunch.

After a fulfilling lunch, consisting of roast beef sandwiches and salad, Tammy and her mother decided to take a walk down the road to the local pub. Tammy needed some time alone with her to have a heart-to-heart chat and see where she stood with the move.

Once at the pub, they found a quiet corner booth and sat across from each other. It was still early afternoon so the pub was relatively quiet, which pleased them both given the somber circumstances. Within a few minutes, a young waitress with a blonde ponytail approached their table and took Tammy's order of two glasses of wine.

Rose purposely avoided eye contact with her daughter and stared down at her glass with a forlorn expression while circling the rim with her index finger as she spoke. "So, this time tomorrow, you'll be on an airplane on your way to the States."

"Mom, I know you're not entirely happy about this, but you've also known this is something I've wanted for such a long time." Tammy reached for her mother's hand. "I'm going to miss you so much, and I promise you I'll keep in touch...even though you're afraid I won't," Tammy said, trying to reassure her.

Rose looked up to meet her daughter's eyes and spoke softly. "Tammy, sweetheart, don't get me wrong. I'm really happy for you." She paused, closing her eyes briefly. "It's just so sudden. In the back of my mind, I've always known this day would eventually come, but now that it's here and everything is happening so fast...well, I'm having a hard time dealing with it." Rose swallowed the lump in her throat and quickly continued before Tammy had a chance to respond. "Little by little, I'm losing my family. First your father, then Donna, and now my youngest. Jenny is the only one left. And that's another thing. Jenny is going to be furious when she finds out you left without saying goodbye to her."

"I'll write her a long letter. I promise. I'll make it right, Mom." This wasn't easy, Tammy thought. She hated to see her mother hurting, especially since she was the cause of her pain. Wishing she could make it easier, but not knowing how, frustrated Tammy beyond reason. Squeezing her mother's hand harder, she tried desperately to cheer her up with smiles and by speaking with a more confident and happy tone. Then, suddenly, she remembered her father's promise. "Hey, Dad said he would buy you a plane ticket to come visit me next year. You've never been to the States, Mom. I bet you'll love it!"

Rose huffed at her daughter's comment. "I'm not going to hold my breath, Tammy. Knowing your father, he's just saying that to make me feel better."

Rolling her eyes, Tammy sighed. "Oh, come on, Mom...I'll make sure he sticks to his word." Wanting to sound sincere and convince her mother that everything was going to be okay, Tammy repeated herself. "I promise."

Her mother wasn't buying it and remained stubborn, shaking her head from side to side as she spoke. "Honestly, Tammy, I just don't like the idea of you being so far away. I know you're all grown up now and you've lived on your own for quite some time, but you're still my youngest daughter. You're my baby! I'm sorry, I'm just having a hard time letting you go."

"Mom, I'm going to be living with Dad. Doesn't that make you feel a little better? It's not like I'll be all by myself in some strange country. To be perfectly honest, it's going to feel weird living with a parent again."

"I know. It's just me being me, and I'll deal with it the best I can. I'm not trying to make this harder for you or make you feel worse than you already do, but I'm going to miss you so much when you're gone. I know Donna was much younger when she went to go live with your father and got into all sorts of trouble. I just hope you're more mature and won't make the same mistakes she did." Tears began to roll down Rose's cheeks. "It tears me apart not knowing where she is or what's happened to her. I ask myself every day. Is she still alive? Does she have a home?" Pulling a tissue from her handbag and wiping her eyes, Rose continued to speak between sobs. "Why doesn't she write to any of us to let us know she's okay? Is it because she's dead? I don't know what to think anymore, Tammy, and I'm afraid I may lose you next."

Tammy walked around the table and hugged her mother from behind. She couldn't stand to see her cry. "Oh, Mom, I'm sure she's okay. Whatever reason she has for not contacting us, I'm sure it's a good one. I'm certain we'll hear from her all in good time."

Her mother wiped her eyes again with her now saturated tissue and squeezed her daughter's hand. "I'm sure you're right, dear. It's just the not knowing that's driving me crazy." Attempting to gather her composure, Rose shook her hair and raised her head. She let go of Tammy's hand and dabbed her eyes one last time. "Okay, enough of this talk. Let's enjoy the rest of our visit. My train leaves in a few hours, so I want to make the most of what little time I have left with you."

Tammy admired and appreciated her mother for being strong for her benefit; despite the obvious hurt she was feeling. "Okay,

Mom, you've got it," Tammy said with a smile while picking up the two empty glasses. "Why don't I get us a couple more drinks?"

"That would be nice. Thank you."

The next hour proved to be much better. Finally, Tammy was coming to terms with and feeling more comfortable about leaving her mother. Yes, it was going to be hard, but Tammy promised to shorten the distance between them with as many phone calls and letters as she could.

When the time came to return to the train station, Rose surprisingly managed to keep herself together. Only a few departing tears were shed as Tammy and her mother said their goodbyes. Standing on the platform while waving at the departing train, Tammy knew she and her mother were both going to be okay.

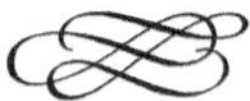

Two months had passed since Tammy left England. Now she was settled and living with her father and step-mother, Joanne, in the small town of Lonesridge, located in Northern California.

Joanne had a feeling she would be returning with John. They had discussed the idea before he left, so it was no surprise to her when he called with his arrival times and casually mentioned that he had a companion with him. She knew right away it was Tammy. Excited to finally be meeting John's youngest daughter, she made every effort to make her feel welcome and at home.

Her father's house was an older two-story, five-bedroom, two-bath home perched high on a hill overlooking Lonesridge. The outside of the home had white siding, black trim, and a large front porch that spanned the full width of the house. Stone steps led up to a heavy wooden front door and pots filled with mums and pink roses were placed sporadically around the porch. Three white ceiling fans spanned the area for hot summer days. A white wicker loveseat and matching chairs with colorful flowery cushions made it an inviting and relaxing place to lounge around and read a good book.

A beautiful rock wall surrounded the grassy lawn in front and continued around to the large back yard. More grass carpeted the garden with surrounding apple, plum, and apricot trees. Blackberries and raspberries made their homes along the back wall.

Originally, the house had had three bedrooms and a bathroom on the ground floor, and three more bedrooms and another bathroom upstairs. John had turned one of the upstairs bedrooms into his office, and Joanne had done the same with one of the bedrooms downstairs. To make the living room bigger, they'd knocked out a wall to one of the other bedrooms, leaving one bedroom and bathroom overlooking the backyard on the ground floor. This was Tammy's room.

As the focal point of the open-plan living room and dining room, an antique cast iron wood stove stood on a stone hearth against the east wall. Both John and Joanne were avid book readers, evident with the floor-to-ceiling bookshelves that lined every room, including the bedrooms. Her father still didn't have a TV, which reminded Tammy of her childhood days. She grew up with her father preferring the company of a good book to watching television. Although, occasionally, he gathered the family around the dining room table to play board games instead.

Tammy and her mother had always welcomed game night. It was a time for bonding and spending quality time with the otherwise busy man of the house. Rose would spend hours in the kitchen preparing a delicious feast while Tammy settled down at the table, eager to learn new board game strategies from her father. Always feeling intimidated by their father's strict working conditions when he was home, Donna and Jenny couldn't warm up to their father so easily. For them, game night was an order by their father, not a choice.

Like her mother, Joanne stayed home and took care of Tammy's new half- brother, Andrew. With the pressures of raising a toddler, Joanne struggled to keep a clean house; dishes were constantly piled in the sink, toys were scattered throughout the house, and dirty clothes were always piled high on the tiled floor of the laundry room.

Because Tammy had entered the States on a visitor's visa, she was unable to work. Being her sponsor, her father had filed papers with the Immigration Department to change her status to a green card within a week of her arrival. Once approved—which could take months if not years—she would finally be able to not only work but also learn to drive. In the meantime, she was happy to help Joanne around the house and watch Andrew when needed.

Being a writer, her father insisted on peace and quiet most of the time. Now with a toddler in the house, that had become impossible, except during nap times. Frustrated, he decided to rent an office above a store in town and was now working outside the home much of the time.

On the increasingly rare occasions he was home, Joanne and Tammy tried their best to keep the house quiet, but they often failed. Like most toddlers, Andrew frequently had temper tantrums. During such incidents, they would first hear the heavy footsteps of her father marching across the office floor above them, and then they'd hear the office door slam and the stomping of his feet down the stairs. In a heated state, he'd give them a snarl followed by a string of grunts and moans as he stormed out of the house, slamming the door behind him.

Once he was out of the house, Tammy and Joanne would simply look at each other, shrug their shoulders, smirk a little bit at his child-like behavior and continue on with their business. To Tammy, this was all too familiar. "Some things just never change," she often chuckled to herself.

Following these incidents, they both knew he would probably spend the night at the office, only to return the next morning, chirpy and happy, acting as if nothing had happened. For Tammy, it was like history repeating itself, but Joanne had learnt to accept his moods and never question them—just like Tammy's mother had done.

Surprisingly, Tammy sometimes found herself homesick for England. She missed her friends, her independence, and even her ex-boyfriend. With nothing exciting to report, she hadn't kept her promise to write to her friends. Because she couldn't work or drive, she hadn't been anywhere or met anyone new. Although it saddened her to say it, her life had become boring. It was nothing like she had imagined or hoped for, and she was feeling somewhat disappointed. The truth was, she had no friends, no social life, no boyfriend, and her sex life had been non-existent since her arrival.

The hunt for Donna was at a dead end with nothing to go on. She had made inquiry phone calls to the children's home and to the detective in charge of the case, but they weren't able to tell her anything she didn't already know. They were waiting for some kind of lead to pop up, but so far, nothing had. Tammy asked if there was anything she should be doing, but the police said they'd already done everything possible. Despite photos being strung throughout the Boston area and the staff and older children from the home having been interviewed extensively, no one seemed to know anything. Now all they could do was wait.

She wrote only to her mother and Jenny, but lied by telling them she was happy and loving her new life in the States. Her relationship with Jenny had become strained since she left without saying goodbye. Tammy tried to make amends with a long letter filled with numerous apologies, but Jenny never acknowledged them or officially accepted her apology. In the time she had been in the States, she had only received one letter from her, and that was just to say how disappointed she was that Tammy had upped and left without a word. She understood Jenny's anger and blamed only herself.

Tammy found adjusting to living back with parents beyond difficult. After living on her own, she now had to live by their rules and respect the eleven o'clock curfew they had given her. So, especially without a car, she was limited on where she could go.

Being a small town, Lonesridge had no bus or taxi service, but Main Street was within walking distance of the house. As the core of the town, with a variety of restaurants and shops, it was here where she spent many afternoons strolling and browsing. Her favorite place to go was the small park at the top of Main Street. An area of shade trees and green grass scattered with wooden park benches and picnic tables. It was a place visited by daily shoppers taking a rest, children playing on the grass, and proud dog owners walking their pets. On the days Joanne didn't need Tammy's help, she often spent time alone at the park under a shade tree with a good book.

While spending one such afternoon at the park engrossed in her latest read, she lost track of time. Glancing down at her watch, she saw it was almost dinner time. Knowing Joanne would be needing her help, she gathered up her things and headed home.

Upon entering the house, the essence of a home-cooked meal filled the air. Damn, what smells so good? Tammy thought while drawing more of the aroma through her nose.

After setting down her bag in the most convenient place, which happened to be the couch, she made her way toward the already set dining room table where she noticed another plate had been added. She smiled down at her little brother and watched him playing contently with his wooden blocks in the playpen.

She heard Joanne in the kitchen, who obviously hadn't realized Tammy was home, and called in her direction. "Hi, Joanne, I'm home. Do you need help with anything?"

Amongst the clatter of dishes, she heard Joanne reply, "Hi, Tammy, no thanks. I think I have it under control. We're having meatloaf for dinner. Just keep an eye on Andrew for me, if you wouldn't mind?"

"Sure, no problem." Tammy bent down and gathered Andrew in her arms; he was still amused by the one block he was holding.

Tammy took a seat at the table and bounced him on her knees while he continued to play.

"I see there's another place set for dinner. Are we having company?" Tammy asked.

"Yes, Raymond is joining us," Joanne replied as she came out of the kitchen, wiping her hands with a dish towel and taking a seat at the table across from her.

"Who's he?"

"Oh, he's a good friend of your father. He owns the contracting company that did the renovations on this house."

"What about his wife? Won't she be coming?"

Joanne shook her head and chuckled. "Oh, Raymond isn't the marrying kind. He's a few years younger than your dad, but he has no kids and has never been married. In my opinion, I don't think he ever will. He likes to play around too much." She then added in a whisper, "Between you and me, he seems to have a different woman every month. Although him and your dad are very good friends; his personal life is really none of our business."

Amused by her comments, Tammy laughed. "Ahh, I see. What time is he coming over?" Tammy asked while putting Andrew back in his playpen.

Joanne glanced down at her watch. "In about an hour. Which gives me just enough time to shower and freshen up before he arrives." She quickly stood up and removed her apron. "Mind if I leave you in charge of Andrew? Maybe you can take him out in the backyard for a while and let him play outside before dinner?"

"Of course. Go take your shower." As Joanne headed upstairs, Tammy turned to her little brother. "Come on, big fella. Let's go play outside," she cooed, heading out the back door.

While watching Andrew play in the green turtle sandbox, Tammy hadn't heard her father come home. Startled by his presence at the back door, she jerked her head in surprise when he called out across the yard.

"Hi, Tammy, where's Joanne?"

"Hi, Dad, I didn't hear you come in. She's upstairs taking a shower."

"Oh, okay. I'm off to take one too. Can you listen for the front door? Raymond is coming for dinner tonight."

"Yes, I know. Joanne already told me. I'll take Andrew indoors so I can hear him knock. He's beginning to get bored with the sand- box anyway."

"Thanks. I won't be long."

Tammy picked up Andrew, brushed the sand off his clothes, and headed for the living room. He smiled and made a chorus of loud baby noises as she placed him down on a blanket in the middle of the room and showered him with wooden blocks and colorful books. Feeling content, she watched him happily while she waited for their guest to arrive.

CHAPTER 10

Fifteen minutes later, there was a knock at the front door. Keeping an eye on her brother, Tammy left him to play while she answered it. When she opened the door, she froze. Time stood still. Subconsciously, her jaw dropped. Before her stood an extremely handsome man holding a bottle of red wine. This was Raymond? Dad's friend? Was her first thought.

He was tall with short brown hair, a broad, dark mustache, and high cheekbones that looked chiseled into his somewhat chubby cheeks, which had a slight distinction of redness to them—in an attractive way. Tammy wasn't sure if he was cold or just blushing, but as she stood in the doorway staring at him, Tom Selleck came to mind. She lost herself in his deep blue eyes, framed by long, thick black eyelashes. When he flashed a heart-warming smile, she found herself being drawn in even more. He wore blue jeans, blue loafers, and a blue and white checked shirt with the top buttons undone, revealing a few dark chest hairs.

Joanne had told her that he was just a few years younger than her father, but he seemed a lot younger. She could feel her heart rate increasing and soon realized she'd been staring at him in silence with her mouth drooped open like a puppy dog.

He spoke softly, albeit with a hint of nervousness, in a manly, alluring voice. "Er, hi. Is John home? You must be his daughter. Tammy, right?"

"Oh, yes. I'm so sorry. Hello," she said, feeling utterly stupid and embarrassed for gawking at him. She pushed the door open with the back of her body and motioned him inside with her hand. "Come on in. My dad and Joanne will be down shortly." She led him toward the couch. "Please have a seat on the settee. I'm just watching Andrew for a moment."

As he walked by her, she couldn't help noticing the pleasant scent of masculine cologne trailing behind him like an invisible shadow. Tammy's eyes continued to follow him as he took a seat on the brown leather couch. After making himself comfortable, Tammy saw he was still holding the bottle of wine. "Here, let me take that from you," she said while reaching for the bottle.

"Thanks," he said as he handed it to her. His friendly smile and perfect white teeth warmed her. Casually, she walked over to the dining room table and set the bottle down.

Since arriving home from the park, Tammy hadn't had a chance to freshen up or change. She felt under-dressed in her blue jeans, black cowboy boots, red t-shirt, and minimal makeup. Feeling nervous, she avoided eye contact with Raymond and took a seat in the armchair across the room next to Andrew, who was still happily playing on the blanket. With a moment of uncomfortable silence, Tammy took the edge off by twiddling her fingers and directing her attention to her little brother. Finally, Raymond broke the silence.

"So, how do you like living here in the States?"

Trying to act normal and not let her racing heart control her, Tammy forced a calm voice. "I love it. It's a lot different from England though, and I'm still trying to get used to all the changes."

Raymond gave her another one of his warm smiles. "I'm sure

it's quite a change. I spoke to John a few weeks ago. He mentioned you were here but, of course, being your dad, he didn't tell me how pretty you were."

Surprise by his comment, Tammy brushed it off as him merely trying to be polite and thanked him with a subtle shy smile.

He continued to compliment her. "I love your red hair. We don't see too many redheads over here." Feeling more at ease, Raymond leaned back in his seat, rested his elbows on the arms of the chair and smiled. "And that English accent of yours is mighty fine too, if you don't mind me saying."

Feeling herself blush, Tammy lowered her head and thanked him again. Uncomfortable with his praises, she needed an excuse to leave the room so she could compose herself. Secretly, she was wishing her father and Joanne would just hurry up. Using Andrew for an excuse, she quickly leaned over and picked him up. "Will you excuse me for a minute? I need to wash this little boy's hands and face before dinner."

"Sure, no problem."

But, before Tammy had a chance to leave the room, Raymond stood and walked over to her. She watched as he put his hand out to Andrew nestled in her arms. He and Tammy chuckled when Andrew grasped one of Raymond's fingers with his tiny hand and gave them both a goofy grin.

"He's growing so fast. Hey there, buddy. How are you doing?" Raymond said in a playful voice while Andrew continued to pull on his finger.

Tammy hadn't expected him to approach her. His masculine hands caught her attention as he played with Andrew. Again, she smelled his cologne and took a deep breath, inhaling the delicious scent. Strangely stirred by his presence, she began to back away. "Er, will you excuse me? I won't be long." And, without looking back, she hastily left the room, leaving Raymond by himself.

Relieved to be out the room, Tammy needed some time to pull herself together and calm her pounding heart. She argued with herself about how absurd it was to be attracted to a man twice her age, especially one that was a dear friend of her father.

With haste, she closed the bathroom door behind her and sat Andrew down on the closed toilet seat before grabbing a soaked wash- cloth and began to wash his face. Andrew tried his best to pull away and fuss. "Hush, little guy. I'm almost done," she said as she battled with him to open his hands. While uncurling and wiping down each of Andrew's tiny fingers one by one, Tammy tried to think of a logical reason why she was feeling flustered around her father's friend, but couldn't explain any of it and refused to accept the fact that she might be attracted to him.

A few minutes later, she heard voices coming from the living room. "Thank God," she whispered out loud, releasing a sigh of relief. Dad and Joanne must have finally come downstairs. Picking up Andrew, Tammy took a deep breath and returned to the living room.

Joanne looked attractive in her black slacks and red turtleneck sweater. She had let her long black hair flow freely down her back, which she seldom did, and she had applied some light makeup, which was another rarity. She was standing in the middle of the room talking to Raymond, while her father, who looked comfortable in his tan slacks and beige sweater, poured wine at the table.

Joanne and Raymond ended their conversation and glanced over at Tammy when she entered the room.

"There you are," Joanne said while walking toward her and taking Andrew in her arms.

"Sorry, I was just giving Andrew a wash before dinner."

"Raymond tells me you've already met," Joanne said as she nestled Andrew in her arm.

"Yes, we have," Tammy, replied, giving Raymond a courteous smile.

Joanne glanced over at John, who was still at the table. "Well, it looks like your father has poured the wine. Why don't I go serve up dinner so we can eat?" she said with a satisfied smile. She then proceeded to walk toward the table, where she strapped Andrew into his high chair and disappeared into the kitchen. Raymond took a seat across from John. Within a few minutes, they were sipping on their drinks and engaged in a deep conversation over John's latest book.

The sun was beginning to set outside, and a slight breeze caused the lace curtain to flap like a sail. Irritated by the noise, Tammy walked over and closed the window.

Happy to see her father had poured her a glass of wine, she reached over and took a huge gulp to help calm her nerves. Pausing their conversation for a moment, her father and Raymond watched with amazement as Tammy downed her drink with a single swig before setting the glass back down on the table. With a smirk, she glanced over at Raymond. "Good wine," she said. And quickly added, "Well, I'm going to go help Joanne in the kitchen." Giving neither of the men a chance to speak, she quickly vacated the table.

With the aroma of meatloaf invading the air and dinner served, Joanne took a seat next to Andrew's high chair so she could feed him while Tammy sat across from Raymond, next to her father. Enjoying how the wine was soothing her, Tammy reached over and poured herself another glass.

The strong friendship between her father and Raymond was clearly noticeable during dinner. Throughout the meal, they talked and laughed about various topics. John had some questions about the house, and Raymond wanted to hear all about his books and what was next.

Having been quiet throughout the entire meal—mainly to let her father and Raymond catch up—Tammy was uncertain what to say when Raymond directed a question at her. "So, Tammy, what are your plans now that you're here?"

With no hesitation, her father quickly answered for her. "Well, I'm hoping she goes to college and gets a degree behind her," John said, glaring intensely at his daughter.

Tammy turned toward her father, giving him an evil but playful stare. "I just got here, Dad. There's plenty of time for me to go to college. Right now, you're teaching me to drive and I'm busy helping Joanne with Andrew. Once I have my driver's license then I'll look in to college."

With a puzzled look, Raymond asked Tammy another question. "How old are you?"

Tammy took a sip of wine. "I just turned eighteen not so long ago."

"But you're drinking alcohol," Raymond stated, still looking puzzled .

"I've been drinking since I was sixteen. It's so different over here. In this country, I can only drink at my dad's house. In England, you can drink beer or wine with a meal at sixteen in a restaurant, so long, as it is ordered, by an adult. You can legally drink in a bar when you turn eighteen. I've been drinking in bars since I was seventeen and never been asked for my ID. But, over here, I just don't get it. You're legally an adult at eighteen, you can marry, become a parent, go off to war and fight for your country, but you can't celebrate any of those accomplishments with a drink because the drinking age over here is twenty-one. It makes no sense to me."

Both John and Raymond nodded. "Makes no sense to me either," her father replied.

"Well, have you seen much since you've been here? Have you been to the small Gold Rush town?" Raymond asked. "That's not its real name by the way, but it's what we all call it around here."

"Er, no, I haven't seen much yet. Dad is busy working and Joanne has Andrew. I plan on doing some sightseeing once I'm able to drive."

"Well, I can take you to the old gold mining town tomorrow if you'd like? It's only three miles away." Raymond paused and looked over at John. "If that's okay with you, John? You're a busy guy, so I'd be happy to show Tammy around."

Tammy didn't know what to say. Shocked that he may be asking her out on a date, she waited to reply, wondering if her father was going to speak for her again.

Not having an immediate answer, her father turned to Joanne for some insight. A simple shrug of her shoulders suggested she wasn't going to offer any help on the matter, so John opted to put her on the spot. "Well, Joanne, what do you think? It's really up to you. Do you need help with anything tomorrow?"

Joanne narrowed her eyes at her husband. She didn't like the decision being left up to her and hesitated before answering. "Er, no, I should be fine if she wants to go." She turned to Tammy. "Do you want to go?"

Well, this is awkward, Tammy thought to herself. Of course she wanted to go. It would be nice to do something different for a change, but she still wasn't sure if it was such a good idea.

Since Raymond's arrival, her head had been in an all-out tailspin. She didn't know what to do. What if she was attracted to him? How uncomfortable would it be if she decided to go? She thought for a moment and concluded that whatever she was or wasn't feeling didn't matter; Raymond would never be interested in her anyway. She was twenty years younger than him and she was his friend's daughter, so she figured it would be okay. Feeling a little tipsy from the wine, she gave Raymond a smile. "Yes, I would love to go. I think it will be fun."

"That's great! What time shall I pick you up?" Raymond cheered with excitement lingering in his voice.

Tammy took another sip of wine. "How about eleven? That'll give me enough time to help Joanne with breakfast and get myself ready."

"Sounds good. I'll be here at eleven."

Tammy gave him another smile and stood up, pushing her chair away with the backs of her knees. "Great. Well, if you'll all excuse me, I'm going to go on the front porch for a cigarette."

A look of surprise blanketed Raymond's face. "You smoke?"

With a contented grin, he added, "So do I. Mind if I join you? I've never liked being the only smoker at the dinner table." With an affirmative smile from Tammy, he excused himself from the table and followed her out the front door.

It was a cool, refreshing evening with just a slight chill in the air, and hundreds of twinkling stars lit up the dark, moonless sky. The wind had finally died down, the air was still, and the trees rose like soldiers standing to attention across the horizon. Tammy took a seat on one of the wicker chairs, lit her cigarette, and took a long, much-needed drag. The smoke rushing down to her lungs instantly satisfied the deep craving she'd had for some time and delivered a sense of calmness throughout her entire body. Never could she imagine quitting. What else could be more satisfying?

Raymond remained standing with his back to her, looking up at the skies from the porch. With one hand nestled in his front jean pocket, he looked like a natural smoker. "What a beautiful night this is. It's so peaceful. I don't even hear the crickets," he said, exhaling smoke and turning around to face her. Saying nothing, he stood motionless and stared at Tammy, taking deep hits on his cigarette.

Tammy looked up and stared back. After a few minutes of uncomfortable silence, she finally asked him. "What? What are you looking at?"

Raymond let out a small laugh and looked her straight in the eyes. Leaning back against the pillar of the porch and folding his arms across his chest, he spoke with a grin. "You're going to do well over here. You're different and you stand out. You really are quite striking."

"Striking? What are you talking about? You're being silly," Tammy remarked, trying to brush off the fact that he might be flirting with her.

"It's that red hair of yours and your fair complexion and freckles. And oh, that English accent, I could listen to it all day," Raymond confessed.

"That's bloody rubbish. After a while, people will get used to it."

"Nah, not here. I think you must be the only English girl in town. Trust me, all Americans love the English accent."

Meanwhile, back in the house, her parents were having their own discussion at the table.

"So are you okay with Tammy going with Raymond tomorrow?" Joanne asked John while rocking Andrew to sleep in her lap.

John sat across from her, looking down at his glass of wine as he curled his fingers in a circular motion around the stem. He looked a little concerned but tried not to show it when he answered. "Sure, why not? I'm sure it'll be fine. Raymond is only trying to help. He knows neither one of us have time to play tour guide with her."

Joanne knew he wasn't being entirely honest with her or himself. Surely he must have some concerns. "Are you sure about that? You know how he is with the ladies."

Irritated by her remark, he replied with a sharper tone. "Oh, come on. I don't think he'll try and hit on my daughter for Christ's sake. He's twice her age. Will you quit worrying so much?"

To help calm him down, Joanne softened her voice. "I'm not worried, John. I'm just a little concerned. But if you think it's okay, then I do too."

Before John could say any more, Raymond and Tammy returned from outside. John didn't want to admit it, but the luring smile Raymond gave his daughter as he closed the door behind them made him quite uncomfortable.

"Brrr, it's getting rather chilly out there," Tammy said, blowing into her cupped hands and rubbing them together.

Raymond looked down at his watch and then over at Joanne and John at the table. "Well, it's getting late. I guess I should get going." He turned to Tammy. "So, I'll pick you up around eleven?"

"Sounds good. And, thank you, I'm looking forward to it," Tammy answered as she sat back down at the table to finish her wine. John got up and walked Raymond out while Joanne went upstairs to put Andrew to sleep.

As Tammy sat at the table alone, thoughts of what she should wear tomorrow entered her head. But what was she thinking? This wasn't a date. This was just a friend of her father's showing her the town. She stood up, shook her head, and laughed at herself and her thoughts as she began to clear the table.

After Tammy had washed the dishes, she spent the rest of the night playing scrabble with Joanne. John retired to his office. Nothing more was mentioned about her day tomorrow with Raymond, but the questions and confusion constantly whirled around Tammy's mind.

CHAPTER 11

With the anticipation of spending the next day with Raymond, Tammy had a sleepless night of staring at the ceiling from her bed. She wanted to break away from what reminded her of a high school crush, telling herself repeatedly that tomorrow she must act mature, stay calm, and not make a fool of herself. She couldn't let Raymond know about the absurd feelings she was having toward him.

Tammy woke the next morning feeling fatigued because of her lack of sleep. She glanced over at the clock and saw it was already after eight. She sat up when she heard the clanging of dishes coming from the kitchen. After rubbing her eyes, she swung her legs out of bed, stretched, and stood up. She reached for her light blue housecoat hanging on the closet door, wrapped herself in it, and headed for the kitchen.

Joanne was now sitting at the table in her red bathrobe with her hair tied back into a ponytail. Andrew sat in his high chair next to her, wriggling with excitement from head to toe every time she fed him a spoonful of oatmeal.

"Morning, Joanne, want some coffee?" Tammy asked, followed by a yawn.

"Sounds great. I've already made a pot," she said while coaxing another spoonful of oatmeal into Andrew's mouth.

Tammy disappeared into the kitchen for a few minutes. With two mugs of hot coffee in hand, she reappeared at the table and placed the mugs in front of them. Tammy wrapped her hands around the warm cup and took a sip. The hot liquid felt good against the back of her throat. She thought the first cup of the day always tasted the best. "Where's Dad?" she asked in between sips.

"He already left for the office. I guess he wanted to get an early start. Looks like it's going to be just me and the little guy today since you're going sight-seeing with Raymond."

Tammy took another sip of coffee, savoring the flavor before answering. "It was really nice of him to offer to take me. I'm really looking forward to it."

Joanne tried not to show her concerns. "Yes, it was," she agreed. "I'm sure you'll have a great time," she added, wiping Andrew's mouth.

"Thanks. After my coffee, I'll take a shower...unless you need help with anything?"

"No, I'm fine, you go ahead. I can put Andrew in the playpen while I get dressed."

After her shower, Tammy faced the dreaded task of figuring out what to wear. She wanted to grasp his attention and look attractive yet not reveal too much or dress too skimpy. She'd heard on the radio it was going to be a warm day of above-average temperatures in the seventies, with blue skies and no wind. For October, that was good.

After some major deliberating, she finally decided on wearing a blue denim mini-skirt, brown cowboy boots, and a light blue tank top that showed off just a hint of cleavage. She would bring her short denim jacket for later in the day. Her makeup was light but just enough to accentuate her high cheekbones and green eyes. She took a quick glance in the full-size mirror; happy with her appearance, she smiled at herself, tossed her hair back with a flirty swing, and glanced down at her watch. It was ten thirty. He would be here soon, she thought with excitement. Nervous with the anticipation of his arrival, she had just enough time to step out on the front porch and smoke a cigarette to calm her nerves.

The cool, brisk air felt good against her skin, and the sun glistened through the trees against a backdrop of cloudless, bright blue skies.

She had been sitting contently for a few minutes enjoying her cigarette, feeling more relaxed, when she noticed a silver metallic Ford Pick-up truck pull up in front of the house and park. After the driver door swung open, Raymond stepped out. While the shadows of the porch were hiding her from Raymond's view, she could already see him clearly. She liked what she saw. She couldn't deny it. He looked sexy, wearing dark shades and jingling his truck keys in his hand as he walked toward the house. His faded blue jeans fit his body like a glove, accentuating every curve in his muscular, toned legs. His gold- tone belt buckle glistened in the sun, and his long-sleeve denim shirt, with the sleeves rolled up mid-way, was tucked loosely into his jeans. Beneath his jeans, the toes and heels of cowboy boots peeked out.

As he approached the front gate, she stood and walked over to the top of the steps. She took a long hit of her cigarette and exhaled a hurried cloud of hazy blue smoke. "Hi. You're early," she said with a soft, alluring smile.

He paused at the bottom of the steps and looked up in her direction. He removed his sunglasses slowly and smiled. Stunned by her appearance, he ignored her comment. "Wow! Don't you look nice? May I join you?" he asked jokingly.

"Sure, like I said, you're early."

"Well, I just couldn't wait to see you again," he teased as he quickly strode up the steps to join her.

When he reached the porch, he stood close to her. He was tall, over six feet, and that familiar cologne wafted through the air to greet her yet again. It was the same as the one he had worn the night before. Without saying a word, he reached into his shirt pocket, pulled out a pack of Marlboro Reds cigarettes and lit one.

They both began to breathe a little heavier as they stood staring at each other in silence. The strong attraction was palpable, but neither one wanted to admit it. At that precise moment, Tammy wanted him to take her in his arms and kiss her passionately. Instead, he guided her back to reality. "Well, are you ready to go?" he said hastily, trying to brush aside the unforgivable thoughts he was having.

Tammy quickly shrugged off her fantasy. "Yes, I am. I just need to grab my purse," she replied before stubbing out her cigarette in a nearby ashtray and turning toward the front door.

"I'll wait right here," Raymond said with a grin.

Tammy felt herself being drawn into him by his gorgeous smile. Anxiously, she opened the door, rushed inside, and leaned against the cool wood of the now closed door. She inhaled a long, hard breath, causing her to tremble as air rushed deep into her lungs. Pull yourself together, Tammy, jeez, she snapped at herself. Almost forgetting what she came in for, she headed toward her bedroom and grabbed her brown purse from the bottom of the bed. Happy that Joanne had already gone upstairs, she hollered up from the bottom of the stairway.

"Joanne, I'm leaving now. I'll see you later."

"Okay. Have fun!" was the faint reply from upstairs.

"I will!" Tammy shouted as she went back outside onto the porch.

Raymond stood up from the wicker chair where he had been sitting. "Ready?" he asked.

"I am," she replied, skipping down the steps toward his truck.

Once Raymond fired up the engine, the radio instantly came to life playing Kenny Rodgers, *The Gambler*. Tammy found herself liking the western cowboy lifestyle in this part of the States. She enjoyed listening to the country music and loved how everyone dressed in jeans and cowboy boots and hats. It seemed much more laid back than the disco music, glitter, and big hair found back in England.

They took Route 49 north and headed toward the Gold Rush town. It was a beautiful scenic drive through the country. The road was narrow and windy, hugging the twists and turns of the hilly countryside. Blackberries, which were succulent and ripe this time of year, grew in masses along both sides of the road. It was October, early fall, and many trees had already lost their leaves, but there were still a few that had glorious shades of reds and yellows that glistened in the sun.

During the ten-minute drive to their destination, Raymond filled her in with some history of the town. He explained how it was a gold rush town in the 1850s and was now a State preserved historical park and a National Historical Landmark. Tammy was fascinated by the history and couldn't wait to see it for herself.

They parked in a lot behind Main Street, since no driving was allowed beyond that point. After Raymond locked the truck and stuffed the keys in his front pocket, they casually strolled side by side toward Main Street.

Tammy stood and stared down at the small town. She could see to the end of the road, about a half-mile away. It was like stepping back in time into an old western movie. All the buildings were made of red brick or logs, and each had a wooden porch and benches in front for shaded resting spots. Handmade store signs hung from chains; she imagined them swaying noisily in the breeze on a windy day. Chalkboards stood in front of many stores, promoting the daily specials, and thanks to the main road being made up mainly of dirt, clouds of dust kicked up into the air with each step as Tammy and Raymond walked along together.

A finely polished, red and gold antique fire truck from the 1850s sat at the top of the street with a golden plaque describing the town's history displayed in front. Tourists were scattered throughout the area, popping in and out of stores and clicking their cameras at the various sights.

While walking through the town, Tammy noticed two hotels and several saloons with squeaky saloon-style doors. A variety of eateries from ice cream parlors, coffee and pastry stores to fancy sit-down restaurants lined the street, along with a selection of gift stores. During their walk, they watched hard candy being made and a blacksmith making horseshoes. They bought homemade jellies and jams for Joanne, and Raymond bought Tammy some homemade scented candles.

Tammy was having a wonderful time, but no matter how she looked at her day with Raymond, she felt like she was on her first date. She found him easy to talk to and there was never a moment of silence between them. He walked her through all the stores, excitedly pointing out all the historical artifacts and photos.

Tammy loved how all the merchants wore 1850s-style costumes. The women wore long dresses and white aprons with their hair pinned up in a simple bun. The men wore long overcoats and pants, white shirts, black neckties and cowboy hats. There was even a place where you could have your picture taken while dressed in costume.

As soon as Raymond saw the sign, he said, "Let's have our picture taken, it'll be fun!"

She looked up at the sign and read it out loud. "Twentieth-century photos taken in nineteenth-century costumes." Tammy agreed it would be fun and so they both entered the store, laughing like over-excited children about to have their photo taken in Santa's grotto.

The walls inside were decorated with seductive red and gold wallpaper. Photos of previous tourists dressed in costume hung in rows. A tall blond skinny man, also dressed in costume, appeared and raised his hat to them as he welcomed them to his establishment. After giving them a tour, he showed them a rack of costumes they could choose from for their picture. After at least twenty minutes of giggling and joking around, they both decided what outfit they wanted to wear and left to go change.

Raymond came out first, wearing a black tailcoat, black pants, a white shirt with a black neck tie, a black top hat, and a black cane swinging from his right hand.

A few minutes later, Tammy appeared from behind the purple curtain of her dressing room, wearing a floor-length light blue dress with long sleeves, ballooned shoulders, and a large blue bow tied in the back. The collar was high and trimmed with white lace. Delicate white-lace shoes and a white-lace umbrella completed her attire.

Feeling the effects of his costume, Raymond decided to do a little role-playing. He rose from his seat, removed his hat, and bowed to her.

"Well, hello, my lady."

Tammy giggled and gave him a slight curtsy. "Good day, sir," she said, flaunting her best impersonation of the Queen's English.

The storeowner suddenly reappeared, interrupting their fun, and asked if they were ready to have their picture taken.

With a nod, Raymond gestured his arm to Tammy. She happily accepted and hooked arms with him as they followed the merchant to the camera. When they posed for their picture. The photographer had Tammy sit on a chair with the closed umbrella held in both hands upside down in front of her. He then had Raymond stand behind her, slightly to her left, with one hand on her shoulder. As soon as Raymond touched her, he gave her shoulder a slight squeeze, which sent a flutter of shivers down her spine.

They ordered two sets of prints and laughed hysterically when the storeowner handed them over. Once back in their normal clothes, they walked outside to have a cigarette. Tammy walked to the side of the building and leaned her back against the wall. With one knee bent, she placed the sole of her foot on the wall for support and closed her eyes.

After a few moments, she felt Raymond's warm breath on her face. She slowly opened her eyes and almost froze when she found his face within inches of hers. He leaned into her and rested the palm of his hand on the wall above her left shoulder. "God," he said, "I could get into some serious trouble with you."

Before she could answer, he was kissing her. His kiss was hard and passionate as his weight pushed her back against the wall. Tammy didn't resist. Instead, she moved away from the wall and wrapped both her arms around his neck, pulling him in closer, kissing him with the same passion. Raymond leaned into her body and pressed his muscular chest against hers while snaking his fingers around her narrow waist, deepening his lustful kiss.

Suddenly, he pulled back. Breathing heavily, he managed to say, "Let's get out of here." Not waiting for a reply, he grabbed Tammy's hand. "Come on!" he yelled as he began to run, pulling her behind him.

In a state of confusion and running at an uncomfortable pace that her feet couldn't keep up with, Tammy asked, "Where are we going?"

"I don't know, Tammy. But this isn't good!" He was yelling and sprinting through the town, clearly in a state of panic. Tammy, almost choking on the dust kicked up by Raymond's speeding boots in front of her, was left with no choice but to follow.

When they finally reached the truck, Tammy all but collapsed against the passenger door, desperately trying to catch her breath. Confused by what had just happened, she waited for Raymond to unlock the truck. Momentarily, she heard the lock release and turned around to open the door.

"Hurry up! Get in!" he hollered from inside the truck.

Raymond was already in the front seat. He didn't look at her; it seemed he couldn't look at her. "What have I done? This is so wrong. What was I thinking?" he mumbled to himself while hunched over the steering wheel. Feeling the anger boiling up in the pit of his stomach, he grabbed the wheel with both hands and squeezed it hard, causing his knuckles to turn white. He could feel the beads of sweat forming on his brow. He wanted to leave. Now. He needed to get away. "Hurry up, Tammy!" he yelled again.

"Okay! Okay!" She yelled back, grabbing the handle and yanking the door open.

Once in the truck, Raymond said nothing. Looking straight ahead, he turned the key, hit the gas, and skidded out onto the main road. Tammy cowered on her side of the bench seat, afraid to speak, feeling confused by his actions and unable to fathom why he was so upset. He continued to drive in silence, only staring at the road ahead. Moments later, he pulled off to the side of the road under a large oak tree and turned off the truck.

An uncomfortable silence followed. Raymond reached for his cigarettes sitting on the dash and fumbled to get one out of the pack. With shaking hands, he managed to lift one up to his mouth and light it. He leaned back in the seat, closed his eyes, and inhaled deeply on the cigarette. Tammy remained motionless and silent, still afraid to move or speak.

Raymond finished his smoke in a matter of minutes, stubbing it out viscously in the ashtray before running his hands through his hair and pulling at it with his fingers. Still grasping his hair, he lowered his forehead onto the steering wheel and looked down at his lap.

"Whatever happened back there; never happened! Do you understand me?" he ordered in a cruel and angry tone.

Tammy could feel tears forming. Not wanting to cry in front of him, she swallowed hard to push them back. She still didn't understand why he was so angry and upset. "What do you mean?" she asked, still struggling to keep back the tears.

He turned his head toward her and glared at her with dark, narrow eyes. "I MEAN it NEVER happened...and you will tell NO ONE about this. Do I make myself clear?"

Tammy spoke softly, trying to calm him. "We only kissed Raymond. It was no big deal. Will you please just calm down?"

"What? Yes, it actually was a big deal, Tammy! I have no idea what I was thinking. You are my friend's daughter, for God's sake! I'm old enough to be your father. Christ! What the fuck was I thinking?" Still shocked, he raised his hands. "What would John think? This is insane. I can't do this. Can you imagine how your father would feel if he found out?"

Unable to hold back the tears anymore, Tammy felt a warm trickle down her cheeks as she tried to reason with him. "I don't understand why you are making such a big deal out of this. We like each other, don't we?" She wiped away her tears. "And as far as my dad is concerned, we don't have to tell him." She paused. "Not yet anyway."

"We can *never* tell him, Tammy! Don't you understand? It would destroy our friendship. I can't even begin to imagine the anger he would feel toward me. No, I'm not willing to take that risk, regardless of how much I'm attracted to you."

In her heart, she knew he was right; her father would never accept it. Not only would Raymond be jeopardizing their friendship, she also risked her father disowning her. Devastated by what was suddenly at stake, her tears began to flow heavier.

To comfort her, Raymond placed his hand on her shoulder, giving it a slight squeeze as he spoke in a softer tone. "Come on, stop crying. I'm sorry I got angry. I'm not angry with you. Just myself for allowing this to happen."

Even though she knew the risks, she refused to give up. With her eyes now swollen and red from her tears, Tammy looked up at him. "I'm as surprised as you are about what happened back there, but I felt the chemistry between us when we kissed. I know you did too. You can't ignore something like that and just pretend it never happened."

Raymond wrapped an arm around her shoulder, hugging her tightly. "Oh, Tammy, I'm flattered that a girl of your age finds me attractive and wants to be with me. You're young, beautiful, and vibrant. Why on earth do you want to be with an old guy like me?"

She smiled and placed her hand on his knee. "Because you're a real man and I feel safe with you. The guys I dated in England were just boys, young, immature, and stupid."

He laughed at her remark, still hugging her while he spoke. "As much as I like you, I can't hurt your father. He would never forgive me for dating his daughter."

"Yes, I know, but can I ask you something?"

"Sure."

"Did you think this would happen? I mean, if you're attracted to me but have no intentions of us dating, why did you invite me here in the first place? I'm sorry, but today has felt like a first date to me. Especially when we kissed."

"I have to admit that yes, I was attracted to you, even before I knew your age. But I thought I had it under control. I invited you with the intentions of just having some fun and making a new friend. I didn't expect it to go this far. You're right, though, there is chemistry between us. I felt it back there too. It consumed me, but I have to fight it and resist the temptations I'm feeling because...because of your father."

Tammy released herself from his hold and reached for her handbag by her feet. She pulled out a pack of cigarettes, took one from the pack and lit it. Leaning back in her seat, she looked over at him with sullen eyes while she smoked.

Thoughts entered her mind. What she felt back there was electrifying. Refusing to let go of something so real and so strong before it had a chance to blossom, Tammy decided to play along but with ulterior motives. "I promise not to say anything. I understand, and like you said, it never happened. Let's just forget it," she said in her sweetest voice.

"Tammy, this isn't easy for me. When I'm with you, you make me feel young and full of life. It's like I'm living my youth again. I've never felt that before with anyone. Then again, I've never dated any one as young as you and to be honest, it scares the hell out of me... and so does your father."

Knowing he was unaware that his hand was now on her knee while he spoke, Tammy stubbed out her unfinished cigarette in the ashtray and reached for his hand. Caressing it softly, she raised it to her mouth and kissed each finger one by one. He didn't pull away. She shifted her body closer to him, placed his hand over her breast, and gave it a gentle squeeze.

Raymond followed her hand with his eyes, admiring her cleavage, feeling her heart beating rapidly beneath his hand. With light fingers and a feathered touch, he began to massage her breast in a slow circular motion. Aroused by his touch, Tammy inhaled a sharp breath and closed her eyes before arching her back and pushing her body closer to him.

Raymond knew this was wrong for so many reasons, but he could no longer resist. Surrendering to his unforgivable desires, he pulled her toward him with force and kissed her with greater passion than before. Tammy welcomed him and matched his passion with a burning hunger and desire of her own. They both needed to stop for air, but neither could let go. There was no going back now. Unable to control himself, he reached up under her tank top and fondled her breasts, squeezing her nipples with his fingertips. He felt the delicate skin harden under his touch as she moaned with pleasure.

While still locked in a kiss, she slid over to his side of the seat and straddled him. Raising her mini skirt to the tops of her thighs, she locked her arms around his neck and pushed his head farther back into the seat. She felt the hard skin of his hands grazing over her legs and up under her skirt. His touch wasn't gentle. The touch of a man, she thought. Filled with lust, he clamped his fingers around the muscle of her buttocks and nuzzled his head between her breasts. Tammy gasped. With one swift move, she peeled her top up over her head and threw it to the passenger side. Now faced with her naked chest, Raymond devoured her, tantalizing each of her nipples with his tongue before engulfing them with his mouth. His hunger for her had overtaken his senses and he was fast losing control.

Feeling the same hunger, Tammy lowered her hand onto the rising bulge beneath his jeans. It began to throb as she massaged it with her palm.

Raymond was at his peak. Setting his hands free from underneath her skirt, he unzipped his pants, adjusted her panties, and entered her in one rushed motion. With an animalistic growl that vibrated from deep inside his throat, he grabbed her by the hips and thrust his manhood inside of her. Tammy lunged onto his lips, locking him in a kiss as he brought them both to climax simultaneously.

Out of breath, her heart beating fast, she remained still on his lap and rested her head on his shoulder, listening to his heavy breathing slowly subside to a normal pace.

After a moment of silence, Raymond shifted awkwardly in his seat beneath her. "Oh shit, Tammy, what did we just do?" There was a hint of remorse in his voice.

"Shhhh, it's okay. It can be our little secret," Tammy said as she pulled her skirt back down and tried to get back in her seat.

"Man, that was intense. I need a friggin' joint," Raymond confessed.

Tammy wrinkled her brow. "You need a what?"

"A joint...pot...marijuana? Don't tell me you've never heard of pot?" Raymond asked in disbelief while fumbling with his zipper.

"Nope, never. What is it?" she asked.

"Oh, Christ, you are so young and naive. I can't believe I'm telling you this. It's like a cigarette, but it makes you feel good and relaxed. It calms you. I don't know how else to describe it. But it's what I need right now."

Intrigued by what he'd just described, Tammy was anxious to try it. "That sounds great! I'd love to try some. Where is it? Let's smoke some now."

Amused by her innocence, Raymond chuckled. "I don't carry it on me, it's illegal. It's known as a drug and I only smoke it at home. It's not like cocaine or anything but it's still illegal."

Tammy was horrified. "It's a drug?" She had heard about drugs and how addictive they could be, but she'd never known anyone that used them.

"It's not as bad as it sounds. Let's go back to my place. I really do need one after what just happened. If you want to try it, that's up to you, but don't feel you have to," he told her as he straightened out his jeans and started up the car.

"Okay, we'll see," Tammy, replied with an innocent smile.

CHAPTER 13

Fifteen minutes later, they were pulling into Raymond's long driveway, which was shaded by trees and bushes on either side. Tucked away from the street was his single-level duplex. Tammy was relieved to see he lived across town from her father's house and not close by.

During the drive, Raymond told her he was the property manager for the three duplexes in the building. In return, he got free rent. A young couple lived below him, and a single guy lived in the duplex behind him.

Once the truck was in park, Tammy picked her purse up from the floor, exited the car, and joined Raymond at the double glass doors where she found him fumbling with his keys. She chuckled at his nervousness and waited patiently while he struggled to open the door.

Once inside, she set her purse down on the long wooden table that separated the kitchen from the living room. Scattered across it were numerous coffee cups partially filled with stale coffee, a dirty ashtray, and a couple of empty soda cans. In the center was what Tammy assumed was Raymond's work area, consisting of building plans, a desk calculator, pens, and numerous business cards.

The off-white walls were in desperate need of a paint job, and the musty brown carpet with a few coffee stains had seen better days, too. Pictures of wildlife and outdoor scenes hung at random intervals on the walls. Both sides of the room had floor to ceiling windows, spanning the full length of the room. A faded beige couch sat in front of one window, while the other windows looked out onto a deck, with views across the main highway into Lonesridge. The focal point of the room was a red brick fireplace. A television and an old comfy-looking chair with worn out tanned cushions were placed to its right.

Tammy quickly scanned the room before checking out the rest of the duplex while Raymond listened to his messages on the answering machine.

Walking through the main room and adjoining kitchen, she passed an office on the left and a bathroom on the right. At the end of the hallway was a dingy master bedroom. Chocolate-brown curtains were drawn closed, preventing natural sunlight from entering the dark space. She flicked the light switch on and saw it was a simple room with an unmade king-size bed against the back wall, which had oversized wooden tables on either side of it. A matching dresser and mirror sat across from the bed, disarrayed with loose change, odd socks, papers, and a variety of keys. The dirty laundry scattered on the floor amused her. Typical man, she thought.

When Tammy returned to the living room, she found Raymond sitting at the table talking business on the phone. She walked behind him, crossed her arms over his chest, and began nibbling on his ear. Unsuccessfully, he tried to brush her off while she quietly giggled behind him.

The odor of the cigarette smoldering in the ashtray next to him caught her attention. Now craving a cigarette herself, she released her hold on Raymond and grabbed his pack of Marlboro Reds sitting on the table, along with his yellow lighter. She left him to finish his work and made herself comfortable on the couch. Picking up the glass ashtray from the coffee table, she then lit the cigarette, inhaled deeply, and leaned back to savor the moment.

Raymond eventually ended his conversation and hung up the phone. Without saying a word, he disappeared into the kitchen and returned a few minutes later with a mason jar and a sheet of newspaper. He sat himself in the comfy chair, placed the newspaper on his knees, and twisted the lid off the jar.

"What's that?" Tammy asked, stubbing out her cigarette.

He smiled, held the jar up to the light and said, "This, my dear, is pot."

Intrigued, Tammy left the couch and knelt in front of him before leaning her arms on his knees to take a closer look. The jar was filled with light-green flakes of what looked like crumbled leaves. It reminded her of sage. She watched closely as he took a few pinches of the pot and placed it on the newspaper. From his top pocket, he took a pack of thin papers, pulled one out, and held it between his fingers.

"What are you doing?" Tammy asked.

"Making a joint."

With fascination, she continued to observe the process as he picked up pinches of the pot and sprinkled it evenly along the center of the paper. When he was finished, he moistened the edge with his lips, rolled it up like a cigarette and sealed it.

"Wow! That's cool. Can I try some?"

"Yeah, but not too much. Don't forget, I've got to take you home later." he said, smiling and pointing at her accusingly. "Let me show you how to smoke it. It's not like a cigarette. Watch me."

Tammy watched closely as he lit the end of the joint and inhaled deeply. "After you've taken a hit, hold your breath for a couple of seconds," Raymond instructed with a tight voice, indicating the smoke was still in his lungs. Then, he slowly exhaled while passing her the joint.

"Okay," she said, looking at the strange cigarette-like object between her fingers. She held it up to her nose and sniffed. "I love the way it smells," she said, wafting the scent into her nostrils like she'd just found a new favorite perfume. With a last curious glance at the joint, she slowly raised it to her lips, sucked a tentative drag, and inhaled deeply. Per Raymond's instructions, she held her breath.

Noticing the reddish tinge appearing on Tammy's puffed-out cheeks, Raymond said, laughing, "Okay, okay, you can let it out now! I only said a couple of seconds!"

After exhaling, she began to cough uncontrollably. "My god! That stuff is harsh," Tammy said, gasping for air.

"Don't worry. You'll get used to it," he said as she took another hit.

Tammy scowled at him in confusion. "I don't feel any different. What's supposed to happen?"

Raymond took the joint from her and finished it. "Give it a few minutes."

He was right. Shortly after, she began to feel the effects of the drug. Paranoia consumed her first. Feeling inexplicably fearful, she didn't like the sudden onset of insecure, unsettling emotions she was experiencing. Afraid to move or stand, she sat motionless on the floor, her knees up high under her chin, her legs locked in her arms.

She wanted to ask Raymond when would it end but was unable to speak, afraid her words would sound jumbled and not make any sense. Losing all her self-confidence and the ability to perform simple tasks, she yearned to feel normal again. *Why do people enjoy smoking this stuff when it makes you feel so awful?* Tammy decided she'd had enough. Feeling scared, she secretly made a promise to herself. *If I make it through this alive, I promise I will never smoke pot again.*

Next came the remorse and guilt. Knowing she was smoking an illegal drug, and therefore committing a crime, stunned her to the core. The notion that she may be caught and thrown in jail threw her head into a petrifying tailspin of horrific thoughts. Feeling ashamed, she wondered how she would ever face her father again. Still frozen by the drug, she kept reminding herself it would be over soon and everything would return to normal.

Slowly, after what seemed like an eternity, things were beginning to make more sense. Feeling more grounded thrilled her. She was able to move her arms and legs without fear and no longer felt threatened or scared. She felt like a warrior; triumph and victory had replaced her fears. She had preserved and beat the drug. She had won!

She turned her body to face Raymond and propped herself up on her knees. Feeling confident and strangely aroused, she leaned in and kissed him passionately on the lips. Then, it happened—triggered by the kiss—every nerve in her body exploded. She surrendered herself entirely to him. Her sexual energy and appetite was beyond anything she had ever experienced.

For a few moments, they caressed each other with force and hunger, but it wasn't enough. Within minutes, she lay naked on the floor, smothered by his sweat and scent, pinned by the weight of his body. "I want you," she whispered in his ear.

Hastily and with dynamic energy, Raymond thrust himself into her. Tammy released a loud, satisfying moan. Molded together as one, limbs intertwined, they quickly peaked and climaxed at the same time. But neither wanted it to end; they still had an appetite for more.

Tammy was now loving the drug and beginning to understand why people smoked it. She realized, now she'd worked her way through all the bullshit, that the resulting feeling was amazing. She didn't want it to end.

For the next couple of hours, they fondled, played, and explored every inch of each other's bodies. Tammy had lost count of the number of orgasms she'd had. She just knew she was feeling incredible. "Wow!" Tammy said breathlessly while lying naked in

Raymond's arms, trying to recuperate from yet another sensational climax. "That was amazing! Now I see why you like to smoke pot," she said, trying to contain a fit of giggles.

"It does have its advantages," Raymond chuckled. "God, Tammy. Your father can never find out about us. He would friggin' kill me," he added in a more serious tone.

"Does my dad know you smoke pot?"

"No, he doesn't. I guess there's a lot your father doesn't know about me."

"Well, Joanne seems to think you're a ladies' man. She told me you have a different woman every month. So, am I the flavor of the month?" Tammy teased.

"Oh, she does, does she? I didn't know she was paying that much attention to my love life. And no, silly, you're not the flavor of the month." Again, Raymond turned serious. "But we do have to be careful. We can't let anybody find out about us. Do you understand?"

Tammy sat up on her knees and faced him. "Don't worry, I won't tell anyone. I promise." She gave him a quick peck on his cheek and rose to her feet. "Now, come on. Let's get dressed so you can take me home."

Over the next three months, Tammy and Raymond continued with their secret affair. Neither one dared to tell her father of their flourishing relationship, fearing his predictable, angered reaction would destroy all existing friendships.

Whenever Joanne didn't need Tammy's help, she would joyously skip the fifteen minutes across town to Raymond's place. He was always happy to see her. Never failing to greet her with a passionate embrace and a smile that warmed Tammy's heart. They cherished their secret afternoons together, never knowing when the next one would be.

Their meeting place was always at his home, never venturing out, afraid they may be seen by someone who knew her father. They made the most of their time together by drinking wine, smoking pot, and making love three or four times in an afternoon. They laughed and giggled like high school kids. For the first time since moving to the States, Tammy was finally having some fun.

But, a few days later, the fun came to a sudden halt. Tammy was facing a nightmare. "This can't be happening," Tammy cried out loud. She had bought three different brands and each one showed the same result. After lining them up on the bathroom counter, all of them revealed a pink "plus" sign. All three pluses jumped out at her from the thin plastic tubes—they may as well have been flashing neon signs—telling Tammy she was pregnant.

Feeling like she was going to faint, Tammy collapsed onto the seat of the toilet like a discarded rag doll. "Oh my god, how did this happen?" she whispered to herself. Of course, she knew how it happened, but she was on the pill and took one every morning. Then again, there was that one morning. It was about six weeks ago; Andrew fell, right before she was about to take it. She'd heard him scream from the living room and raced in to find he'd fallen into the coffee table. Joanne had got to him before she did.

The cut above his eye was deep so, fearing he may need stitches, they stopped whatever they were doing and rushed him to the hospital. In all the commotion, she'd forgotten to take her pill and didn't realize her error until the next morning when she saw she'd missed one. She took two that day to try and compensate, but it hadn't helped—obviously.

After having the three required stitches and returning from the hospital, Andrew slept most of the day, so Tammy had taken advantage and visited Raymond. She remembered they'd definitely had sex that afternoon, more than once. And now, here she was, eighteen and pregnant with his baby. She was too young to be having a child. She wasn't ready for this. She was just having some fun; it was never meant to be anything serious. What was she going to do? She had to tell him. How would he react to becoming a father?

She gasped out loud when she thought about her own father. Tammy knew she could never tell him, but how was she going to hide the pregnancy? The only person she could talk to was Raymond. She had no other friends. Feeling scared and completely alone, her mind raced a mile a minute with endless questions, to which she had no answers.

It'd been over six months since she arrived in the States. This was not how it was supposed to be. She came here on a mission to find Donna but was feeling deflated with nothing to go on and no new leads. Frustrations were at their peak. She had expected to have her independence, a car, a job, and a place to call her own by now. Tammy never imagined she would still be living with her father. But she didn't have a choice. She was still waiting for that damn green card. Without that, she couldn't work or drive. Now she found herself pregnant by her father's friend. Oh, what a mess her life had become.

Worried about her future, Tammy cradled her head in her arms and began to sob. Subconsciously, she rubbed her stomach, thinking of the tiny life growing inside of her. She had to think fast and decide what she was going to do. She needed to tell Raymond as soon as possible and ask his advice. They were in this together whether he liked it or not.

Tammy immediately knew an abortion was out of the question. The thought petrified her on so many levels. Adoption was not an option either. Never could she carry a child inside of her, feeling it grow and move, only to hand it over to complete strangers to raise as their own. No. Having this child was the only choice she had. Raymond would either support her or not. Tammy would just have to wait and see; either way, she was going to have this baby.

She realized, sadly, she could no longer live under her father's roof while pregnant with Raymond's child. She wasn't ready to tell him anything just yet, but when she did, the tension would become unbearable. Her only choice was to move in with Raymond.

Predicting her father's rage when the time came to tell him she was moving in with Raymond, Tammy decided to hide the pregnancy from him for a while; or at least until things had calmed down. Tammy could foresee her father feeling betrayed by Raymond, and probably her, too. She hated the thought of causing him pain. Over time, she hoped her father could forgive them and accept the child she was now carrying as his first and only grandchild. Suddenly, a loud knock at the door snapped her out of her thoughts.

"Hey, Tammy. Are you okay? You've been in there for a while. I need you to watch Andrew while I run to the store to get some milk," Joanne said from the other side of the door.

Startled by the intrusion, Tammy jumped up from the toilet seat in a panic and began scraping together all the pregnancy tests and packages that were spread across the counter. "Yes, I'm fine. I'll be out in a minute," she replied.

Tammy stared at the empty boxes, wondering where she could hide them. She had an idea. Bending down quickly, she opened the cupboard doors beneath the sink and grabbed the trash bag liner from the bin. She stuffed it with the rubbish she had accumulated and then tied the top into a knot. Placing the sealed bag on the counter momentarily, she checked herself in the mirror. Her eyes were reddish and she looked as white as a sheet, but all things considered, she didn't look too bad.

She splashed her face with cold water, applied some lipstick, and gave her hair a quick brush while trying to pull herself together. Satisfied with her appearance, she picked up the trash bag and slowly opened the door. Quietly, she peeked her head out and scanned the corridor left and right. Joanne was not in sight. Letting out a sigh of relief, she scurried to her room and stuffed the bag under her bed. She would deal with it later.

Feeling slightly more composed; she headed to the dining room, where she found Joanne sitting at the table bouncing Andrew on her knee. He was happily feasting on a cracker while spreading crumbs all over Joanne's lap.

Joanne stood up and handed Andrew over. "Thanks, Tammy. I won't be long," she said, brushing cracker flakes off her pants.

"No problem. I'll read him some books while you're gone."

As soon as Tammy heard the back door close, with Andrew still in her arms, she ran over to the kitchen window and looked out. From the window, she could see the garage clearly. The taillights came on and she heard the engine running. She watched and waited. A few minutes later, she saw Joanne back out of the garage and drive down the road into town.

Satisfied that the coast was clear, she quickly ran into her bedroom and gently placed Andrew on the bed while she knelt underneath and grabbed the trash bag. With her other hand, she scooped Andrew into her arm, resting him on her hip, and ran through the house to the back door.

She hurried down the steps to the metal trash cans lined up against the house. Removing the lid from the first one, she buried her bag of secrets among the others and replaced the lid. "Phew. That's done," she said, feeling relieved. She turned to her brother and held her finger up to her mouth, nuzzling his face with her nose as she whispered, "Shhh, it's our little secret. Okay?"

Andrew simply chuckled and smiled, apparently approving of the new game.

Feeling confident that the bag wouldn't be found, Tammy returned inside to read to Andrew.

CHAPTER 15

That night, unable to sleep, Tammy tossed and turned with endless thoughts about how her life had changed forever. Not only had she let herself down but also her father too. She dreaded seeing the dis- appointment on his face when she broke the news to him about her relationship with Raymond.

Ever since she was a child, his approval and praises have always been important to her. She yearned to see the pride in his eyes and smile. Like her father, Tammy had high hopes of going to college. The dream was now crushed due to her pregnancy. Disgusted with how her life was turning out and mortified that she was pregnant, she felt herself spiraling into a depressive state. She had no choice but to accept the new version of her life and the consequences it would bring regarding the relationship with her father.

With no sleep and her emotions in turmoil, Tammy was determined to see Raymond early in the morning and break the news to him about the baby. His possible reaction feared her. She wasn't expecting him to be thrilled.

The next morning, Tammy dressed herself in jeans and a long-sleeved white cotton shirt, applied a little makeup, and brushed her hair. Not wanting to join Joanne for their usual morning cup of coffee and small talk, she needed to think of a reasonable excuse to leave early.

As predicted, Joanne was already sitting at the table reading the newspaper. She looked up when Tammy entered the room. "Hi, coffee is ready," she said with a smile.

Tammy stood nervously, fidgeting with her fingers. "Thanks, but I'm actually just on my way out."

"It's only nine o'clock," Joanne replied after glancing at her watch with a puzzled expression. "Where are you off to so early?"

Tammy thought quickly and blurted out the first thing that popped into her head. "I'm off to the library."

Annoyed with her lame excuse and anticipating the questions that would be likely to follow from Joanne—like why she needed to go to the library when they had so many books of their own—Tammy stalled. But, surprisingly, and thankfully, Joanne simply nodded and smiled.

She was tired of lying, especially to those close to her. The secret love affair she had with Raymond only existed because of her lies. It was the only way she could see him. At least if she moved in with Raymond, the lies would stop.

Relieved to be standing on the front porch with the door shut behind her, Tammy closed her eyes and took in a deep breath, feeling the cool, crisp air tingling her face. Bracing herself for the upcoming talk with Raymond, she found her confidence and began her walk.

Fifteen minutes later, she was knocking on his front door. With no answer, she tried the doorknob and found it unlocked, meaning he was home. Letting herself in, she heard the shower running from the bathroom. She peeked down the hallway and saw the bathroom door was slightly ajar. Clouds of steam from the shower hovered up high around the light. She chuckled while she listened to him bellowing the popular song *Yellow Submarine*. He sounded happy.

Tammy wondered if she was about to spoil his joyful mood. Or might she possibly enhance it? Remembering why she was there, a feeling of nausea crept over her, so she decided to wait for him outside on the deck to get some much-needed fresh air. A place where she could also contemplate how she was going to tell him the news of their child.

Sitting in the oversized wooden deck chair and smoking a cigarette, Tammy was lost in her thoughts. A tap at the window brought her back to reality. She turned to see Raymond looking out of the window, dressed in a blue bathrobe with a white towel draped around his neck. With a smile, he motioned for her to come inside.

Tammy forced herself to return the smile, stubbed out her cigarette, and left the deck to join him. Embracing her in his arms, Raymond gave her a light kiss on the cheek.

"What a pleasant surprise. Do you want some coffee?" he asked.

"Sure, that would be great. Thanks."

Raymond walked over to the kitchen and poured two cups of coffee while Tammy took a seat on the couch. Wondering how the hell she was going to tell him, she tried to make herself comfortable for the upcoming confession.

With two cups in one hand, Raymond took a seat next to Tammy and placed one of the mugs in front of her on the coffee table. "I thought I wasn't going to see you until tomorrow afternoon?" he asked before taking a sip of coffee.

Deciding not to beat around the bush and just tell him, Tammy ignored his question and dove right in. "Raymond, we have to talk."

Anticipating bad news and in fear of spilling his coffee, Raymond returned his mug to the table. "Okay, I'm listening. What's up?"

Before Tammy could reply, Raymond's body stiffened and his eyes opened wide with fear as he gasped. Thinking he had already guessed what she was about to tell him, Tammy nervously waited for his reaction. Sounding desperate, he grabbed her arm. "Don't tell me John knows about us. Please, don't tell me that!"

Tammy sighed; disappointed she'd still have to break the news.

"No, that's not it. But he's about to find out."

Raymond began to panic and tightened the grip on her arm.

"What do you mean? Who knows about us?"

"No one knows." Tammy took a long, deep breath to brace herself. "Raymond, there's no easy way to say this so I'm just going to come out and say it, okay? I'm pregnant." She sat in silence, watching every minute detail of his expression, waiting for him to say some- thing. Anything.

He pulled his hand away from her arm and let his body flop back against the couch. With a look of hopelessness, he simply stared straight ahead, stunned by the news. He said nothing.

After a few moments of silence, she nudged his knee with her hand.

"Raymond. Please say something."

Without reaching out to her or offering any kind of comfort, he finally spoke. "How did this happen? I thought you were on the pill."

"Well, yes, I am on the pill, but I missed one about six weeks ago. I tried to double up the next morning, but it obviously didn't help because...well, because I'm now pregnant."

"Can you get pregnant by missing one pill?" Raymond asked, looking puzzled.

"It sure looks like it, doesn't it?"

"Are you sure?"

"Yes, I'm sure. I brought three different tests and they all came up positive. What are we going to do?" Tammy asked, trying to hold back the tears. Seeking some kind of reassurance or support from the father of her unborn child, she reached for his hand. He simply brushed it away without saying another word.

Raymond stood and began pacing the room with both hands buried in his bathrobe pockets. "Let me think for a minute," he snapped, rubbing his forehead with the towel still draped around his neck. In an angered state, he began rummaging around and looking under papers on the dining room table, tossing them to the side by the handful.

"What are you looking for?" Tammy asked.

Raymond snapped again, "Where are my fucking cigarettes?"

"Here, have one of mine," Tammy quickly said, trying to calm him down. Reaching into her purse, craving a cigarette herself, she pulled out two and lit them both. She walked over to Raymond and handed him one. He took it from her with a hint of gratitude and sat at the table, pulling deeply on his smoke.

Tammy turned a chair to face him and slid into it with apprehension. Wanting to be closer to Raymond, she placed both her hands on his knees and leaned forward. "Before you do too much thinking, I should tell you that I've already decided I'm keeping the baby."

If he tried to hide his feelings of shock, it didn't work. Raymond's questions fired out in one long breath. "You are. But what about your dad? Do you honestly think he's going to accept a grandchild fathered by his friend who happens to be old enough to be his daughter's father? What do you think he's going to say about all this?" Raymond raised his voice a notch. "Come on, Tammy! There's no way! Admit it, we fucked up," he said, shaking his head in disbelief.

Tammy met his tone. "This isn't about my father anymore. This is about me, and the baby—*our* baby. I'm tired of trying to please him all the time. Of course he's not going to like the fact that I'm pregnant by you. It's not like I plan on telling him anytime soon. I'll be able to hide the pregnancy for a while. If you want nothing to do with me or the baby, that's fine, I understand." Tammy added a hint of sarcasm to her tone. "After all, you have a reputation in town to keep. I wouldn't want to embarrass you."

The fact that he was more concerned about her father's reaction angered her, but she still felt compelled to tell him her plan. "I've decided I'm going to have to move out of my father's house. There's no way I can stay there and have this child."

"And what do you plan on telling him?" Raymond asked.

"Well, I was hoping I could move in with you. In all honesty, I'm disappointed that you haven't asked me yet. I'm willing to tell my dad we're seeing each other and suffer the consequences. He'll probably be angry for a while, but give him some time and I'm sure he'll get over it. Living here with you, I'll be able to hide the pregnancy for a few months and give my dad some space to eventually accept us as a couple."

"You've given this some serious thought, haven't you?" Seeming calmer, he touched her for the first time since hearing the news. Leaning in toward her, he took her hands and held them tight under his chin before kissing her lightly on the forehead.

Tammy let out a huge sigh of relief. The kiss, no matter how small, meant so much to her at that moment. It told her he cared. "I really don't know what else to do. Do you have any ideas?" Tammy asked. Feeling she needed to remind him, she quickly added, "I won't have an abortion or give up the baby for adoption. I'll tell you that right now."

"I would never ask you to do that unless you wanted to. It seems your mind is made up. I guess I'm going to have to get use to the idea that I'm going to be a father. I've never imagined myself as one. Especially not now, at my age."

Raymond rested his arms on Tammy's shoulders and locked his hands behind her neck. Looking deep into her eyes, he unknowingly told her exactly what she had wanted, needed to hear. "Tammy, we're in this together. I'm on your side and I agree with you. Yes, I think it's a good idea that you come live here with me. But I must confess, it's going to be quite an adjustment for me. I've lived alone all my life. Your father, on the other hand, won't be okay with any of this. But, like you said, this is no longer about him. It's about us and the baby."

Listening to him speak, especially when he used the word *us*, brought tears to her eyes. As they trickled down her cheeks, Raymond softly wiped them away with his thumb. Tammy spoke, using a softer voice. "Thank you for being here with me...for me. It means a lot."

She wiped her moist cheeks with one of her hands and kissed Raymond softly on the lips. Caught up in the moment and stirred by the feeling of his tender lips on hers, she said, "I love you" for the very first time. Not sure if she truly meant those three little words, Tammy remained silent, anticipating Raymond's response.

He didn't acknowledge her confession. "It's okay," he said, wiping a loose strand of hair away from her eyes. "Have you thought about when you want to tell your father?"

Giving herself some more time to think about the answer, Tammy walked over to her purse and pulled out two more cigarettes before lighting them and returning to the table. She handed one to Raymond, which he gratefully accepted. "Joanne is a lot easier to talk to than my dad. Maybe I should talk to her first. Honestly, my dad scares me. She'll probably give me some good advice on how to approach him. What do you think?"

Raymond didn't know what to say. The only thing he could do was to agree with her. "Sounds like a good idea to me."

Tammy continued with her plan. "I think it's best I do this on my own. No offense, but I'm sure they won't want to see you for a while."

Relieved at knowing he wouldn't have to face John, Raymond agreed without so much as a second thought, just in case she changed her mind. "I'm the last person your father will want to see. Once you tell him, our friendship will be destroyed forever."

"I know. I'm sorry. Collateral damage, I guess." Not wanting to dwell on that particular subject, Tammy added to her plans. "So, I'm going to talk to Joanne as soon as I get home. Hopefully, my dad will still be at the office. I want to get this over with as soon as possible and get out of there. I know, once I tell them, I'll have to leave right away. It'll just be too unbearable to stay any longer." She took his hand and squeezed it hard. "I know we can make this work, Raymond. I know I can't get a job right now, but I can help you manage the duplexes here and—"

Raymond raised his arm, interrupting her. "Whoa, slow down, girl, one step at a time. Let's get through the hardest part first, which is telling your dad and moving you in here, before we start making any more plans. Okay?"

"Yes, okay. You're right. You're right. I'm getting ahead of myself. Sorry." She feigned a slap across her wrist and laughed nervously. "Oh no! I just had a thought."

"What?" he asked, suddenly looking worried.

"How am I going to get my things over here? My dad sure as hell won't help me and I can't ask Joanne." She paused, letting the realization sink in. "Oh jeez, you're going to have to come get me."

"Me!"

"Yes, you. I don't know anyone else." Seeing the look of horror on his face, Tammy tried to reassure him. "You won't have to come in the house. You can just wait in the truck."

Raymond became panicked again. "Oh, Jesus Christ! This is getting harder by the minute." In a flustered state, he stood and began pacing the room. He stopped in mid-stride and turned and faced Tammy. "You're just going to have to leave when John isn't home. If he knew I was waiting outside, he'd come out and probably kill me!" He walked back to the table, stubbed out his cigarette and immediately lit another one from a pack he found among the piles on the table.

"Good idea! I'm going to have to call you when it's time for you to come pick me up. God, I'm dreading this. I can't wait till I'm here with you and all this is behind us."

Seeking comfort, Tammy left her chair and walked over to Raymond. He welcomed her into his arms and held her tight. Fearing what lay ahead, neither of them wanted to let go. With eyes closed, they stood in silence, holding each other for some time until Tammy forced herself to back away, knowing she had to leave and face the music.

"I'd better go," she said as she began searching for her purse, which she found by the couch and slung it over her shoulder. "Oh! I've just remembered I need to stop at the library."

"The library? You're thinking about reading books at a time like this? Can't it wait until you've moved out?"

"No, it's not that," Tammy laughed. "I'm covering up another lie. It's a long story, and I need to get going. Listen, I'll call you later and tell you how it went, okay?" She paused. "Wish me luck."

At the door, Raymond held her in his arms once more and kissed her gently on the lips. He couldn't help but think about the volcano that was about to erupt as he watched her walk down the driveway. Before long, she'd be on her way to his soon-to-be-loathed-by dear friends, John and Joanne. No longer will he be welcomed in their home. News of his relationship with his daughter would soon spread throughout the town. Fearing the locals' reaction, he knew without a doubt that his relationship with Tammy was going to cost him many more friendships.

His life was about to change forever. He was going to be a father, but not by choice. He only agreed to Tammy moving in with him because it was the right thing to do. In his entire life, he had never lived with a woman. The idea of sharing his world and his private space didn't appeal to him in the slightest. Joanne was right. He was a player. Having a serious relationship—or worse, marriage—scared the hell out of him.

Wondering what he had gotten himself into, he didn't know if he could do it. Raymond questioned why she declined the option to have an abortion. It certainly would have prevented this whole mess. Feeling trapped and pushed into a corner against his will, he couldn't help but feel this was the biggest fuck-up of his life.

Tammy turned and waved one last time as she disappeared from the end of the driveway into the street. He unconsciously waved back, forced a smile, and returned inside to wait for her call.

In no hurry to return home, Tammy spent the afternoon wandering aimlessly around the town, mainly contemplating how she was going to break the news to Joanne. She shuddered at the thought of her likely reaction. After procrastinating for a few hours, she finally found the courage to head home. Once on the front porch, she took a deep breath to calm her rattled nerves before opening the door.

Inside, she found Joanne sitting at the dining room table reading a book.

"Hi, Joanne," Tammy said softly, not wanting to startle her.

Removing her glasses, Joanne looked up. "Hi, hon, how was the library?"

"Oh, I didn't go in the end. Is Andrew taking a nap?"

"Yes, I just put him down." Sensing something was wrong, Joanne looked closer at Tammy. "Are you okay? You look upset."

Tammy joined her at the table. Sitting across from her she realized Joanne knew her too well to try and cover up any more secrets and lies, Tammy knew it was time to tell the truth. "Is Dad home?" she asked, wanting to make sure they were alone before she went any further.

"No, he'll be in his office all day. He has a deadline to meet." Joanne was visibly worried. "What's going on, Tammy?"

Thankful that her father wasn't home, she took the plunge. "Joanne, I have to tell you something." She paused, trying to choose her words carefully. "Well, Dad too, but I want to tell you first. Dad scares me." She chuckled, trying to add a little humor to their otherwise awkward conversation.

Joanne laid down her book, giving Tammy her full attention. "Okay, what's up?"

Trembling to her core with nerves, Tammy extended her arms out on the table and clenched her fists. With a forlorn look, she began her speech for the second time. "There is no easy way to say this, so I'm just going to come out and say it."

"Okay," Joanne said, sounding both concerned and suspicious.

Tammy took another deep breath. "I've been seeing Raymond," she blurted. There, she'd said it. It was now out in the open. Letting out a huge sigh of relief, Tammy felt her body being drained of the all-consuming secret she'd been keeping for months.

They sat in silence while Tammy anxiously waited for any reaction from Joanne. Surprisingly, Joanne didn't flinch a muscle. When she spoke, her tone was flat, measured, and her voice was calm. "Seeing him in what way? Are you friends? Are you dating? Have you had sex with him?"

Tammy hesitated. "I've been seeing him since he took me to the Gold Rush town. And yes, we've had sex." Each time she released another secret, her shoulders felt a little lighter as the weight of the burden continued to drain away.

Joanne remained calm. "I see. Although, I must admit, I've had my suspicions."

"You have?" Since when?" Tammy felt heat rising over her cheeks.

"Since your first outing together. When you came home, you seemed...different. Your mannerism was different, your..." Pausing mid-sentence, she changed her tone, raising it a notch. "Okay, I'll be blunt. You looked like a woman that just had sex."

Shocked by Joanne's raw honesty, Tammy was unable to find any words. She listened to Joanne explain her reasoning.

"I could read triumph and satisfaction all over you. And you walked around with a stupid smirk on your face, acting silly and much happier than usual. In fact, there have been many times you've come home acting that way."

Tammy knew part of her silliness was due to smoking pot. But she'd be happy to keep carrying the weight of that particular secret.

She still had more to tell Joanne. "I'm sorry for lying to you, but I've been afraid to tell you and Dad...especially Dad. The reason I'm telling you now is because I want to move in with Raymond."

Up until now, Joanne had managed to stay calm through Tammy's confessions. It hadn't been easy, but she could feel herself slowly losing control. She had to talk some sense into the girl. "Oh my, Tammy, I wasn't expecting to hear that. Have you talked to Raymond about this?"

"Yes, and you probably figured out some time ago that I wasn't at the library today. I was with him, discussing how I was going to tell you guys."

"I don't understand. Why the rush to move in with him? Do you love him?"

Tammy didn't answer and instead looked down at the table.

"Well, you can't love him if you have to think about it." With a short intake of breath, she suddenly sat bolt upright in her chair. She stiffened her lip and used a sharper tone. "Wait, Tammy. Are you pregnant?"

"Absolutely not!" she said, raising her voice slightly to add drama to her reply. So much for letting go of all the secrets and lies, she thought.

Joanne relaxed back in her chair as her anxieties dropped a few levels. "Well, that's a relief. I can't imagine what this is going to do to your father. He'll probably never want to speak to Raymond again. What was he thinking? He's old enough to be your father, for Christ's sake," she said, shaking her head in disbelief.

"It wasn't entirely his fault, please don't blame him," she begged, squirming slightly in her seat. "We never planned for any of this to happen. It just did. He feels terrible, and he's already quite certain Dad will never speak to him again, but we can't pretend nothing happened."

Joanne was still confused. "Well, why the rush to move in with him? Why upset your father?"

Tammy had to think quickly, her answer needed to sound convincing. "To be honest, I'm tired of sneaking around and lying to you both. To come out and tell you wasn't easy for me, but it needed to be done. And, now that you know, it's going to be too uncomfortable for me to carry on living here. I wouldn't be able to mention his name or talk about him. Besides, I need my independence back. It's been hard living with parents again." Unable to hold back the tears anymore, Tammy's body began to tremble as the sadness she was feeling poured out of her. "We never meant to hurt you or Dad, but we think it would be best if I moved in with him."

Joanne felt her pain and at least showed some sympathy by retrieving a box of tissues from the bookshelf and placing them in front of Tammy. Crying uncontrollably, Tammy pulled out a tissue and hid her face in shame. Knowing she had disappointed the two most important people in her life brought her to a crumbling state. After dabbing her eyes, Tammy spoke, her voice weak. "Thank you. I'm so sorry. I don't know how I'm going to tell Dad. You're much easier to talk to, and look at me, I'm already a wreck."

Seeing the poor girl so distraught, Joanne felt the need to console her. Reaching out, she gave her shoulder a tender squeeze.

"Don't you worry about your father for now, okay? But, I must be honest with you, I think you're making a huge mistake."

Tammy sniffed and looked up. "You do?"

"Yes, I do. You're so young. You've just turned eighteen. You have your whole life ahead of you. You've been in this country for less than a year and you want to be with some guy who is twice your age and move in with him for all the wrong reasons. When you decide you want to share your life with someone, it's because you love them, and want to be with them. You haven't even said you love him. Neither I, nor your father can tell you what to do. I just hope you realize how foolish you're being." Joanne knew her words were harsh, but it was her last attempt to talk some sense into her.

Refusing to make eye contact, Tammy held her head low; listening closely to every word Joanne was saying and knowing they were true.

Joanne's tone became softer. "You know, your father may not show it, but he thinks the world of you and your sisters. He feels guilty for being away so much when you were younger. He has always wanted the best for all of you. He's haunted by Donna's disappearance and blames himself entirely."

"Why does he blame himself?" Tammy asked, finally looking at Joanne.

Joanne leaned forward. "Think about it. If he had never brought Donna to the States, she wouldn't have run away."

Tammy never realized how much her father was hurting. He was not one to express his emotions, but strangely enough, it appeared he had shared some of his feelings with Joanne. Tammy knew she would be adding to his pain by moving in with not just a guy, but a man he had trusted. A man he thought was his friend but was now dating his youngest daughter. Tammy couldn't suppress the guilt descending on her conscience. She couldn't deny her fear of possibly becoming estranged from her father. But what choice did she have? She was pregnant with Raymond's child.

Joanne interrupted Tammy's internal dialogue. "And I hate to tell you this, but your dad will probably blame himself for this too."

"Why would you say that?" Tammy asked, confused by her remark.

"Because he brought you here, just like Donna, and he introduced you to Raymond."

"I'm sorry, I just don't know what else to do. I want to keep seeing Raymond, but I can't if I continue to live here. It's not Dad's fault and I don't want him to think it is."

"I know, sweetheart, and if this is what you really want then, well, we can't stop you." Joanne reached out and gently squeezed her arm. "Leave it to me. I'll talk to your father."

"You will?" Tammy questioned, surprised by her gesture.

"Yes, I will. But, honestly, I don't think you should be here when I do."

"You don't? Why not?"

"Because I don't want your dad to say something to you that he may regret. I'm not sure how he's going to react to all this. Why don't you go back to Raymond's tonight? You can call me in the morning after your dad has left for the office. I think that will be best."

"Joanne, I hate to leave this all up to you. I've made such a mess of everything." Unable to control another wave of tears, Tammy reached for a dry tissue from the box.

Caving into Tammy's distraught manner, Joanne left her seat to console her. Tammy stood, reaching out with her arms to welcome her caring hug.

"Shhh, it's okay, everything will be okay," Joanne said, stroking Tammy's freshly mangled hair.

Rising from her tears, Tammy shook her head to compose herself. "Thanks for everything. I love you," she told Joanne.

"I love you too. Now, Andrew will be waking up soon. Why don't you go pack a bag and head over to Raymond's? I'll speak to you in the morning."

Without hesitation, fearing her father may soon return, Tammy hastily grabbed a few things from her room, said goodbye, and left.

On the other side of the closed door, Tammy's emotions peaked. Thinking of the terrible possibilities that lay ahead and slowly becoming hysterical, she sprinted through town, oblivious to the innocent members of public she mowed down along the way. Thankfully, her tears shielded her from the startled looks of disgust on the faces of those in her path.

She arrived at Raymond's in just eight minutes, exhausted and out of breath. Relieved to find the door unlocked, Tammy rushed inside.

"Raymond! Raymond! Are you here?" she yelled, kicking the door closed with her foot and throwing her bags on the dining room table.

Alarmed and scared, Raymond came rushing down the hallway. Meeting him halfway, Tammy raced into his arms. "Oh, Raymond, I've made such a bloody mess of things."

Raymond tried to console her as she continued to cry heavily on his shoulder. "Hey now, calm down. Tell me what happened," he said in a soothing voice.

Letting her tears subside, Tammy wiped her reddened eyes on

her sleeve, pulled herself together, and began telling Raymond about her conversation with Joanne.

"It was horrible and I feel bloody awful about everything. Joanne offered to tell my dad. I couldn't say no," Tammy confessed. "She also thought it would be best if I stayed here for the night. I hope that's okay?"

"Of course it's okay. You don't have to ask me. Do you want a beer?" Raymond asked, craving one himself.

"I shouldn't really, because of the baby, but it will help calm my nerves," she replied.

Taking a seat on the couch, Tammy leaned back and closed her eyes. After grabbing two beers from the kitchen, Raymond placed them on the coffee table and joined her. He stared at her with pity. She looked lost and withdrawn. Wrapping his arm around her shoulder, he was glad to see Tammy welcomed the hug and leaned into his body, resting her head on his chest.

Embraced together in silence, they consoled each other while trying to process the current events unfolding in their lives. Both unsure of their futures and questioning their now fragile relationship with Tammy's father, they were feeling ashamed and embarrassed. Tammy fearing she may lose her father and Raymond wondering how he could ever face John again. His once great friendship was now dissolved because of his stupid, selfish actions. He knew John would never be able to forgive him. Neither Tammy nor Raymond chose to share their private concerns with each other. Instead, they remained somber and quiet until it was time to go to bed.

After a restless night of worry, Tammy woke early the next morning. Being careful not to wake Raymond, she tiptoed across the bedroom and wrapped herself in his bathrobe before going to make coffee. She was thinking, by now, Joanne had probably told her dad everything. So many questions ran through Tammy's mind. How did he take it? Should she call him? Will he call her?

Tired of the miserable rut she was in, Tammy forced herself to take a shower and then dressed herself in jeans and a blue tank top. Feely mildly better, she focused on calling Joanne after Raymond had left. She was anxious to hear how her father had reacted, although she feared the worst.

Soon, Raymond was up and talking business on the phone in his office. Tammy kept herself busy by cleaning the kitchen. A half- hour later, he came out of the office and grabbed his jacket from the back of one of the chairs. "I have to go do an estimate. I'll be back in a couple of hours," he told her as he headed toward the front door.

"That's fine. I'll probably still be here when you get back," she replied, ushering him out.

Mid-stride, Raymond turned and gave her a quick peck on the cheek. Tammy returned the gesture and watched him scurry to his truck.

Within minutes of him leaving, Tammy raced to the office, sat at the desk, and dialed her father's house number, praying it wouldn't be him that answered. Holding her breath, she listened to the phone ring a few times and then, to her relief, she heard Joanne's voice. "Hello."

Tammy relaxed and exhaled. "Hi, Joanne, it's Tammy."

"Hi, hon," Joanne said softly.

Not wanting to deal with small talk, Tammy cut to the chase. "Did you talk to Dad?" she asked, anxiously gripping the phone with both hands.

Joanne's voice was flat, telling her what she had feared. "Yes, I did speak to him. I'm not going to lie to you, your father's upset. And, like I suspected, he blames Raymond far more than you. He thinks you're young and naive, but that doesn't mean to say he's not upset with you as well. I won't repeat what he called Raymond —it'll only upset you—but I must say, in all the years I've been with your father, I've never heard him use such language before."

Tammy began to fret. If her father had such hatred based only on the relationship, how was she ever going to tell him about the baby? "What should I do?" Tammy asked. "Should I come over there or should I call him on the phone?"

Joanne sighed. "Well, your father doesn't want to see you right now."

"What?"

"He needs to calm down and accept this in his own time. It may take him a while and, if I were you, I wouldn't rush him. Let him call you when he's ready."

Tammy couldn't believe her father didn't want to see her. "Does he hate me?"

"No, he doesn't hate you. You're his daughter. He's just upset right now. He'll come around eventually. Just give him some time."

Tammy was astonished. She didn't realize how much this was going to hurt her father. Their relationship had always been good and they'd never experienced any conflicts, up until now. Lost in her thoughts, Tammy's head buzzed with questions and fears. Mainly, she feared her father would never forgive her.

"Tammy, are you still there?"

"Yeah, I'm still here," Tammy replied in a solemn voice.

"What shall I do about your things? Your father won't be home until tonight, so you can come by and get them any time before then." Joanne's voice became stern. "But I must ask, out of respect for your dad, that Raymond does not come in the house."

"I understand." Tammy had another thought. "Should I call before coming over?"

"Yes, I think it would be best." There was silence. "Tammy, are you okay?"

Tammy held back her tears. "No, I'm not okay. I didn't mean to hurt you or Dad, and I'm truly sorry. Will you tell him that and tell him I love him? I need to go. I'll call you later."

"Okay. You take care of yourself. We love you, too," Joanne told her, knowing she needed to hear it.

After Tammy hung up the phone, she leaned over the desk and buried her tearstained face in her folded arms.

Later that afternoon, when Raymond returned, they spoke about her conversation with Joanne. For Raymond, it was now real—John had ended their friendship. But he hadn't expected him to take such actions with his daughter. He agreed with Joanne that Tammy just needed to give her father some time.

After Raymond had been updated, Tammy called Joanne to let her know they were on their way to pick up her things. Joanne reminded her again that she must collect her belongings on her own.

Leaving Raymond in the truck, Tammy approached the front door of her father's house. Strangely, it no longer felt like home. Wondering if she should knock, Tammy paused for a moment. Deciding against it, she slowly turned the doorknob and let herself in. Feeling awkward and alienated, Tammy wanted this to be over with as soon as possible. She spotted Joanne, her back toward her, watering plants at the dining room window. "Hi, Joanne."

Joanne turned, placing the green watering can on the table and crossed the room to meet her. "Hi, sweetie, you okay?" Joanne asked while giving her a hug.

Tammy lied. "Yeah, I'm fine."

Reaching behind the kitchen door, Joanne handed Tammy some canvas bags. "Here, you can use these to put your things in."

"Thanks," Tammy said softly before heading to what was now her old room. Thankful she didn't have much to pack, Tammy crammed her belongings in two bags with speed and returned to the dining room with a bag in each hand.

Approaching the table, where Joanne was reading a book to Andrew in her lap, Tammy placed the bags at her feet. "I'm all done. Can I ask you something?"

Joanne removed her glasses. "Sure. What is it?"

Even though Tammy was apprehensive, she had to ask. "I know Dad doesn't want to see me right now, and I respect that, but would it be possible to come visit you and Andrew when he's not home?"

Joanne gave her a smile. "I don't see why not. Why don't you call me in a few days after things have settled down and we'll see what we can arrange. Okay?"

With Andrew still in her lap, Joanne remained seated. Tammy leaned over and gave her a hug. "Thanks, I will." Crouching down lower, she squeezed her brother's cheek. "Bye, little guy. I'll see you soon," she promised.

Joanne took her hand. "You take care of yourself and remember we both love you. Your father just needs some time to adjust."

Shaken, Tammy could only manage a nod. She retrieved her bags and left out the front door, closing it quickly behind her to prevent Joanne from seeing her shiny, wet eyes.

Once in the truck, her tears fell endlessly. Not knowing what to do, Raymond reached over and held her tight. Tammy cried hard, releasing the pain, the regrets of her actions, and the unknowns of her future. When she had no more tears to shed, she released herself from Raymond's arms, leaned back in her seat and stared out of the window, mellowing deep in her own thoughts. If she had stayed in England, none of this would have happened. She wouldn't be pregnant and she would still have a relationship with her father. Filled with guilt and remorse, Tammy wondered if coming to the States was a mistake.

CHAPTER 18

*L*iving with Raymond was not how Tammy had imagined. She'd rarely seen him in the six weeks since she'd moved in. Within days, he had thrown himself into his work, leaving at the crack of dawn and not returning until after dark. It almost felt like he was purposely avoiding her. Rarely did they speak. With no affection or lovemaking between them, the relationship had turned dry and they both knew they were only together because of the baby.

Realizing Joanne had been right, Tammy knew she was with Raymond for all the wrong reasons. She'd let panic and fear guide her and had made the wrong decisions as a result. With the benefit of hindsight, Tammy now realized telling Raymond she loved him was a mistake—fueled only by emotions and impulse—when what they had really shared was nothing more than pure lust. Sneaking around, lying, and the thrill of doing the forbidden, along with the risk of getting caught, had added danger and excitement to their newly founded affair. They smoked a lot of pot, laughed a lot, and had a lot of sex. In the early days, they had enjoyed the peril that came with the relationship.

Tammy had not spoken to her father in over six weeks. Each time the phone rang, her heart skipped a beat in the hopes that it was him. But it never was. She missed him being in her life. She missed being his daughter.

Guessing she was ten or twelve weeks pregnant, Tammy had growing concerns that she hadn't yet seen a doctor for confirmation or the well-being of the baby. Still trying to protect his image, Raymond had insisted they see a doctor in one of the larger towns, south of Lonesridge. The nearest one was about an hour away. With the promise that he would take her soon, Tammy avoided asking him again.

Raymond showed little interest in the baby. He never expressed any sense of joy or excitement, and rarely did he ask how she and the baby were doing. In her heart, Tammy knew it was over. But she was stuck; she had nowhere else to go. She was just buying time until she could figure out what to do next.

After moping around one morning, still dressed in her blue bathrobe and slippers, Tammy decided she was going to make her day constructive. Letting out a groan, she pulled herself up from the couch. With her body feeling suddenly heavy, her legs weak and numb, she used the arm of the couch to stabilize herself before heading to the bathroom to take a shower.

Overcome with dizziness, she rested at the kitchen counter. A sharp, cramping pain in her abdomen caused Tammy to hold her stomach while straining to make it the rest of the way.

She slowly lowered her body into a sitting position on the closed toilet seat. Assuming the pain was part of the pregnancy, Tammy rested her head on her knees, hoping it would ease the pain. "It'll soon pass," she told herself. But it didn't. She began to panic. Something wasn't right. Beads of sweat formed on her brow. Her sweaty palms itched. In need of a towel, she slowly stood up. That's when she saw the blood on the seat of the toilet. Horrified, she looked down at her body and saw the large patch of soiled blood on her nightgown. Trickles of red liquid ran down the insides of her legs and spotted the floor around her feet.

"Oh my god! I'm losing the baby!" Tammy cried.

Overcome with fear and exhaustion from the emotions ripping through her body, Tammy fell to her knees and wept. She wished she weren't alone. Over her tears, she heard the phone ring from the office. Was it Raymond? Knowing she wouldn't be able to make it before the answering machine came on, Tammy managed to calm herself down and subside her breathing so she could focus on listening instead.

After four rings, the machine clicked on and asked the caller to leave a message.

Tammy held her breath. Will they leave a message?

She heard a cough and then... "Hi, Tammy, it's your dad." He spoke in a cold, stiff voice, expressing no emotion.

"Daddy! Oh my god, it's my dad!" Tammy screamed, knowing he couldn't hear her because she couldn't get to the phone. She strained her ears to listen to the rest of his message.

"Your papers came in from immigration and you have an interview with them in two weeks in San Francisco. Because I'm your sponsor, I'll need to accompany you. Joanne has all the details regarding the date and time, so I'd appreciate it if you would give her a call. Goodbye."

The answer machine sounded a final beep, followed by silence.

Hearing that her father hadn't asked how she was and said he wanted her to call Joanne and not him, made Tammy realize he was still angry. If it weren't for the immigration issue, he would never have called.

With increasing pains and nausea, Tammy managed to crawl to the toilet and raise the lid. Still on her knees, she held her gut while she retched violently into the bowl. With great effort and through her agony, Tammy found the strength to run a hot bath. She crawled into the tub to soak her exhausted and bloodied body, hoping to ease the excruciating pain. Being engulfed in the soothing warm water brought a sense of calmness and slowly washed away her aches and pains until she drifted off to sleep.

Having lost all sense of time, the chilled water woke her with a start. Shivering but now with less pain, Tammy stepped out of the bathtub, being careful to avoid the bloody towels strewn across the floor. Her trembling legs still felt weak beneath her as she wrapped herself in a clean towel and slowly made her way to the darkened bedroom to lie down.

CHAPTER 19

Returning home at dusk, Raymond questioned why the house was in complete darkness. He flicked on the light by the front door and threw his keys on the dining room table, surveying the apparently empty duplex. "Tammy, are you home?"

Greeted by silence, Raymond didn't know what to think. Where could she be? She has nowhere else to go. Concerned, he headed to check the bathroom and bedroom. He turned on the light in the darkened bathroom and gasped when he saw the bloody towels scattered in disarray across the floor. Fear and anxiety swept through him. "Tammy!" he yelled. There was no answer. "Tammy!" Still, no answer. Fearing the worst, he stepped away from the bathroom, took a deep breath, and prepared himself for something bad as he made his way toward the bedroom.

Like the rest of the house, the room was dark. He fumbled for the light switch, found it and turned it on, instantly relieved to see Tammy's outline curled under the covers. Not wanting to startle her, Raymond tiptoed across the room, crouched down beside her, and gently shook her shoulder. "Tammy, it's me, Raymond," he whispered. She didn't move. "Tammy," he said, louder this time. "Tammy, wake up! Are you okay?"

Tammy began to stir from her deep sleep. Opening her eyes slowly, she felt the warmth of Raymond's breath on her cheek.

"Are you okay?" Raymond asked again as he brushed the mop of damp hair from her face.

Grabbing his hand, Tammy buried her face in his palm. "No. Raymond, I lost the baby." That was all she managed to say before bursting into tears.

Raymond was alarmed by her news. "My god! What...how... are you okay?" he stammered in confusion as he lay down next to her. He cradled her in his arms, holding her tenderly while she pressed her face against his chest and wept uncontrollably.

It took Tammy a few minutes to compose herself before she was able to talk.

Raymond pulled himself up to a sitting position while still holding her. "Do you need to go see a doctor?" he asked.

Tammy shook her head. "No, I'm okay. It was early in the pregnancy. I should be fine. I managed to take a hot bath and sleep most of the day." Shedding more tears, Tammy gripped Raymond's arm and squeezed it tight. "Oh, Raymond, it was awful. I felt so scared. There was nothing I could do. I feel terrible. It's all my fault. The baby didn't feel wanted. I showed it no love and that's why it left me."

"Hey now, don't be so hard on yourself. It wasn't your fault at all. Unfortunately, these things happen," he said, trying to reassure her. "Hey, do you want a cup of tea?"

The thought comforted Tammy. "Sure, that sounds good. Thanks."

Before leaving, he helped her up to a sitting position and puffed up the pillows behind her back and neck. "There. How's that?" he asked. "Want to watch some TV?" He grabbed the remote from the dresser as he walked by and aimed it at the television. "It will help take your mind off all this crap," he said. Once the TV came on, he tossed the remote to Tammy. "Watch whatever you want. I'll back in a few minutes."

As promised, Raymond returned a few minutes later with a hot cup of tea and placed it on the bedside table. Tammy smiled and leaned over to retrieve the mug, feeling the warmth as she cradled it in her hands. After taking a sip, she closed her eyes and lay back, letting the calming tea soothe her. Mother was right, Tammy thought to herself; she always used to say, "Never underestimate the power of a cup of tea."

Raymond joined Tammy on the bed and cradled her in his arms again. Both lost in their own thoughts and saddened by the events of the day, they lay together in silence. In addition to the guilt that was consuming her, Tammy was feeling a huge void. One she knew could never be filled.

Keeping his thoughts to himself—mainly because he was too ashamed to admit them—he was feeling a sense of relief that Tammy had lost the baby. He'd never imagined himself as a father or family man.

Tammy interrupted his shameful thoughts, speaking in a soft whisper. "My dad called today."

Alarmed, Raymond sat up to face her. "He did? What did he say?"

"I didn't speak to him. I was in the bathroom and couldn't get to the phone in time, but I heard him over the answering machine."

Raymond was getting impatient. "And?"

"He only called to let me know I have an interview with immigration in two weeks and that he must go with me. He wants me to call Joanne and make arrangements with her." Tammy raised her voice, slightly. "Not *him* I might add. He specifically said Joanne. He doesn't care about me. If it wasn't for the interview, he would never have called."

"Well that's good news, isn't it? You've been waiting a long time for an interview." Raymond paused. "At least you won't have to tell him about the baby."

Infuriated by his remark, Tammy raised her voice. "God, Raymond, you are so fucking insensitive! Is that all you care about? Your reputation with my dad? Don't you get it? He hates you. You fucked his youngest daughter! It doesn't matter that I don't have to tell him about the baby. It still won't change the fact that he ended his friendship with you, and trust me, he will *never* forgive you."

Tammy threw the empty cup hard on the floor next to the bed and heard it shatter. She flung the blankets away from her body, pulled herself up, and slid off the bed in a string of deliberately dramatic movements. Placing her hands on her hips, she glared at Raymond. "Are you not the least bit upset that we lost the baby? Or are you relieved, Raymond? Tell me the truth," she snarled at him.

Startled by her sudden anger and with chilling thoughts of what might happen if he told her the truth, he quickly uttered, "I was getting used to the idea of being a father. Yes, granted, I wasn't overjoyed when you first told me. I was in shock. You have to admit, neither one of us planned or remotely thought this would ever happen." He sat nervously on the edge of the bed, anxiously waiting for her next outburst.

Not knowing whether to believe him or not and still consumed with anger, she stormed over to the closet, grabbed her bathrobe from the door, wrapped it around herself, and jerked the belt into a tight knot. "I'm going out on the deck. I need some fresh air." Without looking back, she stormed out of the bedroom and slammed the door behind her.

Feeling a slight breeze from the evening skies, Tammy sat quietly on the wooden chair as she tried to calm down. Leaves ruffled above her head in the surrounding trees and in the distance, she heard the occasional car drive by on the highway. Thinking about how much she had fucked everything up and how fucked up her entire life was in general; she felt her mood transitioning into a depressive state. Not knowing what to do next, Tammy stared aimlessly at the full moon above her.

The squeaking sound of the screen door behind her interrupted her thoughts. Glancing over her shoulder, she saw Raymond precariously holding two glasses of red wine.

"Hey, thought you might like a glass of wine," he said. "It might make you feel better."

Having finally calmed down after her explosive exit, Tammy appreciated his caring gesture and gladly took a glass. "Thank you," she said in a much friendlier tone.

Taking baby steps, not quite sure of her mood, Raymond eased himself slowly into the deck chair beside her and took a sip of his drink before placing his hand gently on her knee. "I'm sorry if I upset you," he said. "I didn't mean to, and yes, you're right about your father. He'll never forgive me. I'm trying to wrap my head around it. We've been friends for so long."

Taking his hand in hers, Tammy gave it a slight squeeze, followed by a tender kiss, knowing he was trying his best to comfort her.

"I'm sorry too," she said. "I was feeling alone and scared. I was angry because you weren't here when I was losing the baby." Not wanting to start another argument, Tammy quickly added. "But it's not your fault. How were you to know?" Tammy paused, thinking carefully about her next words. "And, to be completely honest, I don't know what's going to happen between us now. We both know the only reason I moved in with you is because of the baby. I wouldn't be here if I hadn't got pregnant. Now that I'm not, where does that leave us?"

Raymond stood up and squeezed her hand, followed by a tug, gesturing her to follow him. "Let's not get into that now. You need your rest," he said with a kind smile. "Why don't you crawl back into bed, watch a movie, and I'll bring you some nice warm chicken soup, okay?"

Knowing he was right, Tammy wasn't going to argue. She

gladly took his advice and followed him to the bedroom, carrying the glass of wine in her free hand. Noticing Raymond had cleaned up the shattered cup from the floor, she set her glass next to his on the end table and waited for him to rearrange her pillows before crawling back into bed.

Once she was settled, Raymond leaned over and kissed her gently on the forehead, whispering softly, "Everything will be okay. You're not going anywhere. Stop worrying so much and concentrate on getting better."

Tammy managed a little smile and nodded as she rested her tired body against the pillows. She had her doubts that they would remain together but was too exhausted to argue. Only time would tell, she thought.

Unable to shake the huge void that had taken over her life since losing the baby, Tammy plummeted into a depressive rut. She mourned in bed for two days straight. Raymond tried persistently to raise her spirits with words of encouragement and affection, but all to no avail. Any hopes of their relationship returning to normal seemed like a distant dream.

During the first few days, words of anger and hate fired back and forth between them, only to be regretted soon after. Clinging to the belief that, over time, their passion would return, the anger began to subside and both made the attempt to be civil to one another, agreeing to work through the emotions as and when they arose.

By day four, Tammy was beginning to feel a little better. Physically, much of her strength had returned and her appetite was improving. Finally pulling herself out of her depressive state, she told Raymond of her plans as he served her coffee on the deck. "I think I should try calling my dad today," she said casually as he took a seat next to her. "It's been four days since he called. What do you think?"

Raymond didn't hesitate to answer. Even though there was no hope for him and John to reconcile, he desperately wanted to see Tammy and her father make amends. "I think it's a great idea. I have to go look at a job after this cup of coffee, so you'll have the whole place to yourself to talk to him."

Tammy shifted in her seat. "He actually wants me to speak to Joanne, but if he answers, then we'll be forced to speak to each other. I need him in my life. As nervous as I am, I hope he is able to forgive me."

Raymond reached over and stroked her hand. "I'm sure when he hears your voice, all will be forgiven."

After Raymond left, Tammy paced the living room until she finally felt she had the courage to call her father. Summoning all her strength, she marched over to the dining room table, picked up the phone, and dialed his number.

After five rings, Joanne answered the phone. Subconsciously, Tammy let out a sigh of relief.

"Hello, Joanne speaking."

"Hi, Joanne, it's Tammy. How are you?"

"Hey, Tammy, I'm good, how about yourself?"

"I'm good," Tammy lied. "Dad called here a few days ago. He mentioned something about immigration and asked if I would call you."

"Yes. Apparently, you have an interview with them in about a week and a half. Your father needs to go with you. Hold on a second, let me find the letter and give you the date and time."

Tammy heard a clunk as Joanne put down the phone.

A few minutes later, she came back on the line. Tammy could hear papers being ruffled. "Hi, Tammy, are you still there?"

"Yes I'm still here."

"I have the letter. It states your interview is in ten days at two o'clock in San Francisco. It's going to take you guys at least three hours to drive there. I'd be here at the house no later than ten in the morning," Joanne said.

"Wait. Just Dad and I are going?" Tammy questioned, feeling a rush of panic.

"Well, yes, Tammy. I have Andrew, so I can't go."

Tammy shuddered at the thought of the grueling three-hour car ride alone with her father. "Well, that's going to be awkward. I haven't spoken to him since I moved out. What am I supposed to say? Hi, Dad, I missed you," she said, sarcastically.

"Don't overthink it, Tammy. You'll be fine. It's probably just what you guys need, you know, to work things out with each other."

"I'm not sure. Dad's pretty stubborn. I hope you're right."

"I hope I am, too," Joanne replied, sighing. "Sorry, I have to go. I hear Andrew waking up. We'll see you next week. Remember, we love you."

"Love you, too. Bye," Tammy said before hanging up the phone.

Taking Joanne's advice, Tammy refused to dwell on the trip to San Francisco with her father. Instead, she focused all her energy on the interview and tried to prepare herself for possible questions they may ask. She couldn't believe that after almost a year of waiting, she may soon be granted a green card. A status that would open the door to many opportunities; learning to drive, getting a job, and buying a car were just a few that came to mind.

By the morning of the interview, she had all her immigration papers in order, including her passport and visa. She chose to wear a sophisticated black knee-length skirt and a white shirt with black pumps. She wore little makeup and a simple gold chain around her neck with a matching chain around her wrist.

Having still not spoken to her father, Tammy didn't want to make matters worse by having Raymond drive her to his house. The thought of them bumping into each other terrified her. So, to avoid any potential confrontations, she thought it would be best to walk there. A fight would be the last thing she needed on such an important day.

The walk to her father's house started out pleasant. She felt excited but nervous, and spent some much needed quiet time gathering her thoughts. It was almost springtime with no clouds in the sky, and the air was completely still. Trees were beginning to bud and traces of flowers were already blooming. But, as Tammy neared her father's house, her mood began to change. Dreading the moment she would be face to face with her father, she felt her heart racing against her chest and her palms were beginning to sweat. Unanswered questions were spinning around in her head. What would she say to him? How was he going to act toward her? Tammy hated to admit it but, at this moment, she felt petrified of her father for the first time.

As she approached the front door, Tammy took a deep breath and hesitated before knocking. She tapped the door three times and heard Joanne shout from inside. "It's open."

Tammy slowly opened the door, trying to ignore the fact that her palms were so moist that they just slid off the handle. Joanne was sitting at the dining room table with a cup of coffee and the newspaper, dressed in a casual navy blue sweat suit. Andrew sat next to her in his high chair eating Cheerios. He smiled at Tammy as she approached them.

"Hey, Tammy, you look nice. Want some coffee? Your dad is still upstairs."

"Sure, that would be great. Thanks," Tammy said as she took a seat next to Andrew while Joanne scurried off to the kitchen.

"How have you been?" Joanne asked, returning with coffee in hand.

Once again, Tammy had to lie. "Good. How about yourself?"

"Oh, fine. Your dad shouldn't be too much longer."

"I wish you were coming with us, Joanne."

"Why?"

"Because Dad is still mad at me and we haven't spoken since I moved out. It's going to be so uncomfortable riding with him in a car for three hours," Tammy said, shuddering.

Joanne chose her words carefully. She wanted Tammy to see the positive side of the situation. "Hon, it just might be what the two of you need. You'll be forced to talk to each other and hopefully work everything out so you can be father and daughter again. Sometimes, when you're forced into an uncomfortable situation, it makes you face your fears," Joanne said. She then added some humor in an attempt to lighten the mood. "The problem is, you and your father are too much alike. You're both stubborn."

Tammy managed a half-smile. "I know. It's just that Dad is so angry, and I don't know how to deal with him."

"Yes, he's angry, and I can't say I blame him. But the bottom line is, you're his daughter, no matter what, and he stills loves you very much."

"I know and I love him too. I just don't know how to deal with this ." Tammy paused "Any suggestions?"

"No, Tammy, I don't. When the time is right, you'll know what to say."

Hoping for more advice, Tammy was about to drill her with further questions when she heard footsteps descending the stairs.

"Shit! He's coming," Tammy said in a panic. Suddenly feeling awkward, Tammy stood to greet him, shifting on her feet, unsure of how to stand. Ignoring the sound of her pulse pounding in her ears, she waited in silence for her father to appear.

He paused at the bottom of the stairs, looking sharp in a gray suit and matching tie with a white shirt and shiny black dress shoes. Saying nothing, he gave Tammy a frigid stare.

Feeling herself shrink in size, Tammy was already finding the silence between them unbearable. To avoid his piercing stare, she turned to Andrew for a distraction.

Her father cleared his throat before speaking—something he has always done when he felt uncomfortable. "Are you ready to go?" he asked in a flat tone.

"Yes," Tammy answered.

~

For the first hour, they rode in silence. The tension between them was intense. Her father looked straight ahead at the road in front, oblivious to her presence. Tammy couldn't remember a time in her life when she had felt so disquieted. With her arms crossed and her head turned away, she stared out of her window, frozen, afraid to move or speak.

A feeling of defeat began to creep over Tammy as she realized she might be unable to fix her broken relationship with her father. Then, she remembered what Joanne had said to her; when the time is right, you'll know what to say. All she wanted was for her father to feel proud of her again. She missed the sparkle in his eyes and his smile when he saw her. She missed asking him for advice. She needed her father and desperately wanted him back in her life more than anything.

It was like a switch just went off in her head. Tammy finally understood. She said it to herself one more time; she missed having her father in her life more than anything—that was it! Why hadn't she thought of this before? She needed him much more than she needed Raymond. Tammy realized what she had to do. She knew how to get her father back. It all made sense now. She didn't want to think about whether she was doing the right thing or not; she wanted to act on it now before she lost her courage and gave in to her cowardice.

Smiling, Tammy sat up tall and turned to her father. "Dad, I want to come back home." She held her breath, anticipating his response.

To her dismay, he said nothing. Not even a flinch. He just stared at the road ahead.

"Dad, did you hear me?"

Rarely did her father show emotion, and she wasn't expecting anything different now, but she had hoped for something more than silence.

In his own callous way, not taking his eyes off the road, he finally spoke. "I heard you, Tammy, and I must say I'm pleased to hear you've come to your senses at last." With a slight turn of his head, he flashed a weak smile at her.

For Tammy, the subtle smile meant the world. She felt triumphant. It broke the barrier and put her at ease in an instant.

"I'm not going to ask any questions as to why you've decided to come home," he said. "I'm just happy to hear you are."

As Tammy predicted, her father was straight to the point. She knew he didn't need to hear the details of her relationship with Raymond—thank goodness. It was enough for him to know it was now over and they could begin picking up the pieces of their shattered relationship.

John's face gradually became alive again with brighter eyes and a placid grin. The tension between them had weakened. Tammy knew she had her father back and, for the first time in a long time, she knew she had made the right decision. As their journey progressed, so did their relationship. Conversations of Tammy's plans, if granted a green card, were discussed along with her father offering driving lessons and Tammy's enthusiasm to look for a job. By the time they reached San Francisco, Tammy was feeling more confident about their relationship. As the car came to a halt, she told him she would pack that night and move back home the next day.

Tammy spent two hours with the immigration officers. A grueling period of time spent going through various papers and answering a whole host of questions. When did she arrive? Where was she staying? Did she have any children? That question had been a tough one to answer. No wonder it had taken her so long to get an interview, she thought, if this is how much time they spent with each person trying to gain entry to the country. With the interrogation finally complete, she was overjoyed when the officer said she was going to be granted a green card. Now she could begin getting her life back on track.

On the way home, they stopped for dinner at a restaurant and were back in Lonesridge by early evening. Not wanting to risk spoiling her father's mood by asking him to drop her off at Raymond's, Tammy made the excuse that she had to go to the market and would be happy to walk home. Before exiting the car, she gave her father a light peck on the cheek. "I love you, Dad."

"I love you too, Tammy."

The words brought music to her ears. She never wanted to forget how good they made her feel. Right at that moment, she promised herself that she would never do anything to jeopardize her precious relationship with her father ever again.

Walking up the silent, darkened driveway toward Raymond's house, Tammy felt confident in her decision and suffered no guilt about leaving him. After spending the day with her father, she knew she was doing the right thing. Joanne was right—that car ride was just what they'd needed.

As she approached the front door, she heard the TV blasting from inside. Letting herself in, Tammy found Raymond sitting in the lounge chair drinking a beer and looking overly relaxed watching a western. The smell of pot lingering in the air served as an explanation as to his placid state.

Hearing the door close, Raymond turned his head and greeted Tammy with a goofy grin—one that is only manageable after smoking marijuana. "Hey, Tammy, how'd it go?"

After tossing her purse on the table, she took a seat on the couch, lit a cigarette, and inhaled deeply before answering. "It went great. They granted me a green card, so I'm now officially a permanent resident of the United States of America!" she said, smiling.

In a toast, Raymond held up his beer. "That's fantastic!

Congratulations. Do you want a beer to celebrate?"

"No thanks." Stalling for a few seconds, Tammy took another hit off her cigarette. "Raymond, I've been thinking. I think it's best if I move back in with my dad."

Tammy waited for his reaction. He didn't seem upset or look like he wanted to argue with her. He simply nodded in agreement. "Well, if that's what you want, I can't stop you." He took a sip of his beer. "I guess you and your father are okay now?"

Thankful that Raymond wasn't making her decision difficult, Tammy felt at ease explaining her reasons for wanting to leave. "For the first hour, we didn't talk or even make eye contact. It was bloody awful. I hadn't realized how much I'd hurt him until we were alone in the car together. Seeing nothing but anger and shame in his eyes tore me apart. And then, it just hit me. As soon as I told him I wanted to come back home, we began talking again." Tammy drained the last of her cigarette and stubbed it out. "We both know it's over between us. It has been since I lost the baby. It's the only reason I moved in here, but when I did, it changed everything. It's just neither one of us wanted to admit it."

Without interrupting, Raymond nodded in silence. He knew she was right and admired her for being braver than he would have been if he were in her shoes. He was happy to hear that her and John were now speaking and picking up the pieces, but in the same breath, he knew his friendship with John could never be repaired. For that, he was deeply sorry.

Showing no hard feelings, Raymond gave Tammy a friendly smile. "You're right. Things have changed between us. I just didn't want to admit it. I do have to say, though, I'm going to miss you. I didn't think I could live with someone, but you proved me wrong. It's going to be awfully quiet around here." He took another sip of beer. "When do you plan on leaving?"

"To avoid any awkward moments, I thought about having Joanne pick me up tomorrow while you're at work. Is that okay with you?" Tammy asked.

"That's fine. I understand. I'm curious, though. Did your father say anything about me while you were with him?"

"No, he didn't, and I was afraid to mention your name. I was thrilled when we began talking again and didn't want to say anything to jeopardize it. I'm sorry our little fling cost you your friendship with my dad. Maybe, over time, you guys will be able to work things out."

Raymond shook his head. "I doubt it. I don't think he could ever look me in the face again without being reminded that I slept with his daughter. To be honest, if I were a father, I'd feel the same way. I could forgive her but not the guy. I'd always blame him for seducing my daughter. I can't say I blame your dad. He's acting like any father should."

"Do you want me to talk to him?" Tammy asked.

Her gesture surprised him. "Oh God, no. Just let it be. The damage is already done, but thanks for asking."

Tammy left the couch and walked over to her now ex-lover, still sitting in the chair. With a friendly smile, she leaned over and embraced him.

"No hard feelings?" she asked.

"None. I'm good. It was just a matter of time until this happened, and I'm fine with it."

"Thanks. Me too. I'd better go pack. I want to call Joanne early so I can spend the afternoon looking for a job."

"Wow, you're not messing around, are you?"

Tammy laughed. "Ha! I've been messing around since I got here, but in the wrong way."

Raymond chuckled at her joke and watched her as she headed toward the bedroom. No doubt he was going to miss her, but he was going to miss John's friendship even more. He had always thought very highly of the man and was proud to have called him a friend. Feeling disgraced with himself, he sunk lower into the chair and chugged down the rest of his beer.

CHAPTER 23

It seemed life in the States was finally smoothing out for Tammy after her reckless beginnings with Raymond. It'd been a year since their break up. Having no regrets or remorse; she couldn't be happier. Still living with her father and Joanne, it felt good to have no secrets and to not have to constantly be telling lies. Raymond was a thing of the past. His name was never mentioned and sadly, her father never rekindled his friendship with him.

Occasionally, Tammy would bump into Raymond in town. Each time with a different woman on his arm. He seemed content to have his old life back. With no hard feelings, they would always take time to say hello and make small talk.

For Tammy and her father, it was like old times. Their relationship slowly repaired itself. Together, they discussed her plans and her father expressed his desire for her to go to college. Tammy had agreed, but she also confessed she wanted to postpone it for a while so she could look for work. It had been a long time since she had earned an income and she yearned for some independence.

Within two months of receiving her green card, Tammy had

passed her driver's test. It changed everything for her. Under the condition that she soon buy her own car, Tammy's father loaned her one of his. Being back on the open road gave Tammy the most freedom she had experienced since arriving in the States.

Wasting no time, Tammy found a job as a waitress at the local hotel. Her previous experience proved invaluable; it helped her secure the job with ease. She worked the lunch and dinner shifts five days a week. The money she earned was easy to save because she had no rent or bills to pay. So, within six weeks, she had managed to save five hundred dollars, which she used to buy her first car—a Mercury Zephyr.

That summer, much to everyone's surprise, Tammy's father kept his promise and invited Rose to the States for an all-expenses-paid, two-week visit. Having not seen her mother in almost two years, Tammy cherished every moment.

Joanne was the perfect host, insisting Rose stay at the house. At first, John had his concerns, but they soon subsided after observing the friendship that flourished between Joanne and his ex-wife. To his delight, everyone got along exceptionally well. During her mother's visit, Tammy took her on many day excursions, including the Gold Rush town—which stirred up memories of Raymond—San Francisco, and Yosemite.

Around the dinner table, serious discussions, stories, and fond memories of Donna were shared. The more time that elapsed with no news, the more they all began to fear the worst. With no leads or any word from the children's home, no one had any idea how to go about looking for her.

Not wanting to upset her mother even more, Tammy chose not to tell her about her relationship with Raymond or the miscarriage; there were some things she just didn't need to know.

The two weeks zipped by quicker than Tammy would've liked, and saying goodbye to her mother all over again was difficult. Many tears were shared at the airport and promises of writing were made by both Tammy and her mother. Tammy left with a heavy heart, not knowing when she would see her mother again.

Tammy had been working at the hotel for eight months, making new friends, and was now dating a chef called Steven. Being from a Spanish decent, his smooth skin always looked tanned. He was tall, over six feet, and lean but not muscular. His head of wavy black hair rested on his shoulders, and Tammy had been captivated from the first moment they met by his dark blue eyes, beautifully framed with thick black eyelashes. But it was his smile, topped with a black mustache that drew Tammy in and really melted her heart. He had passed her in the break room and their arms had brushed, which caused her to look up. He said nothing, but simply smiled, followed by a wink of the eye. Tammy smiled back and then he was gone.

The next day, she saw him again. This time, he spoke, introducing himself as Steven and showing off, once again, his heart-warming smile. Instantly, they struck up a friendship. Drinks were shared after work and days off were spent with each other. She grew fond of him quickly, and within a few months, their relationship had grown to the official "being a couple" stage.

Unable to afford his own place, Steven lived with one of his friends in a one-bedroom apartment across town where Steven slept on the couch. He didn't own a car, but Tammy's was at his disposable whenever he needed a ride. If she had to work, she simply loaned him the car.

One afternoon while Tammy was at work, Steven came into the kitchen to start his night shift. He seemed upset. Without giving her a glance, he mumbled a quick "Hi" before dashing over to his locker to put on his apron.

Concerned, Tammy set down the tray she was carrying and followed him. She found him at the lockers with his back toward her. "What's up? You look upset," she asked, gently placing her hand on his shoulder.

Still facing his locker and struggling with the strings on his apron, he eventually turned to face her. With a distressed look on his face, he yanked the ties one last time and pulled the ends into a tight knot around his middle. "Oh, well," Steven started in a raised voice, "my stupid roommate is kicking me out because his girl-friend is moving in." Frustrated, he slammed the metal locker door shut. "I have until the weekend to move out. Some *friend* he is! I can't afford a place of my own, so what am I supposed to do now? I'm really fucked!"

Clearly in a riled state, Steven brushed past Tammy, shoving her out of his way, and grabbed a metal chair out from under the staff table. Tammy covered her ears and winced at the high-pitched screech of metal legs scraping across the tiled floor. Steven flopped himself down on the seat with his folded arms on the table and his brows in a deep furrow.

Alarmed by his anger, Tammy cautiously took a seat next to him, placed her hand on his knee, and gave it a slight squeeze. "Is there anywhere else you could go?" she asked.

For the first time, Steven made eye contact. My god, he looks awful, Tammy thought. His dark, glazed eyes hooded by droopy eyelids made her shift awkwardly in her seat. The look on his face was one she'd never seen before.

In a calmer state, Steven leaned back in his chair and sighed. "I have another friend who is moving out of his place this weekend. I might be able to get that apartment, but I can't afford it on my own."

Tammy knew him well enough to know what he was getting at. "What are you saying? You want me to move in with you, is that it?" Steven took her hand. "It's crossed my mind, yes. But I have no idea how we're going to come up with the deposit. I'm broke until payday."

Tammy pondered the idea for a moment. The subject of becoming roommates had never been discussed before, but she understood Steven was desperate. Plus, the idea of not having to live with parents and having a place of her own was appealing.

"I'll be a good roommate. I promise," Steven said with a grin while batting his long eyelashes at her.

Tammy smirked. "Well, I do have the deposit. I don't pay rent at my dad's, so I'm able to save the money instead. And I have a car, so we'll have transportation. How much is the rent?"

"Five hundred," Steven replied.

"That's not too bad. We both work. I'm sure between us we could come up with that." A large grin blanketed Tammy's face. "So what do you think? Want to be roommates?"

"We're gonna need the first month's rent too. That's another five hundred," he said.

"Well, I've managed to save about two thousand dollars," Tammy said, beaming with excitement. She grabbed his arm, shaking it vigorously. "We have the money, Steven!"

Being unexpectedly surprised and gushing with relief, Steven shared in her giddiness. "You've been hiding out on me, babe! You have two thousand dollars!" he said, looking like the cat that got the cream. With his spirits now shifted into high gear, he reached over and threw his arms around Tammy, blubbering at speed. "Let's go talk to my buddy tomorrow and see how we can make this happen."

"Sure," Tammy answered, thrilled to see him happy again. "I get off at two tomorrow. We can go then if you like?"

"Sounds good to me. I'll call my friend and tell him we're coming over." He pulled her in closer and gave her a passionate kiss. "Thanks, babe. You're the best!"

Tammy smiled. "You're welcome."

"I can't believe we're getting our first place together. I'm so stoked!" With all the excitement, he realized he had lost track of time and glanced at his watch. "Oh, crap! I'd better go clock in. I'm late for my shift. I gotta run. Love you, babe."

"Love you too!" Tammy hollered as she watched him scurry away with a bounce in his step.

The pressures of the night—burned food, irate customers, and those that left no tip—couldn't dampen Tammy and Steven's elevated mood. They unashamedly shared their news with co-workers and Tammy couldn't wait to get home to tell her father and Joanne the unexpected but exciting plans.

❧

Home by nine, Tammy found her father and Joanne drinking wine and playing scrabble at the dining room table. "Hi, guys," she said cheerfully as she pulled off her coat by the door.

"Hi, Tammy, how was work?" Joanne asked, peering over her glasses.

Tammy threw her coat on the couch and walked over to the table. "It was good. Who's winning?" she asked while pulling out a chair and taking a seat.

"Joanne is. She must be cheating," her father joked.

Tammy laughed at his dry sense of humor. Pleased to find they were obviously in good spirits, Tammy wasted no time. "I don't mean to interrupt your game, but I have something to tell you."

Anticipating bad news, her parents quickly lost interest in the game and turned to Tammy with matching worried expressions. "What is it?" Joanne asked.

Tammy grinned. "Don't worry, it's nothing bad. Steven and I may be moving in together." Her father removed his glasses, leaned back in his chair, and folded his arms across his chest. A posture Tammy recognized well—this was his go-to look for when he wasn't pleased.

"Really. What brought this on?" he asked.

"Steven is getting kicked out of his apartment. Apparently, his roommate who leases the place wants his girlfriend to move in. Steven has another friend who's moving out of his apartment and Steven suggested we rent it. We're going to look at it tomorrow after work."

"I didn't know you and Steven were that serious," Joanne remarked.

"We're not. Heck, we've only been dating for about four months. The thing is, he can't afford the apartment on his own and I think it's about time I got my own place anyway," Tammy explained.

"Can you afford it?" questioned her father.

"I think so," Tammy replied. "We're both working and the rent is only five hundred a month, so I think we should be able to afford it between us." She decided not to disclose the fact that she was covering the security deposit and first month's rent. They would only dispute the idea and insist she just pay her half. She didn't want to explain that Steven had no money until his next paycheck.

Unsure on how to handle the sudden news, John glanced over at his wife for reinforcement. Showing no signs of objection, Joanne gave a slight nod and a smile. John replied with a subtle nod and turned to his daughter. Their silent communication never failed to amuse Tammy.

"Well, seems like you have it all figured out." John raised his glass in a toast. "I hope you get the apartment and I wish you guys the best of luck."

Tammy left her chair and walked over to her father. Leaning over the back of his seat, she hugged him around the neck. "Thanks, Dad. I'm pretty excited."

Joanne smiled from across the table. "If you get the apartment, I have extra dishes you can have and probably some extra bedding."

"Thanks, Joanne. That would be great. I know the place is furnished, but items like that we could really use."

After sharing the news with her parents and securing their blessings, Tammy couldn't wait to see the apartment. The idea of beginning a new life in a new place with Steven was exactly what she needed, and she failed to contain her elation as she skipped down the hall to her room.

The next morning, Tammy woke up eager to see the apartment. With only fifteen minutes to spare before she had to leave for work, she decided to make a quick call to Steven to confirm the time.

She dialed his number and his roommate answered after a few rings. "Hello."

"Hi, it's Tammy. Is Steven there?" she asked.

"The lazy bum is still fucking sleeping," the roommate said with an attitude.

Never having met the guy, Tammy was shocked by his tone and rudeness. "Okay, well, could you please tell him I called and to not forget to meet me after work, to look at the apartment?"

The rude man let out a loud, crackling laugh. "You're shacking up with him?"

"Yes, I am. He told me you're kicking him out."

"Your damn right I'm kicking his ass out. Did he tell you why?"

"Yes, he did," Tammy replied.

"And you're still going to shack up with the guy?" He let out another contemptuous laugh. "You're stupider than he is."

Offended by his remark but rushed to get to work, Tammy had no time to play twenty questions. "Look, I have to go. Can you please just give him the message?" Tammy shook her head, baffled by the conversation, and hung up the phone. She grabbed her coat from the couch, yelled goodbye to Joanne upstairs and ran out the front door.

Shortly after two o'clock, Tammy spotted Steven at the staff table talking to another cook. She clocked out of her shift and walked over to him, stunned by his appearance as she approached the table. Wearing a pair of severely wrinkled black pants and an equally crinkled white t-shirt, Tammy assumed he had slept in them all night. His mangled hair splayed out over the top of his head in an uncombed mess, and he clearly hadn't taken the time to shave. When he looked up, she noticed his pale skin and the dark circles cradling his eyes.

"Steven, are you okay?" she asked.

"Yeah, why?"

"Well, you look like you've just crawled out of a bush."

Offended, he raised his voice. "What's that supposed to mean?"

Not wanting to upset him, Tammy refrained from commenting any further on his wardrobe malfunction. "Oh, never mind. When can we see the apartment?"

"My buddy will be home in about half an hour. His landlord is going to stop by too so he can meet us."

"Great! I'm so excited," she squealed before adding. "Um, can you at least brush your hair? We have to make a good impression, Steven."

"Jeez, Tammy! Don't worry. I'll brush it in the car."

Tammy's mood shifted to frustration. "Fine!" she snapped, rolling her eyes. "Wait here while I go cash in my tickets and collect my tips."

Thirty minutes later, they were pulling up to the parking lot of the apartment: A white two-story building with a dozen units overlooking the town. Tammy parked the car, rolled up her window and asked Steven to do the same, which he did after stubbing out his cigarette. Before exiting the car, Tammy glanced in the rear-view mirror, touched up her lipstick, and gave her hair a quick brush. Speaking only with her eyes—words were not needed—she handed the brush to Steven. Annoyed by her gesture, he rolled his eyes, snatched the brush from her hand, and obediently brushed his hair before stepping out of the car.

In silence, they walked up to the door marked 2A, which was located between two other apartments, and knocked on the door. A few moments later, a tall, skinny guy with short blond hair, still dressed in a brown company uniform, appeared from inside.

"Hey, Randy, how's it going? This is my girlfriend Tammy," Steven said while slinking his arm around her waist.

"Hi, Tammy, nice to meet you. Come on in," Randy said as he opened the door and took a step to the side.

"Nice to meet you, too," Tammy replied before following Steven into the apartment.

Inside, they found themselves standing in the living room. Randy closed the door behind them.

"May I look around?" Tammy asked.

"Sure," Randy said, sweeping his arms in a circular motion around the small space. "There's not much to see," he added.

Tammy left the two men to chatter while she went to explore, almost skipping from room to room with excitement. The apartment was small, with one bedroom and a tiny bathroom, but she was happy to see it at least had a bathtub and a shower. The kitchen was galley-style with a small nook off to the left for a dining room table. The living area, the biggest of the rooms, had two sliding glass doors leading out on to a deck with just enough room for two chairs. The awesome view from the deck overlooked the whole town, and Tammy was already picturing it as the perfect place for her morning coffee.

Tammy found Steven and Randy talking on the couch. "I love it!" she announced. "Did you take a look yet, Steven?"

"I've been here before. I don't need to," Steven replied, showing much less enthusiasm than Tammy.

"Randy, where's your landlord? I thought he was going to be here."

"He called just before you guys arrived. He'll be here in about ten minutes," Randy said.

"Okay, good. So, is any of the furniture included with the apartment?" Tammy asked.

"It comes with the fridge, cooker, couch, coffee table, and dining room table. The bed is mine."

"That's not a problem. I'm sure we can find a bed someplace for a reasonable price. Right, Steven?" Tammy added, hoping to include Steven in the conversation and perhaps encourage him to show a bit more interest.

Steven shrugged his shoulders and mumbled, "Yeah, I guess." Disappointed, Tammy walked away to check out the kitchen again.

A few minutes later, they heard a car pull up in the driveway.

"That must be the landlord," Randy announced.

Tammy stood by the dining room table, anxious to meet him. Moments later, there was a knock at the door.

"Come in. It's open," Randy yelled.

The door opened and a middle-aged man dressed casually in blue jeans and a grey sweatshirt entered the room carrying a manila envelope.

Tammy walked into the living room to greet him.

The landlord extended his hand and introduced himself. "Hi, I'm Bill. It's a pleasure to meet you both."

Tammy shook his hand first and was pleased when Steven stood to greet him. Doing most of the talking, Tammy and Bill walked through the apartment while she asked various questions. She asked if the utilities were included with the rent and was happy to hear they were. Correcting herself a few times for calling it a flat, Tammy was amused with Bill's sense of humor when he began calling it a flat, too. Eager to get the apartment, Tammy explained to Bill that her and Steven both worked and could easily afford the rent, adding for good measure that they had no children or pets.

Bill liked her spunk and enthusiasm and believed they would make good tenants. "Normally, I take applications and make my decision after viewing them. But, I like you, Tammy, so I tell you what," Bill said and paused.

Tammy took a deep breath as she waited. "What?" she finally asked after what felt like an eternity.

Bill smiled, enjoying her excitement. "If you have the deposit of five hundred dollars and the first month's rent, the place is yours."

Tammy held her hands together and squealed a high-pitched "Thank you!" to Bill before yelling, "Steven! We got it!" She raced toward the living room and saw Steven had returned to the couch. He couldn't help but cave in to her over-the-top excitement, and he stood to meet her in a triumphant hug.

After retrieving the necessary rental papers from his car, Bill ushered them both over to the dining room table to complete the process, go over the rental agreement, and answer any questions they may have. He informed them that it was a month-to-month lease and explained he would need a few days to clean and paint the place. He concluded they could move in next Monday, which was just four days away.

With no hesitation, Tammy signed the papers and then slid them across the table to Steven. While waiting for him to add his signature, Tammy pulled out her checkbook, wrote a check in the amount of one thousand dollars and handed it to Bill. Bill scanned the check, making sure everything was filled out correctly.

"Well, congratulations to the both of you," he said, extending his hand for another round of handshakes. Checking his watch, Bill slid the papers and check inside the manila envelope. "I'm sorry, but I have to get going. I have another meeting in half an hour."

Tammy and Steven followed suit as Bill stood up and walked to the front door. "Thank you so much, Bill. I can't tell you how happy you've made us." She took Bill's hand one last time. "We promise to take really good care of the place."

"Now, that's what I like to hear!" Bill said with a chuckle. "How about we meet here Monday morning at ten so I can give you the keys?"

"Sure, that sounds great!" Tammy answered.

After Bill had left and the door was closed, Tammy let out a loud triumph "Yes!" while pulling Steven into a victory dance. "I can't believe this place will be ours," she said, prancing around with joy.

Amused by her giddy antics, Steven twirled her in a spin and met her in a kiss. "Me neither, babe. I love you."

"I love you too, honey."

"Get a room, you two," chirped Randy from the couch.

Cheek to cheek, Tammy and Steven, snickered at Randy's remark.

"Thanks for everything, Randy," Tammy said before turning back to Steven. "Are you ready to go? I can't wait to tell my dad and Joanne that I finally have my own place!"

CHAPTER 25

John and Joanne shared in Tammy's excitement over the apartment and, as promised, Joanne loaded her up with sheets, towels, dishes, and silverware.

The night before their big move, John invited Steven over to the house for dinner. Pleased that Steven had taken the time to at least shave, brush his hair, and put on some clean clothes, Tammy thought the evening had got off to a good start. Joanne had prepared spaghetti with garlic bread—one of Tammy's favorites—and John served everyone a glass of white wine with their meal.

Talk of the apartment ruled the table, with Joanne frequently asking if there was anything else they needed. Each time Tammy repeated her gratitude but assured her they were fine. John's primary concerns were their finances, wondering if they could afford the rent every month. Not wanting her father to worry, Tammy tried her best to put his mind at ease by going over what the two of them made each month. But, even after explaining everything more than once, her father still seemed unsettled. Tammy sensed something else was on his mind. Whatever it was, he didn't discuss it.

At the end of the evening, Tammy excused herself to grab a jacket from her bedroom so she could take Steven home. To Tammy's surprise, her father followed a few seconds later and closed the door behind them.

"Are you okay, Dad? What's up?" she asked.

Her father sat on the edge of the bed with his arms folded and a creased expression on his face. Knowing he rarely expressed his feelings, this was confirmation for Tammy that something was definitely troubling him.

"I'm not sure how to say this," he began. "I can't tell you what to do anymore...you're an adult. But I can still look out for you and, as your father, I'll never stop doing that."

"Where's this going, Dad?" Tammy asked, eager for him to get to the point.

"If you must know, it's Steven. I don't know him that well, and he does seem like a nice young man..."

"He is, Dad."

"Yes, I'm sure he is, but there's something about him that makes me uncomfortable. I can't quite put my finger on it. He hardly said a word all night and his behavioral pattern isn't consistent."

"What's that supposed to mean?" Tammy questioned.

"I have to ask...um, do you know if he's on drugs?"

Tammy was horrified. "What! Why would you ask such a thing? Of course he doesn't do drugs. Don't you think I would know, Dad?" Upset by her father's accusations, Tammy punched her arms through the sleeves of her jacket. "Are you being the over-protected dad? Maybe you think no one is good enough for me. Is that it?"

"I don't know. Maybe I am. But his behavior tonight struck me as odd. When he was sitting on the couch, he could barely keep his eyes open. Even when they were open, they weren't focused. It's like he was looking off into space or something."

Tammy thought her father's suspicions were nothing short of preposterous. "I promise you, Dad, he's not on drugs. Like I said, I would know. He's probably tired. I mean, he walked all the way here straight from work. I couldn't pick him up because I was helping Joanne with dinner."

John stood and gave his daughter's shoulder an affectionate pat. "I'm sure you're right, but I had my concerns so I had to ask. That's what fathers do. Anyway, I'll let you go so you can take him home."

Tammy smiled, relieved he didn't want to pursue the subject, and gave him a hug. "He really is a nice guy, Dad."

Her father nodded, but he wasn't convinced. He could only hope his suspicions were wrong.

$\mathcal{A}$fter picking up the keys from Bill, Tammy and Steven were settled in their new apartment within a few days. When it came time to buying a bed, a TV, and other miscellaneous items they needed, Steven confessed he had some unexpected expenses and was now broke. Refusing to wait another week until he got paid and wanting the apartment to be perfect, Tammy reluctantly spent more of her savings and bought the items herself.

Prior to the move, Tammy had suggested to Steven, to make finances easier, that he pay the rent every month and she would pay for everything else, which included the telephone, TV, food, toiletries, gas, and anything else they may need. Steven thought it was fair and agreed.

Over the next few months, their new life together got off to a great start. Tammy enjoyed having her independence back and making a home for them both, and she could finally invite some of her friends over for dinner. But, on several occasions, she found herself embarrassed by Steven's behavior. Glancing over at him while engaging in conversations with friends, she was horrified to find him in a vegetated state, his eyes closed and his head crouched low over the table. Oblivious to those around him, she watched in bewilderment as he mumbled and whispered random words or phrases to himself.

To save herself from any more embarrassment, Tammy would kick him hard on the shin from underneath the table to discreetly jolt him awake. She was often met with a cold, angry glare and creased brows as Steven snapped out of his dream world, to which she would often reply with a fierce stare of her own while fighting to keep her lips tightly closed for the sake of everyone present.

Tammy found herself defending him more and more, just like she had with her father. She always explained to their guests that Steven was probably tired from a hard day's work before quickly excusing him from the table. Tammy desperately wanted to believe this was the reason for his strange behavior. She'd put aside her father's suspicions when she confronted Steven the next morning, only to be swooned with profuse apologies and feelings of embarrassment in return. He promised it would never happen again.

Surprise by how much she enjoyed being a homemaker, Tammy loved spending her days off cleaning the apartment or trying out new recipes for future dinner parties.

Thankful that Steven had to work all day, she had plans to clean the entire apartment with no interruptions. As soon as he left, Tammy began her day's activities by tuning the radio to a country and western station and turning up the volume. After rolling up her sleeves and grabbing her caddy of supplies, she worked her way around each room, cleaning, sweeping, and polishing while singing and dancing to her heart's content.

Being the least favorite, she left the bathroom till last. Before attempting the dreaded task, she decided she needed to properly prepare for the occasion and searched for a pair of rubber gloves underneath the sink. Instead, in amongst the bottles of cleaning products and spare toiletries, she came across a folded brown paper bag. Tammy, given she had always been the curious type, immediately forgot about the gloves and sat on the edge of the tub to do some snooping. She carefully unfolded the bag, took a peek inside, and let out a loud gasp. Lying at the bottom of the bag, she found syringe needles, two teaspoons that were black on the bottom, and numerous small cotton balls. The only illness she associated with needles was diabetes. Having never known anyone with the condition, she had no idea what the blackened spoons or cotton balls might be needed for, but she found herself feeling pity for Steven.

"Oh my god," she whispered to herself. "Why didn't he tell me? Poor Steven, he didn't want me to know. I have to tell him it's okay and that I understand. He needs to know he doesn't have to hide it from me anymore." Feeling sympathetic, she carefully closed the bag and returned it to where she had found it under the sink.

Later that day, Steven arrived home in a seemingly flustered state. He threw his duffle bag on the couch and raced straight to the bathroom. Closing the door behind him, he hadn't even acknowledged Tammy, who had already served their dinner of roast chicken, mashed potatoes, and carrots. Offended, Tammy waited at the table with crossed arms and a furious stare as she watched the food she'd diligently cooked turn cold. Growing impatient, she yelled, "Steven, dinner's ready! What are you doing in there?"

From the bathroom, he shouted back, "I'll be right there. God, Tammy, I just got home! Give me a break, will you?"

Angered by his tone and tired of waiting, she proceeded to eat alone. Pausing with a mouthful of chicken, she soon came to the realization that he was probably taking his medicine. "How could I be so stupid?" she muttered under her breath. "He doesn't know I know." Now that she understood, she let her anger subside and prepared herself to tell him that she knew about his illness.

Ten minutes later, Steven exited the bathroom and joined her at the table. In silence, Tammy uncovered his dinner and slid the plate in front of him.

"Thank you," he said in a much nicer tone. "Are you feeling okay?" Tammy asked, trying to break the ice.

Without meeting her eyes, Steven replied, "Yeah, why?"

"Well, this morning, while I was cleaning the bathroom, I found a brown bag with some needles inside underneath the sink."

Steven froze. His body became tense and a look of fear flooded his face.

Tammy reached across the table and took his hand. "Why didn't you tell me?"

"Tell you what?" he asked, puzzled.

"That you're a diabetic."

Steven said nothing, which led Tammy to believe he was embarrassed. Comforting him, she rubbed the top of his hand with her thumb. "It's okay, Steven. It's nothing to be ashamed about."

Avoiding eye contact, Steven shifted his gaze downward and played along. "I didn't want you to feel sorry for me, and, um, I didn't want to bother you. I'm fine. It's no big deal."

Surprise by his modesty, Tammy let go of his hand. "Yes, it is a big deal, Steven. You're supposed to be watching your diet and sugar intake. Do you take insulin?"

"Can we just drop it? I'm okay and I know how to handle it."

Sensing his frustration, Tammy let it go, but she wondered why he'd never told her about his illness. It seemed she maybe didn't know him as well as she thought she did.

The next morning, Tammy woke up experiencing severe back pain. Steven offered to take the day off and stay with her, but she ushered him off to work and told him she would be fine. Hobbling around the apartment, unable to stand up straight or walk comfortably, she was thankful she had cleaned the day before. Tammy discovered if she lay on the couch with a few pillows, the pain was slightly easier to deal with. Grateful for another day off, she spent most of it lounging in front of the TV, hoping her back would heal itself before she had to return to work.

By the time Steven returned home, Tammy was still lying on the sofa in excruciating pain.

"Hey, honey, how are you feeling?" he asked.

Groaning in agony, she slowly eased herself up to a sitting position. "Not much better, I'm afraid. I may have to call in sick tomorrow. I can't even stand, let alone work."

Concerned, Steven sat next to her on the edge of the couch. "Is there anything I can do?"

"Yes, can you rub my lower back for a bit? It's killing me," Tammy said, inching herself forward.

Hoping to ease her pain, Steven obliged.

"Maybe you should go to the doctors tomorrow," Steven suggested. "I have to work though. Will you be able to drive yourself there?"

"Yeah, I should be okay. It's only a few minutes down the road. I just want this bloody pain to go away. I've done nothing all day but lie on this stupid couch," she said, sounding frustrated. "You're going to have to fix yourself dinner. I can't move."

"Don't worry about dinner. I'll make you some soup and bring it to you."

Tammy had no objections to being waited on. With TV remote in hand, she slowly sank her body back down and rested her head on the pillows while Steven scurried off to the kitchen.

The following morning, feeling as stiff as a board and with her back showing no signs of improving, Tammy called in sick. Despite much resistance from Steven, she insisted he still go to work. As soon as he'd left for the day, she called her doctor and made an appointment for later that morning. Tammy then managed to take a shower, dress, and drive herself to the doctors, all the while struggling with her agonizing pain.

Sue, who often ate at the restaurant where Tammy worked, was at the front desk. "Hi, Sue, I have an appointment with Dr. Davis."

"Hey, Tammy, what's wrong with you?" Sue asked, noticing Tammy wincing as she stood by the desk.

"It's my back. I have this severe pain that won't go away."

"Hang on a second. I'll let the doctor know you're here," Sue replied before marching off through a door behind her.

Tammy decided she was more comfortable standing while she waited to be called. Happy to see no one else in the waiting room ahead of her, she assumed she wouldn't have to wait too long.

A few minutes later, Sue returned to her desk and flashed a

professional smile. "He can see you now, Tammy. It's the first door on the right."

"Thanks, I know the way," Tammy said, feeling relieved. She turned on her heel, albeit very gingerly, and slowly made her way to the double doors of the doctor's office.

She found Dr. Davis sitting on a low round stool with wheels, his back toward her, writing something in a file. She gently tapped on the opened door before entering.

The doctor turned his head and looked over his glasses at her. "Hi, Tammy. Come on in and have a seat on the examination table while I finish these notes. I'll be just a moment."

Not wanting to disturb him, Tammy gave a silent nod and perched as best she could on the edge of the table, letting her legs dangle over the side. She cupped her hands in her lap and waited. Scanning the room, she glanced at a poster on the wall displaying a detailed picture of the human skeleton. Squinting at the smaller poster next to it, she saw it was all about the three trimesters of pregnancy. Tammy gulped; haunted by the memories of the baby she had lost.

After a few moments, Dr. Davis closed the file and set it down on the table in front of him as he stood up to face Tammy. The almost miniature looking stool, now free from the doctor's weight, rattled halfway across the room on its rickety plastic wheels. The doctor smiled at Tammy as he removed his glasses, folded them, and put them in the top pocket of his white coat.

"So, Tammy, what seems to be the trouble?"

She held her side to ease the discomfort. "I'm not sure. I've had a severe pain in my lower back and sides for the last couple of days."

"Hmmm, okay. Let's take a look, shall we?"

Tammy sat up as straight as she could and lifted the back of her shirt. With cool hands, Dr. Davis pressed firmly on various muscles around her back and sides, periodically asking if she felt any pain. Tammy nodded with a yes when she did. After a few moments of poking and prodding, he pulled down her shirt back down and faced her. "Okay, I think you may have a kidney infection. A urine sample will tell me if I'm correct, so I'll send in Sue to take care of that."

"Okay," Tammy replied.

Dr. Davis then left the room, picking up Tammy's chart on his way out. Sue entered shortly after and handed her a plastic cup with a lid. "Here you go, Tammy. I just need a little bit. There's a small metal door in the wall of the bathroom where you can place the cup after you're done. And then just come back in here, okay?"

"Thanks, Sue," Tammy replied before heading to the bathroom. After following Sue's instructions and leaving her sample on the metal ledge, she headed back to the examination room to wait for Dr. Davis.

Tammy sat in silence for a further twenty minutes, which left her wishing she'd brought a book to read to help pass the time and keep her mind off the pain. Dr. Davis finally returned, carrying her file under his arm, and wheeled his wayward stool back to his desk before taking a seat. He retrieved his glasses from his top pocket, slid them on, and began to read her file. Tammy felt like another twenty minutes passed before he closed the file in his lap and glanced up at her over the top of his glasses.

"Well, Tammy, it seems you do have a kidney infection, which is quite common in an early pregnancy."

"Early pregnancy?" Tammy asked, taking a few seconds to process what he'd said. "What are you talking about? I'm not pregnant."

"Indeed, you are, Tammy. I'm quite sure of it."

"But how can that be? I just had my period less than two weeks ago," she explained in an exasperated voice.

"Bleeding is not uncommon in the first trimester. But it's not your period. It's known as decidual bleeding and will probably stop before you enter the second trimester."

Puzzled, Tammy asked. "Decidual bleeding? What's that?"

"Basically, during the beginning of pregnancy, your body hormones can go a little haywire. This causes you to lose part of the lining of the uterus, which normally happens before the lining has completely attached itself to the placenta. It's not a health risk to you or the baby, and by all means, you should have a normal pregnancy," he said with an encouraging smile.

Unable to focus on the doctor's words, she only heard the word *pregnant* bellowing repeatedly in her head like a loud, beating drum. This was too much information for what she thought was going to be a routine doctor's visit to treat a simple case of back pain. She was in shock. Pregnant? She couldn't believe it. She had stopped taking the pill a few months ago because of terrible side effects and had planned on looking at alternative methods, but she had never gotten around to it with being so busy organizing their new apartment. She and Steven had been careful, she thought; but, obviously not careful enough.

"Tammy, are you listening to me?"

Tammy shook her head, forcing herself back to reality. "Er, yes, Doctor. Sorry."

"That's okay. I'm sure this is quite a surprise for you. I'm going to give you some antibiotics for the kidney infection. They're safe to take while pregnant. I'm also going to make an appointment for you at the hospital, for an ultrasound so we can find out just how far along you are."

Tammy gave him an almost imperceptible nod. "Okay, that sounds fine."

With nothing more to be said, Dr. Davis wrote her a prescription and set up an appointment for her in a couple of days at the hospital. After thanking him, she stood up, shook his hand, and left the room.

Back in her car, still shocked by the news, Tammy tried to grasp the notion that she was once again pregnant. She made a promise, right there and then, to love and nourish the baby while it grew inside of her. She wasn't going to let her body reject another child. The initial shock was beginning to wear off, and thoughts of having a child with Steven actually made Tammy smile. They had been dating for some time, and he had expressed that he wanted kids someday. Well, that "someday" was here already; it was here now! As she started up the car, she found herself feeling excited about telling him the news.

Steven arrived home shortly after six, looking tired and flustered. Tammy couldn't help noticing the beads of sweat forming on his forehead, his drenched hair, and his dark, sunken eyes. "Are you feeling okay?" she asked.

"Yes, I'm fine!" he snapped, throwing his duffle bag on the couch and pushing past her. "I'll just be a minute," he called out as he scurried into the bathroom, closing the door behind him.

Tammy had seen the same routine every night and knew he would be at least fifteen minutes. They had never discussed it, but she suspected he was taking his diabetic medicine. It troubled her that he was still embarrassed about it and continued to hide it from her.

While he was in the bathroom, Tammy racked her brain, thinking how she was going to tell him about the baby. With the antibiotics kicking in and her back feeling a little better, she had managed to cook a special roast beef dinner, along with roast potatoes and steamed mixed vegetables. The aroma of the delicious meal lingered throughout the apartment. The only thing left to do was set the table, so she began the task while waiting for Steven.

Nervous about his reaction toward the baby, Tammy had a strong urge for a cigarette. She took a few long, deep breaths to help subside the cravings, determined to conquer her addiction, especially now that she was responsible for the health of their child.

After setting the table, Tammy stood back and admired her work. "Not bad," she said to herself. Along with the polished silverware and folded beige napkins, she had finished the table off with two pillar candles and a vase of fresh daffodils. She joyfully skipped back to the kitchen, humming a pleasant tune, and proceeded to bring out the main course, followed by the vegetables and two glasses of milk. No more wine, she told herself while setting down the drinks.

As she made herself comfortable at the table, she heard the bathroom door open. "Hey, honey, dinner's ready!" she hollered in his direction.

"Be right there."

She heard Steven rummaging about in the bedroom and assumed he was changing out of his work clothes. Now wearing black jeans and a t-shirt, Steven made his way into the dining room and sat down. Tammy admired him from across the table. He was no longer sweating, his eyes were brighter, and he had combed his hair away from his face. Smelling the scent of his freshly applied cologne as it drifted in her direction, she smiled. "You look good."

"Thanks, babe," he replied. Steven's eyes shined with delight as he took in the sight of the feast before him. "Wow! Looks like you're feeling better. What's the occasion?"

Tammy smirked. "I'll tell you over dinner. Come on; let's eat. It's getting cold."

"Okay," he agreed. Anxious to dig in, Steven began carving the roast. "Hey, how did it go at the doctors today?"

She decided to tell him the easy part first. "It turns out I have a kidney infection. The doctor put me on antibiotics."

"Damn...it's a good job you went then!"

Picking up his knife and fork, Steven scanned the table one more time, taking in the lit candles and the neatly folded napkins. "So why the fancy dinner?" he asked with a devious smile.

Feeling the butterflies in her stomach begin to stir, Tammy took a deep breath and laid down her silverware. The moment she had been anticipating for most of the day had finally arrived. "Well, the doctor did tell me something else."

A worried look blanketed Steven's face. "Is it serious?"

Tammy smirked. "That all depends on how you look at it." She looked straight into his eyes with anticipation. "Steven, I'm pregnant." A huge sigh of relief rushed from her lungs as soon as the words left her mouth. She had told him. Sitting motionless, she waited for his reaction.

Steven stared across the table at her in disbelief, his eyes like those of a deer's caught in the headlights of an oncoming vehicle. Seconds later, the huge smile that lit up his face put Tammy at complete ease. Giggling with joy, she watched with amusement as he lifted one hand over his racing heart while the other covered his gaping mouth.

Flustered with excitement, Steven scurried over to her side of the table, knocking his chair over in the process. Glancing down at her, he thought to himself how beautiful she was and how lucky he was to have her in his life. Straining her neck, Tammy looked up to him with a beaming smile. Steven leaned in closer and met her with a passionate kiss. A passion they hadn't shared for quite some time. Cupping her face with the palms of his hands, Steven gazed into her eyes, which were now shining with tears of happiness. "Are you serious? We're going to have a baby?" he said before releasing a scream of pure joy.

Tammy reached for his hand and squeezed it tight. "Yes, I'm serious, and I've been terrified all day about telling you. I wasn't sure how you were going to react or if you'd be okay with having a child."

"Okay with it? Tammy, I'm over the moon!" He wiped away a tear that was now rolling down her cheek. "We're going to have a baby! Oh, sweetheart, I couldn't be any happier. I love you so much and I'm going to be a great dad. You watch."

"I know you'll be a good father. Our baby is counting on it. Now, come on, let's eat before it goes cold."

Affections were high during dinner. Steven moved his chair closer to Tammy's and smothered her with kisses and cuddles while they shared in their joy of becoming parents. Tammy filled him in on the need for an ultrasound to determine her due date and together they pondered over the sex of the baby, possible baby names, and discussed when and how they would tell their parents.

Tammy had never felt closer to him. For the rest of the night, he was clearly ecstatic about the thought of being a father and a joy to be around. They laughed, they cuddled, and they smooched on the couch while watching a romantic comedy before ending the night with amazing sex. Finally, life was good. The thought that they were going to be a happy family made Tammy smile.

The next morning, still riddled with excitement, Tammy couldn't wait to call her father and Joanne and also her mother in England about her pregnancy. Even though she was feeling skeptical about her father's reaction, she was too exhilarated to worry.

After spending most of the morning on the telephone with family, Tammy finally hung up the phone after talking with her mother, who was overjoyed at the thought of becoming a grandmother for the first time and promised to find a way to come visit if her father couldn't help.

Joanne seemed genuinely happy, and she wasted no time in offering Tammy the heaps of clothes that Andrew had outgrown if the baby was going to be a boy. Her father had cordially congratulated her when he came to the phone after Joanne. Tammy had a hard time detecting any sincere excitement from him. She knew he'd always had greater plans for her, and having a child in her early twenties wasn't one of them.

Tammy had yet to meet Steven's mother, who lived alone in the suburbs of Los Angeles. Steven rarely talked about her but told

Tammy she was widowed at an early age because of his dad's alcohol addiction. She never remarried and raised Steven, their only child, alone. The few memories Steven had of his father were not pleasant. Visions of his parents yelling and screaming, followed by scenes of violence and rage, haunted him. His mother had become a recluse lost soul with no friends, spending her days in front of the TV watching soap operas and living off disability checks. Once out of the toxic household, he began a troubled life of his own. Steven had distanced himself from his mother and only called home on the holidays. He had, however, made the effort to call her and tell her about the baby. The conversation was brief, and whether he believed himself or not, he told her they would get down there to visit once the baby had arrived.

The following morning, Tammy was scheduled for an eleven o'clock appointment to have an ultrasound at the local hospital. Steven had switched his shifts so he could go with her. He dressed casually for the occasion, and Tammy, knowing she would have to change into a gown at the hospital, chose to wear loose fitting sweats and a sweatshirt.

With one hand on the steering wheel and the other tightly holding Tammy's hand, Steven drove to the hospital. Baby related chatter and laughter filled the car for the entire journey, with speculation of the due date and the sex of the baby fast becoming a fun guessing game.

When they arrived, they checked in at the reception desk and were told it would be about a fifteen-minute wait. Taking Tammy's hand, Steven led the way to a couple of empty plastic blue seats against the wall in the waiting area. Once seated, Tammy scanned the room, pleased to see it wasn't busy. An elderly man sat alone in the corner, his head buried low, reading a newspaper. A woman, about the same age as Tammy and very pregnant, sat across from them, holding her partner's hand with one hand and rubbing her large round belly with the other. She looked tired, wearing a loose fitting blue smock and sandals. Picturing herself that far along,

Tammy nudged Steven's arm with her elbow. Giggling, she whispered in his ear, "Look, that'll be me in a few months."

He quietly chuckled and leaned over to kiss the top of her head. "I can't wait, babe."

Still whispering, she replied, "Me neither." Feeling extremely happy and content with their lives, Tammy rested her head on his shoulder.

"Hi, are you Tammy Mellows?" asked a young nurse holding a clipboard.

Tammy raised her head to where the nurse stood at her side, sat up straight and smiled. "Yes, I am, and this is my boyfriend, Steven." The nurse shook Steven's hand. "Hi, Steven," she said, smiling warmly. "Will you both follow me?"

"Sure," Tammy answered.

Already on his feet, Steven took Tammy's hand and followed the nurse down the hallway. Midway down the hall, the nurse opened a door on their left and led them in to a room before closing the door softly behind them and walking to a desk along the back wall.

Feeling awkward and not knowing where to sit or what to do next, Tammy and Steven remained standing and nervously waited for instructions. The nurse pulled out a white gown from a drawer underneath the desk and turned to face Tammy.

"Tammy, I need you to get undressed and put this gown on. Make sure the opening is in front. The doctor will be in shortly, okay?"

Placing her purse on the floor in a corner, Tammy took the gown. "Okay, thank you," she replied.

Tammy started to undress as soon as the nurse left the room. "Steven, why am I so nervous? This is just a normal procedure to see how far along I am."

"It's okay," Steven replied. "I think hospitals make most people nervous, no matter what they're here for. Now, come on, let's get you in that gown before the doctor gets here."

Tammy chuckled and handed Steven her clothes as she removed them before slipping into the gown. Amused by the loose-fitting garment that hung well below her knees, Tammy pranced around the room with one hand on her hip, mimicking a model on a catwalk.

"Come on, silly, stop messing around. Let's get you up on the bed. The doctor's gonna be here soon!" Steven said while guiding Tammy in the direction of the exam table.

"Okayyyyy," Tammy answered playfully as she scurried over to the table and hoisted herself up. Steven assisted the best he could by arranging the single pillow behind her back and settling her against it.

Scanning the room, Tammy pointed to a monitor on her left. "Look! That must be where we will get to see the baby. I'm so excited!" she squealed. "This makes everything feel so real. Can you believe this is actually happening to us?"

Standing beside her, Steven lifted her hand up to his lips and placed a gentle kiss on the tips of her fingers. "I sure can now, being in this room."

A few minutes later, a light tap on the door interrupted their idle chat. "Come in," Tammy said. She propped herself up on her elbows and stared in the direction of the door as it opened.

A striking, tall brunette woman wearing a white overcoat entered the room. "Hi, I'm Doctor Leon. I'll be doing the ultrasound this morning," she said as she walked over to Tammy and shook her hand.

"Hi, Doctor, this is my boyfriend Steven," Tammy replied. "Hi, Steven. This must be a pretty exciting time for you both?"

"It sure is," Steven said, flashing a smile at Tammy.

Dr. Leon continued to chat while preparing the equipment next to the exam table. "So, Tammy, how have you been feeling? Any nausea? Weakness or headaches?"

"No, nothing. I feel great."

"Well, that's good to hear. This is a simple procedure and it won't harm you or the baby. We basically want to get an idea of how far along you are. Unfortunately, it will be too early to determine the sex of the baby."

"Okay." Tammy nodded, feeling more at ease by the soothing tone of the doctor's voice.

"Okay, Tammy, before we begin, I want to take your blood pressure. Can you put your left arm straight out for me?"

Tammy watched in silence as the doctor wrapped a black band around the top of her arm. After a few moments, Dr. Leon released the strap. "Good. Your blood pressure is normal. Shall we get started?"

"I'm ready," Tammy replied.

"Now, I want you to lie back and relax. I'm going to put some gel on your stomach that may feel a little cold. It just helps to get a better reading from the transducer."

As she lay back, Tammy glanced over at Steven and smiled. Together, they watched as Dr. Leon folded the gown away from Tammy's stomach and applied the gel. "Oh, you're right, that does feel cold," Tammy said with a giggle.

"Now, you're going to feel a slight pressure while I move the transducer around. The image will appear on the screen next to you."

Both she and Steven waited with anticipation as Dr. Leon began to move the transducer slowly over Tammy's stomach. Looking closely at the screen, the doctor paused. "Ahh, here we go," she said, smiling.

Tammy gasped. "Do you see it?"

"Yes. Here, let me show you." Dr. Leon reached over to the black and white screen and circled the outline of the fetus with her finger. "See, here's the head and here's the body, and you can clearly see the arms and feet." Dr. Leon circled another part of the screen. "And here you can see its nose and ears are beginning to develop."

With squinted eyes, Tammy and Steven leaned in closer to the screen, desperately wanting to see what the doctor was looking at. A confused look between them confirmed they just weren't seeing it.

Then, suddenly, Tammy squealed. "I see it! I see it!" She shook Steven's arm. "Steven, look! It's our baby. Oh, my gosh, that is the most beautiful thing I've ever seen." Shocked by what she was witnessing—her baby growing inside of her—Tammy cupped her cheeks in her hands as tears trickled down freely over her fingers.

With shadowed, teary eyes, Dr. Leon smiled at Tammy's excitement. No matter how many times she witnessed this moment of parents seeing their child for the first time on the screen, it always brought tears to her eyes.

Still struggling to see the image, Steven was now bent over at a strange angle right in front of the screen. He was trying his hardest to see what Tammy was pointing at with her finger. The fact that she was still shaking his arm wasn't helping him focus on the tiny image.

"Look, Steven, there it is! Oh, God, tell me you see it. It's our baby, Steven." She paused to wipe away more tears and then spoke softly to her child. "Hi, baby, it's your mommy and daddy. We can't wait to meet you and hold you, sweetheart. We love you."

"Oh my god, Tammy! I see it," Steven shouted at the top of his voice. "I do, look...there's it's foot," he yelled while outlining it with his finger. "Oh, wow, that's amazing." Still mesmerized by what he was seeing on the screen, Steven took in every detail of his child in silence. It hit him like a ton of bricks; it suddenly became undeniable—he was going to be a dad. At that precise moment, he knew he had to change his life around or suffer the consequences of losing his family.

Dr. Leon walked around to the front of the screen, interrupting Steven's thoughts. He squeezed Tammy's hand as the doctor spoke. "It looks like the baby is developing just fine, and from the size of the fetus, I would estimate that you're about three months along, which gives you a due date around the end of November or early December."

Tammy calculated the time in her head. "Wow! That's only six months away."

"Yes, it is," the doctor replied. "Now, let's listen to the heartbeat to make sure it sounds okay and there are no abnormalities."

Experiencing a love she'd never experienced before—the love between a mother and child—fear suddenly consumed Tammy. "Okay."

Strung with nerves, Tammy and Steven anxiously watched Dr. Leon prepare the equipment to listen to the heartbeat. Holding her breath, Tammy closely watched the doctor's face while she listened to the heart of the baby with some kind of fancy monitor. After a few moments, she smiled and removed the earpiece. "Everything sounds fine. The baby has a nice strong heartbeat, and it is beating normally."

Tammy let out a huge sigh of relief.

"Do you want to hear it?" the doctor asked.

Tammy's face lit up. "Can we?" she turned to Steven and beamed a radiant smile. Steven smiled back at Tammy—both stunned that they were about to hear the heartbeat of their unborn child for the first time.

"Sure. Just be real quiet so we can hear it, okay?" Dr. Leon instructed.

In silence, Tammy and Steven gripped onto each other's hands, anxiously waiting for the sound of their baby's heartbeat to come through the speakers. Seconds later, they heard the soothing, rhythmic beat of its tiny little heart. Sobbing tears of joy, Tammy held her hand up to her chest as she heard the magical sound of her child, alive and well, inside of her. It sounded healthy, just like the doctor had said. "Honey, do you hear that?" she whispered softly to Steven.

"I do, babe. I can't believe it." He leaned over and kissed the top of her head. "I love you so much."

"I love you too, Steven. We're going to be good parents, aren't we?"

"The best. I won't let you down, I promise."

Dr. Leon turned down the sound and smiled. "So, how was that?"

"Thank you, Doctor. That was awesome. It seems so real now. There's actually a baby growing in here," Tammy said, pointing to her stomach. She wiped her eyes with a tissue that Steven handed to her.

"Yes, there is. Which means you must take care of yourself. Watch what you eat, exercise daily, and get plenty of rest." The doctor turned, picked up the clipboard from the counter, and glanced over Tammy's chart. "You're scheduled to see Dr. Davis in a month. Until then, just take care of yourself and the baby. Okay?"

"Oh, I will, Doctor," Tammy said, rubbing her stomach.

"Okay then, I'll let you get dressed, and good luck with everything," the doctor said as she reached over and shook both their hands before exiting the room.

As soon as they were alone, Steven hurried toward the door. "Hey, Tammy, I have to use the bathroom really bad. I'll let you get dressed. Meet me in the lobby when you're done, okay?" he said, bouncing up and down on the spot in the partly open doorway.

"Sure, that's fine," Tammy replied, giggling at his display of desperation to get to the bathroom. Really, deep down, she was feeling disappointed. She'd hoped they would be able to discuss the magical moment they'd just shared together. But she didn't want to spoil the moment by protesting against his leaving, so she simply smiled and waved him on his way.

Pacing the lobby while waiting for Steven to return, Tammy found herself growing impatient. She glanced down at her watch; he had been gone almost twenty minutes. "What could be taking him so long?" she mumbled under her breath. Tired of waiting, she decided to go look for him. Just as she turned to head for the bathroom, she spotted him trotting down the corridor toward her.

Frustrated from all the waiting, she spoke with a sharp tone. "Did you get lost or something? You've been gone for almost half an hour."

"Jeez! Sorry, when you gotta go, you gotta go. I didn't know I had a time limit," Steven replied with a smirk.

With narrowed eyes, Tammy looked at him suspiciously. He seemed different. She couldn't quite put a finger on it. He was acting cocky and rude and his face was smothered with that horrible grin she'd grown to detest. She'd seen this side of him before and had questioned it then, too. Why had his mannerisms suddenly changed? She didn't have answers then, and she had no answers now. "I'm not going to argue with you, Steven. Let's just go. I have to drop you off at work." Tammy turned toward the exit and picked up her pace, leaving Steven to follow behind.

Five minutes into the ride, Tammy turned to him to say something and was surprised to find him sleeping. She nudged his arm. "Hey, are you okay?" Steven didn't stir. Raising her voice slightly, Tammy nudged his arm again. "Steven...wake up!"

Startling Tammy, Steven bolted into an upright position, his upper body standing to attention as he shook his head from side to side and blinked his eyes rapidly before rubbing them with his palms. "What? What! I'm fine!"

"You were sleeping."

"Jeez, isn't a guy allowed to sleep?" he said in the same annoying, cocky voice he used at the hospital. "Must be from all the excitement of today."

"You don't see me falling asleep, do you?"

"Get off my fucking case, Tammy. Okay?" Steven snarled.

God, I'm sorry! No need to bite my head off. This is supposed to be a happy time for us. Why the fuck are we fighting?"

"Look, I'm sorry. I just have a lot on my mind right now," he told her as she pulled up to the back door of the restaurant and yanked the car into park. Without any further explanations or words of apology, Steven flung open the car door and stepped out.

He leaned his head down into the open doorway to face her. "I gotta go. I'll see you tonight, okay?"

"Yeah, okay. Bye." Tammy answered in a flat, emotionless voice and waited for him to close the door.

After dropping Steven off, Tammy decided to go straight home and call her dad and Joanne about the ultrasound. She parked her car in her assigned parking space, grabbed her purse, locked the car door, and walked toward her apartment. From a distance, she noticed there was a note pinned to her front door. Thinking it might be a congratulations note from a friend on the baby, Tammy quickened her pace to read the joyous message. But, to her horror, it was nothing of the kind—it was an eviction notice for non-payment of rent. "What the fuck!" she yelled.

Using one hand, she ripped the notice from the door and read it while her hands shook with anger and confusion. In bold red letters, the words "Eviction Notice" jumped out at her. Wondering how many other tenants had seen the notice, she felt her cheeks flush with embarrassment at the thought. "This has to be a mistake?" she said in a panic while fumbling with her apartment key. After several attempts, she managed to unlock the door and quickly rushed inside, slamming the door behind her. Needing answers, she threw her purse on the couch and immediately hurried over to the phone to call the landlord.

While the phone rang, Tammy tried to calm her heavy breathing. After four rings, Bill answered. "Hello. Bill speaking."

"Hi, Bill, it's Tammy Mellows from apartment 2A. I just found an eviction notice on my front door. Surely there must be some sort of mistake?" she asked, trying not to sound too desperate.

"I can assure you there's no mistake." His tone was sharp and unfriendly. "I've not received any rent from you two since you moved in. I've left phone messages and previous notices on your door but still no payment. I rented the apartment to you on good faith without running any background checks. Now I see that I was a fool. I'll never do that again, that's for sure!"

Shocked by what Bill was telling her, Tammy intervened. "Bill, I swear I had no idea. Steven was supposed to be paying the rent and I assumed he was."

"What about all the previous phone messages and notices I've left? Are you telling me you never received any of them?"

Tammy was becoming frantic. "No, I haven't, I promise. You must believe me," she begged. Suddenly, Tammy had a horrifying thought. Steven must have found the notices and hidden them from her or thrown them away. He must have erased the phone messages too. How could he? Why hasn't he been paying the rent? She didn't understand. "I'll talk to him, Bill. I'll see what we can do."

"No, I'm sorry, Tammy. Enough is enough. I want you both out by the end of the month, which is in just less than two weeks' time. I'm not sure if you're telling me the truth about not knowing anything, but if you are, you need to talk to that boyfriend of yours."

"Please, Bill, I'm having a baby. Can't we work something out? I swear I knew nothing about this." Tammy could hear the desperation in her voice as she continued to plead with him.

"No, I'm sorry, I can't. Please be out by the end of the month. I have to go now," he said, not an ounce of empathy in his voice. He hung up, leaving nothing but silence on the other end of the line.

Tammy was shaking in shock and disbelief. Still clinging to the phone, using the wall as a brace, she slid down on her knees and wept. An hour ago, she'd been on top of the world, feeling elated about the baby and becoming a real family with Steven. Now she felt like she didn't even know him. How could he be so deceitful? It was quite obvious he'd purposely been hiding the landlord's notices and keeping the phone message from her so she wouldn't know he hadn't been paying the rent. Missing a month's rent, she could understand, but they've been in the apartment for three months and Bill swore Steven hadn't paid anything. What was he doing with all his money? It made no sense.

Startled by the loud beeping noises coming from the phone, she realized she'd forgotten to hang it up. Pulling herself up off her knees, she placed the phone back on the cradle and wiped her eyes with her sleeve. She didn't know what was going to happen now. Where would they go? She needed answers from Steven. How could he justify not paying the rent? What was more important to him than their home?

With her head in turmoil, Tammy lulled around the apartment for the rest of the day trying to make sense of it all, but she came up empty. Unable to rationalize Steven's actions, her anger bubbled away inside of her as the day wore on.

Steven finally returned home after ten that evening. Having had all day to stew over her discoveries, Tammy's anger had reached boiling point. With a piercing stare and a frown of disapproval, she glared at him from the couch when he walked through the door. No words were needed to express her apparent fury. Her stony silence, folded arms, and crossed legs were more than enough to convey her feelings.

Steven was in no state to question her about her foul mood. With his hands shaking and sweat beginning to form on his forehead, he needed to take care of himself first. "Hey, babe, I'll be right there. I have to use the bathroom," he said as he scurried past Tammy, careful to avoid any kind of eye contact.

"Fine," Tammy replied in a stern voice, now refusing to so much as even look in his direction.

Fifteen minutes later, he finally emerged. Tammy hadn't shifted from her seat, and Steven approached her with caution, feeling all too aware of the tension between them.

His attention was drawn to a piece of paper lying on the coffee table in front of her. He instantly recognized it as an eviction notice, just like the other three he had torn down from the door and destroyed. "Oh crap...I-I can explain," he blurted out in a breath of hurried stutters. Really, he had no idea what he was going to say next. He couldn't tell her the truth. She just wouldn't understand.

Tammy remained seated with her arms still folded as she leaned back and gave him another piercing stare. "How are you going to explain not paying our rent for three months?" she yelled in a high- pitched voice. "What the fuck was you thinking? Do you know how embarrassing this is for me?"

Unable to look at her, Steven glanced at the floor and sat beside her with a forlorn look. He reached for her hand. "I'm sorry."

Tammy smacked his hand away with a harsh swing and stood up. Enraged, she placed her hands on her hips and began pacing the room. "Where the hell did all your money go, Steven? The only thing you had to pay was the rent. I pay for everything else. How could you be so goddamn irresponsible?"

Steven shrugged his shoulders. "I don't know. It kind of just went."

"On *what* for God's sake?" she screamed, fast losing her patience with his lame excuses. The thought of having to look at him made her stomach churn. She despised him. All this time he had kept this from her. How could he? What was going to happen now? She certainly didn't have three months' rent, and neither did he—obviously. "Answer me! It went on WHAT Steven? You haven't brought anything home that costs nearly as much as even one month's rent."

"I don't know, just stuff," he mumbled, shrugging his shoulders.

"Stuff? What the...I don't get it! How did you not pay our rent? Did you just decide you couldn't be bothered? Did you forget?"

Steven was still looking at the floor and simply shrugged his shoulders again.

"What the hell are we supposed to do now, Steven? Oh yes, I talked to Bill, and guess what? He wants us out by the end of the month. Do you have any idea where we'll go when we're homeless, hmm?" Tammy knew he didn't have any answers. At a loss, she stood in the middle of the room and covered her face, allowing the pent-up frustrations of the day to drain away as she wept into her trembling hands.

Steven knew he had to fix the mess he'd created. This was their first major argument, and he couldn't stand seeing her so upset. He'd planned to catch up with the rent before she found out, but the months and the paychecks came and went so quickly; he just couldn't do it. Knowing he had to do something to comfort Tammy, he raised himself off the couch, walked over to her, and placed his hand gently on her shoulder. "I'm really sorry," he said, his voice riddled with apprehension. "I thought I would be able to get caught up. I swear."

"Don't touch me!" Tammy yelled, shoving him away. "How could you do this?"

Steven approached her again, with a little more caution this time, and attempted to embrace the mother of his unborn child. "Shh, it's going to be okay."

This time, Tammy didn't push him away. She felt herself weakening and melting into his touch. He sounded sincere and genuinely sorry for what he'd done. She relaxed her body and nuzzled her face into his chest as she continued to cry.

"Let me make some phone calls," Steven said, stroking the back of her hair. "I'll see what I can come up with, okay? I'll take care of this, I promise."

She looked up at him, her eyes now swollen and red, her nose running onto her sleeve. "Who are you going to call, Steven? I'm scared. We have nowhere to go and we're having a baby," she mumbled in between sniffs.

He held her face in his hands, gently kissed her on the lips, and brushed away the tears from her cheeks. "I'll think of something, okay? Just leave it to me. I fucked up but I'll fix it. Trust me."

She'd already trusted him to pay the rent in the first place and he'd failed. Could she trust him again? Tammy didn't know. But, right at that moment, she felt she had no other choice.

Trying to keep her stress under wraps while at work or visiting her parents was becoming a challenge for Tammy. As the end of the week drew near, panic was beginning to set in. Steven still hadn't come up with a solution. On the occasions she'd asked him what his plans were, he'd simply brushed her off, telling her not to worry and that he was working on it. But how could she not worry? Time was running out.

Tired of Steven's feeble excuses, Tammy had lost her patience and was finding him intolerable. With only a week left before they had to vacate the apartment, she needed answers and she needed them now. Enough of this bullshit, she thought. She needed to know what he had planned for them. Even though she was fueled by a huge burden of anger and fear, she had to remind herself that Steven was the baby's father and now was not the time to abandon him. They were going to be a family and were in this together.

A few hours later, her questions were answered. Tammy was sneaking in a nap on the couch while Steven was at work, only to be jolted out of a deep sleep by the sound of someone barging through the front door. Startled and still exhausted, she sat up straight, her muscles tense with fear. "God, Steven, I was sleeping," she said as she patted her chest to calm her nerves, quickly realizing she wasn't in any danger. "You scared the hell out of me. Why all the noise?"

Throwing down his duffle bag by the door, he rushed over to the couch and dropped to his knees beside her. "Sorry, babe. Listen, I've got some great news." He beamed. "I've found us a place to live."

He grabbed her hand and squeezed it tight. "We can move in right away!"

Her eyes lost all signs of tiredness and sparkled with anticipation. Now he had her full attention. "Really? Where?"

Steven hesitated. "Seattle."

Flabbergasted, Tammy pushed Steven's hand away as a look of horror masked her face. "Seattle?" she screamed, unable to control her anger. "We can't move to bloody Seattle. Are you out of your fucking mind?" This was by far the stupidest thing she'd ever heard.

Steven grabbed her shoulders in an attempt to hold her interest. "Hear me out, okay. We can make this work. Look at it like a fresh start."

Tammy wasn't going to listen to him. She had no intentions of moving hundreds of miles away to another state. Pushing him away with the palms of her hands, she leapt up from the couch. "I'm not moving to Seattle, Steven. What about our jobs? And my dad? I can't just pack up and leave. It's just ridiculous. You can't be serious, surely?"

But he was serious. She could see it in his eyes. "It's the best I can do. We have no other choice." He stood and inched his way toward her. Still in shock, Tammy stumbled and allowed herself to fall freely into the chair next to her. Again, Steven knelt in front of her and took her hands. "It'll be okay. We can do this."

"Oh, I don't know, Steven. I'm sick of fucking up my life. Since I've been in this country, it's been one thing after another. I came here with the intentions of looking for Donna, but I've not done a fucking thing about it because crap keeps happening in my own stupid life. And now you want me to run away to Seattle? Yet another bloody hurdle."

"Your dad will call you if he hears anything about her. You know that. There's not much you can do because there's nothing to go on. We've talked about it before."

"I know, I know. But moving away from my dad feels like I'm abandoning her in some way. Not only that, like I've already said, we can't just quit our jobs. What are we supposed to live off for Christ's sake?"

A smug smile stretched across Steven's face. "Well, you didn't let me finish earlier, but I have a job waiting for me in Seattle."

Tammy was astonished. "You have a job?"

"Yep, I sure do. I can start as soon as we're settled."

"What kind of job? Is it with a restaurant?"

He hesitated again. "Actually, no. It's in sales."

Tammy creased her brow. "Sales? You've never sold a goddamn thing in your life. What will you be selling?"

Annoyed by her endless questioning, Steven gave her an answer that he hoped would satisfy her inquiring mind. "I don't know. I'll find out when we get there. They said I have the job, so I took it. We have a place to live and I have a job. What more do you want?"

"But, Steven, it's in bloody Seattle! How are we going to move all our stuff? My car's not big enough and we don't have the money to rent a moving van."

Steven rolled his eyes. "Its just stuff, Tammy. Our new place is fully furnished so we only need to take our clothes. We can just leave the rest here."

Tammy dragged her hands through her disheveled hair. "God, Steven I don't know. This just seems so bloody crazy." She couldn't believe she was even considering the idea. The thought of moving so far away with just a bag of clothes terrified the hell out of her.

Steven leaned in until his forehead was touching hers. Not wanting to cave in to his ludicrous idea, Tammy lowered her gaze to the floor.

Steven gave her a friendly shake. "Come on, Tammy, it'll be an adventure. You've always said you wanted to see more of the States. Well, now's your chance."

"Yes, I do. But this is all so sudden and so fast. Can't we find anything else? Something around here?" she pleaded.

"There's nothing. I've looked. Like you said, we don't have much time. I know it's far away, but we'll be fine. I promise."

Saying nothing, Tammy continued to stare at the floor as her mind buzzed with all the consequences they would have to suffer if they went through with Steven's crazy idea. She knew the only alternative she had was to move back to her father's, but she refused to do that again; she had too much pride. Tammy took a deep breath and looked up, her face painted with angst. "Okay, let's do it. Let's move to Seattle."

Steven's mouth fell wide open. "Really? Are you sure?"

"Yes, I'm sure. The hardest part will be telling my dad. I'll have to go and see him in person. I can't just call him on the phone and tell him."

Steven nodded, not wanting to discourage her decision in any way. "Sure, whatever you want to do is fine with me." He would agree to anything she wanted. After all, it was his fault they had to move. "I love you. You know that, don't you?"

Tammy kissed him on the lips and cupped his face in her hands. "I love you too, baby."

❧

Tammy had avoided calling her father for two days, knowing the inevitable conversation wouldn't be an easy task. On the third day, she finally plucked up the courage to call. She told him she had some exciting news and would come over that afternoon.

At her father's house, Tammy sat at the table, her nerves on edge while she watched Joanne pour coffee for everyone. "So, don't keep us in suspense. What's the good news?" Joanne asked before taking a seat across from John, thankful that Andrew was down for a nap.

"Well, Steven was offered a job in Seattle and we're moving there at the end of the week."

Saying nothing, John and Joanne shared a quick glance at each other.

"Isn't that great?" Tammy added to break the silence.

Her father leaned back in his chair and folded his arms over his chest. "You're moving to Seattle?" he asked.

Joanne had her suspicions. Something wasn't adding up. "Why the sudden decision to move, Tammy? You've never talked about moving before today. Has something happened?" Joanne's mind raced with a million questions. Was she running away from something? Was Steven making her move? Was he in some sort of trouble? She had unsettling feelings about him, but Tammy seemed happy with him so she'd had to trust her judgment. This sudden move had her worried.

Tammy sensed Joanne's anxieties and, once again, she found herself covering for Steven. "Actually, we'd talked about it before Steven was offered the job in Seattle. He discussed it with me and I told him to take it. It pays more than what he's making now. It comes with a furnished place and he'll be able to start right away. I know it's sudden, but honestly, we couldn't pass it up."

John listened to his daughter's announcement with narrowed eyes and a feeling of uncertainty stirring in his gut. This didn't sit comfortably with him. "Are you absolutely sure about this, Tammy? You're right, it does seem rather hasty to say the least."

"I'm sure, Dad. Please, don't worry. I know what I'm doing. I'll be fine, and when the baby's born, we'll come down for a visit." She smiled at her father in an attempt to reassure him.

John reluctantly nodded, unfolded his arms, and glanced at

Joanne, "Well, I guess there's nothing more to say than for us to wish you luck."

"I guess not," Joanne agreed, displaying a subtle smile.

Relieved that they hadn't objected, Tammy walked over to her father and embraced him before giving him a peck on the cheek. "Thanks, Dad. I'm going to miss you guys, but I promise to keep in touch and bring the baby down to see you as often as we can."

He held on to her arm. "We're going to miss you, too," he said, an essence of concern still lingering in his voice. He couldn't help but wonder if bringing Tammy to the States was a mistake, just like it was with Donna.

on't you feel guilty for leaving all our stuff behind for Bill to deal with?" Tammy asked Steven as they walked out of their apartment for the last time, carrying only a bag of clothes each. "Don't you think it's kinda rude? I do," she added.

Steven walked in front of her with a bulky duffel bag draped over his right shoulder. "Nah, not at all. Look at it like we're leaving him the furniture in lieu of what we owe him for rent," he said as he approached the car, opened the trunk and tossed his bag freely inside, not caring where it landed.

"Yeah, I suppose so, but I can't help feeling like a criminal. I feel like we're running away and being totally irresponsible." She dropped her bag next to his and closed the trunk before jumping in the car next to Steven. Clearly not wanting to wait around for a second longer than necessary, he was already sitting in the driver's seat and revving the engine. "I still think we should tell work we're quitting. I hate to just leave without saying anything."

Steven began to back out of the driveway, wishing Tammy would just shut up and stop worrying about all the minor details. Unbeknown to Tammy, he owed money to a few people at work. If he showed up and announced he was quitting, there was a chance they'd start asking for their money back in front of Tammy. He couldn't allow that to happen. "It's better this way. I don't want to explain to everyone why we're moving. It's none of their business. Let's just go pick up our checks and get outta here."

Tammy silently rolled her eyes and sighed in defeat. Already tired from the whole ordeal, the last thing she wanted was to start an argument. She had to keep reminding herself this was for the best. They were about to start a new life with a new baby. Soon, this will all be behind them.

Over the course of the next hour, they had picked up their checks and cashed them at the bank before sitting back in the car to discuss their upcoming journey. Seattle was about eight hundred miles away. With few stops along the way, they estimated they could be there in roughly twelve hours.

"I'll drive the first leg because I have to make a quick stop," Steven said.

"A stop where?" Tammy asked, puzzled. She knew they already had everything they needed for the trip.

"It's just a quick stop. It'll only take a minute. Jeez, Tammy. What's with all the damn questions today?"

"Sorry," Tammy snapped, angered by his outburst. "I just didn't realize we had more stops to make."

Driving out of Lonesridge, the reality of what Tammy was doing slowly began to sink in. It reminded her of the time she left England. Leaving behind the securities of having her dad close by and unsure of where her future was headed this time around, Tammy's mind taunted her with doubts. Had her father been right? Had she been too hasty with her decision to leave town and move eight hundred miles away? She knew it was too late to turn around now. She just hoped, once again, she was doing the right thing.

About ten miles out of town, Steven exited the highway and turned left onto a desolate narrow dirt road.

"Where are we going?" Tammy asked.

"This is the stop I have to make. It'll only take a minute. I promise."

Tammy saw nothing but empty meadows and scattered oak trees through the clouds of dust that surrounded the car. As they continued down the bumpy road, she heard the barking of an agitated dog in the distance, which seemed to become louder and clearer as they slowly approached a house on the horizon. Driving closer, she saw it was more of a run-down shack than a house. Who could possibly live out here? Tammy wondered.

What was left of the flaky white paint was now peeling away from the wood. All the windows, a few of which were broken, had faded worn sheets hanging in front of them from inside the house. The German Shepherd, which was tied to a long rusty chain, continued its frenzied barking as they pulled up to the front. "Why have a pet if you're going to chain it up all day? It doesn't seem fair," she said to Steven as they came to a stop.

"I dunno. It's not my dog. Wait here," Steven ordered. "I'll be right back."

"Who lives out here?"

"It's just a buddy of mine. I owe him some money," he replied, fumbling with the door handle.

"Money for what?" Tammy screeched. They barely had enough to get to Seattle, let alone give money away to his so-called buddies. Tammy couldn't understand why he suddenly seemed so worried about paying someone back when he never bothered to pay any rent to their landlord for three whole months. It didn't make any bloody sense.

Steven had hoped to leave the car without being drilled with a bunch of questions, but she wasn't going to let that happen. "When I was short one month, he loaned me a few bucks."

"How much is a few bucks? The money we have is supposed to be for our drive," she protested.

"Quit worrying. We'll have enough," Steven snapped. With his back now toward her, he stepped out of the car and let the door swing shut. Crouching down, he looked at her through the open window. "I'll be back in a minute."

"Fine. Whatever." Tammy folded her arms in disgust, leaned back in her seat and closed her eyes, refusing to look at him.

Half an hour later, Steven returned. Furious, Tammy yelled, "What the fuck took you so fucking long?" She didn't wait for him to answer. "You said you'd only be a few minutes," she hollered as he got back in the car.

With no apology, he gave Tammy that same cocky grin that she'd grown to hate, started the car, and slid it into reverse. "Relax, okay?" he said, giving her knee a gentle squeeze.

Still angry, Tammy quickly slapped it away. "Don't touch me!"

"Oh, come on, don't be like that. I said I was sorry. We got to talking, and I lost track of time. But I'm here now. We have no more stops to make so we can get on the open road. Come on, babe, let's not start the trip like this."

"Well, stop pissing me off then." Tammy began to calm down. "I'm sorry I got mad but jeez, Steven, half an hour is a little more than five minutes. Do you blame me?"

"Yeah, I get it. But now we're going to Seattle! Woo-hoo!" he said with a beaming smile while shaking her arm. Tammy couldn't help but join him with a smile of her own. "That's better." Steven gleamed at her while putting the car in gear and headed for the main road. "Seattle, here we come!" he bellowed out of the window as they sped down the dirt road, leaving a trail of dust behind them.

Fourteen hours later, at three o'clock in the morning, they finally reached the dim streets of Seattle. Both tired from their trip, they decided to seek a motel for the rest of the night so they could get a good night's sleep and freshen up before calling Steven's new boss in the morning.

As they drove through the blocks hoping to find a vacancy sigh, Tammy began to feel uneasy. Homeless people lined the streets on both sides, sleeping in makeshift tents or cardboard boxes. Some were still awake, chugging liquor out of brown paper bags, and she swore she saw a prostitute or two stepping into vehicles on street corners.

"Steven, I don't think we're in a good part of town."

"Don't worry, it's only for one night. We'll be fine," he said, trying to ease her discomfort while scouting the neighborhood through the window. "There has to be a motel around here someplace."

Wanting to get off the streets as soon as possible, Tammy joined him in the hunt. For twenty minutes, they drove aimlessly up and down the darkened streets, their eyes fixed on each of the passing buildings. Tammy breathed a sigh of relief when she finally spotted a green "Vacancy" sign blinking brightly over a shadowed building on her right. "There's one!" she squealed with excitement, sitting bolt upright in her seat.

Steven lowered his head and glared out of her window. "Where?"

"There." Tammy pointed Steven in the right direction. "It's called The Lagoon."

Steven followed her finger. "Oh, I see it now." He pulled into the driveway of the motel, bringing the car to a stop in front of the office. Tammy waited in the car with the engine running while Steven left to get a room.

A few minutes later, he returned with key in hand and put the car in drive.

"Okay, we're in room 118. The guy at the desk said it's in the middle of the row of rooms on the left."

Tammy joined in the search, reading each room number illuminated by the dim lights of the parking lot while Steven inched the car along.

"There it is," Tammy said, pointing in the direction of the room with her finger.

Steven saw the room and pulled into the parking space in front, bringing the car to a stop. After grabbing their bags from the trunk, they both headed to the room, looking forward to crashing on the bed and getting some well-needed rest.

Disappointment flooded Tammy as soon as she entered the dark and dingy motel room. Overpowered by the odor of damp, musty air, she covered her nose and mouth with her hands. "My god, this is bloody awful," Tammy muffled through the material of her sleeves. She glanced at the vile orange and gold wallpaper in horror and then down at the stains covering the bright orange shag carpet. Her eyes turned to the queen-size bed, topped with a thin, faded orange bed- spread. She shuddered at the thought of sleeping in it.

Steven tossed their bags on the bed and the keys on a small wooden table beneath the TV, which was padlocked to a metal rack high on the wall.

If the room itself was this bad, Tammy dreaded the thought of how the other facilities were going to look. Adjusting to the foul smell of the room, she removed her hands from her face and cautiously made her way over to the door she assumed lead to their bathroom. "Jesus Christ! This is disgusting!" she hollered to Steven as she quickly recovered her face. "How could anyone feel clean bathing in this filth?" She walked across the cracked white tiled floor to the single sink, blotched with rust and other questionable blemishes. "Ugh," she mumbled. To her right was a small shower, shielded with a clear plastic shower curtain. At least, it would've been clear if it weren't for the years of soap scum clinging to it. Tammy peaked behind the curtain. "Fucking gross," she grumbled, eying the paint peeling away from the filthy tiles and the blackened mold growing around the edges.

"Are you done?" Steven called from the room. "I need to use the bathroom."

Tammy reappeared. "I don't know that you should go in there… you might never come out alive," she said, laughing, and then she turned serious. "You know, you don't have to go in the bathroom to take your medicine, Steven. I'm okay with it."

"Huh?" Steven looked puzzled, and then he remembered the diabetic thing. "Oh, yeah. No thanks, I prefer it this way."

She raised her hands in surrender. "Sorry, sorry. Just trying to make it easier for you. Go ahead. It's all yours," she said as she slithered pass him and perched on the edge of the bed. "I'm glad we're only here for one night. This place is bloody awful."

"It's not that bad," Steven said with a grin before closing the bathroom door behind him.

Contemplating if she should take off her shoes or not, she quickly opted for the latter when she spotted a cockroach scurrying across the carpet. "Yuck!" she squealed, flinging her feet up on the bed. With the decision made not to remove her shoes or clothes, Tammy lay down on top of the bedspread and cringed as her head sank into the musty pillow. Despite her ill feelings toward the horrendous accommodation, exhaustion soon took over and Tammy drifted off to sleep.

Fifteen minutes later, Steven crept out of the bathroom. The subtle sound of Tammy's light snoring was music to his ears. Letting out a sigh of relief, he uttered, "Finally, she's asleep." Knowing he would need his rig first thing in the morning, he'd taped it above the water line inside the toilet tank; a hiding place he had often used at home since Tammy found his previous spot under the sink.

As the effects of the drug rushed through his veins, an amazing feeling of warmth and calmness smothered his entire body. The drug was telling him that life was good. Staring at the bed, his eyes and head began to feel heavy. He let his body fall like a lifeless rag doll onto the bedspread, not caring where or how he landed, and drifted off into a deep, drug-induced sleep shortly after.

CHAPTER 33

The next morning, Tammy was rudely awakened by the sound of screaming voices coming from the parking lot outside. She raised her arm and squinted at her watch, angered to see that it was only five o'clock. Looking over at Steven, she envied him, blatantly undisturbed by the commotion outside.

"You're a fucking pig!" Tammy heard a female voice scream in a drunken slur.

"Oh, go fuck yourself," a drunken male voice replied.

For the next hour, Tammy lay motionless in the dark. She chose not to turn on the lights or peek through the curtains in fear of being seen.

Frustrated and fatigued, Tammy had had enough and jabbed Steven on the arm with her elbow. "Steven, wake up." She jabbed him again but with more force. "Steven! Wake up! I want to get out of here." After a few more attempts, he finally began to stir.

In a drowsy state, he strained to open his eyes. "What's wrong?" he mumbled.

"Don't you hear that racket outside? It's been going on for over an hour. Let's get out of this dump. This place sucks," she said, jumping up from the bed and grabbing her bag.

Steven pulled his body up to a sitting position and rubbed his eyes, realizing he wouldn't be allowed to go back to sleep. "Don't you want to shower first and freshen up?"

"I'm not stepping foot in that bathroom, it's horrible. Cockroaches are crawling all over the place. I can't stand it here. Come on. Get up," she ordered as she stood impatiently by the door.

Needing a fix, Steven rose from the bed and tried to smooth out his wrinkled clothes with his hands before walking to the bathroom.

"Where are you going?" Tammy asked. "To the bathroom. I'll just be a minute and then we'll go, okay?"

"God, Steven. You're always in the bloody bathroom! Hurry up will you. I hate this place," she barked as she stormed across the room and took a seat at the table, folding her arms in protest.

Not wanting to piss her off even more, he rushed into the bathroom, quickly closed the door behind him, and double checked it was locked securely. The last thing he needed was her deciding he was taking too long and charging through the door in the middle of a fix. He hurried through his usual morning ritual, retrieved the rig, and hid it in the back pocket of his jeans. In record time, he had completed his task and joined Tammy in the room where he found her still brooding at the table.

Welcoming the sudden rush, Tammy's bitter mood didn't faze him—nothing did when he was high. "Okay, I'm ready. Wanna grab breakfast someplace? It's too early to call my boss."

"Sure, but not in this bloody neighborhood."

Steven slung his bag over his shoulder and opened the door. "Will you cheer up? We're leaving. Get your stuff and let's go."

Tammy dragged her bags off the table and followed Steven out the door.

For the next fifteen minutes, Steven hunted for a restaurant that would please Tammy and hopefully bring her out of her foul mood. Having already turned down numerous places due to them looking "dirty," she finally agreed to a Denny's, so Steven spun into the parking lot at full speed before she could change her mind.

Still giving Steven the silent treatment, Tammy tucked her purse under her arm and exited the car, slamming the door behind her.

"Jeez, Tammy, what's your problem? Easy on the car door, will you," Steven yelled, using his response as a distraction while he discreetly placed his rig underneath the driver's seat. Ignoring him, Tammy continued to march toward the entrance. Steven quickened his pace to catch up with her and finally reached her as she was opening the restaurant door.

While they sat and waited for a table, Steven tried to sooth Tammy's mood by taking her hand. "Are you okay?"

She jolted her hand away. "That motel was just horrible. I can't believe you let us stay there."

Steven retrieved her hand, stroking it gently with his fingers. This time, she didn't pull away. "Relax, babe, okay? It's behind us. We were both exhausted and took the first place we saw."

"I know. It just gave me the creeps. I've never stayed in such a filthy place before."

"Me neither," Steven lied.

"It's okay," Tammy said, sighing. "It's behind me. I'm sorry."

"I'm sorry, too," Steven replied, finishing with a make up kiss on her lips. Once seated and in better spirits, they feasted on a hearty breakfast of pancakes, eggs, and sausage.

"Hey, babe, I need to go make a phone call to see where we need to go," Steven said to Tammy after finishing their meal.

"Okay. I'll wait here. In fact, after you get back, I should call my dad and Joanne and let them know we made it to Seattle. It was too late to call from the motel last night. They'll be worried sick if I don't."

"Good idea. I'll be right back." Confident she wouldn't leave the table, Steven left to find a phone booth.

"Hey, Rick, it's Steven. How's it going, man?"

"Hey, man. You guys here yet?"

"Yeah. We're somewhere in downtown Seattle."

"Oh, you're not too far away then. I'd guess about seventeen miles. You just need to head north on Highway 99 and take the exit for 212th Street." Rick continued to give directions while Steven made notes on a scrap of paper he had found in his pocket.

"Great, thanks, man. We should be there shortly. And, Rick, one more thing." Steven turned his head, confirming Tammy was still at the booth.

"Yeah, what's that, man?"

"Tammy doesn't know what I'm selling. I just told her it's a sales job."

"I understand, man. I gotcha back."

"Thanks, bro, we'll see you soon," Steven said before hanging up the phone and returning to the table. Steven slid into the booth and took a sip of the now cold coffee.

"Hey, babe, we're not too far from where we need to go. It's about another seventeen miles. We should be there in about half an hour."

"Great!" Tammy slid out from the booth. "I'm going to call my dad and Joanne. Can you get me a refill on the coffee? I won't be long." she said before leaving to make her call.

After a ten-minute call with Joanne describing their long drive, leaving out the horrible motel details, Tammy returned to the table and took a seat.

"I wonder what our new place is like. I hope it's nothing like that motel."

Steven had no idea, only that Rick had told him they could stay with him. "I'm sure it won't be. It's in a town called Knottsby. Apparently, it's a small waterfront town."

"Oh, wow, I can't wait to see it. I've never lived by the water. Isn't that where all the rich people live? Come on, let's go," she said as she jumped from the booth. "I'll meet you at the car."

"No, wait...um, I don't have enough money to pay for this," Steven confessed.

Tammy turned and glared at Steven. "What do you mean, you don't have enough money?" she asked in a loud, angry whisper. "You just got paid, for Christ's sake!" She quickly scanned the restaurant to make sure no one overheard.

Steven followed her whisper. "Yes, and it's gone. I owed that guy money, remember? Then there was gas and the motel room..."

"You only paid for gas once, I paid for the rest. How much did you give that guy? Oh, do you know what, never mind. I don't want to know. Just give me the bloody check," Tammy snarled as she snatched it from his hand. "I'll meet you outside." She stormed off to pay the check, shaking her head in disgust.

With tension between them once again, Tammy sat in silence for the most part of the journey. She was trying to calculate in her head where Steven's money had gone—it wasn't adding up. "So, how much did you give that guy? I can't believe you've spent *all* your money."

Refusing to look at her, Steven tilted his head back and rolled his eyes; he didn't want to have this conversation. "I don't remember. It doesn't matter anyway."

"You don't remember?" she asked, puzzled. "It was just yesterday! How can you not remember? And yes, it does matter, Steven. We have no more money coming in until you get paid from your new job, and who knows when that will be."

Tired of her nitpicking and unable to explain that he'd had to buy some tar to make the trip to Seattle without going through withdrawals, Steven tried to reason with her. "I'll be making some money tomorrow. Will you stop worrying? We'll be fine," he said, hoping she would just drop it and shut up.

But she wouldn't. "I just can't believe you spent it all. You had more than I did, and I still have half of my check left."

Again, Steven rolled his eyes. Losing his patience, he tightened his grip on the steering wheel and let his temper flare. "God, Tammy, will you fucking shut up! I told you, I'll be working tomorrow and I'll have some money. Now can we please just drop it?"

Surprise by his rage—never had he expressed such venom toward her—she stared at his dark, hollow eyes and watched his body tremble with anger. She feared he might strike out at her if she said anything more, so she retreated her voice to a much calmer state. "Fine," she mumbled. Tammy folded her arms and stewed in her seat without saying another word for the rest of the journey.

Twenty minutes later, they pulled into the driveway of a modest single-story home and parked behind a black Chevy van. Tammy opened her door and stepped out, welcoming the fresh, cool breeze, especially after sitting in a stale car with no air conditioning for the best part of the last twenty-four hours. Scanning the street, she liked what she saw. It seemed like a quiet neighborhood, with modest, single-family homes in decent condition on either side of the road.

With their long journey finally coming to an end, the argument between them was soon forgotten. Elated to have arrived, Steven walked around the car with a joyful skip in his gait to join Tammy. He grabbed her hand and pulled her toward the front door. "Come on, let's go find Rick."

She followed close behind Steven as he led the way to the front door and knocked. When the door opened, they were greeted by a heavy-set guy, wearing Levis and a white t-shirt. His long black hair was tied loosely in a ponytail and reached the middle of his back.

"Steven, my man! You made it," Rick cheered, pulling Steven into a hug and slapping his back with a meaty hand.

Rick was not how Tammy had imagined. She had pictured him thinner with short hair, clean-shaven, and having a more professional wardrobe—maybe a suit and tie. After all, he was in sales;

his rather rough-looking attire didn't seem appropriate for his line of work.

"Rick, dude! It's been a long time, man."

Rick glanced over Steven's shoulder in the direction of Tammy. "And this must be the beautiful Tammy I've heard so much about?" he said with a smile aimed at her.

Tammy smiled back and nodded, shuffling her feet towards Steven.

"Yeah, this is my Tammy," Steven said proudly, wrapping his arm around her shoulder and pulling her in closer.

"Nice to meet you, Tammy."

"You too, Rick," Tammy replied.

"Well, come on in, guys," Rick said, gesturing them inside with a sweep of his muscular arm. He led them through a dark hallway to a small kitchen at the back of the house, which looked slightly bigger than it was due to the white painted cupboards and the two windows looking out onto the back yard. He pulled out two chairs from the table in the middle of the room.

"Here, have a seat. Can I get you guys a beer?" Rick asked while opening the door to the fridge.

"Sure, I'll take one," Steven replied. "No, thanks...I'm pregnant. Do you have any juice?"

Rick looked up from behind the fridge door. "You're pregnant? Steven, why didn't you tell me?"

Steven flashed a playful wink at Tammy. "I dunno. Figured I'd surprise you."

"You certainly did that. Wow!" Rick said, rooting through the fridge again. "I only have apple juice. Will that do?"

"Yes, that's fine."

Rick placed a bottle in front of her on the table. "Here ya go."

"Thank you."

Rick popped the caps off the bottles of Budweiser and joined them at the table. "I love your accent. British, right?"

Tammy finished her sip of apple juice. "Yes, that's right. I can't seem to hide it," she said, chuckling.

"Oh, don't ever do that," Rick replied.

"I won't," she said. "I like your home by the way."

"Oh, it's not mine. It's my parents'. They're in Alaska for three months. So, right now, I have the place all to myself," Rick said, nudging Steven's elbow.

Tammy guessed he was probably in his mid-thirties and found it odd that he still lived with his parents, but she tried not to act too surprised. "Oh, I see."

"Yeah, works out great. It means you can stay here until they get back. That should give you enough time to find a place."

"Yeah, that's cool, man. Thanks," Steven said.

"Can I see where we'll be staying?" Tammy asked.

"Sure, it's out back." Rick scooted his chair away from the table, grabbed his beer, and headed toward the back door. "Follow me."

Tammy wrinkled her forehead. "Out back?" she whispered to Steven.

Steven shrugged his shoulders and proceeded to follow Rick.

Tammy followed in silence. They stepped out onto a large wooden deck while Rick held the door open. Off to one side was a round plastic patio table and four chairs, all of which looked like they might have once been white. Tammy glanced over at the dozens of empty beer bottles scattered on the table and shuddered at the sight of at least half a dozen tuna fish cans full of cigarette butts. They followed Rick down the wooden steps from the patio and walked across the grass to the far corner of the yard. A silver-colored travel trailer came in to view behind the broken remains of an old storage shed. Rick opened the door to the trailer and stepped inside.

"It's not much, and it needs a bit of a cleaning I'm afraid, but I'm sure it'll work for a few months."

Horrified by what Rick was proposing, Tammy froze outside the doorway and gasped. "You can't be serious? It's a bloody caravan!"

"It's a what?" Rick asked, sticking his head back out the door.

"A caravan. People go on holidays in these things. They don't *live* in them!" Tammy squealed, still stunned.

Steven reached for her hand. "Over here, babe, we call them travel trailers."

Tammy quickly pushed his hand away in a temper. "I've never heard of living in a bloody caravan. There's not enough friggin' room for starters."

Rick yelled from inside. "It's not that bad, Tammy. Come on in and take a look."

Reluctantly, Tammy climbed the skinny metal steps and entered. She saw straight away that it was even smaller than she had imagined. Gulping down her anger, she began to walk through what was to be her new home. A strong musty smell lingered in the air, making her cough, but she soon realized her sudden bad chest might have been caused by the thick layer of dust coating every surface. The pasty yellow color of the cabinets and couch made her feel like she was stepping back into the sixties. The kitchen was the tiniest she had ever seen, with only enough standing room for one person, but it did have the necessities: a single sink, a small white fridge, and a built-in cooker with a small oven.

Walking to the end of the trailer, she passed a small bathroom, consisting of a yellow toilet, a tiny yellow shower, which she had no idea how she was going to fit into once her bump got bigger, and a miniature stainless sink tucked in the corner.

She reached the back of the trailer in no more than an extra three strides and found herself standing in the bedroom. With the bare mattress taking up most of the floor space, she stood still and glanced around the rest of the poky room. Overhead cabinets hung from the back wall with two brass sconce lights on either side. In earlier days, the drapes throughout the living space probably had a yellow floral print that looked quite pretty. But now, they were torn, rotten, and faded from years of being exposed to the sunlight. The carpet wasn't any better, fraying in most places and blotched with a patchwork of stains.

Rick took a sip of his beer and turned to Tammy, who was now standing in the area of the trailer known as the kitchen—she couldn't see herself ever calling it a kitchen. "See, it's not too bad," he said.

Steven was waiting by the door to the trailer, opting to keep quiet and trying to avoid the solemn look on Tammy's face.

Tammy leaned against the sink and folded her arms. "Does the plumbing work? Is there even running water?"

"I'm afraid not. It's not hooked up. But the back door to the house is always open, so you can shower and use the bathroom over there," Rick said cheerfully before chugging down more beer. "The stove doesn't work either, but you can cook in the kitchen of the house if you want."

"I guess we don't have a choice." Tammy scowled and turned to Steven. "Do we, Steven?"

"Come on, Tammy. At least it's a roof over our heads."

"Oh, hush Steven. If I'd known you expected me to live in a bloody caravan, I would never have come here in the first place."

Thinking they needed some privacy, Rick butted in. "I'll leave you two alone," he said before quickly exiting the trailer.

Tammy nodded and continued where she left off. "I'm not raising our child in a goddamn caravan, Steven. I'll tell you that right now."

"We won't be. It's just temporary," Steven said in a reassuring voice.

"You're damn right it's temporary!" Tammy shouted. "Even if it means I have to look for a place on my own...a place with running water, I might add." Holding her nose and coughing, Tammy headed to the door. "I have to get out of here, it stinks."

Steven was left behind to wonder how on earth he was going to fix his latest mess.

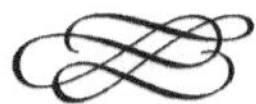

Tammy spent the next three days scrubbing the trailer from top to bottom, lugging buckets of warm, soapy water from the main house. Rick had given her a pile of sheets and pillowcases, some of which she used for the windows after pulling down the old curtains.

By the third day, she had managed to wash all the walls and clean all the cupboards inside and out. The place was at least livable now, if not somewhat cozy. The only area left to clean was the bathroom. After emptying everything from the cupboard below the vanity, she spent a few hours washing the walls, the shower stall, and the small sink. She then bagged up all the items from the vanity, which included an old hairbrush, a rusty can of shaving cream, old razors, and a plastic storage bag. Before tossing the bag, she opened it and peered inside. Sticky black tar with a strong odor of vinegar caused her to hold her breath. "Ugh, disgusting!" she said, whipping her head in the opposite direction.

Feeling satisfied with the much cleaner state of the bathroom, Tammy grabbed the large black trash bag and headed out to the driveway. Pleased to see the trash truck was at the house next door, she waited by the curb and waved to the guy standing on the back of the truck.

As it pulled up in front of her and came to a stop, Tammy held up the bag and yelled, "Can you take this one please?"

The man jumped off the truck and approached her. "Sure, darling," he said with a cheeky grin and a wink.

Ignoring his flirtatious manner, Tammy handed him the bag. "Thank you," she said before heading back up the driveway.

Happy with her progress on the trailer and not expecting Steven to return until after dark, she decided to treat herself to a shower and some lunch.

Since arriving at Rick's, Steven had changed dramatically. Rarely did they see or even talk to each other. Using her car, they left early in the morning before she was awake, and Steven would always leave a twenty-dollar bill on the small dinette table. She used the money to buy cleaning supplies and lunch for herself from the small market at the end of their street.

Always returning home after dark, usually in a delirious state, Steven never said more than few words to Tammy. She watched from afar as he flopped onto the couch with his eyelids drooping halfway over his reddened eyes. He invariably nodded off on the couch with his head bent forward in a drowsy state as Tammy looked on in disgust. Sometimes, straining to stay awake, he'd jerk up in a moment of panic, but within a few seconds, he'd nod off again, incoherent and oblivious to Tammy's presence. Appalled by his appearance and erratic behavior, Tammy often slept in the bed alone. By the time she woke up, he was gone again.

On her way to take a shower the following morning, Tammy couldn't avoid the dirty dishes piled high in the sink of the main house and decided to wash them. Above the clatter of dishes and cutlery, she thought she heard a noise coming from the back yard. Slowly raising her hands out of the soapy water and giving them a brisk shake, she stood in silence and listened intently for any more sounds outside. A few seconds went by before she heard the roaring holler of a male voice and what sounded like objects crashing against a wall.

Puzzled, Tammy ran to the back door and out into the yard. "What the hell is going on?" she grumbled. Turning her head from side-to-side, she scanned the entire area and tried to tune in on where the commotion was coming from. Another round of shouting confirmed the noise was coming from the trailer.

From inside, she heard Steven yell, "Where the fuck is it?"

Alarmed, Tammy ran as fast as she could to the entranceway and nervously peeked her head through the door. Horrified by what

she saw, she slapped her hands over her open mouth and gasped in shock. The trailer she had just spent three days diligently cleaning and trying to make a home out of, had seemingly been destroyed in a matter of minutes. Every drawer had been pulled out and their broken contents were now scattered across the floor in a state of disarray. The once neatly organized stacks of plates and cups now lay in ruins beneath her feet, and the few cupboard doors that hadn't been torn from their hinges were open and swinging freely.

Steven, still unaware of Tammy's presence, was now in the bedroom with his back facing her. As Tammy raced in his direction, fueled with hatred, she could see the bed had been torn apart. Sheets and blankets were tossed into corners, and the mattress lay on its side against a wall. In a blind rage, Steven was pulling everything out of the cupboards above the bed and launching their belongings around the room.

Diving between the flying objects, Tammy ran over to him. "Steven! Stop! What are you doing?" she yelled while grabbing him by the shoulders and pulling him back.

He spun around with a fiery glint in his eyes and locked his fingers around her arms. "Where is it, Tammy? What did you do with the bag?" Steven screamed as he rattled her body back and forth under his tight grip.

Bracing against the pain of his fingernails digging into her flesh, Tammy cried out, "Steven, you're hurting me!" Terrified, she looked into his eyes, shadowed by a haunting darkness of a man she no longer knew.

"WHERE'S THE FUCKING BAG, TAMMY?"

"What bag? I don't know what you're talking about," Tammy sobbed.

"The bag that was underneath the sink in the bathroom. I know I left it there but now it's gone." Steven shook her harder. "What did you do with it? ANSWER ME!" he screamed in Tammy's face so loud that spots of spittle flew out of his mouth and landed on her pale skin.

"Steven, you're scaring me." She was choking on her words, trembling with fear. "There was nothing under there but trash."

Unable to see through the veil of unshed tears, she sniffed hard to clear her nose. "The only bag under there was a plastic bag with some old brown stuff in it."

Steven froze. His eyes shot wide open with hope. "That's the one! What did you do with it?"

"I...um...I th-threw it away. I thought, um...I thought it was rubbish."

As a wave of panic flushed through him, he released his grip on Tammy and spun around before storming back through the trailer, scanning the wreckage for any kind of trash bag. "Where's the trash bag you put it in?" Digging through piles of clutter, he yelled louder, "Where is it, Tammy?"

"I gave it to the trash man. He pulled up right when I was walking out to the driveway."

"You did...fuck...you did what?" As a look of horror descended over Steven's face, he raised his right hand high above his shoulder and swung it down across the left side of her face.

From the unexpected force of his strike, Tammy collapsed against the wall and slid down to the floor. Cupping her cheek in her hand, she felt a hot throbbing pain beneath her skin. Petrified by his enraged state and unable to understand what had come over him, she cowered beneath the shelter of her shaking hands. "I'm sorry, I didn't know," she whispered, her voice trembling with fear.

Steven's shadow loomed over her, his eyes blazing and his nostrils flaring with anger. He mocked her by impersonating a female voice. "I didn't know..." Before Tammy realized what he was doing, his left foot barreled hard into her stomach.

Squealing in pain, she curled up into a fetal position and held her stomach tight. "My god, Steven! The baby!" she screamed as a cascade of tears poured down her face.

Ignoring Tammy's anguish, Steven jabbed her sharply on the shoulder and snarled, "That was five thousand dollars' worth of stuff. I was going to use it to get us outta here. Now what are we going to do?"

Tammy had no idea what he was talking about, nor did she care. Her only worry now was about the baby, unlike Steven, who showed no concern whatsoever. Through her sobbing, she heard someone enter the trailer and the thud of heavy footsteps making their way toward them. In silence, Tammy gushed with relief.

"Hey, Steven, you in here?" she heard Rick call.

Steven held a finger up to his lips, instructing Tammy to be quiet. "Not now, man."

She ignored his request. "In here, Rick!" she hollered back.

Rick appeared in the doorway just in time to see Steven punishing Tammy for not keeping her mouth shut by slapping her across the back of her head. Horrified by what he witnessed, Rick rushed over to Steven, grabbed his arms, and yanked him away from Tammy. "Whoa, man. What the fuck's going on?"

"The stupid bitch threw away the bag, man," Steven moaned, struggling to break loose from Rick's firm hold. Ignoring Steven's protests, Rick turned to Tammy, who was still sobbing on the floor. "Are you okay?"

Afraid to speak again, Tammy simply nodded.

"I'll be right back," Rick said as he began to walk Steven out of the room. "Come on, man, let's get you some fresh air. You need to calm down."

Outside the trailer, with enough distance between them and Tammy, Rick let Steven go.

"I'm so fucked, man!" Steven griped while fumbling for a cigarette in his jean pocket.

"Don't sweat about the stuff right now. Jeez." Rick took a cigarette from Steven, lit it, and inhaled deeply. "Why'd you hit her? She doesn't know what's going on. Damn, man." He drew a few more deep hits off the cigarette and stomped it out on the ground. "Stay here while I go talk to your girl."

Rick found Tammy still curled in the fetal position on the floor, sobbing and holding her stomach. Kneeling beside her, Rick took her in his arms. "Shh, it's going to be okay."

Tammy welcomed his embrace and huddled her head against his chest. Rick held her tight, letting her cry until she was ready to speak.

"I don't know what I did wrong, Rick. There was nothing but trash under the sink." She pulled herself away from his arms and leaned against the wall before stretching out her legs and placing her hands back over her stomach. "I've never seen him so angry. No one has ever hit me before, not even my father. I'm worried about the baby, Rick. He kicked me in my stomach."

"I'm sure the baby's fine. Do you have any cramps or pain?"

Tammy shook her head.

"And you're not bleeding. Right?"

Again, she shook her head.

Rick knew he had to come clean with her; she had a right to know. He placed a hand on her knee. "Tammy, the stuff in the plastic bag that you threw away was five thousand dollars' worth of heroin."

"It was what?" she asked, puzzled.

"Heroin," he repeated. "It's a narcotic drug...and, um, Steven is selling it for me. He should've told you all this before dragging you up here. We go way back. We've known each other since high school and used to get high together."

Tammy stared at Rick in shock. She couldn't believe what he was telling her. "Steven uses drugs?"

"I thought you knew." He was stunned that she didn't. "Haven't you noticed the tracks, or I guess you can call them scars, on his arms? Haven't you found any needles?"

"I did find needles once in our old apartment back in Lones-ridge." Suddenly, it hit her. Steven had been lying to her from the beginning. "I confronted him, but because I didn't really know what they were for, I asked why he never told me he was a diabetic."

Rick chuckled. "Sorry, I don't mean to laugh. You really thought he was a diabetic? And I guess Steven played along, hmm?"

Tammy nodded, but she still wasn't totally convinced. "But diabetics do use needles, and he has the scars to prove it."

"Honey, insulin shots don't leave scars. Those scars are from using heroin. I hate to tell you this, but Steven's been shooting up heroin for as long as I've known him."

"Shooting up? What does that mean?" Tammy asked.

"I'm sorry. It's a term used for getting high with needles."

Tammy frowned. "You mean like...injecting drugs to get high?"

Rick nodded.

"Do you shoot up?" she asked.

"I stopped about four years ago. Now I just sell the stuff."

"And you offered Steven a job?"

"Steven contacted me a while back. Said he needed to get out of town and asked if I was still selling. When I said yes, he said he wanted in. He said he was bringing his girl with him. I assumed you knew everything, so I told him I'd set him up and that the both of you could stay here for a while."

"He hadn't paid our rent in over three months. That's why we got kicked out. He told me he had a job in sales."

"Well, he wasn't lying about that. He just didn't tell you what he was selling."

"I can't believe I never knew he was a drug user." Tammy thought for a moment. "What if I tell him I don't want him to use or sell drugs anymore. Do you think he'll quit?"

Feeling sorry for her, Rick shook his head. She was so naive and clearly had no idea what she was up against. "Tammy, he's an addict...a junkie. Some people are addicted to alcohol. Steven is addicted to heroin, but the addiction to heroin is a hundred times worse than being addicted to booze. Heroin is one of the most powerful and addictive drugs out there. He's not going to be able to just quit. It's not that easy. He'd risk suffering from life-threatening withdrawals."

Tammy knelt on her knees and faced Rick. "But you quit, so why can't he?"

"I spent over three years going in and out of rehab before I became clean. I couldn't have done it alone. I needed help. With medication and counseling, I gradually weaned myself off the drug, and I can tell you now that it was one of the hardest things I've ever had to do. It's dangerous of me to still sell the drug, and yeah, I'm not gonna lie, the temptation is still there, but every day I get a little bit stronger. Now it's all about the money. I make damn good money selling the stuff. More than I could ever make doing a normal job."

Tammy pulled herself to her feet and began pacing the room, combing her hair with her fingers, deep in thought. "Well, what am I going to do? I don't want my baby around drugs, or living in this trailer for that matter. Surely, the baby will make him want to quit."

Rick rose to his feet and walked over to her, placing his hand on her shoulder. Tammy met his gaze. "Look, Tammy, I can't tell you what to do. You need to make your own decisions. But you're right, a kid shouldn't be raised in this kind of lifestyle. I hope he can quit for the sake of the baby, and for your sake, too. But, the sad part is, neither one of us can make him quit. He has to do it on his own."

Trying to comfort herself, Tammy folded her arms. "And what about the stuff I threw away? I'm so sorry, Rick, I had no idea what it was. I honestly thought it was trash."

"Don't worry about it. I'll work it out with Steven." He didn't want to tell her that Steven would have to give him a higher cut on future batches to cover the lost until the five thousand was paid back. Right now, he was just thankful he had some extra cash stashed away to pay the dealer for the batch she had thrown away. "Well, it looks like you have a lot of thinking to do. I'm going to leave you alone. Are you going to be okay?"

"Yeah I'll be fine, and thank you."

Still feeling sorry for her but knowing there was nothing more he could do, Rick left the trailer to go find Steven. After a quick lap of the yard and the house, Rick realized he was nowhere to be found.

Left alone in her thoughts, Tammy questioned why she hadn't seen the signs of Steven's drug use. Reflecting back, they all seemed so clear now; his constant mood swings, falling asleep in the middle of the day—sometimes in front of company—the needles under the sink, his frequent long visits to the bathroom and how he seemed much happier when he came out wearing that awful smirk she detested, the fact that he never paid rent yet still had no money. She also realized now that the stop they'd made to see his "buddy" outside of Lonesridge was a place he needed to stop at to buy drugs—no wonder he wanted her to stay in the car.

Maybe she didn't want to know. Maybe she was in denial. Perhaps the hardest part to accept was that her father had known the whole time. He'd even tried to tell her, warn her, but she'd refused to listen. Steven had been lying to her for months. She was having a baby with someone she didn't even know. Today, she had seen the monster within. No matter what she did, she couldn't get through to him. His one and only concern was the drugs; not her, not the baby.

Tammy found herself fearing him, afraid of what he may be capable of when under the spell of the drug. She could no longer trust him and would have to tread carefully to ensure she didn't cause him to explode. She needed time to think. Was she willing to give him another chance? She didn't know right now. Her priority was to find her and the baby a better home and a better life.

She had to take the reins to get her life back. She had to stand up for herself and not allow herself to cower under him. Tomorrow would be a new start. She would begin by taking her car back so Steven could no longer use it for drug deals. She would spend the day looking for a job and wouldn't return until her hunt proved successful.

Even though Tammy was still sore from being kicked in the stomach, she somehow managed to clean the whole trailer again following Steven's rampage. She put items back in the cupboards and threw away anything that was broken or destroyed. She struggled with the mattress on her own and pulled it back on the box spring before remaking the bed, hanging all the clothes back in the closets, and putting the cushions back on the sofa. Rick popped in from time to time to check on her, making sure she was okay and to see if Steven had returned, but he had not.

By nine o'clock, Tammy was exhausted, both physically and emotionally. Her body ached from head to toe and her stomach was still sore to touch. Periodically, she rubbed it gently to sooth the pain. Relieved she hadn't bled or bruised, she was certain the baby was okay.

Shortly after settling on the couch with her feet up, a pillow behind her head, and a magazine in her hands, she saw the reflection of bright headlights from a car pulling into the driveway. She listened as the engine came to a stop. A few seconds later, she heard the creek of the car door open and then a thud as it was closed. With attentive ears, she listened to the sound of heavy footsteps, growing louder as they approached the trailer. Knowing it was Steven, she wondered if he was still angry and felt a rush of adrenaline as her body switched into fight or flight mode. Should she have fled before he came home? No, she couldn't. She had nowhere to go and besides, he had her car.

Hearing the thud of his boots on the metal steps, Tammy froze. Holding her breath, she watched the handle of the door move down as Steven pulled it open from the other side. Her heart pounded with dread as she waited for him to enter. When he appeared in the doorway, her heart instantly melted. She felt crushed. Never had she seen a man look so sad. His swollen red eyes told her he'd been crying. His hair was in disarray, his pants were dirty, and damp stains blotted his white t-shirt from his tears.

He took one look at Tammy and fell to his knees next to the couch, sobbing loudly. "I'm so sorry, Tammy," he cried. "I don't know what came over me. Please forgive me."

With tears of her own, Tammy reached out and cupped his head in her palms. Softly stroking his hair as he nestled his head on her stomach, she felt pity toward him. He was crouched before her like a little lost boy. "Shh, it's okay. I know," she said, holding him tight.

With tears rolling down his cheeks, Steven pulled himself up to meet her eyes. "I love you, Tammy. I never meant to hurt you. It will never happen again, I promise."

With her eyes scrunched closed, Tammy kissed him long and hard on the top of his head before burying her face in his hair. She saw the remorse in his eyes. She had to believe him. They still had a chance to be a family. She wasn't going to give up so easy. "I forgive you," she whispered. Releasing her hold on him and pulling herself together, Tammy sat up and patted the cushion next to her. "Come on, get off the floor and sit next to me. We need to talk."

Sniffing back a tear, his head hung low, he silently obeyed her.

Tammy took his hand. "I love you too, Steven, but you scared me today...more than I've ever been scared in my whole life. All this time you've been lying to me about the drugs and your new job in *sales.*"

"I'm sorry I lied to you, but I didn't know how to tell you. I was afraid you'd leave me if you knew."

"I want to trust you, Steven." She took a deep breath. "I'm willing to start over and put all this behind us if you will too, but..." Letting go of his hand, Tammy sat up straight with a serious frown.

"But what?"

"In order for me to stay, there have to be some changes." She gazed into his sorry eyes, telling herself not to give in. "I won't raise our child in this trailer and I want there to be no more drugs. I don't want you selling them and I don't want you using them. Do I make myself clear?"

She had no idea what she was asking from him. Nevertheless, Steven gave a silent nod.

Tammy rose from the couch and began pacing the room. "I mean it, Steven. Tomorrow, I'm going to look for work. I'll be taking my car and I'm not coming home until I have a job. And you can do the same. Go out and get a real job. You can tell Rick in the morning that you're done. He knows I'm having a baby. I'm sure he'll understand."

Steven's agitation was niggling at him. He loved her and didn't want to lose her, but she had no idea about the drug world and the addiction he was living with, day in, day out. If he could quit tomorrow, he would, but it wasn't that easy. Just thinking about the withdrawals turned his stomach into knots. The last time he tried to quit—when he first met Tammy—he was violently sick for days on end. He had called her and told her he had the flu. Once he got a fix a few hours later, he was instantly well again and hadn't tried to quit since.

He couldn't explain to her that, because of her fuck-up, he now had to pay Rick back five grand in lieu of the heroin she'd thrown away. And now he'd have to front more stuff from Rick just to keep himself well. Unsure how he was going to sort out the mess he was now in, he decided buying some time until he had an opportunity to really think things through was the best solution. "Sure, Tammy, whatever you want," he said, smiling.

*A*nxious to start her quest to find employment, Tammy woke early the next morning. Careful not to wake Steven, she snuck quietly into the main house to take a shower. After applying her makeup, she dressed professionally in navy slacks and a white long-sleeved shirt.

When she returned to the trailer, she found Steven still sleeping. Not wanting to disturb him, she left him a note on the kitchen counter, asking him to wish her luck and telling him she'd be back later that day—hopefully with a job. She grabbed her car keys from the small table, took twenty bucks out of his jean pocket and left.

She figured a waitress job would be the easiest to find. There were many restaurants in the area and she had the right experience. She also liked the idea of the daily tips to top up her paycheck. Not knowing the roads too well, she pulled out of the driveway, drove down the street and turned left onto the main road, following it south. Her plan was to stop at every restaurant she saw and ask if they were hiring.

Five restaurants later, she was becoming discouraged. Each had told her to fill out an application and that they would call her if anything came up. Having no phone of her own, she'd left Rick's number hoping he would give her the message if they ever got in touch.

By three o'clock, Tammy had lost count on how many restaurants she'd stopped at and how many forms she'd filled out. Desperation was beginning to sink in. Just when she feared she was fast running out of time and options, she spotted a shopping center on her left and pulled into the parking lot out front. It didn't look like the sort of location where she'd find any restaurants, but she slowly scanned all the businesses from left to right, reading all the names out loud one by one. To her surprise, she spotted one called Connie's Diner. "Yes! Might as well give that one a try." She shut off the engine, grabbed her purse and exited the car.

Tammy entered the lobby with her fingers secretly crossed behind her back. It was now after three, so the lunch rush was over and the restaurant was fairly quiet. Soft guitar music played in the background and scenic pictures of harbors and lighthouses hung in neat rows on the walls. A few feet away, a pretty young blond stood behind a hostess station organizing menus. She looked up and smiled as Tammy approached.

"Table for one?" the girl asked.

"Er, actually no. I was wondering if I could speak to the manager."

The girl returned the menus to a slot at the side of her desk. "One moment please," she said before disappearing into the bar area behind her.

Tammy waited nervously by the hostess station, her palms sweating and her skin itching while she silently prayed they were hiring. A few minutes later, the girl returned, smiled, and gestured for Tammy to follow her. "Right this way please," she said with a professional tone. Tammy nodded and followed, giving her hair a quick comb with her fingers.

It was a small room with six round tables, each with four

chairs. Mirrored walls behind the bar reflected the rows of bottled liquors. Sitting on one of the eight bar stools was a short, chubby woman who looked to be of Latino descent. Surrounded by mounds of receipts and fully engaged with a calculator, she hadn't heard them enter.

"Connie, this is the lady that wishes to see you," the hostess said as they approached her. "If you need anything, I'll be out front," she added before leaving.

The woman removed her glasses, placed them on the counter, and gave Tammy the once-over.

Brushing aside her nerves, Tammy extended her hand. "Hi, I'm Tammy."

Connie took her hand and noticed right away she had a good firm grip. "Hi, I'm Connie, the owner. What can I do for you?"

"I was wondering if you were hiring."

Connie pushed the receipts aside. "Here, have a seat. Would you like a soda or something?"

Surprised by her friendliness and feeling more at ease, Tammy sat on the stool next to her. "Sure, a Coke sounds good. Thank you."

Connie left her seat to pour Tammy a drink from the soda fountain. "So, what kind of work are you looking for?"

"Well, I was hoping for a waitress position."

Connie grabbed a napkin and placed it in front of Tammy with the drink on top. "Have you had any experience?"

After taking a sip of the refreshing fizzy drink, Tammy answered, "Yes, I have. I worked in a hotel in Lonesridge, California."

Connie leaned back against the bar and casually folded her arms across her chest. "I like your accent. Where're you from?"

"I'm originally from the north of England, where I was also a waitress. From there, I moved to California." Still able to hide her pregnancy, Tammy decided not to mention it as part of her life story.

"What brought you to Seattle?"

Tammy hesitated. "My boyfriend's job."

"Ah, I see," Connie replied, returning to her seat. "Well, it just so happens..." She paused and smiled. "I had a waitress quit on me just this morning. Your timing couldn't be more perfect. I'm willing to give you a try."

Elated and feeling relieved that her search for a job had finally come to an end, Tammy was unable to contain her excitement and gratitude. She jumped up from her stool to give Connie a tremendous hug, almost knocking her off her seat in the process. "Thank you! Thank you so much!" Tammy squealed.

Amused by her excitement and having seen this kind of reaction many times before, Connie welcomed her embrace. "Now, keep in mind this is just a trial run. Let's see how you do. If you say you have the experience, then there shouldn't be a problem and the job will be yours," she said, peeling herself free of Tammy's arms.

"I won't let you down. I promise," Tammy assured her, smiling from ear to ear.

"I just need you to fill out an application with all your contact information and your social security number. I'll have Stacey at the front desk bring you one. How about you come in tomorrow for the breakfast and lunch shift and we'll see how it goes."

"That's sounds great. What time should I be here?"

"I need you here by six in the morning. I'll have a uniform ready for you. You can pick it up at the front desk."

"Okay, thank you," Tammy answered, excitement still lingering in her voice.

Connie liked her. She liked her enthusiasm and hoped she'd be a good waitress. "Okay then, I'll see you in the morning," Connie said, extending her hand.

Tammy grasped Connie's hand and shook it with every ounce of enthusiasm in her body. "I can't thank you enough for this opportunity. Again, thank you!"

"Don't thank me yet." Connie chuckled. "Show me what a great waitress you are first. Then you can thank me." She motioned with her hand pointing to the lobby. "Now, go tell Stacey to give you the application. When you're done, you can just leave it with her and I'll see you in the morning."

"Thanks, I will." Tammy trotted away to go find Stacey.

Fifteen minutes later, she pulled into the driveway behind the trailer that she reluctantly called home. "This job is going to get us out of this dump once and for all," she said before exiting the car. In a joyous mood, she skipped all the way to the trailer door, excited to tell Steven her good news. She swung the door wide open and leaped inside, yelling, "Steven!"

Standing in the living room, she quickly scanned around the small space before her eyes came to rest at the couch. In an instant, her excitement was absorbed and replaced by disappointment, sadness and anger. Steven was sprawled on the couch, sleeping. Groaning in disgust, Tammy threw her purse onto the floor, marched over to him and nudged her fist firmly on his arm, causing him to stir.

"Steven? For Christ's sake, Steven, wake up," she yelled. Still not awake, she nudged him again. "Steven!"

When he opened his eyes, Tammy's suspicions were confirmed; by his dark, dilated pupils. He was on drugs.

"Hey, baby, you're home," he slurred. "I was just taking a nap."

Tammy stood over him and glared at him with nothing but hatred oozing out of every pore of her body. She fixed her hands on her hips and snarled at him. "Oh, don't give me that crap. You're high. You were supposed to be out looking for a job like I was. You make me sick, Steven!"

He propped himself up on wobbly elbows as he struggled to bring himself up to a sitting position. Tammy watched, repulsed, while he strained to keep his eyes open and fought to keep his head up—just like he had a few nights before.

"Now hang on a second, baby, the day's not over yet. I still have time," he garbled in a sleepy tone.

"You can't go anywhere in the state you're in, and I can't stand to even look at you. Just go back to sleep. I'm leaving." But, before she could finish, he'd crumpled back on the couch in a heap and was fast asleep once again.

Feeling her skin flush a shade of red from anger, Tammy stared at the lifeless figure slumped on the sofa. She no longer felt pity for him, just repugnance. He wasn't going to take her down with him. Steven was making empty promises; she knew that now. Might he change once the baby is born? She wondered. As much as she hated him at that moment, she wasn't ready to give up on him just yet. She decided she would give him the chance to prove himself and show her that he could be a good father to their child.

Over the next few months, Tammy worked as many hours as she possibly could. Sometimes, she picked up extra shifts by covering for the other waitresses, which earned her a little extra money. By buying just the necessities, Tammy managed to save some money—without Steven's knowledge, of course. With the trust gone, she hid her savings in a coffee can that she kept buried in the yard.

She was now almost seven months pregnant, but because she was tall and had gained little weight, she had been successful in hiding it. Being on her feet all day was beginning to take its toll on her already exhausted body, but she continued to push herself, knowing she had only two more months to find an apartment before the baby arrived.

To Tammy's dismay, Steven made no efforts to change and continued to not only use but also sell heroin. They were living under the same roof but leading separate lives. She left him to his despicable lifestyle and refused to take any of his drug money, no matter how broke she was. Her only hope was that he would change once the baby was born. She continued to work hard, determined to get them out of the trailer as quickly as possible; she accomplished her goal just six weeks before her due date and felt triumphant about her success.

In between her shifts, Tammy spent her time scanning the classifieds and had found a one-bedroom apartment just five minutes from work. It was going to be tough, especially because she wasn't counting on any help from Steven. She had enough money saved for the down payment and the first month's rent, but little money for anything else. She was told they could move into the apartment in two days. Unfortunately, it wasn't furnished, but it did have a refrigerator and a stove, which was a start. She could shop at the local thrift stores for the other things they needed, and little by little, just like she had with their last apartment and even the trailer, she would make it a home. Not for Steven, but for the baby.

After signing the lease, Tammy stopped at a few stores in search of boxes and brought home a car full. She wanted to start packing right away. Although she hadn't yet told Steven about their impending move, she was quite sure he wouldn't object to leaving that horrible trailer.

With not much to pack other than clothes, books, and toiletries, Tammy had most of it done by the early evening. She stacked the completed boxes neatly in the front room. Within minutes of taping up the last box and standing back to admire her work, she heard Rick's van pull up in the driveway. Tammy listened to them chatting outside but couldn't make out what they were saying until Steven said, "Night, man," and walked toward their door.

With butterflies fluttering in her stomach, Tammy stood in the kitchen and patiently waited for the door to open. She watched in silence as he entered and stopped in his tracks at the sight of the pile of boxes. "What's this?" he asked, a puzzled look creeping over his face.

Refusing to fear him, she stood tall with her back straight and proudly made the announcement. "We're moving. We can finally be rid of this bloody trailer. I found us an apartment, and I only hope you're as excited as I am." The look on his face told her right away he wasn't.

"Moving? Why? We live here for free."

His pathetic reasoning astounded her. "As I've told you many times before, I'm not raising our baby in a caravan, Steven. Or a bloody *trailer* as you call it. I found us a nice apartment close to my work, and if you get a real job, we'll be able to afford it comfortably."

Steven took a seat on the couch and crossed one foot over his knee. "Don't you think we should have talked about this first? I'm not ready to move."

"This isn't about you, Steven, it's about the baby. How can you be so goddamn selfish?" Tammy threw him a sarcastic laugh. "I actually thought you'd be excited about getting out of here. Instead, you're giving me stupid, lame excuses, and I can't figure out why."

"I can't just move, Tammy," Steven said defensively.

"Why not? I did when we left California, remember?" Tammy folded her arms and huffed. "You don't have to do a bloody thing except load the boxes into the car. I've already paid the rent and packed everything up, and I've already been told we can move in the day after tomorrow. What possible reason do you have for not wanting to leave?"

"What about Rick?"

"What about Rick? You don't need his fucking permission."

"I work for the guy. I can't just leave," Steven protested, raising his voice slightly.

Frustrated, Tammy yelled back louder, "Yes, you can. Selling drugs isn't a *job*; it's a crime for God's sake! Moving now will give you enough time to find a real job and get away from all this crap." Tammy shook her head in disbelief. "I can't believe I'm having to talk you into leaving this pit-hole."

Steven mulled over in his head all the things he couldn't tell

Tammy. He depended on the gig with Rick, not only to make some money but also to get his fixes. He wasn't ready to quit. He had to prepare himself to be gradually weaned down. He had to psyche himself up to face months, if not years of living hell as he transitioned through the painful phases of withdrawal. He needed time. Otherwise, he felt he might as well just kill himself there and then.

"Let me think about it. Okay?"

Tammy couldn't contain her fury. "Think about it? What's there to fucking think about? The place is ours. Tell you what, Steven, you can *think about it* all you fucking want, but I'm moving in. You can stay in this dump if you want. I don't care. I'm getting the hell out of here." She yanked her purse from the counter, flung it over her shoulder and stormed toward the door. "I'm going for a walk. While I'm gone, why don't you ask yourself, Steven...what's more important? Your fucking drugs or your child?"

"Wait, Tammy," he pleaded as she opened the door to leave.

"No! I need to get out of here. I can't believe you're saying you have to think about this." Without looking back, she stomped out of the trailer and slammed the door behind her.

Steven sat in despair, knowing full well his world was falling apart. No matter what he decided to do, he was about to lose the two most important things in his life—Tammy and his child. He loved her so much, and yet he knew how much he was hurting her at the same time. If he left Rick's, he could probably get enough stuff to tide him over for a week, but after that, the violent withdrawals would begin. Tammy would never be able to handle it; she'd freak out and probably leave. And, if he stayed at Rick's, then he'd already lost her.

CHAPTER 38

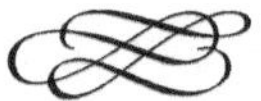

With so many uncertainties of what lay ahead, Steven reluctantly moved into the new apartment with Tammy. He couldn't abandon her and the baby. He had done some really shitty things already, so she didn't deserve to have to deal with that too. Rick had given him enough stash to get by for about a week, but only if he controlled his uses and made it last. What he would do after that week concerned him the most.

Steven watched as Tammy skipped and twirled in a joyous dance around their empty apartment, spreading her arms out wide as she shrieked and squealed with delight. When she passed by him, she beamed him a glorious smile—something he had missed more than he realized. It warmed his heart to see her happy again. Unable to match her enthusiasm, he idly leaned against the wall of the hallway and chuckled as she whisked by him again, this time on her way to check out the bathroom and the bedroom.

"This is perfect for us," Tammy squeaked like a little child. "We'll have it fixed up in no time. Just in time for the baby. I have so many ideas," she said, still beaming a smile. "There are some really good thrift stores around here. I bet we can find a lot of stuff there. What do you think?"

"Sounds great, honey."

Suddenly, Tammy had an idea. "Hey, you know what. I don't have to be at work for a couple more hours. Let's go to the thrift store now!" she suggested.

Steven wasn't feeling up to it; he could feel the stuff wearing off, but he had to hold it together for a few more hours. Maybe shopping would help take his mind off it. "Sure, we can do that."

"Oh wait, we still have a few more boxes in the car. Can you grab them?"

Steven knew he didn't have the strength to carry the boxes up to their second-floor apartment. Not without taking a fix early. He'd make up the time with the next one, he convinced himself. "Yeah, okay, but let me use the bathroom first."

Tammy suspected he was going to use drugs but avoided questioning him. She didn't want anything to spoil her mood. "Okay, I'll wait for you."

Over the next few weeks, Tammy diligently saved money to buy furnishings for the apartment, including a couch, a television, and a dining room table and four chairs. She bought pictures for the walls and filled the kitchen with cookware, dishes, and silverware.

But the brief happiness she'd experienced with Steven deteriorated rapidly as the novelty of their new apartment began to wear off. The trust still wasn't there. Obsessed, wondering if he was still using, Tammy found herself constantly looking for evidence. She'd look closely at his eyes to see if they were dilated, knowing now that dilated pupils were a common sign. She'd watch him walk across the room, waiting for him to stumble. If he sat down, she'd stare at him out of the corner of her eye to see if he nodded off. As part of her daily routine, she'd search all the cabinets, under the bed, and down the sides of the couch cushions for drug paraphernalia, needles, tar, cotton balls, or spoons. Surprisingly, she found none, but she convinced herself it was because she just hadn't found his hiding spot yet.

The times his body language told her he was high; Tammy chose to say nothing. Now in her third trimester, she didn't want the added stress of fighting a losing battle. Fearing his anger, she'd reasoned that silence was the best solution. She needed to get through the pregnancy first. Then she'd figure out what to do. So far, her pregnancy had been an easy one. She'd had no morning sickness and had only gained twelve pounds, which allowed her to remain active and keep on at work. The doctors were not concerned about her lack of weight gain; they reassured her the baby was doing fine and seemed healthy. Because she was tall—almost six feet—the pregnancy still wasn't showing as anything beyond a slight bump, which could easily be hidden with a baggier shirt, so she hadn't felt the need to confide in anyone at work that she was expecting.

Tammy's suspicions of Steven's drug use were confirmed when he came home in a frantic state one day and demanded twenty dollars from her. When she refused, he charged at her with a vengeance and cornered her in the kitchen, his body trembling with anger, his pale face highlighted with blotches of red creeping up from his neck. Tammy, afraid he may strike out at her if she didn't, caved in and handed him the money. Within seconds, he fled through the door, leaving Tammy drenched in her own tears.

When he returned later that day, wearing his signature smirk, he apologized profoundly and promised it would never happen again.

But, it did—just two days later. It was the beginning of a vicious cycle.

Steven's addiction was spiraling out of control. No longer on easy street with Rick, the hunt for the drug consumed him from morning till night. Having a two-hundred-dollar-a-day habit, his days were spent stealing all kinds of merchandise, finding buyers for stolen goods, cashing in, and then—the ultimate reward—buying the drug.

Tammy was now living with a complete stranger. The once happy, funny, and loving Steven had been replaced by a person that repulsed her. A man, that had no dignity or ambition. His long, matted hair acted as a daily reminder that Steven no longer had any pride. His clothes hung like rags from his skeletal frame, and his skin, the color of a corpse, showed what a sick man he was. No one could help or save him; this was his battle, not hers.

The thought of returning to her father's had crossed her mind on more than one occasion since moving into the new apartment, but an unexpected phone call crushed that idea before it even had chance to get off the ground. Her dad broke the news that he and Joanne were moving to Florida at the end of the month and may also be living in Ireland for part of the year. The thought of both parents being thousands of miles away made Tammy nervous and, for the first time, she experienced a sense of utter loneliness. She had too much pride to ask her father for help. It was up to her to somehow find a way to break loose from Steven once the baby was born so she could give her child the life it deserved.

After working late one night, covering a cocktail shift, Tammy returned home exhausted only to find Steven passed out on the couch. Sickened by the sight of him, she simply shook her head and left him in his drugged-out state before going to bed alone.

She tossed and turned for hours, experiencing severe stomach cramps that prevented her from getting off to sleep. Frustrated, she glanced at the illuminated clock and saw it was three in the morning. "Damn it!" she barked while reaching over to turn on the bedside lamp. She threw back the blankets in a fit of annoyance and grabbed her bathrobe from the end of the bed. Tugging aggressively at the ties, she wrapped herself in the pink terry-cloth robe and headed to the kitchen to get a glass of water.

But she only managed to make it as far as the bedroom door before she felt a warm gush of fluids run down her legs. Instantly, she knew her water had broken and the baby was coming. Holding onto the door handle for support, she bent over in excruciating pain as she experienced her first contraction. "Oh my god!" she yelled in agony, hoping it would soon pass.

With the pain subsiding, Tammy fumbled to open the door and yelled down the hallway, "Steven! The baby is coming!" There was no response. She waited for the contraction to fully pass and, while grasping her stomach and using the walls for balance, she slowly made her way down the hall. When she reached the front room, she flicked on the lights. Steven was not on the couch. She looked down and saw he had rolled off and was now passed out on the floor. In desperation and unable to bend down, she fought her pain and kicked him in the gut. "Steven, wake up. The baby is coming."

"Ouch! What the fuck," he yelled, placing a limp hand over his stomach.

"Get up, Steven. I need you to drive me to the hospital. I'm in labor."

"Oh shit!" In an instant, he suddenly appeared normal and sober. Dragging his fingers through his hair, he jumped to his feet in a frenzy and began to walk circles around the room. "What do we do?"

"First, I need you to calm down. Then I need you to get my overnight bag from the bedroom while I call the midwife."

"Okay." Without another word, he hurried off to retrieve the bag while Tammy stumbled for the phone.

With a fear of drugs embedded in her, all thanks to Steven's usage, Tammy had chosen in advance to deliver by natural childbirth. Like the rest of her pregnancy, the delivering went smoothly and quickly with no complications. Just two hours after her first contraction, she gave birth to a beautiful baby boy, weighing in at seven pounds, four ounces.

Surprisingly, Steven stuck around during the delivery, holding Tammy's hand and telling her to breathe during the contractions. But, as soon as the baby was swaddled in her arms, he made an excuse to leave. Tammy knew the real reason why he had to abandon her and his newborn child less than twenty minutes after welcoming him into the world, but she let him go without protest.

When he returned, the signature smirk confirmed what he'd needed the bathroom for. He might be high, but Tammy wasn't going to let anything spoil the magical moment she was experiencing. Bonding with her son cradled in her arms, she was already madly in love and totally amazed by his perfection. Up until that moment, she had not thought of a name, but now, as she looked down on him, the name suddenly came to her. Tammy smiled and kissed his tiny forehead. "Hi, Matt."

"Who's Matt?" Steven asked.

"Our son. I'm naming him Matt. Not as in Matt, short for Matthew, just Matt, and his name is not up for debate."

Steven didn't argue. "I like it. It's fine with me."

Tammy gave her new son a little squeeze. "Isn't he beautiful?"

Steven stroked Matt's full head of black hair. "He sure is." He then looked at Tammy and smiled. "I'm going to be a good dad. You watch."

It meant nothing to her. She'd heard his promises too many times before, all of which had been broken. "Don't just say it, Steven. Show me. The most important thing in my life now is this little boy. If you can't be there for him, we'll be just fine on our own. I mean it, Steven. I'm not going to subject him to a life surrounded by drugs and crime."

Looking down at his son, Steven knew he was in serious jeopardy of losing them both. He couldn't let that happen. He needed help and he needed it fast.

CHAPTER 39

"What do you mean you had a baby? You weren't pregnant last night."

Tammy giggled down the phone. "I'm sorry I never told you, Connie. I was afraid you wouldn't hire me if you knew. And I was able to hide it pretty well. I'm sorry I'm laughing, but I would love to see your face right now."

"No, I just don't believe you. Listen, I know you worked late last night...if you're tired, girl, just let me know and I'll give you the day off. But don't lie to me."

Again, Tammy laughed. "Connie, I'm serious. I'm not lying. I had a baby boy less than three hours ago. There's no way I can come into work today. If you don't believe me, I'm at Northwest Hospital. Come down and meet our new son Matt."

"I think I'll just do that. I'll see you soon! Bye for now," she said with uncertainty and hung up.

Within the hour, Connie was by Tammy's bedside and chattering away with baby talk to Matt. Tammy was happy Steven had left. She probably wouldn't see him for the rest of the day, and she needed to talk to Connie anyway.

"Where did you hide him, girl? He's so precious. I can't believe I didn't know. You're going to have to take some time off. How much do you need?"

"Actually, I kinda wanted to talk to you about that."

Connie, was all ears. "Sure. What's up?"

"Well, Steven isn't working right now and money is tight. If I can find a sitter, I want to come back to work in the next couple of days. I feel great so I'm sure I'll be fine."

Connie had grown close to Tammy over the last few months. She wasn't sure what was going on, but she had an intuition that it wasn't all roses at home for Tammy. "Well, maybe I can I help."

"You? How?"

"Well, you know I live above the restaurant. I could watch the little guy there while you're working. And, not only that, I must confess that I absolutely love babies." Connie chuckled while gently squeezing Matt's cheek.

Tammy was surprised by her gesture. "Oh, Connie, I can't ask you to watch Matt for me, it's just—."

"You didn't ask. I'm offering." "I...I don't know what to say. Thank you!"

Connie patted Tammy's shoulder lovingly. "No need to thank me. I'll put you on breakfast and lunch so you can be at home with him in the evenings."

"That would be great, thank you. I really don't know what I'd do without you."

Tammy did what she intended to do and returned to work just two days after giving birth to Matt. With no help from Steven— whose days were still consumed by drugs—she couldn't afford not to.

By the end of the month, after working as much as she could, Tammy felt she had failed her son. Despite saving as much money as possible, she only had half the month's rent and was going berserk with worry as she contemplated what to do. She returned home, feeling utterly exhausted, and laid her sleeping son in the middle of her bed before straightening his blankets and putting him into his crib.

Satisfied that he was safe and sound asleep, she turned toward his crib and pulled back the small mattress. She let out a sigh of relief; Steven hadn't found it. Tammy retrieved the white envelope she had stashed and slid it open with her finger. To her absolute horror, she discovered it was empty. "No...No...NO!"

In disbelief, Tammy checked the envelope again. She shook it and turned it upside down. It was empty. She gently slid her hand under the mattress to check it hadn't slipped out. Nothing. Steven had found her stash and taken the money she had been saving for rent. Shaking uncontrollably, she fell to her knees and sobbed. "How could he? How could he do this to us? What am I going to do now?" Crying, Tammy crawled over to Matt and gathered him in her arms, being careful not to wake him. With soft kisses to his forehead, she spoke to him in a soft, comforting voice. "It'll be okay, Matt. I'll take care of you. I love you so much. I'll figure something out, I promise."

Later that night, unable to sleep with worry, Tammy heard the front door open and close. She glanced at the clock illuminating the darkened room and saw it was just after midnight. She ripped the bed covers away from her body, leaped out of bed, and charged down the hallway into the living room in a rage.

She turned on the lights and found Steven standing in the middle of the room, swaying from side to side. Inching closer to him and seeing his eyes were closed, she watched as he struggled to hold his head up. Tammy knew instantly; he was high.

He turned his head with what looked like an almighty effort and gazed at her through half-open, sunken eyes. "Hey, honey," he slurred. "I didn't know you were up."

In a fury, Tammy marched toward him until she was within an

inch of his spaced-out face. "How could you!" she yelled, shoving him backwards as hard as she could.

From the force of her unexpected push, Steven lost his balance and fell onto the couch behind him, where he erupted into a fit of giggles.

"How could I what?" he mumbled in a squeaky voice, seeming to assume Tammy was playing some sort of game.

Tammy took a step back as Steven struggled to his feet in front of her. "You've stolen the money I had stashed away. That was for our fucking rent, Steven!" she screamed, feeling her anger intensify. "I hate you!" She raised her hand and slapped him hard across his cheek. Her hand stung, but it felt good to blast her rage at him.

Steven's head whipped around, causing him to fall back onto the couch again. Rubbing the red mark that was now forming on his face, he hollered back, "Fuck! I'm sorry, okay. I was sick. I just happened to stumble across the envelope and temptation got the better of me."

"You didn't *stumble* on that money. You hunted high and low for it until you found it. I'm sick of your fucking lies!" Tammy hollered before kicking the sole of her foot into his shin.

Steven winced and leaned forward to rub his leg. "Goddammit! Quit hitting me, okay. I said I was sorry. Let's talk about this in the morning. I'll get the money back."

Tammy let out a sarcastic laugh. "You'll get the money back, will you? You're a fucking loser, Steven. I used to feel sorry for you, but now, I totally despise you and I just can't wait till I'm free of you."

In an instant, Steven was alert. Taking Tammy by surprise, he grabbed her arm and pulled her down within inches of his face while squeezing her arm tight and digging his nails into her skin.

Tammy shuddered with fear as her body tensed up from the pain.

With a piercing stare, he growled, "If you ever try to leave me and take my son away from me, Tammy, believe me, I will find you. I will hunt you down and you'll wish you never had." He tightened his grip around her arm. "Do you understand me?"

Tammy winched from the pain. "Yes," she whimpered, uncertain of what he might do if she tried to argue.

Steven released his grip, leaned back against the couch and smirked.

"Good. Do we understand each other now?"

Tammy rubbed her arm to ease the throbbing pain spreading over her skin. "Yes, we do." Wanting only the comfort of her son, she ran down the hallway with tears swelling in her eyes. Closing the door behind her, she let the tears fall. Through her watery eyes, she looked down at Matt innocently sleeping in his crib. She was relieved to find their shouting hadn't woken him.

Seeing the rage in Steven's eyes when he threatened her had made her realize he was more than capable of harming her. But would he hurt his own son?

The next morning, Tammy was woken by the sound of Steven's stern voice while he shook her arm. "Come on, get up. We're going to my mother's house."

"What?" she asked, still in a sleepy state.

"You heard me. We're going to my mother's." He ripped the covers away from her body. "So, get up and just grab what we need."

"I can't just leave! What about my job?"

"You'll get another."

"But your mother lives in Los Angeles!" She heard Matt stirring in the crib and got up from the bed. "Out of my way. Matt's waking up," Tammy said while gesturing with her hands for Steven to move aside. She picked up Matt and rocked him in her arms. "So, we're going to run away again? Leave everything behind again? That's your plan?" she asked, her voice laced with sarcasm.

"Well, do you have a better one? My mother will put us up for a while, and besides, it's about time she met her grandson, don't you think?"

After last night, she didn't want to piss him off—especially in front of Matt. "Fine, I'll start packing after I've fed Matt."

"Good. I'm going out for a while. I'll be back in a couple hours. I want you and Matt ready to leave when I get back."

Knowing he'd probably left to score drugs with the rent money he'd stolen, it crossed Tammy's mind to leave with Matt while he was gone. But he had taken her car, and she feared the consequences of being found if she tried to escape. For now, she'd have to go along with his plan. She would know when the time was right to leave.

While sitting in the rocking chair feeding Matt, Tammy made the difficult phone call to Connie. After two rings, a female voice answered the restaurant's phone. Tammy recognized it as the hostess, Stacey. "Connie's Diner. How may I help you?"

"Hi, Stacey, it's Tammy. Is Connie available?"

"Hey, Tammy. One second, let me transfer you to the bar."

"Thanks." Tammy listened to a moment of soothing classical music while her call was transferred.

"Hello, Connie speaking."

"Hey, Connie, it's Tammy."

"Hi, Tammy. How's my little man?"

"He's fine. Listen, I hate to tell you this with such short notice..." She hesitated and took a deep breath. "I won't be able to work for you anymore. I feel awful about it, Connie, and I'm so sorry. You've been so good to me."

"Is everything okay?" Connie asked, concerned.

Tammy lied. "Yes, everything's fine. Steven's mother is sick, so we're going to move in with her for a while so he can take care of her. She lives in Los Angeles."

Connie wasn't buying her story but didn't want to intervene. "I'm so sorry. I'm going to miss you, but I'm going to miss little Matt even more."

"I know, I'm going to miss you too, Connie. Is it okay if I come in later today and pick up my final check?"

"Sure, I'll have it ready for you. And, Tammy?"

"Yes?"

"If you ever need anything, I'm here."

Tammy read between the lines perfectly well and knew she was reaching out, but she couldn't possibly involve Connie in her twisted world. "Thanks, I will." She sighed and hung up the phone.

Tammy knew she should probably call her dad and Joanne with the disturbing news that she was moving yet again. But, not knowing the address of Steven's mother, she decided against it. She didn't have any answers to the concerning questions they'd probably have. Once she was settled, she'd call them with the same excuse she gave Connie.

Once Matt had fallen asleep, she placed him in his crib and began to pack.

Two days later, Tammy and Steven pulled into an apartment complex in San Gabriel, a suburb of Los Angeles.

"Wow, I haven't been here in over five years but it still looks the same," Steven said as he parked the car and opened his door.

Tammy stepped out, opened the back door, and lifted Matt out of his car seat. "Can you grab the diaper bag from the trunk? I need to change him," Tammy asked, her voice flat.

Once they had what they needed, Tammy followed Steven through a narrow passageway toward the apartments. Straight away, Tammy noticed the white metal bars on all the windows. "What's with all the bars? It's like living in a jail."

"It's to stop people from breaking in," Steven answered.

"Can't be a very good neighborhood if you have to bar up your windows."

"It's fine, Tammy. My mom's lived here for over fifteen years and has never had a problem. Why do you always have to find fault with everything?"

"I'm not finding fault. I was merely observing. It's the first place I've ever seen with bars on the windows. That's all."

He shook his head. "Whatever."

Steven approached apartment number 102 on the first floor and banged on the metal screen door, causing it to shake and make a rattling noise.

"Steven! Not so loud," Tammy hissed. "She's hard of hearing. It's you that needs to be quiet. Jeez."

Tammy stood behind him holding Matt, nervously anticipating meeting his mother for the first time. A few moments later, the door behind the screen opened and a frail old lady, using a cane to steady herself, peered through the mesh.

"Hi, Ma, it's Steven!" he yelled.

The old lady looked confused. "Steven?"

"Yes, it's me. Open the door."

His mother fiddled with a few locks and latches on the inside of the door and finally managed to unlock it. Both Tammy and Steven took a step back as she pushed it open toward them. Tammy was astonished by her age; she had to be at least seventy. Then, Tammy remembered Steven telling her she'd had him when she was forty-five.

"Ma!" Steven bellowed, pulling Tammy in closer to him, causing Tammy to cringe. "This is my girlfriend Tammy, and this is your grandson Matt."

Unable to hide her look of shock caused by their unannounced visit, Steven's mother clasped her bony frail hands in front of her face. Tammy noticed the prominent purple veins crisscrossing her skin like a web. "Oh my goodness! Hi, Tammy, I'm Elizabeth. Come in."

"Hi," Tammy said softly with a kind smile.

Following Steven inside, Tammy saw it was a simple two-bedroom apartment, darkened by the closed drapes. Every available surface was cluttered with dusty knick-knacks and photos.

Gaudy, gold framed pictures of flowers and fruit bowls hung from almost every inch of the walls.

Tammy settled herself on the burgundy couch with Matt and watched with pity as Elizabeth struggled to sit next to her. Every movement seemed to cause her discomfort and pain. Tammy turned to Steven, who seemed oblivious to his mother's troubles, and whispered with disbelieving sarcasm. "Will you help her? I can't believe I have to ask you to help your own mother."

Dumbfounded by her request and feeling awkward at the idea of having to help his ailing mother, he complied reluctantly and steadied her with a hand on her arm as she slowly lowered herself onto the couch.

"Oh, he is so precious," Elizabeth, said, staring into her grandson's eyes. "Why didn't you call me and let me know you were coming? I would have fixed us something to eat."

"We wanted to surprise you, Ma." Steven paused. "In fact, we were thinking about staying for a few days." He looked over at Tammy. "Right, Tammy?" he asked with a persistent tone.

Tammy looked away from his stare and turned to his mother. "Err, yes, if it's okay with you, Elizabeth. We don't want to impose on you."

Before Elizabeth could answer, Steven had left the matching burgundy chair and was at his mother's side. He placed a gentle hand on her shoulder. "It's no trouble. Is it, Ma? You want to spend time with your grandson, don't you, Ma?" His leering smile made Tammy shift uncomfortably in her seat.

His mother reached up and patted her son's hand. "Of course I do. You can stay here for as long as you want. You can have the spare bedroom. You may have to clean it up a bit, I've not been in there for quite some time."

Tammy felt sorry for her. She seemed so frail and lost. Steven didn't seem at all concerned about his mother's failing health, only with what she could give him. Shelter, food, and—most importantly, Tammy assumed—money. "Don't you worry about it, Elizabeth. I'll be happy to clean the room," Tammy said.

"Are you sure?" Steven's mother asked.

"Yes, I'm sure. It's the least I can do." Tammy gave her a friendly smile. "And thank you."

Within less than twenty-four hours, Tammy witnessed Steven coaxing money from his elderly mother. Whatever stories he told her were probably lies but, from that day forward, his mother gave him cash every morning. With money in his hand and a smirk on his face, he left, not to be seen until after dark. Insisting the car be left with her because of Matt, Tammy would stare from the kitchen window, which looked out onto the main street, and watch Steven jump into a black beat-up sedan before speeding off down the street.

His mother was oblivious to his drug use. He was an only child, and in the eyes of a mother, her son could do no wrong. Tammy was afraid to tell her, knowing it would break her heart.

Left alone all day with Matt, Tammy soon became friends with Elizabeth's neighbor, Natalie, who was a stay-at-home mom with two young boys aged two and three. They frequently spent the afternoons together in the courtyard, letting her two boys play while Matt got some sun and fresh air. Some days, Natalie watched Matt for a couple of hours while Tammy looked for work. After a week of searching, she found a job as a waitress at a local diner.

Thrilled for Tammy, Natalie relieved one of Tammy's biggest concerns and offered to watch Matt while she was at work.

That night, while Elizabeth and Matt were sleeping, Tammy told Steven about her successful job hunt. As usual, he'd arrived home well after ten o'clock wearing the smirk she despised. After a quick "hi," he grabbed a beer from the fridge, took a seat on the couch, stretched his legs out on the coffee table and fixed his eyes on the television.

Dressed in her bathrobe, Tammy sat in the chair across from

him. "I thought you should know I got a job today. I start tomorrow."

"Why?" He asked, not taking his eyes off the TV.

"Well, we can't stay here forever. I don't want your mum supporting us. Don't you feel bad taking money from her every day?"

Steven laughed. "It's not that much. Besides, she loves me."

Tammy hated his cocky laugh. "Well, it bothers me. I want to contribute."

Steven steered his eyes away from the television. "Who's going to watch Matt? Surely not my mother?"

"No! I wouldn't dream of asking her. I've become friends with Natalie next door. Not that you would know, being away all day. Anyway, she's going to watch him."

"Well, it looks like you got it all figured out. Does this mean you'll get tips every day?"

Tammy could tell he was mulling something through in his head but wasn't going to ask. Whatever it was, it wouldn't be good. "Yes, and it will help with diapers and stuff for Matt." Tammy shifted in her seat. "You know, it wouldn't hurt for you to find a job. Matt is your son too, you know?"

Steven threw back his head and scrunched his eyes closed. "Oh, don't start with me, Tammy. I'm working on something. It takes time."

"You always have an excuse, don't you, Steven?" She stood up and marched towards their bedroom. "I'm off to bed." Just like she did every night, she went to bed alone feeling nothing but hate for the man in the other room.

Now that Tammy had money coming in, she desperately wanted to get Steven away from his mother before he drained her completely. Secretly, she opened a saving account, but struggled to put much away because of Steven's constant demands. Knowing she'd have tips after being on the floor for a few hours, he'd made it a daily habit to show up at her work and force her to give him all the money she had. He'd regularly back her into a corner and pin her against the wall, leaving Tammy with no choice but to give him some cash. She couldn't risk causing a scene that may result in her losing her job.

During her lunch break one day, she scoured the classifieds for apartments but found they were all well out of her price range. Feeling discouraged, even more so by the pouring rain, she finished her shift, grabbed a newspaper to shield her head, and made a dash for her car.

A few blocks away, Tammy was surprised to see one of her co-workers, Judy, standing at a bus stop with no umbrella or hat. She quickly veered her car off to the side of the road and pulled up alongside of her. Tammy leaned over toward the passenger side of the car and rolled down the window. "Judy," she hollered. "You're getting soaked. Do you want a ride?"

Judy approached the car and peered in through the open window, her nose and cheeks flushed from the cold raindrops trickling down her face. Her flat, lifeless hair framed her face in a mangled mess. "Oh, hi, Tammy. Sure, that would be great. Thanks," Judy said with gratitude. "If you don't mind. I don't live too far from here."

Tammy reached over and pushed the door open. "Sure, no problem. Hop in."

Judy lowered herself into the dry, warm car, relieved to be out of the rain. "Thanks," she said again.

"My god, Judy, you're drenched." Tammy turned her head and searched the back seat. "I know I always keep a towel in here. I never know when I may need one, especially when my kid is riding with me." She scanned some more and then spotted the corner of it peeking out from under a bag. "Oh, here it is." With one hand, Tammy pulled it up between the two seats and handed it to Judy.

Judy smiled. "Thanks," she said and began dabbing her face.

"Where do you live?" Tammy asked while pulling away from the curb.

"Oh, not too far. About three miles down this road, at the Clifford Motel."

"You live in a motel?" Tammy questioned. "Isn't that expensive?"

"Actually, no, it isn't. I pay by the week. They never asked me for a deposit and the utilities are included."

Tammy was intrigued. "What about cooking?"

"I have a little fridge, a microwave, and a hotplate. It's amazing what you can do when you have limited space."

"Would you mind if I come take a look at your place? I've been looking for an apartment, but everything in the newspapers is so damn expensive."

"Sure, if you don't mind the mess. I have two kids so it gets kinda cramped."

Tammy couldn't hide her look of surprise. "You have two kids? I had no idea."

"Yeah, I don't talk much about my personal life at work."

Tammy understood. She, too, hadn't shared the fact that the father of her child was a drug addict, or that she was supporting him while they lived with his elderly mother in her small apartment. She wondered what else there was to know about Judy. How did she end up living in a motel? And where was the father of her children?

A few minutes later, Judy instructed Tammy to pull up in front of a pale blue two-story building with white trims, scattered palm trees, and lush green lawns.

"This is it," Judy said as the car came to a halt.

Tammy was impressed. "It doesn't look too bad," she remarked as she got out of the car. Closely inspecting every inch of the building and grounds as she looked around, Tammy followed Judy up the pathway and through a tall metal gate.

"It's not. But it's not the best either," Judy said with a laugh.

Tammy ducked her head inside the collar of her jacket in an attempt to avoid the rain hitting her face. She liked the central courtyard with the benches and tables, even though they'd been soaked with the day's terrible weather. To the left, she spotted a gated community pool, which was unsurprisingly deserted because of the rain. Tammy envisioned it filled with sunbathing moms capturing every moment of peace while their children squealed and frolicked in the pool. Walking past the rooms, Tammy heard television sets blasting loud, children playing, couples fighting, and parents yelling at their kids. It wasn't a quiet place, Tammy noticed.

"This is a busy place," Tammy stated as they approached room number 109 on the first floor.

"Yeah, most of the people live here full time, like me. Mainly single moms and families on welfare," Judy replied while pulling out a bunch of keys from the front pocket of her uniform. She unlocked the door and motioned with her head for Tammy to go inside. As Tammy stepped through the door, Judy threw her keys down on top of the TV set and opened the drapes to let in some light. "Well, this is it. Told you it wasn't much, but it's home to me and my babies."

Tammy glanced around the small, cluttered motel room. Protruding out into the middle of the room were two unmade queen-size beds with very little space between them and much less to walk around the edges. Piled on both beds were toys, clothes, and two laundry baskets filled with towels and even more clothes. Across every surface, various items were piled on top of each other in a jumbled mess. The single sink counter was stacked high with diapers and groceries, but she spotted a microwave and a hot plate among the clutter. Beneath the counter was a small black fridge, and to the right was a closed door, which Tammy assumed was the bathroom.

Judy walked over to the sink, grabbed a towel hanging from the wall, and gently dabbed her damp hair. "Do you want a towel?" she asked.

"Nah, I'm fine. Thanks."

After giving her hair a quick brush and checking it in the mirror, Judy untied her apron and flung it on the counter. "I have to pick up my kids. Do you mind hanging out here for a bit? I'll just be a few minutes."

"Do you need a ride? It's still raining. I don't mind taking you."

"No, but thanks. My babysitter, Maria, lives here on the second floor."

"Oh, well that's convenient," Tammy remarked.

"Yeah, it sure is. Especially since I don't have a car right now." As Judy headed toward the open door, Tammy darted in between the two beds to allow her to get by.

"I won't be long. Make yourself at home."

Tammy sat on the edge of one of the beds and scoured the room, picturing her and Matt living in such a place. Funnily enough, Steven wasn't in the picture. She liked that. She thought how perfect it would be, and at least it was something she could afford on her own. She wondered about the babysitter on the premises and imagined how convenient that would be, too. If the motel had vacancies and the sitter was taking more kids, this could be a way out for her. The thought excited her. Maybe this was the solution she'd been looking for.

In less than ten minutes, Judy returned carrying a sleeping baby boy in her arms and holding the hand of a shy four-year-old girl.

"Hi, what's your name?" Tammy asked the small girl.

"Tell her your name, sweetie," Judy said, giving her daughter's hand a gentle shake.

The little girl smiled. "It's Kate."

"Hi, Kate, it's nice to meet you. My name is Tammy."

Kate hid behind her mother. "Hi, Tammy."

"And this little guy is Christopher. He just turned nine months." Tammy saw she was heading toward the bed and quickly jumped up.

"Here, let me help," Tammy said while placing the laundry baskets on the floor.

"Thanks." Judy smiled and laid her son in the middle of the bed before covering him with a blanket. "Hey, Kate, how about you play with some of your Barbies over on the floor by the sink while your brother sleeps. Okay?"

"Okay, Mommy." Kate scooped up an armful of her dolls and skipped over to her designated spot.

Tammy smiled and sat back down on one of the beds as she watched Kate organizing her dolls. "Aww, she's so cute."

Judy sat across from her next to her son. "Thanks. As you can see, it gets pretty cramped in here, but we make do."

"How long have you lived here?" Tammy asked.

"About six months."

Tammy wanted to know more. "Where's the kids' dad? Does he live here too?"

Judy looked down at her son while she spoke, rubbing his stomach gently. "No, he doesn't. He's in prison and won't be out for a while."

Tammy gasped. "In prison? For what?"

"Oh, the usual. Drugs, selling drugs, using drugs. It's not the first time. He's always in and out of jail. I'm used to it."

Astounded that her husband seemed so much like Steven, Tammy was curious and had to ask. "Why do you put up with it? Why not leave him?"

"I don't really know. I know I should, and I tell myself that every time he gets arrested and goes back inside. I just can't seem to do it. Plus, I don't want to take the kids away from their daddy. They would be heartbroken. He's not the best father, but he's all they have." And then, with a heavy sigh, she added, "And I guess, deep down, I'm hoping that the next time he gets out of jail, he'll change and start being a good husband and a better father to our kids." She paused and smiled. "Ha! I'm still waiting for that day."

Tammy detected her sarcasm. They both knew her husband was never going to change, but she continued to stay and tolerate his behavior because of the kids. Tammy felt like she was looking at her own reflection. Like Judy, she was just making excuses for Steven and it sickened her.

"But it never happens, does it?" Tammy said, looking down at her clasped hands on her lap.

"No, it doesn't," Judy replied, unable to hide the disappointment in her voice. "But I keep holding onto that dream," she added, her eyes now misty.

"You know, I can relate to what you're going through," Tammy said, reaching out and gently patting Judy's leg.

"You can?" Is your husband in jail too?"

"No, but it's just a matter of time." Tammy paused briefly, wondering whether or not to disclose any more. "I've never told anyone this before. I think it's because I've never met anyone that could understand me or understand what I'm going through. But you can."

"Go on," Judy urged. She glanced across the room at her daughter to make sure she wasn't listening, but Kate was still happily engrossed in Barbie world.

"For the record, I'm not married. But the father of my child, Steven, is a drug addict. He doesn't work. We've been living with his mother for almost two months, and I think it's just a matter of time before he ends up in jail." Tammy took a deep breath. She had just opened the gates to her troubled personal life and let someone in for the very first time. The emotions flooding through her were exhilarating; a feeling of hope and a sense of release. She felt like she'd just unblocked a valve and all the built-up pressure was bursting to freedom.

No longer feeling alone in her nightmare, she now had someone to talk to and share it with. Tammy folded her arms and embraced herself with the new comfort she was experiencing. "When I look at you, I see me. I see myself living here with Matt. But I must confess, unlike you, I can't tolerate Steven's lifestyle. I want to leave him. Even though he's my son's father, I'm afraid for our safety. He's been violent toward me in the past. If I stay, I truly believe he's more than capable of doing serious harm to the both of us."

"Oh, wow..." Judy was shocked. She had no idea Tammy was hiding such a secret. "Dave, my kids' father, isn't a violent man. He's never raised his voice or his hand to me or the kids. There are many nights, though, where I've held my kids tightly and cried alone while my husband is hauled off to jail...again. He's a drug addict, yes, and I feel sorry for him. He truly wants to quit and I believe him when he says he does. I tell myself that, one day; he'll beat this addiction and be the husband and dad he truly wants to be. I must hold onto that dream. It's what keeps me going, which is why I'm always here when he gets out. If he ever hit me or the kids, though, I'd be gone in a heartbeat."

Kate trotted back across the room, climbed onto her mother's knee, and nestled in her arm. Judy kissed her daughter's head before turning back to Tammy. "Why not see if they have a room available here? You said you liked it."

Tammy beamed. "I would love to live here. Anything's better than living with Steven's mum. Every day, I have to watch her own son constantly harass her for money. She has no clue what's going on. In her eyes, Steven's an angel. I can't bear to watch it anymore."

"Well, if you want, we can go down to the office and ask if they have any vacancies."

"Really?" Tammy said excitedly.

"Sure, I'll take you as soon as Christopher wakes up. In the meantime..." Judy leaned over and tickled Kate. "I need to feed this little girl."

Kate giggled, got up from her knees and followed her mother to the counter, where Judy made a peanut butter and jelly sandwich for Kate, and a cup of coffee for herself and Tammy.

Tammy left the Clifford Motel feeling hopeful. In the matter of an afternoon, everything was falling into place. She got the last room available on the second floor. It was identical to Judy's with two beds, a small fridge, cooker, microwave, and a bathroom—everything included but without the clutter. Fearing it may soon be rented, she'd jumped on it and took the room for one hundred fifty dollars a week, paying a week's rent in advance.

Judy also took her to meet her babysitter, Marie, a nice Hispanic woman who spoke good English. Tammy liked her right away. She had the experience and offered many references. Best of all, her rates were affordable. After discussing her hours, Marie agreed to watch Matt once she had settled in.

Already late for picking up Matt, Judy walked Tammy down to her car, accompanied by Christopher in her arms and Kate holding tightly onto her hand. The rain had finally stopped and people were beginning to filter out of their rooms with their kids. "I'm forever grateful for your help. In one afternoon, my life has completely changed for the better, and I owe it all to you."

"You're welcome. I'm looking forward to having you for a neighbor. We can help each other."

"I'm at your mercy," Tammy said with a laugh.

Tammy leaned in and gave Judy a light hug, being careful not to squish her son. "Bye. And, again, thank you." Before stepping into her car, she knelt in front of Kate. "Bye, Kate."

"Bye," Kate replied before hiding behind her mother again. Tammy laughed at the shy little girl.

Driving home, Tammy's thoughts turned to Steven. The last obstacle left before she could move. How was she going to handle him? She didn't want a scene in front of Matt or his mother. Tammy was certain Steven wouldn't want to leave the comforts of his mother's home or, more importantly, her money.

But would he let her leave? She had the idea to leave before he returned home but soon scratched it, knowing he would only show up at her work the next day and cause chaos. She couldn't risk losing her job. The only option she had was to tell him when his mother was present; in the hope Elizabeth would be able to keep him calm. Tammy shuddered as she imagined what his reaction might be.

After picking up Matt, Tammy headed home to share her news with Elizabeth. Bounding through the front door, Tammy was shocked when she found Elizabeth sitting on the couch, sobbing into a white cotton handkerchief. Still cradling Matt in one arm,

Tammy rushed to her side. "My goodness, Elizabeth. What's happened?"

Her crying intensified as Tammy wrapped her free arm around her shoulders. In between sniffles, Elizabeth wiped her eyes and said, "Oh, Tammy! Steven called me."

"And?" Elizabeth shook her head and cried into her handkerchief again.

"Is he okay?" Tammy asked.

"He's been arrested," she replied. "He's in jail. He said he was arrested for selling drugs. My boy doesn't sell drugs!"

While comforting Steven's mother, Tammy was silently rejoicing. It took all her strength to refrain from dancing across the room and screaming "YES!" out of the window. Unbeknown to Elizabeth, Tammy was thrilled he was locked up—she just hoped it would be for a long time. Now she wouldn't have to listen to his protests. For her, the timing couldn't have been more perfect. The final obstacle had been resolved.

CHAPTER 43

Not wanting to leave Elizabeth while she was so distraught over Steven's arrest, Tammy waited a few days before taking the plunge into single motherhood.

Steven had called collect at his mother's house the day after his arrest. With the security of jail walls safely between them, Tammy told him she was moving.

"So, now that I'm locked up, you decide to move," Steven yelled down the phone. "And what about my mother? You can't leave her by herself," he added, still yelling.

With his mother in her own bedroom, Tammy yelled back, hoping Elizabeth wouldn't hear her. "This has nothing to do with you being locked up. I got the place before I even found out you'd been arrested. Matt and I need our own space. And what about your mother? She's been on her own for years, yet suddenly you're concerned? You're just using that as an excuse. Don't worry, I'll pop in and check on her occasionally, which is more than you've ever done in the past five years."

"And what the fuck is that supposed to mean? Are you telling me I don't care about my mother?"

Tammy rolled her eyes. "Steven, you can interpret it however you want. I'm not going to argue with you. You either like it or you don't. I really don't fucking care anymore." She was done explaining herself to him. "Your mother will be fine. I gotta go."

"Wait, bitch! Don't you hang up on me!"

She'd had enough of his bullying. Placing the phone back on its cradle, she beamed with a satisfied smile.

Steven was charged with the selling of narcotics and being under the influence of a controlled substance. He was sentenced to ninety days in jail and would probably end up serving forty-five.

Within twenty-four hours of being locked up, his withdrawals came on strong. First came the intense headaches, followed by the dizziness and nausea. A few hours later, the shakes began. Steven watched his hands tremble uncontrollably while trying to beat the sweats and his dripping nose. Feeling like his body was being turned inside out, the pain in his gut became unbearable and brought him to his knees, causing him to scream in constant agony.

For the first two nights, he didn't sleep; he tossed and turned in wrenching pain, his calls and cries ignored by the guards. They had seen and heard it all before. Other inmates laughed and told him to take it like a man.

By the end of the week, the pains began to subside and the withdrawals were easier to handle and happened less frequently. Once again, Steven told himself he was done with drugs. God had given him another chance and he was now a new man.

After prying his mother for Tammy's phone number, he called her and explained all about the new person he'd transformed into and swore he'd learned his lesson. Tammy had heard it all before and no longer believed his empty promises. While locked up, he had no choice but to stay sober, but she wasn't convinced he would remain clean once released. The temptations would always haunt him, and the cravings would still exist as a constant reminder of the power drugs had over him. She knew without a doubt that he would eventually cave into that power and would yet again become submissive to the drug. To her, it was just a vicious cycle that she no longer wanted to be a part of.

It's been two weeks since Tammy moved out of Elizabeth's and took up residency in the Clifford Motel. Being away from him was like a breath of fresh air. As the days turned into weeks, Tammy was adapting to and enjoying the role of being a single mother. Gone were the days of having to walk around on eggshells in fear of Steven's mood swings. Her money was hers, and hiding it was no longer necessary. For the first time in such a long time, she had control of her life again and she wasn't going to let anyone take that away. The motel wasn't much, but it was home to her and Matt.

Having Judy close by was comforting. They spent many hours sharing each other's stories and giving one another support, each agreeing how much the fathers were missing out on their kids' lives because of drugs.

Tammy cherished the quality time she got to spend with Matt on her days off, even if parts of those days were spent catching up with the laundry and cleaning the room.

She had just returned from the community laundry room with a basket of clean clothes under one arm and Matt cooing in the other when the phone rang. She placed Matt in his playpen and answered the phone. "Hello?"

"Hi, Tammy. It's your dad."

"Dad! What a surprise. How are you?"

"Good, listen, I have some great news."

Tammy quickly picked up on the excitement in his voice. "You do? What is it?"

"I just received a phone call from The Boston Police Department. You're not going to believe this but..."

Tammy heard her dad choking up on the other end of the line.

Growing impatient and now concerned, Tammy urged him on. "What, Dad? What is it?"

He took a deep breath and said, "Donna has been found."

"What!" Tammy screamed as she fell to her knees in disbelief, consumed by an overwhelming surge of emotions.

"Is she okay? Where is she?" She had so many questions that she couldn't get them out fast enough.

"From what I understand, she's going to be fine. She's in the hospital right now."

"The hospital? Why? What happened?" Tammy needed answers. "Is she going to be okay?"

He took a deep breath before repeating to Tammy what the police had told him. "Apparently, she was found in an alley about a week ago. She was beaten up pretty bad."

"Beaten up? Oh no," Tammy shrieked.

"Calm down, she's going to be okay. I have to tell you, though, whoever beat her up had left her to die. It was a homeless woman that found her and called the police. She had a pretty bad concussion, some broken ribs, and bruises all over her body. At the hospital, she told the police who she was and that she had run away from the children's home five years ago. It was the home that gave my number to the police."

With tears of joy flooding down her cheeks, Tammy gasped. "My god, Dad. She's alive. I can't believe it!" She glanced over at Matt, who was lying happily in his playpen, and smiled through her tears. "Matt, your auntie Donna is alive!" Tammy hugged the phone. "Oh, Dad, I can't tell you how long I've been waiting for this day... to hear the news that she is still alive. With all the years that'd passed, I was beginning to think for sure she was dead, but with no leads from the police and no proof, I just couldn't ever bring myself to believe it."

"I know, Tammy, I had the same thoughts."

"So where has she been all this time? Do the police know? Do they have the son of a bitch that beat her up and left her to die?" She couldn't hide the fury in her voice. How could anyone be so malice to another human being? She just couldn't fathom it. She felt the rage rush through her body. It was the same kind of rage that she continually felt with Steven. The anger and disgust felt the same.

"That's all I know, Tammy. I spoke to her for a little while this morning."

"You spoke to her? How did she sound? Did she sound okay?"

"Surprisingly, yes, she sounded okay. A little weak and emotional of course, but who wouldn't be after what she's been through. She kept apologizing for running away. I told her it doesn't matter. I'm just relieved to have her back in our lives. I'm going to fly out there at the end of the week. I bought your mother a ticket and a hotel room. We'll see her together."

"Thanks for bringing Mom out, Dad."

"No need to thank me. She kept asking about you and Jenny though. I gave your mother the number of the hospital and she'll give it to Jenny. Do you want it too?"

"Yes! Yes, of course I want it. Hold on a sec, let me go find a pen."

"Okay."

Tammy set the receiver on the floor and started hunting for a pen and paper. Matt, who seemed to have sensed the excitement, was beginning to fuss. "Hold on, sweetie, I'll feed you in just a minute." Tammy found a pen and notepad by her bed, grabbed it, and returned to the phone.

"Okay, Dad, I got one. Go ahead."

With her hands still trembling, she carefully wrote down all the information her dad relayed to her. "Thanks, Dad. I'll call her as soon as I've fed Matt and put him down. He's starting to get fussy. I gotta go. I love you."

"Love you too, Tammy. Bye now."

Tammy quickly hung up the phone and set about attending to Matt.

Twenty minutes later, after a good feeding and a diaper change, Matt was sleeping soundly in his playpen, which doubled up as his crib. Confident she would have no more interruptions, Tammy prepared herself to call Donna. Just thinking about it was enough to bring tears to her eyes. For years, she'd anticipated receiving a phone call that Donna had been found dead. Where had she'd been all this time? Why hadn't she called anyone? It didn't make any sense. The only way to find out was to call her. With a quick shake of her head and a deep breath, Tammy composed herself and dialed the number to the hospital.

After two rings, a female voice came on the line. "St John's Hospital, how may I direct your call?"

"Yes, hi, can you put me through to room 202 please," Tammy, asked politely.

"One moment please."

With a racing heartbeat and what felt like a whole swarm of butterflies darting around inside her stomach, Tammy listened to the phone ringing, waiting to hear her voice.

"Hello."

The voice sounded weak and tired, but Tammy recognized it immediately. Pools of tears flooded her eyes. "Donna?"

"Yes."

Unable to hold back her sobbing, Tammy choked up. "Donna, it's Tammy."

"Oh my god! Tammy. I've missed you so much."

"I've missed you too." Unable to hold it together, both girls wept over the phone, unable to speak, unable to breathe, engulfed in pure bliss at the thought they had finally found their sister.

"Where have you been, Donna? What happened to you? I honestly thought you were dead." Tammy had so many questions. "I've missed you so much."

For the next hour, Tammy sat on the floor with the phone

glued to her ear, horrified as she listened to Donna describe the past five years of her life. She began by telling her that, when she ran away from the children's home, she met a man who told her how beautiful she was and managed to coax her into going back to his place with him.

Within less than a few weeks, he had her strung out on cocaine and was pimping her out as a prostitute on the streets of Boston. Because she had nowhere else to go, she became dependent on him for drugs and a place to live. He dictated her life for the next five years, working her every night till the early hours of the morning and keeping all the money she earned. Anything Donna needed, she had to get down on her knees and beg for it. Whether it was a bar of soap or a pack of cigarettes, it didn't matter, he made her plead and pray for it. Fear consumed her morning, noon, and night. Not a day went by where she wasn't slapped or punched across the face or beaten to the floor and kicked in the stomach. She lived with constant reminders that if she ever tried to leave, he would hunt her down and kill her. She meant nothing to anybody and wouldn't be missed.

The night she was found in the alley, he had come to pick up the money she'd made while standing on the street for three hours turning tricks. She'd tried to explain it had been a slow night and she'd made nothing, but he spat in her face and told her he didn't believe her. When she tried to reason with him, he slapped her across the cheek and called her a lying piece of shit. The more she protested and swore she had no money, the more he hit her. As she fell to the ground, Donna recalled, he continued to kick her in the head and stomach until she finally passed out. The next thing she knew, she was waking up in the hospital.

There was silence on the phone. "Tammy, are you still there?"

"Yeah, I'm still here," Tammy replied in a somber tone. "I just can't believe what you've been through."

"I'm so sorry I never called any of you guys. I hope now you can see why. I just couldn't, he would have killed me, I'm sure of it.

Oh, and by the way, I didn't tell Dad any of this. I don't want him to know, so please don't tell him."

Tammy was still having a hard time grasping Donna's horrible story. Still in a daze, she spoke softly. "Yeah, that's fine. I understand. You don't have to worry. I won't say anything. Have you talked to Mum or Jenny yet? Are you going to tell them?"

"No, I haven't talked to them yet but I do intend to tell them. I just don't want Dad to know. Not yet anyway."

"Hey, are you going to file charges against the guy that did this to you?"

"God, no!" Donna said without hesitation. "If I do, he'll probably come looking for me, and he'd make sure I was dead the next time he beat me up. I did give the cops his name and address, but I won't testify. I just want to get as far away from him as possible." Donna hesitated for a moment. "I want to come live with you, Tammy. He'll never find me in California. I'll finally be safe, and more importantly, I'll finally be with you."

Tammy almost dropped the phone in surprise. "You want to come live out here?" She paused. "With me?"

"Yes. I can't stay here. It would be okay, wouldn't it?" Donna asked.

Tammy wasn't about to say no to her sister, especially after what she had been through. She scanned her room, wondering where Donna would sleep. The extra bed was an array of clothes, toys, and groceries. "Yes, yes, of course you can stay with me. Why wouldn't it be okay, silly?" Tammy said with a light chuckle. "When will they release you from hospital?" Tammy needed to know how much time she had to prepare for her arrival.

"I'm not sure. I think in about a week. Do you think Dad will pay for my ticket? He and Mom will be here in a couple of days. I can't wait to see them, but I'm afraid to ask him for anything."

"Of course he will," Tammy assured her. "I'm sure he's not going to let you stay out there all by yourself. Not after what's happened to you. Let me talk to him, okay?"

"Okay...and thanks." The line went quiet. Tammy could hear her sister crying again. "I've missed you, Tammy. There were so many times I wanted to call you, but I was too scared." Donna sniffled into the phone. "He would have killed me if he found out. I'm really sorry for not calling you or the others. Can you forgive me?"

"Of course I can. Why don't you get some rest, and I'll call Dad to see when we can get you out here, okay?"

"Okay. I love you, sis." "I love you too, sis. Bye, I'll talk to you soon. And, Donna?" "Yes?" "Welcome back," Tammy said with a smile. "Thanks, it's good to be back." After hanging up, Tammy held the phone in her shaking hands as if she were embracing her long-lost sister. She was unable to hold back the intense tears of joy that drenched her face. After all these years of questions, concerns, and heartbreak, she was about to see her sister again. She was alive but had been living a nightmare. Tammy glanced over at the playpen and was relieved to see Matt was still sleeping, which meant she had time to make a few more phone calls.

After pulling herself together, Tammy called her father. He answered the phone almost right away. "Hello?"

"Hi, Dad, it's me again." "Hey, Tammy. Did you talk to Donna?"

"Yes, I did. Gosh, it was wonderful to hear her voice. I'm so happy she's okay. Anyway, the reason I'm calling is, um, she wants to come live out here. She doesn't feel safe in Boston. I can't say I blame her. So, we figured she could come live with me."

"That's a brilliant idea," John replied, clearly elated.

"Yeah, I think so. Anyway, Dad, is there any chance you can buy her a ticket? She has no money and I certainly can't afford to buy one."

"Of course! Consider it done. I'll let you know the details in a day or so."

"Thanks, Dad. You're the best."

They continued to share their joys of Donna's return for a few more minutes before saying their goodbyes and hanging up. Tammy was left with the unbelievable realization that, in about a week, she would be seeing Donna, her beloved sister, for the first time in years.

CHAPTER 44

That evening, Steven attempted to call Tammy, but she refused the collect call. It had been such an amazing day with Donna now back in her life, not to mention the anticipation of seeing her next week, so there was no way she wanted it ruined by him.

Three days later, he called again. Tammy was rocking Matthew to sleep, but she reluctantly had the call put through. As soon as it was connected, she was deafened by Steven's joyous squeals. "Tammy, baby, it's me. I'm out. Come pick me up."

Shocked, Tammy's body instantly became rigid. "You're out? But you've only done five weeks. How is that possible?"

"I know. I can't believe it either. Apparently, they're overcrowded, and I'm one of the lucky ones they let go." He chuckled. "Anyway, just come get me, baby. I have no money for a bus, so I'm standing outside the jail and I'm freezing my ass off."

Tammy's heart sank to the floor. Still fearing him, she had no choice but to give him a ride. "Okay, but I need to get Matt dressed. I'll be there in about an hour."

"Okay, I can't wait to see you. I love you," Steven shouted down the phone. Tammy hung up without replying. She could pretend some things for the sake of her own sanity, but she couldn't pretend to love him anymore. She would never say those words to him again.

"Fucking great," Tammy barked after placing Matt in his playpen. She tossed various items into his diaper bag as she continued her rant. "He's not living here. I won't have it! This is my place. I paid for it and he's not going to bloody well ruin it for me again. As far as I'm concerned he can go live with his mother." She turned to Matt. "Right, Matt?" Her son smiled and cooed at her, kicking his feet in a happy gait. His sweet innocence instantly melted her heart; he had a funny little way of unknowingly comforting her when she needed it the most. She smiled back at him, gently gathered him in her arms, and kissed his tiny forehead. "Come on, big boy, let's get your stupid dad."

An hour later, she pulled up in front of the jail. Before she'd even had chance to park, she spotted Steven galloping toward her car. The streetlights illuminated his scruffy wardrobe, consisting of black sweats, a stretched out gray sweatshirt, and a pair of slip-on sandals over his bare feet. As he approached the car, she began to fully appreciate his fresh-out-of-jail appearance. He looked awful. His hair was matted and dirty and in dire need of a good brushing. A short, scruffy black beard hid his chin, and his ever-present mustache needed a generous trim. His taut, pallid skin stretched over his prominent cheekbones; an indication of his drastic weight loss.

As he stepped into the car, he glanced over at his son who was sleeping soundly in his car seat. He then turned to Tammy and gave her a peck on the cheek. She quickly turned her head and covered her nose as she reached for the car window handle. "God, Steven, you stink!" she yelled, winding down the window as if her life depended on it. Taking in a lungful of fresh air, she gladly welcomed the cool breeze from outside.

"Geez, sorry, Tammy, not exactly the Ritz Carlton in there you know. Come on, let's go home so I can take a shower."

Tammy pulled away from the curb with a huge smile on her face. "I have some great news," she said.

"Oh yeah, what's that?" Steven asked while fidgeting with his sandals that had slipped off.

"My sister Donna has been found. Can you believe it? She's coming out here in three days. I'm so excited, I can't wait!"

"Wow! That's awesome, Tammy. Didn't I always tell you she was going to be okay?"

"Yeah, you did," Tammy agreed, avoiding eye contact, knowing what his next question was going to be.

"Where's she staying?"

With her eyes fixed on the road ahead, she gripped her hands firmly on the steering wheel. "With me," she replied, loading her voice with as much confidence as she could muster.

"What? The place you have ain't big enough for three people and a baby."

"You're right, it's not. Which is why I need you to stay with your mother."

"What? I just got out of jail for fuck's sake! What the fuck are you talking about? Live with my mother."

Tammy tried to reason with him, only for the sake of not wanting to start a fight with Matt in the car. "It'll only be for a little while. My sister has been through a lot, Steven. I just want to help her out and get her back on her feet."

"What about me? I've been through a lot, too, you know? I just got out of fucking jail!" He thought for a moment. "Wait. Are you dumping me?"

Her immediate reaction was to yell "YES!" at the top of her voice and be rid of him once and for all. But, once again, she told him what he needed to hear in order to keep him calm. "No. I'm trying to help my sister, that's all."

Steven shuffled in his seat. He really wasn't keen on the idea of going back to live with his mother. But, in reality, what was more important right now, what he really needed, was a fix. Staying with his mother would be easy money. Especially tonight, with the novelty of having her beloved son back home after the injustice of being locked up for something he didn't do. He was exhausted and wasn't up to hustling. His mother was a perfect alternative.

"Fine. Take me to my mother's. I'll see you tomorrow," Steven said, pretending to feel like he'd had his nose pushed out.

Tammy wasn't about to argue with him. Getting him to stay at his mother's had been easier than she'd thought. Beneath her mask of anger and hatred, she was glowing with endless delight and self-satisfaction. She sped up a little bit and happily waved goodbye as she left him standing in the parking lot outside his mom's place.

CHAPTER 45

The day Tammy had relentlessly hoped and prayed for over the last five years had finally arrived. She was pulling into the busy Terminal Six parking lot at LAX airport to pick up Donna.

Thankfully, she had only seen Steven once since he was released from jail. He'd turned up at her apartment two days ago; using the excuse he wanted to see Matt. Tammy wasn't surprised to see he paid no attention to him once inside the room. She noticed right away he was high, showing the usual signs of dark, sunken eyes, the smirk, and the occasional nod while sitting. She'd also caught him scouring the room. "There's nothing of value here, Steven," she'd warned.

"What are you talking about?" he said defensively. "I was just checking out the place. Give me a break."

"Yeah, right. You'd sell the shirt off my back if you could get a good price for it."

"No, I wouldn't. Hey, I'm starving, can you give me some money so I can get a bite to eat?"

Tammy threw out a laugh. "I'm not giving you any money. Do you think I'm that bloody stupid? I have food, go make yourself a sandwich. I'm not falling for your little scheme."

Angered that he couldn't coax her into giving her a few bucks, he'd said a few choice words and left, slamming the door behind him. With all thoughts of Steven pushed to the back of her mind, Tammy concentrated on parking the car. She never believed she'd see the day when she was reunited with Donna. For the past three days, she had thought on nothing else. Tangled up in a ball of emotions from anxiety and anticipation to excitement and joy, she was now nothing more than a bundle of nerves.

After trying on five different outfits that morning, she'd finally settled on a pair of cream-colored pants, matching heels, and a beige silk shirt. She had even splurged and bought Matt a rather expensive pair of denim overalls and a blue and white- checkered shirt along with a matching baseball hat.

Tammy had a million "what if" questions zipping through her mind. What if they didn't get along? What if Donna wasn't how she remembered her? What if Donna didn't like her?

Brushing her fears aside, Tammy smiled at her son. "You always give me strength, Matt, and you help me push myself through my troubles. I love you sooo much." She leaned in and kissed him on his cheek. Matt squealed and laughed. "Come on, big boy, let's go meet your auntie Donna."

Tammy scurried through the covered parking lot while looking in all directions. Cars zipped by her in the hunt for a parking space, others backed out, not paying attention. Twice she banged on the trunks of cars yelling "Hey!" before they almost plowed into her. Once outside, she shielded Matt's eyes from the unwelcome glares of the bright sun. She only enjoyed the heat in moderation and was quickly growing tired of Southern California's constant heat waves. She missed the four seasons. L.A. seemed to have just one: summer all year long.

Tammy spotted terminal six across the road. Lost in the crowd of people waiting to cross, Tammy watched the bustle of tourists, cars and taxis traveling in all directions. Manners simply didn't exist. Cars honked and people yelled and bumped into each other as they rushed to get to their destinations. The airport was a place of confusion, hostility, and rudeness, sparing no consideration for others. Holding Matt tighter, she crossed the road when the light turned green and hurried inside the terminal.

Finding the inside to be a much calmer environment, Tammy breathed a sigh of relief and made her way over to the area of the airport marked as "Arrivals." She stood on her tiptoes to see above the heads of others as she searched the monitors for Donna's flight; it was landing in fifteen minutes. She then followed the signs leading to the baggage claim area. Now at six months old, Matt's weight felt heavy in her tiring arms. She wished she'd grabbed his stroller from the trunk.

Tammy wondered what Donna looked like. Too much time had passed since that now tattered photo of her was taken; the one she carried everywhere in her wallet. Donna had told her that her hair was now long and dyed blond, which Tammy had a hard time picturing. For the purposes of spotting each other in the airport, Tammy let Donna know her hair was still red and still the same style. Wavy, shoulder length, and feathered bangs.

For the next forty-five minutes, while bouncing Matt on her knees, Tammy anxiously waited for Donna to appear. She honed her eyes in on every blond female that walked through the gate, searching for some sort of recognition. After frantically scanning what felt like hundreds of arriving passengers, finally, she saw her. Donna spotted Tammy at the same time. They both gasped. Donna froze. With Matt resting on her hip, Tammy rose slowly from her seat, raised her hand high in the air and waved hysterically. Donna waved back and broke out a smile, tears swelling in her eyes. Her nightmare had finally come to an end. She was safe. Jordon could no longer hurt or threaten her. Ready to start her new life, Donna quickened her pace as she approached her baby sister.

Face to face, Donna looked skinny, wearing a tight black mini dress, black nylons, and black high heels. Tammy suddenly felt like a bit of a plain Jane in her boring beige suit. Donna's makeup was heavy, with a thick layer of mascara, a ruby-red lipstick painted perfectly over her lips, and a matching red nail polish disguising her badly chewed nails.

"Donna!" Tammy squealed.

"Tammy!" Donna screamed back. Embracing her sister with her free arm, Tammy held Donna tight against her.

"Oh, I've missed you so much."

"I've missed you too," Donna cried in between her gush of tears. After a few moments of not wanting to let go of their long awaited reunion, they finally parted. Still holding hands, both sisters took a step back to absorb the glorious sight of each other. Neither could believe they were actually standing face to face with the other.

"You look good, Donna."

"So do you, sis." Tammy turned her hip so Matt was facing her sister. "This is your nephew. His name is Matt. Matt, meet your auntie Donna." Donna reached out and squeezed Matt's cheek. "Hi, Matt. You're so frigging cute!" She looked at Tammy. "Can I hold him?"

"Of course you can." Tammy leaned into Donna and bundled Matt into her arms. Never having held a child before, Donna felt a little awkward at

first but soon warmed up when Matt shone her a huge smile. "Oh, you're so precious. It's so nice to meet you, Matt." Donna glanced over at Tammy. "I can't believe you're a mother."

"It's an amazing feeling, and so is watching aunt and nephew meet for the first time." Tammy beamed with pride. "Now, come on, let's go get your luggage," she said while locking arms with her sister and chuckling. "I'll let you have the pleasure of carrying Matt."

"It will be my pleasure."

~

Over the next few weeks, the two sisters spent endless hours catching up on their lost five years. Tammy hadn't noticed over the phone, but Donna no longer spoke with an English accent. For entertainment purposes, she had tried speaking with one but had failed miserably.

Donna recalled how she'd shared a tearful reunion with their father and mother at the hospital. Tammy laughed when Donna told her that Mom had refused to stay at the hotel when she arrived. Instead, she had insisted on sleeping on a cot in Donna's room until she was well enough to be released.

Donna went on to tell Tammy that, after she'd left the hospital, they all stayed at the hotel and Mom and Dad treated her like a queen. They both took her shopping and bought her an entire wardrobe, and Mom even took her to have her hair done. For Donna, the three days at the hotel went by far too quickly. She shared with Tammy how saying goodbye at the airport had been really tough. She desperately wanted to spend more time with them but understood Mom and Dad had to get back to their lives. More importantly, she had a new one to begin in California.

Donna choked up when she talked about her emotional reunion over the phone with her twin, Jenny, and discovered she had missed her wedding. They had talked for hours. Donna understood that Jenny couldn't take time away from her work—caring for the elderly—at such short notice without jeopardizing her job or losing pay. "As soon as my status is sorted out here in the States, I promise I will come visit you and Mom in England," Donna had told Jenny.

When Donna spoke of Jenny, sadness crept over Tammy, too. She hadn't seen her since she'd left England. They wrote occasionally and exchanged photos, but the distance between them had grown. In some ways, Tammy felt she had found one sister but lost another.

Tammy explained to Donna that the motel was temporary while Steven looked for work and that Steven was staying with his mother so she could stay with Tammy.

Donna wasn't convinced that Tammy was telling her everything.

After meeting Steven for the first time, which consisted of a brief fifteen-minute visit where he was oblivious to his son playing in the playpen and herself reading a magazine on the bed, Donna's instincts had been proved right. She'd seen enough drug addicts to recognize one when she saw one.

With only one mission in mind, Steven had pulled Tammy outside to exchange some private words. Donna couldn't hear the entire conversation, but she knew what they were discussing. He wanted money from her. Stand your ground, sis, don't give into him, Donna thought when she overheard Tammy say "NO" in a strained, loud whisper.

"Why not?" she heard Steven ask, his voice frustrated.

Donna sat up to listen more closely. If Steven became violent, she was ready to rush out and butt in. She'd had her fair share of being bullied and wasn't about to let it happen to her sister. Fortunately, there was no need. Tammy had stood her ground and re-entered the room while Steven, she assumed, had left. Probably racking his brains and trying to think who else he could hit up for money.

"Okay, Tammy, what's going on?" Donna asked in a stern voice.

"What do you mean?" asked Tammy, checking on Matt as a distraction.

"Oh come on, Tammy! He's on drugs. He was high as a kite. I've been around the block a few times so I know when someone is using drugs. So, what's the deal? What's going on? Is that why you're living in this dump? Because of his drugs?"

Tammy knew she could no longer fool her sister. "Yes, he has a drug problem." But then found herself defending him yet again. "But he's trying really hard to quit."

Donna rolled her eyes. "You honestly believe that? Are you that stupid? If you keep allowing him to come around, he's gonna keep harassing you for money. Jeez, Tammy, wake up!"

Tammy knew she was right, but she still continued to make excuses. "I know that, Donna, but I have his child. I don't want Matt to grow up without a father."

Donna tried desperately to talk some sense into her sister. She knew Tammy was fighting a losing battle. She had seen the same scenario repeatedly back in Boston. Many of the other prostitutes had children and were trying to support not only their kids but also the dad, who was invariably a drug addict or an alcoholic.

She looked directly into her sister's eyes and spoke sternly in a louder voice as a serious look blanketed her face. "This is no joke, Tammy. Quit defending him. He's a deadbeat dad. What has he ever done for you and Matt? What do you mean when you say you don't want Matt to be without a father? He'd probably be better off without him. I can't tell you what to do, Tammy, but I can tell you what I think, and I think you're a fool if you stay with him."

Tammy lowered her head in shame, embarrassed that Steven was Matt's father; not that she would ever admit it. Even though she no longer had feelings for him, it wasn't that easy to just pack up and leave. Donna didn't know that he'd threatened to hunt her down and kill her if she left him, and she wasn't about to tell her, either. This is something she was just going to have to figure out on her own.

"It's not that simple, Donna. You don't understand." She didn't want to have this conversation. Not now. "Listen, can we talk about this later. I have a bad headache. Can you watch Matt for a half hour? I'm going to take a bath."

"Sure. But taking a bath ain't gonna solve your problems," Donna said sarcastically.

For the first time since Donna arrived, Tammy raised her voice at her. "Damn it, Donna! I said *not now*. Can we just drop it please?" Tammy glanced at the playpen when she heard Matt beginning to stir. He gurgled a few times and then went back to sleep. She lowered her voice. "When I'm ready, I'll do something. Now is not the right time."

"It never is, baby sis. It never is."

CHAPTER 46

Tammy eventually shared her troubled times with Donna and confessed that Steven was a heroin addict. She told her about his lying and stealing and how she struggled to make ends meet by spending money she'd worked hard to save. She confided in her about her fears of walking away and what he may do to hurt her and Matt if she did.

Donna understood her fears. She, too, had been waiting for the right moment and building up the courage to escape her pimp so she could take her life back. In the end, he had done it for her; albeit by almost killing her and leaving her to die in an alley. She didn't want that to happen to her sister. It seemed Tammy needed her as much as she needed Tammy, and Donna was determined to find a way to get her and Matt away from that monster of a man.

Although Tammy never complained about taking care of Donna, feeding her, or buying her clothes at thrift stores, Donna didn't want to be a burden and wasted no time in finding a job. Her choices were limited, having run away as a minor and never becoming legalized in the States. She walked up and down the streets of the neighborhood when Tammy was at work and, within a week, was hired as a stripper at a club a few blocks away.

"A stripper!" Tammy screeched in shock when she heard the news. "Couldn't you find anything better? How can you even do that?" she asked, horrified by the thought.

"What choices do I have, Tammy? I'll tell you something, it's a lot safer than turning tricks on a corner and having to answer to a goddamn pimp. It's a legit business. They have security, and the girls' welfare is always a top priority. How do I do it, you ask? After a few beers, I loosen up. I become numb and I just do it. Do I enjoy it? No. It's a job that pays well and will give me some independence. It's all I can do right now, and I'm sorry if you don't like it but there's nothing else I can do," Donna said defensively.

Tammy instantly felt guilty. "I'm sorry, I have no right to judge you."

Donna was right. It was a vast improvement from turning tricks on the street and, much to Tammy's surprise; she made more than a decent enough living. Tammy welcomed the help Donna offered with rent and food, something she'd never experienced with Steven. In addition, Donna was able to save some money in the hopes of getting her own place someday. Tammy objected profusely when she discovered she was stashing the savings in her suitcase.

"I really wish you'd let me keep your money in my bank where it'll be safe," Tammy pleaded as flashbacks of finding the empty envelope zipped through her mind.

"It's fine in here. It ain't going nowhere. Besides, if I need some, I don't have to bother you to go to the bank. Don't worry about it. Okay?" Donna said as she closed the suitcase and pushed it back under the bed.

Donna had come a long way in the short time she'd been in California. Tammy admired her strength and how she'd managed to pick up the pieces of her broken life so she could live life on her own terms. She was proud of her. But Tammy got some unexpected news when Donna returned home one night, carrying a bouquet of roses.

"Wow! Aren't you special. Who's the lucky guy?"

Donna pranced into the room like a teenager experiencing her first crush. "His name is Jason and he's gorgeous. He works as a ranch handler somewhere outside the city. He's strong, muscular, and beautifully tanned. I spotted him as soon as he walked into the club. I was pretty stoked when he asked me out," Donna announced, followed by a glorious laugh. "I've been seeing him for a few weeks and it's amazing. Tammy, I'd never been on a real date before. It felt awkward at first. I was expecting him to throw dollars at me." Donna laughed again. "But he treats me like royalty. I think I'm falling in love with him."

"That's great, Donna." Tammy smiled, genuinely happy for her sister. "How come you've never told me about this guy?"

"I dunno. I didn't know where it was going at first, I guess. Anyway, I'm telling you now. Be happy for me, sis."

Tammy walked over and hugged her sister. "Donna, I'm over the moon. If anyone deserves to be happy, it's you. Here, hand me those flowers and I'll put them in a vase for you."

Within a month, the relationship between Steven and his mother had become strained to the point where Elizabeth was insisting he leave. Having more than outstayed his welcome, and with his mother beginning to see the dark side of her son, she ceased giving him money. In desperate need to feed his addiction, Steven started paying Tammy surprise visits to her work every day. Knowing she wouldn't want a scene, he had been successful in demanding some cash out of her every time.

But his luck was about to change. Tammy was walking round the corner from the kitchen one day when she saw her manager, Paul, meet Steven at the entrance of the restaurant. Tammy ducked back behind a doorway to watch from a distance. Blocking the doorway with his full rounded body, Paul prevented Steven from entering. Paul glared at him, expressing only anger. "I know exactly what you're up to. Tammy may be afraid of you, but I'm not. I've watched you come in here every day, tormenting her and taking money from her," Paul snarled.

"Hey, man, Tammy's my girl, and it ain't none of your fucking business, okay?" Steven snapped back.

Paul leaned forward within inches of his face. "Yes, it is my business when you come in here and upset my waitress while she's on my floor. I make it my business. You got that, punk?"

Steven took a step back. "If my old lady wants to give me money, that's up to her, not you. Who the hell do you think you are?"

"Listen, asshole! I don't want to see your scrawny assed face around here ever again. You got that? If I do, I'm calling the cops and having you arrested. Now get the fuck outta here, you fucking jerk!"

Steven kicked open the door to the restaurant and left in fury— empty handed. Now what was he going to do? Tammy had been his last resort. As he stomped off down the street, it came to him. He had an idea. He knew how he could get some money and get it fast.

CHAPTER 47

Before Steven stormed off, Tammy knew he'd spotted her because he threw her a menacing stare over Paul's shoulder. Tammy quickly turned the other way. For a few minutes, Paul stood by the open door to make sure Steven had left the property. Once confident the bastard was gone, he closed the door and approached Tammy. Noticing she was shaken by Steven's presence, he gently placed his hand on her shoulder. "Are you going to be okay? I eighty-sixed the guy from the restaurant. If he ever steps foot in here again, I'll have him arrested."

"Yeah, I'll be fine. I'm really sorry, Paul. I've told him so many times not to come here."

"Tammy, there's no need for you to apologize. This is not your fault. You need to get away from that guy. He's no good for you. If he causes any trouble for you tonight, you come right here. Do you understand?"

Tammy was touched by his offer. "Thanks, Paul. I'll keep it in mind, I promise."

After seeing the rage in Steven's eyes, Paul was concerned for her safety. "Make sure you do, okay? We're here for you. All of us.

Why don't you take a ten-minute break? I'll have the other girls cover your shift."

"Thanks, Paul. I think I will," Tammy said before giving him a hug.

When Tammy finished her shift, Paul reminded Tammy to come back to the restaurant if Steven gave her any trouble.

She picked up Donna from the club on her way home and listened patiently as she dominated the whole conversation, giving Tammy no chance to tell her about Steven. "Guess what?" Donna asked.

"What?"

"Jason has asked me to move in with him! Can you believe it?"

Tammy faked her happiness. After seeing Steven's outburst, the thought of being alone terrified her. "That's great. When are you moving?"

"I haven't given him an answer yet. It's all happening too fast, don't you think?"

Tammy released a subtle sigh of relief, knowing she was going to be around at least a little while longer. "Yeah, you're probably right. Don't rush into anything," she said as she pulled into her parking space. "Hey, I gotta pick up Matt from the sitter. I'll see you at the room, okay?"

"Okay. Love you, sis," Donna replied as she skipped out of the car and blew her a kiss.

A few minutes later, with Matt in her arms, Tammy headed back to her room. As she neared the apartment, she could see the door was wide open and she could hear Donna yelling from inside. "What the fuck?" Tammy mumbled to herself as she tightened her grip on Matt and hurried toward the door.

Rushing inside, she gasped. Tammy couldn't believe what she was seeing. Her room had been trashed. Everything that could be broken, was. Dishes, chairs, the table; even the mirror above the sink had been shattered. Any items of value had been stolen. The toaster oven, the microwave, and the radio were all gone. She noticed the TV was still there, but only because it belonged to the motel and was bolted to the wall. Tammy stood in the doorway in disbelief, looking at all her wrecked belongings. Donna was knelt on the floor next to her open suitcase.

"Oh my god! What the hell happened?" Tammy cried.

"I'll tell you what fucking happened. Some motherfucker broke in here and stole all my money. Six hundred fucking dollars! It's all gone."

"Oh my god, no! It can't be." Tammy panicked and began scouring the piles of clutter around the room while still holding Matt. "It must be here somewhere."

Donna slammed the suitcase shut and jumped to her feet. "Nope, it's all gone. What the fuck am I going to do now? That was all the money I had." Stepping over broken toys and dishes, Donna sat on the edge of the bed. "Who would do this to you? You have a child. Couldn't they see all the baby things around? And another thing, what the hell does everybody do around here? Didn't anyone see someone break in? Didn't they hear anything when the place was being turned upside down?"

Tammy went silent for a moment, on the verge of tears. "I don't think anyone thought we were being robbed, Donna."

"What do you mean?"

"Think about it. There was no sign of a break in. No windows or locks were broken. Whoever came in here knew how to pick a lock and has been seen here before. I bet you Steven knows how to pick a lock and break in without causing suspicion. People have seen him here, so why would they suspect anything?

"And you think he did this?"

"No, I don't think he did this. I know damn well he did this." Tammy sat of the edge of the bed with Donna and placed Matt between them with a few unbroken toys. She stared in disbelief at the mess surrounding her. How could he do this? she thought.

"He's a drug addict, Donna. He'll do anything for a fix. It doesn't matter who he hurts, his mother, you, even Matt, or me.

He's out of control. You've been around them, so you know. Today, he came by my work, which he has been doing all week, by the way. He usually corners me and demands I give him some money. He knows I'm not going to cause a scene and that I'd rather cower and give it to him so he will go away. Well, today, my boss intervened. He stopped him at the door and wouldn't let him come in the restaurant. In fact, he eighty-sixed him and threatened to call the cops if he ever showed up again."

"Wow! You never told me he was harassing you at work."

"I tried to on the way home today, but you were so excited about Jason I didn't want to put a damper on your mood. Anyway, I saw the anger in his eyes when he left. He looked directly at me and stared me down. It scared me, Donna. He came here in a rage and stumbled on your six hundred dollars in the process. I plan on paying you back, by the way."

"No you will not!" Donna insisted. "You didn't steal it. It's not your responsibility. It's my own fault for leaving it here. You kept telling me to put it in the bank. I should have listened to you." Donna picked up Matt, who was beginning to fuss. "But what are you going to do? This was your home. It's destroyed. I can go live with Jason, but I can't leave you here like this."

Tammy squeezed her sister's hand as tears rolled down her cheeks. "I'll be fine. My boss said he would help me. I'll go talk to him in the morning. It's over between Steven and me. I'll never forgive him for this. For what he did to our home and even more so for what he did to you." Tammy's crying intensified. "I'm so sorry, Donna, please forgive me."

Donna wrapped her free arm around her baby sister and let her cry. "Shh, it's okay. It's not your fault. Come on, it's almost dinnertime and Matt's hungry. Why don't I take you guys out for dinner and we can figure out what we're going to do about this mess, hmm?"

CHAPTER 48

Over dinner, Donna called Jason and told him what had happened. He insisted they all stay at his place for the night. Not wanting to go home or be alone with Matt, Tammy gladly accepted his offer.

After a sleepless night of worry, wondering what on earth she was going to do, Tammy woke early, bundled up Matt, and left before Donna and Jason appeared. She left a thank you note on the kitchen counter and wrote that she'd be in touch soon.

Her first mission was to find a phone booth and have it out with Steven. Within two minutes, she spotted one on her right and pulled up alongside it. She turned to check on Matt and saw he was sound asleep and opted to leave him in the car while she made the call. Reaching over, she pulled Matt's blanket up under his chin, grabbed her keys, and stepped out of the car. After entering the call box, she peered through the glass to check she could see Matt clearly. With nowhere else to go, Tammy assumed Steven would be at his mother's and dialed her number. A sleepy male voice answered the phone. "Hello?"

Hearing him made Tammy cringe. "You fucking bastard!"

Tammy screamed down the phone. "You destroyed the only home Matt and I had, and you stole from my sister." She didn't need to wait for a reply; she knew he was guilty. "How could you do this? I fucking hate you!" Tammy hollered in a rage.

Steven didn't even try to deny what he was being accused of. "Well, what was I supposed to do? I have no money. You know damn well I need a fix every day so I don't get sick. My mother won't give me any more money. Your stupid boss banned me from the restaurant. Who the hell does he think he is anyway? Your sister shows up in town and you kick me out. So, yeah, I went over to the motel to see what I could find. I was sick, Tammy. I came across your sister's money, and yeah, I took it. I needed to get well, but you just don't understand that, do you?"

Tammy was furious. She couldn't believe he felt no remorse and truly believed he had a good reason to do what he did. "You make me sick, Steven. I never want to see you again. That was your son's home. It wasn't much, but it was all he had. All I had. How could you do this to us?"

"Oh, come on, Tammy, I'll make it up to you. I was desperate. I wasn't thinking straight. You're just upset and acting irrational. Everything's going to be okay. You just need to stop acting silly and saying stupid things. Things you don't even mean."

She didn't want to hear any more of his excuses or listen to him trying to make amends. Deciding she was done with him, she slammed down the phone, got back in her car, and drove to her work.

Tammy arrived at the restaurant during the busy breakfast shift in floods of tears. She stood helpless in the doorway, holding Matt tight, unmoved by the many eyes looking her way. From across the floor, Paul spotted her and immediately walked away from his business, shattered by Tammy's distraught demeanor.

"He destroyed our home. I have nothing. I don't know what to do," Tammy sobbed.

Holding out his arms, Paul embraced Tammy in a tight hug.

With Matt sandwiched between them, he tried to console her. "Shhh, it's going to be okay. We're family here. We'll get you some help."

"Thanks, Paul. I'm so sorry, I didn't know where else to go. I can't believe he did this."

"Don't apologize. You came to the right place. Now, come on, let's go in the back and get you a hot cup of tea and some milk for Matt. Then we'll figure out what we can do for the two of you."

Word traveled fast through the restaurant about Tammy and her troubles with Steven. Everyone pulled together to help her. Marco, the head chef, made them a breakfast fit for royalty. Louise, another waitress, held an impromptu collection and managed to collect over five hundred dollars.

After the breakfast rush was over, most of the staff joined Tammy in the break room to discuss her options and find out what they could do to help. Already feeling overwhelmed by their generosity and the unexpected donations, Tammy felt she couldn't take any more from them. Ruth intervened her objections. Ruth was the oldest waitress—in her sixties—and like a mother to the rest of the girls.

"Stop with your protests, Tammy. I've thought about this, and I'd like you and Matt to come stay with me for a while."

The rest of the staff cheered at Ruth's invitation, but Tammy quickly silenced them. "Oh, Ruth...thank you, but I couldn't."

Offering a caring smile, Ruth sat next to Tammy and took her hand. "I'm not taking no for an answer. I'd love to have you. You know too well my husband passed away recently, and I gotta tell you, I've been pretty lonely. Having you and Matt around will help me, too. We'll be helping each other."

While Tammy bounced Matt on her knees, Ruth took a hold of his tiny hand and spoke baby talk to him. "What do you say, little fella? Wanna come live with me?"

"Oh, Ruth, I don't know what to say. Thank you so much." Tears of happiness filled Tammy's eyes.

With the decision made that she would be staying with Ruth, Paul had some other concerns and wanted to run them by Tammy. Sending everyone back to their stations and asking one of the girls to entertain Matt, he closed the door to the break room. "I don't want to scare you, but there's a good chance that asshole will show up here looking for you. Even though I kicked him out, he'll still come back. I could call the cops, but he may even wait across the street for you when you've finished your shift. You can't be here when that happens. We need to be able to tell him you no longer work here."

A look of worry crossed Tammy's face. "Are you firing me?"

"No, no, of course not...but Steven will think you were."

Tammy creased her brow. "I don't understand."

"You're going to have to go into hiding for a few months. Stay away from anywhere or anyone you had in common with him, like friends, restaurants, and stores. Like I said, he's bound to come here at some point. And when he does, I'll tell him you never showed up for work one day and I fired you. He may come back a few times, but eventually, he'll get the message and give up."

Tammy shook her head in protest. "Paul, I can't afford to take a few months off."

A sly grin appeared over Paul's face. "Don't you worry. I have it all figured out. This is just between you and me, okay?"

Tammy nodded her understanding.

"I'm going to continue to clock you in every day. That way, you'll still get a paycheck each week. You won't get any tips, but at least you'll get a little money coming in."

"You can't do that," Tammy objected. "You could lose your job if you get caught."

"You're forgetting, Tammy, I'm the boss. My job will be fine. Don't you worry. I'll have you make up the hours when you return. We'll work something out."

She rose to her feet. "Thank you, Paul. I owe you one."

Wanting to protect her, Paul wrapped his arms around her. "You're going to be okay. I promise."

After their discussion, Paul left Tammy alone to make some phone calls using the pay phone on the wall. Not wanting her sister to worry, she tried calling her at Jason's first, hoping she was still there.

Thankfully, she was. "Hello?"

"Hey, Donna, it's Tammy."

"Tammy! I've been worried sick about you. I woke up and you were gone. Are you okay? Where are you?"

"I'm fine. I'm at work. Everyone here has been amazing. I'll tell you all about it later. I'm going to be staying with one of the waitresses."

"Tammy, you can stay here."

"Thanks, Donna, but you and Jason are just starting out. I don't want to ruin it for you guys. Having a baby around may scare Jason off." Tammy laughed.

"Okay, if that's what you want. But if it doesn't work out, you're always welcome here. Just remember that."

"I will. Thank you. Hey, listen, I'm going to call my neighbor, Judy, and tell her what happened. I'm hoping she can watch Matt for an hour while I go and salvage what I can from the room. Do you and Jason want to meet me there so you can grab your things? I'd love it if Jason comes in case the asshole shows up."

"Sure, we can do that. What time?"

Tammy thought for a moment. "How about noon?"

Donna agreed to the time and told her she loved her before hanging up the phone.

Just as Paul had predicted, Steven showed up the next day, demanding to know where Tammy was. He was dressed in grunge jeans and a stinky t-shirt that clung to his greasy body. His hair was uncombed and matted and his face was unshaven. Paul felt no pity toward him, only fury. He went along with his plan and told Steven that Tammy never showed up for work and had been fired as a result. After peering around the restaurant in search for her, he bellowed a few choice cuss words and stormed off. The following day, Steven returned. This time, Paul called the cops and had him escorted off the property. After that, he stopped coming by.

Ruth was the perfect host and welcomed Tammy into her spacious three-bedroom, two-bath home. She gave Tammy and Matt their own bedroom and bathroom, situated at the back of the house, and refused to take any rent. Tammy insisted on paying her way somehow and helped with the groceries and cleaning the house.

Every room was bright and cheerful with yellow painted walls and floral prints on all the drapes, tablecloths, chairs, and couches. Ruth's entire house was a showcase for the many framed pictures of her three daughters, one son, and eight grandchildren.

Tammy enjoyed sharing her evenings with Ruth and listening to her stories about her husband, Jack. Ruth reminisced about how they met and his time in the marines. She told Tammy she didn't have to work, Jack made sure of that, but she still did it for the company and to get herself out of the house.

Most nights, when Matt had gone to sleep, they'd open a bottle of wine and spend the evening playing board games and enjoying each other's company. For once, Tammy felt at ease. She'd forgotten what that felt like. Most of all, she enjoyed spending her entire days with Matt. She was around to watch him take his first steps, learn new words, and try new foods.

Donna and Jason came by frequently for dinner, and Tammy was pleased to hear that, after a month of living with him, Donna had quit the stripping gig and was now living the life of a happy homemaker.

Judy also visited often. Along with Ruth, she kept Tammy in

the loop of any gossip happening at work, but the latest gossip was about Judy herself. Her husband had been released early from jail and took a swing at her the same day. Over money, of course. Judy had packed her bags, got a restraining order on him, and was now living at her mother's with the kids. But she wasn't sure how long she could last.

"Judy, why don't we join forces and get a place together? It would be ideal. I've been at Ruth's for almost two months now. Although she's been fantastic, I can't stay here forever and I need to get back to work. If we ask Paul not to put us on the same shift, we could watch each other's kids. We could seriously help each other out if we did it right."

Judy pondered over her suggestion. "That's not a bad idea. I'm game if you are! I have some money saved. It's not a lot, but if we're splitting everything, I think I can swing it." Judy raised her Coke bottle in a toast and shone a huge grin. "Sure, let's be roommates."

Sitting on the couch together with the kids playing on the floor in front of them, Tammy matched her grin and hugged her soon-to-be roommate. Tammy hoped this would be the last time she'd be starting over. But, with Steven finally out of the picture, everything was on her terms.

That night, Tammy told Ruth about her and Judy's plans. Even though Ruth said she'd be sorry to see her leave, she knew it was time for her to move on. Excited for Tammy, she joined in on their hunt for a new home and insisted they use her as a reference and a co-signer to give them a better chance of finding a place.

All three women spent every spare moment of the next week scanning the classifieds and viewing rentals. By the end of the week, Tammy and Judy were holding the keys to their new two-bedroom, two-bath house in Pasadena, which was a convenient ten-minute drive from work. A three bedroom would have been nice, but with the fenced yard and a quiet street, it was perfect for the kids—and it was affordable. Tammy gave Judy and her kids the bigger bedroom with the en-suite bathroom, and Tammy and Matt took the smaller one with the bathroom at the end of the hallway. The kitchen was spacious with white cabinets, a stove, a fridge, and a large dining area where a table big enough to seat everyone would fit. The living room had French doors overlooking the backyard and a cozy brick fireplace in the corner.

Paul agreed to put them on different shifts, and because Tammy had a car, he gave her the nights. Once again, everyone at work offered to help by donating most of their furniture, including beds for every one, a couch, a dining set, dishes, pots and pans, and toys and clothes for the kids. The only things they needed to buy were a TV and a telephone.

As per Paul's Plan, Tammy had gone into hiding for two months and hadn't heard anything from Steven. The plan had worked. She was now ready to start her new life and was due to return to work in two days. Tammy had agreed with Paul to take a small cut in her hourly wage to begin paying back the funds she was fronted while in hiding.

For the first few days, Tammy's anxiety level was high. Every time the door to the restaurant opened, she spun around and expected to see Steven. But, over the next few weeks, her uneasiness subsided and she began to embrace having normality in her life.

After returning home from a busy dinner shift, Tammy kicked off her shoes and flopped onto the couch like a wet rag.

"You look exhausted," Judy remarked. "Want a glass of wine?"

"Yeah, that sounds great. How was Matt?"

"Oh, he was great as usual," Judy, hollered from the kitchen before returning with two glasses of white wine. "Here you go," Judy said as she handed Tammy a glass and took a seat next to her, placing her glass on the coffee table.

Tammy took a large sip. "Oh, that's good. Thanks."

"You're welcome. Hey, I'm off tomorrow, want to take the kids somewhere?" Judy asked.

"Sure. Do you—"

Judy quickly stood up, interrupting Tammy, and held her hand up in front of her. "Shhh, did you hear that?"

Tammy froze. "No, I didn't. What was it?" she whispered.

"I could have sworn I heard footsteps," Judy said quietly, feeling worried.

Suddenly, a loud crash came from the front door as one of the eight glass panes shattered to the floor. They both shrieked and Tammy jumped up from the couch to join Judy. Terrified, they clung to each other and watched as a gloved hand reached through the white mesh curtain, searching for the lock.

"Oh my god!" Tammy screamed.

Judy broke herself free from Tammy's grasp and grabbed the poker from the fireplace.

"Where are you going?" Tammy screamed.

"Hurry! Call nine-one-one!" Judy yelled back as she raced through the kitchen toward the back door.

"Judy, don't go out there..." But she was gone. While fumbling with the keypad on the phone, Tammy screeched at the intruder, "Go away! I'm calling the police." Not fazed by Tammy's threat, the imposter continued to search for the deadbolt. "I'm calling them right now," Tammy yelled.

A female dispatcher came on the line. "Nine-one-one. Is this an emergency?"

Holding the receiver tight as if it were her only lifeline, Tammy bellowed into the phone, "Someone is trying to break into my house! Hurry! They've broken my door. I have glass everywhere."

"Stay calm, ma'am. Help is on the way," the woman explained in a calm voice.

Still clinging to the phone, Tammy heard a loud thud and then a muffled groan. Staring at the door, she saw the gloved hand disappear back through the broken glass and fall away on the other side of the door. Fearing for Judy's safety, she threw down the phone, leaving the dispatcher talking to herself. Tammy screamed, "Judy!"

Driven by adrenaline, her only concern being her friend, Tammy rushed to the front door. Avoiding the broken glass sprayed across the floor, she unbolted the lock and yanked the door open. Panting and listening to the sound of her pulse beating in her ears, Tammy found herself face to face with Judy. The intruder lay face down on the ground between them. Standing with her feet apart, holding the poker in one hand, Judy released her grip on her weapon and let it crash to the ground.

Tammy raced to Judy's side and held her tight. "Oh my god! Are you okay?" she looked down at the motionless body at their feet. "Jesus, did you kill him?"

"No, I just gave him a good whack across the back of the head and knocked him out cold." Judy smirked as she walked around to the other side of the man and crouched down. "Come on, let's see who this bastard is."

Tammy leaned down on the other side and took hold of the medium-built limp body with two fistfuls of his jacket. With one final shove, they managed to roll him over.

Tammy immediately jumped back. "Fuck...Its Steven!"

Still crouched, Judy took a closer look at the scruffy, bearded face. "Damn. It sure is. I only saw him once when he came into the restaurant to bug you, but even with that beard sprouting out of his chin, I'd never forget that ugly, scrawny face."

Tammy and Judy turned their heads in unison at the sound of sirens coming closer to the house. Judy rose to her feet and approached Tammy with open arms.

"How the hell did he find me?" Tammy said. "He's like a friggin' nightmare that won't go away. What am I going to do? I can't keep running from this creep."

Rubbing Tammy's shoulders, Judy led her over to the steps of the front porch. "Sit here while I go check on the kids. The cops should be here any second, they sounded pretty close."

"Okay." Tammy eased herself into a sitting position against the cool front wall of the house.

Judy returned just as the patrol car pulled up, illuminating the front yard with its flashing lights. "Amazing, the kids slept through the whole thing. They're all sound asleep. I'll be right back. I'm gonna go talk to the cops," Judy said as she scurried to meet the officers stepping out of the patrol car.

Tammy scanned the street while she waited. Neighbors were now standing on their front lawns dressed in pajamas and bathrobes. She spotted others peeking through their curtains. Embarrassed by the scene unfolding in front of her house, Tammy avoided their curious stares.

Moments later, the two officers approached Steven, who was still out cold on the ground. Tammy watched with slight amusement as they brought him to a conscious state by slapping him across the cheeks a few times. "What the fuck!" Steven hollered as he started to come to. Not giving Steven an opportunity to lash out, the two policemen immediately brought him to his feet and handcuffed his hands behind his back. One of the officers led him to their patrol car while the other stayed with Tammy.

"Are you okay?" Judy asked her as she slid down next to Tammy and held her hand.

"Yeah, thanks."

When the officer approached them, both girls stood to greet him. "How are you doing?" the cop asked Tammy.

"I'm okay, just a little shook up."

The cop smiled at Tammy. "Well, you can relax now. He won't be bothering you for a long time. Apparently, he just robbed a liquor store a few blocks from here. We have eyewitnesses. He also has numerous outstanding warrants. He's obviously under the influence of drugs and he's carrying a loaded firearm, which I'm sure he doesn't have a license for. We also now have him for trespassing and breaking and will be charged anyway, whether you do or not."

Tammy shook her head. "No, I just want him to go away. How much time do you think he will get?"

"I'd say at least six years," the officer replied, followed by a smile, knowing he was giving her good news.

With a huge sigh of relief, Tammy let the tears trickle freely down her cheeks. She was finally free of Steven and, without a doubt, she had her life back. She glanced over at the pathetic excuse of a man sitting in the back of the patrol car—a man she no longer knew. A man, whose mind was consumed by drugs. An addiction so powerful that it cost him his family and his son.

Because of their twisted love affair, Tammy had lost one love to drugs, but she gained an even greater one the day Matt was born. She and Judy watched from the porch as the patrol car pulled away. Tammy knew that chapter of her life was closing. It was time to take her life by the reins and turn these reckless beginnings into happier, better endings.

IT TOOK A NEW
LOVE TO DISCOVER
HER DEMONS ...
TINA HOGAN GRANT
BOOK TWO IN THE TAMMY MELLOW SERIES
BETTER
ENDINGS

To my husband Gordon
& my son Mark
You are my Better Endings

PROLOGUE

At the tender age of seventeen, Tammy left England and moved to the States, leaving behind her mother and her other older sister Jenny. Her main objective was to find her older sister Donna—Jenny's twin—who, at the time, had been missing for three years. But Tammy's own poor choices led to a troubled life, full of turmoil and frustrations that kept getting in her way.

First, there was her secret affair with Raymond, a man twice her age and a good friend of her father's. After becoming pregnant by him, she revealed her affair to her father, shattering the friendship the two men shared and almost destroying her own. She ended up losing the baby and soon after, the relationship with Raymond dissolved.

She then went on to meet Steven, but it turned out he carried a dark secret. She discovered while pregnant with his child that he was a drug dealer and heroin addict. Determined to be a family and for her son to have a father, she remained with him, even while he continued to beat and steal from her. She tried relentlessly to change him, to give him a chance to be a father, but her efforts were to no avail. The drugs and his lifestyle consumed him.

After years of living in despair and fearing for the safety of herself and Matt, she finally plucked up the courage to leave him. But not without the help of many friends from work and by going into hiding for two months.

Her best friend Judy, whom she had met during this time, was also going through similar troubles with her husband. He too was a drug addict and was always in and out of jail, leaving Judy to raise their two young children, Kate and Christopher, alone. Kate was now eight and Christopher was close to Matt's age. Judy's relationship with her husband ended when he hit her for the first time, and Judy made sure it was the last time by leaving him.

Together, Tammy and Judy finally managed to rent a two-bedroom house in the outskirts of Los Angeles. It gave their children the home they deserved, but it also gave both women the support they needed.

Life was beginning to look good, until Steven somehow managed to find her—she has no idea how he did, even up to this day. Armed with a gun and high on heroin, he attempted to break into her home during the late hours of the evening, only to be confronted and knocked out by Judy.

The police were called and he spent eight years in jail for numerous charges, including armed robbery and being under the influence of a narcotic drug.

She doubted she would ever see him again.

During her troubled times, Tammy's sister Donna was found in an alley in Boston, beaten and left to die by her pimp. Once recovered from her injuries, their father bought her a plane ticket to California, where she lived with Tammy until she met Jason and eventually moved in with him. Jason was good for Donna and treated her like a queen, taking care of her every need. She never had to work. Jason owned his own business as a tree trimmer and provided enough for the both of them. For Donna, life was finally good. Not only had she found a good man but also her baby sister.

When Donna moved in with Jason, she didn't go far, just an

hour away to Whittier. Jason had inherited his four-bedroom, three-bath house after his father's death and owned it free and clear. Bills were light and money was plentiful for the two of them.

After supporting each other through their troubled times, Tammy and Donna nourished their rekindled sisterhood and visited each other frequently. Donna had also bonded with her newfound nephew Matt and once in a while went over to babysit him.

Tammy's mother Rose remained in England close to Jenny, which comforted Tammy, knowing her mother was not alone. After the divorce from Tammy's father John, Rose dated other men for a while but never remarried. Her mother was content being on her own and in the comfort of her little flat, twenty minutes from Jenny.

John kept his promise and had flown Rose out to the States every year for the past four years to visit Tammy and Matt. Tammy wanted to make sure her mother got to do what every grandmother should do while visiting their grandson in California, including visits to Disneyland, Knottsberry Farm, LA Zoo and of course the beaches. She saved hard before her mother's visits by picking up extra shifts at work. But, sadly, her other older sister and Donna's twin Jenny were now estranged.

Because Jenny was on her honeymoon when Tammy left England, neither had gotten to say goodbye and it scarred their relationship beyond recovery. Tammy couldn't afford to buy plane tickets for her and Matt on her waitress salary or take any time off from work to go visit. Likewise, Jenny had no desire to visit the States, so they had grown apart. They kept in touch with the occasional letters, giving updates on their lives and sharing photos. Jenny was still married to her high school sweetheart and now had two children, a boy and a girl, but it seemed Tammy had gained one sister and lost another. Tammy had told herself since arriving in the States, one day she would make it back to England and rekindle her relationship with Jenny.

Even though it was hard being a single mother and raising Matt on her own, she wouldn't have it any other way. No one was going to dictate her life or put her and Matt's life in jeopardy ever again.

To make ends meet, she worked long hours at the restaurant, sometimes picking up extra shifts when others called in sick. She felt guilty leaving Matt in the care of Judy or the daycare center for many hours a day, but she justified it by reminding herself that the reason she worked so much was so she could be a good provider for Matt and give him a good home and maybe one day meet someone that could be a good father to him. Something he'd never had for the first four years of his life.

Thankfully, Tammy's future was beginning to look a little brighter. But this wouldn't be a story about Tammy without some more drama to cope with along the way.

CHAPTER 1

ammy tried to open her eyes, but the bright lights from above forced her to quickly close them again. She tried once more, allowing her eyes to adjust slowly to the piercing lights. She could only manage a squint. *Where am I?*

Then she felt the excruciating pain coming from her head. Wanting to rub it and relieve some of the discomfort she was experiencing, she tried to reach up with her right hand but discovered she couldn't move her arm. Something was holding it back. She only heard metal banging against metal every time she tried to move it. Without turning her head, she managed to look down in the direction of her hand and saw with disbelief that she was handcuffed to the rail of the bed.

"What the fuck?" she whispered out loud.

The repetitive beeping noise from her left distracted her thoughts. Even in pain, she managed to turn her head slowly in the direction of the annoying sound. With her eyes now fully adjusted to the lights, she saw she was hooked up to a monitor and an IV.

She scanned the room and saw an empty bed on her right, which was next to a large picture window with the shades drawn.

On the wall facing her was a television mounted up high. To the left of the TV was a door, which Tammy assumed led to a bathroom, and the other door in the room probably led to the way out.

I'm in a frigging hospital. What the hell happened? She scanned the room again. *How long have I been here?*

Confused and in a state of panic, she yelled, "Hello! Hello! Anyone hear me?"

Suddenly, the door opened, and an officer of the law appeared.

"Who are you? And where am I?" Tammy lifted her cuffed hand. "And why am I handcuffed?" she asked, still in a state of confusion.

The officer remained by the door. "You've been in a car accident. I need you to remain calm, until a nurse arrives to check you out," he said, using his tone of authority.

"But why the handcuffs? My head is killing me." She leaned her head back in the pillow, distraught. "What the hell happened?"

"I'll explain everything to you in just a moment." The officer peeked his head outside the door. "Here she comes now," he said, sounding relieved. "I'm going to leave you alone with her. I will be right outside the door."

Once he had left, Tammy's head went into a tailspin. *Car accident? Was anyone killed? God, why can't I remember?*

While deep in thought, the door opened again. This time it was the nurse with a clipboard in her hand. She was an older lady, skinny, and probably in her late forties. She had dark chestnut hair tied in a ponytail, and she gave Tammy a small smile as she approached the bed.

"Hi, welcome back. You've been out for a while." She stood by Tammy's side. "How are you feeling?"

"I am so confused. I remember nothing." Tammy strained to keep her head up. "My head is killing me, I'm handcuffed to this damn bed, and no one is telling me anything. How would you feel?" she replied sarcastically.

"All's I can tell you, is that you came in late last night with severe head injuries after being in a car accident." She turned to look at the monitor. "Your vitals look good." She looked down at the chart in her hand. "It says here that you had eleven stitches across your forehead, which is now bandaged. No broken bones and no internal injuries. I don't think you'll be here too much longer." She finished with another comforting smile.

Tammy tried her hardest to remember the night before. "Hey, what's today's date?" she asked.

"January first. Not exactly a great way to start out 1990 now, is it?" the nurse joked, followed by a chuckle.

"It was my birthday last night. New Year's Eve. Oh my god! That's right, I went out with some friends." Tammy closed her eyes, trying desperately to remember the night before. "We went to…oh, god, I don't remember. We went to a few places and drank all night." She cracked a laugh. "Well, I'll never forget my twenty-fifth birthday, that's for sure." Ignoring the pain in her neck, her body stiffened and her eyes grew wide. "Oh, shit! My son! I never went home." She looked over at the nurse, fear consuming her face. "My roommate Judy must be worried sick! I have to call her! She's watching my son."

The nurse tried to calm her. "I'm sure we can arrange for you to call her after the officer has spoken to you. I'm going to call him in now, and then I'll leave you two alone." She patted Tammy's free hand. "I'll see what we can do about that phone call, okay?" The nurse made her way to the door and opened it enough to call through, "Officer, you can come in now." Opening the door for the officer to enter, she stepped outside and closed the door behind her.

Tammy had a horrific thought and wasted no time asking, "Am I going to jail?" She didn't wait for his answer; she had to explain why she couldn't. "I can't. I have a son at home with my babysitter. He's only four," she pleaded.

The officer ignored her question and approached the bed with a stern look. Chilled by his presence, Tammy cowered back against her pillow.

He gave her a speech, in a manner like a father would give to a child. "You are a very lucky young lady. Do you realize you could have killed yourself?" Tammy nodded. "I'm surprised you don't have any more serious injuries," the officer added.

Tammy didn't want a lecture. She needed answers. "Can you please tell me what happened?" She paused and softened her tone. "Am I going to jail?" she asked again.

The officer continued in a stiff voice. "It seems you attempted to drive a vehicle last night while under the influence of alcohol. You apparently blacked out at the wheel and in the process hit five parked cars. When we received the call, you were found unconscious, stooped over the steering wheel with a large abrasion across your head. You were brought here by ambulance, where a blood sample was taken to measure your blood alcohol level. The results showed it to be 0.11, which is above the legal limit of 0.08. Therefore, you are in our custody for driving while intoxicated. Which is why you are handcuffed to the bed."

Tammy listened in disbelief. "Oh my god! I fucked up big time." She wanted the officer to believe her and tried to sound sincere when she spoke. "I honestly thought I was okay to drive, Officer."

He released a slight chuckle—the first facial expression since he had entered the room. "Everyone does, ma'am," the officer told her.

Tammy dreaded asking the next question, but she needed to know. "Can you tell me if anybody else was hurt?" She took in a deep breath. "I didn't kill anyone, did I? Oh, god, please tell me I didn't. I couldn't live with myself if I did."

The officer delayed his answer for a few seconds, letting her stew over the possibility. "Luckily, no one else was hurt. Just yourself."

Tammy held her hand up to her racing heart while briefly closing her eyes. "Oh, thank god," she gasped.

"And, like I said, you're very lucky to be here." He waited for Tammy to compose herself after hearing she hadn't killed anyone before continuing with his report. "Your car is totaled and has been impounded. They had to use the Jaws of Life to remove you from your vehicle, and I'm here to serve you a DUI." He paused for a moment and pulled out a yellow piece of paper from the top pocket of his shirt. "While you've been here, we ran a report on you. You have no priors or outstanding warrants. It seems this is your first offense."

Tammy spoke quickly. "Yes, it is. I've never been in trouble before."

"Because you've had no priors, we are releasing you on your own recognizance."

Tammy let out a huge sigh of relief, knowing she wasn't going to jail. "But," the officer stated, "you have to appear for your arraignment in two days at the court specified on this ticket I'm giving you to sign. If you don't appear, a warrant will be issued for your arrest."

"Oh, I'll be there. I promise," Tammy said eagerly.

"Okay then, before I remove the handcuffs, do you have any questions?"

"Will I be able to drive again?"

"The courts will explain everything to you. Being a first offense, they will probably suspend your license. But get another DUI and they won't be so lenient, and you will go to jail. I can promise you that."

"Oh, Officer, I've learnt my lesson. I'll never get behind the wheel drunk again. I promise."

"That's good to hear. Now I'm going to remove the cuffs and I'll need you to sign this citation."

"Okay."

Tammy watched as the officer walked to the right side of the bed and freed her wrist from the cuffs. Feeling relieved, she rubbed her now stiff, tired arm with her other hand.

"Thanks."

"No problem," he said while reaching into his top pocket for a pen. He turned and slid the bed tray in front of her and laid the ticket and pen down. "Here you go. Once this is signed, I'm all done here and the nurse will be in shortly to advise you on when they will be releasing you."

Tammy took the pen, and without reading the citation, signed her name. "Thank you, Officer. I promise you it won't happen again."

The officer took the pen, placed it back in his pocket, removed a copy of the citation and gave it to her while holding onto his copy. "I hope not. You have a good day now." He paused and smiled. "Oh, and happy new year."

Tammy chuckled. "Thanks. You too," she replied as she watched him walk out of the room, leaving her with her own thoughts.

She remembered nothing about the accident. She vaguely remembered getting in her car after saying good night to her friend Hailey, a friend from work. Judy, her roommate and best friend, had offered to babysit so she could enjoy her birthday. Hailey was also a single mother and wanted to take Tammy out after work.

Tammy thought of her son. What a terrible mother she was. Poor Matt must be wondering where Mommy was. Not to mention Judy. God, she fucked up this time. She needed to call home and apologize to Judy.

While deep in thought, the same nurse entered the room. "How are you feeling? I hear you've been released from custody. You're a very lucky lady you know."

"Yeah. I know. The cop told me the same thing."

The nurse walked to the side of the bed and checked the vital machine.

"I can't believe how stupid I've been. I'm a mother. I'm not supposed to be acting this way. I feel like such a failure to my son," Tammy confessed.

"I'm sure he's fine. You can use the phone next to the bed to call home. Just dial nine for an outside line then dial the number. I'll be back in a few minutes."

"Thank you! Oh, wait, what hospital am I in?"

"Huntington Memorial in Arcadia."

"Okay, thanks."

Before the nurse had left the room, Tammy already had the phone in her hand and was dialing home. After three rings, she heard Judy's voice on the other end.

"Hello?" she heard Judy say.

"Judy, it's Tammy."

"Tammy! I've been worried sick about you. Are you okay? Where are you?"

"I was in a car accident last night. I'm so sorry. I feel terrible."

"Oh my god! Are you okay?"

"Yeah, I'll be fine. I totaled my car though. I don't remember anything, and I woke up to find I was handcuffed to the bed."

"Handcuffed?"

"I'll tell you everything when I get home. Is Matt okay? God, I'm a terrible mother."

"No, you're not," Judy said in a harsh tone. "Don't you say that. He's fine. Do you need me to come get you?"

"I haven't been released yet. But I'm sure I will be soon. If you can, that would be great. I'm so sorry." Tammy paused to remember the name of the hospital. "I'm at Huntington Memorial. Thanks, Judy, I owe you one."

"Don't you worry about it. Matt loves going for car rides." Judy laughed. "I'll see you soon."

CHAPTER 2

Tammy was released from the hospital a few hours later. Not wanting to let go of her son, she opted to ride in the back seat with him for the journey home.

Having to explain to him why Mommy had a bandage on her head was difficult, but she explained as best she could. *"Mommy had a car accident, and they had to say goodbye to the car because, like Mommy, it got hurt and couldn't be fixed."*

Now, because of her stupidity, Tammy found herself without a car. Thank god Judy had one.

Over the next few days, remorse began to sink in. Tammy appeared for her arraignment before the judge and was ordered to attend twelve AA meetings. Her license was to be suspended for thirty days and she would have to pay a $1,500.00 fine.

Surprisingly, none of the owners of the cars that she'd hit threatened to sue her. They were all simply relieved she was going to be okay and told her their insurance would take care of any damage.

She could handle the court orders from the courts, but the $1500.00 fine worried her. She had no idea how she was going to come up with that kind of money. The judged gave her the option to do community service, but she couldn't afford to take the time off work so the judge gave her three months to pay the fine instead.

Feeling like a failure was taking its toll. She was a single mother and now, because she had chosen to be reckless and irresponsible, she found herself with no transportation for her and her son. She was back to taking the bus everywhere or hitching rides from Judy until she figured out how to buy another car, which probably wouldn't be until she got her tax refund in April—another four months away.

Tammy knew it was time to quit drinking. It was slowly destroying her life. Since Steven, the father of her child, had attempted to break into her home three years ago, alcohol had become her companion and her escape from the everyday stress of raising a child alone.

She knew she was sliding down a destructive path. She drank almost every night after work with Judy and was a regular at the British pub across the road from her job. She had been through a lot since arriving in the States from England over seven years ago, but that was no excuse to drink.

Tammy had no desire to start dating anytime soon. She was enjoying every free moment she had with the only man she wanted in her life: her four-year-old son Matt.

For the next four months after the accident, Tammy struggled with not having a car. She couldn't rely on Judy all the time, and hustling with a child just to get groceries was taking its toll. What used to be an effortless chore with a vehicle, sometimes took hours. From waiting for the bus, walking to the store from the bus stop, doing the actual shopping and carting the groceries back to the bus stop and from there lugging them home with a child in tow, there was no longer any such thing as a quick run to the store. It was something she had to make time for and plan in her day.

Getting to work was also a hassle. She had to leave an hour earlier just to get there in time, and if Judy couldn't watch Matt, she had to leave at least two hours earlier to take Matt to the day care center and from there, take a bus to work. And, of course, she then had to do the same thing all over again on the way home.

. Finally, when April rolled around, Tammy filed her taxes as soon as the state allowed her to and used the entire $2,500 refund to buy a used car in the first week of May. With no other money saved, she returned to the court to ask for an extension on the fine from the accident. To her relief, the judge gave her an extension of eight weeks, telling her to return to court on May 25th.

Busy raising her son and trying to get her life back together, she wasn't looking for love or any kind or a serious relationship. When the time was right or when she felt she was ready, she knew it would find her.

And it did.

A few weeks after buying her car and with life now much less stressful, except for the huge fine hanging over her head, Tammy was working the dinner shift and had just taken an order for a party of five in a corner booth. Satisfied she had all their orders correct, she headed back to the kitchen station to pin the order to the chef's wheel. Halfway across the restaurant, she sensed somebody standing behind her and then felt a light tap on her shoulder.

"Excuse me, miss, may I give you my order?"

Tammy came to a sudden halt. The voice she heard made her knees almost buckle from beneath her. It was deep and assertive. It exuded power, strength and masculinity. As he spoke, she felt his warm breath on the back of her neck. She was afraid to turn around. How would she react if she turned and faced him? Would she be disappointed by what she saw, or would she just melt before him and act flustered and foolish like a high school teen?

"Miss?" she heard again.

She braced herself and slowly turned to face him. She was now staring at all six feet of him, and to her relief, she wasn't disappointed. She was greeted with the friendliest smile she had ever seen on a man. It warmed her and welcomed her into his space.

He had shoulder-length blond hair that feathered back away from his face, and she was immediately captivated when she stared into his ocean-blue eyes, finding herself lost in their gaze. And even though his blond mustache was tattered, it suited him. If it had been trimmed and groomed, it wouldn't have looked as good.

The skin on his arms and face was well tanned and rough, telling her that he liked the outdoors. He didn't overdress; in fact, he looked comfortable in his faded Levi jeans and white tee-shirt that enhanced his muscular arms.

Tammy returned the smile, but it was no ordinary smile. It was one of her cuter ones that revealed her dimples just above her cheeks. She wanted to get his attention. She wanted him to be attracted to her, just like she was to him. "Sure, I can take it for you," she said in a flirtatious manner, tossing her red hair back with a subtle swoop of her head.

Her flirting seemed to be working, as he was staring at her with his mouth slightly open. She wondered what he was thinking at that very moment. Did he like what he saw? She followed his eyes as he took in her whole being from her head to her toes, and when he smiled again, she sensed his approval.

"I'm sorry, what?" He had obviously forgotten his original question. "Oh, yes, my order." They both laughed at his forgetfulness, both knowing the reason why. "Yeah, I'm sitting at the counter over there." He pointed. "Can I get a Pepsi and a cheeseburger?"

"Sure, no problem, I'll bring it over when it's ready," she informed him while jotting down his order on her notepad.

But he wasn't ready to end the conversation. "I detect an accent. Where are you from?" he asked.

"England, and you? Where is your accent from?" Tammy said with a hint of sarcasm.

"Me, nah, I don't have an accent. Born and bred right here in California."

"You have an accent to me. It's not English," she replied with a smirk.

He chuckled at her sense of humor. "Got a point there, I must admit." He paused. "I love your accent. It makes you sound very posh."

"Ha! Trust me, I'm far from posh." She threw him a cheeky grin.

He chuckled again at her witty comment. He liked this girl. She had spunk.

As much as she wanted to continue talking to him, she had to get back to work before she got into trouble with the manager. "Well, if you want to eat, I'd best get your order in for you. It shouldn't take too long. Go ahead and have a seat and I'll bring your Pepsi over."

"Great, sounds good."

Tammy watched as he turned and walked toward the counter, admiring how well his jeans fit him. His body was well toned and muscular, and he walked with confidence, holding his head up high with his back straight. "Man is he cute," Tammy whispered to herself before scurrying off to the kitchen to fetch his drink.

She returned a few minutes later with Pepsi in hand and placed it in front of him on the counter. He looked up and smiled at her. "Thanks."

Tammy felt her cheeks blush. "You're welcome." There was a moment of awkward silence while they continued to stare at each other. *Should I stay and try to talk to him or should I go?* She chose to stay for just a moment. "So I've never seen you in here before. Do you live around here?" she asked.

"Nah, I just dropped off my son at his mother's."

"Oh, you have a son?" She couldn't hide the hint of disappointment, assuming this also meant he was married.

"I do. His name is Justin. He lives with his mother, and I visit him on weekends or he comes and stays with me on my boat."

He's separated...yes! "Wow! You have a boat! Impressive. I have a son too," she confessed. And quickly added, "His dad isn't around. It's just me and my boy."

"Really? How old is he?"

"He'll be five in a few months. His name is Matt. How old is your son?" Tammy asked.

"He's seven."

The chef from the kitchen interrupted their conversation.

"Number twenty-six. Order up!"

"Oh, that's mine. I gotta go. I'll bring your food out shortly," Tammy said, even though she wanted to stay and chit-chat with him some more.

"That's fine. I'm not going anywhere." He gave her a suggestive wink as she walked away.

Since being on her own, she hadn't met anyone that she truly wanted to get to know. Yes, she had dated the occasional guy, but they were meaningless relationships and for her just physical. Since her horrific relationship with Steven, she was afraid to let anyone into her world. She had been hurt and lied to and had issues with trust.

But this guy was different. The physical attraction was definitely there, but unlike other guys that had crossed her path, she had a desire to get to know him more. Deep in thought while picking up her order, she turned her head discreetly in his direction and was shocked to find him glancing her way. She blushed and gave him a quick subtle smile before picking up the rest of her order and scurrying off to deliver the meals to a party of four across the restaurant.

Five minutes later, the cute guy's order was up. Feeling a little flustered, she managed to pick up the single plate and headed to the end of the counter where he was sitting. She felt his eyes on her as she approached. Standing before him on the other side of the counter, she gave him one of her best smiles. "Here you go," she said as she placed the plate in front him. "Can I get you anything else?"

He glanced at his plate and then back at her, ignoring her question. "You know, it just occurred to me that I don't even know your name."

"It's Tammy. And you are?"

"I'm Dwayne, and it's a pleasure to meet you, Tammy," he said with an alluring smile.

Tammy tried hard to suppress the butterflies fluttering in her stomach. "Likewise, Dwayne." Feeling more at ease, she rested a hand on the counter, inches from his, and leaned in a little closer. "So, Dwayne, you know what I do for a living. What do you do?"

"I'm a commercial fisherman. I fish for lobsters," he said with a hint of pride.

Tammy was intrigued. She had never met a commercial fisherman before. The thought excited her. "Really? Well, that's something you don't hear in LA every day. I would love to know more." She paused for a moment, not wanting to seem too forward. "I've never been on a boat before. How exciting that must be."

Dwayne threw her a flirtatious smile, catching Tammy off guard. "I think we'll have to do something about that. When's your next day off?" He didn't wait for her to answer. "Come on down and check it out and I'll buy you lunch."

Tammy couldn't hide her enthusiasm. "Wow, that would be awesome. I would love to."

Dwayne chuckled at her excitement before surprising her again. "Hey, when do you get off? I can give you directions to the boat and my phone number. I don't mind sticking around. Maybe we can go play a game of pool or something."

Caught in his web, Tammy beamed a radiant smile. "I would love that." She checked her watch. "I get off in about an hour. That's not too long, is it?" She held her breath, nervously waiting for his answer.

"That's just fine with me. After I've eaten, I'll go grab a paper while I'm waiting."

"Great!" Tammy replied, her feet frozen to the floor. Not wanting to tear herself away, she realized she felt at ease with Dwayne. Something she hadn't felt in a long time, and it felt good. "Well, I guess I should get back to work," she said, disappointment lingering in her voice. "Let me know if I can get you anything."

"I'm good," Dwayne replied, followed by his alluring smile.

Oh, I know you're good. Tammy headed back to the kitchen, thinking this was going to be the longest last hour of work ever.

CHAPTER 4

Tammy lost count of the amount of times she checked her watch during the final hour of her shift. Eight o'clock couldn't come fast enough. Sometimes, only five minutes had passed in between checking her watch.

For the rest of her shift, Tammy failed miserably at trying to concentrate on the tasks at hand and put herself on auto pilot as she went about doing what she'd done for years without putting a lot of thought into it—filling the ketchups and condiments, folding napkins, replenishing the salad bar and making fresh coffee.

Periodically, she'd glance over at Dwayne and admire him from afar. Hunched over the counter while reading the paper on the counter, his blond hair cascaded down to his shoulders and his biceps bulged slightly over his bent elbows. She had to quickly look away a few times when he slowly raised his head and looked over in her direction, but she didn't miss him throwing her a warm, sensual smile. Caught off guard and embarrassed that he'd seen her staring, she could only give him a nervous smile before returning to her duties.

When her shift finally came to an end, she pulled off her apron and skipped over to Dwayne. "Hey, I'm all done. I just need to go in the back really quick, grab my things and call my roommate to let her know I'll be home a little later. She's watching my son."

Dwayne raised his head and met her eyes. "No problem. Go right ahead. I'll wait here for you."

"Thanks. I won't be long."

With her heart racing, Tammy scurried off and disappeared behind the swinging kitchen doors. Before retrieving her things from her locker, she decided to call Judy first and headed to the payphone in the lunchroom.

After two rings, Judy came on the line. "Hello?"

"Hey, Judy, it's Tammy. How's my little man?"

"Oh hi, Tammy. He's fine. He just got out of the tub and is now watching a movie with Kate and Christopher. What's up? Are you on your way home?"

Tammy ignored her question. "You're not going to believe this. I've met this amazing guy. He's absolutely gorgeous."

"What! Tell me more. I'm all ears."

"He came in the restaurant a few hours ago and he's still here, waiting to take me out for a game of pool." An excited giggle burst from Tammy's lips. "I can't believe he's waited here this long."

"Wow. Well, you must go. Don't worry about Matt. He's fine. Go have a good time. You can tell me all about it when you come home. Oh, by the way, I'm off tomorrow, so you can tell me about it tomorrow if you end up spending the night with him."

Tammy shrieked into the phone, "Judy! I'll be home tonight. Yes, it might be hard to pull myself away, but I can promise you I'll be home."

"Hmm, I'm not so sure. I've not heard you sound this excited over a guy before. Now go on, don't keep the guy waiting any longer. Love ya."

"Love you too. Hugs to the kids. Bye."

"Bye."

With the night now hers, Tammy hung up the phone and

skipped over to her locker to retrieve her things. After applying a fresh coat of lipstick, a splash of perfume and a quick brush of her hair, she did a quick check in the mirror on her locker door before closing it and throwing her purse over her shoulder. After taking a deep breath, she smiled to herself and headed back out to the restaurant to meet Dwayne.

With butterflies still stirring in her stomach, Tammy approached Dwayne from his side of the counter. The scent of his masculine musk cologne captured her attention as she stood beside him, her arms folded nervously in front of her. "Hey, I'm all set. Ready to go?"

Dwayne looked up from where he sat and beamed her a smile that melted her heart. "I sure am. Now where's there a good place to play pool?"

"Actually, there's an English pub right across the street. They have a couple of pool tables. We can walk there."

Dwayne nodded his approval and slid himself off his stool. "Sounds good. Lead the way."

Tammy led him through the restaurant toward the main entrance, staying a couple of footsteps ahead of him. As she passed the hostess station, Paul, her manager who had helped her through the dark times with Steven and was now somewhat protective of her, raised his head from the cash register. "Night, Tammy. See you tomorrow. Where are you off to?"

When Tammy paused at the station where Paul stood, Dwayne came to a standstill next to her. "Oh, I'm off to play some pool with Dwayne." Tammy turned and rested her hand on Dwayne's shoulder. "Paul, this is Dwayne." Tammy swayed her arm between them while introducing them. "Dwayne, this is my boss Paul."

Both men nodded their heads and shook hands before Tammy scurried Dwayne out of the restaurant. "See you tomorrow, Paul."

Once outside, Tammy checked her watch. "It's only a little after eight and a week day. The pub shouldn't be too crowded. Sometimes on weekends you have to wait over an hour for a pool table to open up."

"I guess you're a regular." Dwayne chuckled.

"It's the closest place from work. I sometimes come here with my co-workers after my shift." Tammy turned to face Dwayne. "Not every night, I might add," she said with a cocky grin, not wanting to reveal that she was a regular.

Dwayne raised his hands in a joking manner. "Hey, I'm not judging. So where's this pub? I don't think I've ever been inside an English pub before."

"Oh, you're in for a treat." In a mad dash before any cars came around the corner, Tammy grabbed his hand. "Come on, follow me." Halfway across the road, it hit her that she had made the first move by taking his hand. His strong fingers felt good wrapped around hers; his palms felt rough and his grip was strong. Tammy squeezed his hand a little tighter as they approached the other side of the road, and to her delight, he tightened his hold in return. Tammy pointed to the left. "It's right over here."

Dwayne followed her finger and saw the green and black sign of "The Tudor Pub" illuminated by two floodlights.

Still holding hands, with Tammy leading the way through the heavy black door, they entered the pub.

They were immediately greeted by a middle-aged man wearing a long white bar apron and rolled up green shirt sleeves. "Hi ya, Tammy," he said with a thick British accent.

Feeling embarrassed that the bartender knew her name, Tammy shied away from his stare. "Oh hi, Mike," she replied while quickly scanning the bar for a table across the room.

As she had predicted, the pub wasn't busy. Better yet, she didn't see any of her regular drinking buddies present. Tammy glanced around the room and led them over to a quiet table in the corner next to the two empty pool tables.

"Not a regular, eh?" Dwayne said with a hint of sarcasm.

"I told you I come here sometimes," Tammy replied in a defensive tone.

When they reached the table, she was surprised when Dwayne pulled out a chair for her. "Wow, a gentleman too," she said with a pleasing smile while taking a seat.

Dwayne laughed. "Must be one of my good days."

Tammy chuckled at his joke and then scanned the bar again. A couple sat across the room, holding hands and whispering to each other; three single guys stood at the bar, and over at the juke box stood a young lady, holding a glass of wine while debating which tune she should play next.

Still standing, Dwayne looked down and met Tammy's eyes. "I should get us a couple of drinks. What are you having?"

"You know, if you've never been in an English pub, I bet you've never had Guinness. Want to try one?"

"Oh, I don't drink. I'm going to have a Pepsi."

Tammy's jaw dropped. "You don't drink? Wow! That's a first. I don't think I've ever met anyone that didn't drink before."

Dwayne let out another chuckle. "Yeah, I tend to get the same reaction whenever I mention it. What shall I get you?"

Feeling somewhat flabbergasted, along with a tinge of uneasiness, Tammy felt she had to ask. "Do you mind if I have a beer?"

"No not all. Draft okay?"

"Sure, that's fine. Thanks."

As he headed to the bar, Tammy's eyes followed him, admiring his rear end that fit so well in his jeans. Then she watched as he perched one foot up on the brass foot rail and rested his elbows on the surface of the bar. Tammy moistened her lips with her tongue, watching his jeans grow tighter as he leaned in to give the bartender his order. "Damn, he's cute," Tammy mumbled to herself. Feeling her attraction intensifying by the minute, she shook her head to compose herself and fumbled in her purse for a cigarette.

She had managed to quit smoking while pregnant with her son

and for a year after his birth. But she fell into the nicotine trap again three years ago.

After pulling almost everything out of her purse and setting the contents on the table, she finally located her pack of Marlboro lights at the bottom. With a sigh of relief, she pulled out a lighter and hastily took a cigarette out of the pack and lit it. She took a long drag and enjoyed the instant satisfaction it provided. Still holding the cigarette in her mouth, Tammy quickly tossed the contents of her purse back into her bag before Dwayne returned.

With just a few seconds to spare, she took another hit of her cigarette and sat back to enjoy watching Dwayne striding back to the table with their drinks.

"Here you go," Dwayne said while setting their drinks in the center of the table and taking a seat.

"Thanks. Do you want a cigarette?" Tammy asked while picking up the pack.

Dwayne picked up his can of Pepsi and took a sip. "No thanks. I don't smoke."

For the first time, Tammy became self-conscious and slightly embarrassed by her habits and hastily slid the pack of cigarettes back to her side of the table. "Oh, I'm sorry. Will it bother you if I smoke?"

"No, not all at. Go right ahead. I used to smoke, but I quit about two years ago. Hardest thing I've ever done."

"I know what you mean. I quit a few years back when I was pregnant with my son. Now look at me. I'm back at it." Tammy laughed before taking another hit. "So why'd you quit drinking?"

"Oh. I'd had enough to last me a lifetime by the time I was twenty-four," he said. "Can't believe I lived through it. That was almost eleven years ago."

"You're thirty-five?"

"Yep. Does that bother you?"

Tammy shook her head. "No, no," she quickly replied, realizing he was ten years older than her.

"So tell me about the fishing. I've never met a fisherman before. In fact, I've never been on a boat." She laughed. "What a way to make a living. It must be awesome."

"It can be at times, but it's a lot of hard work. Labor intensive. I grew up around boats. My dad sold yachts for a living and owned a couple of boats himself. It's in my blood."

Tammy wanted to know more. She found herself fascinated by the whole fishing thing. "I want to see it all," she said with a huge grin, her eyes beaming with enthusiasm. "I want to see your boat, the ocean, and I want to know everything there is to know about fishing. Will you show me?"

"Sure, but it's not as glamorous as it sounds." He leaned in closer, his elbows resting on the table. "How about you come down this weekend? You and your son. I'll take you both for a boat ride."

"Really? That would be awesome! I can't wait." Tammy reached over and squeezed his knee. "Thank you!"

"Don't thank me yet. You might hate it."

Suddenly, the song *Every Breath You Take* by The Police blasted from the jukebox. It seemed the woman had finally made her choice. Tammy began to tap her fingers on the table to the beat of the music. To make sure he was heard, Dwayne leaned in closer, his lips almost brushing Tammy's ear. This caused Tammy to flush as she felt his warm breath tickling the side of her face.

"So how good of a pool player are you?" he asked.

"Oh, you have nothing to worry about. I'm sure I won't be much of a challenge for you."

Dwayne scooted his chair back, stood up, squeezed his hand into his front pocket and pulled out a handful of change. "Let's find out," he said, retrieving two quarters and returning the rest of the change to his pocket.

"Okay." Tammy smiled and followed him over to the pool table.

She watched with admiration as Dwayne picked out two cues and handed her one. "Thanks."

Standing off to the side, Tammy allowed Dwayne to set up the table. While holding her cue and swaying her body to the beat of the music, she watched and admired him as he slowly took one hand and ran it through his long blond hair before bending down to insert the change into the coin slots. Tammy took a deep breath; she liked what she saw. Dwayne excited her.

The sudden clatter of the balls dropping snapped Tammy out of her thoughts, but she continued to watch closely as she waited for Dwayne to set up the game.

During what turned out to be four games, two of which Tammy won but with suspicions that Dwayne let her, Tammy found herself milking her beer. Having never been around someone that didn't drink before, she suddenly found herself conscious of how much she was drinking. After playing pool for a few hours, she realized she could have easily had five beers instead of just the one. Even at this early stage, she could tell Dwayne was good for her. It was the same with the cigarettes. She found herself not wanting to smoke in front of him and dismissed the urge each time it crept up.

The chemistry between them couldn't be denied. Her heart often skipped a beat when he brushed against her, and he always smiled before taking his position for his next shot. She returned the favor by sliding by him, allowing her breasts to gently glide across his chest, and she noticed he didn't move back. As their bodies touched for that slight moment, Tammy paused and met his eyes. She felt at such ease with Dwayne.

When they returned to their seats, Tammy glanced at her watch and was saddened to see it was almost midnight. Not wanting the night to end, she frowned and turned to Dwayne, who she noticed had slid his chair next to hers.

"I'm really sorry, but I have to go."

Dwayne reached over and squeezed her thigh. "I was afraid you were going to say that."

She grabbed his hand and added, "I don't want to. But I must."

He leaned in to meet her gaze, leaving just inches between their lips. "I know. I feel the same way. I'm having such a good time with you."

"Me too." She attempted a cute smile.

Mesmerized by his eyes, she found herself lost in his stare and welcomed the flushes of heat she was feeling. While still holding her hand, he lifted his other hand and gently brushed the side of her cheek. Tammy closed her eyes and breathed in heavily. She felt his warm breath on her lips, telling her he was close. Seconds later, he placed his lips softly upon hers. With the warm sensation from his kiss, followed by the tickling of his blond moustache, Tammy could do nothing but surrender and kiss him back.

While still locked in a kiss, Dwayne cupped his hands around Tammy's neck and pulled her in close. As the passion of the kiss intensified, both became oblivious to the rest of the world. The kiss was everything Tammy had hoped for—passionate and sensual. When they finally broke free, she was left with the desire of wanting more.

"Wow!" was all she managed to say while catching her breath.

"My sentiments exactly," Dwayne said while rubbing her thigh. "Come on, I'll walk you to your car."

Reluctantly, Tammy rose from her seat, grabbed her purse and took Dwayne's hand.

They walked back to her car arm in arm, their bodies close, holding each other tight, neither wanting to let go. Tammy felt safe with him and more importantly, she felt she could trust him. Something she'd not been able to do since breaking up with Steven.

When they reached her car, Tammy stalled before opening the door. Instead, she leaned her back against it and pulled Dwayne in closer. Dwayne smiled and pressed his body against hers, pinning her to the car with his hands wrapped around her waist. Tammy let her purse fall to the ground from her shoulder and locked her hands around his neck. She pulled his lips to hers, where they met in another passionate kiss

This time, the kiss was longer and harder as they explored each other's mouths with their tongues. While savoring the taste of her lips and his heart now beating like a hammer, Dwayne slid his hand down over Tammy's shirt until it rested over one of her breasts. Tammy had to break away from the kiss for a second, gasping from his touch. When she returned to the kiss, Dwayne cupped her breasts and squeezed her now protruding nipples before massaging them deeply with his palms.

Panting, Tammy had to break away from the kiss again. As turned on as she was, and as much as she wanted Dwayne, she didn't want to have sex in her car, especially not with it sitting in the middle of the parking lot. "Fuck! What are you doing to me? I'd better go," she said, her chest still heaving with desire.

Dwayne rearranged the pronounced bulge in his jeans and let out a cocky laugh. "What are you doing to me, more like? I stop in a restaurant for a bite to eat, and yet I'm still here hours later."

Tammy tossed her head back and laughed. "And I was supposed to be home hours ago." She gave her hair a good shake and tried to run her fingers through it. "Will I see you again?" she asked.

"Only if you'll let me," he replied. "Besides, you want to see my boat, don't you?"

"I do, yes."

Dwayne reached into his back pocket and pulled out a black wallet, from which he took a business card and handed it to her. "Here's my pager number. I don't have a phone on the boat. You can call and leave a message when you want to come down and I'll call you right back and give you directions."

"Great. I can't wait. Is this weekend good?" Tammy asked, not wasting any time.

Dwayne laughed at her enthusiasm. "Yes, it is. Now, before I have my way with you, I best let you go."

"If we weren't in a parking lot, I'd probably let you." She failed to hide her devilish grin.

Dwayne smacked her playfully on the butt. "Come on, get in the car. You're killing me here. I'll see you this weekend."

Tammy turned and opened the driver's door. "Okay. I'm going, I'm going." She giggled as she jumped in and started up the engine. Winding down the window, she leaned her head out to meet Dwayne in another kiss. In a failed attempt to release herself from him, she squeezed out her words with his lips still on hers. "Okay, I'm backing up now."

She put the car in reverse and eased onto the gas.

Dwayne didn't let go and instead walked with the car, still kissing her as Tammy slowly backed out of her parking space. Tammy muffled a giggle and with force, unlocked her lips from his. "Okay. I'm gone." She beamed him a bright smile. "I'll see you this weekend!"

Dwayne patted the top of her car. "I can't wait. Drive safe."

"I will. Bye for now."

As she put the car in drive and began to inch forward, she blew him a kiss and waved to him in the rearview mirror. Her head had been in a tailspin since their first kiss, and her heart was beating like a drum so much she couldn't calm it down. She'd forgotten how it felt to be totally smitten. It had been a long time, and now she couldn't wait to get home and tell Judy all about it over a glass of wine.

*J*udy was anxious to hear all about the new guy Tammy had met. She didn't want to wait until the morning to hear all the juicy details so had decided to stay up and wait for her. She knew she'd be sorry in the morning, having to work the breakfast shift, but this was big news. It would be worth it.

It reminded Judy of the time she'd met her boyfriend Joel, just over a year ago. She too had met Joel at work and, like Tammy, she couldn't wait to get home and tell her best friend the news. They shared everything, and she knew how excited Tammy was feeling. It was the first time Judy had heard Tammy being overly excited about a guy since they had decided to join forces over three years ago and raise their kids together. Judy knew Tammy deserved this.

After Steven, Tammy had become gun shy about settling down with anyone, but from the moment Tammy burst back through the door to their home, Judy could tell Dwayne was different. There was a sparkle in Tammy's eyes that she hadn't seen before.

Tammy sat next to her on the couch while nursing a glass of white wine. "I'm falling for him really fast," Tammy said before even taking a sip of her drink. "I need to slow down. I've just met him. But he seems so perfect." Tammy turned to face Judy with wide eyes. "You know he doesn't drink or smoke?"

Judy's jaw dropped. "What! You're kidding me."

"Nope, I'm not kidding. I've never met anyone that didn't drink. Non-smoker, yes, but not non-drinker. What are we supposed to do for fun?" Tammy allowed her body to flop back against the couch. "Every time I've gone out with a guy, we've always gone to the bar for drinks. I honestly have no idea what else to do."

"Damn, Tammy. Me neither. It's what Joel and I always do unless we're here at the house with the kids. Even then, we have a bottle of wine going." She snickered while nudging Tammy's elbow.

"This is all new to me. You know, when we were at the pub tonight, I was so self-conscious of my drinking and smoking. I didn't really notice before Dwayne came along how much I would normally drink. I could easily have had four or five beers, but tonight I had just the one. The same with the cigarettes. Maybe I should think about quitting?"

Judy let out a loud, cocky laugh. "Yeah, right. You, quit drinking? Who are you kidding? You almost killed yourself in a car accident from being drunk and you're still drinking. I don't think some guy who happens not to drink is going to make you quit anytime soon."

Tammy listened to Judy's words carefully. Even though she said them in a friendly manner, she knew she was right. She HAD almost killed herself and was still drinking. But before meeting Dwayne, she really hadn't thought about it. Maybe Dwayne was what she needed in her life.

Her court date was coming up the following week and Tammy already knew she wouldn't have the money for the fine. Yet again, she was going to have to plead with the judge for another extension. But Tammy didn't want to think about that right now so brushed it aside. Her thoughts were all about the upcoming week-end, when she would finally see Dwayne again and he would get to meet Matt for the first time.

The next three days couldn't go by fast enough. Consumed daily with thoughts of Dwayne, Tammy desperately wanted the week to end. There were many times she wanted to call him, but she refused the urge because she didn't want to seem like she was coming on too strong.

Finally, when Friday rolled around, she waited until she was home in the afternoon and had fed Matt before dialing his beeper number. After hearing the two beeps, Tammy entered her phone number and hung up. Clasping her hands together, she stared at the phone, waiting anxiously for it to ring. After what began to feel like an eternity of silence, Tammy started having terrifying thoughts. *What if he doesn't call me back? What if I never see him again?*

As the minutes ticked by, Tammy started to convince herself that there was a possibility he may never call back.

A pain staking two hours passed by with no call. Tammy tried to stay positive and keep busy by entertaining Matt outside. Of course, she left the front door open so she could hear the phone if it were to ring. With her ears and mind focused elsewhere, she halfheartedly played catch with Matt.

And then she heard that joyous sound—the ring tone of the phone. In a rush to reach it in time, Tammy grabbed Matt's hand and pulled him along behind her. "Come on, buddy, let's go inside. The phone's ringing."

She slammed the door closed and raced across the room to get to the phone.

She took a second to catch her breath before picking up the receiver. "Hello?"

"Hey, Tammy, it's Dwayne. Sorry I didn't get back to you right away. I was out working on a boat and there wasn't a phone booth close by."

Tammy closed her eyes and heaved a huge sigh of relief, warmed by the sound of his voice. "That's okay," she said, trying to calm the butterflies churning in her stomach. "I just called to see about coming down tomorrow."

"Oh, you bet," Dwayne almost screeched. "I've been looking forward to it all week. I've missed you."

"Really?" His confession took her by surprise.

"Yes. Really. What, you haven't missed me?"

Tammy hugged the phone. "Yes, I have actually."

With their feelings clearly mutual, Dwayne gave Tammy directions to the boat yard where his boat was docked, and they made plans to meet at ten the next morning. After ending the call, Tammy carefully folded the piece of paper and tucked it securely in her purse.

~

Having already packed everything for her weekend getaway the night before, she was up bright and early the following morning. She'd picked out a denim miniskirt and a blue tank top to wear. After hugging Judy goodbye and giving Kate and Christopher a peck on the cheek, she headed out the door to put Matt in his car seat.

Heading south, she took the 110 freeway to the 10 freeway, west onto the 405 freeway and finally the 90 freeway, which took her into the heart of the marina. Being a weekend, the traffic was light and the drive took just over an hour. In less than a couple of minutes of pulling off the freeway, she turned into the parking lot of the Anchors Boatyard.

She smiled to herself when she saw Dwayne standing by the main gate, dressed casually in tanned shorts, a white T-shirt and loafers. His perfectly tanned arms and legs glowed against the light colors of his clothes.

"Damn, he's fine," Tammy mumbled under her breath.

Dwayne, upon seeing Tammy pull in, beamed her a smile and waved, and then he wasted no time in rushing over to the car to open her door and greet her.

"You made it," he said with another heartwarming smile as he reached out his hand.

Tammy took his hand and stepped out of the car. "I did." She smiled when she noticed a slight ocean breeze combing through her hair.

Still holding her hand, Dwayne gazed into her eyes, leaned in and kissed her. With his warm breath coating her mouth, Tammy closed her eyes and kissed him back with greater force, using her tongue to explore beyond his lips. Dwayne let out a little moan and cupped his arm around her waist.

"Damn, I've missed you," he muffled through the kiss.

"I've missed you too," she said before reluctantly breaking away. "I have to get Matt out of the car," she said between panted breaths.

Dwayne licked his lips, savoring her taste. "That's right, I get to meet your son."

"Yes, you do." She straightened out her miniskirt before walking around the car to let Matt out of his car seat. She held his hand as they walked over to Dwayne and then knelt beside him with her arm around his waist. "Hey, sweetie, this is mommy's friend, Dwayne."

Dwayne knelt down to Matt's level and took his hand. "Hi buddy. It's good to meet you."

Matt had never been a shy child and beamed Dwayne a big smile as he replied, "Hi."

Dwayne leaned in a little closer. "So do you want to see some boats, Matt?"

Matt's smile got even bigger. Letting go of Tammy, he jumped up and down with his arms flying in the air. "Yes!"

Tammy and Dwayne laughed.

"I guess that's a yes," Dwayne said while taking Matt's hand. "I'll get your bags." he added.

Tammy took Matt's other hand and together they walked over to the main gate. After entering a code on a number pad, Dwayne swung open the gate and led them into the boatyard.

Not only was this the first time for Matt to be around boats, it was also Tammy's first time. In all her twenty-six years, she had never stepped foot on a boat. She scanned the huge and busy yard as they walked toward the docks. For as far as she could see, boats of all shapes and sizes stood in neat rows on metal stands. Sailboats, power boats and fishing boats. Each one had a set of large metal ladders next to it so the boat could be accessed while it was being worked on.

It was a noisy place with radios blasting from the various workstations, crews sanding the bottom of some boats, some were drilling, others were hammering. To her left, cranes lifted boats in and out of the water. Throughout the entire yard, chatter was loud, but the laughs were even louder. Fascinated by her new surroundings, Tammy took her time walking down to the docks. She wanted to take it all in, this world that she never knew existed, and for reasons she didn't quite understand, she knew right away she wanted to be a part of it.

Tammy was impressed by the friendly atmosphere. She couldn't help but notice the skew of waves and smiles Dwayne received as they walked through the yard. It was a gesture she never saw in the city, a place where everyone kept to themselves and no one ever smiled or said hello.

Dwayne led them down a ramp onto the floating docks. Tammy paused for a moment to steady her feet, but the wobbling of the dock took her by surprise and caused her to let out a giggle.

Dwayne turned to face her. "Are you okay?"

"Yeah, I've never walked on a dock before. It moves!" She laughed and tried to balance herself with an outstretched arm. " Even Matt is walking better than me."

"Oh, you'll get used to it. Hang around with me and you'll have your sea legs in no time."

Wobbling her way down the dock, Tammy marveled at the rows of boats, most of which were white, all of which were squeaky clean and glistened in the sun. The rigging on the masts of sailboats rattled in the breeze. She looked out at the inviting sparkles dancing on the surface of the ocean to her left. Beyond the water on the other side of the channel, she noticed a park with more boats hugging the docks. The cheerful sounds of kids playing and adults laughing could be heard, even from where Tammy stood. She was surprised how clear the sounds could be heard from so far away.

Tammy looked out beyond the dock on which they were standing and saw several large boats cruising the marina at a slow speed. Most had music blasting from them, and quite a few boasted beautiful, bikini-clad women with perfectly slim bodies dancing and sunbathing across the deck and bow of the boat. Everywhere Tammy looked, she saw people were having fun, living life to the fullest. She couldn't help but think what a great place it would be to live.

Dwayne led them down to the third slip, where a medium sized power boat with a large deck was docked. "Welcome to my humble abode," he said, motioning his hand toward the vessel.

Unable to hide his enthusiasm, Matt pulled away from Tammy's hand and raced to Dwayne's side. "A boat! Can we go on it?" he asked with wide eyes.

Tammy and Dwayne chuckled at his excitement, but Dwayne wasted no time in sweeping Matt off his feet and lifting him up onto the boat. As fast as his little legs could run, Matt disappeared down into the cabin. "Mommy, come see. There's a bed in here."

"I'm coming." Tammy was promptly escorted onto the boat by Dwayne's extended hand. The rocking on board was even more intense than on the dock and took her by surprise. Afraid of losing her balance, Tammy reached for the rail and held on until her feet steadied.

Dwayne laughed at her uneasiness, and was equally amused that little Matt wasn't fazed at all by the experience and was still in awe down in the cabin.

It was a simple boat with a large, spacious deck, which Dwayne explained was ideal for stacking and hauling gear. The helm, where the steering wheel and radio equipment were positioned, were on the starboard side of the boat, which Tammy soon learned meant the right-hand side. Three wooden steps to the left led down to the small cabin below, which had all the amenities one would need while out at sea. A bed, a table with two benches, a small sink and the smallest bathroom Tammy had ever seen. The sight of it ignited a flashback to the horrible trailer she had lived in with Steven when they moved to Seattle. Even though the boat's cabin was small, it was still far better than the trailer.

Tammy peeked into the tiny cabin and giggled when Matt waved from the bed, where he appeared to be testing its bounciness.

"You live in here?" Tammy asked Dwayne.

"Yep, I sure do. I don't need much, and you can't beat the view."

Tammy had to agree with him. People would pay thousands for an ocean view like this.

He went on to tell her the history of the boat, and Tammy listened intently. It was an old wooden 1959 Drake Baywatch lifeguard boat with twin 440 Chrysler gas engines. Dwayne told her with an added snarky laugh that they were gas guzzlers and not ideal for fishing. Most commercial vessels had diesel engines, which were a lot more efficient to run. But he loved the size of the deck for hauling gear, so when the boat was retired from service in 1988, he bought it and converted it into a fishing boat. The boat was already called *Baywatch,* so he simply changed one letter and named her *Baywitch* instead.

Dwayne had what was called a doublewide slip, which allowed

tow boats to be docked in it. While he was telling Tammy the story about the *Baywitch*, he pointed to a small gray boat next to them. "That's mine too," he said proudly.

"You have two boats?"

"I do. That one over there, I built myself. I found the hull in a field behind a boat repair shop. It was being used as a dumpster. I liked the shape of it and asked the owner if he'd sell it to me. To my surprise, he said yes, as long as I took all the trash away that was piled in it. Of course, I jumped on it and hauled it away." He looked over at it with pride shining from his eyes. "It took me about three years to build. She's a 19 foot outboard skiff. I added the little cabin. It has just enough room to camp down for the night if I need to."

"What did you name that boat?" Tammy asked.

"Little Boat," Dwayne replied with a smirk.

"Well, that's original." Tammy laughed. "Why do you need two boats?"

Before Dwayne could answer, Matt raced out of the cabin. "Mom, this is so cool!" he squealed with excitement.

Tammy held out her arms and stopped him in mid-stride. "No running on the boat, honey."

Dwayne approached Matt and just like in the parking lot, he knelt to Matt's level. Dwayne's way of handling her son really impressed Tammy. He took Matt's hand. "Hey, buddy, how would you like to go for a boat ride?"

"Really!" He looked up at Tammy with the eyes of a child left alone in a candy store. "Mom, can we?" he pleaded.

Tammy was just as excited as her son. "Dwayne, that would be amazing. We would love to."

Dwayne clapped his hands together. "Okay then. Consider this your first boating lesson. And I'll tell you why I need two boats while we're cruising the marina. I don't think Matt wants to wait any longer."

Having no clue what to do on a boat, Tammy stood aside, held

Matt's hand and watched Dwayne's every move, taking everything in. After putting a life jacket on Matt, Dwayne went to the helm and fired up the boat. The roar of the motors took Tammy by surprise, and she soon discovered that yelling was the only way to be heard over the noise.

While still at the helm, Dwayne glanced over at Tammy and shouted, "I'll let you untie the boat."

"Me?" Tammy hollered back, shocked.

"Yes, just untie the two ropes around the cleats. Jump off the boat and do the front one first. Then come back on the boat and untie the one on the stern."

Tammy was slowly making sense of all the boating terms Dwayne was throwing at her. *Cleat, bow, stern, helm, hull.* She soon realized she had a lot to learn. She let go of Matt's hand and told him in a stern voice to stay put. She then stepped off the boat and instantly found she needed to brace herself for a few seconds while the dock rocked beneath her feet. After regaining her balance, she walked to the front of the boat to find the rope.

While fumbling with the rope tied around the cleat, she was thinking there must be a simpler way to do it and struggled for some time before finally untying it and throwing it on the boat.

Once she was back on the deck, Dwayne instructed her to take the rope from the front and lay it on the edge of the deck alongside the cabin so it didn't fly out. Tammy followed his instructions and then headed to the stern—the back—of the boat, where she made eye contact with him and waited for the signal that he was ready.

Dwayne nodded, giving her the sign she was waiting for. The second time around, the rope was easier to untie from the cleat and without being told, she tucked it safely on the deck of the boat.

"See, the two rubber fenders hanging over the sides?" Dwayne hollered while pointing in their direction with his finger. "Those stop the boat from rubbing on the dock. Go ahead and flip them over into the boat. No need to untie them."

Tammy located the fenders and followed Dwayne's orders precisely.

Dwayne smiled and gave her a thumbs up.

Feeling pleased with herself, she took Matt's hand and joined Dwayne at the helm.

She watched as Dwayne put the boat in reverse, using a throttle on his right, and the boat began to putter and release smoke from the stern. With ease, he maneuvered the boat out of the slip and turned it around so it was facing the main channel. Being her first time on a boat, Tammy braced herself by holding on to the dash while her legs found their balance. Again, Tammy watched Dwayne's every move and was impressed how easily he drove the boat, although she had no idea how he did any of it with no brakes.

Puttering at five knots, they headed out to the main channel. Matt was placed in the captain's chair between where Dwayne and Tammy stood, holding hands, while Dwayne steered the boat one-handed.

As they cruised down the channel, Tammy took it all in. Sailboats tacked in front of them caught the wind in their sails as they zigzagged toward the open ocean, the heavy material flapping in the breeze. Power boats chugged through the water, abundant with fishermen, families and partiers. Some seemed to be returning to their slips after a morning on the ocean, while others were leaving to see what the open waters had to offer. Scattered throughout the channel were kayakers and little dinghies, some with motors and others being rowed.

Tammy was in a new world. She had no idea that such a lifestyle existed just an hour away from home. To her, the place smelt like money.

As they cruised closer to the open waters, they passed high-rise condominiums overlooking the water's edge. Mega yachts were docked on the end ties, and large party boats with disco music blasting were beginning to meander into the channel. Tammy pointed all the things out to Matt who, like her, was also taking it all in. Only he was being much more vocal with high-pitched squeals of excitement.

"I could get used to this," Tammy said over the sound of the motors into Dwayne's ear.

Dwayne nodded. "Yeah, it's not a bad way to live. I have no complaints."

As they passed the break wall, which was the entrance to the marina, Dwayne sped the boat up to a comfortable fourteen knots, causing Tammy to force herself up against the captain's chair for support. More squeals came from Matt as he too clung on to the chair.

Fearing she may lose her balance, Dwayne locked his arm around her waist and gave her a smile. Thankful for the extra support, Tammy looked up and smiled back.

The spray of sea water kicked up by the boat felt cool and refreshing against the exposed skin of her arms and legs. She loved the feeling of the wind rushing through her hair and across her face. The city quickly felt like a distant memory, one she was in no rush to return to.

As they headed out to sea, Tammy listened to the sound of the water crashing against the boat as the vessel plowed its way through the water. She watched the seagulls flying above, following the trail of the boat in hunt of a free meal or a place to land. She spotted boats far away on the horizon and in the other direction, people frolicking in the waves on the beach.

Dwayne leaned in close to her ear so he could be heard above the motors. "How are your sea legs? Are they getting any better?"

"Yes. I'm still standing." Tammy laughed.

Suddenly, he let go of the wheel and stood back. "Come on, you drive," he said with a devious grin.

Tammy gasped. "What! I don't know how to drive a bloody boat. Are you insane? What if I hit something?"

CHAPTER 6

*D*wayne scanned the ocean, wearing a sarcastic grin. "What are you going to hit? The nearest boat is five miles away." He returned to the wheel and pulled the throttle toward him to slow it down to a comfortable eight knots. "Out here is the best place to learn to drive a boat. Come on, give it a try," he said, standing away from the wheel again.

Enjoying Dwayne's new game, it didn't take long for Matt to take sides. "Come on, Mommy, you can do it," he squealed while banging the arms of the chair with his palms.

With no one at the wheel, Dwayne threw Tammy another playful smile. "Better hurry up, the boat isn't going to drive itself."

Obviously having no say in the debate, Tammy shook her head, released a nervous smile and approached the wheel. "So what do I do?"

"Well, for starters, you can take a hold of the wheel." Dwayne looked to be trying to suppress a chuckle.

With apprehension and feeling somewhat intimidated by the cold metal wheel, she grasped it with both hands and locked her fingers securely around it until her knuckles turned white.

A squeal of delight roared from Matt's lungs. "Yeah, Mommy is driving the boat!"

Afraid to take her eyes off the ocean, Tammy threw Matt a quick smile.

"Easy now," Dwayne said. "You don't have to hold it so tight. It's not going anywhere." Dwayne stood next to her and pointed dead ahead. "See that island way out there on the horizon?"

"Yes."

"That's Catalina Island. Aim the bow of the boat for that."

Seeing it was slightly to her left, Tammy steered the wheel toward it, but nothing happened so she tried again. This time, the boat turned too much, so she steered in the other direction to try and correct the problem. Instantly, the boat began to zigzag.

Tammy let out a nervous laugh. "I don't know what I'm doing. I'm steering but it's not working."

Dwayne rolled his eyes. "What you're doing is oversteering. Don't worry; it's a common mistake for first-time boaters. The key is that you have to remember a boat doesn't steer like a car. A car steers from the front, whereas a boat steers from the back. It takes a while for the boat to recognize the wheel has been turned. When you turn the wheel, it takes a few seconds for the boat to begin turning. If you try and correct it then you get the zigzags. Does that make sense?"

Tammy smiled. "It actually does."

"Okay. Good. Now, aim for Catalina again." Dwayne turned, picked up Matt and sat him on the ledge next to the wheel where he could hold him steady. "Matt and I will watch," he said with a wink.

Tammy was beginning to understand the steering part of a boat a little better, and she adjusted the wheel to point the bow in the direction of the island. Dwayne stood in silence next to her, letting her get the feel of the boat. He was impressed with her eagerness to learn, but he could still see the frustration on her face as the boat continued to sway from side to side across the water.

"It takes time to get a feel for it and know when not to over-steer. You'll get it. You're off to a good start." He didn't want her to feel discouraged.

"It's a lot harder than it looks," Tammy announced, her eyes still fixed straight ahead.

"Do you want to try speeding up the boat a little?" Dwayne asked.

"Yes! I want to go fast," Matt screeched in delight.

Tammy laughed at her son's enthusiasm. "When Dwayne is driving, we will go fast. Okay?" She turned to Dwayne. "We can go a little faster but not much. How do I do that?" She looked down at the controls while waiting for an answer.

"See that silver throttle next to you on your right, the one with the red knob on the end?"

Tammy looked across. "Yes."

"If you push it forward, it speeds up the boat; put it in the middle, you'll be in neutral, and all the way back toward you is reverse. So, to go a little faster, push the throttle forward—SLOWLY."

Tammy listened to his instructions and with a gentle touch, just like he had instructed, she pushed the throttle forward. The boat instantly picked up power and speed and as the noise from the motors increased, Tammy couldn't help but feel pleased with herself.

"Well done. Now you can cruise at that speed for a while. Let yourself get comfortable and just concentrate on keeping the boat straight," Dwayne instructed her.

Tammy nodded.

Dwayne lifted Matt off the ledge. "Come on, big fella, let's go to the back of the boat and see if we can see any dolphins."

Tammy felt a rush of panic. "Don't leave me! What if I crash? Where are the brakes?"

Dwayne laughed. "Crash into what? And there are no brakes on a boat."

"What?" Tammy said with a look of horror. "Then how do I stop the bloody thing?"

"You use the throttle to slow it down. Give it a go. Pull the throttle back easy until you are in neutral."

Tammy followed his instructions and smiled when the boat slowed down and began to idle. "Oh, okay. Can I speed it up again?"

"Sure! You're in control of the boat right now. Come on, Matt," Dwayne replied before leading Matt to the stern.

Tammy had discovered a new lifestyle. Never in her wildest dreams did she ever think she'd be driving a boat. The freedom she was experiencing out on the open ocean was exhilarating. She looked at the coastline of Santa Monica and beyond, at all the other cities clustered together. Where people lived liked ants, all on top of each other in concrete cities while dealing with the chaos and stress that ran their lives. There was none of that out here. For the first time, she felt disconnected from all her worries as a single mother and trying to make ends meet. Out here, she felt completely free.

She glanced over at Matt and Dwayne, and what she saw warmed her heart. The smile on her son's face said it all. Curled over in a protective manner, Dwayne was pointing to a school of dolphins following the boat. This is what her son needed, a male figure in his life.

Since leaving Steven, it'd always been just her and Matt. She'd done her best to provide for him and had given him a good home, but she could never give him that male influence that a young boy needed. Being on the boat, watching Dwayne with her son, just felt right. She hated to admit it so soon, but she felt like a real family. Was she setting herself up to have her heart crushed?

They spent the whole day on the boat. Dwayne had obviously planned ahead and surprised them with an ice chest full of sodas and lunch. In one afternoon, Tammy and Matt had experienced so many new things, and so many new doors had been opened. For the first time, she got to see her son fish, and the excitement that masked his face when he caught his first mackerel would be forever planted in her mind. Like herself, he was eager to learn and was a natural on the boat.

Tammy also gave fishing a go. It was another first for her. She admired Dwayne's patience as he showed her how to bait the hook with live anchovies that he pulled out of a bait tank. Tammy soon discovered that there was an art to grabbing one of the slippery creatures from the tank and keeping hold of it so it didn't slip through her hand. After a few attempts and giggles from Matt and Dwayne, she succeeded. She cringed a little when she hooked the anchovy to the line, but that soon passed when she caught her first sea bass. After that, she was eager to get the line back in the water in the hopes of catching another.

They stayed out until the sun began to set over the horizon. Before heading in, Dwayne turned off the boat, leaving just the calming sound of the sea splashing against the hull. "Hey, guys, I want to show you something," he said while holding out his hand.

Not questioning him, Tammy had Matt take Dwayne's hand and followed them both to the bow of the boat. "Here, have a seat," Dwayne said while pointing to the bow.

Wrapping an arm around Matt, Tammy followed his directions and then looked out to sea. She gasped at the breathtaking view of the sunset in front of her. The sky was now a brilliant shade of orange, entangled with streaks of red and yellow. The surface of the water danced and shimmered from the glow, and a feeling of peace engulfed her as she watched the ocean and the night sky slowly going to sleep in its own magical way.

"Oh my god, that is absolutely amazing. I've never seen anything like it," Tammy said, her hand held to her chest in awe.

Dwayne took a seat next to her and curled his arm around her shoulder. Tammy welcomed his embrace and nuzzled her head into the crook of his neck.

"You don't see that in the city, now, do you?" he said in a soft voice.

"No, you don't."

Mesmerized by the beauty that surrounded her, Tammy had never felt such calmness in her life. Back home, she was always on the go, chasing the almighty dollar, struggling to make ends meet and focusing entirely on providing for Matt.

She looked down at her son. Worn out from the day's events, he had fallen asleep nestled in her arms. "Look, he's sleeping," Tammy whispered.

Dwayne leaned in and peeked at Matt. "I guess he had a good day."

"He did, thanks to you. You showed him so much today." She let out a light chuckle. "And me too." She paused and gave him a sweet smile. "I had a good time. Thanks."

Dwayne returned the smile while brushing her hair away from her face with his hand. "You're welcome."

Moved by the gesture, Tammy held his palm close to her cheek before kissing it tenderly. Embracing his masculine scent, she leaned in and met him in a kiss.

As she sat back and watched the sun set, she realized she didn't want the day to end. Everything was perfect and felt so right. She had a strange sense of belonging. This was the life she wanted. But did Dwayne want the same? She knew she was thinking too fast and needed to slow down. She'd made so many hasty mistakes in the past. First, there was Raymond, who almost cost her her relationship with her father, and then there was Steven the drug addict. Just thinking about him made Tammy cringe. She had only just met Dwayne and knew absolutely nothing about him, except for the wonderful life he led.

Dwayne stirred her from her thoughts. "Hey, what are you thinking about?"

"Oh, just how beautiful it is out here. It's so peaceful. You're so lucky to wake up to this every day. I envy you."

Dwayne gave her shoulder a light squeeze and pulled her in closer. "You and Matt can come down here anytime you want."

"Don't say that, you'll never get rid of me." Tammy laughed.

"I have no objections."

Hearing him say that warmed Tammy's heart. She knew she was falling for him fast, but she didn't know how to put on the brakes. Much like the boat, it appeared she didn't have any.

Although Dwayne seemed perfect in every way possible, because of her wrecked relationships in the past, she was expecting the inevitable bomb to land in the middle of her happiness at any moment. So far, it had not. But the past she had lived reminded her to tread carefully.

They lay in each other's arms for the next half hour, cuddling and sharing kisses while Matt slept soundly in Tammy's arms. For her, life couldn't get any better. She didn't want it to end but knew she should get her son home and into bed at a reasonable hour. Plus, she had to work in the morning. Tammy let out a big sigh. "I guess we should get going."

Dwayne ran his fingers through her hair, stroking it over her shoulders. "I was afraid you were going to say that soon."

Tammy strained her neck and looked up at him. "Believe me when I say I don't want to. But this little guy needs to be in his bed, and unfortunately I have to go work tomorrow. It's been an amazing day and I honestly hate to see it end."

Dwayne squeezed her tight while kissing the top of her head. "It's been an amazing day for me too. But as they say, all good things must come to an end." While releasing his hold on Tammy, he shifted his body to allow himself to stand up. "I'll fire up the boat and take us back to the dock. You can stay here with Matt, I'll drive slow. We are only a few minutes out of the marina's main channel."

After a few minutes with the engines idling, Dwayne returned with a blanket. "Here, you can cover Matt with this. There might be a chill when the boat starts moving."

Tammy looked up and smiled as she took the blanket. "Thanks."

Within ten minutes, they were tied up to the dock and the night returned to a tranquil silence after Dwayne shut off the motors. Amazingly, Matt didn't stir during the ride back to the dock.

Once the boat was secured, Dwayne returned to the bow of the boat and held out his hand to Tammy. "Come on, let's get you to your car. I'll carry Matt for you."

Being careful not to disturb Matt from his sound sleep, Tammy rose slowly and stood precariously on her feet as she handed Matt to Dwayne. Once he was safely in Dwayne's arms and thankfully still asleep, Tammy headed to the deck of the boat while guiding herself with the rail. After searching for her purse, which she found on the table in the cabin, she threw it over her shoulder and took Dwayne's free hand. With Dwayne already on the dock, she stepped off the boat into his arms.

A few minutes later, they had Matt secured in his car seat and covered with his favorite blanket. Tammy stood next to her car, wrapped in Dwayne's arms and not wanting to leave. "Thank you for a fantastic day. I'll never forget it," she said while gazing up into his eyes.

"Hey, you say it like we're never going to see each other again." He brushed his lips against hers, lingering for a moment as his breathing became deeper.

Feeling his warm breath close to hers, Tammy pulled him in to her lips and saturated her mouth with his as they locked in a sensual kiss. Tammy latched her hands around his neck and gave way to the subtle moans escaping her throat. She suddenly gasped when she felt his hand slide up under her shirt and gently massage her breast.

"Oh god, I want you," Tammy panted between breaths.

"I want you too," Dwayne whispered as he broke away from the kiss and slid his tongue delicately across her neck, smothering her with kisses.

With a heaving chest, Tammy closed her eyes and leaned back against the car while holding Dwayne's head close to her breast. Rotating his hips, he pushed his body hard against hers as he worked his lips down to the V between her breasts.

"Stop…" Tammy reluctantly moaned between baited breaths. "Matt's in the car. I really should go."

Still breathing heavily, Dwayne lifted his head and stood before her, his hand still cupping her breast. "I know." He kissed her gently on the lips and released a slight chuckle. "We need a weekend alone."

Tammy placed her hand on his and squeezed it before pulling it away from her breast. She smiled and kissed him back. "I agree. I can't wait. When do you suggest?"

With the passion between them now subsided, Dwayne retrieved his hand from under her shirt and wrapped his arms around her waist while staring into her eyes. An inquisitive smile appeared across his face. "Well, I'm entered in a shark tournament this weekend. Want to join me? Can always use an extra hand on the boat."

Tammy's jaw dropped. "A shark tournament? As in, you catch sharks?"

Dwayne laughed out loud, amused by the look of horror that had invaded her face. "Yes, I catch sharks," he said with a smirk.

"And you're not afraid they will attack you?" She shook her head in disbelief. "Are you insane? I've never heard of such a thing."

Even though he was enjoying Tammy's reaction, Dwayne felt he needed to explain a little further. "It's a competition I enter every year. In fact, I've won for the past two years," he said with a hint of pride. "The prize money is twenty five hundred bucks."

"Wow!" Tammy shrieked.

"We can only catch Mako sharks—which, by the way, are delicious—and all others are thrown back. The shark isn't wasted; it's caught for consumption. The tournament lasts two days, with the biggest fish winning the prize money." He folded his arms and grinned at Tammy. "So do you wanna go?"

"Wow! This I gotta see," Tammy said, her eyes beaming with enthusiasm. "I've never seen a shark up close before. Only on the TV and even then, they look too damn scary. To see one up close on a boat, well, that's just too crazy to miss." Tammy raised her voice and added, "Hell yeah I want to go. I can't wait! Let me talk to Judy and see if she can watch Matt this weekend."

Dwayne loved her spirit. "Great! Page me this week. Okay?"

Tammy planted another kiss on his lips before stepping in her car and firing it up. "I will." She leaned back into her seat and stared up at Dwayne. "Oh, I really hope Judy has the weekend off. Wait till I tell her I'm going shark fishing." Her eyes became wide again. "I can't wait to see the look on her face!"

Dwayne tossed his head back and let out another laugh. "You'll have to tell me all about it. I hope you can make it." He leaned through the window and gave her one last kiss before stepping away so she could back up.

"One way or another, I will make it," she said with a beaming smile. "There's no way I'm going to miss shark fishing."

CHAPTER 7

Tammy didn't pull into her driveway until close to eleven and was thrilled to see the lights were still on. After putting the car in park and shutting off the engine, she turned to check on Matt and found he was still sound asleep. She quickly grabbed her purse and other bags off the front seat and after exiting her car, she skipped across the grass to the front door and burst into the house. She found Judy stretched out on the couch, dressed in her usual evening attire of blue pajamas and fuzzy black slippers. With her kids in bed, she was doing her favorite things—watching black and white movies and sipping on a glass of white wine.

"You're up!" Tammy squealed while tossing her bags on the foot of the couch next to Judy's feet.

"Of course I'm up," she said with a sarcastic roll of her eyes. "Joel just left and I want to hear all about your day on the boat. How was it?" Judy swung her legs onto the floor and sat up. "I'm dying to hear."

A huge smile blanketed Tammy's face. "Oh, Judy, I can't wait to tell you." Tammy glanced quickly at the open front door. "I have to get Matt out of the car and put him in bed, and then I'll be right back to tell you everything."

"Oh, this sounds like it's going to be good." Judy laughed while making her way across the room to turn off the TV. "I'll go pour you a glass of wine. Then I'll be waiting right here."

"Great. I'll be right back. I've not had a drink all day."

After Matt was tucked into his bed, Tammy did a quick change of clothes into her favorite comfortable white pajamas and joined Judy on the couch. "Come on. Have a seat," Judy pleaded while handing Tammy a glass of chilled wine.

Before spilling the events of her day, Tammy inhaled a huge gulp of wine and smacked her lips. "Damn, that tastes good."

"I can tell you had a great time. You can't stop smiling." Judy patted Tammy's knee. "Come on, tell me. I want to hear all the juicy details."

Tammy lit a cigarette, took a long drag and threw her head back into the pillows of the couch. "Oh god! It was amazing. I don't know where to start. Dwayne just seems so perfect, and he was totally awesome with Matt." Tammy took another sip of wine. "He has a son too, so it makes sense he'd be good with kids, right?"

Judy nodded and gave Tammy's arm a nudge. "Go on. Tell me more."

"Matt had so much fun; he really likes Dwayne," she said while putting her feet up on the coffee table. "Do you want to know something?"

"What?" Judy asked.

"Today was the first time I saw my son fish, and the look on his face when he reeled in his first catch was absolutely breathtaking. It brought tears to my eyes." Tammy let her head fall back against the cushions. "Oh, Judy, what am I going to do?"

Judy creased her brow. "What do you mean? What are you going to do?"

Tammy sat up and stubbed out her cigarette while she spoke. "I really like him, and yet I'm scared. I don't know if I'm ready for a serious relationship. What if I get hurt again?"

Judy understood where Tammy was coming from. They had both made poor decisions in the past when it came to men, which is how they ended up living and raising their kids together.

Judy tried to give Tammy some advice. "Who says it has to be serious? Just have some fun, girl. After all, you deserve it." Tammy listened and nodded. "You've been working so hard, raising Matt and giving him everything he needs. And doing a damn good job, I might add. It's time you started thinking about yourself. Maybe this guy is just what you need."

Tammy let out a sigh. "Oh, Judy, I don't know. Why am I so petrified? I've gone on the odd date or two in the past, but Dwayne is different. I feel so comfortable when I'm with him, and the lifestyle he lives, well, I want it. It's like a different world down there. Everyone waves and talks to you. There's no traffic like there is here. And people are actually nice to each other." Tammy shifted her body, unable to hide her excitement. "And, get this, I drove the boat! All by myself."

"What!" Judy almost choked on her wine with the shock. "Wow!"

Tammy couldn't contain herself. Rising from the couch, she began walking in circles around the room. "Judy, I loved everything about the boat and found myself wanting to learn everything Dwayne showed me. I want to learn more. I'm fascinated by it all." A devious smile grew across her face. "In fact, he's invited me to go shark fishing this weekend and I really want to go."

Judy almost fell off the couch. "Shark fishing! Are you fucking nuts?"

"That's what I said to Dwayne. But I can't explain it. I'm honestly excited by this whole fishing and boating thing. I've never been exposed to such a lifestyle before and I'm totally intrigued by it. I want to learn everything about it. Please say you'll watch Matt this weekend. It will be the first time I've ever been away from him overnight, but I really want this and I know he'll be safe with you."

Judy's eyes lit up. "Oooh, so you'll be spending the night, will you? And we all know what that means!"

Tammy reached over and slapped Judy's shoulder. "Stop! Tell me you can watch Matt. Please?"

"Of course I'll watch him. I have the weekend off and I'll have Joel spend the night here." She laughed and added, "Which means we'll both be getting some nookie."

Tammy slapped her again. "You're terrible."

"Nah. Just honest. Don't worry about Matt. He'll be fine. Just go have some fun, okay?"

Tammy embraced her friend, who had always been her rock in the past. "Thank you so much!"

After finishing her wine, Tammy set down her glass on the coffee table and looked at Judy with a frown.

"What's up?" Judy asked, looking puzzled. "Everything okay? You suddenly went from bloom to gloom."

"Yeah, I'm okay. I just realized I have to go back to court this week and ask the stupid judge for another extension to pay my fine. What if he says no? Will they take me to jail right then while I'm in court?"

Seeing the worried look on her friend's face, Judy tried to ease her mind. "I don't think so, hon. I think you're entitled to three extensions."

"But you're not sure, are you?"

"Well, no, I'm not."

Wearing a worried look, Tammy leaned in closer to Judy and placed her hand or Judy's knee. "Judy, I need to know, if they take me to jail, that Matt will be okay with you." She gave Judy's knee another squeeze. "Can you promise me that? I know it's a lot to ask but I have no one else to turn to."

Judy took Tammy's hand, followed by a warm smile. "Don't you worry about Matt. He will be just fine. Now come on, let's have another glass of wine and get back to talking about Dwayne. Enough of this legal bullshit crap." Judy paused before adding, "Hey, does Dwayne know about your accident and the courts?"

"Oh, god no! I don't want to scare him off." She laughed. "I'll try and hide it from him as long as I can. By then, he'll hopefully like me enough to forgive me."

Judy nodded. "I like your way of thinking, girl. Now, off I go to get us some more wine," she said, pulling herself up off the couch.

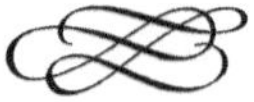

Dressed in the best outfit Tammy could find, which consisted of a beige knee-length skirt and a white shirt, she returned to court on May 25th to face the judge one more time.

Once her name was called, Tammy made her way to the front of the court room. She nervously rubbed her sweaty palms on the sides of her legs while she waited for the judge to speak, and the piercing stare he gave her over his glasses caused her to shudder.

"Miss Mellows, do you have the one thousand five hundred dollar fine?" the judge asked in a stern voice.

Tammy swallowed the lump that was now invading her throat and tried to calm her racing heart. "No, Your Honor, I do not."

The judge was silent while he picked up her case file and began to read. Again, he looked up and gave Tammy a cold stare. Tammy clenched her hands in front of her, trying to control their shaking.

"Well, Miss Mellows, the fine was due today."

Trembling, Tammy struggled to speak. "I know, Your Honor, and I apologize. I…um…would like to know if I could get an extension."

The judge pursed his lips and again looked at her file. "You've had two extensions already, Miss Mellows."

"I know, Your Honor. I have a young son and I had to buy a car."

"I don't want to hear your excuses," the judge snarled.

Tammy cowered before him, her knees feeling like they were about to buckle. "Sorry, Your Honor," she replied in a timid voice.

Before speaking, the judge removed his glasses and squinted his eyes over at Tammy. "Miss Mellows, I will give you one final extension."

Tammy released a huge sigh of relief as all the worries of going to jail began to subside. "Thank you, Your Honor."

"I'm not done yet," the judge quickly added. "I'm giving you until August 15th to pay the fine. On your next court appearance, you must pay the fine or do jail time. This is your final extension. Do I make myself clear, Miss Mellows?"

"Yes, Your Honor. I understand," Tammy replied. She was unable to hide her smile but at the same time, she was counting in her head that she had roughly ten weeks to come up with the money.

The judge closed her file and put it to the side. "Miss Mellows, you are dismissed. We will see you back here in court on August fifteenth."

"Thank you, Your Honor," Tammy answered before quickly exiting the court room.

For Tammy, the following weekend couldn't come fast enough. She paged Dwayne earlier in the week to tell him she would be able to make it for the shark tournament. He had called her back within five minutes and sounded beyond excited when he spoke to her over the phone. "That's fantastic! I can't wait to see you. I hope I get a shark this year so you can see one up close and personal," he had said.

When Friday finally rolled around, Tammy was ready. She had packed her bag the night before and couldn't wait to rush home from work, take a shower and grab her things.

Saying goodbye to Matt wasn't easy. Trying to hold it together for her son, she held back her tears and swallowed the lump in her throat. But Matt didn't seem fazed at all. When she knelt to his level in the driveway to say goodbye, he simply locked his arms around her neck and gave her a quick peck on the cheek before rushing off back to the game he was playing with Judy's kids. Left alone, Tammy remained on her knees and watched him for a moment as she brushed away the few tears that had escaped and rolled down her cheeks.

"Don't you worry. He'll be fine," Judy said from her spot on the front porch.

Tammy approached her friend and gave her a firm embrace. "I know. I love you, girlfriend, and thank you."

"You're welcome. Now go on, get out of here." She shooed Tammy away.

By four o'clock, Tammy was on the road heading to Dwayne's.

With the infamous LA traffic, it took her two hours to reach the boatyard. Once the car was in park, she grabbed her bags from the back seat and checked her car was all locked up. She let herself through the gate with the code Dwayne had given her over the phone and headed toward his boat. While walking through the yard, she was greeted with smiles and waves from people she recognized from the previous week. God, she loved this place and how friendly the people were.

When she reached Dwayne's boat, she was stunned to see all the stuff packed on the deck and the hatches to the motors lying open. Dwayne was nowhere in sight. She scanned the docks in search of him but had no luck.

"Dwayne?"

Tammy almost fell backwards when she heard a voice coming from down by the engines. "Hey, Tammy! Hold on, I'll be right there," Dwayne hollered from beneath the deck.

A few minutes later, his head popped up from the open hatch in the deck. "Hi. You made it," he said with a smile that creased the motor oil stains on his cheeks. "Just making a few last minute checks before we head out in the morning. Making sure the motors are okay."

His droopy eyes were a dead giveaway, not to mention the huge yawn. "You look tired," she said, sounding concerned.

"Yeah, I've been up since five getting the boat ready. There's always a ton of things to do when you want to go fishing. It's never an easy task."

Tammy scanned the boat. "I can see that. What's all this stuff?"

Dwayne pulled himself out of the engine hatch and wiped his hands with a towel before pointing to various objects on the deck.

"Well, over there, we have our six fishing poles rigged with heavy test line and shark hooks. We have boxes of mackerel for bait. Over on that side, we have white buckets of chum." He looked over at Tammy and beamed her a smile. "And we have two chairs and an ice chest full of food." He pointed to the back of the boat. "That large gray box is full of ice to keep any sharks we may catch cold until we get back into port, and this pile of stuff next to me is mainly tools and replacement parts in case we have mechanical issues with the boat. I still need to put them away."

"I had no idea so much went into fishing," Tammy said, still looking at the gear stacked neatly around her.

Dwayne laughed. "This is nothing. Wait until I go lobster fishing in a couple of months. Then you will really see what fishing involves." A warm smile blanketed his face as he held out his arms. "Come here. I've missed you."

That's all it took for Tammy's heart to melt. She returned the warm smile and stepped on the boat. After dropping her bags on the deck, she welcomed Dwayne's open arms and met him in a warm sensual kiss.

"Man, you taste good," he said before giving her a devious smile. "You know, I could take a break. Do you want to join me?"

Tammy looked around where they stood. "And where do you take a shower? I've never seen one on the boat."

Dwayne pointed to a gray building just off to the left at the top of the ramp. "Over there. It's a community shower." He gave her a smirk. "Don't worry, it has a lock on it."

Tammy playfully slapped his chest and gave him a peck on the cheek. "I'd love to join you."

"Great! Let me grab my shower bag and a couple of towels and some clean clothes."

"Okay. I'll wait right here," Tammy replied, feeling a twinge of excitement.

Once Dwayne had gathered their stuff, he took Tammy's hand and led her up the ramp to the gray building he had pointed at. She stood behind him, holding his hand while he used a key to open the door.

After entering, Dwayne had a quick look around. "Good, it's empty," Dwayne whispered before locking the door behind them.

Tammy took in their surroundings while she waited for Dwayne to put their things on a wooden bench and run the shower. There wasn't much to the place. The walls flaked with dull gray paint, large white tiles covered most of the floor, and there was just one shower stall and one sink. Tammy held her hands up to her mouth and began shivering.

"It's cold in here," she muffled while blowing warm breath into her hands.

Dwayne turned to face her, his arm stretched out. "Come here. I'll take care of that."

Tammy didn't hesitate and nestled herself into his embrace, allowing the warmth of his body to overshadow the chill lingering in the air. She snuggled against his chest, feeling the faint beat of his heart against her ear.

Dwayne squeezed her tight, lowered his head and gazed into her eyes before kissing her passionately, exploring her mouth deep with his tongue. He had an unexpected fresh salty taste from the ocean air that Tammy found refreshing, and she soon found herself melting beneath him. With force, she pushed her body into his while locking her hands around his neck and gripping the ends of his blond hair.

This was the first time they had been alone, and both felt the long anticipated hunger building once again between them. Dwayne ran his hands up and down her body, squeezing her skin between his fingers and kneading her curves with the palms of his hands. Untamed and consumed by lust, he ravished her voluptuous breast through her shirt and moaned at the touch of her perked nipple.

Feeling his masculine strength take control, Tammy gasped as her chest heaved from his touch. She pulled away from his mouth, sucking in a lungful of much needed air. Dwayne continued to kiss her on the neck, sucking her flesh with his lips and tracing her jaw line with his tongue. Tammy let out another gasp as she tossed back her head and stretched her neck, welcoming the moist touch of his heated breath.

Pressed hard against each other, their bodies merging as one, Dwayne reached up and entwined his fingers in Tammy's hair before engulfing her mouth once more.

"Let's get in the shower," he panted between short gasps of air.

Tammy could only manage a short "Yes!" before being smothered by his lips once more. Her body became invaded by his heavy caresses.

Dwayne struggled to unbutton his jeans while keeping his lips locked on hers. With fumbled fingers, he managed to unsnap the button and pull down the zipper. He released a satisfying moan as his now erect manhood revealed itself from his pants. Craving to be inside of her, he reached down and began stroking his aching member.

With his heart now pounding, Dwayne reluctantly pulled himself away from Tammy, leaving her panting for air. "Come on, let's get undressed. I want you." He wasted no time in tearing his jeans away from his body.

In a passionate frenzy, Tammy pulled her t-shirt over her head and threw it on the ground.

Dwayne paused for just a second while he admired her full breasts peeking out of her sheer white bra. "God! You are beautiful. Hurry up. Take off your pants," he urged while freeing himself from his shirt. Tammy met him in his rushed state and peeled her jeans off her body.

Intoxicated by her standing before him, wearing only a bra and white lace panties, Dwayne couldn't resist and pulled her in to his chest once more. He devoured her mouth while smothering her breasts with his hands.

Overwhelmed by his scent and the jabbing of his manhood between her legs, Tammy wrapped her arms around his neck and latched on to his lips with fury, exploring every inch of the inside of his mouth with her lips and tongue.

Dwayne reached down between her legs and grasped the sheer material of her panties. Charged by his touch, Tammy released a high-pitched shriek while taking in a deep breath and gasping for air. In one swift movement, Dwayne had her underwear at her feet. Tammy hastily stepped out of them without breaking away from his lips. Still latched together, their breathing intense, Dwayne reached around and unsnapped her bra, freeing her breasts from the sheer material. Tammy inched back, allowing the last piece of clothing to fall to the floor.

Still locked in a heated kiss, unable to break away, Dwayne used his strength to guide Tammy to the shower while stumbling over their clothes scattered across the floor. They clumsily stepped inside the now steamy stall and, still using his body, Dwayne pushed Tammy against the cold tile of the shower wall and pressed her back against it. The chill stunned her for a moment and she let out a shrill squeal before closing her eyes to the shower of warm water drenching her face.

Pressed against the wall, Tammy clasped onto Dwayne's now wet body, digging her nails into his shoulders as he deeply massaged her buttocks, pulling her closer to him and thrusting his hips. The anticipation of this moment was finally here and neither wanted to waste any more time. Feeling him thrust into her, Tammy wiggled her body to welcome him inside of her and both released loud simultaneous moans of pleasure and satisfaction as they devoured every moment of pleasure they were sharing.

After the heated sweat of an intense orgasm and no longer feeling the cold, Tammy clung to Dwayne's limp body with loose arms, trying to catch her breath after their shared climax. A satisfied smile spread across her face.

Dwayne raised his head from her chest, cupped her face in his palms and smooched her lips. "Damn, girl. What did you do to me? I can't feel my legs." He shuffled his feet helplessly around the stall floor, trying to regain his balance.

Tammy laughed and shook her head before breaking away from the wall and loosening her hold on him. "Come on. I need a cigarette after that," she replied before squeezing past Dwayne to exit the shower and get dressed.

"Hang on a sec. I'll join you."

Tammy froze while putting her jeans on. "What! You quit smoking."

"Well, that was until I met you."

A look of guilt invaded Tammy's face. "That's not funny, Dwayne. You've not smoked in over two years. I don't want to be the person that made you start up again. Do you know how awful that would make me feel?"

Dwayne reached for a towel on the counter and swabbed his body before picking up his jeans from the floor. "It's not your fault. It's the sex. Sex hasn't been that good in a long time. I'm blaming the sex, not you, silly." He shuffled his body into his jeans before grabbing his t-shirt.

Tammy frowned. "I don't care. I still feel bad."

Amused by her guilt, Dwayne chuckled. "Well, I haven't had one yet. I may change my mind by the time we get back to the boat." He gave her a loving hug and a peck on the cheek. "Now come on, let's go. You're craving a smoke and I want a Pepsi."

A few minutes later, they were back at the boat with their hair still damp and their bodies slightly chilled from the cool evening air. Dwayne went down into the cabin and grabbed himself a Pepsi from the compact fridge buried under one of the counters. Tammy stayed on the deck and lit a cigarette.

"Let me have one," Dwayne said as he approached her, breathing in the smoke that she exhaled.

"No!" Tammy shrieked, turning her body away from him in an attempt to keep the cigarette she was holding out of his reach.

Dwayne looked around the boat and spotted her pack sticking out of the top of her purse.

"Ahh ha!" he bellowed in triumph while heading toward it. "Would it make you feel better if I got my own instead of you giving me one?" he asked with a devious smile.

"No, it doesn't. No matter how you look at it, Dwayne, if I wasn't here, the thought of smoking would never have crossed your mind. I'll feel awful if you have one." She was trying her best to convince him not to do it, but he ignored her requests.

With apprehension, hoping he would change his mind, Tammy watched him reach into her purse and take out a cigarette and her red lighter.

"Don't do it, Dwayne," she pleaded.

He paused for a moment and turned to look at her. A cheeky smile covered his face as he held the cigarette up to his nose and breathed in heavily. "Been a long time since I held one of these," he said.

Tammy closed her eyes, praying he wouldn't light it. But the sound of the flicker from the lighter and the sudden bout of coughing told her he did. "Damn it, Dwayne! Why did you do that?"

After releasing a few more coughs, he laughed and said, "Will you stop feeling so guilty? This isn't your fault. I've missed these for a long time and it feels damn good." He took in another long hit, this time with no coughs. "I've forgotten how good this feels. I've not had one in so long that I'm getting dizzy."

Tammy approached him and gave him a light slap on the chest. "Oh, stop it. I still feel terrible."

Dwayne rolled his eyes before giving her a playful squeeze.

"Well, I can't help that. Tell you what. Why don't I take you out for dinner before we head out?"

Tammy was shocked. "We're leaving tonight?"

"We sure are. We gotta claim our spot and get some chum in the water."

Tammy creased her brow. "Chum? What's that?"

"Well, if you must know, it's buckets of fish waste and guts to attract the sharks."

"Yuk! That's just gross."

Dwayne laughed at Tammy's expression and couldn't help thinking about what an interesting trip lay ahead. He stubbed out his cigarette and downed the last swig of Pepsi in his can. "Come on, let's go eat. I know a good seafood restaurant across the marina."

Tammy curled her upper lip in disgust. "Yuk. I don't like seafood."

Dwayne started coughing again at her reaction. "What! You're dating a fisherman and you don't eat seafood? Well, we're going to have to do something about that. You're English. You like fish and chips, right?"

"I do," Tammy replied.

"Great! Well, they have that. Come on, let's go. I'm starving." He grabbed Tammy's hand and led her away for a seafood supper.

They returned to the boat shortly after ten, with their bellies full and Tammy slightly tipsy from the three glasses of wine she had over dinner. Dwayne did one last check on his gear and supplies before announcing to Tammy they were ready to head out. Remembering their last trip and wanting to help as much as she could, Tammy saluted Dwayne, followed by a cute smile. "Aye, aye, Captain. I'll untie the boat."

Amused and impressed, Dwayne played along while she got into position at the front of the boat and stood to attention, ready to untie the rope on the bow. Dwayne fired up the engine. "Go ahead, First Mate!" he yelled.

Tammy remembered the routine like clockwork and repeated the same process at the stern, and without being told, she flipped the fenders into the boat before joining Dwayne at the helm as they drove out of the harbor under the night skies.

When he noticed Tammy rubbing her shoulders from the chill of the cool air, Dwayne reached for his jacket hanging on the back of his captain's chair and wrapped it around her. With a smile, she leaned in close to his chest and snuggled against his warm body. Life couldn't get any better than this. That was until they pulled out of the harbor into the dark open water of the Pacific Ocean.

Mesmerized by the beauty of the full moon reflecting off the calm water, Tammy pulled away from the comfort of Dwayne's chest to take it all in. She breathed in deeply, moved by the tranquility and peacefulness that surrounded them. "Wow! It's absolutely gorgeous out here." Tammy looked up at the dark sky. "Look at all the stars above us. I've never seen so many."

"It's one of the reasons why I love being on boats. You don't get this in the city."

"Oh, Dwayne. You don't know how lucky you are." Tammy did a 360. "I mean, look at this. We are the only ones out here for miles. I've never experienced such freedom. If I wanted to, I could strip off all my clothes and run around the boat naked."

Dwayne laughed. "Be my guest."

"Ha! You would love that, I'm sure."

Dwayne pulled her back into his arms. "I'm so glad you like boats. They take some getting used to."

"Like them?" Tammy's eyes widened. "I love them. I'm hooked, trust me."

For the next hour, they putted along at a comfortable eight knots. Tammy stayed close to Dwayne's side, even taking the wheel a few times. Her zigzags were becoming fewer and further between, but they were still there. Dwayne was impressed by how she managed to stay on course by following the dim light of the compass on the dash.

When they finally reached their spot, just outside the shipping lanes, Dwayne brought the boat to a stop and turned off the motors.

"Do you hear that?" Tammy whispered.

Dwayne pinned his ears. "I don't hear anything."

A large grin appeared across Tammy's face. "Exactly! Absolute silence, and it sounds friggin' wonderful. All's I hear is the water softly splashing up against the hull." She looked up at the sky one more time. "It's just you, me, the moon and the stars, and I love it."

"You really do like it out here, don't you?"

Tammy beamed. "I do!"

Dwayne went on to explain to her that they were in five thousand feet of water, and because it was too deep to set anchor, they would be drifting through the night. He continued to explain to her what he was doing as he prepped the boat for shark fishing. Tammy watched intently, following his every move. After turning on the flood lights on the deck, she paid close attention when he tied the chum buckets to the back of the boat and let them hang in the water. A few minutes later, she saw the blood ooze out of the holes from the buckets into the water, making a trail around the boat.

"See, they are making a scent that will attract the sharks. It's called a chum line," Dwayne explained.

"Aren't they going to come a little too close to the boat though?" Tammy asked, wearing a worried look.

"Well, we can't catch them way out there," Dwayne said, laughing.

Not sure how to react to the thought of sharks being next to the boat, Tammy simply nodded.

After completing the necessary tasks before they could actually put their poles in the water and start fishing in the morning, Dwayne let out a loud yawn while stretching his body.

"You look tired," Tammy said.

He yawned again. "I am. I was up most of the night and now I'm running on fumes. I haven't got much sleep in the last few nights. Would you mind if I went and lay down for an hour?"

"No, not at all. Go get some rest. Is there anything I need to do?" Tammy asked.

"Not really. Just keep watch. We're drifting, so keep a look out for other boats, especially large ones. We're close to the shipping lanes so wake me up if you see anything."

Tammy took a seat on the deck chair, and before Dwayne headed down to the cabin, he reached inside and grabbed a blanket off the bench and covered Tammy's legs. "Here you go," he said, planting a soft kiss on her lips.

Tammy looked up and smiled. "Thanks."

She watched him as he made his way down into the cabin, leaving the door open and crawling onto the bed. Within a few minutes, she heard the faint sound of snoring.

She chuckled and made herself comfortable in the chair, snuggling into the blanket and gazing up at the stars. The view took her breath away and for the first time in her life, she saw a shooting star and wished Matt was with her to witness it.

Tammy hadn't realized it, but she must have dozed off and was woken by a flapping sound in the water. Upset with herself for not doing the one thing Dwayne had asked her do and keep watch, she jumped up from her chair in a state of panic, letting the blanket fall to her feet.

In a frenzy, she quickly scanned the horizon for any other boats and let out a huge sigh of relief when she saw there were none. She glanced at her watch. It was 2:00 a.m. She'd nodded off for at least an hour. Peering down into the cabin, she heard snoring, telling her Dwayne was still asleep. Figuring there was no need to wake him just yet, she decided to let him sleep a while longer. He needed all the rest he could get.

The flapping sound continued from the stern and sparked Tammy's curiosity. With apprehension and feeling somewhat fearful of the unknown, she picked up the blanket and wrapped herself in it before slowly tiptoeing to the back of the boat. She peered into the dark water, illuminated only by the flood lights on the deck, and gasped.

"Holy shit!" Leaping back, she couldn't believe what she had just seen. Consumed with adrenaline and her nerves piqued, she inched her way over to the stern to take one more look. "Fuck! Look at them all," she whispered out loud, afraid they might see her. She'd never seen even a single shark up close, and now she found herself peering over the stern at a dozen of them splashing in the water, swimming in circles around the boat.

"Holy fuck!" She watched with horror as they swam in a frenzy, their tails hitting and splashing the surface of the water. Their bodies moved in circles as they fed off the scraps of fish and guts oozing out of the chum buckets. Finding a little more courage, although still stunned by what she was seeing, she strained her neck to get a closer view while still holding her body back. On the swim step, she noticed there were eight cardboard boxes. The bottom ones were now crushed and soaked from the weight of the top ones and were also seeping blood into the water.

Tammy watched with a dropped jaw as the sharks bit on the swim step, trying to get to the boxes of bait. She was horrified and stepped back away from the stern, afraid they might jump on the boat. Having no clue what to do, she yelled out to no one in particular, "I've gotta wake up Dwayne!"

In a mad dash, she headed down in to the cabin where she found Dwayne in a deep sleep, his face covered with the blankets. Tammy nudged his shoulder. "Dwayne! Dwayne! Wake up!"

His body stirred. "Huh? Is the boat okay?" he asked in a delirious mumble.

"Yes, it's fine. But there are sharks all around the boat. Wake up." She shook him again, using more force. "Come on, Dwayne! Wake up."

He hadn't heard the part about sharks. He only heard her say the boat was fine so, exhausted from a lack of sleep in the past twenty-four hours, he rolled his body away from her. "I'll be right there," he said before starting to snore again.

Realizing her attempts to wake him had failed, she stopped shaking him and decided to let him rest. She knew the boat was in no danger and she was certain the sharks wouldn't jump on board. With her decision made, she covered Dwayne's bare shoulders with the blanket. He moaned and curled his body to the welcome warmth. Tammy stroked his shoulder, which was now covered with the blanket, and smiled. "Get some rest. Everything's fine," she whispered before heading back out onto the deck.

Still hearing the commotion and splashing in the water, she tip-toed her way to the stern and again strained her neck to glance over the side. The scene was just how she had left it. The out-of-control school of sharks were still feasting on the chum in a mad feeding frenzy. Tammy whispered out loud, "Wow!"

For a few minutes, she stood motionless, watching the scene before her. The sharks were unaware of her presence as they continued to feed on the blood infested waters, snapping their jaws at the pieces of chum floating on the surface while exposing their razor-sharp teeth. Their smooth, wet bodies glistened in the glow of the floodlights, and their tails slapped on the surface in excitement.

Tammy turned her head while shading her eyes from the glare of the floodlights and stared into the cabin. From where she stood, she could tell Dwayne had not moved and had returned to a deep sleep. Tammy knew there was nothing she could do about the situation so inched her chair away from the stern, grabbed her blanket and cigarettes and took a seat.

After inhaling a long, much needed smoke, she heard the splashing sounds becoming quieter and less frantic. To confirm, she pulled herself up and while still wrapped in her blanket, peeked over the side. Yes, there were fewer sharks and less chum in the water. Relieved, she returned to her seat and after a few minutes began to drift off to sleep.

CHAPTER 11

Unsure how long she had been asleep, Tammy was woken by the soft whisper of Dwayne's voice in her ear and a slight shaking of her shoulder. "Hey, kiddo, wake up. The sun's about to come up. It's time to go fishing."

Still haunted by the night's events, Tammy jumped up from her seat, startling Dwayne. "You're up!" she shrieked.

Puzzled by her outburst, Dwayne cautiously answered, "Yes. Are you okay?"

"Shit, Dwayne! I tried to wake you. There were a ton of sharks right next to the boat last night, feeding on that chum stuff. It was crazy! I've never seen anything like it."

"What! Holy shit! You're kidding me? And I slept through the whole thing?" He raced to the back of the boat and peered over the side. "Oh, damn. They did a number on the paintwork of the swim step." He looked at the few remaining boxes. "I left the boxes of bait back there too. They were feeding on the soaked boxes. I was so tired I forgot to bring them onto the boat. Here, give me a hand with these."

Tammy walked over and helped him bring the remaining four boxes onto the deck.

Standing with the boxes between them, Dwayne took count. "Wow, we lost four boxes of bait, but we still have enough to fish with. I can't believe I missed all the excitement. I must have been really tired."

"I tried to wake you but it was impossible. It was amazing. I watched them for a while. There were some big ones too."

Dwayne laughed. "I don't need to hear that. That may have been the winning fish that got away. Let's hope they come back for more chum." He chuckled while scanning the horizon and saw there were a few other fishing boats in the distance. He glanced at his watch. It was just before 6:00 a.m. and the sun was almost up.

"How are you feeling? Did you get any sleep?" he asked.

"Oh, I feel fine. Just thirsty, that's all."

Dwayne turned around, opened the lid of the ice chest behind him and pulled out an orange juice. "Here you go."

Tammy swiped it from his hand and quenched her thirst.

"So are you ready to go shark fishing?" Dwayne said with a smirk.

Tammy beamed him a smile. "I sure am. After seeing all those sharks up close, I can't wait to see you catch one."

Dwayne rubbed his hands together, eager to get started. "Okay then. Let's get the gear ready and try to catch the winning shark."

Not having a clue how he might go about catching a shark, Tammy watched Dwayne's every move with intrigue and listened carefully as he explained what he was doing. First, he tied off two more buckets of chum to the back of the boat and hung them in the water.

"We need another chum line. Why don't you open one of those boxes of bait and see if the mackerels are defrosted?"

"Okay," Tammy replied, anxious to help. When she had the box open, she pulled out one of the top fish from the uniformed stack and gave it a gentle squeeze."Yep, it's definitely defrosted. It feels kind of squishy between my fingers."

"Great, hand it to me." Dwayne couldn't help but chuckle at Tammy's look of disgust.

Trying not to let the fish slip between her fingers, Tammy used both hands to pass it to him. When she looked up, she saw he was now holding a large fishing pole equipped with a huge reel and a hook that glistened in the sun. She watched as he pierced the mouth of the dead mackerel with the hook and secured it into place.

"Eww. That's disgusting," Tammy squealed.

"No, that's fishing." Dwayne laughed. "You'll get us to it. People always get grossed out the first time they see it."

Tammy continued to hand Dwayne four more fish for the remaining poles, each one getting easier to handle. She watched with fascination as he took each pole, baited it and let the line out into the water before placing each pole in a holder around the boat.

After the last pole had been rigged, Tammy leaned over the side of the boat, rinsed her hands in the cool water and dried them off with a rag.

"What's next?" she asked with enthusiasm and a big smile.

After washing his hands, Dwayne grabbed one of Tammy's cigarettes from the pack sitting on the deck, lit it and took a long drag. "We wait."

"Wait for what?"

"For a shark to take the bait." He rolled his eyes at her innocence.

But Tammy was still confused. "How do we know when that happens? We can't see anything."

"Oh, trust me, you will know."

Tammy walked over to the dash and joined Dwayne in a smoke. After taking his last hit, he had an idea.

"While we're waiting, let's chop up some of the mackerel and throw the bits in the water. That should attract the sharks."

"Okay!" Tammy agreed, thrilled there was more to do. Sitting idle was not her thing.

Dwayne walked to the other side of the deck, grabbed a large plastic chopping board and a knife and handed them to her.

"Here, set these up on the back of the deck and I'll pass you the fish to chop up. You just need to cut them up into small chunks and I'll throw them overboard."

Eager to get started, Tammy claimed her spot and began chopping while Dwayne scooped the pieces into a bucket and began tossing them into the ocean. Within a few minutes, a flock of seagulls appeared, squawking and hovering above the boat while diving into the water after the chunks of fish.

"Damn seagulls," Dwayne hollered.

"Where did they come from?" Tammy laughed. "They weren't here a minute ago and we're in the middle of nowhere."

"I swear they can spot a fish a mile away. Just keep cutting. The sharks will eventually smell it."

"Okay, Captain," she said with a salute before returning to the task.

After improving the chum line and having cereal for breakfast, Dwayne had Tammy help him clear a space on the deck in the hopes of bringing a shark on board.

"It's been two hours. Maybe they're full from their feeding frenzy last night," Tammy said while pushing a box of bait off to the side with her foot.

"Oh, they'll be back. I promise."

Another hour passed and Tammy had just about had enough of the idle time when suddenly, one of the poles began to make a loud buzzing sound and the line was being pulled out from the reel at high speed. In a flash, Dwayne was on his feet yelling, "Fish on!"

"Really?" Tammy squealed, leaping to her feet.

In one quick movement, Dwayne grabbed the pole and pointed

to a fishing harness off to his side. "Quick, grab that, put it around my waist and snap the buckle into place."

Fueled by adrenaline, Tammy asked no questions and followed his directions. Once the harness was in place, Dwayne lifted the pole and set it in the holder on the front of the harness. Unable to contain the sudden rush of excitement, Dwayne's voice was loud as he explained the process to Tammy.

"This is what's called a fighting harness. It gives me support while I'm fighting the shark. Right now, I'm letting the shark take the bait. I want it to be completely in his mouth before I set the hook. See how the line is still going out? He's running with the bait. I'll give him a little more time before I set the hook."

Tammy watched from his side, not wanting to get in his way. It seemed the sudden commotion had left her lost for words, as only a murmur of agreement left her lips.

Dwayne continued to holler instructions. "I want you to go around and reel in the other lines. Last thing I need is another shark to get hooked." He let out a sarcastic laugh. "Unless you want to reel it in?"

"Ha! If I knew what I was bloody doing, I might consider it. But I've never handled a fishing pole. What do I do?"

Suddenly, Dwayne yanked the rod he was holding and began reeling. "Hold on!" he yelled. "I just set the hook. Now I need to wear him out."

Tammy watched with her eyes wide as Dwayne began to work the line, reeling it in a little at a time, using his back and knees for support. "This feels like a big fish!" he said with a huge smile. "Okay, take each rod and reel the line in with the handle. Once the mackerel is out of the water, push the button on the side to lock the line and just let the mackerel dangle. Place the rod back in the holder."

Tammy understood his instructions and proceeded to reel each line in while Dwayne continued to work on tiring out the shark. Once done, she stood to the side and watched in amazement as

Dwayne's pole almost doubled over with the weight of the catch. Dwayne used all his strength to reel in the line a little at a time, but the shark was clearly putting up a tremendous fight beneath the water.

"How do you know it's a shark? We can't see anything."

"Only a shark will take the whole mackerel. Hopefully, it's not a blue shark. We can't eat those," Dwayne yelled, still driven by adrenaline.

Tammy watched with admiration as each well defined muscle flexed under his tight skin. She moistened her lips, stood back and enjoyed the view. *Now that's a real man.*

"I want you to go grab me that blue rope at the back of the boat and that long gaff lying along the side. It's the wooden pole with the large hook at the end," Dwayne yelled while still fighting the shark.

Tammy scanned the boat and quickly spotted the items he needed. She dashed over to retrieve them and brought them to his side. "Here you go."

Dwayne held on to the fishing pole tight with both hands and looked to be struggling to reel in the line. He didn't take his eyes off the water while he spoke. "Hold on to them. I'll tell you when I'm ready."

"Okay."

For the next thirty minutes, Tammy watched with fascination as Dwayne continued to work the line to wear down the fish. At times, she thought the pole was going to snap because of the way it was bent over, but Dwayne told her they were made to handle such tension and weight. Suddenly, Tammy squealed.

"Oh my god! I see it's fin! It's right there!" she yelled while jumping up and down, full of excitement and pointing in the direction of the huge fish circling and splashing in the water.

Dwayne began to work the reel harder. "This feels like a big one."

"I've never seen anything like it. That is unfucking believable."

After twenty more minutes of fighting the shark, Dwayne finally managed to tie off the tail, gaff it and bring it on the boat.

While still flapping around on the deck in a frenzy, exposing its razor sharp teeth as it snapped its jaws repeatedly, Tammy took a step back and couldn't help but wonder how they were going to get the huge creature back to shore without it doing them or the boat some serious damage. Her question was soon answered when she saw Dwayne pulling a large knife from a leather sheath hanging by the helm. She knew what was about to happen. It was one of the realities of shark fishing, a necessary evil, but it was one she wasn't ready to stand and watch first hand—not yet, possibly not ever. As Dwayne approached the shark and lifted the knife, Tammy turned her head and walked as far away as she could within the confines of the boat.

After the dreaded task was done, the shark laid lifeless, no longer a threat. Still panting and out of breath but wearing a huge smile, he removed the harness and bent over to catch his breath. "That's a good size fish. We may just have the winning shark," he said, beaming.

No longer feeling threatened by the beast, Tammy's mood lightened and she soon realized this was probably a chance in a lifetime photo opportunity. No one was going to believe her without a picture as proof. "Where's my camera? I need to take a picture. Judy is never going to believe me, and I want to show Matt too."

While Dwayne dealt with securing the shark, Tammy dashed down to the cabin in search of something to capture this momentous occasion with. A few minutes later, she returned waving her disposable camera in her hand. "Found it!" she yelled from a distance as she started to snap a few pictures.

"I bet you this is a 150 pound mako," Dwayne said with pride. "I heard on the radio that the biggest fish weighed in so far is a 120 pounds."

"Really? You mean you may win this thing?"

"Yeah. If I'm right about the weight and no bigger fish is caught by tomorrow afternoon, then yep, I win the 2,500 dollar prize money."

"Wow! That's awesome."

Dwayne checked the shark one more time. Satisfied it was secured, he began clearing off the deck. "Only way to find out, is to head back in and get this puppy weighed. Let's clean up the deck and head back to the marina. We're done fishing in the tournament." He couldn't hide his contented smile.

"Okay!" Tammy beamed.

An hour later, they were pulling into a slip back at the marina and were greeted by dozens of spectators standing on the docks. A couple of guys helped tie off the boat to the cleats. Within minutes of Dwayne turning off the motors, they were surrounded by a crowd of people who had spotted the shark from a distance and hurried over to get a closer look.

Conversations were loud and eyes were wide, and everyone congratulated them on their successful catch, patting Dwayne on the back as he stepped off the boat wearing a huge grin. It took three guys plus Dwayne to get the shark over to the scale.

With anticipation, Dwayne stood with his arm around Tammy's waist, circled by the many onlookers waiting for the official weigh-in. Everyone fell silent while the officials of the tournament hoisted the huge shark up onto the scale and took notes. After what felt like hours, the announcement was made. "157 pounds!"

No sooner had the weight been announced, loud cheers erupted all around them and the crowd swarmed in closer, all wanting to congratulate them personally. Tammy squealed and planted a big kiss on Dwayne's lips while others reached out and patted whatever part of his body they could reach. Tammy felt like they had just won the super bowl.

While the crowd continued in a frenzy of cheers, snapping pictures of each other standing next to the giant catch, the officials clarified that Dwayne currently had the biggest fish. Now all they had to do was wait out the tournament until it ended at 5:00 p.m. tomorrow and hope that no other boat caught a larger one. Tammy and Dwayne both agreed it was going to be a long weekend.

Once the shark was returned to Dwayne's boat and put on ice, Tammy left the crowd in the hunt for a phone booth. Being away from Matt was taking its toll and she desperately wanted to hear his voice. As she walked up the ramp, she chuckled to herself when she overheard Dwayne telling the crowd the events of the catch. She never knew fishing could be so much fun.

After a long chat with Matt, who sounded his usual happy self, Tammy realized she was probably having a much harder time being separated from him than he was. Judy came on the phone and confirmed her suspicions, assuring Tammy that Matt was fine. After going over the fish story and telling Judy she had photos to prove it, Tammy hung up the phone in better spirits.

When she returned to the boat, she found Dwayne still surrounded by an excited mass of people, all wanting to hear how and where he caught the shark. Tammy watched from a safe distance, feeling proud to be his girlfriend.

His face glowed with joy as he repeated the story of the catch to any new people that approached the boat. It was a fishing tale that would stay with him for years. With wide eyes and gaping mouths, the spectators listened. The other fisherman, however, merely scowled with envy, giving him only a cordial congratulation.

For the rest of the day, they hung out on the docks of the tournament, where Tammy mingled with the crowds and made new friends. She could get used to this lifestyle of chatting with friendly boaters, sipping on cocktails and walking barefoot wherever she pleased.

By five o'clock, no larger shark had been caught and Dwayne was still in the lead. With fingers crossed that he would still hold the record by tomorrow evening, they drove *The Baywitch* back to the boatyard and tied it up in Dwayne's slip. Shortly after, friends from the tournament joined them for a mako feast, barbecued by Dwayne. It took a lot of coaxing from the group to get Tammy to try the fish, but when she eventually did, she loved it and wanted more.

The next morning after having breakfast in a nearby restaurant, they headed back to the docks of the tournament where they planned on hanging out all day to witness other catches being weighed in. At noon, a fishing vessel radioed in that they had a big shark and were bringing it in. As the news spread that the fish may be bigger than Dwayne's, anticipation filled the air and Dwayne, who spent his time pacing the dock, was unable to hide the worried look on his face.

An hour later, the vessel pulled into a slip and like yesterday with Dwayne's boat, it was met by a crowd of people eager to see the shark. Tammy and Dwayne held hands while looking on from a distance. There was no doubt it was a good size fish. Dwayne knew it was going to be close. With clenched fists, they followed the crowd to the scale and waited for the weight to be announced. The crowd became silent as they watched the officials compare notes and nod their heads in agreement. Finally, the weight was announced. "133 pounds."

The crowd turned to Dwayne and Tammy, and cheered.

"You're still in the lead," Tammy squealed in excitement.

Dwayne let out a loud "Yes!" while picking up Tammy off her feet and spinning her around in his arms. Tammy screamed a

joyous cry of relief as the crowd circled them, leaving the disappointed fisherman alone with their catch.

Tammy checked her watch. It was almost two o'clock. They still
had another three antagonizing hours to wait until the tournament was officially closed. There was still time for another large
shark to be caught. And Tammy learned if someone calls in a catch
at five minutes to five and they are an hour out, that shark can still
be brought in to be weighed and would still be entered because
they called it in before the deadline.

For the next three hours, they hung around the docks mingling
with others to pass the time. Dwayne constantly checked his radio
for the latest fish report updates, each time feeling relieved when
nothing was reported. But Dwayne knew from past experiences
that could easily change.

By four thirty, Dwayne was already receiving congratulating
handshakes by those that already believed he had won the contest.
But Dwayne refused to acknowledge it until it was officially five
o'clock. For the next thirty minutes, he and Tammy held each
other's hands tight while counting down the minutes and pacing
the docks. It was the longest thirty minutes Tammy had ever
known.

At the five o'clock hour, the sound of a loud horn quieted the
noise of the crowd and echoed throughout the marina, closely
followed by one of the official's voices booming over the loud
speaker. "We have a winner! With a magnificent weight of 157
pounds, Dwayne Carson is this year's winner of the annual mako
shark tournament. Congratulations! Come on up here, Dwayne."

In a buzzing frenzy, Dwayne and Tammy were swarmed by the
crowd with hugs and pats as they made their way up to the
podium. Tammy had never felt so proud of anyone other than her
son, and at that very moment, she felt honored to be by Dwayne's
side.

Wearing a huge grin, Dwayne walked up to the announcer, still
holding Tammy's hand, and the crowd cheered them on when he

was handed a blue ribbon and $2,500 in cash. In triumph, Dwayne waved the cash above his head while being swarmed by photographers. It truly was a momentous occasion.

As much as Tammy didn't want the weekend to end, she knew she had to get back to her life in Pasadena. The thought depressed her. She wished she could give Matt Dwayne's lifestyle. He would learn so much about boats, fishing, the ocean and so much more from living in the marina. After procrastinating leaving as long as she could, she couldn't avoid it anymore when seven o'clock came around. Reluctantly, she pulled Dwayne away from the crowd, where he was still telling the great fishing story, and with a solemn look told him she had to go.

"Already?" he asked, glancing at his watch.

"Yes. I have to watch the kids tomorrow morning and take Judy's daughter to school. She's working the breakfast and lunch shift. I work tomorrow night. I'm really sorry. I would love to stay."

Dwayne took her in his arms. "It's okay. You don't have to apologize. I'll take you back to your car at the boatyard. Let me tell these guys I'll be back shortly and we'll get going. Okay?"

"Sure, that's fine. I'll come say goodnight too."

Fifteen minutes later, after retrieving her things from Dwayne's boat, they were standing by her car ready to say goodnight.

Embraced in his arms, her arms wrapped around his waist, Tammy gave Dwayne a loving smile. "Thank you for an amazing weekend. It was incredible. I can't wait to tell Matt and show him the pictures I took. I'm going to take the film in tomorrow to get it developed."

"Cool! Get a couple of copies. I'd love to have a set."

"Sure. I hope they turned out good." She paused for a moment and gave him a tender kiss. "I gotta go. Call me?"

"Better yet, I may be up your way this week. I didn't see my son because of the tournament, so I may go up one night this week after he gets out of school. If I do, I'll definitely give you a call."

"That would be great!" she said with a huge smile. Before entering her car, she met him in another sensual kiss. "Bye," she whispered, leaving his arms.

"Bye," he echoed.

Tammy returned home to the welcome sight of her son running out the front door as fast as his little legs could carry him, dressed in his blue pajamas with his arms wide open. After smothering him with motherly kisses in the driveway, she scurried him inside to tell him all about the shark stories. They were going to be so much better than any children's book she had ever read to him.

Over the next few days, Tammy's mind was flooded with thoughts of Dwayne. She constantly talked about him to Judy and anyone else who was willing to listen to her at work. Judy never got tired of listening. The sparkle that shone in Tammy's eyes said it all and lit up the entire room. She had never seen Tammy so happy. Since she had returned from her getaway with Dwayne, she hadn't complained about her job, the long hours she worked or the stress of raising a child alone. Then it occurred to Judy that she too had quit complaining about her woes in life when she had met Joel. Somehow, life just seemed much easier when you had a good guy by your side.

Miraculously, Tammy and Judy both had the following Friday

off. Judy took advantage of Tammy being home and disappeared into the bathroom to dye her hair, something she had wanted to do for weeks. Finally, she had worked up the courage to go blond after letting her hair grow back to its natural light auburn color a few years ago.

Tammy had only heard from Dwayne once since seeing him last week. With him only having a pager, she couldn't pick up the phone whenever she felt like it and call him. She pretty much had to wait for him to call her. To her disappointment, he never made it up in the middle of the week to see his son. He had a big job on a boat to finish and just couldn't get away. But he made up for it by calling her unexpectedly that Friday afternoon.

"Hey Dwayne," she said with an accelerated heart rate.

"Hey Tammy. How's it going? Sorry I've not called. I've wanted to but by the time I get done with work, I always think it's too late to call."

"It's fine, Dwayne. You're calling now." She paused before adding, "I've missed you."

"I've missed you too. Which is why I'm coming up."

"What? You mean now?" Tammy asked, unable to hide the sudden panic in her voice.

"Yeah. I'm leaving here in ten minutes. It's okay, isn't it?"

Tammy scanned the living room, seeing the kids' toys scattered across the floor, the empty beer cans on the coffee table and the laundry piled high on the couch waiting to be folded. It was a real mess. "Um, yeah, sure, that's fine. I can't wait to see you."

"Well, I had an idea. I'm picking up my son and having him for the entire weekend. How would you and Matt like to join us?"

"Really? That would be fantastic! I can't wait to meet Justin. I'll be ready by the time you get here."

"Wonderful. We can all ride in my truck. There's enough room on the front seat. I'll swing by and get Justin first and then come by and pick you guys up." He suddenly laughed.

"What's funny?" Tammy asked.

"It just dawned on me, I've never been to your house. I need to know where you live."

Tammy joined him in the laughter before giving him her address.

As soon as the call ended, panic set in and in a frenzy, she began dashing around the house yelling, "Judy! Judy!" There was no answer. Only the sound of the radio blasting from the bathroom. "Damn it!" she said to herself, realizing it was probably going to be left to her to clean the house before Dwayne's arrival.

Tammy quickly popped her head outside the back door to check on the kids before making a start on the house. Engulfed in a game of tag, they hadn't even noticed her so, satisfied they were fine, Tammy returned inside and began yelling for Judy again. This time, she heard a reply, closely followed by Judy appearing from the bathroom with her hair now wet and blond. "Everything okay?"

Seeing her hair for the first time, Tammy came to a sudden halt. "Wow, that looks good. I love the color on you."

"Thanks. What's up?"

Tammy shook her head, remembering her predicament. "Oh, shit, yeah. Dwayne is on his way here. I've got to get this place cleaned up. Can you help me? The kids are playing in the back. They're fine."

"Fuck! You mean now? Um, yeah, sure, but let me get dressed first." She quickly scurried past Tammy to her room.

Tammy first tackled the dishes in the sink while still holding a conversation with Judy who was hollering from her room, "I can't wait to finally meet him."

"I'm sure you'll like him."

A few minutes later, Judy appeared wearing jeans, a red-t-shirt and a new hair color. "Okay, what do you want me to do?"

We gotta get rid of all these beer cans and empty wine bottles. I don't want Dwayne to see how much we've been drinking. He knows I drink but damn, Judy, when you start looking around, there's quite a few empties. It looks pretty bad."

"What am I supposed to do with them?"

"I don't know. Put them in the neighbor's trash can? I'll help you. They aren't home."

Judy threw her a devious smile as she began scooping up empty cans. "Good idea!"

It took a few minutes to fill up the trash bags and during the process, a concerned look appeared on Tammy's face.

"Are you okay?" Judy asked.

"I really need to quit drinking, Judy. Look at this. I never realized how much I drank until I started dating Dwayne. I can't keep hiding this from him. It's not a good way to begin a relationship." Tammy threw a few cans in the trash bag. "I've gotta tell him about my accident and my upcoming court date in August."

Judy approached Tammy and placed the last can in the open bag. "Whoa, girl, slow down. Don't be so hard on yourself. I drink too you know. This isn't all you. If you want to come clean with Dwayne, I suggest you do it when you're alone and not with the kids."

Tammy thought for a moment. "Yeah, you're right. I'm gonna go sneak over to the neighbor's yard with this trash and check on the kids. Can you help me fold the laundry and pick up the toys? He's going to be here soon."

"Sure, I'm on it."

After bathing Matt, Tammy was just putting the last pieces of clothing in her bags when she heard the rumbling of a truck pulling up in front of the house.

"They're here!" she hollered from the bedroom.

Judy shouted back, "Okay! I'll be out back with my kids so you can be alone for a while. But make sure you come out and introduce me before you leave."

"I will," Tammy replied while rushing to the front door with Matt by her side.

Before opening the door, she took one quick glance around the room. Satisfied with how it looked, she took a deep breath and headed outside.

Dwayne was already out of his truck and standing next to him was a young boy. He too had blond hair and was the spitting image of his father.

"Hey, Tammy, I want you to meet my son, Justin."

Tammy approached him slowly. He seemed shy. "Hi Justin." She turned to Matt. "This is my son, Matt."

He spoke only one word in a soft voice, his eyes focusing on the ground. "Hi…"

Matt came to the rescue. After saying hi to him, he took his hand and led him into the house saying, "Come on, let me show you my toys."

Now in each other's arms, both Tammy and Dwayne laughed as they watched the two boys scurry off into the house.

"How sweet is that?" Tammy chuckled. "I'm all ready to go. I just need to grab our bags from the bedroom. Oh, and my roommate is dying to meet you."

"Uh-oh. Is this the moment where you're seeking her approval?"

Tammy gave him a playful slap on the chest. "No, silly. She's heard so much about you. It's about time she met you." She grabbed Dwayne's hand. "Come on. She's in the back yard."

Tammy proceeded to lead him through the house and out the back door, where they found Judy sitting in a lounge chair smoking a cigarette. Tammy had known her for a long time and had gotten to know her body language pretty well. From her smiles and subtle nods, Tammy knew after just a few minutes that Judy liked Dwayne.

That weekend, Tammy couldn't help but feel like a real family. Something she had never experienced before. Matt looked up to Justin like an older brother and followed his every move, and Justin protected him like a younger sibling. The whole weekend was all about the boys and making sure they had a good time. Matt experienced so many first time events that Tammy had never been able to give him before.

After a successful Saturday morning fishing trip, they all headed to the rocks of the main channel, where they spent the afternoon searching for mussels and digging for small sand crabs. The evening was spent on the boat, barbecuing steak and mako, and Dwayne gave everyone rowing lessons around his boat in his dinghy.

Sunday was spent at the nearby Venice Beach, where the boys frolicked in the surf with boogie boards and played with frisbees on the sand and before heading home, Dwayne took everyone out on the dinghy again.

Like previous times, Tammy didn't want her stay to end and had a hard time leaving him, especially when she didn't know when she would see him again. Living an hour away and leading separate lives was becoming increasingly difficult as time went on. She wanted to be with him all the time, but his lifestyle of fishing and her job in Pasadena prevented that.

Before packing up her car, Dwayne told her that lobster season was only four months away and every spare minute he had would be spent preparing for the season. He explained to her that this was the busiest time of the year for him. After working on boats all day, he would be working late into the night getting the gear ready for fishing lobsters. It was intense and it wouldn't leave much time for them. He didn't know when he would make it up to Pasadena again to see his son. During this time of year, it wasn't as often as it had been, maybe once a month if he was lucky.

Tammy's heart sank. She couldn't bear the thought of seeing

him only once a month and surprised him when she eagerly squealed, "I want to help!"

A puzzled look spanned Dwayne's face. "You want to help? With getting the gear ready?" he asked.

Tammy couldn't contain her excitement. She had loved every minute of being with him shark fishing and being on the boat. She was fascinated that he was going to be fishing for lobsters next.

"Yes! I want to know everything there is to know about lobster fishing. I would love to come down here when I'm not working and help you. I won't be in your way, I promise."

Dwayne was surprised by her eagerness and her genuine interest in the industry, but he was also thrilled that she wanted to learn about it. "Really? I would love to have you come down. But I have to warn you, it's a lot of hard work and long hours. It's hard on the body. You'll go to bed with aching bones and tired muscles. Are you really up to it?" he asked with a soft smile.

"Yes. I'm up to it. I've never been afraid of hard work." But there was one thing that would prevent her from getting on board, and she needed Dwayne to know. "I have to ask though. Would I be able to bring Matt sometimes? I can't leave him with Judy all the time. And not only that, I don't want to be away from him. I'd make sure he wouldn't interrupt your tight schedule."

"Of course, that's fine."

Tammy suddenly had an idea. "Hey, I could pick up Justin too. He's only a short distance from my house."

Dwayne shook his head. "Nah. I don't think his mother would go with the idea of my current girlfriend being at her house. She's one of those jealous kinds. But thanks for the offer. I'll make time to see him."

Tammy jumped in the air like a little school girl before running into Dwayne's arms. "Oooh, I'm so excited. I'll page you this week and let you know when I can come down."

That weekend, Tammy left the marina with a feeling that she was leaving a part of her behind. She had gotten to know

Dwayne's son and everyone had bonded. She had a sense of belonging. It was a lifestyle that Tammy wanted her son to have. He had grown and learnt so much over the past few days because of Dwayne's influence. She also realized that Dwayne was good for her too. She hadn't drunk any alcohol over the entire weekend. There were a few times where she craved a beer or two, but with all the fun they were having, the cravings soon subsided.

But Tammy knew she'd have to come clean with Dwayne soon and tell him about her upcoming court date. She didn't want to jeopardize what they had by keeping secrets from him.

A painful two weeks went by before Tammy could finally plan another trip to Dwayne's boat. She and Judy relied on each other to rotate watching the kids and working, and Judy hadn't had the last two weekends off so Tammy was stuck at home babysitting. But since spending time in the marina, home didn't feel the same.

As soon as she had returned, all the stresses of living in the city and the constant pressure of bills and being a single mother haunted her. For the first time, she had a sense of not belonging. She was living her life in auto-mode, doing what she needed to do just to get by. Day in, day out, the routine was the same. There were no waves of excitement or breathtaking views to lose yourself in. She missed the clean air of the ocean and being able to look up and see the stars. She no longer wanted the life she was living. Dwayne's lifestyle offered so much more, not only for her but also for Matt.

But Tammy had to keep reminding herself there might be a possibility that Dwayne wouldn't want anything to do with her once he found out about her accident and the upcoming court date. She feared his reaction when he discovered how long she had been keeping it from him. He would have every right to be angry with her; after all, you don't begin a new relationship with secrets. She had prepared herself for the worst—the fact that Dwayne may just break up with her over this. If he did, she was willing to accept it and would have to make the best of her life in the city, just like she always had before meeting him. She simply hadn't realized up until now that it wasn't the life she wanted.

Tired of not being completely honest with Dwayne, Tammy was anxious to tell him and come clean. She had arranged to leave Matt with Judy the next weekend so she could talk to Dwayne alone. As much as she was dreading it, she couldn't postpone it any longer. Her court date was just two months away and she no idea when she could get another weekend alone with him.

After packing her bags and saying goodbye to Matt, she left feeling hesitant about her trip for the first time. Not knowing what the outcome would be after telling Dwayne, she couldn't help but wonder if it was going to be her last trip to the marina.

She arrived at the boatyard around noon, but Dwayne was nowhere to be found. She checked his boat, the office, and his truck that was parked in the lot before finally asking one of the guys working in the yard. They had all become familiar faces, giving her a wave and a smile whenever they saw her. This man she knew as Jose. He directed her to one of the far corners of the yard away from all the boats and told her Dwayne was working over there. Tammy thanked him and headed in the direction he was pointing.

She found Dwayne, shirtless, wearing just a pair of Levis. His tanned back was facing her as he stood in front of a large work bench cutting a humungous roll of wire. Admiring the view, Tammy moistened her lips with her tongue. A radio perched on a wooden stool was blasting a Rolling Stones song and Dwayne was unaware of her presence. Tammy stopped for a moment to enjoy the sight of him working while he was oblivious to his surroundings.

She noticed beads of sweat forming on his back from the intense heat of the sun, and she watched as they began to trickle slowly down over his parched skin. His blond hair shimmered and rested on his shoulders, gently blowing from the subtle ocean breeze. As he cut the wire, she was drawn to his muscular arms, flexed and well toned. God, she was a lucky woman. She only hoped he would still feel the same way by the end of the weekend.

Not wanting to startle him while he was using sharp cutting shears, she approached the bench slowly to make her presence known. As soon as Dwayne spotted her, he threw down the shears and greeted her with a bear hug and a passionate kiss.

"Hey gorgeous! I've missed you."

Tammy squeezed him tight. "I've missed you too." While still in his arms, she scanned the area and saw five more rolls of wire stacked away from the bench and a mound of white buoys lying on the ground along with five large reels of rope. More piles of various supplies and an array of tools were also stored haphazardly around his bench. "What's all this stuff?" she asked.

"This stuff, as you call it," Dwayne said with a chuckle, "is all the material needed to make lobster traps. I need to make a hundred fifty of them within the next month. And that's on my spare time when I'm not out hustling and working on boats. Wanna help?" he said while tickling her side.

Tammy darted away from his invasive fingers. "Wow! That's a lot of traps you've got to make." She threw her purse off to the side and placed her hands on her hips. "You bet I want to help! Put me to work."

Tammy never failed to impress Dwayne with her dedication and enthusiasm. "Tell you what, I'll start you off with something easy. You know how to paint, right?"

"Yes," Tammy replied, her voice dripping with sarcasm.

Dwayne pointed to the pile of white buoys. "Good! All those

buoys over there need to be branded with my numbers and then painted with my colors, which are a red and black stripe. The numbers are so Fish and Game know who the traps belong to if they ever decide to pull it up and check it, and the colors help fishermen identify their traps while out pulling their gear."

"I never realized so much went into fishing." She tilted her head inquisitively. "And normally you would do all this by yourself?"

Dwayne nodded. "Yep."

"Wow. That's a lot of work."

"Well, this year I'm going to San Clemente Island. I've never been there but I hear the fishing is really good. In the past, I've only fished locally, and I came home every night. But San Clemente is much farther away, so I'll be spending at least a week out there and to make the trip worthwhile, I'll need a lot more traps. In fact, I'm doubling the amount I normally fish with, so technically, I've doubled my work."

"And you'll be out there all by yourself?" She shuddered at the thought. "For a week?"

"Yep." Dwayne pulled her in close and whispered in a husky voice, "It will get lonely out there you know."

Tammy's heart skipped a beat. Thoughts of being alone with Dwayne, miles away from civilization, on a boat in the middle of the Pacific Ocean for an entire week sounded appealing. She couldn't believe she was actually considering going with him. She didn't reveal her thoughts to Dwayne. It was too soon. Plus, she had Matt to think about, and her job. Who could take care of Matt for a whole week? And how could she ever afford to take a week off from work to go fishing?

Tammy knew she tended to act on impulse and not follow things through with any kind of consideration. She could feel herself doing it again. But this was the chance of a lifetime, and she honestly didn't want to pass it up. Even though Dwayne hadn't officially asked her to go with him, he just dropped the biggest hint by telling her how lonely he was going to be. There had to be a way to go with him. She was going to somehow figure it out and surprise him. She couldn't wait to see his reaction when she told him.

But the daydream didn't last long. It suddenly occurred to her that she still needed to tell Dwayne about her court date and that she might possibly have a drinking problem. It's funny how just the thought of telling him ignited her cravings for a drink.

It suddenly occurred to her that she got a lot of her courage from liquor. Whenever something was bothering her, or life was too stressful, she'd open a beer or have a shot of whisky to numb her feelings. For the first time, Tammy was looking at her drinking habits in a different light. No longer did she believe it was a fun social habit; instead, she realized she depended on alcohol to get her through most of the struggles she faced in life. Yet the problems she was trying to avoid by drinking never went away and were never resolved. Alcohol just temporarily numbed them.

When she left Steven, she turned to alcohol for comfort. Ironically, unbeknown to her until she met Dwayne, she was still depending on it. Tammy was finally understanding herself but needed to gather her thoughts some more before explaining her new discovery to Dwayne.

She didn't know how long she had been self-absorbed in her thoughts, but it must have been a while because she heard Dwayne's voice calling through the fog of her reverie.

"Tammy? Tammy, are you okay? You look like you're miles away."

Tammy shook her head to clear it. "Yeah. Sorry. I was just thinking about Matt. I miss him already."

Dwayne took her hand and led her over to the buoys. "Well, let's put you to work. That will take your mind off him."

Tammy followed him and together they hung a length of rope up across the back of the workspace, and after Dwayne branded each buoy with his fishing numbers, Tammy threaded them onto the rope and spent the next two hours painting them.

Her previous thoughts were soon forgotten and her craving for alcohol quickly subsided. She was enjoying doing something other than waiting on tables and tolerating rude and impatient customers. Instead, she was working outside next to the ocean and learning so much with a fantastic guy. They were a team, working together, side by side. There was no clock to pay attention to, no boss to answer to, and she was working in shorts and flip flops. It couldn't get any better. She began to wonder if she could actually make money from doing this like Dwayne.

They continued to work until the sun went down. Tammy was eager to learn and quickly picked up on all the tasks Dwayne threw at her, from cutting the wire, clipping the traps together, and making funnels to go inside the traps. To Dwayne, she was a natural. Impressed by the amount of work they had accomplished between them, Dwayne told her he was going to treat her to a fancy dinner in the marina. Tammy loved the idea, but in reality, she knew it would also be a good time to tell him about the accident and her upcoming day in court.

CHAPTER 15

After another heated session of lovemaking in the shower, Dwayne took Tammy to a high end steak and seafood restaurant that overlooked the main channel of the marina. The male host led them to a secluded window table with spectacular views over the water. From their table, they could see the entire marina, where endless rows of powerboats and sailboats shimmered under the dark starlit sky. There were no cars, no crowds of people or noise. It was the most peaceful place Tammy had ever experienced.

Once they were seated at their table and the host left them to browse the menus, Tammy leaned back and took in the view. "Gosh, it's so beautiful and peaceful here. You're so lucky to wake up to this every morning. I just love coming down here."

Dwayne smiled and reached for her hand across the table. "I'm glad you like my lifestyle. I feel pretty lucky." He browsed over the menu. "Order whatever you want. It's on me. They have the best steaks here."

A few minutes later, a waiter arrived and asked them what they wanted to drink. Tammy didn't hesitate and ordered a glass of white wine. She'd gone all day without alcohol and was feeling the effects. And she convinced herself she'd need it to tell Dwayne about the accident. It seemed like a pretty good excuse.

Dwayne didn't comment on her choice of drink and she appreciated it. After Dwayne ordered himself a Pepsi, the waiter left them alone to browse the menu some more. Tammy took Dwayne's recommendation and ordered a sirloin steak, and as usual, Dwayne ordered a seafood platter.

After seeking the support of three glasses of wine and with dinner almost over, Tammy finally had the courage to tell Dwayne what had been on her mind for weeks. She took the last bite of steak and before laying down her fork, she took in a deep breath. "Dwayne, there's something I have to tell you."

For a moment, he stopped eating and looked up. "Uh-oh. This sounds serious." Unsure of what she was about to tell him, he released a nervous laugh. "Let me guess, I worked you too hard today and you saw how hard lobster fishing really is and you want nothing more to do with it. You're breaking up with me. Is that it?" he asked, his nerves hidden behind an anxious smile.

Tammy quickly shook her head. "No. No. I love everything about what you do. This is about me." She paused and looked down at the table. "There's something I've been hiding from you and I think it's time you knew."

Sensing this was hard for her, Dwayne reached over the table and took her hand in a firm hold. "You can tell me anything, Tammy. Surely it's not as bad as you are thinking."

Tammy gripped his fingers for support and began the dreaded task of telling him.

"Before I met you, I got into a car accident. My car was totaled and I woke up in the hospital. Thankfully, no one else was hurt, but it could have been a lot worse."

Dwayne looked puzzled. "Why are you afraid of telling me about a car accident? Is it because it was your fault?"

Consumed with guilt, Tammy looked away to avoid his eyes.

"Yes, it was my fault. I was drunk. It was my birthday and I had too much to drink. I know that's no excuse, but I drove while intoxicated and could have killed someone because of my stupidity. The thought haunts me every day."

"Go on," Dwayne urged, sensing there was more to the story.

Tammy took in another deep breath. "When I woke up in the hospital, there was an officer there and he gave me a DUI. I've been to court twice to try and take care of the fine, and I have to appear again in August. It's my final extension and I'm not sure what will happen. I'm not asking for your help; I just think you should know." Tammy waited nervously for Dwayne's reaction.

He didn't answer right away. Instead, he mulled over Tammy's confession. "Is there more you want to tell me?"

Tammy creased her brow. "What do you mean? No, that's it."

Dwayne chose his words carefully. He admired her honesty and wanted to keep her on track. "Okay, so is it a concern of yours that you continue to drink even after the accident, and the fact that you could have killed innocent people doesn't stop you from drinking?"

Tammy felt herself sinking into her seat. She hadn't admitted to him that part of the story but he clearly understood her. Feeling embarrassed, she answered while again avoiding eye contact. "Yes."

Dwayne tilted his head to try and catch Tammy's eye. Showing his continued support, he didn't let go of her hand. "Do you think you have a drinking problem?"

Tammy could feel the tears beginning to pool in her eyes. She felt ashamed and unworthy of him. Finally, she looked up and met his stare. "Yes, I do." She let her tears flow and wiped them away from her cheeks. "And I don't know what to do. I'm an awful person and I don't deserve you."

Dwayne spoke to her like he had spoken to many others, all of whom had come to the realization that they were alcoholics. "Tammy, you took the first step. You admitted to yourself and to me that you have a drinking problem. Do you realize how much courage that takes?" He squeezed her hand. "I'm so proud of you."

Tammy took in a deep breath and smiled through her tears. She knew she had nothing to be afraid of. Dwayne wasn't going anywhere.

"That means a lot. Thank you."

Dwayne knew exactly how she was feeling. After all, he'd been there over ten years ago when he found himself in the same predicament and had decided to quit drinking. Knowing she needed a shoulder to cry on, he left his seat and took the empty one next to her. Tammy welcomed his embrace and buried her face in his shoulder while allowing her tears to drench his shirt.

"What am I going to do?" she asked between sniffles.

"Well, I think you already know the answer to that. You tell me. It's not up to me to tell you."

Tammy was quiet. He was right; she did know the answer. "I don't want to drink anymore. But why am I so scared? Why does the thought of not drinking petrify me? My biggest fear is that you won't like me anymore. That I may be too boring."

Dwayne laughed. "Do you hear yourself? Do you realize how dependent you are on alcohol? Think about it. I don't drink. Am I boring?"

Tammy soon realized how pathetic she sounded and all she was doing was trying to find excuses to drink. Dwayne was right. If anything, she'd probably be a better person if she didn't drink. The problems and insecurities she was experiencing all stemmed from her drinking habits. It was like a light bulb switched on in her head. She suddenly saw herself from another perspective and it all made bloody sense.

She raised her head in triumph and for the first time, she was excited about her future. "You're right! I don't need alcohol. I can do this. From now on, I'm not going to have another drink. I'm done." She turned to Dwayne and kissed him passionately on the lips. "Thank you."

Dwayne gave her a warm smile. "You don't have to thank me. I just listened. You are the one making all the decisions. You've got this. I can tell you, at times, it won't be easy, but I'm here for you. Whenever you want to talk, I don't care if it's in the middle of the night, you know how to get hold of me. Talking instead of drinking is the key."

Determined to be successful and now having made the commitment not to drink, Tammy proudly pushed away the glass of wine in front of her and smiled. "I think I'll have a cup of coffee."

Dwayne smiled back and flagged down the waiter while pushing her glass to the edge of the table to be picked up.

Tammy managed not to drink for the rest of the weekend, but she never realized up until that point how much she craved a beer or a glass of wine throughout the day. At times, she felt herself becoming irritated and found herself snapping at Dwayne for no apparent reason. Thank god he understood it was the absence of alcohol that was causing her mood swings. Once the cravings had subsided, she made a point of apologizing, and he made the extra effort to take time out and talk to her about what she was feeling. He was giving her all the support she needed. Tammy wondered how she was going to handle the cravings once she was back home and Dwayne wasn't around.

She saw how easy he picked up smoking again when she smoked around him. A wave of guilt swept through her at the thought. She knew she would be returning home to Judy who, like herself, loved to drink. She would have to be a lot stronger and not cave in to the addiction. She couldn't let it be more powerful than her own determination.

By the end of the day, she was feeling exhausted. Not only mentally from the head trips of no alcohol but also physically. She and Dwayne had spent all of Sunday working outside in hot temperatures on the lobster gear. Her muscles were sore, her body ached and her hands were stiff from endless hours of cutting and bending wire. She'd used muscles she never knew she had, and in an odd way it felt damn good. Never had she worked so hard and had such a feeling of accomplishment. She was proud of herself, not only for not drinking but also for doing what most would call 'a man's job.' And she had loved every minute of it and couldn't wait to return and do some more.

By the end of the day, they had fifty traps built, all the buoys painted, one hundred and fifty bait jars prepared, rope cut to the appropriate lengths and more wire cut to start on the next fifty traps.

"I want to come back next weekend," Tammy said while packing her bags on the boat.

Dwayne couldn't get over her enthusiasm. It excited him every time. "Sure! I'd love it if you would. I can't believe how much we got done this weekend. We make a great team." He walked over to her, pulled her away from her bag and took her in his arms. "You're a natural. You're good at this stuff. Damn, you might even be better at it than me some day. You're a fast learner and you never cease to amaze me."

Tammy stayed in his arms, loving the security they brought her. "Oh, I could never be better than you. But I love this stuff! I mean, my nails are a mess." She held her hand out flat. "Look, they're all broken. My hair is all matted from working in the sun and I'm sweating like a pig. My body is the sorest it has ever been but as weird as it sounds, I feel bloody fantastic. I'd take this any day over waiting on tables."

"Well, there's still plenty of work to do. I still have another hundred traps to build so I could use all the help I can get."

Tammy beamed him a smile before breaking away. "Great! I can't wait. Can I bring Matt? I promise he won't be in the way."

"Of course you can bring him." He leaned down and grabbed Tammy's bag off the bed. "Come on, I'll walk you to your car."

Always hating this part of her visit where she had to say good-bye, Tammy hesitated before putting the car in reverse. She looked up at Dwayne, who was standing by her window leaning down and looking in. "I'll miss you," she said.

"I'll miss you too. Now remember, you can call me whenever you want if you're having a hard time with the not drinking thing."

"Thanks. I will. It's going to be tough with Judy drinking, but I'll be strong. I've got this."

Dwayne squeezed her shoulder. "I know you do. You'll be fine. I'll see you next weekend."

"I can't wait," Tammy replied before reluctantly putting the car in reverse. It was time to return to the life in the city where she no longer wanted to be.

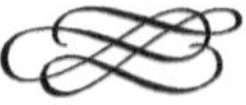

Tammy arrived home after dark, feeling exhausted and regretting she hadn't taken a shower at the boatyard. But she had already left later than she had intended to and wanted to see Matt before he went to bed.

"My god, woman, you're a mess," Judy said as soon as Tammy walked through the door. Judy was sat in her usual spot on the couch nursing a glass of wine. All three kids were sat together on the floor engrossed in a movie.

Tammy laughed while closing the door behind her. "Ha! Thanks. I love you too."

The minute he heard his mother's voice, Matt was up off the floor and ran into her arms. "Mommy!" he squealed.

Tammy gave him a huge smile as she knelt to greet him and swallowed him up in her arms. "Hey buddy. I've missed you too," she said while planting a big kiss on his cheek.

Judy rose from the couch. "You look like you need a drink."

Matt soon returned to his movie, allowing Tammy to stand. "Actually, nope. I've quit drinking."

Judy froze, her mouth agape, stunned by Tammy's announcement. "What? Why? We always have wine together. Is it because of Dwayne? Did he tell you to quit?"

Upon hearing Judy thinking Dwayne was to blame, Tammy raised her hand to cut her off before she went on a rampage. "No, it's not because of Dwayne. He has nothing to do with this. I've just been doing a lot of thinking, and I think it's stupid that I've continued to drink after I almost killed myself while driving drunk. Next time, I might not be so lucky."

Judy shook her head in disbelief. "You can't be serious? You don't even drink that much. It's not like you wake up in the morning and drink all day. Don't you think you're overreacting a little bit?"

Tammy was disappointed by Judy's reaction. Instead of being supportive like Dwayne, she was actually trying to find fault with her decision. "Judy! I almost killed myself, and if you think about it, I drink every day after work and on my days off, I drink even more. I'm a mother and I need to be more responsible. I don't want to ever risk doing that again. I drink to escape my crappy life, but I don't want it to turn into a full-blown addiction where I need alcohol every day, which is where it's heading. I'm nipping it in the bud now so it doesn't slowly begin to consume me. I've seen how addiction can destroy someone's life. So have you for that matter. The fathers of our children lost us and their kids because of their drug addiction. Alcohol can do the same thing. I'm not going to let that happen."

Judy had never seen Tammy so defiant about something. "You're serious, aren't you?"

"Yes, I am. No more alcohol. I'm done. And I know this is your home too, but I'd appreciate it if you'd not drink in front of me for a while until I can get a grip on not wanting that glass of wine that is sitting in front of you."

Judy was suddenly flooded with guilt by Tammy's words. She looked down at her glass and quickly picked it up. "Oh, sure. Not a problem." She scurried out of the room with the glass. "I'll empty it down the sink. I've had enough anyway."

"Thanks. I'm going to take a quick shower and then cozy up with my little man before he has to go to bed."

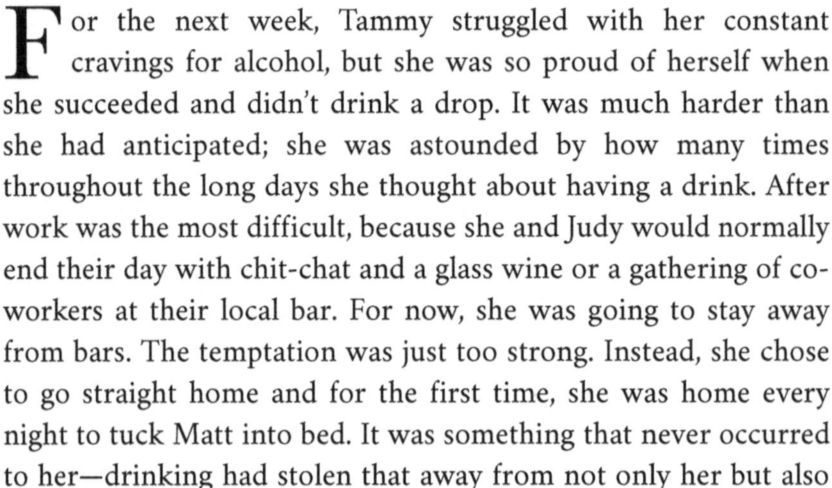

For the next week, Tammy struggled with her constant cravings for alcohol, but she was so proud of herself when she succeeded and didn't drink a drop. It was much harder than she had anticipated; she was astounded by how many times throughout the long days she thought about having a drink. After work was the most difficult, because she and Judy would normally end their day with chit-chat and a glass wine or a gathering of co-workers at their local bar. For now, she was going to stay away from bars. The temptation was just too strong. Instead, she chose to go straight home and for the first time, she was home every night to tuck Matt into bed. It was something that never occurred to her—drinking had stolen that away from not only her but also her son.

She suddenly found herself more productive. No longer did she lounge on the couch sipping wine. Instead, she had quality time with Matt, playing games, going for evening walks, cooking home-made meals, reading stories to Matt and even reading books for herself, which was something she had always loved to do. She soon realized it had been a long time since she had picked up a book.

Tammy found herself wanting to keep busy to keep her mind off drinking and in the process, she discovered how much she was missing out and how much she had been neglecting Matt.

She even made a spontaneous trip with Matt on her day off in the middle of the week to visit her sister Donna, who she hadn't seen in months. She always had lame excuses for her absence, but in reality, she was too busy sitting at the bar or hanging out at home nursing a beer or a glass of wine.

Her sister lived only an hour away so it was inexcusable that she hadn't made the effort to see her more often. Donna never learnt to drive and depended on Jason for rides, but he had recently started his own tree trimming company and was working ten to twelve hour days; it was close to impossible for Donna to get him to take her to Tammy's house. Tammy understood that and blamed only herself for not visiting more often.

Tammy had other motives for visiting Donna. Still in the back of her mind was the idea of going fishing with Dwayne to San Clemente Island. Matt was only four and wouldn't start school until next year. She would need someone to watch him full time while she was gone for at least seven days, according to Dwayne, and she thought of asking Donna. But the idea soon crumbled when Donna reminded her of the one and only time she had ever watched Matt, which turned out to be a disaster. It was the year before, close to Christmas, and Tammy was visiting her sister. She saw the opportunity to get some Christmas shopping done without Matt and decided to leave him with Donna for a few hours.

While in the care of Donna, Matt took a bad fall, which resulted in his lip getting split open. Tammy returned to find Donna, in floods of tears and clearly in a panic, sitting on the couch with Matt while holding a cold washcloth to his lip. After cleaning off the blood, which made it look worse than it was, Tammy inspected the cut and didn't feel it was necessary to take him to the hospital.

But, as a result of that event, Donna was now too afraid to watch Matt for any length of time, afraid he may get hurt again while in her care.

For the first time on this most recent visit, Tammy shared with her sister about the car accident and the shame she felt.

"Why did you wait so long to tell me, Tammy?"

"I'm sorry. I've been so embarrassed by the whole thing. I can't believe how bloody stupid I was."

Donna got up from the couch where they were sitting and grabbed her cigarettes off the kitchen counter. "Well, you're really lucky you didn't get more seriously hurt." She held out the pack of cigarettes. "Do you want one?"

"Sure, thanks," Tammy said. "Yes, I am lucky. But one good thing came out of it."

"What's that?' Donna asked between drags.

"I quit drinking."

Donna returned to the couch and gasped. "You're kidding? Wow! I was wondering why you hadn't asked for a beer yet. I was about to offer you one. Sure glad I didn't now," she said with a laugh.

Donna had been her only hope. She couldn't ask Judy because she had to work. Only then did it occur to Tammy that poor Judy would have to find someone to watch her own kids if Tammy did manage to find a way to go to the island. Although she and Dwayne had agreed Matt could go along for the weekend, there was no way she could take him with her for a full week. It would be too dangerous. Dwayne had explained to her that he would be living on the boat for the entire time because the Navy owned the island and there was no access to the public. Tammy knew there would be no way she could keep Matt confined to a boat for a week.

Tammy was determined to find a solution. But she also realized she couldn't make any concrete plans until she learnt the outcome of her court appearance, which was coming up in the next few months. She knew if she didn't pay the fine, there were no more extensions and she would probably be facing jail time. She had no idea how much time the judge would sentence her to, but there was a possibility she might be in jail when it came time for Dwayne to go fishing. The thought petrified her.

She wanted to go to San Clemente Island more than anything. She was learning everything there was to know about preparing for lobster season, listening to Dwayne's stories about his previous adventures and how much fun it was to pull up traps and find them loaded with lobsters. He said it was better than Christmas. After spending hours prepping the gear with Dwayne, Tammy wanted to experience that gratification first hand.

She called Dwayne every day during the week to give him a progress report on the no-drinking project and also for moral support. He had a way of talking to her where everything made sense. The times she had broken down on the phone and told him she couldn't do it anymore, he knew exactly what to say and put everything back in perspective.

There was one time she had called him late in the evening. It was after Matt had gone to bed and there was nothing on the TV. Judy was out with her boyfriend and their friends, and she was home alone babysitting. She had tried to focus on reading, but the cravings were super strong. And she knew Judy's beer was in the fridge. Three times she had opened the fridge and just stood there staring at the cold cans, listening intently as they screamed at her to pick them up and take them back to the couch.

Not knowing what else to do and not wanting to give in to her cravings, she lit her fourth cigarette and called Dwayne. He stayed on the phone with her for an hour, talking to her about anything. What had she done that day? How was Matt? How was work? What was she wearing? That last one got a chuckle out of Tammy.

He didn't let her hang up until he was convinced she no longer craved a beer and promised she would go straight to bed. She kept her promise and after hanging up the phone, she turned off the lights and went to sleep. Her last thought was about how lucky she was to have Dwayne in her life.

CHAPTER 17

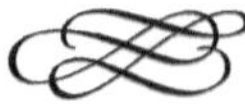

Over the next month, Tammy switched her days with other servers so she and Matt could spend every weekend with Dwayne. Their productivity was much slower now that they had a four-year-old to keep occupied, but Dwayne wasn't concerned. He was still way ahead of where he would have been without Tammy's help.

They spent the first two weekends cutting wire, making traps, painting buoys and cutting ropes. By mid-July, Tammy felt like she belonged in the community and received a lot of admiration from the crew working in the boatyard as she worked alongside Dwayne.

Many stopped by the corner of the yard on their breaks to watch the duo in action. Some even helped by entertaining Matt. He had become the little buddy of many, and the guys seemed genuinely excited to see him when he came dashing through the yard, anxious to see Dwayne and all the boats.

Everyone in the boatyard knew Dwayne was on a tight schedule to get ready for lobster season so they all pulled together like one big family, eager to help by taking time out from their own jobs to spend some time with Matt. Some played soccer with him in the middle of the yard, some showed him the boats they were on and gave him little easy jobs. Others brought him a cheeseburger and spent their lunch hour with him. Like Tammy, Matt was beginning to enjoy being in the marina more than at home and couldn't wait until the next weekend arrived.

By the end of the second weekend, all the traps were built and stacked neatly in the corner of the yard. The piles of wire scraps had been tossed, the ropes were coiled and hung up and buoys were stacked along the side wall. Tammy stood back, leaning against the workbench to admire their work while Matt bounced a buoy around at her feet. "Look at that. It's only mid-July and you have all your traps built. What are you going to do for the next month?"

Dwayne laughed at her comment. "Sweetheart, those traps aren't even close to being finished. When you come next weekend, we're going be unstacking fifty of them, cementing them and dipping them in tar. We can only do fifty at a time because we have limited space in the yard. And, trust me, it will take all weekend to do fifty."

Tammy cocked her head in confusion. "Wait. What do you mean by cement and dip them?"

Dwayne released another laugh as he approached her and gave her a playful hug. "The traps have to be weighted so they will sink to the bottom of the ocean. That's what the cement is for. And I dip them in tar—just like what's on the roads—so they don't rust and will last longer in the ocean."

Tammy stood for a moment while she tried to work out the process. "So you mean to tell me we have to unstack all these traps again?"

"Yep. By the time you get here next week," he said, pointing to the space at the end of the work bench, "there will be a cement mixer over there and next to it will be a large dip box full of tar. The best bit? You get to play with both cement and tar. So prepare to get messy. Oh, and be sure to bring some long pants and long sleeve tops. The older the better. You can't be dipping in shorts. The tar is really tough to get off your skin."

"Oh boy, I can't wait. I'm sure Matt's going to love it too."

Thinking she had learned everything there was to know about building lobster traps, Tammy muddled the next part of the process for most of the following week. It actually sounded like fun. For weeks, it had been the same repetitive chores, so she was looking forward to doing something different. Even if it meant getting covered in cement and tar.

Yet again, she found herself anxious to be a part of the fishing industry and couldn't wait for the next weekend to come around. Matt mirrored her excitement, to the extent that her days in the city were now spent listening to Matt asking when they were going to the boat again. It seemed neither of them enjoyed the city life anymore.

Per Dwayne's request, Tammy and Matt arrived at the boatyard super early on Saturday, just in time to see the sun come up. He wanted to get the dipping part done before the day got hotter so the dip would have time to dry. Dressed in her oldest worn-out jeans and an already stained shirt, she found Dwayne at the corner of the yard amongst twenty plus bags of cement and a shiny new orange cement mixer. Tammy gasped. "God, that's a lot of cement. Are we going to use all that?"

Facing away from Tammy and Matt, Dwayne was startled by her question and was almost knocked over by Matt's enthusiastic hug when he rushed over and locked his arms around Dwayne's legs. "Yep, we certainly are," he said, bending down to give Matt a loving hug. "We might even need more."

She turned and looked at a large plywood box. It stood as tall as her waist, was at least four feet wide and wasn't there last week. "What's that?"

"That's the tar dip."

"I can't wait," Tammy said sarcastically, even though she was intrigued by the whole operation. Eager to get started and learn something new, Tammy rubbed her hands together. "Okay, tell me what to do. I'm all yours."

"All mine, eh? I like that." Dwayne laughed before getting down to business and giving Tammy the rundown on what needed to be done. He walked her over to a huge blue tarp that was lined with rows of dipped traps. "I had the afternoon off yesterday so I was able to get these dipped. They're pretty light without the cement." Dwayne touched one and rubbed his fingers to check they were still clean. "They're dry now so we can cement them."

Being early, the yard was quiet, which meant no one was around to entertain Matt, but Dwayne had a way of making it fun for him so he enjoyed being involved. At this stage of the building process, being just wire, the traps were super light to handle and Matt was made to feel important by helping Dwayne carry a trap over to the dip box.

Wanting to beat the rising temperatures, Dwayne wasted no time in turning on the cement mixer and getting Tammy to help him hoist up the first 100 pound bag of cement and empty it into the mixer.

"Fuck, that's heavy," Tammy yelled over the din of the motor. Once relieved of its weight, she stood back and watched Dwayne cut the bag and pour the contents into the mixer. As soon as he did, a large cloud of dust blew out of the opening and settled all over Dwayne's face.

Dwayne quickly turned his head and shouted, "Hold your breath. Don't breathe this stuff in."

Tammy only needed to be told once. She quickly pulled Matt away and gave him a pile of buoys to play with; they always seemed to entertain him.

They repeated the process and lifted another two bags into the mixer, and then Dwayne added water using a long hose that stretched through the yard from the nearest faucet. After a few minutes, Dwayne felt comfortable that the cement was mixed to the right consistency and turned off the mixer. Tammy's ears struggled with the sudden silence as Dwayne grabbed two five-gallon buckets. "Now the fun begins." He winked at Tammy with a playful smile. "Here, hold one of these buckets under the mixer as I pour some cement into it. I'm only going to fill it halfway, otherwise they will be too heavy."

Using both hands, Tammy held the bucket tight, but the sudden weight of the added cement being poured in caused her to almost lose her grip. "Damn it!" she yelled as she quickly adjusted her grip to compensate for the extra weight. She lowered it to the ground with a thud when Dwayne was done pouring. "Now what?" she asked.

"Grab the other bucket. We're going to fill that one too."

After the buckets were filled, they each took one over to the traps. Dwayne then showed her how to pour a little cement into each corner of the bottom of the traps until the wire on the base was covered with cement. Two buckets did three traps. Already feeling the strain in her back, Tammy stretched her muscles and scanned the rows of remaining traps. "Only forty-seven more to go."

It took most of the day to complete the task, working under the cruel heat of the sun with no shade and few breaks. Again, the community of the boatyard came together and helped by keeping Matt busy. Lifting the cement bags, carrying the weighted buckets and bending over each trap was so back wrenching that by the time they had reached the last trap, Tammy struggled to move.

With a joyous sigh of relief, she threw down the bucket, grabbed an ice cold water from the cooler and collapsed on the ground next to the workbench. "I can't believe we got them all done," she said as beads of sweat poured down her face and glistened in the sun. Enjoying the cool sensation of the cold water gliding down her throat, she poured some over her head to break the intensity of the heat rushing through her veins. "God, that feels good," she said while shaking her head. Matt, who was now with them, laughed at his mother drenching herself in water, her hair soaked.

Dwayne joined her on the ground, patting her wet hair as he lowered his body. "It was a team effort. There's no way I could have gotten all of them done on my own." He gave her a peck on the cheek. "Thank you."

Tammy lowered her head on his shoulder but quickly pulled it back. "Ouch! God, even my neck is sore. My entire body is one big sore." She laughed. "And you don't have to thank me. Even though my body aches, my muscles are beyond strained and I feel like I have no fingerprints left, I love doing this stuff."

"Well, I'm glad you do. I don't know too many women that would do this. You are an exception. Even the guys in the boatyard are amazed by your strength and stamina. No pun intended, but you're quite the catch."

"Awww, you are too, and I truly mean that."

Still exhausted from their day of intense labor, they decided to do absolutely nothing for the rest of the evening except take showers and hang out on the deck of the boat with Matt until, at around nine o'clock, they were too tired to stay awake.

The next morning, Tammy could barely get out of bed. Holding her back, she pulled herself upright and released a moan of agony. "Man, I feel like I've been run over by a train."

Dwayne and Matt were nowhere to be found in the small cabin, and no clock hung on the wall so she had no idea what time it was. She struggled some more to get her wounded body out of the bed. Her joints creaked as if they needed oil, her hands were rough like sandpaper and her neck and shoulders hurt from the inside out. When she finally managed to stand, which was a long drawn out process consisting of repetitive moans and sharp screams of pain, she made her way up on to the deck and scanned the boatyard and slips.

She heard Dwayne's voice off in the distance.

"Hey! You're awake," he yelled.

Tammy turned her head in the direction of his voice and spotted him fishing off the dock with Matt. What a way to wake up—coffee and fishing. It couldn't get any better.

An hour later, around eight, they were back at the corner of the yard. After two large cups of coffee and keeping herself moving, Tammy's body was beginning to loosen up and she was ready to face another day of intense labor. Dwayne didn't seem fazed by yesterday's strenuous tasks and was raring to go.

After taking a sip of his coffee, he led Tammy far across the yard to another stack of traps.

"These are traps from last year. We have to dip these too."

Tammy stared at the pile. "But these already have cement on them. Aren't they going to be heavy?"

Dwayne nodded and gave her a smirk. "Yep, 'fraid so. It's gonna take the two of us to dip these." He looked at the stack and folded his arms. "These are gonna take a lot of dip, so I think we should dip them before we finish the new ones."

Tammy let out a huge sigh. "Okay, let's get to it. Where are we going to put them? You're taking up half the yard already."

"That's okay. It's the weekend." He looked over at the traps they dipped yesterday. "We can lay a tarp next to those and line them up alongside."

It took them well over an hour to unstack the traps and lay them in a row on the ground, by which time, Tammy's back was already beginning to hurt again.

"God! How much do these things weigh?" she asked while rubbing her side.

"About seventy pounds. You going to be okay?"

"Yeah, I'll be fine. Let's do this."

Dwayne had Tammy help him remove the heavy plywood lid on the dip box. Tammy looked inside and scrunched her face at the black gooey liquid.

"Eww. This looks like it could be messy."

Steering an eager Matt away from the box, as he was anxious to look inside, Dwayne laughed. "Yeah, you could say that." He handed Tammy a large pair of black rubber gloves. "Here, put these on. You don't want to get any of this stuff on your hands."

With the oversized gloves now in place, Tammy couldn't help but feel like the mad scientist. "Okay, what are we doing?"

After setting Matt up with buoys and blocks of wood to keep him occupied, she'd given him strict instructions to keep away from the wet traps. Dwayne handed Tammy a rod of rebar. "We first need to stir the tar up really well, and then we're going to dip each trap into the tank and put them back on the tarp to dry overnight."

"Wow! This will take a while; it's so much work. I sure hope you catch some lobsters after all this."

"Fishing is the easy part. Getting ready to fish is the hard bit."

"No kidding. I had no idea there was so much involved," Tammy said as she began to stir the thick black liquid, being careful not to splash any on her clothes.

After a good thirty minutes of stirring, they were finally ready to dip the first trap. Anxious to get the first one in the box, Tammy attempted to lift a trap on her own but quickly changed her mind. "Damn! These are heavy."

"Yep. The cement just added another thirty pounds of weight to them. Each trap now weighs about sixty. Come on, we'll both take an end and lift them together."

Tammy couldn't imagine how she was going to feel by the end of the day after lifting all these traps, and she decided it was best she didn't think about it. After setting the first trap on the edge of the box, they slowly lowered it into the dip box until it was completely covered. Tammy watched as the liquid gurgled and the trap sunk beneath the surface. It reminded her of quicksand. "That's pretty cool. Now, how do we get it out?"

Dwayne raised his gloved hands. "With these."

"Seriously? And I thought the cement part was messy."

Dwayne looked at Tammy as he took his place at one side of the box. "Ready?"

"Let's do this," she replied as she positioned herself on the other side. Next, she reached inside the box and slid her gloved hand into the tar in search of the top of the trap. "God, it's so thick."

"It has to be so it will stick to the wire."

Suddenly, she felt the trap and quickly wrapped her hand over the wire, making sure she had a good grip and hoping her glove wouldn't slip off. "A-ha! Found it," she yelled in triumph.

"Good. Now, hold on tight. We're going to pull it up together and rest it on the side of the box to let all the excess tar run off."

"Okay. I'm ready."

"One, two, three…and lift."

Using all her strength, Tammy lifted at the same time as Dwayne and was amazed at the effort it took to get the trap up onto to the edge. As they pulled, the liquid tried to suck the trap back down; she thought it would be easier if they were pulling it out of quicksand. By the time it was out of the tar and dripping, Tammy was leaning over trying to catch her breath.

"Man, that was heavy." She glanced at the rows of undipped traps. "And we have to do all these?"

Dwayne threw her a cocky smile. "Yep. Come on, let's walk this one over to the tarp and grab another one."

Because it was Sunday and most of the workers took the day off, the yard was empty besides them. Thankfully, though, Matt was doing a really good job of entertaining himself while they dipped the traps. Sometimes riding his bike that Tammy had brought down, or playing with his ball or the buoys or eating snacks. The boatyard was like a huge playground he had all to himself, and he never once seemed bored. More importantly, he stayed where they could keep an eye on him at all times.

By noon, they had managed to get thirty-five of the traps done and Tammy's body was feeling it immensely. Not only did every part of her body ache to the core, but her clothes from the waist down were caked with dry tar along with smears of it on her face where she had unknowingly wiped it with the glove. Parts of her hair were even glued with tar. "God, I'm a mess," she proclaimed. "I need to take a break."

"I think you look cute. But sure, I need a break too. I'm having a hard time keeping up with you. I thought you'd never ask."

Tammy groaned as she removed her gloves and walked her aching body over to a lounge chair, where she called Matt over for a snack and some juice. A few minutes later, Dwayne's pager went off with a high pitched beep. He pulled it out of his front jean pocket and looked at the display. "I gotta make a phone call. It's one of my clients. I'll be right back."

"Okay, I'll be right here. I'm not moving." Tammy took a sip of cool water and lit a cigarette.

Dwayne returned ten minutes later with a distraught look on his face.

"Everything okay?" Tammy asked.

"No. Not really. I gotta go. A client of mine is in a sailboat race tomorrow and his bilge pump isn't working." His face flushed with anger. "Damn it! I really wanted to get these traps done before the yard fills up with workers tomorrow. I was hoping to get them all stacked in the morning after they've had a chance to dry and before the boatyard opens." He looked over at Tammy, who appeared stunned from his sudden outburst. Clearing his throat, he continued in a calmer voice. "Maybe it won't take that long and we'll have time to finish up when I get back. I need to get out of these dirty clothes and change. Will you guys be okay until I get back?"

"Of course. Do what you have to do. We'll be fine."

Tammy understood his annoyance and disappointment; after all, she was feeling it too. They were on a roll and could have probably knocked out the last batch of traps in an hour and been done for the day.

After Dwayne left, a feeling of defiance crept over her. She refused to be defeated by the fact that Dwayne had to leave. Plus, it would be fun to surprise Dwayne if she could dip the traps by herself. She began to toil with the idea in her head. The main obstacle would be lifting them out of the box. She'd have to use her upper body strength for leverage and brace the trap against her stomach to move them on to the ground to dry, which meant she really would be covered in tar. Then she had an idea.

Determined to complete the task singlehandedly, she pulled out a roll of oversized, extra strong black trash bags and tore one off the roll before holding it lengthwise in front of her body. It reached below her knees. "Perfect! This will work." She then proceeded to make a hole, just big enough for her head in the sealed bottom, and two on the sides for her arms. Once she was satisfied with her creation, she pulled it over her head and slid her two arms in like a smock. Her entire body was now protected. Matt laughed at her new idea of fashion.

"You look funny, Mommy." He chuckled as Tammy made her way over to the traps. Using both hands and all her strength, she heaved one of the traps over to the dip box and up on to the edge. Out of breath already, she had to pause before lowering it into the box. "I can do this," she proclaimed between gasps for oxygen. After catching her breath, she lowered it into the tar and watched it sink beneath the surface. "Okay, now how the hell am I going to get this thing out and over to the other traps to dry?"

On her first attempt, she failed miserably. It was just too heavy and she soon found herself exhausted. A couple of minutes later, she had an idea. She tried picking the trap up by its short end and standing it on its side while still in the dip. From that angle, she had more leverage and could pivot the trap out of the dip and onto the top corner edge. Once there, she could let it sit and drip while she caught her breath again.

Pleased with her progress so far, she now how to figure out how to carry the trap over to the drying area without wiping most of the tar off. She couldn't hold it against her body because the side touching her would be wiped clean of tar, and again she thought about using the short side, just like she did when it was in the dip box.

Using the wonders of gravity, she inched the trap to the edge of the box and grabbed the two short sides. While holding it, she pulled it way from the box and allowed gravity to take over until the trap was just inches from the ground. From this position, even though it was a struggle, she was able to walk the trap over to the others and slowly lower it onto the ground to dry.

Matt cheered at her success. "Do another one, Mommy," he hollered from his spot in the deck chair, amused by his one-man-team mother and her terrible attire.

Now that she had the system down, Tammy knew she could get the rest of the traps done on her own. She knew she'd probably regret it afterwards and would be hurting for days to come, but she was driven by wanting to see the look on Dwayne's face when he returned and saw all the traps were dipped and laid out to dry. It would be well worth it.

He returned a few hours later, just when Tammy was dipping the last trap. Matt rushed across the yard on his tricycle to greet him. The shock on Dwayne's face was priceless as he scanned over at all the dipped traps.

"You've got to be fucking kidding me! How the hell did you manage to do all those? And what are you wearing?" He looked up and down at the trash bag now soaked with tar covering her body.

Tammy beamed him a smile. "It's a trash bag, and it worked great to protect me from the tar. Now watch," she said, excited to show him her method as she began pulling out the last trap from the box.

Fascinated and amazed, Dwayne watched as she completed dipping the last trap and set it down to dry. "Wow! You're amazing! I can't believe you did all those by yourself. Come here and give me a kiss."

"You're welcome. I knew I could do it. And now you don't have to worry about getting the rest dipped before tomorrow. They'll all be dry by the morning. I'm just sorry I won't be here to help you stack them," she said as she slowly tore the sticky bag away from her body and tossed it into the trash can.

"Oh, don't worry about that. I'll manage. You've done enough," he said, still in shock over what she had done. "Now, where's that kiss?" he asked while taking her into his arms.

"Ooh…ouch!" Tammy screeched as Dwayne squeezed her tight. "Not so hard. My shoulders are killing me."

"Oh god, you're going to be hurting later. I wish I could be home with you to give you a full body massage later. You're going to need it."

"I know. I'm going to soak my body in the tub as soon as I get home. I'm beginning to feel the pains of my labor already. Speaking of which, and I hate to say it because of how much I want to stay here and help you, I must return to my boring life in the city. I have to go to work tomorrow. But I'll be back next weekend."

"Great! Because it's gonna be just like this weekend. We're going to dip fifty more traps."

A genuine smile blanketed Tammy's face. "I'm actually looking forward to it. Call me crazy, but this beats waiting tables any day." She rubbed her back. "By then, my body should be healed and ready for the next round."

It was becoming harder to leave the marina when it was time for her to go home. She was returning to a life where she felt she no longer belonged and had absolutely nothing to look forward to.

As usual, she found Judy on the couch, and Tammy immediately zoned in on the glass of wine on the coffee table and a sudden craving for alcohol began to poke at her mind. For the entire weekend, she had been too busy to think about drinking, but as soon as she walked through her front door, the temptations were all around her. Judy followed Tammy's eyes and instantly felt the tension between them as Tammy quickly looked away from her glass.

"Sorry, I'll get rid of it," Judy said as she scurried away to the kitchen.

Exhausted from the weekend, Tammy simply nodded. "Thanks."

But she was starting to realize that she and Judy were beginning to take different paths in life. It was a realization that she didn't want to confront so instead, she headed to the bathroom for a soak.

CHAPTER 19

ammy and Matt returned to the marina the following
weekend and just as Dwayne had warned her, it was
exactly like the previous one where they spent both days
cementing and dipping another fifty traps. And, just like before,
her body was screaming with pain by the time they were finished.

Judy wasn't home when she returned. She and her kids were
spending the weekend at her boyfriend's house. But she promised
she'd be home later that night to watch Matt the following day
while Tammy worked. Tammy was expecting Judy to announce
any day now that she was moving in with Joel—that's how much
they'd grown apart. They only saw each other to drop off their
kids when one of them needed to work.

Tammy had no idea how she would manage on her own if Judy
moved out. She depended on her for a lot of things, from child
care to splitting the bills, and with her upcoming court date that
had been constantly occupying her mind, she was relying on Judy
to take care of Matt if needed.

That date was coming up fast. She only thought about it when
she was home, just like all the other worries that consumed her.

But she still hadn't managed to save any money for the fine. How could she? She was barely making enough to make ends meet as it was. During her recent visits with Dwayne, she never mentioned it to him because she always tried to leave her problems behind. Otherwise, her weekends would be ruined.

When the eve of her court date was upon her, Tammy still didn't know what to tell the judge. She knew she was out of extensions and would be facing either jail time or community service.

Feeling the urge to have a drink to calm her nerves, Tammy decided to call Dwayne, who always seemed to make her feel better during testing times. She paged him and waited for him to call her back, which he did within ten minutes.

"Hey, you okay?" he asked with concern.

"Yeah. I just wanted to hear your voice. It's a rough night. I've got court tomorrow and I'm a nervous wreck, so of course I want a drink. Because, as we both know, alcohol fixes everything." She laughed.

Dwayne sounded shocked. "It's tomorrow? Why didn't you tell me?"

"Yes, it's tomorrow, and I'm telling you now," Tammy said with a hint of sarcasm.

"But I want to be there. What time is your hearing? And which courthouse is—"

"Now wait just a minute, Dwayne. What do you mean you want to be there? What if I don't want you there? I'm kind of embarrassed by the whole thing as it is, and I'm not sure if I want you seeing me standing in front of a judge."

"Oh come on, Tammy. You're being silly. I want to give you some moral support. Can you at least allow me to do that?"

Feeling guilty for her stupidity and realizing he was willing to take time out of his busy schedule to be with her, she immediately softened her tone.

"I'm sorry. You just took me by surprise. I had no idea you

wanted to be there. Thank you. That's really sweet of you. Have you got a pen? I'll give you the details."

After giving him the address of the court, they remained on the line for a while longer until Tammy's cravings for alcohol subsided. Once she'd hung up the phone, she decided to watch the news before turning into bed. It was then that she came to a decision on what she would tell the judge tomorrow.

One of the headline stories was about Civil Brand, the women's jail in downtown Los Angeles. Apparently, they were releasing many inmates early due to an excessive problem of overcrowding. Some were only doing ten percent of their time. Tammy was glued to the set, a seed of an idea growing as she told herself what she was going to do. She just needed Judy to get home so she could talk to her. After all, she was part of the plan.

Struggling to stay awake, Judy finally arrived home sometime after eleven. Before she even had a chance to take off her coat or peek in on her sleeping kids, Tammy stopped her in her stride. "Sit down. I need to talk to you."

"Can't it wait? I just got home," Judy stated in an irate voice. The odor of alcohol resting on her breath didn't go unnoticed either.

Tammy ignored her request and motioned her to sit down on the couch. "The kids are fine. They are all sleeping. This is really important."

Judy rolled her eyes. "Fine. What's up?"

"I'm going to jail and I want to make sure you'll be able to take care of Matt."

Judy's jaw dropped. "What? Are you crazy? What do you mean you're going to jail?"

"I know it sounds crazy but I've been watching the news. They're releasing people early because of overcrowding. If I turn myself in tomorrow, I bet I'll only do a few days."

"And if you don't? What if they keep you in for most of your sentence? Which, by the way, might be weeks or even months for all you know. I'm sorry, but your idea sucks." Judy had heard enough. She shook her head in protest before attempting to leave the couch, but Tammy grabbed her arm and pulled her back down.

"Hold on a second, Judy. I have no other choice. I can't do community service. That would take up endless hours of time and I can't afford to take so much time off from work. If this goes to plan, I'll only miss a couple of days. Tell me you can watch Matt?" Tammy pleaded.

"Matt will be fine. I'll work it out with Joel. Between us, we'll be able to take care of the kids. If worse comes to worse, I can always ask my mother. But I can't believe you are seriously considering this. What does Dwayne think?"

Tammy lowered her head. "I've not told him." Then she raised her voice a notch. She was not going to argue about this. "And I'm not going to tell him. He will only try and talk me out of it like you're doing. My mind is made up."

Judy raised her hands in defeat. "Okay. It's your life. I just hope your plan works. They might keep you in for weeks. You know that, right?"

"There's a slim chance that might happen, yes. But as long as I know Matt will be okay, I'll get through it."

"Tammy, you've never been to jail. You have no idea what you're in for. I hope for your sake you're not there too long." Realizing Tammy had made up her mind and there was no more to be said, she again attempted to stand. This time, Tammy didn't stop her. "Okay then, I guess I will see you when I see you. Call me from the inside when you can, and good luck. I'm off to bed."

"I will, and thanks," Tammy said as she took Judy's hand. "You're a good friend."

Judy scuffed the top of Tammy's hair. "And don't you ever forget that." She laughed before leaving the room.

Tammy pondered her decision for a few moments and told herself she was okay with it. She was tired of the fine hanging over her head. It had been dragging on for almost eight months. She wanted to be done with it so she could move on. This was the only way.

Other than going to jail, her only other anxiety was how was Dwayne going to react. He'd only find out Tammy's plan when she told the judge.

Tammy had to be in court by 9:00 a.m. She gave herself plenty of time in the morning, to shower and get ready. She wore her best jeans that were not faded and free from any holes. Knowing she was going to jail she wanted to be comfortable. She chose not to wear any jewelry, considering the fact that she was turning herself in, and she told Matt a little white lie, that she was going to be gone a few days with Dwayne. At first, he was upset but only because, of course, he wanted to go too, but Tammy bribed him with a movie date when she returned.

She arrived at the court building a half-hour early and after parking her car, she began scanning the parking lot for Dwayne's truck. But it was a huge lot with tons of white trucks just like Dwayne's so she soon gave up. After entering the court building, she glanced down the corridors at the crowds of people sitting on wooden benches along the walls. Some were reading official documents, others were talking to well dressed men and women—who Tammy assumed were their attorneys—and many were pacing up and down the corridors with excessive nervous energy.

Tammy was disappointed to see there was no sign of Dwayne.

She thought maybe he got an emergency call from a client. And then it suddenly occurred to her that there was no way to call him from jail. He only had a beeper. She hoped he would call the house and Judy could fill him in.

While waiting for the courts to open and with no empty seats, Tammy stood against a wall and kept to herself. At the end of the hallway, a woman was crying as she clung to who Tammy believed was her husband. The man tried to console her but failed miserably, and more people began to stare in her direction as her cries became louder and more frantic. Tammy wondered if he was going to jail today also.

Distracted by the woman's cries, Tammy hadn't noticed Dwayne walk in, and she jumped when he squeezed her shoulder. "Fuck! You scared me," she roared while holding her chest.

Dwayne chuckled. "I'm sorry. I thought you saw me."

"That's okay." Tammy leaned in and gave him a peck on the cheek. "Thanks for coming. But you didn't have to, you know?"

He wrapped an arm around her shoulders and pulled her in close. "But I wanted to be here. You don't have to thank me." He glanced down at his watch. "It's almost nine. You should be going in soon. Are you nervous?"

"Yes, I'm nervous. I just want this to be over."

"And it will be," Dwayne reassured her.

Tammy considered telling him her plan, but after no more than a few seconds, she decided against it. She knew he'd only protest and would try every possible way to talk her out of it. Once in the courtroom before the judge, she knew he couldn't say anything.

A few minutes later, the doors of the courtrooms were opened and people began to shuffle in. Tammy swallowed the lump in her throat and tried to calm her accelerated nerves. "Ready?" she asked Dwayne while taking his hand.

He squeezed her hand tight. "You'll be fine. I'll take you out for a fancy lunch afterwards."

Tammy knew he wouldn't be able to, but she simply nodded as

they walked hand in hand into the courtroom and took a seat near the back next to a much younger man and an older couple, who Tammy assumed were his parents. For the next five minutes, Tammy watched as people of all races and ages continued to file in and claim their seats, all waiting to hear their fate from the judge.

The noise level steadily increased as people took their seats and talked with each other and their attorneys. Tammy and Dwayne remained quiet. Occasionally, Dwayne gave Tammy a comforting rub on the shoulders and asked if she was okay, and Tammy gave him a simple nod.

A few minutes later, everyone stood and the room fell into complete silence as the judge entered and took his seat of authority. Tammy swallowed another lump in her throat before sitting again. Her nerves were now at their peak, but she managed to hide them successfully from Dwayne.

For the next hour, they listened to cases mostly about traffic violations—speeding, parking violations, and DUI's like Tammy's case. One girl cried before the judge as she stood next to her attorney—something Tammy couldn't afford—and listened as the judge gave her a final extension. Tammy wondered if she too would be turning herself in to jail in three months.

Another guy said he could pay the fine, sending vibes of jealously through Tammy, and the last guy chose community service and was required to do 500 hours. Tammy gasped and calculated the amount of days that would be. She whispered in Dwayne's ear, "Wow! That's over twelve weeks."

"Maybe he had priors?" Dwayne whispered back.

"I don't think so. Not with a DUI."

Suddenly, Tammy heard her name echo through the courtroom. "Shit, I'm up," she said under her breath into Dwayne's ear while handing him her purse.

Dwayne gave her arm a gentle rub as she squeezed past him and made her way to the front of the courtroom, feeling all eyes upon her. She stood in silence before the judge as he peered over his glasses and read her case. She could do nothing but wait for him to speak.

As she waited, a thousand questions raced through her mind, none of which she had no answers to. *How will Dwayne react? Will Matt be okay? Will I still have a job?* She hadn't told her boss because he had the next two days off and was hoping she'd be out of jail by the time she had to go back.

The judge interrupted her thoughts and gave her a stern look as he read the DUI charge to her. Then, with a cold, harsh stare, he asked, "What is it going to be, Miss Mellows? Today, you must either pay the fine, do community service, or do jail time."

Tammy hesitated before answering. Was she doing the right thing? She had no other choice.

"Miss Mellows?" the judge asked again.

Tammy looked straight ahead, not taking her eyes off the judge. "I'll…um…I'll do jail time, Your Honor."

Suddenly, Tammy heard an outburst from the spot behind her where she knew Dwayne was sitting. "What!" he screeched, along with gasps from many others.

Tammy didn't look at Dwayne. She couldn't. She would only weaken, and she couldn't allow that to happen.

The judge ordered silence and stated, "So be it, Miss Mellows. I sentence you to twenty-one days in the county jail."

Tammy was shocked by the amount of time the judge had ordered her to serve. It was much more than she had anticipated. What had she done? She would never be out in a few days with that much time to start with.

There was another outburst from Dwayne. "Wait. I can pay the fine!" he yelled. Tammy turned and saw him pulling out a wad of bills from his front pocket and holding it up to show the judge.

The judge gave Dwayne an angry stare. "One more outburst from you and I'll hold you in contempt of court."

"But…" Dwayne said in a softer tone as he returned to his seat, realizing the judge was not going to listen to him.

Tammy felt her eyes beginning to mist. Struggling to hold it together, she quickly turned back towards the judge. If she looked at Dwayne again, her knees would just buckle beneath her and she refused to let him see her that way. She committed the crime, and there was no way she was going to allow Dwayne to bail her out. She had to take responsibility for her own actions.

Once the court was back in order after Dwayne's outburst, the judge focused on Tammy again. "Miss Mellows, did you want to begin serving your sentence immediately or do you need some time to arrange things at home and turn yourself in at a later date, which I would set today?"

Again, while rubbing her sweaty palms across her stomach, Tammy hesitated and swallowed hard before answering. "I would like to begin my time immediately, Your Honor."

Again, Dwayne couldn't refrain himself. "What! Tammy, you—"

"Silence!" the judge ordered before turning to the bailiff and instructing him to take Tammy into custody.

Tammy couldn't hold back her tears any longer and allowed them to fall as the bailiff approached her. Showing no sympathy, he ordered her to put her hands behind her back. Waves of whispers rolled through the courtroom as Tammy felt the cold metal of the handcuffs grasp her skin. She shuddered when she heard them snap closed.

Without looking back, her heart tore at what she was putting Dwayne through, leaving him to witness her being led out of the courtroom in handcuffs. She wished now she had insisted he hadn't come. What thoughts would be going through his head as he drove home alone with only her purse sitting next to him? Tammy wouldn't blame him at all if he didn't want to see her ever again.

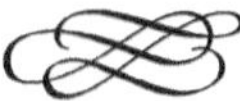

*D*wayne was numb from what he just witnessed, and for the next hour he sat lifeless in the courtroom with images of Tammy in handcuffs haunting his mind.

She knew all along she was going to turn herself in. Why didn't she tell me? Why didn't she let me pay the fine?

He looked over at her purse, alone on the chair next to him where Tammy had been sitting just a short while ago. He pictured her sitting in a cell, crying and scared. He wasn't angry with her. He was disappointed that she hadn't confided in him or asked for his help. He knew she was independent and hard-headed, but yet again her pride got in her way. She didn't have to go to jail. They could have worked this out.

Oh, Tammy, what have you done? How am I supposed to go back to my life knowing you are locked up for the next twenty-one days?

Lost in his thoughts, the distant voice of the judge calling, "Court is dismissed," followed by the loud knocking of the gavel on his wooden desk brought Dwayne back to reality. He hadn't been expecting to leave the court alone. He wasn't prepared for this. He didn't want to abandon Tammy knowing she was probably still somewhere in the courthouse. But she had left him no other choice.

Before standing, he took one last look at the door where she had been led away and with a heavy heart, he picked up her purse and forced himself to leave for the lonely drive home.

Once Tammy had been escorted out of the courtroom, she let her tears fall. The tears weren't from fear of what lay ahead for her. They were for Dwayne. The thought of him sitting alone, oblivious to her plan and watching as she was taken into custody, unable to do anything about it. It pulled at her heart strings. She knew she had hurt him and regretted now not telling him. It was selfish of her for putting him through that and she wondered if he would ever forgive her. Did she just destroy the best thing that had ever happened to her? Sadly, she wouldn't know until she was free again. The not knowing was going to be harder than being locked up in jail.

She was led to a room where some other female inmates of various nationalities sat waiting. Some were Hispanic, two were of color, and the remaining four were white. Tammy was relieved the guard had removed the handcuffs before locking the door behind him.

She was greeted by silent nods and screening stares from the other females. She nodded back and made her way to a desolate corner and quietly took a seat, keeping to herself.

She remained in the room for the next four hours. Two other women were brought in during that time. One was Hispanic and crying, and the other was a petite blond who Tammy knew was high just by looking at her dilated eyes. Past experiences had taught her that was a dead giveaway. She had seen the look too many times with Steven.

Not knowing what to expect, Tammy remained tense for the

entire time she was in the room. The constant sound of her heart hammering against her chest prevented her from talking. A couple of the women nodded in her direction, usually followed by the words, "Hey, what are you in for?" After she had told them a DUI, they again nodded and left her alone while they chatted with other women. Tammy got the impression it wasn't their first time in jail.

The room where they were being kept was small, and the lack of air quickly became apparent. Many of the women, Tammy included, began wiping their sweaty brows with their sleeves. Others walked back and forth, complaining of the heat while fanning their faces with their hands. Outer layers of garments were removed and tossed in corners, and everyone expressed a need for water to quench their elevated thirst. As the hours dragged on, some of the women became irritated and began yelling.

"Hey, we need some water here!" one shouted from the other side of the tiny room.

"This is fucking bullshit. I wouldn't keep my dog in these conditions," another shouted with her face pressed against the door.

But nobody came.

Tammy cowered in the corner as their ranting continued. A young Hispanic girl sat next to her and they both muttered a few words, each sensing they were not a threat to one another. They remained seated next to each other for the rest of their time in the room.

When the sound of footsteps could be heard approaching the door, silence swept over the room and smiles of relief replaced the frowns on most faces. With anticipation, all eyes focused on the door, waiting for it to open. Two sheriffs entered the room, both with their hands cupped over guns hanging from their hips, ready to grab them if necessary. "Okay, everybody form a single line."

Immediately, all the women stood to attention and faced the officers. Tammy was at the back of the line and watched as each girl was handcuffed with their hands in front of them before being led out in single file. Tammy cringed when she felt the familiar sensation of the cold metal touching her skin and the snap of the cuffs binding her wrists.

They were led out into a narrow corridor, with one of the sheriffs in front and the other at the end of the line behind Tammy. After a maze of corridors and locked double doors, they ended up outside at the back of the courthouse. Tammy breathed in heavily, filling her lungs with the welcoming fresh air that greeted them. Parked at the curb was a black and white jail bus with all the widows barred. One by one, the women were instructed to board the bus in single file. Just like the room, the bus was hot and stuffy. Tammy took an extra moment to breathe in and fill her lungs one more time with the fresh air before being told to "move it" by the sheriff standing behind her.

The noise level on the bus was deafening. All the women seemed happy to finally be out of the hot room, and the small amount of fresh air they'd managed to grasp in transit seemed to have perked them up and put them in better spirits. Tammy quickly scanned the bus for the girl she sat next to in the holding tank and spotted her in the middle on the right. She was relieved to see the seat next to her had not been taken and quickly scurried over to her. The woman smiled when she recognized Tammy and patted the seat next to her with cuffed hands.

Within two minutes, the engine of the bus began to roar and the doors slid closed. The two sheriffs at the front exchanged a few words before the driver put the bus in gear and drove out of the covered parking lot, onto the main street and into congested traffic.

While sitting idle at the traffic lights, Tammy looked out of the window over her new friend's shoulder and noticed all the people in the cars surrounding them. She found herself envious of their freedom. They were going about their daily lives, traveling wherever they pleased and whenever they wanted with no restrictions.

Some were with friends or loved ones. Others had their children in the back seat.

Tammy thought of her son. Was he missing his mom as much as she was missing him? What was he doing right now? She choked back her tears at the thought of not being there at night to tuck him into bed. *I'm sorry, Matt. Mommy will be home soon.* Tammy remained silent with her thoughts as the bus meandered through the traffic on its way to Civil Brand, the women's county jail.

Tammy guessed it took about an hour to arrive at the back entrance of the jail. Once the bus had come to a complete stop, the doors were opened and the women were ordered to exit. They were led by the two same officers, again one at the front and one at the back, through a large metal gate and then through several sets of double doors, all of which had to be buzzed opened. Standing on the other side were two hefty female guards dressed in brown uniforms. They stood straight, with their feet apart and their fingers curled around the leather of their belts. Their stares were cold and their bodies were stiff. Immediately, one of them took authority and yelled at the women.

"Okay, ladies! Follow me in single file and there will be no talking."

Obeying her orders, the women fell silent and followed her down the cold lime green hallway. They had to go through three more locked metal gates before they reached the holding tank where they would wait until booked. A guard stood at the doorway of the holding tank and removed the handcuffs from each woman before she shuffled away.

When it came to Tammy's turn and her wrists were free, she began rubbing them vigorously to relieve the constant urge to itch that she had been experiencing for the past hour. The room was about the same size as the one at the courthouse but painted the same ugly lime green like the hallways, and like the other holding tank, it had no windows. Concrete benches hugged the walls, and there were just enough seating spaces for the dozen or so women, although a few chose to stand in the middle of the room.

Tammy sat across from the same woman as before and nodded when she saw her. The woman nodded back and then folded her arms and closed her eyes. Tammy tried again to keep to herself, but a colored woman sitting next to her, dressed in a skimpy black dress, black stiletto heels and wearing heavy makeup, nudged her arm. "Whatcha in for, girl?"

Tammy felt the lump rise in her throat but swallowed it before answering. Unable to hide the nervousness in her voice, she softly answered, "DUI."

"Your first one?"

"Yes."

The woman nudged her arm again. "They got me for prostitution. Third time I've been 'ere in a month." Again, she nudged Tammy's arm. "A woman's gotta make a living, right?"

"Right," Tammy quickly agreed, wishing the woman would leave her alone.

"So what's your name, girl?"

"Tammy."

"You're a shy one, ain't you?"

Tammy didn't reply. Instead, she looked down at her feet and rubbed her arm, which was now sore from the constant nudges she had been receiving.

"Everyone calls me Raven," the woman said before letting out a loud laugh and putting her face close to Tammy's. "That's because I'm dark and mysterious." To block the stench of alcohol coming from the woman's mouth, Tammy quickly turned her head and held her breath. She rolled her eyes as Raven continued to talk. "You'll be fine, girl. Just keep to yourself and don't piss anybody off. They ain't gonna keep you here long. Before you know it, you'll be out."

"Thanks. I hope so," Tammy replied before folding her arms

against her chest and closing her eyes, hoping the woman would sense she wanted to be left alone.

To her relief, she did, and she began talking to the woman on her other side.

Finally left to her thoughts, Tammy sat quietly, her eyes still closed and her mind filled with thought of all the things she took for granted: her son, her home, Dwayne, and most of all, her freedom. She wondered how long it would be before she would be able to experience any of that again.

She was overcome with shame when thoughts of family entered her head. Her father, Joanne, her mother, and her two older sisters. What would they think of her if they could see her now? She didn't want to know the answer to that. She had let everyone down, including herself. Once she got out of this wretched place, she was going to make sure she'd never be back. Even though she had managed not to drink alcohol for almost two months, she now knew for certain she would never touch the stuff ever again.

She didn't know how long they were kept in the holding tank, but it felt like hours. She had lost all track of time. She had no idea if it was still daylight outside or night time. She was hungry, her mouth was dry from her long-suffering thirst and her body was stiff from sitting on the hard, cold benches. When a few of the women were called and escorted out of the room, Tammy wondered where they were being taken. Were they released or being moved to another part of the jail? Every time a guard entered the room, the chatter of the women ceased in the hopes they would hear their name called. Tammy held her breath, wondering if she'd be call next. Utters of disappointment and a few cuss words were exchanged amongst the women when they were left behind. Tammy's heart sank at the notion that she was to remain in the same room for much longer. Being idle for so long was killing her. She wasn't use to wasting her days away by just sitting in one spot for hours on end.

Tammy wasn't sure how much time went by until a guard entered the room again. "Tammy Mellows," she heard through the fog in her mind. All heads scanned the room, looking to see who the name belonged to.

"Here," Tammy said nervously while rising to her feet.

"Come with me," was all the guard said.

As Tammy made her way to the front of the room, some on the women patted her on her shoulder as she walked by.

"Bye, girl," she heard from Raven.

She was led down a maze of corridors and through more metal gates until they reached a counter with a small window at head height. The guard instructed her to stand by the window. Tammy did as she was told and remained motionless, afraid to make any sudden moves that might startle the guard. A middle-aged woman, heavyset with dark brown hair and dressed in the same uniform as the others, appeared at the window and handed Tammy a plastic bag.

"Place all your valuables in the bag. Jewelry, cash, wallet, purse."

"I have none," Tammy quietly said.

The woman retrieved the bag. "Okay then." She looked Tammy over. "What size are you? About a medium?"

"Yes, I think so," Tammy replied.

The woman disappeared and returned a few minutes later with an orange jumpsuit and handed it to Tammy. "Here you go. This should fit. Follow the guard down the hall."

Tammy picked up the jumpsuit and proceeded down the hallway behind the guard. Her stomach rumbled as she walked. She wondered when they were going to feed her. She hadn't eaten or drank anything in hours. What she wouldn't give for a glass of water right now.

The guard led her in to a room on the left, where another guard with glasses and blond hair pulled up into a bun was waiting. The room was painted in the same lime green, and a wooden desk sat in the center, piled high with papers. The box of rubber gloves sitting on the edge didn't go unnoticed. A pile of large plastic bags sat on the floor next to the desk, and a black and white chart showing measurements in feet hung on the back wall.

The guard that had brought Tammy in nodded to her co-worker.

"I'll take it from here," the co-worker said while looking at a file. She paid no attention to Tammy.

After the other guard left, Tammy stood in the middle of the room, her heart pounding beneath her skin, her bones rattling from the cold, desolate room. The guard still hadn't looked at her. She might as well have been a crumb on the floor.

"Are you Tammy Mellows?" the guard finally asked while continuing to look at the papers in her hand.

"Yes."

"Okay then. Approach the desk."

Tammy did as she was told and waited for the next order.

The guard opened one of the desk drawers, pulled out a fingerprint kit and a book and laid them on the surface of the desk. "I need your right hand," the guard said in a flat tone.

Tammy lifted her hand and allowed the guard to maneuver it across the ink. But the guard struggled to get it in the exact position she wanted. "Relax your hand," she commanded.

Tammy tried her best, but she could still feel the tension in her muscles as she watched the guard first roll her index across the ink and then her thumb.

"That's good enough. Now go stand against the wall in front of the chart and face me."

With nothing to wipe her inked fingers on, Tammy rubbed them across her jeans as she walked over to the wall. She blinked as the flash of a camera took her by surprise. She didn't need to ask what she looked like in the picture, but she didn't dare ask for a re-take.

"Okay, I need you to strip down and put your clothes in here." The guard handed Tammy one of the plastic bags.

"You want me to take *all* my clothes off?"

"That's what I said, isn't it? Now come on. I've not got all day."

Tammy was horrified that she had to remove all her clothing and stand naked before this woman. How humiliating. Up until now, she had managed to hold it together, but this was the worst feeling in the world. She had never felt so degraded and unimportant. This was just wrong. She felt the tears welling up in her eyes as she slowly began to undress, first her shirt, and then her jeans. She folded them carefully and placed them in the bag along with her tennis shoes and socks. She felt a sudden chill, as her skin was now exposed to the cold, damp air of the room. Hesitating, she remained standing in only her bra and panties, and she slowly lifted her arms to cover her chest.

"Come on. I need the underwear too." The guard seemed agitated.

Tammy looked away and closed her eyes, trying to stop the tears from falling. Taking a deep breath, she removed first her bra and then her panties. She dropped them in the bag, her hands now shivering from the cold.

The guard set down the papers and pulled a flashlight out of her back pocket. "Open your mouth," she instructed as she strode across the room, flashlight in hand.

Tammy obeyed and looked up while the guard shone the bright light into her mouth and then into her eyes. Next, with a puzzled expression, Tammy watched as the guard put on a pair of rubber gloves. "Now face the wall and spread your legs apart," she said as if it were a perfectly normal request.

"What?" Tammy squealed in disbelief.

"Just do it."

Tammy wanted to do nothing but run into a corner and hide. Never had she felt so humiliated and violated by another human being. She realized now they were searching her for drugs. Wanting to get this over with as quickly as possible, she walked over to the wall with her arms covering her breasts and did what the guard instructed. Once the intrusion was over, she heard the words she'd be longing to hear. "Okay, you can get dressed now."

Tammy couldn't pull the white cotton underwear and orange jumpsuit on fast enough. She wrapped her arms around the ugly suit, enjoying the protection from nakedness it gave her.

Once dressed, the guard led Tammy out of the room, where another guard was waiting beside the door. She was once again led through a maze of corridors and brought to a huge hall full of cots. There must have been at least fifty of them. Each had one flat pillow and a brown blanket. At the entrance of the hall was a booth surrounded by glass and a small hole to speak into. Inside the booth, Tammy saw four female guards.

"This is where you'll be spending your time. You're assigned to bed twenty-eight." The guard pointed to the middle of the room. "Over there."

Tammy scanned the room. There were only three other inmates inside, and all were looking her way.

"But where's everyone else? This place is empty," Tammy said with uncertainty.

"Yep. We did a bunch of early releases this week. Now, go claim your bed. They'll be calling you for dinner pretty soon."

Tammy's heart sank and tears gushed down her cheeks.

What have I done? They've already done all the early releases. I may be in here for weeks, Oh god...Matt, Dwayne, I'm so, so sorry.

CHAPTER 22

Dwayne didn't know how long he sat in his truck in the parking lot of the court. In fact, he didn't even remember walking to his truck. When he'd left the courtroom, he was feeling so numb that he was oblivious to everything around him. He remembered staring out of the window of his truck and just looking over at the courthouse, knowing Tammy was still in there somewhere.

He believed she wasn't aware how much she had hurt him. She had obviously put some thought into turning herself in today, because he knew she would've had to arrange for someone to watch Matt while she was locked up. Dwayne assumed it was Judy. So, if Judy knew what she was going to do, who else knew? "Why didn't you talk to me, Tammy?" He crashed his fist down on the dash and looked over at her purse before yelling some more. "You should be sitting here next to me. We were supposed to go have lunch!" He couldn't help but feel disappointment toward her. He thought their relationship had reached a level where she could trust and confide in him. Obviously, he had been wrong.

He was steered away from his thoughts by a screaming mother, who was chasing a young child through the parking lot while yelling at him to stop running and wait for her. Dwayne watched as the child turned and looked at his mother, laughed, and then began running again. He waited until they were far enough away from his truck and fired it up. He turned and looked at Tammy's purse one more time, shook his head, put the truck in gear, and pulled out of the parking to head back to the marina. Alone.

Tammy was lying on her assigned bed with her stomach in knots from hunger and her mouth so dry that she was finding it hard to swallow. A loud female voice suddenly came over an intercom.

"Stand up next to your beds. Dinner is in fifteen minutes."

The thought of food and liquid gave Tammy an instant boost. She jumped to her feet and realized she must have dozed off when she saw there were now at least a dozen other women in the hall, some she recognized from the holding tank.

The guards followed the same procedure as before and led the women in single file, one in front and another in the back, to a massive food hall two hallways down. The fowl stench of the food hit Tammy's nostrils as soon as she entered the room. It reminded her of the smell of school dinners, something she always used to hate. She gasped at the number of inmates crowded in the hall. There must have been hundreds of them, all wearing orange jump-suits, sitting twenty to a table, ten on each side. Tammy tried not to make eye contact with anyone as her group was led to the front and made to stand in line with a plastic plate. But she could feel the daunting stares as she nervously walked by, keeping her eyes fixed to the ground.

Tammy watched with disgust, curling her lip, as dollops of

mashed potatoes, creamed corn, and what she thought was some sort of meat dish in a disgusting tanned color sauce was plopped on her plate. Not to mention the three cooks drenched in sweat that were responsible for serving it. The last cook handed her a carton of milk and a bottle of water. With her food in hand, her group was led to a table near the back of the room and ordered to sit.

Tammy sat next to an Asian girl who seemed harmless enough and nodded in her direction as she took a seat. The Asian girl rolled her eyes, muttered something under her breath and then turned the other way.

Tammy felt hurt by being shunned; she was just trying to get along with whoever crossed her path while locked up in this hell-hole. Tammy decided to give her the same treatment and ignored her for the rest of mealtime.

The girl across from her, who she found out was called Charley, seemed okay. She smiled at Tammy when she sat down, said hello and immediately asked her name. She was about Tammy's age and was in for shoplifting. Apparently, it was her fourth time committing the same crime.

Consumed with hunger, Tammy cleaned her plate of the vile looking food within minutes. She would have eaten a frog if it was put in front of her. She gradually felt the stomach pains begin to subside and after drinking the bottle of water in one continuous gulp, she was beginning to feel like herself again.

After her meal, she chatted some more with Charley before being interrupted by the same guard that had brought her and the group to the hall. She stood at the end of the table and instructed them to pick up their plates and stand. Tammy said a quick goodbye to her new friend and followed the guard and the others to the trash bins to throw away their plates before being led back to their beds.

When they returned to the hall of beds, Tammy thought she was in a different place. The room was now over half full with inmates. Some were curled up sleeping, others were grouped on beds laughing and singing, and a few sat on their own sobbing. Tammy couldn't believe how quickly the room had filled up in just a few hours. Her spirits were suddenly lifted with hope. *Maybe there is a chance of getting an early release after all.*

She spotted her friend from earlier sitting on the edge of a bed, talking to another girl. She saw Tammy walk in and waved her over. Relieved to have someone to talk to, Tammy immediately took her up on the invite and scurried over to join them. Conversations between them were light and friendly. She found out the other girl's name was Amelia. Oddly enough, it was the first time in jail for all of them. Six unpaid parking tickets for Amelia, and a DUI for the other new girl called Sandra—who, ironically, also swore she would never drink again.

Suddenly, an outburst from the back of the hall startled Tammy and the rest of the women

"You, fuckin' bitch! I'm gonna kick your ass!" a rough-looking fair skinned woman yelled at the top of her voice to a petite young colored woman.

Everyone else froze and turned to watch the commotion in silence. Only the two women could be heard. Tammy watched in horror as the heavyset woman grabbed the other woman by her hair and threw her to the ground.

Others close by began to chant, "Fight! Fight!"

"Isn't anyone going to stop them? They'll kill each other," Tammy shrieked to Amelia and Sandra.

Within a few seconds, a loud horn went off and an angry voice came over the intercom as five guards hurried out of the booth.

"Back to your beds. Now!" the voice yelled.

Tammy leapt to her feet and dashed over to her bed and sat on the edge. She watched as the guards raced over to the two women, who were still in a raging fight on the ground, and yanked them apart.

"Okay! Break it up!" one of the guards yelled.

Tammy was astonished it took all five guards to break up the fight and drag the two women out of the hall.

With the commotion over, the room soon began to return to normal and sounds of chatter and laughter filtered around the remaining women. But a few minutes later, the angry voice came over the intercom again.

"Okay. You ladies don't know how to behave. Lights out in five minutes."

Tammy heard the protest from many of the women around the hall, yelling cuss words and using finger gestures to express their disapproval. But they were ignored and in five minutes, as promised, all the main lights went out, leaving just a few dim ones to illuminate the room. Tammy curled up in her bed and fell asleep listening to the whispers and subtle giggling of the few that refused to go to sleep.

~

She wasn't sure how long she had been sleeping and thought she was dreaming when she heard loud voice calling her name.

"Tammy Mellows! Wake up!"

Tammy stirred in her sleep but still hadn't opened her eyes.

"Tammy Mellows!" the voice shouted again.

She realized she wasn't dreaming and remembered where she was. Groans and complaints came from the other women, as they too were now awake from the yelling of the guard. Tammy sat up and rubbed her eyes, and then she spotted the guard standing two beds away.

"Get up, Mellows. You're going home."

"What?" she asked. But she didn't need to be told twice and jumped out of bed as fast as a bolt of lightning. "Are you serious?"

"As serious as I am standing here. Get up and follow me."

With her eyes now focused and adapted to the dim lights, Tammy scanned the beds and saw every single one was occupied. *My god! This place filled up in a matter of hours.*

"Come on! Move it!" the guard yelled.

"Coming. Coming," Tammy quickly replied, her heart racing with excitement.

As the guard marched toward the door, Tammy hurried to catch up with her. Once in hearing range, she found the courage to ask, "What time is it?"

Without looking back, the guard replied, "A little after midnight."

Tammy calculated in her head that she'd only served under twelve hours from the time she was first handcuffed in the courthouse until now. She chuckled to herself. That worked out to be over a hundred dollars an hour of her fifteen hundred dollar fine. Unlike before, she was now chuffed to bits about her decision to turn herself in. No one could argue with the outcome. Finally, the DUI that had been hanging over her head for months was now finally behind her. She had done everything the courts had requested her do and now she could move forward with her life.

Lobster fishing was the first thing that came to mind. She was now free to figure out a way to go fishing with Dwayne. That is if he still wanted to be with her after the stunt she pulled in the courtroom.

The release process took a few hours, but by 2:00 a.m., Tammy found herself standing on the streets of Los Angeles at the back of the jail. She was happy to see it was a full moon, the night air was warm and the street was well illuminated with lights.

To her right, she saw a row of phone booths, conveniently placed for the newly released inmates like herself. But panic consumed her at the sight of the phones. She hadn't thought this far ahead in her plan. She had no money! She couldn't call Dwayne, as he only had a pager and couldn't call collect on it. The only option she had was to call her house and wake up Judy, but she couldn't expect her to pack all the sleeping kids into the car and come to pick her up. She didn't want to put Judy or the kids through that. Tammy thought long and hard.

She had an idea and walked over to one of the phone booths and reluctantly dialed zero to call the operator. After two rings, a woman's voice came on the line.

"This is the operator; how may I help you?"

"Yes, I'd like to make a collect call," Tammy quickly replied.

After giving the woman the number to her house, Judy answered the phone after a few rings in a sleepy voice and had apparently accepted the charges.

"You're now connected," the operator confirmed before leaving the line.

"Judy! Judy, it's me. I'm so sorry to wake you, but there was no one else I could call. I'm out! Can you believe it?"

Judy snapped out of her drowsy state. "What? You're kidding me?"

"Yes! My plan worked. How is my baby boy? I can't wait to hold him. Listen, I want you to page Dwayne and punch in this phone number when it alerts you for a call back number. I don't want you to wake the kids to come get me."

"Sure, not a problem."

"Thanks. It's late, so I'm not sure if he will return the page tonight. He may think it's a job and wait till morning. I'll give him twenty minutes. If he doesn't call me by then, I'm going to have to call you back and I'm afraid you'll have to come pick me up."

"That's fine. I'm just glad you're out. Will you be coming back here?"

"Yes! I want to see Matt in the morning." Tammy then proceeded to give Judy Dwayne's pager number and the number to the phone booth.

"Okay, I'll make the call and then I'm going back to bed. Call me if you need me."

"Will do, and thank you."

After hanging up the phone, Tammy looked at her empty wrist and realized she wasn't wearing her watch. "Damn it!" she whispered under her breath and began pacing the sidewalk, desperately hoping the phone in the booth would ring soon. Knowing Dwayne would have to get dressed and walk across the boat yard to return the call, Tammy gave him some time.

After what seemed like hours, although it was probably only ten minutes, the phone still hadn't rung. "Come on, Dwayne. Call me back," Tammy pleaded out loud as she huddled her body in her arms and continued to pace back and forth to keep warm.

Suddenly, a car pulled alongside the curb and a window wound down.

"Hey! You need a ride?" yelled a male voice from inside the car.

Tammy froze. "No, I'm good. Thank you."

"It's awfully cold out here. I can take you any place you wanna go," said a young colored man, who Tammy guessed was probably in his late twenties.

"I have a ride. Thanks again."

The man leaned out of the car window. "I don't see no car here."

Suddenly, a loud ring came from one of the phone booths. "That's him. I gotta go." Tammy rejoiced before dashing over to the phone. In the distance, she heard the car speed off and released a huge sigh of relief.

She swiped the receiver off the hook so fast she almost dropped it. "Dwayne! Dwayne! Are you there?"

"Tammy! Yes, I'm here. How are you able to call me?"

"I'm out! I'm standing outside the jail and I need a ride. Can you come get me? I'm all alone and it's pretty creepy out here."

"You're out? Oh my god! Yes! Yes! Of course I can come get you. It's going to take me a while to get there. Hang tight, okay?"

"Okay…and, Dwayne?"

"Yes?"

"I'm so sorry for not telling you I was going to turn myself in."

"It's okay. You can explain later. Let me get on the road. I'll see you soon."

"Okay, and thank you," Tammy replied in a soft voice before hanging up.

Tammy knew it would take Dwayne at least an hour to get to the jail from the marina and spent her time pacing the sidewalk to stay warm, hoping no more strangers would stop to offer her a ride. She kept herself occupied by trying to think of ways to go fishing with Dwayne in September—if he allowed her to, that was. Tammy racked her brains, trying to come up with a solution on who could watch Matt. *There has to be a way!*

Suddenly, after what seemed like an eternity, she saw bright headlights coming down the road. Unable to see the vehicle, Tammy shielded her eyes from the glare and backed away from the curb with uncertainty, not knowing if it was another stranger.

As it approached the curb, Tammy clearly recognized it as Dwayne's truck and raced over to meet him. Once it was in park, she saw Dwayne lean over and unlock the passenger side. Tammy yanked open the door and immediately saw her purse sitting on the seat. She picked it up and hugged it. "My purse! Thank you for taking it," she said while hopping into the truck.

"Well, you left me no choice." Tammy sensed his sarcasm and knew he deserved an explanation. He leaned over and gave her a hug. "Welcome home," he said with what Tammy felt was a forced smile. It wasn't the welcome she had hoped for and felt she needed to smooth things out before they could move forward in their relationship.

Dwayne put the truck in drive and casually said, "I'll take you home."

With no mention of him spending the night, Tammy felt the tension between them. She reached over and placed her hand on his thigh. He didn't reciprocate, which had Tammy worried.

"Dwayne, I'm sorry I didn't tell you I was going to jail. I knew if I did, you'd talk me out of it somehow and I couldn't let that happen."

He turned and gave her a stern look. "Why would that have been so bad, Tammy? You didn't even give me the chance to help you. I had the money. This could have been prevented. You didn't have to go to jail. And yeah, my feelings were hurt. I thought you could talk to me."

"I know that now. You know the crap I went through with Steven. I've always had to figure out stuff for myself, and I guess I've become hard-headed because of it. I'm so used to my one-man army that I don't know how to ask for help. And besides, why should you pay for a crime I committed? That's not right."

Dwayne released a slight chuckle, which lifted Tammy's spirits a little. "First of all, I'm not Steven, and second, I would have made sure you paid me back. I wasn't going to make it that easy." He reached over and took her hand. "From now on, if something's bothering you, know that you can talk to me about it. Okay?"

Tammy finally relaxed in her seat. He was right. She should be able to trust him and reach out to him. "I'm sorry. I'll try and change my stubborn ways."

Dwayne laughed. "That's better. Now come over here and give me a kiss. I've missed you, woman. Don't ever pull something like that again."

"I won't. I promise." With a huge grin, she hastily scooted over to his side, snuggled into the embrace of his arms and gave him a hard kiss on the cheek. It felt good to be close to him again. She breathed in his scent and knew this is where she belonged. She thought for a moment and with hesitation decided she was going to share what was troubling her. "You know, there is something that is bothering me. It has for a while and I don't know what to do about it."

"Really?" Dwayne sounded pleased she was about to confide in him. "Well, go on, tell me. Maybe I can help. It begins by sharing. See?"

The butterflies she was feeling were somewhat calmed by his humor. "I don't think you can help, but maybe you have some ideas that will help me." Tammy took a deep breath. "You know, for the past month or two, I've been working really hard with helping you get ready to go fishing and I've loved every minute of it." She stalled for a moment.

"Go on," Dwayne urged her.

"Well, I'd like to be there when you start reaping the rewards."

Dwayne took his eyes off the road for a second and looked at her. "You mean you want to go fishing with me?"

"Yes, if you'd let me."

"I would love it! Why should that bother you? Do you think I wouldn't want you to come with me? I was actually going to ask you this week. But apparently, you had other plans of going to jail." He laughed, but Tammy could hear the excitement in his voice.

"Really? I would love to go!"

"Tammy, I love the idea of you being out there with me. It gets so friggin' lonely. So what's the problem? Why does it bother you? Do you think I was going to say no after you've been right there next to me, working just as hard as me? I wouldn't do that."

"No, that's not it. I can't just take off for a week. Who's going to watch Matt, and what about my job? That's what's been bothering me. I have no one to watch him and my job isn't going to allow me to take a week off. Not only that, I can't afford to lose a week's pay."

Dwayne's tone suddenly became flat. "Oh, I see what you mean. That is a problem. Hmm, we're going to have to think about this one."

"I've been thinking for weeks now and can't come up with a solution. Judy can't watch him; not only will she have to work, she will have figure out who will watch her kids if I do go. I thought about asking my sister, but she's afraid of watching him ever since he fell at her house one time and split his lip. There is no one else. And I can't take him with us. It's too dangerous."

Dwayne suddenly mentioned an idea that hadn't occurred to Tammy. "What about your parents?"

"My parents? You mean my dad and Joanne?" Tammy creased her brow. "You do know they live in Florida, right?"

"I know. Maybe they would like to spend some time with their grandson. When was the last time they saw him?"

"Oh, I don't know, Dwayne. That's an awfully long way to go, and I'd have to put him on a plane. I don't think I can do that. And besides, there's still the issue with my job."

"Well, that's easy. Just quit. You'll get a cut of the money we make fishing, so you'll still be getting a paycheck."

"Quit?" Tammy was horrified by his suggestion. "I can't quit! What will I do when I get back?"

Tammy suddenly realized they were pulling into her driveway. She had been so busy talking about her hopes of going fishing that she hadn't been paying attention to their drive. Once the truck was in park, Dwayne turned to her and gave her a passionate kiss on the lips. "You know there really is a simple solution to this."

"There is?" Tammy replied with her eyes narrowed.

"Sure. Quit your job, you and Matt come live with me on the boat, and you can become a commercial fisherwoman. There are only a handful in California, you know?"

"Is that a word? Fisherwoman?"

"It is now!" Dwayne laughed.

Tammy was stunned by his idea. Quit her job? Leave Judy and move in with Dwayne on a boat? She had to think about this. "Oh, Dwayne, I don't know. It all seems so sudden. I've been known in the past to make hasty decisions. And it still won't solve the problem with Matt for the fishing trip. And do you think there's enough room on the boat for all three of us?"

"Sure there's enough room. The dinette table folds down into a bed. Matt could sleep there. I'll admit, it will be a little cramped, but hey! It will be an adventure." He laughed and gave her a cheeky wink. "Call your parents. I'm sure they'd love to have him over for a visit."

Tammy shook her head in despair. "Can we go inside and talk about this? I'm freezing sitting out here. You're spending the night, right?"

"You bet I am." He laughed. "I need to talk some sense into you."

I f felt good to be home. Dwayne and Tammy tip-toed through the house so as not to wake anyone, and before running a much needed bath, Tammy quietly stood over her son as he slept and gushed at the sight of him. Overjoyed to see his innocent face, she carefully leaned over and gave him a gentle kiss on his forehead. "Mommy's home. I've missed you, buddy," she whispered softly.

Dwayne joined Tammy in the bath, where together they erased all lingering scents of the jail from Tammy's body and quietly made love. Afterwards, they huddled on the couch until 5:00 a.m., where they finally fell asleep in each other's arms, discussing Dwayne's idea in whispered voices.

Tammy still couldn't wrap her head around upending her life so drastically and suddenly. She needed time to think about it. But time was running out. Dwayne would be leaving to set the first round of traps in a month.

Even though he was exhausted from little sleep, Dwayne had to leave the next morning for work. He left Tammy with her thoughts and in the company of her son, who screamed with joy when he saw his mommy sleeping on the couch.

Over the next few days, Tammy's life began to fall back into its normal routine of waiting on irate customers, babysitting kids and picking up toys. She needed more out of life than this and made the decision to at least mention Dwayne's idea to her dad. She convinced herself it couldn't do any harm. *Dad will probably be too busy with his writing anyway*. But she finally picked up the phone.

After three rings, he answered. "Hello, John speaking."

"Dad, it's Tammy."

"Tammy! How have you been?"

"Good. Hey, listen, I have this crazy idea and thought I'd run it by you."

John's tone suddenly changed from joyful to serious. He'd heard too many crazy ideas from Tammy in the past. "Go on."

Noticing the sudden change in his voice, Tammy stalled, wondering if this was a bad move. "Well, you see, I've met this guy and I want to go fishing with him." After blurting out the first thing that popped into her head, Tammy realized how stupid she sounded.

"Fishing? Since when have you liked fishing?" her dad asked in a questionable tone.

Tammy couldn't hide her enthusiasm when he asked and began to ramble on excitedly. "Oh, Dad, I love it! It's amazing! I'm not talking about regular fishing with a rod. This is commercial lobster fishing. That's what Dwayne does, the guy I've been seeing, and for months now I've been helping him get ready for the season and I absolutely love it. He's taught me so much and well, you see, I want to go pull the lobster traps with him. But the thing is, he fishes off an island sixty miles out at sea and stays there for a week. I can't go unless I have someone to take care of Matt."

"My daughter wants to go fishing sixty miles out at sea." John laughed. "Well, Tammy, you never cease to surprise me. Have you thought this through? What about your job? Have you talked to them? And where do I come in?" John asked, assuming she might be asking for a loan so she could take time off from work.

Tammy didn't want to mention the rest of the idea or that she might be quitting her job so she ignored that question. "Dad, I wanted to ask if you and Joanne might want a visit from Matt?" There was silence. "Dad?" Tammy asked nervously. "Dad, are you there?"

"Yeah. Yeah, Tammy, I'm here. Well, I can tell you genuinely like this fishing thing. How long are we talking about?"

Tammy was surprised that he was even considering it. "I think a week. I'd have to check with Dwayne."

"Hold on a second. I'm going to put Joanne on the phone. She's the one you'll have to ask. After all, she'll be the one that would have to watch him, and Andrew already keeps her busy enough as it is."

Tammy waited with her heart pounding in her chest, wondering if this was a bad idea. A few moments later, Joanne came on the line and again Tammy recited what she had just told her father. Joanne was just as amused as her father when she mentioned her quest to go fishing, and she showed her motherly concerns regarding Tammy's typically hasty decision.

"What if you don't like it, Tammy? You said you've only helped him get the traps ready but you've not actually gone fishing. You'll be stuck out at sea with no way to get home. You can't ask your boyfriend to stop what he's doing to bring you back, you know, especially when you're that far out."

Tammy understood Joanne's concerns, but her recent shark fishing trip came to mind. "If it's any consolation, I went shark fishing with Dwayne not so long ago and absolutely loved it."

Joanne gasped. "Did you say shark fishing?"

Tammy giggled at her reaction. "Yep, I sure did, and it was an amazing experience."

"Well, I wasn't expecting to hear that." She laughed. "Oh, Tammy you are full of surprises. Maybe you have found your calling."

"I know I'll love it, Joanne. I can feel it."

"Tammy, I do know one thing. When you've made up your mind about something, it's impossible for anyone to change it." She paused for a moment. "Sure, we'll watch Matt."

Tammy sensed the smile in Joanne's voice. "Really?"

"Yes. Besides, it's about time Matt met his uncle." Joanne laughed. "Doesn't that sound odd? But Andrew is Matt's half-uncle, even though he's only two years older."

Tammy chuckled at the thought. "It does seem kind of weird."

Tammy spent the next few minutes thanking Joanne many times for agreeing to watch Matt if she decided to go with Dwayne. She explained that there were other issues to iron out before committing herself completely but she would keep her posted.

After hanging up the phone, Tammy remained stunned on the couch for a few minutes. She hadn't expected her parents to say yes. The only thing holding her back now was her job. She asked herself how much she actually enjoyed her job. And if she quit her job, would that mean she'd have to move onto the boat with Dwayne? Was she ready for that? Could she really live on a boat? She had so many unanswered questions.

She had a few more days to think things through properly, which was something new for her. She wasn't going to make any drastic decisions this time. She had to be sure this was something she and Dwayne both wanted and that their relationship was going places. Without a doubt, she knew she loved him, but she had never confessed her true feelings to him. Not yet. Was it because she didn't know how he felt about her?

It also occurred to Tammy that if she did this, she'd be giving up everything. Her and Matt's home, her job, and most of all her independence—all things she had worked really hard for. If it didn't work out between her and Dwayne, his life would just go on like it did before they'd met. He'd still have his boat, his home and his jobs, whereas Tammy would have to start over yet again. She'd lost count of how many times that had occurred in her life because of stupid decisions. She didn't want this to be another one.

CHAPTER 25

By the time Friday rolled around, Tammy still hadn't decided what to do. She had too many 'what ifs' tormenting her head. She needed some reassurance from Dwayne that he was in their relationship for the long-term. This weekend, she intended to find out. Dwayne had warned her that it was going to be another intense weekend of getting the last of the gear built and dipped. He only had three weeks left before he headed out to the island to drop off the first round of traps, and he still had a ton of work to do on the boat.

Tammy was anxious to get back to the familiar surroundings of the boatyard and the friendly people, so as soon her shift was over at three, she hurried home to change and pick up Matt. In no time at all, she was back on the road and heading for the marina.

She found Dwayne shirtless, looking as sexy as ever at the corner of the yard, and wasted no time diving into the work that needed to be done. Matt knew the drill and busied himself with riding his bike around the yard.

They worked hard into the night, allowing Matt to stay up late and gaze at the stars he never got to see in the city.

Tammy hadn't mentioned anything about talking to her dad. She'd wanted to wait until she had Dwayne's full attention. Once their work was done for the night and Matt was finally asleep on the boat, she felt it was time to talk. She grabbed a blanket from the bottom of the bed and laid it out on the deck before Dwayne returned from his shower.

When he came back, wrapped in his bathrobe, he found Tammy stretched out on the blanket, staring up at the sky with its stars like jewels. He immediately joined her and snuggled his body next to hers. Breathing in the fresh scent from her recent shower, he embraced her and looked up. "Beautiful, isn't it?"

Tammy laid her head on his chest and embraced him. "It's absolutely stunning and so peaceful. I love how the water glistens from the moon and the sounds the ripples of the water makes. I hate leaving this place."

Dwayne rubbed her shoulder and kissed the top of her head. "Well, you don't have to, you know."

Tammy sat up and placed her hands on his chest. "I talked to my dad about watching Matt."

Dwayne's eyes shot wide open. "You did? And?"

Tammy beamed him a smile. "They said they would love to watch Matt. I couldn't believe it. You know what this means, don't you?" she said excitedly without waiting for a reply. "I can go fishing with you."

"So what's stopping you? I know you'll love it, and you're so good at building traps. We'll have a blast out there. Pulling the traps is the easy part."

"Oh, Dwayne, I really want to go but I need to know that this is not just a fling we are having. I'd be giving up everything to do this."

Dwayne sat up and took Tammy's hand. "Tammy, I don't ask every woman I've dated to move in with me. She has to be pretty special." He laughed. "And you are. I've never told you until now, but I love you and would love nothing more than to share my life with you."

Tammy heard what she needed to hear. "I love you too," she replied before closing her lips on his and folded her arms around him. There was no going back. This was the life she wanted and it was where she felt at home. She was going to take the plunge and move in with Dwayne. She broke away from their now passionate kiss and sat up. "I'm going to do it!" she said excitedly. "I'm going fishing with you! But not just that. If the invitation is still on the table, I want to move in with you and live my life with you."

Dwayne's eyes beamed with happiness. "Really?"

"Yes! I belong here, and so does Matt."

Dwayne pulled her in close and kissed her hard on the lips. "You won't regret it. I promise."

"I know. This feels right. I've never been so sure about anything in my life. The hardest part will be sending Matt off to Florida. Joanne suggested having him stay there until Thanksgiving. She wants me to make sure I really want to commercial fish for a living."

Dwayne nodded. "I think she's right. A week isn't enough."

"But Thanksgiving's over two months away. I'm not sure if I can do that."

Dwayne felt the uneasiness in her voice. "Tammy, he'll be with family, and he will probably love spending time with his grandpa. It's likely you will have more of a hard time than him. Kids adjust real easily."

She knew she was doing this for their future, but she had to be sure this was what she wanted to do for a living and Joanne was right, a week wasn't enough. "Okay! I can do this! I'm calling my parents tomorrow," she exclaimed excitedly while throwing herself into Dwayne's arms.

"Oh, Tammy, I love you so much. Go grab another blanket so we can get hide beneath it and get frisky under the stars." His devious smile had returned.

"Okay!" Tammy said cheerfully as she hurried down into the cabin in search of a blanket.

~

With her mind made up and feeling excited about the future, Tammy left the marina with a spring in her step. She had three weeks to get everything in place before heading out to the island with Dwayne. Her first concern was telling Judy. They'd been through a lot with each other, and she couldn't deny the sadness and the sense of guilt she was feeling, knowing she was abandoning her.

Since Tammy quit drinking, they no longer had their midnight chit-chats over a glass of wine. In fact, Tammy couldn't remember the last time she had an in-depth conversation or just joked around with Judy. With all the sudden realizations while driving home, Tammy knew it was time to move on.

When she arrived at her house, Judy was still up in her usual spot with a glass of wine and immediately rose from the couch to go pour it down the sink. Tammy hated that she made her feel that way.

"It's okay. You don't need to do that. I'm fine," Tammy told her. "Sit down. We need to talk. I'll just go and put Matt down."

"Okay," Judy said, looking worried as she returned to her seat.

A few minutes later, Tammy entered the room with a chilled Pepsi and sat on the couch next to Judy. With her curiosity piqued, Judy spoke first.

"So, what's up?"

Tammy stalled with her reply by circling the rim of her can with her fingertips. "Dwayne has asked me to move in with him." She took Judy's hand. "And I really want to, but I hate the idea of messing things up for you. You are my best friend, and we've always had each other's backs. I feel like I'm abandoning you. But I also think we're beginning to go our separate ways. Am I right when I say that? You've been seeing a lot of more of Joel, and I've been spending more time with Dwayne…"

To Tammy's surprise, Judy started laughing.

"What's so funny?" Tammy asked.

It took a moment for Judy to calm herself and wipe the tears from her cheeks. "I'm sorry. It's just that Joel and I have been talking about moving in together too, but I just didn't know how to tell you. Well, you just saved me the trouble." She laughed again.

Tammy eyes became wide. "You're kidding me!" she yelled before joining Judy in her laughter. "Oh, so I have nothing to be worried about? Have you guys found a place yet?"

"No. We were planning on starting after I had found the courage to tell you. So I guess we can start right away. His place is too small; it's only a one bedroom so we can't live there."

Tammy thought for a moment. "Well, wait a minute. Why doesn't Joel just move in here after I've moved out? There's no reason for you to move, Judy. This is your home."

Judy suddenly realized how everything was falling into place. Releasing a satisfactory smile, she eased back into the couch. "You're right! It will work out perfect for everyone. There's just one downside to all of this."

Tammy looked worried. Had she overlooked something? "What's that?"

"I'm going to miss the hell out of you. Come here and give me a hug."

"Aww, we'll still see each other. I promise. After lobster season, I'll see if Dwayne will take us all out on the boat."

"Really?" Judy squealed. "The kids have never been on a boat. They would love it."

Tammy went on to tell Judy all about her plans for the big move, which included quitting the restaurant and becoming a full-time commercial fisherwoman.

"You and Matt are going to live on the boat?" Judy asked,

sounding skeptical. "Is there enough room for all of you? And what about all your stuff?"

"It will be cramped, but we'll make it work. I've lived in worst places, as you well know. It's beautiful in the marina, and it'll be worth sacrificing the house just to be able to wake up in the middle of such a magnificent environment. Matt will love it. I know he will. He's adapted so well to the boat life and has learnt so much. It will be tough having my parents watch him for a few months, but it's something I need to do if I'm serious about giving this lobster fishing a try."

Judy shook her head. "Damn, girl! I can't believe you're gonna be a frigging fisherwoman. Who'd have thought? I'm really happy for you and if anyone deserves to be happy, you do." She held out her arms. "I need another hug."

"We both deserve these changes in our lives. I'm excited for you and Joel as well. You are about to start a new life together too."

Both girls felt the tinge of sadness lingering in the air. It was an emotional and scary time for them. The Tammy-and-Judy era was slowly but surely coming to end. Neither knew what the future held, but they were anxious to find out.

Over the next week, Tammy knuckled down with organizing everything so she would have her life and her belongings in place by the time Dwayne left for his first trip to the island. It wasn't the first time she had made a quick decision to move; in fact, she was somewhat concerned that this seemed to be a common occurrence in her life. First, there was her rushed move to the States from England, and then the expedited decision to be with Raymond when she discovered she was having his child. When her thoughts switched to Steven, Tammy shook her head in disgust. She'd lost count of how many times she'd had to move with him.

Her last shift at work was done and the day she officially moved out of the house had finally arrived. She'd already put most of her belongings in storage, leaving all the furniture for Judy—much to Judy's protest. But Tammy got her way and after one last family meal with the kids and a tearful farewell, Tammy and Judy's path together had finally come to an end.

She spent what she thought was going to be an emotional night with Matt on Dwayne's boat before taking him to the airport the following morning, but he was so excited about flying on an airplane for the first time that the only person having anxieties was Tammy. All three of them stayed up late telling stories to Matt under the bedcovers via flashlight until Matt finally fell asleep in their arms, which is where they huddled together until sunrise.

It was just a short ten minute ride to LAX airport from the marina, and Tammy had a hard time containing Matt's excitement over his upcoming plane ride and the only tears that were shed, were Tammy's. Once they were checked in, they were greeted by a flight attendant who assured Tammy that she would be sitting next to Matt for the entire trip and would be personally handing Matt over to Joanne at the other end.

Tammy watched through her tears as her son disappeared through the crowd. Once he was out of sight, she let the tears fall uncontrollably while burying her face in Dwayne's chest. "Oh, Dwayne! Am I a terrible mother for doing this?"

Surprised by her outburst, Dwayne held her tight. "No, you're not. Now don't be saying that about yourself. He's going to be fine. He's visiting family so Mom can learn a new career. You're doing this for him."

As always, he had a way of making her feel better and helping her take note of the brighter side of situations. "Thank you," she whispered while wiping her now swollen eyes.

"Let me take you out for breakfast. Tonight, we can call your family and you can talk to Matt. Okay?"

The thought brought a smile to her face. "I'd like that. Come on, let's go. I'm hungry."

～

For Tammy, living on the boat was like an endless camping trip, except they were on water. Tammy didn't deny that their living quarters were cramped, but she really didn't feel the effects because they spent all their days outside, evenings were spent relaxing on the deck with other fellow boaters and meals were cooked on the barbeque. It was a lifestyle she knew she would never get tired of.

Sending Matt to Florida for the next few months was going to be difficult, but she couldn't deny that she was enjoying her temporary freedom from motherhood. For the first time in four years, she could do as she pleased without worrying about Matt. But her biggest relief was her money anxieties. Once she moved out of the house, they had all disappeared. She suddenly found herself free of rent and all the other overwhelming obligations that came with living in a house. Tammy embraced it and gave one hundred percent of herself to Dwayne and helping him get ready for the season.

With only two weeks left until they were due to head out with the first load of traps, they worked around the clock finishing up the gear and stacking it so it was ready to be loaded onto the boat when the time came. Dwayne spent hours going through both boats thoroughly, making sure everything was running smoothly and that he had extra supplies and tools to fix anything that may go wrong while out at sea.

It was too late to get Tammy a commercial lobster permit for the current year so instead, Dwayne got her a deck-hand permit, which allowed her to be on the boat and participate in the actual pulling of the traps. Having not considered it before, Dwayne thought it was probably a better idea for her first year. The deck-hand permit was much cheaper and it gave Tammy a chance to see if she liked it before committing to the expense of a commercial license.

Everything was going to plan and they were right on schedule. The last two days before their departure, Dwayne took Tammy on an amusing shopping excursion for her official bright orange slickers, rubber boots and matching rubber gloves. They also shopped for groceries and filled the boats up with fuel. The only thing left to do was to load the traps onto the boats, which ended up taking most of the last day.

Each trap weighed close to sixty-five pounds, but between them, they loaded fifty traps on to the *Baywitch* and ten traps onto the *Little Boat.* Once all the traps were tied down and secured, leaving them with no deck space whatsoever, Tammy dropped her exhausted aching body onto the dock next to the boats to admire their work while Dwayne returned the handcart to the corner of the yard.

When he returned, she had a question for him. "So how are we going to take out both boats? Are you going to be towing the little boat?"

Dwayne chuckled because he knew she'd be asking this question. He just thought she would have asked it much sooner. "Nope. I can't tow a boat with a load of traps. That's too dangerous."

Tammy thought for a moment. "So who's going to drive the *Little Boat?*"

A devious smile appeared across Dwayne's face. "You are."

Tammy never rose to her feet so fast. Even with her sore body, she had to talk some sense into Dwayne immediately. "Are you insane? I can't drive that boat to the island. It's over sixty miles!" she protested in a panicked state.

"Yes, you can, and you will." He held a slight firmness to his tone. "On the next trip, we will just take the *Baywitch*, but this is my first time to the island and I want to use the *Little Boat* to explore. I can't do that with the *Baywitch* because it doesn't go in shallow waters, which is why I need you to drive the *Little Boat*."

As much as Tammy appreciated his confidence, she wasn't feeling it. "No, I can't! I've never driven a boat that far. That's a long way." She began pacing the deck as her nerves started to take over. "I've only driven the *Baywitch* a few times outside the harbor, and that's been with you on board. I've never even driven the *Little Boat* before. And you expect me to drive it by myself, sixty miles across the goddamn ocean? I can't do it, Dwayne!"

Dwayne approached her as she continued to pace the dock and stopped her in her tracks by placing a firm grip on her shoulders.

"If you want to commercial fish, you're going to have to learn how to drive a boat. It's part of the trade. You can't fish by car."

Tammy slapped his arm and shoved him away. "This isn't funny. It's sixty bloody miles. That's a long way. I have no idea what to do and not only that, I'll be by myself. What if something goes wrong?" She didn't wait for an answer and continued to express her anger. "You're telling me this now. Why didn't you tell me sooner so I could have at least prepared myself?"

"This is exactly why I didn't tell you until now. If I had, you'd have been stressing over it the whole time and working yourself up into a frenzy, just like you are doing now. Yes, sixty miles is a lot of ocean, but it's also a great opportunity to learn how to drive a boat. By the time we get to the island, you'll be a pro." He approached her and grabbed her hand, speaking in a softer tone. "And as for you being alone goes; you will be following me, and I won't let you out of my sight. If it makes you feel any better, we will be in radio contact, and we can talk on the radio the whole time if you want." He shook her hand vigorously. "You can do this. I know you can."

"Oh god, I don't know, Dwayne. I'm scared. I'll be driving the boat for nine hours. That's a long time."

"That's nine hours of practice time. Like I said, you'll be a pro by the time we reach the island. There's nothing but open ocean. You can make all the mistakes you want. You're not going to hit anything. Look at it like a big adventure. Come on, what do you say? You'll be fine."

Tammy folded her arms across her chest. "Well, it looks like I don't have a choice. But I'm still not happy about it."

Dwayne pulled her in and gave her a hard kiss on the lips. "That's my girl. Now come on, let's get some sleep; we have a long day head of us tomorrow."

"Okay...I guess we will see how I do tomorrow." Still feeling concerned, she followed Dwayne into the cabin of *Baywitch.*

Tammy understood why he hadn't told her sooner about

driving *Little Boat*. He was right. She'd spent a sleepless night worrying about it and was now afraid she wouldn't be able to stay awake for the entire crossing. After four cups of coffee and an obscene number of cigarettes, her nerves were still getting the better of her. Feeling the chill of the morning air, she left to use the bathroom for the last time, knowing a bucket would be her only source of relief for the next few days. Dwayne fired up both boats while she was gone.

When she returned, Dwayne met her at the bottom of the ramp and led her over to the *Little Boat* and took her to the helm. "The only thing you need to know about is the throttle. It works just like the *Baywitch*. Forward, neutral and reverse. You'll be following me so you won't need to read the compass, but pay attention to it and take note of the direction of where we're heading for practice." He lifted the mic from the VHF radio. "This is the radio. You can call me anytime by pushing this button and talking into the mic. Release the button to hear me talk and press to talk again when you're ready. Got it?"

Tammy nodded. "Got it."

I'm going to pull the *Little Boat* out of the slip and put it on the end tie so you don't have to deal with steering it out of the slip. Once I've passed you on the *Baywitch*, you simply untie the boat from the cleats, push yourself off away from the dock and follow me slowly out of the harbor." Dwayne saw the worried look on her face. "You'll be fine. Give me a kiss and go wait for me at the end of the dock."

Tammy leaned in and welcomed his affection before heading over to the end of the dock to wait for him. Left in her own thoughts for a few moments, she tried desperately to calm her escalating nerves. *You can do this, Tammy.*

She glanced at her watch. It was almost ten. She knew they were leaving later than intended, but last-minute details had set them back. Tammy calculated the time of the crossing and knew they wouldn't arrive until after dark. The thought of driving the boat into the night didn't help matters.

The sight of seeing Dwayne turn out of their basin and head toward her snapped her out of her daydream. With ease, he pulled alongside the dock where she stood and threw her a line. Despite her shaking hands, Tammy caught it and tied off the *Little Boat* onto the cleat. The outboard motor rumbled as Dwayne stepped on to the dock and gave Tammy's shoulders a firm squeeze. "Are you ready?"

"As ready as I'll ever be."

"You'll be fine. I know you will. Give me a few minutes to get the *Baywitch*. As soon as I pass you, simply untie the boat and follow me slowly out of the harbor." Dwayne gave her a lingering kiss on the lips. "I'll see you at the island." And before she could summon any further protests, Tammy suddenly found herself alone on the dock.

She stepped on to the boat—her boat—and stood motionless for a few seconds to steady herself as the boat rocked from her presence. Her body trembled viciously, and it wasn't from the cold. *Come on, Tammy, pull yourself together. You've got this.*

But as hard as she tried, she couldn't control her fear or the high levels of anxiety she experienced while waiting for Dwayne.

About ten minutes later, she heard Dwayne's voice over the radio. "You should see me coming out of the basin in about a minute."

"Okay," Tammy hollered, but then she remembered Dwayne's instructions about pushing the button to speak. She shook her head at her stupidity and lifted the microphone out of the cradle before pushing the black button on the side. "Okay," she hollered again, remembering a few moments later to release the button. "This is going to take some getting used to," she said to no one in particular.

Dwayne's voice crackled over the radio again. "You got me, Tammy?"

"Yes."

"There you are. You've got to remember, it's not like a regular phone. To hear me, you have to release the black button."

The sound of his voice brought a smile to her face. "Yeah, I know. I'll get used to it. Where are you at?"

"You should be seeing me in just a few seconds. As soon as I've passed you, untie the boat and ease away from the dock. The *Baywitch* has a heavy load so we will be going slow the whole way. It will give you plenty of practice time."

Tammy chuckled at his comment. She needed all the practice she could get. Standing at the helm, she fixed her stare at the basin where he said he would be coming and sure enough, she spotted him almost immediately as he turned into the main channel. The *Baywitch* was a much larger boat than the one she was driving and looked even greater with traps stacked five high on the deck. The *Little Boat*, on the other hand, sat low in the water. In fact, Tammy could reach over and put her hand in the chilled water if she wanted to. She patiently waited for Dwayne to pass her, and he waved and gave her a huge smile as he slowly eased by. Tammy waved back, took a deep breath and proceeded to untie the boat. Once free, she gently pushed away from the dock with her hand. "Here we go!" she whispered nervously before scurrying over to the helm and gently easing the throttle into gear. "Fuck! I can't believe I'm doing this."

The zigzags started as soon as she began inching forward to follow Dwayne.

"You're oversteering," she heard Dwayne say. "Don't try and compensate by steering the other way. That's why you're zigzagging. Give the boat a minute to respond."

With both white knuckled hands clenched on the steering wheel, Tammy didn't want to let go to pick up the mic of the radio. "Yeah, yeah, I know. Give me a minute," she hollered into the air, not that there was a chance of Dwayne hearing her over the roar of both motors. Feeling thankful no wake was allowed inside the harbor, Tammy continued to follow Dwayne at the slow pace of about four knots, zigzagging the whole time.

Along both sides of the channel was a bike path, where joggers, dog walkers and bicyclists roamed. Many stopped to look at the boats leaving or entering the harbor. Some waved at Tammy as she passed but, not wanting to let go of the wheel, Tammy simply nodded and threw them a nervous smile. But she couldn't help feeling a sense of pride as these people watched her driving a boat.

"How are doing back there?"

Realizing she had no other option, she let go of the wheel with one hand and picked up the mic. "Fine. Trying to get use to this steering. I'm still zigzagging."

"You're doing great. You've got sixty miles of open ocean to practice. By the time we get to San Clemente, you'll be driving as straight as an arrow."

Tammy laughed. "I'm not too sure about that. This is really hard. My hands are already tired and we've not even left the harbor yet."

"It will get easier. It's only because you are oversteering right now. Hang in there. I'm going to let you go so you can concentrate."

"Okay," Tammy replied before hanging up the mic.

It took about fifteen minutes to exit the harbor but even then, Tammy wasn't feeling any more relaxed. Still clinging onto the wheel, she gave the boat a little more speed as they came around the break wall and into open waters. She instantly felt the choppiness of the waves beneath her, which intensified the rocking motion of the boat. "God damn it!" she yelled, trying to steer the boat in anything that might resemble a straight line. But she was losing her battle fast. The wind was much stronger and cut through her hair with force, blowing it back away from her face. Sitting closer to the water than the *Baywitch*, she actually felt the spray of water against her face and arms. On the brink of tears, she kept trying to compensate her steering as if she was driving a car, which only resulted in more zigzagging. "I can't do this!" she cried in desperation. Looking at the compass on the dash, she assumed it was obviously just as confused as she was on the course she was trying to keep.

Frustrated with her attempts so far, Tammy took a deep breath and stopped steering, allowing the boat to straighten itself out. Dwayne was probably about five hundred feet in front of her. She envied how he handled the *Baywitch*. She wanted to be just as good as him but also realized he'd spent his entire life around boats.

Once the boat seemed to be going in something like a straight line, Tammy took the wheel again and paid close attention to her steering. She looked at the compass and saw they were on a course of 180 degrees and used that as her guidance. Concentrating and watching the compass seemed to help, and she soon noticed she was keeping on course and doing less of the zigzagging. "I'm getting this!" she squealed triumphantly. But as soon as she became more relaxed, she found herself going off course again. "Fuck!" she yelled before correcting her steering for what seemed like the hundredth time.

Tammy had been so engrossed in her steering and the wheel that she hadn't paid much attention to her surroundings. Feeling a little more comfortable, she scanned the ocean. There were a few sailboats in the distance off to her port and starboard side, and numerous fishing boats anchored off shore. She looked behind her and saw the coastline of Santa Monica and Venice in the distance. She could make out the Ferris wheel on the Santa Monica Pier and people lazing around on the beach. She wondered when she would be walking on land again.

About an hour into the trip, Tammy was feeling a little more confident and extremely proud of herself. She was driving a boat all by herself across the Pacific Ocean. "Fuck, this feels great!" she yelled at the top of her voice. The sense of freedom she was feeling was exuberating and she wanted to share her joyous mood with Dwayne. After picking up the mic, she held down the button and hollered over the sound of the motor, "Dwayne! You got me?"

A few seconds later, he replied, "I got you! How's it going back there? I've been watching you. You're doing much better. Looks like you're getting the hang of it."

"I am! This is fucking awesome! How far have we gone?"

"Oh, I'd say about eight miles. And, Tammy, watch your language. This is an open channel. Every boater on this channel can hear you out there."

"Oops…sorry. Hang on, only eight miles? It feels like we've gone a lot farther."

"It always does on a boat. We're only going about eight knots. We won't get there till after dark."

"Yeah, I know. Not sure how I'm going to like driving at night."

"Don't think about it right now. That's hours away. Just enjoy the ride and keep up the good job."

Over the next few hours, they conversed over the radio periodically. Hearing Dwayne's voice comforted Tammy and instantly put her at ease. She was no longer zigzagging and was able to keep on course pretty easily without even thinking about it. It was beginning to come naturally for her. Dwayne was right. This was the perfect opportunity to learn how to drive a boat.

By the third hour, she had the radio turned up full blast and found herself screaming out the song "I am sailing" by Rod Stewart when it played over the speakers. While enjoying the feeling of confidence and complete freedom, she noticed something splashing in the distance on the starboard side of her boat. It wasn't just one splash; it was hundreds of them, and they were moving closer to the boat. "What the hell is that?" she asked herself. When the splashes came close enough, she suddenly realized they were dolphins and squealed with delight before calling Dwayne on the radio. "Dolphins! On my right. I'm going to go check them out," she hollered over the radio.

Being a smaller boat, it was easier to steer, so Tammy took a detour and headed over to the school of dolphins while Dwayne slowed down the *Baywitch* and waited for her. In one swift movement, Tammy gave the wheel a sharp turn and headed off to the right where she had seen the splashes. Within minutes, she found herself surrounded by a school of dolphins racing through the water and jumping two to five feet out of the water. There must have been at least a hundred of them. Many came up alongside the boat, where Tammy could actually reach into the water and touch them as they swam by playing and following the wake. "This is amazing!" she cried out loud as she watched in awe the beauty before her. *This is what it's all about!* As she lost herself in the world of dolphins, she became a part of their world for just a moment.

After they had blessed her with their presence and moved on, Tammy called Dwayne on the radio. "Did you see that? That was amazing. I've never seen anything like it."

"I saw with my binoculars. That was pretty cool. You'll be seeing a lot of that in the future. Ready to keep going?"

"Yeah. I'm back behind you," Tammy confirmed.

She had taken Dwayne's advice and kept her jacket and snacks handy on the dash to grab and eat while she drove, but her arms and hands were beginning to tire from steering for so many hours and she was in desperate need of a bathroom break. She looked behind her at the mainland and saw it was now only a speck on the horizon. There were no longer any boats close by; it was just her and Dwayne. The vast size of the ocean suddenly hit home and she wondered how anyone could possibly find them if something happened out here; how would they ever survive? The ocean would just swallow them up in a matter of minutes. Tammy shuddered at the thought and while doing so, suddenly spotted land up ahead in the distance. *Surely we can't almost be there already?*

Tammy picked up the mic. "Dwayne, you got me?"

"Yeah, I got you. Everything okay?"

"I see land up ahead. That's not San Clemente, is it?"

"No, that's Catalina Island. I'll take you there sometime. There are all kinds of fun things to do like snorkeling, scuba diving and beach combing. You'll love it. We'll be passing the west side in about an hour."

"That would be great. We could bring Matt too. Listen, I really need to take a break and give my arms a rest. Is that possible?"

"Sure! Catch up to me and put your motor in neutral. Then you can shut off the boat and we'll bob around for a little while."

Tammy followed his instructions and beamed a huge smile when she could see Dwayne waving at her from the helm of the *Baywitch*. She waved back and shut off the motor. The sudden silence brought her peace. After hearing the constant roaring of the outboard motor for several hours, a welcome calmness embraced her. She stood for a moment and listened to the sound of the ocean crashing against the hull of the little boat. She would never get tired of the vast sense of freedom the ocean always brought. She loved the way it smelt, the constant breeze in her hair and most of all she loved being away from the pressures of the city.

After being confined to one spot on the boat for hours, Tammy took the liberty to stretch her legs and paced back and forth around the helm and either side of the boat. Even though there wasn't a lot of room, it made a huge difference to be able to walk a few steps up and down.

She was close enough to the *Baywitch* to holler and be heard without using the radio. "I'm gonna use the bucket," she shouted while laughing.

Dwayne gave her thumbs up. "Okay!"

They conversed while eating tuna fish out of a can, along with some crackers and fruit before firing up the boats twenty minutes later to continue with the crossing. Dwayne told Tammy they had another five hours to go before they reached the island. He reminded her to let him know if she needed another break. She agreed and put on her jacket before putting the boat in gear.

The small break made a huge difference and totally rejuvenated her. She now felt she had enough energy to complete the trip, but a few hours later when the sun began to go down and the sky began to darken, an eeriness crept over her. She suddenly felt so small and vulnerable amongst the ink-black sea, which was now only lit by the glow of the moon and the twinkles of the stars. She could no longer see any land, and the only part of the *Baywitch* that she could see was the small white light above the helm and two white lights on the stern.

Bracing both hands on the wheel, she held tight as the little boat cut through the waves. Afraid to take her eyes off the lights of the *Baywitch*, Tammy strained to stay focused, fearing if she turned her head for a moment she'd lose him. The ocean no longer felt like a friendly place. Images of sea monsters and what lay beneath haunted her mind. It was a different experience than driving during the day. A frightening one and a reminder just how deadly the ocean could be. If she went overboard, she would be lost for good. Dwayne would have no idea unless he tried to call her on the radio to check in, and by then, there could be miles of ocean between them. The thought petrified her, so she called Dwayne on the radio to seek some comfort and reassure herself that he was still on the *Baywitch*. "Dwayne, you got me?"

"Yep, I got you. How you holding up? You doing okay?"

"Yeah. Just a little spooked since it got dark. How much farther do we have to go?"

"We should be approaching Northwest Harbor at the island in about forty-five minutes."

Tammy released a joyous cheer. "Hallelujah!"

"You've done great, Tammy. I'm really proud of you. I knew you could do it!"

Feeling proud of herself, Tammy did a little jig while she talked to Dwayne for a few more minutes. It was the longest, most nerve-wracking ten hours she had ever experienced. But she did it. She'd driven a boat solo, sixty miles across the Pacific Ocean, and she was feeling pretty damn good about it. Despite the darkness surrounding her, she sang her heart out to the tunes on the radio for the remainder of the journey.

Thirty minutes later, Dwayne came back on the radio. "Hey, Tammy?"

"Hey," Tammy replied after picking up the mic.

"Once we get into the harbor, I'm going to need to set the anchor. It will take me about fifteen minutes. Just put the *Little Boat* in neutral until I'm ready. When I'm done, I'm going to have you come alongside the *Baywitch* and I'll tie the *Little Boat* up against it."

A sudden gush of panic swept through Tammy. "I don't know how to pull up alongside the *Baywitch*. What if I hit it?" she asked, raising her voice.

"You'll do fine. I'll walk you through it over the radio. Hold tight. I'll come back on in a bit."

With a fresh wave of elevated nerves, Tammy hung up the mic and tried to envision in her mind how she was going to approach the *Baywitch*—in the dark—but she had no clue and knew she could only wait for Dwayne's instructions. Once inside the harbor, she slowed the boat and then put it in neutral. She could make out the silhouette of the island ahead of her and wondered what it would look like in the day time. With no other boats in the harbor, she could hear the waves crashing against the shore.

Tammy wasn't sure how long she'd been bobbing around but was relieved when Dwayne came back on the radio. "Okay, Tammy, I'm ready for you."

"Okay," Tammy replied, unable to hide the nervousness in her voice.

"Put the boat in gear and slowly make your way toward the port side of the *Baywitch*. When you are close to the stern, put the boat in neutral and let the current of the water drift you toward me. Make sure you have a rope tied to the cleat on the stern. You're going to throw that to me so I can tie you off."

Tammy listened carefully to everything he had said and

followed his instructions precisely. Inch by inch, she headed toward the *Baywitch*, which was much easier to see since Dwayne had put the flood lights on the deck. With her heart racing and her palms sweating, Tammy put the boat in gear and slowly nosed her way toward the *Baywitch*. Feeling thankful that the water was calmer inside the harbor, Tammy was able to steer the boat with ease and when she was within ten feet of the stern of the *Baywitch*, she put it in neutral. Just like Dwayne had said, the current drifted her alongside his boat.

Dwayne had already gotten two rubber fenders in place along the side and instructed Tammy to throw him the line, which she did right on cue. It landed in Dwayne's hands, and he rushed to tie it off before racing to the front of the boat where he and Tammy repeated the process with a second line. "You made it!" he hollered. "Go ahead and shut off the boat and come over here and give me a big hug."

Beaming like a Cheshire cat, Tammy gladly turned off the boat, stepped up onto the *Baywitch* and almost fell into Dwayne's arms.

"Oh my god! That was nerve-wracking and exhilarating all at the same time. I can't believe I did it."

"You were great. I knew you would be," he cheered before giving her a much needed celebratory kiss on the lips.

Tammy remained in his arms. "I'm so tired. My arms and legs are killing me.

Please tell me we get to lie down soon."

"We sure do. We need plenty of rest before we dump this gear off tomorrow. Everything is secure. Let's go down below and make ourselves a cup of hot chocolate and call it a night."

"Sounds good to me," Tammy said with an exhausted smile.

Tammy soon discovered that sleeping on a boat in the middle of the ocean was not an easy task. Between the constant rocking and rolling of the boat and the sounds of the water slapping against the hull, she got very little sleep and was envious of Dwayne, who didn't stir the entire night.

When she finally did drift off to sleep, seemingly hours after Dwayne, she was rudely awakened by the roaring of male voices somewhere off in the distance. Forgetting she was on a boat, she jumped up, startled by the noise, only to bang her head on the low ceiling of the V-berth where they slept. "Ouch! God damn it!" she seethed while rubbing her head to sooth the throbbing pain.

Dwayne stirred in his sleep, "Are you okay?"

"No, I'm not okay. I've hardly slept, I just banged my head, and there's a bunch of noise outside."

Dwayne sat up and pinned his ears. He too heard the yelling of male voices from outside. "What the hell is that? We're anchored at a desolate island!"

Being on the inside of the bed against the wall, Tammy began to climb over Dwayne, keeping her head low so as not to bang it again. "I don't know, but I'm going to go check it out."

With her feet finally on the floor, she steadied herself from the continuous rocking of the boat by grabbing a hold of the edges of the table. She glanced at the watch on her wrist. "It's only four in the morning," she grumbled while making her way to the cabin door. Once there, she inched it open and peeked through the gap, only to be startled by the sound of an airplane flying above them. "What the hell? Where the hell are we?"

Being his first time on the island too, Dwayne was also confused by all the noise and climbed out of bed to follow Tammy onto the deck. He waited patiently while Tammy precariously climbed the steps, holding onto the sides as she pushed through the cabin door. She stepped out onto the deck, leaving Dwayne down below, and started looking around for something else to hold on to. After a moment of fumbling around in the dark, she curled her fingers around the wire of one of the traps and finally found her balance.

The chill of the air made Tammy wish she was wearing more than just a t-shirt. She crossed her arms and rubbed them with her hands to try and block the cool air from hitting her skin. Suddenly, she heard the roar of an airplane again and strained her eyes toward the black silhouette of the island. That's when she saw the flashing lights of a jet as it took off from the island and disappeared into the sky. The sound was deafening, causing Tammy to cover her ears. "Wow!" she hollered once the plane had passed over them. "Dwayne, you've got to come see this."

"I'm coming," she heard him holler, and soon he appeared carrying a blanket. "Here, wrap this around you. You've got to be freezing."

Shivering, Tammy beamed at his thoughtfulness and turned her body so he could wrap the blanket around her.

"Thanks," she said, embracing the instant warmth. "Sssh. Do you hear that?"

Dwayne listened closely and could hear the sound of men hollering in the distance, from the direction of the island. He nodded, not taking his eyes off the coastline where the sounds were coming from. He pointed with his finger. "Look over there. It's a bunch of navy seals in the water."

Tammy followed his hand and immediately made out several dark shapes scurrying along the coast. Screaming and shouting, the figures ran down the beach and into the cold waters before swimming out to rubber dinghies waiting just offshore. Tammy watched in both amazement and confusion as they then climbed in and began rowing like their lives depended on it.

"Good god! Are they nuts? That water has to be freezing. What are they doing?"

"Looks like they are training. After all, the island is owned by the government. I guess this is where the navy seals train and practice their take-offs and landings, which explains the planes. We can fish off the island but we're not allowed to go on it."

Tammy continued to watch the seals for a few minutes, impressed by their agility and strength. "Damn! Pretty impressive. That would toughen up any guy." She cocked her head back in awe as another plane flew above them.

With the rude awaking of the noise explained and now wide awake, they decided to start their day. The sun was beginning to rise and for the first time, Tammy got a glimpse of the island. It looked almost deserted with only a few buildings and trees dotted around its otherwise barren landscape. Behind her, she saw nothing but open ocean and way off in the distance, she could make out Catalina Island. But there was no mainland in sight and no other boats in the harbor. They were completely isolated from the rest of the world, other than the Navy Seals on San Clemente Island. It was an eerie realization for Tammy. A small sandy beach, the one where they'd seen the Navy Seals, sat at the far end of the harbor, and a vista of rocky cliffs spanned much of the visible coastline. Tammy was looking forward to seeing more of the island when they dropped their gear.

Once they were dressed in jeans, sweatshirts and rubber boots, Tammy managed to boil some water—holding the handle of the pan on the cooker the whole time so it wouldn't slide off from the constant rocking of the boat. While trying to keep her balance, she made two cups of coffee and poured two bowls of cereal.

Before heading out to drop the traps, Dwayne spent an hour setting a mooring so he wouldn't have to drop an anchor every time they returned to the harbor. Tammy helped with the task and because the *Little Boat* went faster and Dwayne wanted to explore, he intended to use that boat to unload the traps.

Before loading more traps onto the *Little Boat*, Tammy put on her rubber slickers for the first time. She immediately felt like an official commercial fisherwoman and giggled at her attire.

By 6:00 a.m., they had a full load of fifteen traps on the *Little Boat* and Tammy was already feeling fatigued from all the lifting. But she fought through it, and with snacks stored in an ice chest, they were ready to take off with the first load.

Dwayne explained that he would be driving the boat so it would be up to Tammy to bring a trap over to the trap table. She was then to take out the rope and buoy and clip the door open so any sea life that entered would be able to escape. On his command, she would drop the trap in the water and toss the rope in behind it. Then she'd do it all over again when he drove to the next spot. Tammy understood and gave him a nod above the noise of the motor roaring behind them.

"Go ahead and untie us from the *Baywitch*," Dwayne hollered while warming up the engine.

Having untied boats so many times now, it came naturally to her, and she did as Dwayne asked without even having to think about the task at hand. Once they were free of the *Baywitch*, Dwayne sped out of the harbor to explore his options on where to drop the gear.

The island was fifty-three square miles and twenty-one miles long. They were only allowed to fish the backside of it and noticed buoys were already in the water from other fishermen. Dwayne had to make sure he didn't drop his gear too close to the others, so he spent some time scanning the coastline before carefully choosing his spots.

Once he'd figured out the area, it didn't take long to drop the gear and return to the harbor for a second load. It took three trips to dump all sixty traps, and they were done by noon. The warm weather had worked in their favor, with a clear blue sky and a calm, flat ocean. They were perfect conditions for making the task easier, but it wasn't going to remain that way. Dwayne pointed to a gathering of darker clouds looming on the horizon. With a storm brewing, Dwayne wanted to leave and get back to the mainland to beat the weather.

"I have to drive the *Little Boat* in a storm?" Tammy said, feeling horrified.

"No, I want you on the *Baywitch* with me," he replied. "I don't know how big this storm is going to be. The *Little boat* is empty now so we can tow it." Seeing he'd just eased Tammy's mind, he beamed her a loving smile.

"Phew! Thank god for that."

But, as Dwayne pulled alongside the *Baywitch*, he noticed a large orange flag up on the hillside of the harbor.

"Do you see that?" he asked Tammy while pointing in the direction of the flag.

"I do. What's that for?"

"I have no idea. Want to go check it out real quick? The *Little Boat* can get close to shore in the shallow waters."

Always eager to explore new things, Tammy answered with enthusiasm. "Sure. Let's go."

Curious about the orange flag and never having seen one in a harbor before in all his years on boats, Dwayne sped toward it. Within a few minutes, they were hugging the coastline in shallow waters beneath the flag. It was at least three feet across and stood midway up the cliff. Dwayne strained his eyes to see if he could make out any writing on it but saw nothing. He turned to reach for his binoculars while Tammy leaned out from the helm to see if she could make anything out.

"I don't see any kind of markings on it," she hollered. "I wonder what it's for."

As Dwayne lifted the binoculars to his eyes, an almighty boom erupted from the hillside where the flag stood, showering dirt and rocks into the waters below and barely missing the *Little Boat*.

"Holy shit! What the hell!" Tammy screamed.

"Jesus Christ!"

As Dwayne slammed the boat in reverse and revved the engine to its full capacity, Tammy ducked her head behind the windshield to take cover. They continued to watch in horror as the hillside collapsed before their eyes. Rocks and boulders, followed by mounds of dirt and rubble tumbled into the water like the aftermath of an avalanche.

Once they were a safe distance away, Dwayne put the boat in neutral and released the lungful of air he'd been holding. Tammy laughed nervously. "Damn, that scared the shit out of me!"

"Well, now we know what an orange flag means. I think it means stay clear because an explosion is about to happen." They both burst out laughing. "What else do the Navy Seals practice here?" he added sarcastically. "Come on, let's go pack up the boats and get out of here. I'm not looking forward to making the crossing in a storm."

It took them about an hour to secure everything on the *Baywitch* and rig up the *Little Boat* to be towed. It was two o'clock by the time they headed out of Northwest Harbor, and they passed another fishing boat heading in, loaded with lobster traps. Dwayne grabbed his binoculars and peered at the boat. "I know that boat. They fished Malibu last year. The captain's name is Mitch."

Tammy looked over and saw the name of the Boat was *Sea Life*. "Cute name for a boat. Nice boat too."

"Yeah, he's been fishing for decades. I had no idea he was fishing out here this year. He's a really nice guy. If we had time, I'd buzz over and say a howdy and introduce you, but we have to get out of here. Maybe we'll see him on the next trip. In the meantime, I'll give him a shout on the radio."

Dwayne continued to steer the boat with one hand while reaching for the mic of the radio. "Sea Life. Sea Life. You got me? *Baywitch* here. Over."

A few seconds later, Mitch came over the radio. "Hey, Dwayne. How's it going? You fishing out here this year? Over."

"Yeah, I am. Thought I'd give it a shot. We just dropped sixty traps. Now heading back. We're trying to beat the storm. Is this your first time fishing out here? Over."

"Yep. I hear it's supposed to be pretty good. We're gonna drop our first load in the morning. You be careful heading back. You might get caught in the storm. It's moving faster than they predicted. Over."

"Thanks, man, we will. Oh, and hey, stay away from orange flags on the hillsides. We almost got blown up." Dwayne laughed. "There's all kinds of crazy Navy Seal drills going on over here. Over."

"Someone else told me about that shit. Said a rock hit their boat. They also said that the navy do underwater explosions inside the harbor. Over."

"Really? I hope they give the boats some kind of warning. Over."

"Let's hope so, man. Thanks for the heads up. I'll catch you on your next trip. Have a safe crossing. Over."

"We will. Thanks. Over and out."

Once the exchange ended, Dwayne hung up the mic and pulled Tammy into his arms. "How are you doing, sweet stuff?" he asked before planting a kiss on her lips. "You did really good out here. I'm proud of you." He flashed her that smile that always melted her heart.

Tammy leaned into his embrace. "I'm doing good. I'm having a really good time. I love it out here. Hey, I have a question."

"Sure, what's that?" Dwayne asked, keeping his eyes focused ahead.

"When you were talking to Mitch on the radio, you both kept saying 'over.' What does that mean?"

"You don't miss anything, do you?" Dwayne chuckled and yet, at the same time, he was impressed by how much attention she paid to the details. "Well, you see, radios aren't like regular phones. Remember you have to push the black button on the side to speak and release to hear the other person talk. Well, saying 'over' let's the other person know you have finished talking. And when we say 'over and out,' that lets the other person know you are ending the call."

"Aaah, okay. That makes sense. You never told me that when we were talking."

"You're right, I didn't." He smiled. "Well, now you know."

Having left the harbor and with the weather still looking to be on their side, Dwayne let Tammy drive the boat so she could have more practice staying on course by reading the compass. He used the time to go around and made sure everything was tied down securely.

The labor intense day was beginning to catch up with Tammy. Her arms ached from lifting the sixty traps around the boats and throwing them overboard. Her feet and calf muscles were sore from a combination of standing all day and fighting to keep her balance on the rocky boat. She was super hungry from only eating snacks throughout the day, her skin was dry, and her hands were chapped and sore from the salt water. And now she had to endure a ten hour boat ride, possibly through a storm, but her spirits were still high. She had been working alongside Dwayne for over three months now, learning everything she could about the trade, and she was loving every minute of it.

They would soon be setting the traps and reaping the rewards of their labor. The anticipation pushed Tammy to work harder in the hopes they would be successful. But she couldn't help feeling that fishing was a gamble. They had put in so much time and effort, and she knew Dwayne had spent quite a bit of money on the gear in preparation for the season. And all of it was in the hopes they would catch a good haul of lobsters at an island Dwayne had never fished before.

What would they do if their catch was poor? Dwayne told her that he had to have a successful trip in order to catch up on the bills, which he had let slide so he could buy the gear. He was two months behind on the boat slip fee, a month behind on his truck payment, and other bills were beginning to pile up too. He also had to buy supplies for the first trip, plus bait and fuel that ran at least another fifteen hundred dollars. Everything depended on their first trip; they needed to make enough money to buy more supplies for the second trip. To say the least, Tammy was somewhat concerned about their finances. She didn't realize until now the risks that were involved.

Knowing she'd be able to call Matt as soon as they docked at the mainland made her feel much better. By the time they reached the marina, it would have been three days since she last spoke to him. She had never gone that long before and it was beginning to take its toll. She couldn't wait to hear his little voice and hear what he had been up to. Occasionally, since she said goodbye to him at the airport, rushes of guilt had consumed her. But, now that she was learning the industry, she was looking forward to introducing Matt to it and hopefully having him on the boat with them.

Two hours into the crossing, the sea began to take a turn and Dwayne took the wheel. The sky had become darker and white caps were now beginning to crest on the ocean. Tammy could no longer walk across the deck without constantly holding on to something.

"Damn! It's getting rough out here," Tammy hollered as she fought with the ice chest lid, which kept slamming shut as she tried to grab two Pepsis from inside.

Dwayne turned his head to make sure she was okay. "It's just starting. It's going to get a lot worse than this. The swells are only about four feet right now, but when the boat is down in the trough of the wave, it's double, which makes it eight feet." He put one of his hands out, palm up, around the outside of the helm. "Now it's beginning to rain. Come stand next to me after you've gotten the sodas and stay dry."

"Okay," Tammy hollered, but she was concentrating on balancing the drinks in the crook of her arm so she had a free hand to hold on to the rail while making her way back to the helm. Suddenly, the boat became airborne as the bow of the boat rose high and crested over a wave, and then it slammed back down and smacked the surface of the water. On impact, waves crashed over the side of the boat, knocking Tammy off her feet. "Damn it!" she yelled. Grabbing the leg of the trap table, she watched in despair as one of the soda cans fell from her grasp and rolled away from her before coming to a stop against the side of the boat and exploding.

Dwayne turned his head in horror. "Are you okay?" he hollered, rushing over to help Tammy to her feet.

Using all her strength to stand up, she had no choice but to let the other soda go, and that too exploded like the first. She grabbed his aiding hand to pull herself up as gushes of water continued to pool around her. "It's a good job I still have my slickers on," she yelled above the roar of the ocean. "I'd be drenched if I didn't. So much for some refreshments."

Dwayne held onto her hand tight. "Never mind the drinks. Let's get you over to the helm where it's dry and safe. I need to get back to the wheel," he shouted while ducking his head away from the now pouring rain.

By the time Tammy reached the helm, her hair was drenched and beads of water dripped down her face. While holding onto the rail of the dash, she licked the excess water running over her lips and wiped the drops of water falling over her eyes from her bangs. She looked behind her at the downpour of rain and could barely make out the *Little Boat* being towed behind them. It rocked violently from side to side, taking on water from each crashing wave.

"Is the Little Boat going to be okay? It's taking on a lot of water," Tammy yelled.

Dwayne looked back over his shoulder. "So far, it's doing okay. The scuppers that allow excess water to run out of the boat seem to be working fine, but the waves are getting bigger by the minute. I'm guessing they are at about six to seven feet right now. When we are in the trough, that's twelve to fourteen feet of water above us. Hold on, okay? I don't want anything to happen to you."

Tammy gripped the rail until her knuckles turned white. She looked out through the windshield of the helm and saw nothing but an angry ocean, with waves constantly crashing over the bow of the boat. At each breaking wave, they became airborne and Tammy had to brace for impact when the hull slammed back into the ocean. It took all her strength and every muscle in her legs to remain standing.

By nightfall and still with six hours left of their journey, the storm became ruthless and showed no mercy. The jet black skies shielded the stars from view, and the winds howled at fifty miles an hour, throwing the downpour of rain at high speed against the windshield of the helm. The wipers couldn't keep up with the floods of water pouring down the glass. The seas had increased another foot. Each time they dipped down in the trough, Tammy cringed as the wall of water on either side of the boat crashed down over the deck. Anything that had been loose on the deck was now washed away.

Tammy looked over at Dwayne, who was at the wheel about two feet away. She was scared and wanted to be held by him, but that wasn't an option. It was impossible to move even an inch on the boat without losing her balance. Dwayne had braced himself against the side wall of the helm and was using both hands to steer the boat as best he could through the terrifying storm.

"How do you even steer in this weather?" Tammy hollered.

While turning the wheel back and forth, Dwayne yelled back, "It's not that easy, but I've spent most of my life on boats and have had plenty of practice." Suddenly, he grabbed the wheel hard with both hands and held it tight. "Shit, here comes a big wave. Hold on tight and bend your knees on impact."

Tammy looked ahead and screamed. She saw nothing but a fast approaching, solid body of water about to crash over the boat. "Oh my god! I don't want to die out here."

"Hold on!" Dwayne yelled.

Within seconds, the wave crashed into the boat and completely consumed the bow and the windshield. Sprays of water came around the sides and into where they stood, and Tammy ducked her head from the sting of the rain pelting her skin. She wanted to shield her ears from the angry roar of the ocean but was unable to let go of the rail. She turned her head just in time to see another deluge of water washing over the deck. "Oh my god!" she screamed. "There's the *Little Boat*. It's alongside of us. It's supposed to be behind us!"

Dwayne quickly turned his head and yelled, "Fuck! It's racing down the wave, causing a slack in the line."

"Is it going to be okay?" Tammy shouted back.

"As long as it doesn't hit us, it should be okay. When it's ridden the wave, the line should get tight again and pull it back behind us. Keep an eye on it."

"Okay."

Fearing the worst—that the *Little Boat* may crash into them—Tammy remained focused on it, waiting for the line to tighten like Dwayne said it would. But for the next few minutes, it remained alongside them as if in competition to beat the storm. "It's not going back!" she screamed.

"Give it a minute," Dwayne hollered while fighting with the wheel.

A few seconds later, Tammy saw the boat beginning to fall behind and released a huge sigh of relief. "There it goes."

Dwayne glanced over his shoulder. "Keep checking on it. If we get another big wave like that, it could happen again." No sooner had he said that, he yelled, "Hold on!"

Tammy looked ahead and saw yet again another huge wave about to hit them. "Fuck!" she screamed, scrunching her eyes closed. Both she and the boat got another drenching as they rocked violently back and forth. While still trying to recover from the impact, Tammy strained to check on the *Little Boat*. "It's alongside us again, but this time it's leaning right over."

Dwayne looked over and saw the side of the boat almost submerged. "Oh shit! It may roll." Panic blanketed his face as he continued to watch the *Little Boat*. "Come on. Get back up," he shouted at the *Little Boat* with urgency in his voice.

Both he and Tammy continued to watch the *Little Boat*, which was now almost on its side as the waves continued to crash over it.

"Come on!" Dwayne yelled again.

Tammy held her breath. There was nothing either one of them could do but hope the *Little Boat* would straighten itself out once the wave had passed. If it didn't, it would be a huge disaster and both boats could go down.

Dwayne yelled again, "Come on! God damn it!"

Tammy's eyes were now clouded by a mixture of seawater and tears. For the first time, she was afraid for their lives. She didn't know how to react or what to do. She was scared. She didn't want to die, especially not out here. The thought of drowning and falling to the bottom of the ocean never to be found again, absolutely terrified her. They were sitting ducks, helpless against the force of nature and what it may throw at them.

Images of Matt haunted her mind. She wanted to be with him and hold him. For the first time, she questioned herself and her recent decisions. What was she doing out here? In a panic, she yelled to Dwayne, "Isn't there anything we can do?"

"No!" He hollered back. "Just pray it gets back up."

They continued to watch for what seemed like an endless amount of time. Eventually, they both cheered and yelled, "There she goes!"

Tammy squealed "Yes!" as she saw the side of the boat lift away from the water. A few minutes later, the line slowly tightened and the *Little Boat* began to fall back behind the *Baywitch*. "Oh my god. I thought we were goners," she said while catching her breath. But in a matter of seconds, the *Baywitch* was back in the air and Tammy lost her balance again. Taken by surprise and with nothing to hold onto, she was thrown backwards onto the deck like a discarded ragdoll and swept to the back of the boat. She came to a stop when her spine slammed into the stern.

"Arghh!" she hollered, wincing as pain shot up and down the length of her back.

Because they had been so preoccupied with the status of the *Little Boat*, they hadn't seen the next humongous wave about to slam into the boat and Tammy had failed to brace for it. Luckily, Dwayne was still wedged against the wall of the helm and managed to avoid the brunt of it. He looked in horror at Tammy, who was scrunched against the back of the boat surrounded by pools of water. He watched helplessly as she ducked her head out of the howling wind and the fierce downpour of rain beating upon her.

With one hand, she held on to the back of the boat while trying to use the other hand for balance as she pulled herself to her feet, but the force of the boat surging back and forth made it impossible.

"Tammy, are you able to get up?" Dwayne yelled over the roar of the wind.

Unable to look up, she hollered back, "No, the wind is too strong and the boat is rocking too much."

"Hold on!" Dwayne yelled back.

While still keeping one hand on the wheel, Dwayne reached over to where he had some line on a hook and pulled it loose. Despite needing to keep the boat under control at the same time, he skillfully tied a loop knot and threw the end to Tammy. "Here, grab the line."

Straining to see the line through the pouring rain, she missed on the first attempt. "Fuck!"

Dwayne quickly pulled it back in and threw again.

"Got it!" she yelled.

"Okay. Hold on tight to the line. I'm going to pull you in."

"Okay!" Tammy yelled, grasping the line tight with both hands and wrapping it around her fists. Using the line for leverage, Tammy was finally able to pull herself to her feet and using all his strength, Dwayne began pulling her in. As she inched her way back to the helm, she could feel the line cutting into her flesh. As soon as she was within reach, Dwayne grabbed her and pulled her into his arms and held her tight. She was a mess. Her hair was soaking wet and matted, streams of water were running off her slickers and her cheeks were ice cold.

Dwayne took a hold of the wheel with one hand while still holding onto Tammy with the other. "My god, are you okay?"

Tammy fought to loosen the rope from around her fist. "No, I'm not okay," she cried, letting the tears stream down her face. With one last tug, she finally broke free of the rope. In a rush of fear and frustration, she bundled it up in a ball and threw it on the dash before fixing her cold, numb fingers back on the rail again.

She leaned in to Dwayne, who squeezed her tight and said, "You're okay now."

Tammy buried her face in his chest, trying to seek warmth from the frigid cold of the stormy night. "I was so scared and I'm freezing. I can't even feel my hands."

Dwayne rubbed her shoulders and pulled her in even closer, not wanting to let her go. "I'm so sorry that happened to you. You're safe now, I promise."

Still holding the wheel, he strained his eyes to see out through the windshield. Even though gushed of water still pounding against it, he couldn't miss what was coming. Releasing his hold from Tammy, he held on tight to the wheel and yelled, "Hold on with both hands and don't forget to bend your knees on impact. A big one is coming."

"God! I'm sick of this! When is it going to end?" she screamed while gripping her hands around the wooden rail of the dash. "I'm exhausted."

Within seconds, they became airborne as the *Baywitch* rode over the wave. Tammy braced herself for the impact; she didn't know how much more her body could take. She wouldn't be surprised if she had bruises the following day from the beating the ocean was giving her. As the *Baywitch* plunged into the water, Tammy let out a loud, painful grunt to ease the force of the impact. She turned her head to check on the *Little Boat* and saw it had snuck up closer but wasn't alongside them this time.

"You okay?" Dwayne shouted once the wave had passed.

Too tired to speak, Tammy gave him a nod and continued to look straight ahead.

For the next ten minutes, the boat continued to rock viciously and sprays of water continued to flood the deck, but the waves seemed to be decreasing in size.

"I think we're through the worst of it," Dwayne shouted from the wheel.

For the first time in a while, a slight smile breached Tammy's face. "God, I hope so. I was seriously scared for my life back there."

Dwayne could tell she was still concerned about their safety and left the wheel for a moment to embrace her. "I'm so sorry that your first experience out here was a life-threatening event. Trust me, I would never let anything happen to you. I knew we had a storm coming, but it traveled a lot faster than I anticipated and it was much stronger too. But, Tammy, you've been a trooper and handled it better than most people I know."

Tammy hugged him back, enjoying the security of his masculine arms around her. "It's okay. You can't control nature. I feel safe with you. I know how experienced you are, and I wouldn't be out here with anyone else but you." She chuckled.

Dwayne leaned in and gave her a wet, salty kiss on the lips. "I love you. You're the best."

"I love you too."

Feeling better and with the seas beginning to die down, Dwayne took the helm again, and Tammy returned to holding the rail and looking straight ahead.

By the time they were about an hour out of the harbor, the storm was behind them. It was around ten o'clock in the evening. Clouds still lingered in the sky, allowing a few stars to appear, but the rain had stopped and the wind was only a slight breeze. The waves were now a comfortable three-foot swell, and the *Little Boat* was where it was supposed to be, in tow behind them.

Tammy's body ached from head to toe. She couldn't wait until the boats were tied up to the dock so she could do a complete body check and look for bruises. She had a feeling she would find a few. Her hands were sore from clenching onto the rail for hours, to the point that it was too painful to move or bend her fingers, and every muscle in her legs ached and her feet were numb from standing for the entire trip.

Looking for any kind of relief and wanting to be close to Dwayne, she snuggled close to him for the last hour at the wheel. He held her close and rubbed her tired body with his free hand while she tucked her head onto his shoulder.

"I'm so tired. I can't remember ever feeling this exhausted," Tammy said in a sleepy voice.

Dwayne kissed the top of the head. "We're almost there, sweetheart. As soon as we're tied up, you go crawl into bed, okay? I'll take care of the *Little Boat*."

"No argument from me." But then a thought occurred to her and she raised her head. "You know, it just dawned on me that we're already home. We live and work on this boat. When we tie up, we don't have a home to go to. It's here. That's a strange feeling."

Dwayne nodded. "Yep, you're right. It kind of takes the stigma away of actually going home."

"It does. It feels kind of weird. Depressing in a way. No big bed to go home to or the space that a house offers. Something else I'll have to get used to I guess. It just never occurred to me until now."

She confessed to herself that the idea wasn't so appealing.

They finally pulled into the dock around eleven o'clock, where the waters were calm and the winds were non-existent. Tammy dragged her feet and struggled to step onto the dock to help tie off the boats. She giggled when her feet came into contact with the hard surface of the dock. Even though they swayed a little bit, it was nothing like being on a boat for the past two days. She had to stand for a moment to become reacquainted with dry land. Her legs felt like jelly and she had to think before putting one foot in front of the other.

"This feels weird." She laughed while cleating off the *Baywitch*.

"You'll get used to it. Wait until we come back after being out for seven days." Dwayne laughed while shutting off the engines of the *Baywitch* and jumping off to deal with the *Little Boat*.

Once both boats were secured, Dwayne joined Tammy in the cabin. Having wasted no time, she was already undressed, wearing only her bra and panties and was busy inspecting her body on the edge of the bed.

"God, no wonder my body hurts. Look at me. I'm a mess!" she said while twisting her leg at obscure angles to see her thigh.

"Here, let me take a look." Dwayne leaned in to help. "Damn, girl! You're not kidding."

After a closer look, they found a total of eight bruises on Tammy's body. The worst being on her back and upper thighs, which probably happened when she fell and slid across the deck. Her back was scraped up from the rough finish of the non-skid on the deck, and the thigh that had slammed onto the surface was bruised a deep purple. She had more bruises on her hips where she banged into the dash of the helm a few times, and a couple more on her arms.

"God, Tammy, I didn't realize you got so banged up," Dwayne said while rubbing the back her thigh softly. "Are you going to be able to go back out?"

Adamant about not being a quitter, Tammy became defensive. "Of course I'll be able to go back out. Nothing a good night's sleep can't take care of." She softened her tone and kissed Dwayne on the lips. "They're just bruises. I'll be fine."

"Okay. I just worry about you. Come on, let's get you into bed and I'll massage you until you fall asleep."

The next morning, Tammy could barely move. She turned her head on the pillow and saw Dwayne was already up and busy making coffee. It was the sweet aroma that had woken her. Rolling to the edge of the bed, she winced in pain every time she had to move a muscle. "God, doesn't your body ache? I feel like I've been run over by a steam roller." She reached round to rub the small of her back, but she pulled away again when her arm flinched in pain.

"I'm a little sore, but I didn't get thrown across the boat like you." He turned and took Tammy's hands. "Here, let me help you."

Slowly, Tammy raised herself to her feet. "Ouch!" she screamed, followed by grunts of pains. "Oh man, I wish you had a bath tub. You have no idea what I would do to be able soak in a tub right now."

Dwayne helped her up on to the deck and into a chair before bringing her a cup of coffee. "Are you sure you'll be able to go back out? I don't want you to overdo it. I care about you." He seemed genuinely concerned about the agony she was going through.

"I'll be fine. I just need to loosen up a bit. After my coffee, I'll get dressed and walk a few laps around the yard."

Dwayne leaned in and gave her a gentle kiss. "Okay. If you're sure. I know how stubborn you can be." He chuckled.

After a few sips of her coffee, Tammy was already feeling the magical effects of caffeine and feeling more alert. "When do we leave again?" she asked.

"Tonight."

A look of shock blanketed her face. Tonight!"

"I'm afraid so. We only have a week to get all these traps out. We need to do two more trips. But we're only taking the *Baywitch* this time. I wanted to take the *Little Boat* on the first trip so we could explore the island. I figured we'd go get fuel and groceries today and when we get back, we can load traps on to the boat and do a night crossing. We'd leave here about six and get to San Clemente around three in the morning. There are no storms in the forecast, so it should be a nice crossing," Dwayne added, knowing how anxious Tammy must be about going back out there again. "We can rest up for a bit before the sun comes up and then go dump the traps." A devious smile appeared on Dwayne's face as he knelt in front of Tammy and began rubbing her thighs. "Tell you what. Why don't I take you up to the showers and caress those bruises of yours? I can gently wash every inch of your body. How does that sound?"

Tammy beamed a radiant smile. "Hmm, that sounds wonderful. But after the amazing shower that you are promising me, I want to call Matt. I can't wait to hear his voice. That will make me feel better."

"Good idea! I want to say hi to the little guy too, and I'll give Justin a call while we're there." Dwayne took her hand. "Are you ready?"

"I am. Let's go."

～

Over the next week, Tammy and Dwayne made two more trips to the island. Both were much easier than the first. A friendlier ocean and taking only one boat allowed them to trade off driving and take breaks so they could actually sit down for a while. But each trip was made back to back, and the work was intense from the minute they tied up at the dock to the time they left again. There was so much to do when they returned that there was little time left for sleep.

On one of the trips, Tammy finally got to meet the captain of *Sea-Life*. He was about the same age as Dwayne but heavier set and wore a red baseball hat with the name of his boat on it. His arms and face were tanned from spending endless days on the ocean. He was friendly toward Tammy and welcomed her to the fishery. He wished her luck and offered his help to them both if they ever needed it.

After making the last trip and returning in the early hours of the morning, they managed to get a good night's sleep of at least seven hours. It was the most they'd had in over a week. But then they had to gear up for the actual fishing trip, which was scheduled for the first Wednesday in October. They had only five days to get ready. This is what Tammy had been waiting for and just the thought was enough to energize her. She couldn't wait to get started.

As always, her priority at the beginning of each day when they were on land was to call Matt, which always put her in a better place. He had adjusted quickly and well and was enjoying his new playmate Andrew. Tales of him doing new things that Tammy hadn't yet seen tore at her heart. She laughed with tears while Joanne told her about the day he got stuck up in a tree. It was his first time climbing a tree. Another time, her father said Matt had been helping him to plant some bulbs. Tammy had never done any gardening with Matt, but it brought back forgotten memories of gardening days with her dad.

That morning, Tammy and Dwayne moved with great difficulty. The grueling week had finally caught up with them, and they tried to capture as much rest as possible before going at it again. After Tammy's phone call to Matt, they spent a few quality hours together on the deck of the *Baywitch*, enjoying the morning rays of sun with an overdose of caffeine.

Even though the time spent together was short, it was something they both needed and had missed. While working on the boat, it had been nothing but intense labor from sun up to sun down and a few hours in between to catch some sleep. Tammy savored every minute of Dwayne's affection and cuddles, knowing as soon as they got up, they wouldn't stop again until the traps were baited and set at the island.

Dwayne had explained what needed to be done before they headed out, and the list was long. They had just enough money to make it back out, but after buying all the supplies, he told her they would be broke. Everything relied on a successful catch.

The first task was to fuel up both boats, and they would also need extra barrels of fuel on the boat to fill up the *Little Boat* while they were out at the island. Next would be a trip to downtown LA to pick up 500 pounds of frozen bait and load it onto the boats. A week's worth of groceries needed to be bought, and twenty-five lobster receivers needed to be stacked onto the boat.

"What are those?" Tammy asked.

"They are plastic crates that float in the water and are tied up to the *Baywitch* in the harbor. We use them to put the lobsters in and keep them alive until we return. We only get paid for live lobsters, so keeping them healthy is critical. After a few days, I'm hoping a few of the crates in the water will be full of lobsters."

It took two days to get all the tasks completed, but now that the last knot was tied and everything was secured on the boat, they had just enough money left over to treat themselves to a nice dinner at the nearby steak house. It would be their last big cooked meal for seven days, Dwayne reminded Tammy.

At the restaurant, they sat side by side. Tammy cuddled in Dwayne's arms as she devoured every last morsel on her plate, enjoying the simple pleasures of a hearty meal.

"That was delicious. I'm stuffed," she said as she pushed her plate away. "And I'm so tired."

Dwayne pulled her in closer and gently pulled her hair back away from her face before kissing her softly on the cheek. "How are you holding up? Are you sorry you decided to go fishing with me?" He added a nervous chuckle, not sure of her reply.

Tammy pulled herself up away from his chest and turned to face him. "Oh gosh, no. Never! I'm loving every bit of it. Even our victory at sea." She laughed. "I love spending our entire days and nights together, working with you and learning all these new things. I just hope we catch some bloody lobsters after all this hard work."

"Hearing you say that makes me happy. You're a trooper, Tammy. I've never met anyone like you. I was afraid I'd worked you too hard and probably scared you off. I thought you'd never want to fish again. Having you around makes fishing enjoyable. I love you."

Tammy leaned in and met his kiss. His lips felt rough from being on the ocean but she didn't care; she loved everything about him. "I love you too."

Their kiss lingered for a few minutes and grew passionately with their tongues exploring each other's mouths. Holding her tight in his arms, Dwayne broke away in a panted breath. "Come on, let's go back to the boat. I want to make love to you. It might be the last time for a whole week."

"Sounds like a beautiful way to end the day," Tammy replied in a soft voice.

The next morning, they left before the sun was up, feeling refreshed and fully rested. They rode together on the *Baywitch* with the *Little Boat* in tow. The ocean remained their friend and granted them a glorious crossing with calm waters, blue skies and plenty of sunshine. They made good time and reached the island by three o'clock, and they found they were no longer alone in the harbor. There were six other boats already anchored.

Tammy recognized the *Sea-Life* and Dwayne pointed out three others that he knew: *Patience, Lobster Fest* and *Out to Sea.* He had gotten to know them when he had fished Malibu but hadn't seen any of the captains since last season. "We'll have to go for a cruise around the harbor so I can introduce you after we've cut up all the bait and gotten organized."

Remembering how friendly Mitch was at their introduction, Tammy liked the idea of meeting the other captains. She agreed with great enthusiasm.

By five o'clock, Dwayne and Tammy had all the bait cut, the bait jars filled and everything ready to start baiting and setting the traps tomorrow. They had just enough daylight to go and say hi to the captains Dwayne already knew, and to introduce themselves to the others. They jumped on the *Little Boat*, which was easier to maneuver, and drove off.

They stopped first at the *Patience*, a boat about the same size as the *Baywitch* but with a bright red hull. Patrick, the captain, walked to the stern of the boat as Dwayne pulled up. Tammy saw he had one other crew member who was busy coiling up line and gave Dwayne a nod before returning to his task. Patrick was also about the same age as Dwayne, in his thirties, and he gave them both a friendly smile. Much to Tammy's surprise, he made her feel welcome.

"It's nice to finally see a woman out here. I'm sure you'll show us how it's done and put us in our places," he hollered across the water with a hearty laugh.

Tammy couldn't help but laugh back. "I'll do my best!"

To Tammy's disappointment, the captains on the other two boats, Tom on the *Lobster Fest* and Lester on the *Out to Sea*, weren't so friendly. She sensed their doubts regarding her ability, and she felt a little hurt when they both told her they'd be surprised if she lasted the season.

"I've never seen a woman fish out here in all my forty years. There's a reason for that you know," Lester said.

"Well, she's not like other women," Dwayne corrected. "She's going to be just fine out here. You watch. She surprised the hell out of me and she will do the same to you." He threw Tammy a smile as he bragged about her.

"I'm curious to see how long she'll last. Well, good luck to you both," he said before they took off.

With the sun setting fast, they made it to one other boat to say hi to the eldest of the captains called Dale. His boat was named *Dreaming*, a boat Dwayne didn't know. He didn't seem too happy to see them and was also surprised to see a woman out at the island. Tammy could tell he doubted her abilities to fish and live on a boat for five days straight, which is what they would be doing once the traps were baited and set. He asked her the typical questions. Had she ever fished before? Does she know what she's in for? All his questions were followed by a sarcastic laugh.

She could tell he had spent his entire life on the ocean fishing. He was probably in his sixties, with a crew of three deckhands handling the traps stacked on the boat. His skin had clearly been exposed to years of sunlight, having a look of tanned leather. Deep wrinkles and crow's feet surrounded his eyes, his nose was peeling and his lips were dry and chapped. As he spoke from his boat, his shoulder-length, mangled gray hair blew in the wind. He also stroked his gray beard the entire time, which Tammy thought was a little creepy. But she wasn't going to allow herself to be intimidated by anyone. She knew she was capable of handling anything that was thrown at her, and she would prove herself to the rest of the fleet fishing the island.

During the interrogation, Tammy was grateful Dwayne had her back and beamed him a smile when he began bragging about her to Dale while holding her tightly around the waist. Dale seemed surprise by Dwayne's praises and had backed off a little by mumbling, "Well, all's I can say is good luck."

Dale went on to tell them he'd been fishing San Clemente for over ten years, and more boats showed up every year. He complained that pretty soon the island would be fished out. "There's not enough lobsters for all these damn boats."

Dwayne took it all in his stride. Being one of the new boats Dale had complained about, he didn't want to be on the old timer's shit list. He'd heard many stories of angry fisherman who had been known to cut off your traps if you fished too close to his, or if he was envious of your catch, he would steal them for himself, or even worse, pull your line and open all the doors to your traps.

Life as a commercial fisherman was competitive and at times ruthless. Dwayne wanted no trouble; he just wanted to fish, and even though the guy came across as an asshole, Dwayne bit his tongue. "Sorry you feel that way. We just stopped by to introduce ourselves." Dale had already turned his back on them and proceeded to move gear around on the deck of his boat. "We'll let you get back to work," Dwayne hollered before steering the *Little Boat* away. "What a jerk," he whispered in Tammy's ear.

By the time they got back to the *Baywitch*, the sun had already set and the night sky was dominated by a full moon, which Dwayne liked because, according to legend, it made the lobster crawl.

Bright deck lights from all the other boats illuminated the harbor while Tammy sat on the deck, surrounded by boxes of fresh-cut bait and frozen mackerel.

"God, this bait stinks," she said to Dwayne.

"That is the smell of money," he said, inhaling a lungful of the stench through his nose. "I love that smell. Wait till the end of the week when most of this lot has defrosted."

"Speak for yourself," Tammy tried to say while holding the end of her nose closed.

Dwayne took her hand and rubbed it softly. "I'm so happy you're out here with me. I'd be so lonely if you weren't. Thank you for coming."

"You don't have to thank me. I want to be here. I'm loving every minute of this new adventure you brought me on. And you are a great coach by the way."

"You have gone far beyond my expectations and you never cease to amaze me. As for the guys on the other boats, don't let them get to you. They can be real assholes at times."

Tammy shook her hair and held her head up high in defiance. "Oh, I won't. I'll show them."

While enjoying the little time they had to relax, they spent the rest of the evening watching the crews on the other boats doing their last-minute chores before the big day of baiting and setting traps. Like Dwayne, some were finished and could be seen hanging out on their decks, the sound of their laughter carrying across the water.

Dwayne went over their plan for the next day. They would be using the *Little Boat* every day. He would be driving the boat and Tammy had the job of deckhand. As Dwayne pulled up to each buoy, her job, he explained, was to hook the line using a long-handled gaff and wrap the line around the pulley. Dwayne would then work the pulley wheel and pull the trap up. Once it was on the table, Tammy would bait it and close the door while Dwayne drove the boat to the desired fishing location. Once at the spot, it was up to Tammy to push the trap overboard and throw out the line and buoy. They had a hundred fifty traps to do. They worked well together and both were confident they could get them all done by the end of the day.

The next morning, before sunrise at four thirty, Dwayne and Tammy were the first to leave the harbor. Dressed in their slickers, rubber boots, gloves and a layer of t-shirts with a sweater beneath, they took off in the chilled darkened morning for the first trap. It was only five minutes away on the east side of the island, where it was always calm for the first half of the day.

With her gaff in hand, Tammy stood alert behind Dwayne, looking out for the first buoy floating on the water. A few minutes later, she spotted their red and black colors and squealed while pointing with her finger. "There it is at two o'clock!"

Dwayne followed her finger and as they approached it, he slowed down the boat to allow Tammy to gaff it, but she missed and yelled, "Damn it!"

"That okay. You'll get the hang of it after doing this all day," Dwayne said as he began turning around and coming back up on the buoy. "Okay, try again," he hollered while trying to keep the boat steady.

With one swing of the gaff, she nailed it. "Got it!" she yelled in triumph.

"Great! Now grab the rope, wrap it around the pulley and throw the buoy on the deck."

It didn't take Tammy long to bait up the trap and seal the door closed. By the time Dwayne was at the fishing spot, she was ready to drop it back in the ocean and on command, she pushed it overboard and tossed out the line and buoy.

Dwayne gave her a high-five. "Good job!" he shouted over the noise of the outboard. "Hold on, we're gonna speed up to the next one. 149 more and we'll be done."

As they headed toward the next trap, Tammy hollered to Dwayne, "Look over there! It's a sea lion. He's following us," she squealed with excitement.

"Yeah, he's after the bait. Whatever you do, don't feed him, otherwise we'll never get rid of him."

They hustled all day, and with no time to rest in between each set of traps, they snacked on whatever they could grab and ate quickly before they reached the next trap. Tammy missed with the gaff a few more times, but like Dwayne had said, she soon got the hang of it. Periodically, she noticed the seal was still following them and when Dwayne wasn't looking, she tossed him a mackerel. *What harm can it do? The poor guy is hungry.*

By mid-afternoon, they had succeeded in baiting and moving one hundred twenty traps, but the last thirty were becoming a challenge. The wind had picked up and the swells had increased. Keeping the boat steady to allow Tammy to gaff the rope wasn't easy, and the time spent at each one was becoming longer. They were beginning to tire; their bodies were sore and their feet ached from standing all day. Tammy found she had to brace her knees hard against the hull of the boat to steady herself from the increased rocking of the boat as she leaned over to hook the line.

The *Little Boat* had low sides that only came up above their knees and, afraid she might fall overboard, Dwayne held onto the back of her sweater as she leaned over. "I gotcha!" he hollered each time she swung out the gaff.

By the time the sun was setting over the horizon, they were pulling up to the last trap. Feeling rejuvenated that their quest was finally coming to an end, and that they had accomplished what they had set out to do over fourteen hours ago, they pulled up on the final buoy cheering at the top of their lungs. "Don't miss!" Dwayne laughed. "I don't want to prolong this anymore."

"Got it!" Tammy cheered.

"That's my girl!"

Once the last trap was back in the water, Dwayne turned off the boat and made his way over to Tammy. "Give me a kiss, partner. You were fantastic today."

Tammy held up her hands. "Don't get too close. I'm a slimy mess." She looked down at her slickers, now coated in blood and what she could only describe as gunk. "Look at me. I'm covered in fish guts."

Dwayne ignored her warning and took her in his arms. "You smell like money." He laughed before giving her a hard kiss on the lips.

Tammy welcomed his affection and smothered him in wet, salty kisses. "Thanks. You weren't too bad yourself. I can't wait to see what we have tomorrow. You're right, this is just like bloody Christmas Eve."

*W*hen they returned to the harbor, it was nightfall and the moon was just as bright as it had been the night before. The sky was clear and hundreds of stars glistened above them. "Man, what a beautiful night," Tammy said, admiring the illuminated skies above her from the deck.

Most of the boats were already back in and anchored down for the night. Dwayne and Tammy waved as they cruised by toward their mooring.

"I gotta find a way to clean up. I stink," Tammy proclaimed while tying up to the cleat of the *Baywitch.*

"I wouldn't bother until we've scrubbed down the little boat and cut up enough bait for tomorrow's pull. That's gonna take a few hours."

"Damn…does it ever end? Tell you what, I'll chop bait while you take care of the *Little Boat.* I'm already stinky." She laughed.

Dwayne was right. It took them another two hours to do the last remaining chores of their long day, by which time, Tammy was beyond desperate to find a way to clean herself up. There was no shower on the boat, or any hot water for that matter.

"I'm going to go say a howdy to Mitch on the radio before it gets too late and see how his day went. You can always dip a towel in the ocean and use that to wash yourself off with."

"I'll think of something. Say hi to Mitch for me."

Ten minutes later, while Dwayne was involved in a conversation with Mitch on the radio, he heard a loud splash from the back of the boat and quickly turned his head, just in time to see a spray of water hit the boat. "What the hell?"

Mitch came over the radio. "Was that your girl I just saw jump into the water naked?"

Hearing cheers and whistles from the other fisherman echoing from the surrounding boats, Dwayne dropped the mic and left it dangling by its cord while he rushed to the stern to see what all the commotion was about. With a confused look, he peered over the side and saw Tammy raise her head out of the water.

"God, this feels bloody fantastic!" she yelled with a huge grin painted across her face.

Dwayne was stunned. "Are you crazy? What the hell are you doing?"

"I'm taking a bath. It feels wonderful. Want to join me?"

"No!" Dwayne said defiantly. "Great whites swim in that water. Come on, get out."

Behind them, the other fisherman continued to cheer and raise whatever drink they had in their hand. Dwayne looked up and laughed at the excitement from the growing audience of guys, who were probably enjoying a memorable moment of seeing a naked woman swimming in Northwest harbor for the first time in their lives. "Well, that's one way to get the guys to like you." He chuckled. "They're never going to forget this. You're crazy, girl!"

"Ha!" Tammy squealed while floating on her back with her breasts protruding toward the stars. "I feel liberated. You gotta try it!"

"No thanks. I'm good. Besides, I'm enjoying the view like

everyone else," he said with a mischievous wink. "Isn't the water cold?"

"Nah. It's feels great. Sure you don't wanna come in?"

Dwayne shook his head again. "Thanks. I'm sure."

Tammy rolled off her back and continued to tread water as she spoke. "Okay, but you're missing out. I'm going to go for a swim. I'll be back in a bit."

"Stay close to the boat where I can see you. I'm going to stay right here and watch you. I'm sure everyone else will too," he added.

Tammy granted Dwayne's wishes and didn't swim too far away. Periodically, she waved to the loud fishermen, some of whom were now viewing the spectacle through binoculars. She liked the attention, and it seemed Dwayne was getting a kick out of it too. She swam around for a good ten minutes before the chill started to set in, so she made her way back to the swimstep where Dwayne stood anxiously with a towel in hand. As she pulled herself out of the water, her naked body on full display, the whistles and cheers grew louder.

"Well, you've certainly made their night," he said with a grin. He handed her the towel over the side of the boat and she quickly wrapped herself in it. "Come on, take my hand, I'll help you up," Dwayne told her.

Once she was on the boat, Tammy started to shiver, so Dwayne took her in his arms and began rubbing her shoulders vigorously.

"That felt good. But damn, I'm freezing now. I'm going into the cabin to warm up." She looked up at Dwayne while still in his arms and gave him a smooch. "I love you."

"I love you too, you crazy woman you." He slapped her behind as she broke away from his hold. "Now go on. Go get warm while I put some soup on for dinner."

Soup was the quickest and easiest meal to heat and eat on a boat, especially when they were too tired to do anything else.

Dwayne knew this from experience and within ten minutes, he had two servings of clam chowder in metal cups ready along with a couple of rolls.

"Soup's ready," he hollered from the deck.

"Coming," she replied from the cabin while pulling a comb through her wet, mangled hair.

A few minutes later, she joined Dwayne on the deck dressed in clean sweats. "I'm bloody famished. The soup smells good," she said, taking the empty seat next to him. She scooped a cup out of his hands and a roll from his lap. "Thank you."

"Let's eat this and call it an early night. What do you say? Tomorrow's the big day. I want to take off around five in the morning."

"Sounds good to me. I'm bloody knackered," Tammy said in between spoonfuls of soup, each one instantly warming her to the core. Other than her quick dip in the ocean, this was the first time she had been still all day, and she cherished the short moment of quiet while savoring every delicious taste of her hot soup. The winds were absent and the boat rocked gently, making it easier to eat. She glanced out at the other boats and noticed a few already had their lights turned off, telling her they also were planning for an early start.

Dwayne had told her that the opening day of lobster season is usually the best. The lobsters hadn't been fished in six months and the crawl should be heavy. It's the day that they should make the most money. After that, it would start to drop off. Every boat was counting on a good catch on that first day, because most were probably in debt, just like they were.

The anticipation of pulling the traps tomorrow was not only exciting but also nerve-wracking. What if they didn't catch enough lobsters to cover their expenses and get caught up with the bills? What were they going to do? She never realized how much they were depending on this first catch until Dwayne had explained their finances.

"I hope there's a bunch of lobsters crawling in our traps right now," she said while taking her last spoonful of soup.

"Me too. Come on, let's go to bed. We will find out tomorrow."

Fifteen minutes later, they were curled up in each other's arms beneath the covers, both trying desperately to fall asleep. But the anticipation of tomorrow's pull prevented them. Lying restless in Dwayne's arms, Tammy thought she heard a loud thud out on the deck of the boat. "Did you hear that?" she whispered to Dwayne.

"Hear what?" Dwayne asked in near sleepy state.

"I think there's someone out there."

After almost being asleep, Dwayne was now wide awake again and feeling somewhat irritated because he knew it would be a challenge to go back to sleep again. He answered with an edge to his voice. "Tammy, we're in the middle of nowhere on a boat. There's no one out there. Now go to sleep."

Suddenly, they were alerted by another loud thud on the deck. They both sat bolt upright, straining their ears for any more strange noises.

"See, I told you there's someone out there!" Tammy whispered.

"What the fuck?" Dwayne whispered back. "Wait here."

Tammy remained in the bed while Dwayne reluctantly ducked his head and crawled out of their tiny sleeping quarters. Flashlight in hand, he cautiously eased his way to the cabin door and again heard another thud. Looking over his shoulder at Tammy, he whispered, "There's definitely something out there."

Unsure of what Dwayne was about to face, Tammy swung her legs out of the bed and sat nervously on the edge, her legs dangling in the cold night air. Dwayne turned on the floodlights of the deck before swinging the cabin door open. Shocked by what he saw, he had only two words. "Holy fuck!" he shouted and quickly closed the door again

Now on her feet, Tammy asked, "What is it?" A loud grunting noise came from the deck. "What the fuck is that?"

"There' a fucking 500 pound seal on the deck of our boat,"

Dwayne hollered back while searching frantically for some sort of weapon to shoo the beast off the boat.

"What? You're kidding?"

Dwayne froze mid search and turned to Tammy with an inquisitive stare. "Wait. Did you feed the seal today while we were baiting the traps?"

Tammy shied away from his stare and chewed on her lip for a moment, contemplating her answer. "Well…maybe a couple of times. There was a seal following us and he looked hungry, so I tossed him a couple of fish."

Dwayne knew he should be angry with her for not following his rules when it came to feeding the sea lions, but he just couldn't. Maybe now she'd understand why. Instead, he simply shook his head and laughed. "Well, your buddy is wanting more fish. Now do you see why I told you not to feed them?"

Showing his impatience, the sea lion bellowed in the direction of the cabin door. Tammy jumped back from the beastly sound while hanging her head in shame. "I'm sorry. I had no idea. I promise I won't feed them again." She looked up toward the cabin door and then at Dwayne. "What are we going to do?"

"We've got to figure out a way to get him off the boat."

"Can we throw a mackerel in the water? Maybe he will jump off to get it," Tammy suggested.

Dwayne chuckled. "No, because he will just come back for another one tomorrow." He began searching the boat again, but he soon realized all his long poles were on the deck.

"What about saucepans? You can bang them together."

Dwayne smiled with an agreeable nod. "Good idea! Hand me a couple." Tammy quickly retrieved two metal saucepans from a drawer and gave them to Dwayne, who inched his way back toward the door. Standing closer behind him, with one hand on his shoulder, she held her breath as Dwayne slowly pushed open the door. Shocked by what stood before them, Tammy almost fell backwards and clung onto Dwayne's shoulder to keep her balance.

"Fuck! He's huge!" she screamed, finding herself face to face with the biggest creature she had ever seen.

The stench that came from his breath as he let out another fierce roar caused Tammy to quickly turn her head and hold her nose. "God, he stinks," Tammy yelled in disgust.

Not wanting to give the beast a chance to enter the cabin, Dwayne wasted no time in furiously banging the pans together while yelling at the top of his voice, "Get out of here! Go on. Go!"

For a few seconds, the seal stayed put in his puddle of water on the deck and simply stared at Dwayne. Seeing Dwayne as the only thing standing in his way of the mackerel, the seal argued his case with another deafening roar. But Dwayne stood his ground. Hitting the pans together harder, he continued to shout and step slowly up to the deck.

Tammy followed close behind, joining Dwayne in his yelling. "Go on! Go!" she growled in a vicious tone.

The seal began to retreat and inch by inch, he slid his body toward the stern of the boat. Dwayne and Tammy continued with their yelling and screaming, backing the seal away. They herded him backwards until he had nowhere to go but over the back of the boat. With one last clash of the pans, the seal roared again before sliding his body around and leaping onto the ledge of the stern. By this time, flashlights from other boats were aimed in their direction, all wondering what the commotion was about.

"Go on! Shoo!" Dwayne yelled, now within a foot of the intruder. Defeated and clearly upset, the seal pushed himself off the ledge and landed in the ocean with an almighty splash. He instantly disappeared beneath the surface.

With a heaving chest and an adrenaline rush still raging through his body, Dwayne bent over and locked his hands on his knees to try and catch his breath. "Damn, that was close."

Tammy flopped into the deck chair close by, her legs limp like a jellyfish, her breathing heavy like Dwayne's. "Man, I've never seen a seal up close like that before. I can't get over how big he was. He was bloody massive."

Dwayne's panting began to subside and his demeanor began to soften. Raising his back, he released a cocky laugh. "Now do you see why I said not to feed the seals?"

"Yes. I'm sorry." Tammy gave him a flirtatious smile to strengthen her apology.

Feeling relieved from the departure of the seal, they headed back toward the cabin to attempt to go back to sleep, but they stalled when they heard Mitch's voice over the radio.

"Dwayne, everything okay over there? Do you copy?"

Dwayne said to Tammy, "Mitch probably heard everything. Sound carries over water. Let me talk to him real quick. He's probably wondering what all the commotion was about. I'll be right there."

Tammy nodded. "Okay," she replied as she headed down into the cabin.

"Hey, Mitch, I gottcha. Over."

"Hey, Dwayne, everything okay? I heard you guys hollering and making all kinds of noise. Are you guys having a domestic?" He laughed. "Over."

"No. A giant seal decided to pay us a visit on the boat. He's gone now. Tammy learnt the hard way about why we don't feed the seals. Over."

"Oh, man. Yeah, they're aggressive buggers. Glad everything's okay. Tell Tammy hi. I'm out."

"Sure will. Thanks for checking in. Over and out."

"Well, that was embarrassing," Tammy said from under the covers as Dwayne entered the cabin. "Now I'm gonna be the laughing stock of the fleet."

Dwayne joined her in the bed and gave her a comforting hug. "No you're not, silly. You're not the first one to feed the seals. Out here, everything is a learning curve. Through trial and error, we learn what to do and what not to do. And you've just had your first lesson on what not to do." He pulled her in closer. "Come over here and give me a kiss. We've got a big day tomorrow, so try and get some sleep and dream of thousands of lobsters crawling into our traps."

After months of preparation and hauling gear across the ocean, Tammy was too excited to sleep. She knew she'd regret it tomorrow, but everything they had worked so hard for led up to the opening day. This is what it was all about, and the anticipation kept her awake most of the night. Afraid of waking Dwayne, who slept peacefully next to her, she lay motionless, staring at the berth's ceiling for most of the night and feeling anxious for the alarm to go off. When it finally did, she shook Dwayne's arm vigorously.

"Dwayne! It's time to get up. We get to go fishing today!"

Startled by her force, Dwayne was awake in seconds. "You're not excited, are you?" he said while rubbing his eyes and pulling himself to an upright position.

Tammy was wedged between the wall and Dwayne. The only way to get out of the bed was to either climb over Dwayne or wait for him to get up and move out of the way. "Come on, get up. I want to get dressed and get our snacks together."

Dwayne laughed at her enthusiasm. "Hold on a sec. Can I open my eyes first?" He chuckled while slowly pulling himself out of the bed.

In a dash, Tammy rolled out and squeezed past Dwayne while grabbing her clothes off the bench. "There's no room down here for us both to get dressed. I'm going on deck, it's still dark out so no one will see me."

"It wouldn't matter if it was broad daylight. Everyone's already seen you naked." He laughed again.

Tammy gave him a friendly slap across his shoulder before heading out to put on her clothes. Within minutes, she was fully clothed along with her slickers and rubber boots. "Are you dressed yet?" she hollered down to the cabin, throwing snacks and drinks into the ice chest on the little boat.

"Yes. I'm coming," he said with a giggle in his voice. "Damn, who needs an alarm clock when I have you?" Once on the deck, he grabbed his slickers and his boots and began putting them on. "What about coffee?" he asked while struggling with his boots.

"No time. I have orange juices and cereal bars on the dash of the *Little Boat*. We can eat those while on our way to our first trap."

Dwayne looked around the boat, checking to make sure they weren't forgetting anything. He had learnt to load the *Little Boat* with everything they would need the night before, which made the morning much easier. "Okay. I guess we're ready to go."

Not wanting to waste another minute, Tammy quickly jumped onto the *Little Boat* and began untying the lines while Dwayne fired up the motor.

"Let's go fishing!" Dwayne hollered as he pushed them off the *Baywitch*. Tammy beamed him a huge smile while scanning the harbor. All the deck lights shone brightly from the other boats and Tammy could see the crews preparing for their day. They were the first to leave the harbor, so she gave them a friendly wave as they drove by.

As they pulled out of the harbor, the waters were calm and the sun was just beginning to rise. "Nice day for fishing," Dwayne yelled from the wheel as Tammy stood close behind him with her gaff in hand, searching for the first buoy.

Within a few minutes, she spotted it. "There it is, at three o'clock." She pointed with her finger.

She grabbed it on the first try and wrapped the line around the puller. In turn, Dwayne worked the puller to bring the trap up to the boat. Peering into the clear water, Tammy squinted her eyes for a glimpse of the trap.

"Oh, the anticipation." She laughed while still looking. "I wonder if it has lobsters in it?" Suddenly, she jumped with excitement. "I see it. Here it comes." Within seconds, it was on the trap table, but to her dismay it was empty. "Not one bloody lobster," she moaned and looked at Dwayne with worry written across her face. "I hope they're not all like this."

While the boat was in idle, Dwayne pointed to the back. "Go ahead and bait it and stack it at the rear of the boat. We'll move it out deeper. There are obviously no lobsters here."

He waited until the trap was secured on the deck and Tammy had her hand on a rail before taking off toward the next one. The next two traps were identical to the first one, empty. Both traps were brought on the boat to be relocated, and Tammy and Dwayne rode in silence to the next one with looks of concern

It took a few minutes to reach it and with hesitation, they brought it onto the boat. Tammy squealed once it was on the table, as inside were a bunch of lobsters. "Yes! We got some."

"Halleluah!" Dwayne cried while doing some sort of happy dance and reaching over to give Tammy a quick smooch.

Having never seen a lobster up close before, she opened the trap with caution.

"They look weird. They look like giant cockroaches."

"Hey! That's what we call them. We call them cockroaches of the ocean."

"I can see why." With the door of the trap now open, she leaned in to take a closer look. The bottom of the trap was covered with them. "Will they bite?" Then she noticed something. "I thought lobsters had claws and they pinch you. These don't have any claws."

"No, these are California spiny lobsters. They don't have claws; they have the long antenna instead, which they use as feelers. But see all the thorn looking things on their back? If you get poked by one of those, it will sting for days. Always wear gloves when picking one up."

"I don't know if I want to," Tammy said with a hint of fear in her voice.

"It's easy once you know how. Here, I'll show you."

Tammy watched closely as Dwayne reached in and grabbed one with his gloved hand, touching only the shell part above the tail. As he slowly lifted it out of the trap, the lobster began flapping its tail, causing Tammy to jump back.

"That's another thing you've got to watch out for," Dwayne warned.

Once the lobster had calmed down, Tammy approached the trap again and watched as Dwayne reached over to the dash and grabbed some sort of metal gauge.

"What's that?" she asked.

"It's a measuring gauge. Every lobster must be measured, and I use this to make sure they are within the legal limit, which is three and a quarter inches. He moved in closer so Tammy could see what he was doing. Tammy watched as he placed the tool between the eyes and over its back, which was the shell part. He wriggled the gauge. "See this? There's movement. This is what we call a short. It goes back in the ocean." With one swift movement of his arm, Dwayne tossed it overboard.

"What?" Tammy protested. "You mean we can't keep all of these?"

"Nope," Dwayne said, picking up another lobster.

The second lobster was thrown back into the water too. "Okay, it's your turn. Try picking one up and handing it to me."

"Ugh. Really?" Tammy hesitated before reaching into the trap. "What if one pokes me?"

"Then you will be hurting for a few days."

After looking at the cluster of lobsters all piled on top of each other, she finally spotted one that she thought would be easy to pick up and slowly placed her fingers around the shell, like Dwayne had showed her. She was careful to avoid the needle-like thorns. "Here's one," she said softly while holding it loosely above the others, her arm still in the trap.

"Well, bring it out then," Dwayne said, chuckling at her nervousness.

In silence, her face scrunched and holding it far away from her body, she slowly raised it out of the trap. The lobster sensed the movement and began flapping its tail. Tammy screamed and held out her quivering arm. "Quick, take it! Before I drop it."

Dwayne laughed as he took the lobster and measured it. "Ahh, a keeper," he said as he tossed it into a barrel of circulating salt water.

"Finally!" Tammy sighed.

"Our first lobster," Dwayne said, wearing a huge grin. "Come on, hand me another one."

It didn't take Tammy long to figure out the correct way to pick up the lobsters or, as Dwayne kept calling them, *the bugs.* By the time they had emptied the trap, she was picking them up like a pro. Each time they got to keep one, she did a little dance across the deck, followed by a cheerful "Yes!" They counted thirty lobsters in the trap, out of which there were nine keepers. Dwayne said that was a good trap, but Tammy had expected there to be more.

Feeling pleased with the trap and their spirits now lifted, Dwayne decided to set the empties they had on the deck close by before heading off to the rest of the gear. As they drove to their next spot, Tammy noticed a sea lion following them. "Fuck," she said under her breath, secretly wondering if it was the same one that had paid them a visit on the boat. She took a quick glance at Dwayne to see if he'd seen it too, but he was facing the other way driving the boat. She waved with her arms and mouthed "Shoo!" at the seal. It didn't do any good, as the seal kept following the wake of the boat. Lost on what to do, she turned and simply ignored it in the hopes it would disappear by the time they reached the next trap. To her relief, it had.

Anxious to see what the rest of the traps held, they hustled all morning to get as many traps as they could pulled and rebated by noon before taking a quick lunch break. They needed to get all one hundred fifty pulled by the end of the day. Leaving lobsters too long in the traps runs a high risk of other critters entering the traps and killing them. By midday, they had managed to pull sixty traps, just over a third of their gear, and they had close to three hundred lobsters. Dwayne was stoked.

"If we keep this up, we'll be out of the red in no time," he said while turning the motor off so they could drift and get a quick bite to eat.

"Sweet!" Tammy replied, now feeling more confident about this fishing adventure she was on. "You know, I've not heard anyone on the radio all morning," she said in between bites of her granola bar. "Every other day, it's been nothing but non-stop chatter all day. Today, nothing. Seems kind of odd, don't you think?"

"That's because the rest of the fleet, including us, have discovered their secret spots for lobsters. No one is going to come on the radio and ask how everyone is doing. Besides, fishermen never tell the truth and let you know how their catch is going. If they did, everyone would swarm their area." He let out a playful laugh. "We are all sworn to secrecy."

"Ha! That makes sense."

"Are you ready to pull more gear?" Dwayne asked after taking his last sip of Pepsi.

"You bet."

It took until sunset to pull the rest of the traps. Tammy and

Dwayne worked well together. Each knew their place on the boat and the tasks they had, making everything run smoothly. Dwayne held his position, driving the boat and working the hydraulics, while Tammy gaffed the line and wrapped it around the pulley. Once the trap was on board, it was up to Tammy to hand Dwayne lobsters to measure and then together, they rebaited the trap and threw it back overboard. Any empty traps, they'd stack until they found another fishing spot. After the last trap was pulled, even though Tammy was covered in fish goo and her feet ached from standing all day, she did her usual happy dance across the deck, which always amused Dwayne.

"Come here, beautiful," he said with his arms out. Tammy skipped over to him to meet his embrace. "You did great today," he told her before smothering her with kisses.

"Thanks. I had a really good time. But man, my body is sore. Please tell me we're done."

"Unfortunately not. Once we're back in the harbor, we have to clean the boat, cut bait for tomorrow and refuel the little boat using a hose. Oh, and we have to eat too."

"Well, looks like we'll be eating soup again tonight."

It was already dark by the time they were securely tied up next to the *Baywitch*, and they wasted no time getting back to work. Tammy noticed all the other boats were in and trailing behind their sterns were the lobster receivers, floating on the surface with their catch for the day. Tammy soon realized it would be a good way to see how much each boat had caught and grabbed the binoculars off the dash. She held them up to her eyes and counted the total number of receivers behind each boat. She saw Mitch on the *Sea-life* had the most with ten. "Damn, he did good," Tammy said while still checking out the other ones. Suddenly, she heard a commotion of flapping lobster tails and glanced over in Dwayne's direction. She saw he was putting their lobsters into receivers and making a train just like everyone else. "Need a hand?" she asked.

"Sure," Dwayne replied while struggling to get one of the

receivers overboard and into the water. In a snap, she returned the binoculars to the dash and rendered him some assistance. The count was good and Dwayne was thrilled. They had caught a total of five hundred lobsters and had eight receivers.

"How much is that worth?"

Dwayne gave her a big grin before answering. "Oh, about five thousand dollars."

"What! I don't make that much in a month, and we made that in one day? Yowza," she bellowed. "Now I really like this fishing thing." Stunned by the value of their catch, she couldn't believe how much these lobsters were worth. "Damn. And we have four more days of fishing before we head back in. This is unfucking believable."

Dwayne stood before her and gave her a loving smile. He was thrilled to see her so happy. Not many women would have the stamina or enthusiasm that she constantly exuded. He truly admired her. "Well, we're off to a good start. But keep in mind we're about fifteen thousand in the red and we still need to make enough to get back out here. Let's hope the rest of the trip is just as good."

"Ugh. Damn. We still need to catch a bunch more lobsters. Well, you just burst my bubble. Come on, let's get our chores done. I want to cuddle up next to you and eat some soup."

"You got it. But first, give me a kiss, partner."

Tammy smiled and melted in his arms. She always felt safe with him, especially out here in the middle of nowhere. She admired his strength and his knowledge of boats and the ocean. She knew from experience that the seas could turn on you at any given moment, but she knew he wouldn't allow any harm to come to her.

As she sat close to Dwayne, finally in comfortable sweats and with a warm hearty bowl of soup nestled on her lap, she knew she was where she wanted to be. This would be her life from now on—Dwayne, boats and fishing. The only part of the equation that was missing was Matt. Being away from him tore at her heart. She thought of him in her sleep and kissed his picture good night before tucking it under her pillow. She couldn't be away from him for this amount of time again. Once he was home, he'd being staying home. Finding a way to come to the island and fish would be a challenge, but Tammy was confident they'd find a solution.

CHAPTER 35

The intensity of the last few days was beginning to take its toll. Tammy and Dwayne were not the first to leave the harbor the next morning. They moved slow and were still tied up to the *Baywitch* an hour after the sun had risen. Tom, the captain of the *Lobster Fest* pulling up to their boat on his way out of the harbor, wearing a cocky grin and wasting ten minutes of their time, didn't help matters either.

"I see your woman is still standing," he said wearing a smirk. "How'd she do?" he asked Dwayne, who was busy making last-minute preparations on the *Little Boat*.

Tammy heard from the deck of the *Baywitch* and didn't like his sarcastic tone. "I did just fine, if you must know. I can't wait to get back out there." She placed her hands defiantly on her hips.

Tom looked surprised to see her and lowered his tone a notch. "Oh, I didn't see you there."

"Obviously," Tammy muttered under her breath.

"Well, I'm glad to see you're still with us. I'll have to check on you at the end of the week. Dwayne here might need help carrying you off the boat." He almost cackled.

"She's doing just fine. Stop giving her a hard time," Dwayne said with a hint of irritation to his voice.

Tammy marched to the rail of their boat, her hands still on her hips. "Why don't you go right ahead and do that?" She'd heard enough and waved him off before putting on her boots. "Have a good day," she added, her voice flat.

The rest of the morning couldn't have gone any better. Other than feeling somewhat fatigued, the fishing was going exceptionally well. They were catching just as many lobsters as the day before. That was until Dwayne suddenly yelled, "Fuck! I have no steering. My steering has gone!" He shut off the motor, feeling thankful they were not in shallow waters.

"What?" Tammy screeched, realizing they were dead in the water. "Now what?"

But Dwayne was already kneeling on the deck below the wheel to try and see if he could locate the problem. Tammy remained quiet and out of the way so he could concentrate. When he yelled the word "Fuck!" again, she knew he had found it.

"The steering cable is broken. We really are fucked!" He was clearly distraught.

Dwayne stood and looked out at the position of the boat, to make sure they weren't drifting too close to shore. He looked at Tammy, his face flushed with worry.

"Without steering, we can't pull the traps. I have to figure out a way to fix this. I don't have another cable, and we can't leave. We've not caught enough lobsters to get us out of debt and get back out here. What the fuck are we going to do?"

Tammy felt helpless. She knew nothing about the mechanics of a car, let alone a boat. "What about the *Baywitch*? Maybe we can get a tow from one on the other boats and use that to pull the gear."

"That's a great idea, except our traps are in too shallow for the *Baywitch*."

"Damn it!" Tammy said, now feeling the same frustrations and anxieties as Dwayne. She continued to think hard while Dwayne got on the radio and called Mitch to see if he had an extra cable, but he didn't. "Shit! We have to find a way to pull our gear in this boat," Dwayne said in a somewhat panicked state. He went to the back of the boat and sat on the hood of the motor, sliding his butt from side to side while pushing down hard at the same time.

"What are you doing?" Tammy asked with a puzzled look.

A smile appeared on his face, making Tammy feel a little more at ease. "I think I can steer the boat this way."

Tammy looked in the direction of the helm. "But the throttle and everything is up front. How can you work those from back there?"

Again, he smiled, but this time it suggested he had a plan. "I can't. But you can."

"Me?" she screamed, unable to hide her shock. "Now hold on a second. Let's talk about this."

"Come on. We can do this. In fact, we don't have a choice. I can sit back here and steer just like I showed you, and you can work the throttle, reverse and neutral from the helm."

Tammy began pacing the small deck. "That's the craziest thing I've ever heard. Driving across the ocean was easy. I didn't have to use reverse or neutral. But this is totally different. I have no idea what to do when we pull up to a trap."

"You don't have to. I will tell you from the back of the boat."

Tammy shook her head. "I don't know, Dwayne. I'm not sure if I can."

Eager to try his idea, he quickly stood and walked toward the helm. "Only one way to find out." He fired up the motor and motioned Tammy to come up to the wheel. "Come stand here and wait for my instructions."

Again, Tammy shook her head as she watched Dwayne take a seat on top of the motor again.

"Okay, put the boat in forward and go slow. You are my eyes.

So when you see the next buoy, slow down some more and we will try and approach it. You are also going to have to gaff it and bring it on the boat. I'll come help once the trap is on board."

"Okay," Tammy groaned reluctantly. "I'll do my best." Once the boat was moving, Tammy scanned the ocean for their next buoy and spotted it within a few minutes. "I see it at two o'clock," Tammy yelled while pointing with her finger. Dwayne sat up as tall as he could and saw it too.

"Okay, slow the boat down and ease over there, and when I say reverse, don't hesitate. Just do it."

Tammy felt the palms of her hands beginning to sweat as she eased the boat towards the buoy, waiting for his command. When they were within a few feet of the buoy, Dwayne yelled, "Reverse!"

Tammy did it on cue while Dwayne steered the boat with his butt. It looked like a tough job to get it to move. The engine was heavy and bulky and he had to push down really hard while moving his hips in the direction he wanted the boat to go. By some sort of miracle, they were on the trap. "Okay! Neutral!" he yelled.

Again, she didn't waste a second and put the boat in neutral. She knew what to do next, and grabbed the gaff and hooked the line on the first try. Next, she worked the puller and brought it up on the boat. It was full of lobsters. "We did it!" she squealed, planting a big kiss on Dwayne's cheek as he approached the trap table.

"I knew we could! But I don't know about pulling like this all week. You'd have to do everything until I get to the trap table and my butt will be killing me by the end of the day."

"I'll be fine," Tammy said, handing him a lobster like she'd been doing it for years.

For the rest of the day, they had no choice but to pull the traps that way. It was slow going and they only managed to pull a hundred twenty traps. That meant whatever lobsters were left in the traps overnight were at risk of being killed by other critters.

This was a concern. They could be losing money while they slept. On the way back into the harbor with a good day's catch, Dwayne was quiet, deep in thought, trying to think of an alternative method. Mitch checked in over the radio, asking how it went and had a good laugh once Dwayne told him what they had to do.

Over dinner that night, consisting of Denny's Beef Stew, they thought hard about their dilemma. They wouldn't be able to get the boat fixed until they were back at the mainland, and there was no way they could cut their trip short.

"There has to be an easier way," Dwayne said, thinking out loud while deep in thought. Tammy didn't have a clue. Unfortunately, if there was another way, it was all up to Dwayne to figure it out. "The hardest part is moving the damn engine with my butt. If there was another way to steer it from the back, it'd be a lot easier." He turned to face Tammy. "You're doing fine on the throttle." Suddenly, his eyes lit up and he quickly rose from his chair. "I know. I have a long, thin piece of metal below the motor that acts as a kelp knife." He mulled over his plan in his head before continuing. "If I can somehow attach that to the base of the motor, I can use it like a tiller."

"A what?"

"A tiller. It's a long stick. You normally see them on dinghies and small boats with engines. The guy will sit at the back of the boat and steer the boat with the tiller."

"Oh, yeah. Now I understand," Tammy said, nodding.

Dwayne was excited with his idea and was anxious to try it out, so, for the next thirty minutes, he struggled with trying to get the kelp cutter off from the motor and finding a way to bolt it to the motor like a tiller. Next, he wrapped the whole length of the metal bar in duct-tape to protect his hands from getting cut. "That should do it," he said, feeling proud of himself. "I guess we'll find out in the morning."

～

Dwayne's idea worked brilliantly. They managed to pull all the traps every day for the rest of their trip. Tammy struggled at times with the extra workload at her end of the boat but, as always, she pulled through like a champ. They had become the talk of the fishery. Word soon spread about how they were having to pull their gear, and within a day they had earned the upmost respect from all the other boats for their perseverance and ingenuity.

Each night, all the boats stopped by to ask how they were doing and to see if they needed anything. Remarkably, they now looked at Tammy with admiration. Not once did they hear her complain or whine. She was always upbeat and wore a smile.

Tammy noticed the change in them and wanted to show her appreciation for accepting her into the fleet. She knew how to get to a man's heart—through his stomach. So, on their last day, knowing the guys would be stopping by on their way in, she surprised them each with a plate of grilled chicken, mashed potatoes and carrots. She knew none of these men had had a home-cooked meal all week, and it was worth the extra effort and hassle of cooking on the boat just to see their beaming smiles when she handed them the plate. In fact, it was also the first cooked meal Dwayne and Tammy had eaten. It made a nice change from a can of soup.

They left the next morning for the mainland, happy and content with over three thousand pounds of lobsters, worth about twenty-seven thousand dollars. When Dwayne told her the dollar amount, Tammy felt like she had just won the lottery. "Holy fuck!" she squealed. "I've never seen that much money at one time. That's more than I make in a friggin' year!"

Nothing could dampen their sprits. They'd pulled through and had a successful trip. They would soon be out of the red and catching lobsters for more profit. Tammy was excited about their future together. They would be back home for just a few days to fix the *Little Boat,* refuel, restock on bait and supplies and call their boys before heading out to do it all over again. Tammy couldn't wait.

*O*ver the next six weeks, Tammy and Dwayne fished hard, and it was grueling to the point of exhaustion. It took a toll on Tammy, but she was determined to be successful and to prove not only to herself but to the rest of the fleet that she could do anything she set her mind to. Not only had it made her a stronger woman but it had also strengthened the relationship she had with Dwayne. They had built a foundation together. They were a team, having been put to the test so many times while living out at sea on a fishing boat for weeks at a time. In such a short time, she had embraced the life of commercial fishing, learning as much as she could about the industry while at the same time, falling deeply in love with Dwayne.

Since beginning this journey, she had noticed huge changes in herself, both physically and mentally. She found living and working on the ocean was a great therapy, especially when she had only recently decided to quit drinking. She no longer had the cravings for alcohol that had haunted her for such a long time. But she was also aware that the addiction would always be a part of her and could well be triggered at any given moment in her life. But, as

Dwayne had said numerous times while giving her words of encouragement to stay sober: *"As long as you don't pick up that first drink, you'll be okay. If you do, it's all downhill from there and you'll have to start all over again."*

Tammy was the fittest she'd ever been. Her arms and legs had defined muscle tone from hauling heavy gear daily, and her abs clearly showed a six pack. Being exposed to the intense rays of the sun while out on the ocean, her skin had become tougher and deeply tanned. Her hair was no longer a rich red color; the sun had bleached it to a natural strawberry blond.

But, unlike the rest of her body, there were some downsides to her newly acquired life. Her hair and hands had suffered the consequences of direct sunlight and being in salt water for days at a time. She couldn't remember the last time she'd styled her hair. It was dry and brittle and hung loosely around her face. And wearing make-up had become a distant memory. Her hands had constant sores and cuts, and blisters were a major problem, taking weeks to heal because of continually being around salt water and heavy equipment. Without fail, no matter how well she tried to protect it, the wound would somehow re-open while working. The skin on her hands was tough and chapped like a walrus. Her nails were no longer painted and manicured. All of them were short, broken or chipped, and feeling the pain of torn cuticles was a daily experience.

Solitude also came with her new lifestyle, which stirred some mixed emotions for her. Dwayne was the sole person she shared her life with. They were with each other twenty-four hours a day, doing everything together. She'd never had a relationship like that before. She no longer had to suppress her feelings behind alcohol, because she knew she could tell Dwayne anything. And the best part was, he'd listen.

While alone on the boat together, they had spent hours curled up in the berth or beneath the stars under a blanket talking about anything that came to mind. Tammy soon realized that being with a loved one, adrift at sea for many days at a time did wonders for a relationship. Tammy really felt like they knew each other.

But she also realized she had made many sacrifices and neglected those that used to be in her life. Being away from Matt troubled her the most. Even though he always sounded happy on the phone and couldn't wait to tell her about his week, the phone call always ended with Tammy having a huge sense of guilt and crying on Dwayne's shoulder for the next hour. She knew, once he was home, she'd never be separated from him again for such a long period of time.

Because her father and Joanne were taking care of Matt, they were still a part of her life too. When she called, she always talked to them first, giving them updates on their trips and any adventures that may have occurred. She could tell her dad enjoyed listening to her stories and she sensed the pride in his voice when he spoke. But she had failed to keep the rest of her family involved.

Each trip out to the island was done with such a quick turnaround that they only spent a few days on the mainland. Tammy would often let too much time pass before calling her sisters or mother, excusing it by telling herself she'd call them on the next trip in. But weeks would go by before that happened, and she felt the distance between them when she finally did call.

Her mother's sentences were short and cold and she often used harsh words. She expressed how sad she was that she couldn't watch her grandson grow up. *"I used to love getting pictures of him. Now I don't even get those anymore,"* she had said. She would also bring up Tammy's sister. *"When was the last time you three girls were in the same room together? It's been years, Tammy. Sisters shouldn't be that far apart from one another."*

Tammy felt the knife twist as her mother continued to fuel the guilt she was already feeling. She never contested her mother's words; Tammy knew she was right. She and her sisters had drifted apart and none of them were doing anything about it.

"When was the last time you saw Donna?" her mother had asked.

Tammy had calculated the time in her head and knew it had been months, but she didn't admit it to her mother. Before hanging up the phone, her mother had ended the call with an unusual request that stuck in Tammy's head. *"My last dying wish is to have all my three girls together in the same room. Is that too much to ask?"*

"No, Mom. It's not," Tammy had replied in a solemn voice.

She used to call her mother at least twice a week and send her pictures of her grandson in the mail every month. She hadn't called her in over two months and couldn't remember the last time she sent her photos. Her mother had every right to be upset with her.

It'd been almost three years since she last saw her. She had come over with the help of her dad for two weeks when Matt had just turned one, and she had stayed with Tammy and Judy at that house they had shared. Tammy had had good intentions of travelling to England with Matt the following year, but she had always struggled with money and with her finances, it just wasn't possible. Her mother refused to ask John for any more help and said she would somehow make it out on her own, but that hadn't happened yet either.

After receiving a reality check from her mother, Tammy spent some extra time at the phone booth and called Donna, only to receive another blow and have more feelings of guilt added to what she was already suffering.

Over the phone, Donna told her that she and Jason had eloped and had recently gotten married in Las Vegas. Tammy felt like she had been kicked in the stomach. *"I tried paging Dwayne to let you know. I was hoping you guys could join us and be at the chapel. But you were probably out on the boat again, as usual. I really hate not being able to call you,"* Donna had said. *"We use to call each other all the time."* Tammy listened with a heavy heart as she wiped away the tears of guilt that were beginning to roll down her cheeks. *"I miss my nephew too. I can't believe he's all the way in Florida,"* Donna had added.

Tammy had no words, just apologies. After everything they had been through together, she should have been present at her sister's wedding. She had missed both Donna's and Jenny's special days, a momentous time that all siblings should share.

Thoughts of Jenny had a clouded her mind as she listened to Donna's complaints. She hadn't seen Jenny in almost eight years. It saddened her to admit that she no longer knew her as a person. Neither one had made the effort to call. The cost of long distance calls was the main factor, and now that her only way to make any kind of call was via a phone booth, it was impossible to call England.

Sisters were supposed to know everything about each other. Tammy didn't even know what Jenny's favorite food was or what hobbies she had. She knew nothing about her husband or their two children. The only thing she had were a few photos that may as well have been the store-bought ones that come with new picture frames, filled with the faces of strangers.

Once she started thinking about her now distant relatives, not to mention her long-lost friends, she found herself adding to the list and right away, Judy came to mind. They had been best friends for years, raised each other's kids together and without fail they had always had each other's back. Tammy hadn't talked to her since she moved out of the house and decided she would try calling her after hanging up the phone with Donna.

She was surprised she still remembered the number. Then again, it used to be her number too. After several rings, a recording came on. *"The number you are trying to reach has been disconnected or is no longer in service."* Tammy hung up the phone with a knot in her stomach. Tammy wondered if Judy had moved. The only way to find out was to call the restaurant where they had both worked. Not giving it a second thought, Tammy picked up the handset of the phone, dug into her pockets for a few more quarters and tried calling the restaurant. A voice she didn't recognize answered the phone and after inquiring about Judy, she was informed she no longer worked there. Tammy was now numb. The one voice she was counting on for some sort of reconnection with her past had slipped away.

Tammy wondered how she could've allowed this to happen. How did she allow those closest to her to become so distant? And how was she going to fix it? It was impossible for her to drop everything and fly off to England for a visit. Even though she and Dwayne had had a good first six weeks, money was still tight after catching up with the mounds of bills, making unexpected repairs on the two boats and paying for fast turn-around trips.

The trips to the island were beginning to wind down. The catch was fewer and soon the ocean would become fierce with the winter storms, making it impossible to fish.

On the last two trips, they began bringing some of the gear home and setting it off the coast of Malibu where they would fish the rest of the season. The fishing wouldn't be as intense. They only needed to pull the gear every three days because, unlike the island, there wasn't a threat of other critters eating the catch. Another upside to fishing Malibu was it was only a thirty-minute boat ride from the dock, not nine hours, and they could be pulled with the *Little Boat* without lugging a week's worth of supplies in the *Baywitch.* This meant Tammy could stay on the *Baywitch* with Matt while Dwayne went fishing alone for three days a week. Of course, there was also the option of taking Matt with them.

She could also begin making crab traps while on the mainland. Lobster season would be ending in March, and for the first time, Dwayne was going to try and fish year round by fishing for crabs off Malibu during the off-season of lobsters. But the fishing required a different trap, so Tammy eagerly volunteered her assistance in the building of them.

But there was a downside to fishing for lobsters off Malibu—the catch wasn't as plentiful as out at the island. Even though they would be letting the traps soak for three days between each pull, they wouldn't catch as much as one day at San Clemente Island.

Tammy knew she needed to make some adjustments in her life, and that would begin with Matt when he was finally home in just a few days.

With the fishing winding down for the Thanksgiving holidays and Christmas and with most of the gear now in Malibu, Dwayne and Tammy were taking two weeks off and spending it with their sons.

Since being back on the mainland for the past few days, Tammy has spent most of her time scrubbing the *Baywitch* from top to bottom in preparation for Justin's visit and Matt's return home. Really, she was trying to keep busy to mask over the nagging guilt that haunted her. And the fact that she had spent far too much money on gifts for the two boys, from new bikes to skateboards and fishing rods.

Living by the beach in California had its advantages. They could pretty much camp anytime of the year and it was decided when the boys were home, that's what they'd do for a week. They needed to reconnect and be a family again.

When the day finally arrived to pick Matt up from the airport, Tammy was beside herself with excitement. She wanted everything to be perfect for the boys. She bought new sheets for the area where they'd be sleeping, which was where the table was in the cabin. Amazingly, it folded down into a double bed. The little cupboard space they had and the fridge were filled with every kind of fun kid food imaginable. Rows of stuffed animals, which Dwayne had never seen on his boat before, lined the benches, and new clothes were squished and hung between theirs in the tiny closet. It would be cramped on the boat with all four of them, but Tammy and Dwayne didn't care—even though that was one of the reasons they decided to go camping. What mattered was they would be with their boys.

They took Tammy's car to the airport so the boys could ride in the back. They would be picking up Justin after they had collected Matt. When they pulled into the busy terminal, Tammy was reminded of the time she'd said goodbye to her mother after her last visit, and before that it was when she had reunited with her sister Donna after she had been missing for over five years.

Curled up next to Dwayne, with his arm hung over her shoulder, Tammy thought back to the emotional day of seeing Donna and how close they soon became, just like two sisters should be.

She thought back to saying goodbye to her mother and how much she took her for granted. She had no idea that three years and more would pass before she would see her again.

Tammy must have been reminiscing for some time because she hadn't realized the car was in idle, parked in their parking spot. "Hey, are you okay?" Dwayne asked, noticing her misty eyes.

Tammy dabbed at her face while sitting up and taking notice of their surroundings. "Yeah, I'm fine. This place just brings back memories of Donna and my mom."

Having talked for hours with Tammy about her reunions with her family members, Dwayne understood completely and pulled her back into his arms. "Oh, sweetheart, come here," he said, wiping a tear that had escaped. "You'll see them again soon."

"I know. It's just hard," Tammy said, fighting back her tears. Determined not to let her son see her upset, she shook her head to compose herself and wiped her face one more time before leaning in and giving Dwayne an affectionate kiss. "I love you. Now come on, let's go get Matt." Saying his name made her smile.

"I can't wait until both boys are riding in the back seat."

"Me neither," Tammy said while stepping out of the car.

Once inside the busy terminal, Tammy firmly holding hands with Dwayne, they checked the screen detailing all the flight information and saw Matt would be landing on time in about half an hour. Tammy glanced at her watch, synchronizing hers with the screen. "This is going to be the longest damn thirty minutes of my life," she whispered into Dwayne's ear as they made their way through the crowds and toward the arriving gate.

Unable to find two vacant seats, they stood arm-in-arm, mesmerized by the vast number of people around them and things one normally doesn't pay attention to unless standing idle for a stretch of time. They looked at the clothes people were wearing, their nationality, the language they were speaking and where they were going. Typical airport idle time.

Tammy lost count of how many times she checked her watch and each time only a few minutes had gone by, until finally, she heard the announcement of Matt's flight. Tammy squealed, "He's here!" and beamed Dwayne a radiant smile before giving him a big smooch.

Unable to stand still, she began tapping the ground with her feet as she anxiously waited for Matt to be escorted off the plane by one of the stewardesses. With her eyes pinned on the passengers walking through the gate, Tammy was once again reminded of the time she stood in the same airport waiting to be reunited with her sister.

After what seemed like an eternity passing by, Tammy finally saw her little boy being led by the hand of a middle-aged blond stewardess. Consumed with excitement and desperate to hold him, Tammy broke away from Dwayne's arms and squeezed her way through the people standing in front of her.

Waving her arms, she yelled, "Matt!"

But he was still too far away and her voice was lost in the crowd.

Dwayne finally reached her and used his louder masculine voice. "Matt!" he yelled while also waving his arms.

This time, Matt heard his name and began searching the mass of people before him.

Tammy waved her arms again. "Matt, over here."

Matt followed the direction of her voice and with a huge smile that melted Tammy's heart, he pointed in her direction while talking to his chaperone. Tammy hugged her chest as her eyes flooded with tears of joy. The stewardess saw her and Dwayne, smiled and waved and started walking towards them.

When there was ten feet between them, Tammy stopped and knelt, holding her arms out wide. Matt tore away from the stewardess's hand and raced towards Tammy, screaming at the top of his lungs, "Mommy!"

Tammy yelled back, "Matt! Come here, big boy."

Within seconds, he was in her arms. Tammy wrapped him tight, kissing him over and over across his face. "Oh, sweetie. I've missed you so much," Tammy cried, unable to control her tears. She couldn't help noticing how much older he looked. She held out his arms and smiled between her tears. "You've gotten so big. Look at you." And then she quickly pulled him back in. "Oh, I love you so much."

"I love you too, Mommy." And then he looked up at Dwayne. "Hi Dwayne."

Dwayne gave him a big smile before scooping him up in his arms. "Hey buddy. We've missed you. Have you got a high-five for me?"

Matt raised his hand and giggled before slapping Dwayne's palm.

While Matt was amused in Dwayne's arms, Tammy wiped her moist cheeks and shook the stewardess's hand. "Thank you for taking care of him."

"Oh, my pleasure. He's a very sweet boy. We enjoyed having him." She handed Tammy a piece of paper. "I just need to see your ID and have you sign this."

"Oh, sure," Tammy said, rooting through her purse for her wallet.

Once all the official business was done, Dwayne and Tammy thanked the stewardess again and Matt waved goodbye before all three of them headed to the car.

On the drive to pick up Justin, Tammy sat in the back seat with Matt, holding his hand tight while she listened to all his stories about his stay with Grandpa. His vocabulary was so much better, and he told her he was reading books too. In the few short months that he had been away, Tammy noticed how much he had grown up. Next year, he would be starting school. *Where has the time gone?*

Juggling fishing and having Matt in school was going to be a struggle, but she and Dwayne would somehow make it work.

As soon as they pulled up to Justin's house, they saw the front door open wide and Justin come running out yelling, "Daddy!"

Tammy leaned forward and squeezed Dwayne's shoulder. "There's your boy. Go get him. I'll wait in the car with Matt."

Dwayne turned his head and gave her a peck on the lips. His eyes misty, he whispered, "I'll be right back."

Tammy stepped out of the car, leaned against the hood with her arms folded and enjoyed the scene before her of Dwayne finally hugging his son. From inside the car, she heard Matt yell, "Justin!" It warmed Tammy's heart to know Matt remembered him and missed him too. Together, the four of them were a family. Matt looked up to Justin as his big brother, Dwayne treated Matt like his own son, and Tammy mothered them like they were both her own.

With her family now established, Tammy knew she needed to fulfill her mother's only wish. Those precious words entered her head again as Dwayne picked up Justin's backpack, took his hand and walked him back to the car.

"My only wish is to have all three of my girls together in the same room..."

WILL TIME BE ON THEIR SIDE?
TINA HOGAN GRANT
BOOK THREE IN THE TAMMY MELLOW SERIES
THE
REUNIONS

To my sisters
Jane & Debbie
Miles apart
but
close at heart

*Don't put off until tomorrow
what you can do today* - Benjamin Franklin

PROLOGUE

Two years ago, not only had Tammy met her calling as a commercial fisherwoman, but she had also unexpectedly fallen in love with Dwayne. A man who showed her the beauty and freedom of the open ocean and lobster fishing skills.

He tolerated her stubbornness and hardheaded attitude as she slowly learned to trust again after being in an abusive relationship that left scars unhealed. She had become dependent on alcohol to numb her wounds, and he was there for her throughout her sobriety. Dwayne believed in her and saw beyond her tattered shell. He was determined to help her rise beyond her troubles and to believe in herself like he did.

He admired her strength, her beauty, and the determination she held to prove herself worthy and rise above her troubled past.

Tammy entered the fishing industry, feeling intimidated and fearful of the unknown. She feared the ocean and its power. Men dominated the fleet, and the opinions they voiced of her had her on edge. They questioned if she would be capable of keeping up with the enduring intense labor expected of her during the six months of the season. But just as Dwayne had expected, she faced every challenge that came her way with an attitude of steel and refused to be defeated. The bigger the challenge, the more she pushed herself to succeed, and she never gave up.

Tammy's love for the ocean was instant, and so was the respect she had for those that worked it. It's one of the toughest ways to make a living, but it drew Tammy to it like a magnet. Dwayne saw her eagerness to learn and taught her everything she knew about commercial fishing and living a life at sea.

Dwayne saw what Tammy couldn't, and because of his patience, he brought the best out in her. She finally had a sense of belonging and a passion that drove her to keep pushing herself and work hard. At the end of each day, her body ached to the core, her muscles were sore, and she could barely move, but she still had a smile on her face because the work, as grueling as it was, gave her a feeling of satisfaction.

After her first year, Tammy earned the respect of the other fishermen. Like Dwayne, they admired her strength and stamina, and let's not forget her homemade chicken dinner, which she had cooked for them one night while they were all anchored in the harbor. By the end of the season, she was considered part of the fleet.

Tammy's son, Matt, was four years old when she met Dwayne, and for the first time in his life, he finally had a father figure. Matt took to the boats, fishing, and ocean as quickly as his mother did. He fished off the back of Dwayne's boat, the *Baywitch*, most nights with Dwayne after he and his mom had moved onto the boat with him shortly after they had met. And even though the boat's living quarters were small, especially when Dwayne's son Justin, visited, they were content and happy and most of all a family.

But all good things came with a price, and Tammy allowed herself to become estranged from her close friends and immediate family. Once she left her job at the restaurant where she worked for most of Matt's life and moved out of the home in Pasadena, she shared with her best friend Judy, Tammy never looked back. Sadly, she and Judy never kept in touch, and she no longer knows where she is.

Tammy last saw her mother Rose five years ago. She rarely writes or calls because of the times she spends on the ocean. She is even more estranged from her sister Jenny, who also lives in England with her husband Stuart and their two children, Tommy and Kate. It saddens Tammy that she had a niece and nephew that she has never met, and Jenny has never met her nephew Matt.

Tammy was seventeen when she last saw Jenny. That was ten years ago. They were sisters by blood, but knew nothing about each other. Calls between them were non-existent. They only shared letters and photos over the holidays. Tammy had often wondered if they were to pass each other on the street, would they recognize each other?

Her father John and his second wife Joanne, still lived in Florida, and Tammy called them often. Ever since her big move to the states, she had remained close to her father and continued to seek his approval. Finally, after numerous embarrassing mistakes, Tammy heard the pride in his voice when she called after returning from the island with adventurous tales of their fishing trip.

Before Tammy took up a life as a commercial fisherwoman, she remained close and saw her other sister Donna often, who was Jenny's identical twin. She lived only an hour away from the house Tammy shared with Judy. But once Tammy moved in with Dwayne on the boat, her regular visits stopped. Tammy was either out at sea or on the mainland for just a few days to sell the lobsters and pick up more supplies before heading back out. There wasn't enough time to make the two-hour drive from the Marina to Donna's place. It's been over a year since she last saw her.

Her mother's only wish was to have her daughters all in the same room one more time, and she reminded Tammy every time they spoke on the phone. It was how she always ended her calls, and each time Tammy's heart tore just a little more. She realized her mother wasn't getting any younger, and she saw the signs of aging were showing on the rare occasions she made it to the States. Tammy wanted to make her mother's wish come true. But how and when?

In a panic, Tammy dropped the Pepsi can she held, ignoring the soda explosion that spilled over the deck of the *Baywitch*. With her heart racing, she ran to the stern of the boat, where her son screamed. Blood poured from his mouth. She predicted the accident before it occurred and couldn't move fast enough. It happened so quickly.

They were at San Clemente Island, anchored in the harbor after dumping a load of lobster traps to prepare for the upcoming season. It was Tammy's third season fishing with Dwayne, and it was the second time they had taken Matt. Last year she refused to send Matt to Florida to stay with her dad and Joanne for three months like she'd done the year before. Being separated from him was just too unbearable.

Somehow, they juggled care for him between the wives of the workers at the boatyard and the mothers of Matt's friends at school. This year they were more organized and hoped things would go smoother.

They knew from experience that dropping off the lobster traps before the season's opening wasn't as intense as pulling the gear, so they took Matt with them for these short turnaround trips.

Last year, Tammy and Dwayne stayed at the island for five to seven days at a time. This year it will be different. They would only be gone weekdays Monday thru Friday.

Tammy became good friends with Louise—a mother from Matt's school and one of Matt's friends. She agreed to watch Matt at her house for the five days they would be gone with the promise that they'd return Friday night. This arrangement would give Tammy weekends with Matt. Even though she knew they would spend the time getting ready for the next trip, Matt would at least be with her and not thousands of miles away in Florida, where she couldn't see him at all.

It was only an eight-week arrangement with Louise, depending on the weather. After that, just like the previous years, Dwayne and Tammy would move all their gear to Malibu and fish every three days. Because Malibu was closer, and they would be home every night, they planned on taking Matt on some trips when he didn't have school.

The first trip to San Clemente Island with Matt on board went great. He was a burst of energy in his orange life vest and took everything in as his mother had on her first trip. He never got seasick and walked around the boat like it was second nature. When the time came to drop the traps, Dwayne sent Matt down to the cabin where it was safe. Periodically Tammy made it a point to check on him. She laughed at how entertained he was with Matchbox cars that moved by themselves across the table inside the rocking boat.

"Look, mom, no batteries," he would say, making Tammy laugh.

Because last year went so well, they took Matt again this year. Everything went according to plan. They had all their gear in the water, waiting to be fished the following week when Tammy and Dwayne would return. Tammy just removed her slickers and rested her tired body while sipping on a Pepsi. Dwayne worked on the *Little Boat*, ensuring everything was cleaned up and secured for the crossing home.

Matt stood at the back of the *Baywitch*, watching an airplane take off from the island.

"Look at the plane, mommy," he yelled as he pointed his finger up to the sky and then quickly covered his ears from the roaring sounds as it took off. The loud sound scared Matt. Tammy knew he was about to run toward her. She saw the puddle of water on the deck and screamed.

"No, Matt, don't run!" But it was too late.

Tammy watched with horror as Matt slipped on the water, and his body crashed onto the deck facedown, and his face slammed into the non-skid finish of the deck. She immediately saw the pool of blood, and his blood-curdling screams tore at her heart.

"Oh, my god!" Tammy screamed as she raced over to her son. "Dwayne! Dwayne! Come quick!" She hollered above Matt's piercing screams, who was still face-down, kicking his legs while his head remained still.

Tammy didn't know how severely Matt was hurt. It scared her. She trembled as she knelt beside him and gently lifted him into her arms. She gasped when she saw his face covered in blood.

The boat suddenly rocked from the force of Dwayne leaping onto it from the *Little Boat*. Tammy steadied her feet until the rocking subsided and noticed her shirt sleeve saturated with blood.

Dwayne saw the panic on Tammy's face and heard the screams from Matt, who coughed from the blood trickling down his throat. He couldn't see Matt's face from where he stood, but he could read the fear in Tammy's eyes.

"What happened? Is he okay?"

Tammy shook her head hysterically as the tears she had been holding back streamed down her face. "No, he fell, and he is bleeding badly," she cried.

Dwayne went to Tammy's side and gently touched Matt's head

as he inspected his face. "Jesus! We may have to call the coast guard."

Tammy held Matt tighter, who was still screaming at the top of his lungs, "Is it that bad?" She tried to comfort him with rubs to his back. "Shh, it's okay, baby," she whispered. Guilt was flooding through her. "There was a pool of water on the deck, and he got scared of the planes taking off. I knew he was going to run over to me. I couldn't stop him in time."

Dwayne tried to inspect Matt's face to see where the bleeding was coming from, but it was impossible to tell with all the blood smeared across his skin. "Hey hon, it's not your fault. Let's get him down below and clean him up. I think he may have knocked some teeth out."

Tammy gasped. "What, oh, no!" She rubbed Matt's back some more. "Come on, buddy. We're going to clean you up and see where you are hurting." "Okay," she said over Matt's heart-wrenching tears that weren't subsiding at all.

Dwayne went down into the cabin first. "Here, sit on the edge of the bed with him and turn him around so I can see his face. I don't want him lying down in case he has a loose tooth that may become dislodged. He could choke on it."

Tammy gently lifted Matt's head off her shoulder and, with care, turned him around and placed him on her lap with the back of his head against her chest.

"No!" Matt protested as Tammy folded his arms in front of him and held them tight.

"Jesus, that's a lot of blood," Dwayne whispered, not wanting to scare Matt. He rubbed Matt's knee. "It's okay, buddy. We're going to help you, okay. Now sit still with mommy while I go find a towel to clean you up with."

Matt nodded and hiccuped some tears back.

"It looks like most of the blood is coming from his mouth. I'll be right back with some fresh water and towels."

Tammy nodded and kissed the top of Matt's head as she rocked him on her knees. His crying continued, but not at the screeching level it had been.

A few minutes later, Dwayne returned with a saucepan of water and towels and kneeled before Matt and surveyed his face. It was hard to tell where the injuring originated from. Dwayne moistened the towel. "I'm going to clean your face, okay, buddy."

Matt darted his head away from Dwayne's hand. "No!" He screamed.

Dwayne looked at Tammy. "Hold on to him while I do this."

Tammy nodded and tightened her grip. "It's okay. Dwayne is going to make you feel better. Relax, sweetie."

After a few shakes of his head, Matt finally allowed Dwayne to gentle dab his face. Dwayne wanted to get his mouth clean where most of the blood was coming from. The blood smeared on his cheeks, and his forehead had no cuts. He could clean those parts up later after determining how severe the wound was around the mouth. Little by little, with care, Dwayne wiped away the blood. Matt was still bleeding, and it seemed to come from his lower lip. His crying now subsided to hiccups and sniffs.

Dwayne wanted Matt to trust him and spoke softly, "Can you open your mouth?"

Matt nodded and slowly separated his lips.

Dwayne was pleased to see all his teeth were in place and felt them with his fingers. "None of his teeth seem to be loose. That's good," he said as he dabbed more blood that was oozing out of his lip. "Bite softly on the towel," he told Matt, which he did.

"I'm going to leave it there for a few minutes to stop the bleeding, Okay buddy?"

Matt nodded.

"It looks like it's just his bottom lip that's cut."

Tammy released an enormous sigh of relief before kissing Matt tenderly on his head. "Thank god! So, he's going to be okay?" Tammy pleaded.

Dwayne crouched down and removed the towel from Matt's

lips, looking at it closely. "Yeah, I think so. There's no need to call the coast guard. It looks like when he fell; his upper teeth bit down onto his lower lip. I see at least three teeth marks."

"I saw him. He hit the deck hard, and his face slammed into it," Tammy said, as she lifted Matt from her lap and looked at his lip. She looked at Dwayne with pity in her eyes. "We can't bring Matt out here until he's older. I thought he'd be okay on these quick turnaround trips, but look what a bit of water on the deck did, and most of the time when we are fishing, this deck is drenched." She shook her head with frustration. "We have to figure something out for next year when we have to dump the gear. You realize that, don't you?" she said as she laid Matt down on the bed.

Dwayne gave her a loving smile, and she couldn't help but notice the sudden sparkle in his eye.

Tammy narrowed her eyes and gave him a suspicious grin. "What?" She turned her head and watched Matt as he crawled onto the bed and laid down.

"Well, I have an idea, and we have an entire year to plan it."

Tammy's eyes became wide. "Well, are you going to share it with me?"

Dwayne sat on the bench at the table and turned his body to face Tammy, who was still sitting on the edge of the bed, rubbing Matt's tummy as he drifted off to sleep.

"Didn't you tell me that the last time you had talked to your mom, she had said she could come visit us next year?"

Tammy shrugged her shoulders. "Well, yeah, but where is she going to stay? She can't stay on the boat with us. There's no room, and besides, when we go fishing, the boats go with us."

Dwayne laughed at her logic. "Well, what if we look into renting a house?"

Tammy leaped up from the bed and into Dwayne's arms. "Really? Are you serious? I love living on the boat, but Matt is growing by the minute, and I think it's time he had his own room. By the time next season rolls around, we'd have lived on the

Baywitch for almost four years." Tammy chuckled. "I'm not sure if Matt will like the idea, though."

Dwayne creased his brow. "You don't? I thought he'd be happy to have his own room and a yard to play in."

Tammy laughed again. "A backyard is no comparison to an entire boatyard to play in and docks to fish off and not to mention a dinghy to go row-about, as Matt calls it. He loves the water and fishing just like we do."

Dwayne nodded. "You have a point, but we would still have to go to the boatyard every day to work on gear, and we'd have the option to spend the night on the boat if we wanted to."

"Don't get me wrong, I enjoy living on the boat, but it would be nice to have a house to go to after spending a week on the ocean." Tammy gave him a dreamy smile. "I could soak in a bubble bath and sleep in a king-size bed where there are no dangers of me banging my head," she laughed, "and besides, Matt is seven now, and I think it's time he had his own room."

Dwayne pulled her in tight and wrapped his arms around her waist, giving her a long lingering kiss on the lips. "Yes, I agree. Living on the same boat that we also use for fishing is not getting any easier. Even for me, who has been around boats all my life," he laughed. "If we rent a house, your mom, who I still have not met, could stay there with Matt while we went fishing."

Tammy squeezed Dwayne's waist and kissed him hard on his lips. "That's a brilliant idea! I know she's going to love you as much as I do, and It's been over five years since she last saw Matt, or me for that matter." Tammy did some calculations in her head. Wow, Matt was only two when she last saw him. That's sad. We miss her so much. I'm sure she would love the idea of watching Matt. It would give her a sense of feeling needed. I know she hasn't felt important since her girls have all grown up and now have their own families. I'm not sure if she watches Jenny's kids in England. I've never asked her." She turned and looked at Matt. "Oh good, he finally fell asleep. I'm going to put a clean shirt on him while he's sleeping." She turned to face Dwayne again. "Are we all ready to shove off and head home?"

"We sure are. The *Little Boat* is all secured. I'm going to fire up the boat and head out of here. Why don't you stay down here with Matt for the first few hours and get some rest, and I'll let you drive once we've passed the west end of Catalina?"

"Sounds good! I can't wait to get back and call mom." Tammy said with a beaming smile. "We're getting a house! I'm so excited."

CHAPTER 2

*N*ight-time came quickly, and they did the rest of the crossing to the mainland guided by the stars. Tammy and Dwayne took turns driving while one of them hunkered down in the cabin with Matt. His lip was healing nicely, and he didn't seem to be in any pain.

By the time they tied up to the Marina dock, it was nearing 4:00 am, Sunday morning. There would be no time to rest. They wanted to be back at the Island by tomorrow morning, which meant they would have to leave that afternoon.

With the eight-hour time difference between America and England, Tammy knew it was a good time to call her mom. She checked on Matt and saw that he was still sleeping. Dwayne was on the deck. "I'm going to call my mom," she said.

Dwayne smiled from the back of the boat while tying fenders to the stern. "Oh, good. I'm eager to hear if she likes my idea."

"I'm sure she will," Tammy said as she stepped off the boat and headed to the phone booth.

After feeding the coin box a ton of quarters, she finally heard the foreign ringtone of an English phone. After three rings, her mom picked up.

"Hello." She said in her thick British accent.

"Hey, mom. It's Tammy."

Tammy instantly picked up on the smile in her voice. "Tammy! What a pleasant surprise. Is everything okay? How's my grandson?"

Like always, she answered the call with many questions but never gave Tammy a chance to answer any of them. Tammy couldn't blame her. Months passed since she last talked to her.

"Everything's fine, mom. We just got back from fishing. Matt is fine too."

"You're still fishing, eh? Are you sure you like it, Tammy?" her mom asked.

Tammy laughed. It was another favorite question of hers. "I love it, mom. I wouldn't do it if I didn't. Listen, I need to make this quick. I only have a few more quarters. After the season ends, we're going to look for a house to rent."

Her mother's tone turned sharp. "Well, it's about time. I don't know how you can all live on a boat. And doesn't your boyfriend have a son too?"

"Yes, he does, but he doesn't live with us. Anyway mom listen," she said, rushing her words.

Suddenly a recorded voice interrupted her. "Please deposit $1.75 to continue this call."

"God damn it," Tammy barked as she fed more quarters into the phone. "Mom, are you there?"

"Yes, I'm here."

"Listen, mom." Tammy couldn't help but smile as she spoke her next words. "How would you like to come over next year and watch Matt at the house we plan on getting while Dwayne and I go fishing?"

Her mom didn't hesitate to answer and squealed into the phone.

"Oh, Tammy, I would love that. Are you serious?"

Tammy laughed. Her mom's reaction was all that she had hoped for. "Yes, mom, I'm serious. You would help us out a lot, and I love the idea of you and Matt bonding while we are away."

"Will I get to see Donna too?" her mom questioned.

"I'll make sure of it, okay? Look, I'm out of quarters. We are heading back out later today. I'll call you when we get back in, and I'll also write to you and explain all the details. I love you, mom."

"I love you too, Tammy. Be careful out there on the ocean."

"I will mom, bye."

Tammy hung up the phone and skipped back down to the boat to find Matt awake and eating cereal at the table. The engine hatch on the deck was open, and Dwayne stood at the edge, wiping his hands on a towel.

"Everything okay?" she asked while looking down at the engines.

"Yeah. Just checking everything before we leave again."

Tammy inched closer to him and gave him a peck on the cheek. "You are so thorough. I always feel safe with you. Even sixty miles out at sea," she told him, followed by a loving smile.

"Gotta take care of my sweetheart," Dwayne said before climbing down between the two engines.

Tammy leaned over to talk to him, "I called my mom, and she is super excited about watching Matt. I knew she would be."

Dwayne looked up and wiped his forehead, leaving a smear of oil on his brow. "That's great! I think it will all work out."

"I do too. It's a brilliant idea you had." Tammy glanced over at the cabin and saw Matt was still eating. "After Matt has finished his breakfast, I'm going to pack his clothes and backpack for school and drop him off at Louise's in your truck. That way, I can go down to Los Angeles and get the bait."

"Sounds good. I'll take the *Baywitch* over to the fuel dock and fill her up, and then I'll take the *Little Boat* over and fill her up too.

When you get back, we'll go grocery shopping. I want to be out of here no later than two this afternoon if we can."

"Okay, I'll be back as soon as I can. I'll see you later. Love you."

"Love you too." Dwayne hollered with his head buried next to an engine.

An hour later, Tammy was on the freeway heading to Los Angeles, where she would hit up the fish markets for their fish scraps, which made excellent bait. She would also buy a thousand pounds of frozen mackerel. All the guys at the markets knew her and made it a habit to save her scraps. Tammy was pleased that it didn't take her much time to collect eight barrels of fresh bait.

After making her last stop where she purchased the mackerel, she noticed she was low on gas and pulled into the next gas station before getting on the freeway. After paying for the gas and a cup of much-needed coffee, she headed back to the truck to pump the gas. She looked over at her truck and saw a middle-aged man, wearing jeans, a black jacket, and a black baseball hat walking around her truck and looking under the rear bumper.

Tammy hesitated before approaching the stranger, knowing she was not in the best part of town. As she drew closer, she made her presence known.

"Hey. Can I help you?" she said with an edge to her voice.

Startled by her sudden appearance, the man quickly stepped away from her truck. Tammy looked at his hands for any weapons. There was none, but she noticed he was wearing a wedding ring and felt less threatened by him. His eyes were wide when he spoke, and there was a slight tremble to his voice.

"Yeah. Did you know there is blood dripping from the back of your truck?"

Tammy sensed the uncertainty in his voice and chuckled to herself. Feeling a little mischievous, she messed with the guy and bent down to look under the truck. "Oh, dear, there sure is." She said with narrowed eyes and a straight face.

The guy took another step back and glanced at a silver SUV at a nearby pump. Tammy assumed it was his "So, what do you have in there?" the guy asked, with his eyes still wide.

Tammy folded her arms and leaned back against her truck, giving him a devious smile. "Wouldn't you like to know?"

The guy's jaw dropped, and his eyes grew to twice their size. Fear masked his face. "Never mind. I have to get to work. Have a nice day." He said in a rushed voice as he raced over to his car without looking back.

Tammy laughed to herself. The poor guy probably thought she was some wife that had just killed off her husband. Then she had a troublesome thought. Shit, I hope he doesn't call the cops and give them my license plate number. She wondered if she went a little too far, making a joke about the barrels' fish blood leaking. But the look on his face was well worth it. Tammy chuckled; he'll probably be talking about the crazy lady at the gas station for years to come. She didn't see him write anything down and assumed he probably just wanted to get away from her as quickly as possible.

Tammy still had a smirk on her face when she arrived back at the boat. She found Dwayne on the deck of the *Baywitch*, making room for the bait.

"Well, you look happy," Dwayne said as he picked up some tools and set them on the dash. "How did it go with the bait? Any problems? I worry about you going down there by yourself. It's a pretty rough neighborhood."

"Oh, I'm fine. I can take care of myself. I told you I wanted to go on my own last time we came in. That way, we can get every thing done quicker. But I think I scared the crap out of a poor guy at the gas station."

Dwayne laughed before he even heard the story. "Oh, crap. What did you do?"

Tammy walked up to him, wrapped her arms around his waist, and gave him a peck on the lips. Dwayne pulled her in and swayed her from side to side as she spoke.

"Well, he asked me why there was blood dripping from the

back of the truck. I knew it was the bait, but to him, it probably looked pretty suspicious. He looked scared too." Tammy laughed.

"So, what did you tell him?"

"Well, I didn't tell him what it was. I just asked him with a devious smile, wouldn't you like to know?" Tammy cracked a laugh and tossed back her head. "Oh, you should have seen the look on his face. He looked petrified."

Dwayne gasped. "No, you didn't. Oh, that poor guy."

"I know. But I couldn't resist. It's the devil in me. What can I say?"

After sharing her story and having a few more laughs, Dwayne and Tammy spent the next hour and a half unloading the bait from the truck, carting it through the boatyard on a dolly, and stacking it on the *Baywitch*. Out of breath and winded, they took a thirty-minute break before going to the market to buy their groceries for their five-day trip to the island. By two-thirty, they untied the boat from the dock, and they were heading back out to sea.

If all goes to plan, they should reach the island early Monday morning when it is still dark, which would give them time to rest for a few hours. They would spend Monday and Tuesday moving and baiting the gear before the first day of the season begins on Wednesday, and because it was the opener, Louise had agreed to watch Matt an extra day. But Tammy had her doubts things would go so smoothly. Something always happens that derails their plans. She just wondered what it would be this time?

CHAPTER 3

What felt like a tornado came out of nowhere? Buckets, slickers, and anything else that was not tied down had been thrown across the deck from the force of the pounding winds. Before the chaos erupted, Tammy had spent the morning pulling traps with Dwayne.

It was their third day of fishing at San Clemente Island and a day after the opener. They had left the mainland like many times before, with no sleep, and took turns driving the *Baywitch* with the *Little Boat* in tow so they could each try to get some sleep. But the boat's noise and rocking made it hard for Tammy to fall into a deep sleep, and she failed to get enough rest.

On this day, fatigue had caught up with her. Her body hurt to the core, her muscles hurt down to her bones, and her hands were chapped and raw to where she couldn't bend her fingers without expressing the piercing pain she was feeling.

They left the harbor in the *Little Boat* before sunrise to begin their day of pulling 150 traps. But by noon, Dwayne grew concerned when he looked over and saw Tammy's face tight, and her eyes scrunched closed from the agony she felt when she heaved a trap across the deck to be stacked and dumped at a better fishing spot.

When she finally voiced her pain with a loud, piercing scream, Dwayne immediately turned off the motor. "Okay, that's it. I'm taking you back to the *Baywitch*," he said as he precariously walked over to Tammy while trying not to lose his balance as the *Little Boat* bobbed around in the vast ocean. "You need to get some rest."

Tammy gripped her hips and tried to stretch her back, but it hurt too much. "I'm fine," she protested. "My body is just a little stiff. I'll loosen up soon," she said as she continued to rub her sides.

Dwayne shook his head. "I'm not taking no for an answer. You've been pushing yourself hard lately, and I want you to take the rest of the day off." He gave her a playful grin. "Captain's orders."

Tammy rolled her eyes and grunted. "Oh, I hate it when you pull rank on me." She knew she didn't stand a chance. When Dwayne made up his mind, he took the authority; there was no arguing with him.

Still keeping his balance as the boat rocked, he approached Tammy, who was now leaning against the stacked traps for support, and started rubbing her shoulders. Tammy closed her eyes and moaned from the sudden pleasures she was feeling. "Oh god, that feels so good," she moaned with her eyes still closed.

Dwayne chuckled from the relief his hands were giving her. "Now, I'm going to take you back to the *Baywitch*, and you're going to rest for the remainder of the day," he insisted.

Tammy tilted her head from side to side to loosen her sore neck as Dwayne continued to massage her, "But you can't pull all the traps by yourself," she protested.

"I'll pull what I can today, and tomorrow when you are feeling better, we will play catch up."

Tammy pouted her lips and folded her arms across her chest, knowing she had lost the argument. "Fine. Take me back to the boat."

They weren't far from the harbor and were at the *Baywitch* within thirty minutes. Dwayne put the boat in idle and approached Tammy, who was still dressed in her yellow slickers and boots. He smiled and took her in his arms.

Tammy giggled as she tried to push him away playfully. "What are you doing? I'm covered in fish goo," she laughed.

Dwayne, also dressed in slickers, moved his hips from side to side and rubbed his belly with hers, smearing the goo some more across their slickers. "Oh, but you look so sexy and smell like money." He said before planting a hard kiss on her lips.

Tammy laughed out loud and pressed the palms of her hands on his chest. "You're nuts. You've been out at sea too long." She changed her tone to a more serious one. "Are you sure you'll be okay by yourself?"

"Yeah, I'll be fine. We will be in radio contact." He scanned the harbor. "And look, you have the whole harbor to yourself. All the boats are out fishing. You could go skinny dipping and wash up if you wanted to," he said, followed by a wink.

Tammy checked the other moorings and saw they were all empty. "Huh. I just might. I smell like bait."

Dwayne held her hand as she stepped onto the *Baywitch*. She turned and watched as he put the boat in gear. "I'll see you just before sunset." he hollered over the roar of the motor. "Get some rest. I may have my way with you tonight," he laughed, followed by a sexy smile and a wink that never ceased to make Tammy's heart flutter.

Tammy continued to watch as he sped off, feeling a little envious that she wouldn't be reaping in the fruits of their labor and feeling the rewards. But it was just for today. She had been pushing herself hard to meet the deadline of the opener. She was grateful for what would be an afternoon of rest.

Tammy watched Dwayne as he disappeared around the point and, for a moment, enjoyed the sudden silence that surrounded her. She only heard the gentle splash of the ocean against the hull.

She took in a deep breath, closed her eyes, and filled her lungs with fresh air. She tilted her head back slightly so the slight breeze could brush against her face. It was exhilarating and immediately made her feel a little better.

Tammy looked down at her slickers and saw the fish goo was already drying. She needed to wash them before the goo became too hard to clean and stepped out of her boots. After sliding the straps off her shoulders and stepping out of the slickers, Tammy removed her socks, threw them down into the cabin, and went barefoot for the rest of the afternoon. It was a favorite of hers and one she couldn't do too often on the drenched decks of the boat. She wasn't going anywhere, and the deck was clean. It felt good to give her feet a chance to breathe and not be scrunched in the rubber boots.

Underneath the slickers, Tammy wore jeans and a sweatshirt. They were still dry, and she left them on. She walked over to the stern with her slickers in hand and stepped over the side onto the swim step. Steadying herself with one hand on the rail, Tammy knelt and dipped the slickers into the ocean and pulled them up and down in a fast motion to wash off the grime. The water felt good on her hands. It was refreshing. Maybe I should go for a quick dip? Tammy thought as she scanned the harbor. No one's here. She put her arm deeper into the water and smiled. Yeah, she was going for a swim; Tammy decided and hastily stepped back on to the boat carrying the slickers and headed to the cabin to undress.

After hanging up the slickers to dry on a hook by the helm, Tammy went down into the cabin to disrobe and returned to the deck a few minutes later, wrapped in a white towel. She checked the harbor one more time and saw it was still empty. She looked out to sea to make sure no boats were coming in. There were none.

Satisfied it was safe to go for a quick dip, Tammy unwrapped herself from the towel and let it fall to her feet. The warmth of the sun felt good against her naked skin. After soaking up the rays for a moment, she headed back to the swim step and dove into the water. It felt better than she had imagined. After coming back up to the surface, she shook her head vigorously and enjoyed being immersed in the cool crispness of the water.

Tammy swam around for a good fifteen minutes before heading back to the boat. She felt rejuvenated and refreshed. Her body no longer ached, and it relaxed her muscles. If Dwayne had shown up at that very moment, Tammy would have insisted she'd go back out with him and help pull the rest of the gear. But she knew the route, and at this time of day, he was probably over at the backside of the island.

The harbor was still empty, but she soaked up some rays on the deck of the boat. A surge of guilt hit her, knowing Dwayne was hard at work, but hey, she's just following the captain's order, right?

After laying out the towel, she laid naked on her back and released an enormous sigh as her body soaked up the heat from the sun. In no time at all, she drifted off to sleep until the tornado winds blasted above the boat.

CHAPTER 4

Tammy released a high-pitched scream and jolted her body up to an upright position. She hollered, "What the hell!" Afraid to move and the fact that she was naked, Tammy remained frozen in place and watched in horror as a white bucket, one of the deck chairs, and her slickers flew across the deck in a fury. Tammy was relieved that they didn't land in the water.

She covered her eyes as sprays of water hit her face and stung her sunburnt cheeks. Tammy heard the motor's loud noise from above, but the powerful winds prevented her from looking up. "What the hell is going on?" she yelled again. The strong winds lasted for maybe a minute until they subsided. They were still present, but not as harsh. Finally, she was able to open her eyes and look up, which is when she broke out into a roaring voracious laugh.

Tammy hollered, "Really?" Even though she knew she couldn't be heard over the loud noise of the helicopter that hovered above the boat. Then she saw the heads of six Navy Seals hanging out of the doorway, waving their arms.

There was nothing Tammy could do but laugh and wave back. *I guess they haven't seen a naked girl in a while.* Their intrusion flattered her on what should have been a peaceful afternoon of rest. She laughed again and gave them a friendly wave and smile. They'd already seen her naked, so she thought it senseless to cover up. As the helicopter ascended, it took the wind with it. Tammy watched and waved as the helicopter and the happy Navy Seals flew off in the distance, leaving Tammy once again in the harbor's calm waters and the glorious warm sunshine.

Tammy waited until they were off in the distance before she stood up and wrapped her body in the towel. She giggled and shook her head at the boldness of the men that had just surprised her with their grand presence. "Well damn, that's one for the books. Wait till I tell Dwayne about this." She snickered and thought it would be a good idea to get dressed in case she had any more unannounced visitors.

Feeling more energized and somewhat guilty for not helping Dwayne pull traps, Tammy wanted to be more productive for the rest of the day and spent the next few hours chopping mackerel for tomorrow's pull. She also surprised Dwayne with a hearty fried chicken dinner, a rarity on the island. After fishing all day, they usually only had enough energy to open a can of soup and butter a bread roll.

It was almost dark when Tammy spotted Dwayne entering the harbor. He was the last boat to come in, and being later than usual, Tammy smiled and released a sigh of relief when she saw him.

She gave him an enormous smile when he slowed down the *Little Boat* and, with caution, eased it alongside the *Baywitch*.

"How did it go?" Tammy hollered over the roar of the motor before tossing him a line.

Dwayne caught the rope and quickly tied off the boat before shutting off the engine. "Great! We did well." He turned and pointed to two large grey barrels full of circulating ocean water and filled with lobsters. "Both barrels are full," he said with a satisfactory smile. "Wanna help me get them into the receivers?" he asked.

Still feeling a tad guilty, Tammy was eager to help. "Sure. How many receivers do you need?"

"I'd say three," Dwayne replied.

Tammy headed over to the stern of the boat where they were stacked and handed them one at a time to Dwayne, who set them on the deck of the *Little Boat*. She then jumped down, grabbed a pair of rubber gloves off the dash, and began pulling the lobsters out of the barrels to give to Dwayne.

"So, how was your afternoon? Did you get plenty of rest?" Dwayne asked as he took a lobster from Tammy's hand and placed it in a receiver.

Tammy gave him a smirk, "Oh, I guess you could say it was interesting."

"How can hanging out on a boat in an empty harbor be interesting?" he said with a creased brow. He looked at her with wide eyes and beamed her a huge smile. "Wait! Did you go skinny dipping?"

Tammy felt her cheeks blush. "I did. But that's not what I'm talking about," she said while handing him another lobster.

Dwayne's eyes lit up. "Ooh, you went skinny dipping, and I missed it. Darn it. So, did someone see you? Is that it?"

"No, it was after my swim when I was lying naked on the deck."

Dwayne's jaw dropped. His eyes remained wide. "You sunbathed naked too? Damn, I should have taken the afternoon off with you. I really missed out," he laughed. "So, tell me what happened?"

"Let's put it this way, me and everything on the boat were almost blown out to sea by the helicopter hovering super low above me with a bunch of Navy Seals straining their necks over the side to get a good view of me sunbathing naked."

Dwayne cracked a loud laugh. "You're kidding me? What did you do? Run down to the cabin?"

"No, I couldn't move because of the force of the wind coming from the helicopter. I figured, screw it. They were harmless and twenty feet above me in a bloody helicopter. What could they do? And I'm sure I made their day."

"Well, shoot, I missed it all. Do you know how many navy seals are going to be jacking off in their bunks tonight while visions of you naked crowd their brain?"

"Dwayne!" Tammy shrieked as she handed him the last lobster.

"What? You know I'm right." He leaned in and gave her a smooch. "I think it's pretty cool that my hot girlfriend diverted the US government's Navy Seals from their training exercise."

Tammy gave him a friendly slap on the arm. "Oh, stop. They probably hadn't seen a naked woman in months. Now come on, let's get cleaned up. With all the free time I've had this afternoon, I made us a chicken dinner."

Dwayne's eyes bulged. "No way! Really? Oh, wait till I get on the radio and ask the other captains what they are having for dinner. They're going to wish they brought their other halves with them too." He released another loud, cocky laugh. "Oh, I love showing you off and bragging about you. Come here and kiss me," he said before they put the last receiver in the water and stepped onto the *Baywitch*.

By the time Tammy exited the cabin with two plates of chicken and instant mashed potatoes, the sun had set, and a full moon appeared on the horizon. It was a glorious evening with very little wind. "God, what a beautiful night," Tammy said as she sat in one of the deck chairs and gazed up to the darkened skies.

Dwayne joined her. "Thanks for cutting all the bait today. Now we get to watch the other guys prep for tomorrow while we eat." He chuckled.

All the familiar captains and boats had returned this year. Dwayne's good friend Mitch on the *Sea-Life*. Patrick on the *Patience* and Tom on the *Lobster-Fest*. Lester was also back on his boat, *Out to Sea*. Tammy remembered him well. He was the one who doubted she would make it through the season. But he had surprised her this year with a friendly wave and smile when they first arrived. Dale on the boat *Dreaming* was still his grumpy self but had warmed up to Dwayne and Tammy after receiving a home-cooked meal from Tammy at the end of her first season.

When Tammy returned for a second season, the captains couldn't hide their look of surprise. She made it through her first year with endurance, and more strength than other fishermen held and had earned their respect with flying colors.

This year there was no rank; they considered her one of them. They treated and spoke to her like they would any other member of the fleet. They'd wave and smile at her as they drove by and included her in the conversations when they pulled up to the *Baywitch* at the end of the day for a quick chit-chat before heading over to their moorings.

Dwayne and Tammy had two more days of pulling traps before they would have to head back to the mainland. They wasted no time and left the harbor before the sun was up and before any other boat. Feeling rested, Tammy was eager to pull the first trap and, like a pro, gaffed it on her first try. She rarely missed a trap now.

They had the system down and made a good team. Dwayne pulled out the legal lobsters and tossed them into a barrel of water while Tammy replenished the bait compartment with mackerel and fish scraps she had gotten from the fish markets.

"Ready?" Dwayne asked. He pushed down on the fish in the bait compartment so he could close the door.

"Yep, ready to dump, captain," Tammy said with a smile.

Dwayne pushed the bait down one more time and then suddenly jumped back. "Ow! That friggin' hurt," he said, ripping off his glove. He let it fall to the deck, so he could inspect his hand, which was now throbbing.

Tammy pulled off her gloves and walked over to Dwayne's side. "What happened?"

"Something poked me in the bait compartment. It stings like hell." He brought his palm closer to his face. "But I don't see anything."

Tammy took his hand. "Let me look." She rubbed over his skin with her fingertips. "Where does it hurt?"

"Right in the middle. That's where I was pressing down on the bait. Damn, it still hurts." He said as he scrunched his eyes and shook his hand.

Tammy looked closer. "I see a little pinprick with a spot of blood. Is that it?"

"That's where it hurts, but now my whole hand hurts. It must have been a fishbone or something. But why the hell is it hurting so much?"

"What do you want to do? Are you going to be able to drive the boat, or do you want me to?"

"I'll be fine. I'll just keep an eye on it," he said as he continued to shake the pain away.

When they pulled up to the next trap a few minutes later, Dwayne looked worried. "I can't feel my arm and look. It's all swollen."

Tammy raced to the helm where he stood. "What!" She gasped when she saw his fingers had swelled to double their size. "Oh, my god! Let me see your arm. Hold it up."

Dwayne tried to raise his arm. "I can't; it's dead." Using his other hand to support it, he pulled it up just enough so Tammy could see it. His wrist disappeared from the swelling, and his arm was twice its size all the way up to his elbow.

"Holy shit! That doesn't look good. What the hell poked you?"

"I have no idea, but I can't feel my arm at all. What the hell are we going to do?"

ammy's face turned pale, and her jaw tightened from the fear she felt. She didn't like it, and it scared her.

With a look of despair, Dwayne looked down at his arm that continued to swell. "I can't have my arm flopping around on the boat like this. It's too dangerous, and we have to pull traps today and tomorrow; otherwise, we won't make enough money to come back out." Dwayne twisted his body in an awkward position so he could turn off the motor. "Let me think for a minute."

Tammy spoke in a stern voice, "Think! What's there to think about? We're going home. You can't fish with one arm, and we need to get that looked at. Look how much it's swollen, Dwayne." Tammy shook her head in frustration. "Why is it every time we come out here something happens? Last year we drove over a line, and it got tangled in the prop. Do you remember?"

Dwayne nodded. "Oh yeah, the water was freezing."

"Yes, you had to jump into a frigid cold and cut off the line. The next day, the Navy Seals decided they would do underwater explosion practices in the harbor and only gave us an hour to vacate with our two boats and the lobster receivers. We had to spend the next two nights anchored out at sea in a rocky ocean." Tammy stomped her feet. "Every year, there is a challenge of some kind. And now this. You can't fish with that arm, Dwayne. It's dead," Tammy insisted.

Dwayne refused to listen to her reasoning. He could be stubborn when he wants to be. "Going home is not an option, Tammy. We won't have any money to come back out. You know how broke we are the first week of the season."

Tammy stomped her feet again in protest. "Goddamn it, Dwayne. This could be serious." She looked around at the vast emptiness of the ocean. "We are in the middle of nowhere. Do you see any hospitals? What if you get sick?"

"I don't feel sick. It's just my arm; that's all."

Tammy raised her voice. "We need to go home, Dwayne. The swelling is growing while we are sitting here arguing."

Dwayne stood up and brushed by her without speaking. He reached over to the far end of the dash and grabbed a rope with his good hand. Using his teeth, he unraveled the line.

"What are you doing?" Tammy said abruptly and with an edge to her tone.

He held out one end on the line to her. "Here, take this and tie my arm to my waist so it won't flop around."

Tammy placed her hands on her hips and creased her brow. "What? Are you crazy? What good is that going to do?"

Dwayne raised his voice, which startled Tammy. "Just do it!"

Tammy grabbed the rope and placed his arm behind it as she wrapped it around his waist. "Fine," she said, feeling defeated.

"Make sure you tie it tight. I don't want my arm slipping out because I'll never know if it does, and I could knock it against something and break it."

Tammy wasn't happy with his solution and let him know by giving the rope an extra hard tug.

"Ouch!" Dwayne yelled.

"Well, you said to make it tight." She tugged again. "So now that you are the one armed fisherman, what are your plans?" she snarled at him, still not happy with his ridiculous plan.

"We're going to keep fishing."

Tammy shook her head. "Seriously! That's the craziest thing I've ever heard. It's obvious that something poisonous poked you, and we need to get it checked. I think it's affected your brain too. I can't believe you want to continue fishing. It might travel through your entire body and kill you."

Dwayne released a slight chuckle while trying to adjust his dead arm. "It won't kill me," he said with a smirk.

Tammy flared her nostrils. "This is not funny, Dwayne. It could be serious. I mean, look at your bloody arm now. It's twice its normal size. You can't fish like that."

"Tammy, we don't have a choice. I'll keep an eye on it, and if I start feeling sick, I'll let you know."

"No, you won't. I know you. Fine, we'll fish, but I'm taking your temperature as soon as we get back to the *Baywitch,* and if you have a fever, we're heading home. Even if I have to lock you in the cabin and get us out of here on my own," She shook her head again. "This is fucking unbelievable, and you call me stubborn." She folded her arms in front of her. "So how are we going to do this, Captain Dwayne?"

Dwayne gave her another smirk, but Tammy wasn't amused and rolled her eyes.

"Look, we only have two more days, and then we head home. I can stick it out until then. I can drive the boat with my good arm and reach over to work the throttle, and you'll be in charge of everything else, including measuring the lobsters. We can do this, Tammy. We fished without steering in the *Little Boat* for five days; we sure as hell can do this."

Tammy grunted. She worried about Dwayne's arm but knew there was no sense arguing with him. Yet again, he had pulled rank, and she had no choice but to go along with his absurd plan, no matter what her opinion was.

While they had been drifting, the swell had increased, and Tammy grabbed the handrail on the trap table to get her balance. "Fine, let's do this. The sooner we get back to the *Baywitch*, the sooner I can take your temperature."

Tammy watched as Dwayne started the boat with his right arm. Being left-handed, she could tell it was awkward for him. He then twisted his body so he could work the throttle and put the boat in gear.

"I'm not sure about this, Dwayne." Tammy hollered above the sound of the motor as Dwayne headed to the next trap.

It took a few traps to get the system down, but they were a good team, and Tammy knew what was expected from her to get the job done. Periodically she insisted that Dwayne let her check his arm. It remained swollen for the entire day, but it seemed to hold twice its normal size and not swell anymore.

By the end of the day, much to Tammy's surprise, they pulled the rest of the gear, and the catch was plentiful.

Dwayne didn't complain of any pain, just that his hand and arm were completely dead, and he couldn't feel anything. Tammy was at least thankful that he wasn't experiencing any pain, but she still didn't like it.

On their way back to the harbor, Tammy discovered she was hurting more than the usual aches and pains she experienced. Her body ached down to her bones, her hands were chapped, and she could barely bend her fingers. Her hair was a matted mess, and she could hardly bend her knees. She took on a lot more tasks and would be for the next two days. She wasn't sure if she'd be able to handle the extra workload.

Once Dwayne had the *Little Boat* alongside the *Baywitch*, Tammy quickly grabbed a line and tied off the boat, but not before letting out a scream of pain.

"Are you okay?" Dwayne yelled after he turned off the motor."

Tammy shook her hand. "Yeah, my hands are so sore, and grabbing that rope didn't help. Even with gloves on."

Once they'd secured the boats, Tammy attempted to jump up on the *Baywitch* to grab some receivers for today's catch, but the leap was more than her body could handle. With one foot on the *Baywitch,* her knee buckled, and she lost her balance. Before she could save herself, she fell backward and crashed to the deck of the *Little Boat,* slamming her back hard on the rough non-skid finish. "Ouch! Goddamn it!" she screamed, wincing from the sudden burst of pain she was experiencing.

Dwayne faced away from her, looking through his binoculars with his good arm at a strange boat on the horizon. He had not seen Tammy fall but heard her scream. In a flash, he turned to find her curled up in pain. "Shit! Are you okay? What the hell happened?"

He set down his binoculars on the dash and knelt beside her, steadying himself with his working arm.

"I lost my frigging balance while trying to step on the *Baywitch.* My knee buckled." She screeched with her eyes closed and a tight jaw. "My bloody back is killing me. God, I'm sick of this shit!" She grunted through gritted teeth.

Dwayne rested his hand on her shoulder. "Are you able to get up?"

"Yeah, just give me a minute."

For the next few minutes, Tammy laid on her back, waiting for the sharp pains that were shooting down her back to disappear. She had her eyes closed and a hand over her brow. She was on the brink of crying but refused to give in to the forces that were continually trying to knock her down. Commercial fishing was dangerous and a constant battle with the ocean, the weather, and the intense labor that would break you if you didn't have the stamina to fight it off. This too would pass, she told herself as the pain subsided.

For the first time since she fell, she moved her legs until they were straight and rubbed her back.

Using his good arm, Dwayne supported her shoulder. "Are you able to sit up?"

"I'm going to try," Tammy grunted while holding out her hand. "Give me your hand and try to pull me up," she moaned.

Dwayne did as she asked and tried not to winch when she squeezed his hand hard and was thankful that her fingernails were short.

Tammy braced herself, and with her other hand, she pushed on the deck as she dragged herself up. "Argh," she screamed at the top of her lungs, trying to fight off the burning pain she was feeling.

Dwayne held her hand tight. "You're almost there! Come on, babe, you can do it," he encouraged her.

Tammy released another cry from the unbearable pain she was experiencing before she could eventually sit upright. Panting and out of breath, she rubbed her side. "Oh, fuck, this really hurts. You are going to have to help me get to my feet."

Dwayne stood and held out his hand. "Take my hand."

Tammy continued to rub her side. "Give me another minute," and then she chuckled.

"Well, I'm glad you're able to see the humor in all this," Dwayne said and joined her in her laughter.

Tammy laughed again, but this time a little louder. "Will you look at us? You with your dead arm, and me with a bad back. We're quite the fishing team, don't you think?"

Dwayne had to agree and laughed again. "Come on, let me help you up. Are you ready?" He asked with his good arm extended.

Tammy reached for his hand and let out another "Argh." She dragged herself up and steadied her feet. "Okay, I'm going to try this again. We need to get these lobsters in the water. I'll be right back," she said, giving her back one last rub while she worked through the pain. After her second attempt to jump on the

Baywitch was successful, she grabbed three receivers and handed one at a time to Dwayne, who lined them up on the deck. It was then up to Tammy to load up the receivers, and using his functioning hand, they both lowered them into the water, and Tammy tied them off.

"Okay, I'm going to take your temperature now." Tammy insisted. Go sit in the cabin while I look for the thermometer."

"I'm sure it's fine," Dwayne contested. "It's been hours since it happened."

Tammy was in no mood to hear Dwayne's protests. She was tired, her back was killing her, and she still had quite a few chores to do before the day was over. "Just do it!" She bellowed.

Dwayne didn't argue and went down into the cabin to wait for nurse Tammy. After taking his temperature, she was relieved to see he didn't have a fever. "Let me see your arm." She said.

Unable to lift it, Dwayne stood up away from the table so Tammy could take a closer look.

"Wow, it's still swollen. Your hand and arm are still twice their sizes."

Dwayne seemed surprised it hadn't gone down at all. "I still can't feel anything either."

"I wonder what the hell poked you."

"I have no idea, but we're not getting any more fish scraps. We'll only be using mackerel from now on. If we still have some scraps, dump them in the water. The fish will love them."

"Good idea," Tammy said, taking hold of the rope that was tied around his waist to keep his arm secured. "Okay, let me help you get out of these slickers, and then I need to go cut up some bait. Why don't you call Mitch on the *Sea-Life* and ask him if anything like this ever happened to him?"

It took a good ten minutes to get Dwayne comfortable and retie his arm to his waist.

"I'm going to have to call you the one-armed bandit," Tammy laughed.

Dwayne cut her off and spiked his ear. "Shh, I hear a boat in the harbor. It sounds like they are coming this way."

"I hear it too," Tammy said as she headed up the steps to the deck. Dwayne was right behind her.

Dwayne looked out into the harbor; none of the other fishing boats had returned yet—so who were those guys? Dwayne questioned as he watched the vessel head their way. He soon realized it must be the boat he saw earlier through his binoculars.

"Shit, it's Fish and Game," Dwayne said as the boat drew closer. "What do they want? I've never been boarded before."

Dwayne explained to Tammy that Fish and Game would board your boat unannounced to check that the fishermen were abiding by the fishing laws and had no short lobsters on board.

"Well, we're not doing anything wrong. Let them do their thing, and then they'll leave." Tammy tried to reason after she noticed how upset Dwayne had become.

"That could take hours. Especially if they want to go through all eight of our receivers and measure every lobster."

"What! They would do that?"

"Sure. It happened to Mitch a few years ago. They were on his boat for five hours. They checked everything."

"Well, that's bloody ridiculous. Don't they realize we are tired, and we still have to get ready for tomorrow's pull?" Tammy watched the warden's pull up alongside the *Baywitch* on the other side from where the *Little Boat* was tied. A warden at the helm leaned out and yelled. "How's it going today? Can I throw you my line?"

With her nerves now peaked, worried they might find something, Tammy rushed to the other side of the boat and braced herself to catch the line. "Sure."

She caught it on the first throw and quickly tied off the boat, and then ignoring the shooting pains in her back, she rushed to the bow to tie the other line.

Dwayne saw two wardens on the boat and waited until the one

driving had shut off the motor before he spoke. "Hey, how's it going?" He said with a forced smile.

Having never dealt with Fish and Game before, Tammy remained quiet and let Dwayne handle the conversation.

"May I come aboard, sir?" a warden asked.

Tammy was impressed that they had asked first.

"Sure," Dwayne replied as he leaned against the dash.

Tammy nodded as they boarded their boat and watched as they held out a hand to Dwayne. "Are you the Captain? I'm officer Peaks, and my partner here is officer Kinsley. Would you mind if we look around your vessel?"

"Sorry, my arm is bound; otherwise, I'd shake your hand," Dwayne said, followed by a nervous smile.

Office Peaks looked down at Dwayne's arm and took a step back. "Good lord. What happened to you? Do you need medical assistance?"

Dwayne shook his head. "No. I'll be fine. I pushed down on some bait in the traps earlier today, and something poked me. I think it was a poisonous fish of some sort. It should be fine in a day or two."

The officer looked alarmed and glanced over at Tammy and then back at Dwayne. "And you're still fishing?" the officer asked.

"I have no choice." Dwayne looked over at Tammy and nodded. "My girlfriend, who is also my deckhand, is carrying most of the load. We only have two more days to fish. We should be able to do it."

The officer looked stunned that Tammy and Dwayne were still fishing despite Dwayne's injury. "Well, listen. Keep an eye on it, and if anything changes, we'll be anchored in the harbor for a few days. Call us on the radio if you need anything."

Dwayne nodded. "I will. Thanks."

Officer Peaks scanned the boat. "Well, everything looks in order here. You take care of that arm, okay."

Dwayne didn't want to question their brief visit and assumed they thought it would be too difficult for him to retrieve the lobsters from the water with only one arm. "Okay, thanks again. Enjoy the rest of your night," Dwayne said with a polite smile.

Tammy helped untie their boat and waited until they were far enough away before she spoke. "Well, that went well," she chuckled.

Dwayne stood across the deck. "Too well, I'd say. That must have been their shortest inspection ever. So, I guess they'll be boarding all the other boats as they come back into the harbor."

Tammy walked over to where he stood and nuzzled herself into his space. He draped his good arm around her neck and gave her an affectionate smooch.

Tammy smiled. "We sure have fun together, don't we?"

Dwayne jerked back his head and laughed. "If this is your idea of fun, then you are easy to please." He laughed again when Tammy gave him a playful slap on his chest.

"Hey, how is your back doing?" he asked in a more serious tone.

Tammy rubbed it. "It's still really sore, but much better than a half-hour ago. I'm going to take it easy for an hour before I cut the bait."

"Good idea." He kissed her again. "Hey, thanks for taking on most of the work today. You did an outstanding job. Are you going to be okay tomorrow?"

"I'll be fine as long as I don't fall again." She rubbed his chest and smiled. "I got this okay. We're in this together. If it were me, you'd be doing the same thing."

Dwayne nodded. "I sure do love you. How did I ever get so lucky?"

"I love you too, babe. Hey, are you going to call the other boats on the radio and let them know Fish and Game are in the harbor?"

"Nah. It's an open channel, and Fish and Game are probably on the same channel. They'll find out soon enough."

Tammy pulled away and grabbed one of the folded deck chairs stored on the side of the boat and unfolded it. "Okay, then. Well, why don't you have a seat and I will make us two cups of hot chocolate, and then we can kick back for a while before I toss the fish scraps over the side and cut up more bait."

"Sounds good," he said with a loving smile.

Dwayne and Tammy pushed through the next two days and got a decent catch before planning their trip home. Dwayne talked to the other captains about his arm, and none of them had ever seen or heard of a fisherman getting injured that way. Curious by what Dwayne had told them over the radio, each captain swung by the *Baywitch* to see it for themselves.

The swelling didn't go down until their last day, and Dwayne finally experienced some feeling in his fingertips. It was a good sign and a tremendous relief for them both. Dwayne was going to be okay, and they were heading home with a good catch, which would pay their bills, as well as pay for their next trip to the island. Tammy hated to admit it, but Dwayne's stubbornness had paid off.

Tammy never liked the grueling ten-hour crossing home, unlike the journey to the island where they were excited to fish and couldn't wait to get there. The trip back to the mainland always seemed much longer. After fishing for a week, she was exhausted, and it was still a struggle. They took turns at the wheel, but she could never get enough rest as tired as she was. The constant loud sounds of the motors and the boat's continuous rocking made it impossible to sleep. And then there was the worry of the *Little Boat*, which they towed behind them.

They pulled into the Marina in the wee hours of the morning, and even though Tammy was eager to see Matt, it was too early to call Louise. She would have to wait at least another three hours until seven when the sun would be up.

"I can't wait to see Matt," Tammy yelled to Dwayne from the dock. "I love fishing, but I hate being away from him," she added as she cleated off the *Baywitch*.

"I know, babe. I miss him too." Dwayne shut off the boat. Tammy embraced the peacefulness of the dock. She closed her eyes, released a heavy sigh, and smiled. "Oh, it's so quiet. I just friggin love it." Tammy tickled her ear with her finger. "But, there is always a ringing sound in my ear after listening to the loud sounds of the engines for the last ten hours." But the ringing was soon forgotten when she looked up to the night skies and smiled at the stars.

Dwayne jumped off the boat and took her in his arms. He looked up to the skies with her. "Yeah. It can't get any better than this. Let me take care of the *Little Boat*. I'll be right back."

"Not before you give me a kiss," Tammy laughed, covering her lips with his and then broke away to inspect his arm. "How's your arm?" She rubbed his skin with her fingertips. "It looks like the swelling has almost gone."

Dwayne ran his hand down his arm. "It's much better. It has most of its feeling back. That was the weirdest damn thing."

Tammy chuckled. "It sure was. No more fresh bait from now on."

When Dwayne returned from tying up the *Little Boat*, Tammy helped him get the lobsters into the water. The receivers were heavy, and it took all their strength to ease them beneath the surface slowly.

"I'm going to go call the fish buyer," Dwayne said while still trying to catch his breath.

Tammy heaved her chest. Lifting the receivers took all her strength. "Okay. I'm going to take a shower and then go pick up Matt."

The highlight of Tammy's return home was holding Matt in her arms and smothering him with kisses. He may be almost eight, but he was still her baby, and he always welcomed her and held her tight every time she picked him up.

Today was no different. She saw Matt looking out the window before she even pulled up in front of the apartment building where Louise lived. Louise must have told him she was on her way. He beamed her a big smile that melted Tammy's heart and waved both his arms. In a flash, she saw the front door swing wide open, and Matt raced down the pathway before she stepped out of the truck. "Mom!" he screamed.

Tears pooled in Tammy's eyes. "Oh, there's my boy," she cried as she met him halfway down the path with her arms wide open.

Matt came to a sudden halt in the embrace of his mother's arms and wrapped his arms around her. "Mom. I've missed you. Did you get a lot of lobsters?"

That was always his first question. Tammy kissed the top of his head and ran her fingers through his hair. "I've missed you too, buddy. We did good, and we got a lot of lobsters," she said with a huge grin.

Tammy held Matt in her arms for a little while longer and thought of Dwayne's idea about renting a house. The idea of Matt being with his grandmother in his own home and bedroom while she was out fishing warmed her heart. The thought excited her, and soon, she would write her mom a detailed letter about their plans.

"Hey, do you want to go out for breakfast? You can have your favorite. Chocolate chip pancakes." Tammy asked Matt as she smiled.

Matt leaped from her arms and spun around. "Yes. Let's go."

After grabbing Matt's bag, they went to a nearby Denny's,

where Tammy shared stories with him about their trip. It was a time where they reconnected. Matt listened as his mom told him about Dwayne's arm and the poisonous fish with bright eyes and pinned ears. He laughed when she joked about always banging her head in the v-berth, and how her hands were covered in poke holes from the lobsters poking her.

After breakfast, she took him with her to downtown LA to pick up bait for their next trip. The guys all knew Matt and gave him a high-five. Tammy told the owner about Dwayne's arm, and he, too, had never heard it happening to anyone before either. They processed so many varieties of fish he had no idea what kind it could have been.

By the time they got back to the dock, the lobsters were sold and picked up by the buyer. Dwayne had called his son, Justin, and smelt fresh from his shower.

He smiled at Matt when he spotted him running through the boatyard towards him.

"Dwayne!" Matt yelled.

"Hey, buddy. It's so good to see you. We've missed you," he said, giving him a high-five. Dwayne waited for Tammy to catch up, who was still walking through the yard.

"Hey," Tammy said with a smile, followed by a kiss on Dwayne's cheek. "I've got the bait in the truck."

"Great. Let's take Matt fishing at the dock for a little while, and then we can all go shopping for our next trip."

"Sounds like a good idea, but I'll only stay on the docks with you guys for a little while. I need to call Donna. I've not called her in over two months."

While Dwayne and Matt had fun fishing, Tammy snuck away to call Donna. She was excited at the possibility of their mom coming out and couldn't wait to tell Donna, who also hadn't seen their mom in over five years. Tammy's thought was that their mom would have two of her daughters in the same room if she took their mom on a road trip to visit Donna. But it still wouldn't fulfill her mom's one wish of having all three daughters together. Tammy was determined to make it happen someday.

After two rings, Donna answered the phone.

"Hello."

"Hey Donna, It's Tammy. How's it going?"

"Tammy! God, I've been trying to call you for the past month. I hate not being able to get a hold of you."

Guilt suddenly swept through Tammy. "I'm sorry. We've been so busy. Lobster season has started, and we're only in the Marina for the weekend, then we head right back out again for a week. We have to make a quick turnaround trip, becaus after a few months, the seas arc too rough to fish the island."

"Who's watching Matt while you're gone?" Donna asked.

"Oh, the mother of one of Matt's friends from school. It's working out great."

"If I knew how to drive and lived closer to you, I'd probably watch him again. But when he got hurt while he was with me, it freaked me. I felt terrible."

"It's okay, Donna. Don't feel bad. So how is everything with you?"

"Well, I have some news for you, which is why I've been trying to call you. It sucks that you don't have a phone, Tammy."

"Yeah, I know. I'll try to call you more often. I promise." It was a promise Tammy had made before but had failed it. "So, what's this news you have for me?" Tammy asked. "I have some news for you too." She suddenly had a thought. "Wait! Are you pregnant? Am I going to be an aunt?" she gasped.

Donna laughed. "No, I'm not pregnant." She took a deep breath. "Jason and I have sold our house, and we are moving."

Tammy's heart sank. "What? Where are you moving to?"

Tammy sensed Donna's hesitation. "Colorado."

"Colorado!" Tammy shrieked. "What the hell is in Colorado?"

"More work for Jason. He's a tree trimmer, and the work is endless out there. He already has jobs lined up that will carry him through to next year. Once we get settled, he plans on hiring a crew."

Tammy shook her head. "This is all so sudden. When are you leaving?"

"It's sudden to you, but we put the house on the market over six weeks ago and took a drive out to Colorado and bought a house. Like I said, I've been trying to call you. We leave this Wednesday."

"What! You're leaving in three days." It crushed Tammy's heart. A few minutes ago, she couldn't wait to tell her about their mom coming over. Now she didn't want to upset her by sharing the news. "So, when I get back from fishing next week, you'll be gone."

"I'm afraid so. Any chance I can see you before we leave?" Donna asked.

"No. We leave tomorrow night and won't be back for five days. We have just enough time to load up the boat before we head out," Tammy said with a tinge of guilt.

"Wow! You spend a lot of time on the ocean, Tammy. Do you ever see anyone anymore? How does Matt handle it?"

"It's only for the first couple of months of the season. We don't fish the island all year. It gets too rough out there. Matt is much better now that I see him on weekends. I'll never send him to Florida again. That was bloody awful."

"So, what news do you have for me?" Donna asked.

Tammy hesitated. "Well, it doesn't matter now because you won't be here, but mom is coming over next year, hopefully."

"Hopefully? What does that mean?"

"Well, Dwayne and I are going to look for a house to rent, and if we do, then mom is going to stay with Matt while we are fishing."

"Really!" Donna squealed. "That's a brilliant idea. Who thought of that?"

"Dwayne did. But it's not definite. We need to find a house first. And I'd have to arrange for someone to take Matt to school and bring him home. Mom doesn't drive, as you know."

"Well, it's about time you guys got a house. I don't know how you can live on a boat. There's no room. Don't you get cabin fever?" Donna laughed.

It was a question she got asked a lot, and for the most part, she never complained. She and Dwayne spent most of their time outdoors. The only time she remembers having a hard time living on the boat was when they had twelve days of non-stop rain, and they were confined to the cabin. Tempers flared, and harsh words were said between her and Dwayne. But Tammy has no recollection of what the trivial arguments were about. "I actually enjoy living on the boat, but Matt is getting bigger, and it's about time he had his own room. Anyway, I was hoping mom and I could visit you if she comes over, but now that you're moving to Colorado, that's not going to happen. I know Mom won't be happy. She asked me if she was going to see you, and I told her yes."

"Yeah, I know. I write to her every so often, but I've never been good at writing letters. You know that, Tammy."

"Do you call her?" Tammy asked. "Every time I talk to her, she always tells me she wants to see all three of her daughters in the same room. I could hear the excitement in her voice when I told her we would visit you. God, now I have to tell her you're moving. That's not going to be a fun phone call."

"I've called her a few times, but she always sounds so pissed off because we are all spread apart. We always argue, so now I just write, so I don't have to listen to her. I know she wants to see us all together, but I don't see that happening anytime soon, and that's all she talks about. She doesn't understand that I can't travel to England because I'm still trying to sort out my status even after all these years in this country. It got all screwed up when I ran away from home."

"What about Jenny? Do you talk or write to her?"

Donna cracked a sarcastic laugh. "Hell no. I've not spoken to her in years. The last time I spoke to her was when I lived with you at the motel. Yeah, she sends me photos of her kids at Christmas time, and I send her a Christmas card every year, but I don't know her, Tammy."

Tammy had to agree with her. "Yeah, I know what you mean. I don't know her either. It's pretty sad, don't you think?"

Suddenly a voice interrupted their conversation. *"Please deposit seventy-five cents to continue this call."*

"God damn it. I'm out of quarters, Donna. I have to go. I love you, and I'm really sorry I won't get to see you before you leave." Tammy said in a rushed voice, afraid the call might end.

"Yeah, me too. I love you too, sis. Call this number when you get in from fishing. It will forward the call to our new one, and the recording will give you the new number. It will only forward for thirty days, so make sure you call."

"I will. I love you. Bye." And then the phone went dead.

Feeling numb from Donna's sudden news, Tammy turned around and lost herself in the view of the hundreds of boats sitting calmly in the docks. There was a slight breeze, and the sound of the rigging rattling on the sailboats always seemed to soothe her.

Regret filled Tammy. She should have called and visited Donna more often when they were in from fishing. If she had, she would have known about her move to Colorado and could have made plans to see her before she left. Now Tammy didn't know when she would see her, and the idea of fulfilling her mom's wishes to have all three of her girls together just became much more challenging.

Tammy kept her promise and called Donna when they returned to the mainland after fishing a week at the island. She wasn't about to let another sister slip away and was tired of not having a phone and keeping a jar of quarters just to make phone calls. It saddened her that she lost contact with so many friends because of not having a phone and was unreachable while on the ocean. Tammy realized that getting a house held another advantage. They could finally get a phone.

The more Dwayne and Tammy thought about getting a house, the more confined they felt on the boat. Dwayne's son, Justin, visited less frequently because, like Matt, he was growing, and the boat wasn't big enough for all four of them. When he visited, it was just for the day, and they took him home by nightfall. But months would go by between each visit. Justin was now a preteen and would much rather hang with his buddies from school than in a boatyard.

As soon as their third season at the island had ended and they were now fishing Malibu, Dwayne and Tammy began the grueling task of looking for a house to rent that was close to the Marina, but they soon discovered everything was out of their price range.

"How do people afford these places? The cheapest we have found is $1,800, and that's without coming up with the first and last month's rent and whatever else they require. There's no way we can afford that," Tammy said, feeling discouraged. They looked at dozens of houses and even a few apartments, which they realized would never work for them. They needed a yard for Matt to play in and space to store their fishing gear. Also on the list was a garage for Dwayne. Tammy couldn't hide the frustration in her voice. "My God, we only pay $300 a month for our boat slip. We'd still have to pay that on top of the rent." Tammy leaned against Dwayne's truck outside the last house they looked at and folded her arms. "What are we going to do? I can't tell my mom to buy her tickets until we have a house, and she's hoping to come out here in September, which is just eight months away."

Dwayne approached her and rubbed her shoulders before giving her a loving kiss. "We still have time. Quit worrying so much. We can look some more tomorrow or later today after we've picked up Matt from school."

Tammy shook her head and raised her hands. "I'm done for today. I don't want to take Matt to different houses and have him ask a bunch of questions. He loves the boatyard, and I'm sure if he could, he would ask for a house in the boatyard." Tammy laughed, checking her watch. "Speaking of which, we should get going. School gets out in ten minutes."

Dwayne nodded and walked around the truck to get in on his side. Tammy hesitated and took one last look at the overpriced home that would have been perfect before getting in herself.

They arrived at the school just as the bell went. Tammy leaned over and gave Dwayne a peck on the cheek. "I'll be right back," she said as she stepped out of the truck. A few minutes later, she spotted Matt exiting from the double doors and waved. He smiled and waved back while adjusting his backpack with a wiggle of his shoulders.

"Hey, buddy. How did school go?" Tammy asked as they walked back to the truck, where Matt gave Dwayne his usual high-five through the open window.

"We're having a career day," Matt said as he got in the back seat. "Can you come, mom?"

Tammy, who was already in the front seat, glanced over her shoulder at Matt and then at Dwayne. "You want me to come to career day? Matt, I'm a fisherwoman," she said with a creased brow.

Dwayne threw her a devious smile. "You should do it. I bet you'd be the only parent that is a commercial fisherwoman." He gave her an encouraging nudge. "Come on, Tammy, the kids would love it."

"Yeah, come on, mom. It would be cool," Matt echoed from the back seat.

Tammy laughed. "Yeah, I could show up in my slickers, carrying a gaff, and I'd also bring a lobster trap."

Dwayne gave her a grin. "There you go. Now you're talking."

"That would be awesome, mom," Matt shrieked.

"So, are you going to do it?" Dwayne asked while giving her another nudge.

Tammy took another look at her son, who beamed at her with hope in his eyes. "Yeah, I'll do. I'll talk to your teacher about it."

Matt shouted out a victory, "Yes!" He gave Dwayne another high-five.

Now that they had settled that, Tammy would do career day; Dwayne fired up the truck and took the side streets back to the Marina to avoid the crowds of parents picking up their kids from school. When they were just a few minutes away from the boatyard, Tammy's outburst startled Dwayne. "Stop the truck!" She yelled while looking out her window. "I see a house for rent."

Dwayne slowed down and peered over Tammy's shoulder. "I

thought you were done looking at houses for the day. Don't forget; we also have Matt with us."

"Oh, but this one looks so cute, and it's so close to the Marina," Tammy said, sounding hopeful.

"Which means it will be expensive," Dwayne reminded her.

Tammy wasn't listening. "There's a parking space. Pull in over there," she said as she pointed out the window.

"Okay, but I'm telling you right now, it's probably going to be too expensive."

"I just want to take a look," Tammy said as she stepped out of the truck and opened the back door for Matt.

Tammy couldn't help but feel a little excited as they approached the front gate. It had a for rent sign on it. It was a one-story house just off the main road on a quiet street and only a few minutes from Matt's school and the boatyard.

"Look, it has a fenced front yard with grass," Tammy said as they all walked through the gate. "And the front door is open," she whispered.

Dwayne knocked on the door. "Hello."

Tammy held Matt's hand as they waited patiently.

"Are we getting a house?" Matt asked.

She squeezed his hand. "No, we're just looking," Tammy told him.

Dwayne called again. This time a little louder. "Hello."

They heard a woman's voice come from inside the house. "Coming."

Tammy and Dwayne smiled at each other and held hands while they waited patiently. A few minutes later, they were greeted by an older woman, probably in her sixties.

"Hello. Can I help you?" the lady asked.

"Yes, we saw the for rent sign on the gate and wanted to ask how much it was," Dwayne replied.

"Eight-hundred." The woman said firmly. It's non-negotiable.

Tammy's eyes grew wide. "Only eight hundred." she gasped.

She beamed Dwayne with an enormous smile. "Can we look? I'm Tammy; this is my boyfriend, Dwayne, and my son Matt."

The lady held out her hand to Tammy and smiled when she shook it. "I'm Sherry. Sure, you can come in and look round, but if it's for all three of you, I don't think it will be big enough. It only has one bedroom."

Tammy laughed, "We've been living on a boat for three years. It's like a bloody mansion."

Sherry stood back to let them in where they stood in a pretty good size living room.

"Oh, look, it has a fireplace," Tammy beamed.

"I'm not sure how often we'll use that," Dwayne chuckled. "We live at the beach in southern California."

Sherry led them through to the kitchen. It was also a good size, and it looked out onto a large backyard and a garage.

"Wow, look at the garden, Dwayne. It's massive, and there's a garage too," Tammy said from the window where she stood.

"Can I go outside, mom?" Matt asked.

Tammy looked over at Sherry. "Would that be okay?"

"Yes, that's fine."

Matt immediately left Tammy's side and ran out the open back door to check out the yard.

Dwayne stood and talked to Sherry in the kitchen while Tammy was too eager to see the rest of the house. There wasn't much left to check out. It disappointed her. At the end of the hallway, she only found a large bathroom and one bedroom with a small closet off from the kitchen. She returned to the kitchen, and Dwayne threw her a smile.

"Sherry knew my dad when he had the yacht brokerage in town," Dwayne told her.

"Really! Wow, small world. He was there for many years, right?"

Dwayne nodded. "Yep. I grew up on boats, just like Matt is doing," he said with pride.

Tammy took to Dwayne's parents, Cathy and Charlie, immediately when she first met them just over three years ago. They were the perfect role model parents, married more years than Tammy had lived on this earth. She first met the entire family, which was huge, on her first Christmas with Dwayne. There were his two brothers, one sister, and a lot of his other relatives, all of whom welcomed and treated her like family. Tammy hadn't been to a family gathering in years, but every time they went to Dwayne's parents, it reminded her of the family get-togethers at her auntie Maddie's house in England.

Dwayne wrapped his arm around Tammy's waist and pulled her in close. "So, how do you like the house?"

"It's cute, but yes, it's small with only one bedroom," Tammy said, wearing a frown.

"That's why it's only eight hundred," Sherry said. "I told you it would be too small for the three of you."

Tammy glanced out the window to check on Matt and saw he had found a soccer ball and was kicking it around the yard.

"Now hang on a second, Tammy," Dwayne said. "Right now, we don't even have one bedroom, so this is a vast improvement. We can let Matt have the bedroom, and we can put a hide-a-away bed or a futon in the living room."

Tammy's frown soon turned into a smile. "I never thought about that."

"Are you saying you would like to fill out an application? I should tell you, though, I have forty applicants already."

"Forty!" Tammy shrieked, sounding discouraged.

Dwayne ignored her. "Yes, we do. Can I do it here and leave it with you?"

Sherry walked over to the counter and handed Dwayne a pen and the application. "Yes, that will be fine. After running your credit check, which will take a day or so, I'll arrange a meeting with you at my house. I like to interview all of my prospective tenants. I'll leave you to it. I'll be out in the garage when you're finished; just bring it out there."

Dwayne nodded while taking the form and throwing Tammy a smile.

"Really! You're going to apply for the house?" Tammy said as she cuddled up to Dwayne and gave him a peck on the cheek.

"Why not? We can afford this place and compared to the boat, it's huge."

Tammy did a little skip through the kitchen, "Oh, I'm so excited. I'm going to take another look while you fill that stuff out."

Dwayne used the counter for a desk and began writing. "Don't get your hopes up too much. There are forty other people after this place, remember."

Dwayne and Tammy didn't hear from Sherry for four days, and Tammy couldn't stop thinking about the house. Dwayne was afraid that she was setting herself up for a hard fall. There were many applicants, and Dwayne knew their chances of getting it were slim. He tried to get her to look at other houses while they waited, but Tammy refused. She had her heart set on that house.

"But what if we don't get it? Don't you want to have some others to fall back on?" Dwayne had said the next day.

Tammy had shaken her head defiantly. "Nope, I don't want to jinx this one. It's the perfect house for us, and the location is ideal. Suppose we don't get it, then we can start looking again." She crossed her fingers and closed her eyes. "Please let us get this one."

Dwayne knew from past debates that when Tammy's mind was made up, he never tried to change it. "Okay, then. I guess we will have to wait and see."

On day four, Dwayne's beeper went off when he and Tammy were in downtown LA selling the lobsters they had caught the day before at Malibu. Dwayne recognized it to be Sherry's number.

"Shit, we have to find a phone booth after we are finished here. That was Sherry beeping me."

"Oh, crap. I think there's one at the gas station right before the onramp of the freeway." Tammy said, sounding alarmed.

After settling the sale with the lobster buyers and with a decent size check in hand, they headed for the gas station and spotted the phone booth straight away.

Tammy waited in the truck while Dwayne made the call. She didn't take her eyes off him, trying desperately to read his body language. But he gave off no clues.

"What did she say?" Tammy asked anxiously when he returned to the truck.

"She wants us to go for an interview this afternoon after we've picked up Matt from school."

Tammy shifted in her seat. "Oh, now I'm nervous,"

Dwayne rested his hand on her thigh. "It will be fine. Points for us, she knew my dad," he said with a laugh. "He was well known and highly respected in the Marina."

"Okay. Well, I hope Matt will be on his best behavior."

Tammy and Dwayne thought the interview went well. Sherry was friendly towards Matt and asked if he liked the house. Dwayne's dad was the highlight of the conversation. They must have talked a good fifteen minutes about his yacht brokerage business, and Sherry mentioned her brother might have bought a boat from him. Their fishing careers fascinated Sherry, and she had tons of questions for Tammy and how she ever became a fisherwoman. So, of course, Tammy had to tell her the story from the beginning when she had first met Dwayne.

The interview lasted about an hour, and Sherry told them she would get back to them in a day or so with her decision.

"God, I'm tired of waiting. Why can't she just tell us today?" Tammy whined as they headed back to the truck.

"She probably has more interviews to do," Dwayne said as he took her hand and glanced over at Matt, who was trailing behind. "Come on, let's have a barbecue on the dock and do some fishing."

"Yes!" Matt yelled as he picked up his pace and raced to the truck.

Tammy's hopes of getting the house dwindled as more days went by. Three days had passed, and they were getting ready to head out to Malibu to pull their gear. That was one thing nice about fishing Malibu—the lobsters were not in danger of being eaten by other critters, and they didn't have to pull the traps every day like at San Clemente Island. It was safe to pull them every two or three days.

Tammy had just dropped Matt off at school and arranged for Louise to pick him up if they were late coming back in. She found Dwayne on the *Little Boat* with the motor already running. He was anxious to go.

"Untie me and jump on," he yelled as she approached the boat.

Tammy flicked him a salute. "Aye aye, Captain." And set the boat free from the cleats before jumping on board.

They only had a couple of months left of the season before it closed for six months in March. They would then pull all one-hundred-fifty traps out of the water and stack them in the boatyard until next season. The summers would be spent making any repairs and building new traps if needed. Tammy was amazed at how many traps they lost each year. And they weren't cheap. Each trap costs roughly sixty dollars to make.

After the season had ended and the traps were stacked, they would fish crabs for the rest of the year, which meant many trips out to Malibu to dump the one hundred crab traps they had made over the years. These were bigger and heavier traps and more of a toll on Tammy's body.

Dwayne knew how much Tammy loved to drive the *Little Boat* and stepped aside when she jumped on board. Tammy happily took the wheel and headed for the main channel. For January, the water was calm, and the sun was out. It looked like the weather would be on their side for the day. Half-way down the channel, Dwayne's beeper went off. Tammy slowed down the boat a notch so Dwayne could steady himself as he reached into his front pocket for his beeper.

"It's Sherry," he said after glancing at his beeper.

Tammy gasped and quickly put the boat in neutral, so they were drifting in the main channel.

"What are you doing?" Dwayne asked with a creased brow.

"We have to go back and call her. What if we got the house? If we don't call her back right away, she may give it to someone else." Tammy put the boat back in gear. "I'm turning around."

"Seriously!" Dwayne said with an edge.

"Yes. I don't want to wait until tonight to call her. We can always head back out after you've called. What's another thirty minutes?"

Dwayne knew there was no sense in arguing with her and nodded in defeat as she headed back to their slip.

With the motor still running, Tammy practically pushed Dwayne off the boat. "Hurry, go call her. I'll wait here."

Dwayne laughed at her urgency and hoped the news would be good. "Okay, okay, I'm going," he said with a smirk.

Tammy turned off the boat and watched as Dwayne walked up the ramp and across the boatyard to the telephone booth. To kill time, she paced back and forth on the dock, waving at boaters as they went by. Ten minutes later, Dwayne returned, but he didn't look happy. Tammy's heart sank, and she felt her dream slipping away.

Dwayne approached and placed a hand on her shoulder. Tammy tried to see a glimpse of a smile, but there wasn't one.

"Well?" Tammy asked and held her breath for his reply.

Dwayne took a deep breath. "Do you still have the newspapers with the rent classifieds in them?"

Tammy felt the wave of disappointment. "Yes, damn it."

Suddenly Dwayne burst into laughter. "Good! Because you can throw them away. We don't need them anymore. We got the house!"

Tammy gasped and shrieked, "What!" She raced into Dwayne's arms. Dwayne pulled her in tight and spun her around before kissing her hard on the lips.

"We got it, babe! We can move in today if we want to. The keys are ready for us to pick up."

"Oh, my god! I want to move in today. Can we?" She begged. "We can fish tomorrow."

Dwayne set her back down on the dock but continued to hold her close. "I was going to suggest the same thing," he said with a loving smile.

When Tammy found out the house was theirs, she was beside herself. They spent the next five minutes cheering, crying, and pacing up and down the dock. Tammy couldn't believe it, and tonight, if she wanted to, she could cook dinner in a full-size kitchen and not on a tiny counter. Tammy smiled, knowing the house came with a full-size oven. For the last three years, they had only a small toaster oven. Her head swelled with meals she hadn't cooked in years and new recipes she'd been wanting to try but didn't have space: roast beef and Yorkshire pudding, a whole chicken with roasted potatoes. The list was growing by the minute. Tammy giggled when it suddenly dawned on her that she could boil potatoes, carrots, and gravy all at the same time and not have any sitting cold.

The house also came with a full-size fridge and a washer and dryer. "Ow wow! No more laundromat." Tammy squealed. "Oh, my god. I'm so friggin excited. I can't wait to tell Matt when I pick him up from school," she smiled big and raced into Dwayne's arms, giving him a long drawn out kiss on the lips. "I'm going to change out of my fishing boots, and then I want to go to storage," Her eyes were wide when she laughed. "Gosh, I haven't seen that stuff in years. I can't remember what's in there."

"Well, it will be like Christmas. But first, we have to pick up the keys and sign the lease." Dwayne reminded her.

Tammy tugged on his hand. "Well, let's go! Screw changing my boots."

Dwayne laughed and followed her lead. He had no idea she would be so excited about getting the house. It made all the headaches and the times they had endured looking for a place well worth it.

"Wait, I have to grab my checkbook," Dwayne said as he pulled Tammy back.

"Okay, I'll meet you at the truck."

Dwayne nodded and headed back to the *Baywitch*.

Within an hour, Tammy held the keys to their new home tight in her hand. "I still can't believe the house is ours." She said as they headed over to their home.

Dwayne rubbed her thigh. "It's ours, babe. We'll be sleeping there tonight if you want to."

"Yes! I know we don't have beds right now, but we'll figure something out."

When they pulled up in front of the house, Tammy rested her head on Dwayne's shoulder and let out a big sigh. "Home sweet home."

Dwayne kissed the top of her head. "Come on. Let's go check it out. We need to break that key in."

Tammy couldn't stop smiling as she opened the small wooden gate and walked towards what was now her front door, and as she turned the key in the lock, she looked over her shoulder at Dwayne and beamed him a huge smile.

She stepped into their living room, which had brand new carpeting, and the entire house had a fresh coat of paint. Tammy looked over at the fireplace. "I want to make a fire tonight," she said as she hugged Dwayne.

Dwayne laughed. "What? It will be in the sixties tonight."

"I don't care. It's our first night in our new home." She had the entire day planned out. "I want to go to storage and bring all of our stuff here. I want to cook a big family meal and light a fire, and I want to do laundry."

"Laundry?" Dwayne said and cracked a laugh.

"Yes. I want to hear the washing machine while I'm cooking dinner. Just like a regular family home."

Dwayne raised his hands. "Okay. Whatever makes you happy."

"And I want to soak for hours in the bathtub," she laughed as she hugged herself and closed her eyes.

Dwayne and Tammy walked through the small house hand in hand, sharing decorating ideas and what they needed to buy. They had no furniture, so they would sit, eat, and sleep on the floor for a few days until they could check out some thrift stores. They had a tiny TV on the boat, which they could make do with for a while.

They stood in the backyard and decided on where to store the fishing gear. Dwayne told Tammy his plans for the garage, and none of them involved keeping the cars in it. Tammy didn't care. It warmed her heart to see Dwayne so happy when he talked about the workshop he would build.

"Okay, let's go to storage and load up the truck," Tammy said eagerly. "And afterward, we can go to the store and buy something for dinner and firewood. I want to make a big spaghetti dinner."

Dwayne laughed at her excitement. "Okay. Let's go." He echoed.

The storage unit was only ten minutes away, and no sooner had Dwayne opened the door, Tammy raced in and began grabbing boxes, hastily throwing them in the bed of the truck.

"You want to take everything over today?" Dwayne asked as she continued to pile boxes on the truck's tailgate for Dwayne to slide in.

"Yes! That way, I can organize it. It's going to be so much fun going through all of this stuff."

Dwayne shook his head. "Okay, then we might as well bring all my stuff too, and I can organize the garage, and we can do away with storage altogether."

"That would be fantastic!" Tammy shrieked. "Now that we are paying rent, we need to save money where we can."

In record time, they made three trips to the storage unit and emptied it. Tammy spent the afternoon going through her forgotten treasures until it was time to pick up Matt from school.

"I wonder if Matt will be as excited as us about getting a house. He loves the boatyard and fishing so much he may hate the idea," Tammy questioned herself as they drove to the school in Dwayne's truck.

After she told him, she saw that her prediction was right.

"But I want to go fishing off the dock like I always do," Matt said from the back seat with his arms folded and a puckered lip.

Tammy's smile soon disappeared. "Sweetie, don't you want to see your room?"

Matt shook his head. "No! I want to go fishing."

Tammy looked over at Dwayne. "Well, shoot, I was afraid of this. He doesn't care about living in a house."

Dwayne chuckled. "Well, I think we saw this coming." He reached over and squeezed Tammy's knee. "Tell you what. Why don't I drop you off at the house, and I'll take Matt fishing for an hour?"

Tammy's smile returned. "That's a great idea. I still want to make us a fire and fix us a big dinner."

"You know what else I'm going to do tomorrow?" Dwayne said with a devious smile on their way back to the house.

"No, what?"

"Buy us a phone and get us a phone number."

Tammy shrieked. "Oh, that's right! We can finally get a phone, and I can call my mom without a bunch of quarters and tell her to book her ticket. Oh, she's going to be so excited." Tammy suddenly had a thought. "I wonder if Donna has told mom that she has moved to Colorado. I had promised mom I would take her to see

Donna, but that was before Donna had moved. And I'll be reminded again how mom wants to see all her daughters together." Tammy shook her head. "Well, I won't worry about it right now. There's too much good going on, and those thoughts will just spoil my mood."

A few minutes later, Dwayne pulled up in front of their house.

She turned and looked at Matt sitting in the back seat. "Are you sure you don't want to come in for a minute and check it out?"

Matt shook his head. "I'll see it when I get back, mom."

"Okay." She leaned in and kissed Dwayne. "You guys have fun."

Dwayne kissed her back. "We will. Love you."

While Dwayne and Matt spent the afternoon fishing, Tammy was in her realm, doing what she could to the house without much furniture. They planned to hit the thrift stores tomorrow and go crab trapping the day after.

By the time the two most important men in her life returned home, Tammy had a fire going and spaghetti cooking on the stovetop. She had most of the dishes put away from the boxes and made makeshift beds out of blankets and sheets, and was pleased to find four pillows in a box.

Matt finally showed some excitement when Tammy showed him his very own room with some early trophies of his sitting on the windowsill and a few of his toys he hadn't outgrown.

That night they sat in a circle on the floor of the living room in front of the fire and ate Tammy's homemade meal, and then she surprised them with one of her finds from storage—Monopoly.

"Matt, you're old enough to play this game now. Wanna play?"

Matt nodded and helped his mom clear the plates to make room for the game.

The night couldn't have gone any better for Tammy. Everything she had missed over the past three and a half years was suddenly all available to her whenever she pleased. Even the luxury of being able to stretch out on a floor while playing a board game was heaven.

Tammy decided she would give Matt the honors of taking the first bath and breaking it in. But only because she had plans to take a long bubble bath surrounded by some candles she had found in storage. Together she and Dwayne would break in the bathtub their way. She closed her eyes at her erotic thoughts and hurried Matt off to take a bath.

The next morning, after Tammy had taken Matt to school and discussed her career day with his teacher, she returned home, anxious for the phone company to arrive. Dwayne had called them first thing in the morning and then went to the store to buy a phone before heading to the boat to do some maintenance work.

It felt strange for Tammy not to go to the boat with him. It had been her home for the past three and a half years, and this was the first time she had spent over twenty-four hours away from it. Tammy soon realized that living in a house again was going to take some getting used to.

By one o'clock, they finally had a working phone and a telephone number. Tammy had a long list of people she wanted to call and tell them the good news that they could now call her.

She called her mom first and gave her the exciting news that she could book her ticket. Dwayne and Tammy already decided that they would buy bunk beds for Matt's room so she would have a place to sleep, and they would buy a foldaway couch for the living room for themselves.

It felt strange not having to feed the phone quarters to make a phone call, and after four rings, her mom finally answered.

"Hey, mom! It's Tammy."

"Hello Tammy, I was just thinking about you. Is everything okay?"

"It couldn't be better, mom. We got a house!" Tammy squealed into the phone.

Tammy heard her mother gasp. "You did. Oh, that's wonderful. I bet you will be glad to be off that boat."

"Actually, I kind of miss it, but I love the house, too. It just feels weird having all the space and a backyard again."

"Oh, you've already moved in?" her mom asked.

"Yes. We moved in yesterday. It's only one bedroom. Dwayne and I sleep in the living room, but it's massive compared to the boat."

"Only one bedroom. Well, if I come over, where am I supposed to sleep?"

"We're going to get bunk beds for Matt's room; you can sleep in there."

"What a good idea. I would never have thought of that. I'm going to book my ticket next week." Her voice dropped a notch. "You know Donna moved to Colorado, don't you? She called me last week."

Tammy knew this was going to be part of the conversation and took a deep breath. "Yes, I do, mom."

"So, I guess I won't see her when I come over?"

"I'm afraid, not mom. Colorado is a sixteen-hour drive, and besides, we'll be fishing most of the time while you are here. You'll be in charge of Matt while we are gone." Tammy added, trying desperately to change the conversation and make her mother feel needed.

"Oh, my little Matt. How is he?"

"He's not little anymore, mom; he's almost eight. He's going to be thrilled when I tell him you're coming over."

"That's if he remembers me," her mom said with a hint of sarcasm.

"Oh, stop it, mom. Of course, he'll remember you. I have pictures of you on my wall."

"Well, I'm still not going to have all my daughters together, am I."

Tammy rolled her eyes. "Mom, You're going to see Matt and

me, and you'll meet Dwayne for the first time. Aren't you excited about that? Someday we will all be together. I promise."

"Of course, I'm excited about seeing you and meeting your fisherman friend."

Tammy chuckled at her mom's remark. "Mom, he's more than a friend; he's my boyfriend." Tammy checked her watch. She wanted to call Jenny in England before it got too late. "Listen, mom; I gotta go. I'm going to give Jenny a call. I've not talked to her in years. Now you can call me whenever you want."

"Jenny never answers her phone, you know. You'll have to leave a message." Her mom told her.

"Then I'll leave a message. I love you, mom. Call me when you have your ticket. I can't wait to see you in September."

After ending the call, Tammy immediately called Jenny's number and discovered her mom was right. Jenny either wasn't home or wasn't answering the phone. It was ten in the evening in England, so she assumed she was home. After five rings, the machine picked up, and after the ear-piercing beep, Tammy left a message. "Hey, Jenny! Guess who this is? It's your baby sister in America. I finally have a phone number. Call me," Tammy looked at the piece of paper in her hand and recited the new number that she had yet to memorize. "I can't wait to talk to you. Love you. Bye."

After leaving a message, Tammy made two more phone calls. One to Donna and one to her dad in Florida. The conversation with Donna was uplifting and pleasant. She and Jason loved Colorado, and they were thrilled and were settling nicely into their new home, but the call with her dad was disturbing.

After the initial hellos and I miss you, he told her his latest news. "We're moving to Ireland at the end of the month."

Tammy was stunned. First, Donna and now her dad. "What?" She shook her head. Trying to grasp what she had just heard. "Why and how long have you been planning this?" She asked with a slight edge.

"Joanne and I have been talking about it for some time, and we took a trip out there last month. I guess you were fishing. Anyway, we found a house, and we're going to make a go of it."

"But dad, why Ireland? I'll never see you."

John released a sarcastic laugh. "Tammy, you never see me now. You won't even know I'm gone. I'll be traveling back and forth to the States."

Tammy knew he was right. She hadn't seen her dad in almost five years. Like the rest of her family, they had become estranged, and she had a long-distance relationship on the phone with all of them. He had two more sons now, and Tammy had yet to meet them. He had done his usual fly-by visits while doing a book tour when Matt had just turned two, and then he saw Matt when he went to Florida the first year Tammy had fished. "Yeah, I guess you're right. Well, when you're in the States, you will have to visit your grandson. He's going to be eight soon, and he hardly knows you."

This time John had an edge to his voice. "And who's fault is that, Tammy? You are the one that chose not to have him come to Florida during the fishing season. Joanne offered to watch him every year."

"I know, dad, but I can't be away from him for three months again. That was horrible. I know he was okay with you, but being away from him that long was almost unbearable."

Tammy and her dad spoke for a few more minutes, but she felt an urgency to get off the phone. Her father's news stunned her, and yet again, her family was becoming more spread across the globe. She believed her mother that her sisters would never be together again. She was determined to prove her mom wrong.

For the remainder of the year, Tammy and Dwayne continued to fish for crabs off the Malibu coastline and did what they could to make their house a home.

Tammy had fun doing career day at Matt's school, and the children loved seeing her dressed in her slickers when she walked into the classroom with a lobster trap and some live lobsters in a bucket of ocean water. Many of the kids had never seen a lobster before, let alone touch one. The expressions on the kids' faces were priceless, and the look of pride that shined on Matt's face made it all worthwhile.

Even though they enjoyed the luxuries of the house, their lifestyles still revolved around the boats, and Dwayne and Tammy had a hard time adapting to living on land. Tammy noticed Matt was too. After school, he still wanted to fish off the docks at the boatyard, which resulted in them having a barbecue for dinner on the dock most nights and returning to the house after dark.

When they were not fishing, they spent their days in the boatyard either repairing or building traps and getting ready for the lobster season coming up in September, which would soon be upon them. But knowing Matt would be in his own home for the first time while she fished, bonding with his grandmother whom he had not seen in over five years comforted Tammy. Tammy had spent the previous months covering every detail for her mother's stay. She wanted it to go flawlessly and be as easy as possible for her mom. Tammy arranged with Louise to take Matt to and from school and leave her number by the phone in case of any emergency. The house had been cleaned from top to bottom, and there was no risk of them running out of food.

"So, are you excited about meeting my mom for the first time?" Tammy asked Dwayne as they waited patiently in the terminal of LAX airport for her arrival.

Dwayne turned to her and smiled. "Yes, I am. The only person I've met in your family is your sister, Donna. I went with you once when you visited her shortly after lobster season a few years ago."

Tammy squeezed his hand. "Yeah, I know. I hate that my family is so scattered. I'm so jealous of you when it comes to your family," Tammy confessed.

"You are?" Dwayne said, wearing a surprised look. "Why?"

"Because you are all so close, and you always have family gatherings on the holidays. I've met your entire family, and you've only met one of my sisters." Tammy released a heavy sigh. "I understand my mom when she tells me she wants to be with all her daughters. The last time she saw us all together was when I was twelve, and my sisters were fourteen. That was sixteen years ago. How sad is that?"

"Wow, that's a long time. No wonder she keeps bringing it up," Dwayne said as he glanced over at Matt. "Where does he think he's going?' Dwayne chuckled when he saw Matt was wandering off too far. He hollered loud above the chatter of people. "Matt!" He waved him back with his hand.

Tammy raised her arms above her head and stretched her stiff body. "Yeah. I'm just glad we're living in a house now, and mom can stay with us and bond with Matt. I can't believe lobster season starts in two weeks. Where has the time gone?" She gave Dwayne a cute smile. "This will be my fourth season fishing with you. Are you getting tired of me yet?" she laughed.

Dwayne took her in his arms and smiled. "I could never get tired of you."

"I can't wait to fish off the *Baywitch II* and see how she handles the season."

"Yeah, me too. I'll miss the old *Baywitch*, but she was just too expensive to run. This year we should have a better profit margin. Our new boat runs off diesel engines—much cheaper than gas, and we were able to build more traps over the summer. It should be a good year for us."

Tammy loved working with Dwayne. They had grown together as one when it came to fishing and knew what they expected from one another. It was a relationship that worked. They spent every hour of every day together, and sometimes that didn't seem enough for the two of them. In two days, they would leave to start the many trips to the island to drop off the gear before the season began.

"Nana's plane has landed," Tammy said with an edge of excitement to Matt, who was now sitting between her and Dwayne.

Matt's eyes grew wide before he jumped up from his seat and did a happy dance. Tammy stood too. "I wonder how long it will take her to get through customs? We've been here for over an hour already."

"Hopefully, not too long. Matt is getting restless. So am I, for that matter." Dwayne laughed.

It took another hour and a half before Tammy finally spotted her mother walking amongst a crowd of passengers. Tammy stood and raised her hand high before she squealed, "There she is!" She then grabbed Matt's hand and headed in her mom's direction with Dwayne close on her tail.

"Mom!" Tammy yelled over the loud noise of the terminal. It took Rose a few minutes to spot her daughter, but her beaming smile told Tammy when she did.

"Tammy!" Rose shouted.

Tammy embraced her mom with misty eyes and held her tight. "Oh, mom, I've missed you."

"I've missed you too, Tammy," Rose said with tears trickling down her cheeks.

Tammy stood back and looked at her mother. She was dressed in black slacks and a light purple sweater. Her hair, which hadn't changed, was still bleach blonde and her well-manicured nails looked perfect as always. "You look, great mom. And I love your hair."

Rose ran her fingers through her hair. "Thanks; I just had it done a few days ago." She scanned the area around them. "So, where is this grandson of mine?"

Tammy noticed Dwayne had held back while she reunited with her mom and motioned with her hand for them to join her. "Here, he is, mom." She said as Matt took her hand. "And this is my boyfriend, Dwayne," Tammy said with pride while squeezing his hand.

Rose pulled Matt in close to her and smothered him with kisses. Tammy laughed as she watched Matt wince from the wet kisses his nana was drowning him in. He had outgrown some of the smothering affections unbeknownst to her mom.

Dwayne approached Rose and held out his hand. "Hi, it's good to finally meet you. Tammy talks about you all the time." He smiled. "She really misses you."

Rose held on to Matt's hand as she looked at Dwayne, taking him all in from head to toe. "Hi, Dwayne. Good to meet you too. So, you're the man that got my baby girl into fishing, eh?"

Dwayne gave Tammy a quick glance and wrapped his arm around her waist. "I sure am, and she's damn good at it."

That night Tammy and her mother cooked a chicken dinner together while Tammy told her some of her fishing adventures.

"You had a sea lion come on your boat?" her mom laughed while setting the table. "Why was it on your boat?"

"Go on, tell her." Dwayne laughed from the couch.

Tammy rolled her eyes and folded her arms. "Because I was throwing him fish from the boat even though Dwayne told me not to."

Her mom laughed louder and clapped her hands. "You still don't listen, do you, Tammy?"

"No, she doesn't," Dwayne butted in.

CHAPTER 11

The next day Dwayne and Tammy gave Rose a tour of the boatyard. Tammy was pleased to see the yard was busy, and her mum could experience it during the regular working hours. Another bonus was that Matt could join them because school was still on break.

As Tammy watched her mother walk precariously down the swaying docks, it reminded her of her first time with Dwayne, and she couldn't refrain from giggling quietly to herself. It was also the first time for her mom.

When Rose stepped onto the *Baywitch II*, she glanced around and looked down inside the tiny cabin; it was close to the size of the cabin of the old *Baywitch*. "You lived there?" Rose said in disbelief.

Tammy laughed. "It was the other boat we lived on, mom, but the cabin was about the same size."

"Good lord, Tammy. Where did you all sleep? And how did you even cook?"

"We managed. It was like we were camping every night."

Her mom shook her head. "I'll say." and continued to check out the boat. Every so often, she'd steady her feet by holding onto the rail. "I don't know how you did it, Tammy."

"I loved it, mom, but Matt is getting older and bigger, and now it is too small for the three of us. But Dwayne and I still live on it when we go to the island. It's kind of like a second home. We often come down here with Matt and spend the night on it because we miss it. Tammy threw Matt a proud smile. "But now that Matt is older, he sleeps in the cabin of the *Little Boat.*" Tammy pointed to the boat docked next to the Baywitch II. "That's ours too."

Rose turned her head and stared at the *Little Boat.* "That's a cute boat."

"It's the one I like to drive. Dwayne built it. There's nothing he doesn't know about the ocean and boats. He's taught me everything I know," Tammy said as she threw Dwayne a loving smile.

Her mom took a seat on one of the deck chairs and took in the view. "Gosh, it sure is pretty here. I can see why you love it."

Tammy glanced down the dock and saw Matt and Dwayne were walking to the end with fishing poles in their hands. Tammy's mind wandered—how did she ever get so lucky to meet such an amazing man? He was everything to her and then some. Lost in her thoughts, she shook her head and turned her attention back to her mom. "I love it here. I fell in love with this place the first time I came down. I knew that day I wanted to be a part of it." Taking a seat next to her mom, they sat for a few minutes in silence, mesmerized by the beauty of the water glistening in the sun and the sight of the occasional sailboat or powerboat cruising by.

T he ocean breeze masked their faces and gently blew through their hair. Tammy leaned back and enjoyed the warmth from the rays of the sun reflecting off her face. She released a big satisfying sigh. Life couldn't get any better.

"I can see why you never want to leave," Rose said as she

became more at ease on the gently rocking boat and eased her head back into the deck chair and closed her eyes.

"Yeah, and Matt loves it too. I can't keep him away from the water. He's a fishing fool." Tammy laughed.

Rose sat up and reached for Tammy's hand. "You've come a long way, Tammy. I'm proud of you. Not too sure about the fishing thing, though. But I can tell you are happy."

Tammy squeezed her mom's hand, "I am a mom. I've never been happier."

"So, when are you leaving?" her mom asked.

"The day after tomorrow. So, Dwayne and I will work late tonight and tomorrow getting the boat ready and loading the traps. Which means you get to watch Matt at the house," she said with a large grin.

Rose matched her daughter's grin. "I'm looking forward to it."

Tammy stood up and glanced down to the end of the dock and saw Dwayne and Matt were still engaged in fishing. "Hey, mom, do you want to give fishing a go?" she asked with a devious smile.

Her mom cracked a sarcastic laugh. "Fishing! You're bloody joking, right?"

Tammy stood and held out her hand. "No, I'm not. It will be fun. Come on, let's join the boys. Matt would love it."

"I've never fished a day in my life, Tammy. Have you gone mad?"

Tammy laughed. "You've never been on a boat before, and look, here you are. Now, come on. It will only be for a short while. Dwayne and I have to get to work if we want to leave on time."

Her mom shook her head in defeat and took Tammy's hand. "Okay, then. I'll give it a try."

"That's the spirit, mom," Tammy said in triumph.

Rose continued to mumble as they walked down the dock. "I can't believe you're making me fish. What if I get one? I won't know what to do."

"Ha! Mom, we will help you, don't you worry."

As they approached the boys, the rocking of the dock from their steps caused Dwayne and Matt to look over their shoulders.

"Nana!" Matt squealed. "I caught two Mackerel. Wanna see?" He said as he reached for a white bucket at his side with his free hand.

Rose peered into the bucket and curled her lip when she saw the two shiny, slimy fish looking up at her with their large round glazed eyes. She took a step back. "Are they dead?"

"Yes, mom, they are dead," Tammy laughed. "We'll use them for bait in the lobster traps. It makes Matt feel like he's doing his part to help." Tammy said as she stroked the top of Matt's head. She leaned in and rested her hands on Matt's shoulders. "Hey, buddy. Do you want to show Nana how to fish? She's never done it before."

Matt looked up with bright shiny eyes. "Yes! Can I?"

"Sure. Why don't you give her your fishing pole?"

Matt stood up from where he had been sitting at the dock's edge and handed her the pole. "Here you go, nana. Now hold it tight, and when you feel a bite, yank it to set the hook."

"Yank it?" Rose asked with a puzzled look.

Matt jerked his pole up and down. "Yes, like this. See."

Rose nodded and took the pole in her hand. Dwayne stepped aside to give her some room and threw her a smile. "If it runs in the family, you're going to be hooked after your first fish like these two." He said as he gave Rose's shoulder a nudge.

"I can't see that happening," Rose said with a smirk. "Tammy takes after her dad. I can see she's not afraid of anything."

Rose stood at the edge of the dock next to Matt while Tammy stood back and took pictures with the disposable camera she had grabbed from the *Baywitch II*. She was sure this would be the only chance she could capture nana and grandson fishing together. It warmed her heart to witness such a moment that she would treasure for years to come, and she was sure Matt would too. Tammy clutched her hands close to her heart as she watched Matt show his nana how to pull the rod up and down in the water to attract the fish.

Dwayne, who still had a rod in the water, glanced over his shoulder in her direction and gave Tammy a loving smile. He knew this was a special moment for her.

After a few minutes, her mom suddenly squealed. "I think I got one!"

Tammy tucked the camera in her jacket's pocket she was wearing and raced over to her mom. She stood behind her and looked in the water from over her shoulder.

"What do I do?" her mom screamed as she held the rod with two hands and took a step back.

"Hold on to the rod tight," Dwayne yelled, wearing a huge grin. He patted Matt on the shoulder. "Show her what to do, buddy."

Tammy gave Matt some room as she watched with admiration her son give her nana instructions on how to reel in a fish. It was the cutest thing she'd ever seen.

"Go slow, nana. Pull the rod up, then wind some line in. Pull the rod up. Then wind some line in." Matt told her over and over, watching her every move.

After a couple of minutes, her mom screamed again. "I see it!"

Tammy looked in the water again and saw a silverfish splashing at the surface. "You got a Mackerel, mom." Tammy squealed as she patted her mom on the shoulder. "Show her how to take it off the hook, Matt." Tammy bellowed with excitement.

Rose quickly handed the rod to Matt. "No, no. Let him do it. I don't want to touch it."

Matt laughed at his nana's queasiness and happily took the rod from her and yanked the line out of the water where the fish landed on the dock in a frenzy. Rose squealed in disgust and dashed until she was a few feet away from the flapping fish.

"Oh, no! There is no way I'm touching that." Rose claimed from a distance.

In a few minutes, Matt laughed and had the fish free from the hook and in the bucket.

Tammy, who was still laughing at her mother's reaction, approached her mom and hugged her. "Well done, mom, you caught your first fish."

"And it will be my last," she said in defiance. "I'm not sure what you see in it, Tammy, but thank you for the experience."

"Well, before you go home, we will have to take you out on the boat. Maybe you will like that."

Rose shook her head. "I don't think so, Tammy. I get carsick. I can only imagine what I would be like on a boat."

"You do? I didn't know that."

"There are a lot of things you don't know about me, Tammy. How could you?"

Her mom's words stung her. Why did she have to continue to twist that knife? She knew what she was doing. Did she get enjoyment from making her daughter feel guilty? Tammy shook it off, just like she had done many times in the past. She wouldn't allow her mother to get to her. "Okay, mom. Dwayne and I have to get to work. I'm going to drop you and Matt off at the house, and we will see you tonight, okay."

"Ah, but mom, I want to stay here," Matt hollered from behind her in protest.

Tammy gave her son a stern look. "No, Matt. You're going home with nana. Now come on. Let's go."

Matt folded his arms and pouted as he walked behind his mom, dragging his feet.

Tammy turned and gave Dwayne a tender kiss on the lips as he stood at the end of the dock holding the two poles. "I'll be back soon. Love you."

"Love you too," he said as he gave her waist a gentle squeeze.

To meet their deadline and leave for the island in just under two days, Dwayne and Tammy worked late into the nights at the boatyard. Traps needed to be repaired and loaded onto the *Baywitch II*. Tammy hadn't seen much of her mom or Matt. They were already asleep when they finally made it home to catch a few hours of rest themselves and left before they woke up.

Worried about how her mom was coping, Tammy called many times throughout the day to check-in. "Hey, mom, I'm just calling to see how everything is going and to see if you guys need anything."

It had been a long time since Tammy had heard her mom sound genuinely happy. She was almost singing when she spoke. "Tammy, this is the fifth time you've called me today, and as I said before, we are fine. I can't believe how grown-up Matt is. We are having a wonderful time together. This afternoon we are going to make Shepherds Pie. It's his favorite." Rose laughed. "He certainly has some British in him."

"Yes, he does, mom. He loves Scotch eggs too. Give him a big hug and kiss. I'm glad you guys are having a great time."

In a flash and with little sleep over the past few days, Dwayne and Tammy were ready to head out with their first load of traps. Tammy spent the early morning going over everything with her mom. Making sure she knew where Louise's number was. How to work the appliances and making sure they had everything they would need.

"I'll be fine, Tammy. Will you stop fussing and get out of here?" her mother said, while practically pushing her daughter out the door.

Tammy laughed. "Okay. Okay, I'm going." She called Matt over and gave him a tight squeeze and a kiss on his cheek. "You be good for nana, okay?"

"I will," Matt said as he wiped the moist spot on his cheek.

The sound of a horn came from the street. Tammy knew it was Dwayne who was waiting in the truck. "Okay, I gotta go. I love you guys. We should be back in late tomorrow night for the second load of gear, and then probably head back out again the next morning," she said as she gave them both one last hug before heading out the door.

"When do you sleep?" her mom asked.

"On the boat, or we may come home for a quick shower and a nap. It depends on how it goes. You are in charge now, mom."

Tammy waved to her mom and Matt from inside the truck, who stood outside the door, yelling goodbye and waving. She leaned over and gave Dwayne a peck on the cheek. "Okay, let's go before I start crying."

Dwayne rubbed her shoulder. "They'll be fine. It's not like your mom has never taken care of a child before. She raised three girls, remember."

"Yeah, I know," Tammy said, giving her mom and Matt one last wave as Dwayne pulled away from the curb.

∼

Their hard work had paid off, and they were right on schedule. Within an hour, they were heading down the main channel on the *Baywitch II*. Tammy was at the helm driving the boat while Dwayne checked that the traps were securely tied down.

For the middle of September, the weather was glorious, with bright blue skies and no clouds. The wind was light, and the spray of salt-water felt refreshing against Tammy's face. She loved the beginning of the season and what would be their first trip out to the island in six months. She still enjoyed the solitude of it and the freedom they inherited being away from the mainland.

"How's it looking back there?" Tammy yelled over the sound of the roaring engine.

Dwayne steadied himself as he headed to the helm to join her. "Everything looks good. I checked the weather, and it looks like it's going to be sunny and calm all day. We should have a nice crossing."

Ten hours later, they were pulling into Northwest harbor at San Clemente Island. They saw Mitch on the *Sea-Life* was anchored with a load of traps. He waved from his deck and then a few minutes later called Dwayne on the radio to say a howdy. They chatted for a few minutes.

"Happy to hear you had a good crossing. Some new boats are showing up this year. One just left the harbor an hour ago to dump gear," Mitch told Dwayne. His tone told Dwayne he wasn't too pleased with more boats fishing the island.

"I guess word travels fast about the good season we had last year," Dwayne said.

"It sure did. I don't think these guys realize, though, that it's a short season out here. As we all know, the weather gets too rough to fish pretty quickly."

Dwayne chuckled. "Well, they'll soon find out."

It took Dwayne and Tammy twelve days and four trips to drop

all two hundred plus traps at the island. Over that time, they made it home twice to take hot showers and check on Matt and her mom. But it seemed Tammy had nothing to worry about. Their smiles told her everything was fine.

On their last trip and with all the traps now at the island, they loaded the *Baywitch II* with all their supplies and had the *Little Boat* in tow.

Tammy sat at the helm and drove while Dwayne checked the towline. It all looked good.

"You know I've been thinking," Dwayne said with a devious grin that Tammy has gotten to know so well.

"What?" she asked with her eyes narrowed. What was he up to now? she wondered. Tammy sped up the boat as they left the main channel and hit the open waters.

Dwayne raised his voice over the elevated noise. "Well, we have fifty extra traps this year, and you've been doing this for a few years now and even have your own permit."

Tammy had a feeling he was setting her up for something. "And?" she said with a piercing stare.

Dwayne threw her a large grin, showing off his pearl white teeth. "How about you run the *Little Boat* by yourself this year, and I'll pull the deeper traps from the *Baywitch II*?"

"What!" Tammy shrieked. She checked the compass to make sure they were on course and then quickly set the autopilot so she could reply to Dwayne's ridiculous idea. "Why do you always do this to me?"

Dwayne laughed. "Do what?" he said while shrugging his shoulders.

Tammy rolled her eyes. He knew what he was doing. "You always put me on the spot like this with no warning. It's how you got me to drive the *Little Boat* for the first time years ago."

"And it worked, didn't it?" Dwayne laughed. "I think this will work too. We have more traps to pull this year, and if you start at one end and me at the other, we'll get them pulled faster."

Tammy made a frustrated grunt. "I don't know, Dwayne. I've never driven the *Little Boat* by myself at the island before, let alone pull traps. I'd have to do everything. Drive the boat, pull the traps, and measure the lobsters. Oh, and let's not forget, we need to re-bait the traps." She shook her head. "That's a lot for one person."

"Yes, it is, and I'll have to do the same." He gave her one of his sexy smiles that always weakened Tammy. "Think of it as precautionary measures."

Tammy creased her brow. "What do you mean?"

"What if I get injured? You need to pull traps by yourself if I can't. Remember my arm. When it went numb, something like that could happen, but far worse. This is our only source of income. We need to be prepared, and I'm surprised at myself for not having thought of it sooner," he said while giving her shoulders another tender rub.

Tammy released a heavy sigh and pulled away from his hands that were still resting on her shoulders. "You always know what to say, don't you?" Tammy said while rolling her eyes. "Okay, I'll give it a go. But we won't meet in the middle; I can guarantee you that. You'll have two-thirds pulled by the time I've only pulled a third."

"Don't underestimate yourself. You're damn good on the boat. It might surprise you just how well you do."

Tammy gave him a loving smile. He always believed in her. "Thanks for the vote of confidence, but I don't know about this."

"I think you'll be fine."

Tammy was pleased to see all the regular boats from the previous years had returned, along with the two new boats Mitch had mentioned.

They were the last to arrive in the harbor, and after setting the mooring and tying off the *Little Boat* alongside the *Baywitch II*, Dwayne got on the radio to say hi to a few of the captains.

Tammy waved at those close by who she now considered friends. "Hi, Tom!" she yelled across the water.

Sound carries well across the water. Tom heard her and yelled back. "Hey, Tammy. Good to see you back for another season."

"I wouldn't miss it for the world," Tammy hollered. Dwayne covered his ears and struggled to hear himself on the radio.

"Tammy! Hush, I'm on the radio."

Tammy rolled her eyes. "That's why I'm hollering at the guys because you are hogging the radio."

Dwayne gave her a sarcastic grin. "Smartass."

The sun was setting rapidly on the horizon, so Tammy fixed them some soup and rolls for dinner after Dwayne had finished talking on the radio.

"That was good soup. Thanks." Dwayne said. "Let's get the *Little Boat* set up for you. We must make sure you have everything you will need. We can load the bait on there too," he added.

"I'm not so sure about this, Dwayne. What if I mess up or if the *Little Boat* breaks down?" Tammy said as she handed him a box of mackerel.

"You're going to be fine, and I also told a few other captains that you would fish on your own tomorrow and to keep an eye out." He nudged her elbow and gave her a wink. "They are pretty impressed by you. If you can't get a hold of me on the radio, they can help. Especially if I'm on the backside of the island where I don't get a signal. You can always call one of them if you need help. Okay?"

Tammy nodded. "Okay."

They worked hard for the next few hours, so in the morning, both boats would be turnkey ready, and by midnight Tammy was prepared to call it a night.

The next morning Tammy woke before Dwayne because of a restless night worrying about fishing on her own. It was a huge step for her to be in charge and make all the decisions. She had always relied on Dwayne to fix things if something went wrong. Tammy realized how much she took him for granted and understood why he insisted on her learning to fish independently. It was a huge responsibility, but she was ready.

Being careful not to wake Dwayne, Tammy tried her best to crawl over him to get out of their confined sleeping quarters but was unsuccessful. As she rolled her body over his, he stirred and pulled her back. "Where do you think you're going?" he said in a sleepy state with his hair in a tangled mess.

"I can't sleep. I'm going to make some coffee. Do you want some?"

He smiled and locked his hand around the back of her neck. "Not before you give me a kiss."

Tammy returned the smile and leaned in until their lips

touched and gave him a long, drawn-out kiss. "Man. You're better than a cup of coffee," she said before kissing him again.

Dwayne lowered his hand and gave her naked butt a playful squeeze. "And sleeping next to you naked every night out here sure brightens my fishing trips."

Tammy laughed and smacked his naked chest. "Okay, before we start anything here, I'm getting up. The sun is coming up, and we need to get a move on."

Dwayne saluted her. "Aye aye, captain. I can call you that now, you know. You're captain of the *Little Boat*."

Tammy pulled herself off the bed and thought about what he had said. "Yeah, I guess I am," she smirked.

Dwayne swung his legs over the side of the bed and sat on the edge as he watched Tammy pull on a pair of jeans and, top. "It feels good, doesn't it?" he said, looking proud.

"Yeah, it does." She giggled. "Captain Tammy. I like that."

Once Tammy was dressed, she left the cabin, so Dwayne had room to stand and do the same. It was still dark outside, but the sun peeked over the horizon. Tammy breathed in the fresh ocean air. She couldn't think of a better way to wake up. A steaming hot cup of coffee while they bobbed around in the middle of the ocean at a remote island. It was something she would never get tired of.

She scanned the harbor and saw floodlights illuminated on the decks of the other boats. Tammy knew how they were feeling. The day before the opening of the season, everyone was eager to get their traps baited in time for the opener. She watched from the deck chair as the other boats' crews did their last-minute chores while she drank her early morning beverage. A few minutes later, Dwayne appeared and grabbed the coffee off the helm that Tammy had made for him.

"So, are you ready to go?" he asked, as he leaned back against the rail of the helm and took a sip of his drink.

Tammy took her last sip and stood up. "As ready as I'll ever be."

"That's my girl," Dwayne said as he approached her and gave

her a peck on the lips. "You'll be fine. I have all the faith in the world. I'm going to make sure you get off okay, and then I'll fire up this beast and head for the far side of the island."

Tammy freed her slickers from the hook at the helm and slid into them. She then grabbed her boots from inside the cabin and put them on. "Okay, I'm ready," she said with an edge of nervousness.

"Damn, you're the cutest fisherman out here. I'm so lucky." Dwayne said before giving her one last hug and a passionate kiss on the lips. "I'm so proud of you."

"Tell me that after today. Let's see how I do first."

Dwayne smacked her butt as she stepped onto the *Little Boat* and fired it up. "Okay, untie me." She yelled.

"Oh, I love it when you talk dirty to me," he chuckled. "Now, you know where you are going, right?"

Tammy nodded. "Yes, we discussed it last night. I'll go over to the east side where the swell is low in the mornings and then head around Castle Rock and meet you somewhere down the line over there."

"You got it. Okay, I'm going to push you off," Dwayne said as he untied the last line at the stern of the boat. "I love you," he hollered as Tammy drove away from the *Baywitch II*.

Tammy smiled and yelled over the motor. "I love you too."

When she was a distance away, it suddenly hit her that she was in charge of the *Little Boat's* entire fishing operation. "Wow!" she said out loud before the sound of a horn startled her. She looked to her right where the other boats were anchored and saw Mitch was standing tall, waving at her. Tammy smiled and waved back vigorously. It felt good to have these guys finally on her side and rooting for her.

With both hands firmly on the wheel, she steered the boat and headed out of the harbor. "You can do this, Tammy," she said out loud, feeling confident.

Tammy was pleased that the weather was on her side for her first day of being solo. The ocean was flat with hardly any swell, and the sun reflected off the surface of the clear water. Today would be a good test for her to handle the boat by herself and retrieve the traps to bait them. Her task was to pull as many traps as she could, fill them with bait, and toss them back in the water. Tomorrow would be the big day, where she would pull the traps for lobsters and do all the tasks independently.

It took her roughly ten minutes to spot the first trap, and she immediately slowed down the boat so she could ease up on it. She took a deep breath, "Okay, here we go. Trap number one."

Tammy had watched Dwayne pull up to the trap hundreds of times and was thankful that she had been paying attention. With her gaff in one hand, she steered the boat with her other and hooked the line perfectly before putting the boat in neutral and wrapping the line on the pulley. "Yes!" She screamed in triumph as she saw the trap break through the surface of the water and land on the trap table. "I knew I could do this!" she squealed as she skipped across the deck to grab some bait.

Still beaming like a Cheshire cat and feeling mighty proud of herself, Tammy plugged the trap with bait and secured the door. Before pushing it over the side, she grabbed the radio microphone. "Dwayne. Dwayne, you got me?"

A few seconds later, she heard his masculine voice over the radio. "Yeah, I got you. Is everything okay? Over"

"I did it! I pulled my first trap. Over."

Tammy heard him laugh before he spoke. "See, I knew you could do it. You should be proud of yourself. Over."

Tammy had forgotten they were on an open channel and suddenly heard the cheers of Mitch coming through the speakers. "Yeah, Tammy! Well done. Holler if you need anything. I'm out."

"Will do. Thanks, Mitch. Over," Tammy replied before getting Dwayne back on the radio.

"Dwayne, are you still there? Over."

"Yeah, I'm here. I'll be out of radio contact in about twenty minutes. Give yourself a big pat on the back from me. I'm so proud of you. I'll see you on the other side. Over," he laughed.

"Okay. Be safe. I'm out."

Tammy returned the mic to its holder and was flattered that Mitch had come on the radio to congratulate her. It was comforting to know that the rest of the fleet knew she was on the boat alone and would assist her if need be. Suddenly she didn't feel so isolated.

After pushing the baited trap into the water, Tammy put the boat in gear and worked the rest of the line without incident and felt like she was ready to fish the traps on her own tomorrow. It took her a good two hours to bait the rest of the line before she headed around Castle Rock, where she would meet up with Dwayne somewhere down the line up ahead.

She was eager to hear his voice. She hadn't spoken to him in hours. She needed to know if he was okay. She didn't like that he was out of radio contact for the first part of the day but felt a little at ease when Dwayne told her a couple of other boats would fish the backside of the island at the same time as him. When she finally heard his voice over the radio, three hours later, she immediately slowed down the boat and put it in neutral.

"Tammy! Tammy! You got me? Over."

"Yes, Dwayne, I got you! I'm so happy to hear your voice. Over."

"So, how did you do? Over."

"Good! There are no problems, and the boat is running fine; I've baited about ten traps on the other side of Castle Rock. Where are you? Over."

"I'm coming down the same line. We should meet up in a few hours. Well done. I'm out."

Tammy couldn't wait to see Dwayne. They had fished side by side for the past four years, and she preferred it to fishing solo. As much as she felt proud of herself for her accomplishments today, she didn't like her loneliness. She missed the laughs she and Dwayne had shared while fishing together, and the adventures they had while exploring new parts of the island. And when she had stopped to take a lunch break before heading around Castle Rock, she found it to be a lonely experience and cut her break short.

Tammy baited another thirty traps before she spotted Dwayne off in the distance and immediately called him on the radio.

"Dwayne! I see you! Do you see me? Over."

"Hey Tammy, I see you! How are you doing out there? Over."

"Missing you. It's lonely out here. Over."

Dwayne laughed. "Tell me about it. Over."

Suddenly Mitch's voice came over the radio. "Get a room, guys," he laughed.

Tammy laughed and hollered into the radio. "The *Baywitch II* will rock tonight. I can tell you that."

"Ha! I gotta love your style of fishing, guys. You have it made. I'm out."

"See ya, Mitch," Tammy hollered.

Tammy couldn't help but feel excited as she and Dwayne's

boats were getting closer. She felt like she had been at sea for days. It was the loneliest day of fishing she had ever experienced. When she was in close range to the *Baywitch II*, she screamed and waved her arms high above her head. "Dwayne! Dwayne!"

Dwayne waved back, wearing a huge smile that melted Tammy's heart, as always. He turned off the boat, leaned against the helm, and waited for her to get closer. "Tammy, I've missed you. How was it?"

When she was near enough that she didn't have to yell, Tammy turned off the motor and beamed Dwayne a big smile. "I've missed you, too. I did okay, but damn, it was lonely out there by myself. I'm not sure if I like this." Tammy confessed.

"Yeah, I hear ya. It's a whole different ball game when you're out on your own." He threw her another smile. "Listen, we are all done. We've baited all the traps between us. Meet me back at the harbor, and we'll discuss it some more."

"Sounds good," Tammy said before firing up the boat again.

Back at the harbor and with both boats tied securely, Tammy couldn't wait to feel Dwayne's muscular arms around her. She had missed him so much.

"I'm so proud of you, Tammy. I knew you could do it." Dwayne said to her after a long, drawn-out smooch. He held her tight as they conversed about their day apart.

"Thanks, it was nerve-wracking at first, but I kept picturing you driving the boat and how you did it, and it helped me a lot."

They were the first to return to the harbor, but Dwayne wasn't surprised since they were using two boats to bait the gear.

Tammy slid out of her slickers and then grabbed two Pepsis from the ice-chest. She scanned the empty harbor and smiled. She loved where she worked. She noticed Dwayne had also pulled off his slickers and was sitting in one of the deck chairs smoking a cigarette. She took a seat next to him.

Dwayne held out the pack of Marlboros. "Want one?"

"Yes, I've only had about four all day. It's hard to have a smoke when you have to do everything yourself." She took a long drag, enjoying every satisfying moment the rush of nicotine was bringing her.

"So, did you have fun?" Dwayne asked.

"Yes and no. I like the sense of pride I felt all day, and knowing I could handle the boat and traps on my own was comforting, but God, the isolation part sucks. I hated it when you were on the backside of the island. I did nothing but worry about you. I was relieved when I spoke to you on the radio and knew you were okay."

"Yeah, I didn't like it either," Dwayne admitted.

"I hated not being able to check in on you, and I miss the fun we had fishing together. We laugh all the time. I didn't laugh once today, and that was a drag too."

"Are you saying you don't want to fish alone anymore?"

Tammy leaned back and rolled her eyes in despair. "I don't know, Dwayne. I don't want to disappoint you, but what if something happens to you on the backside? I would never know. That's a scary feeling."

Dwayne reached over and took her hand. "Tammy, you could never disappoint me. What you did today took a lot of guts. Don't ever say that. Believe it or not, I agree with you."

His confession surprised Tammy. "You do?"

"Yes, I do, and I have an idea."

"Okay, I'm listening," Tammy said as she sat up and anxiously waited for him to tell her more.

"I think you should continue to fish alone for practice." He immediately saw the disappointment on her face. "But it doesn't have to be all day. How about you go and fish the quiet side where it is always flat in the mornings by yourself, and I'll fish up to Castle Rock? We meet back in the harbor, unload the lobsters and fish the rest of the day around Castle Rock and beyond together, on the *Little Boat* and leave the *Baywitch II* in the harbor?"

Tammy jumped up from her chair and threw herself in his lap

as she hooked her arms around his neck. "I love that idea. Yes, it's brilliant."

Dwayne leaned in and gave her a tender kiss. "Great, then that's how we will do it from now on. No more lonely days of fishing."

Tammy smiled and kissed him again. "I sure do love you."

"I love you too, babe."

For the next three years, Tammy was pleased that things ran smoothly for her and Dwayne. Her mom had so much fun watching Matt for the nine weeks they fished San Clemente Island that she came back every year after that. Tammy left worry free. She watched the relationship grow over the years between her mom and son. The love seeped from their eyes when they reunited. What they had was special. But the constant reminder that her mother still yearned to have all her daughters together was something her mom would never let go of.

"I know, mom, but I don't know how that is possible right now," Tammy said during her mom's last visit.

"That's what you always tell me. I've not seen Donna since she moved to Colorado, and I've only met her husband once. It's just awful, Tammy. Families shouldn't be this far apart from one another," her mother ranted. "And when are you coming to England? You've not been back since you left. That was fourteen years ago."

Tammy rolled her eyes. She's had this conversation too many times. "Mom, I can't afford to go to England. It wouldn't be just me. What about Dwayne and Matt? Do you know how much three tickets would cost? And let's not forget, we wouldn't be making any money. Fishing doesn't have vacation pay. We just can't do it, mom. I'm sorry," Tammy told her.

She expected her mom to come out this year again and take care of Matt. It would be her fourth year and Tammy's seventh year of fishing. Tammy was so proud of her son who was almost eleven. Since he was old enough to understand, he had been eager to learn as much as he could about lobster fishing, just like his mother many years ago. He couldn't wait to return home from school and finish his homework so he could help get the traps ready for the season. But what Matt enjoyed the most was when he didn't have school, he would join them on the *Baywitch II* and help pull the traps at Malibu.

Today was one of those days. It was the first week of March, and they were getting ready to wrap up the lobster season and took the *Baywitch II* so they could bring some gear home. Tammy and Matt stacked the traps while Dwayne drove the boat. In between traps, Tammy stood and watched with pride when Dwayne would let Matt have a go at steering the boat.

When they returned to the dock, with the boat loaded with traps, Tammy fell into Dwayne's arms. "I'm exhausted. I wish we were done."

Dwayne glanced at the sun that was setting. "It shouldn't take more than an hour to stack these traps in the yard."

Tammy watched Matt jump off the boat and chase a duck off the dock. "Where does he get his energy? He is not the least bit tired." She placed her hands on her hips. "Okay, let's do this. I want to be home before dark. It's pizza and a movie night."

After taking turns to shower, Tammy ordered the pizza and settled on the couch with her two favorite guys to watch a movie when the phone rang. Dwayne turned to reach for the cordless phone but saw it wasn't in the cradle. "Where's the phone?" he asked. "You're always misplacing the phone, Tammy," he laughed.

Tammy looked at the empty cradle. "Oh, shoot. I think I had it in the kitchen last. I always forget to put it back. I'm sorry."

Dwayne tapped her knee as he stood up. "It's fine. I'll get it." He said as the phone continued to ring.

He answered it before the answering machine kicked in. "Hello. Dwayne here."

Dwayne heard the chirpy voice of his dad. "Hello, son. It's your dad."

"Hey, dad, how's it going?"

"It's going good, son, but your mother and I have been having a conversation, and I wanted to give you a call."

Dwayne couldn't hide the worry in his voice. "Is everything okay, dad?"

"Oh yes, everything is fine, but we were just trying to figure out how long you and Tammy have been together."

"Hold on a sec, dad." Dwayne pulled the phone away from his mouth and hollered to Tammy, who was still in the living room watching the movie. "Hey Tammy, how long have we been together?"

Tammy hollered back, "About seven years."

He repeated her answer to his dad. "Seven years."

"Are you two ever going to get married?" his dad asked.

Dwayne laughed and hollered to Tammy again, humorously. "Hey Tammy, are we ever going to get married? dad wants to know."

"I'm sure we will someday," Tammy replied—distracted by the movie.

"When?" his dad asked.

Dwayne shrugged his shoulders—amused by his dad's questions and threw out a random date. "I dunno. August second."

"Is that okay with Tammy?" his dad asked.

"Is August second, okay?" Dwayne hollered to Tammy.

"Sounds good," Tammy said, still distracted by the movie.

But Charlie wasn't done. "Where?"

"Where what?" Dwayne asked.

"Where will you get married?"

Dwayne thought quickly. "Your house."

"Great!" Charlie shouted away from the phone to Dwayne's mother. "Hey, Cathy, Dwayne and Tammy are getting married in five months at our house. We have a wedding to plan."

Dwayne heard his mother cheer in the background and chuckled.

"I gotta go, son. Your mother wants to talk about the wedding. She is so excited. I'm sure she will call you later. Love you, son. Bye."

Dwayne sat stunned, looking at the now silent phone in his hand. "What the hell just happened?" He chuckled to himself and was still wearing a huge grin when he returned to the couch.

"What are you smiling about?" Tammy asked, as she placed a hand on his knee and made room for him on the couch between her and Matt.

Dwayne's smile got bigger. "I guess we're getting married."

Tammy's jaw dropped. "What? I thought you were joking."

Dwayne shook his head. "Nope. That was my dad. When I told him we'd been together seven years, he asked when we were getting married. You said August second was okay, so that's the date, and it will be at my dad's house."

Tammy gasped. "Holy shit! You're kidding me. We're getting married."

Matt screeched. "you're getting married? Dwayne will be my dad?"

Tammy couldn't contain herself and jumped off the couch and began skipping around the room. "We're getting married. Oh my god! I can't believe it." She raced back over to Dwayne's side and gave him a hard kiss. "Pretty sneaky of your dad, I must say."

Dwayne laughed. "Yeah, it was. He had me propose to you without even knowing it."

Tammy laughed. "You're not regretting it, are you?"

Dwayne cupped her face in his palms and kissed her tenderly. "Oh, hell no. You're the best thing that ever happened to me."

Tammy leaned back against the cushions of the couch. "Wow! I can't believe I'm getting married." She narrowed her eyes at Dwayne. "I only plan on getting married once, you know. You realize you're stuck with me for the rest of your life?"

Dwayne took her hand and gave her a smile. "That's just fine with me."

Tammy let out a loud, cocky laugh. "So not only do we have to get ready for lobster season this summer, but we also have a wedding to plan."

Tammy didn't know how they pulled it off, but with the help from Dwayne's family and some close friends, her wedding day had quickly arrived. Tammy stood outside on the lush green grass of Dwayne's parent's house, where everything looked perfect for the big day. She admired the beautifully decorated tables with white and pink roses for their one hundred guests. The white arbor where she would become Dwayne's wife stood tall and was decorated with ivy, roses and carnations.

Tammy looked off to the edge of the lawn and saw that the caterer and band were busy setting up their equipment and buffet tables. It was early August, and the heat of the sun showed its strength. "Oh, the guys are going to die in their tuxedos," Tammy whispered under her breath as she wiped a bead of sweat from her brow. Tammy glanced at the shimmering water in the pool and thought how inviting it looked.

She went inside and admired the three-tier cake that stood elegantly on the large dining room table, safe from the expected 102-degree scorching temperatures.

Tammy was pleased when she got the news that her dad was

flying in from Ireland for the wedding to give her away, and Donna was also going to make it from Colorado. It was peak season for Jason's tree trimming business, and they buried him in work, and he wouldn't be able to come out with Donna, but he had called that morning to congratulate them.

Tammy's mother Rose flew out a month earlier than her normal time when she normally watched Matt in September to help Tammy with any last-minute plans. Tammy loved having her at the house for an extra month.

Donna also stayed at the house and slept on the living room floor, and their dad, John got a room at a hotel right across the street.

On the eve of the wedding, over dinner with Tammy and Dwayne's families, Tammy wondered if this was as close as it would get to have her mom's three girls together. It saddened Tammy when Jenny had told her they wouldn't make it to the wedding. With the short notice of a wedding, they didn't have enough time to apply for a visa for the family, and then there was the expense and time away from work which was also a factor. Tammy understood but couldn't help feeling the void at the table.

Tammy hadn't seen her parents together since their divorce almost twenty years ago. She admired them from across the room and saw the sparkle in their eyes as they chattered to one another. Tammy was happy to see they had risen above their differences and were now good friends, and knew from their body language and the caring smiles they shared that they carried a special place in their hearts for one another.

Now on the morning of the wedding, with tears in her eyes, Tammy held hands with her mom and Donna, "I can't believe I'm getting married in just a few hours." she cried.

Donna cracked a laugh. "It's about time, sis. I wouldn't miss this for the world. Does Dwayne know what he is getting into?" she joked.

Suddenly Tammy heard the familiar sound of Dwayne's truck

pull into the driveway. Tammy had driven her car to Dwayne's parent's house with her mom and sister. Her dad had stayed behind and rode with Dwayne. "Shit!" Tammy shrieked. "Dwayne's here. I don't want him to see me until the wedding. It's bad luck."

Donna laughed again. "Didn't you see him this morning when you woke up? And haven't you shared his bed for the past seven years?"

Tammy rolled her eyes. "Yes, but that doesn't count. Come on; we gotta disappear," she said, grabbing her mom's hand and hurried them to the east side of the house where the ladies would get ready.

A few hours later, Tammy stood in front of a full-length mirror with her mom and sister on either side. Her long white dress, which flared at the bottom, hugged her body perfectly. If she had brought the dress instead of renting it, it would have cost her $8000, instead of the $500 weekends rental rate. She only planned on getting married once and couldn't fathom spending an obscene amount of money for a dress that would not see the light of day after her wedding.

Tammy's tears flowed when she saw herself in the mirror. She couldn't believe she was a bride.

"Don't cry," her mother whispered, as she tried to hold back her own tears. "You'll ruin your make-up."

"How do you want to wear your hair?" Donna asked.

"Definitely down. I hate my ears and forehead," Tammy laughed.

Donna nodded. "Good choice. You have beautiful hair. Why don't you have a seat, and I'll curl it at the ends?"

Tammy's eyes sparkled, "Ooh, I love that idea." Tammy watched as her sister did her magic. "Wow, that looks great. Where did you learn to do hair?" Tammy asked.

"From other strippers at the club when I lived with you. We all did each other's hair."

"Donna!" Rose gasped.

"What, mom? I'm not ashamed of it. I did what I had to do."

Tammy raised her hands. "Okay, enough, guys." She took another look at herself in the mirror. "Okay, I'm ready. Where's dad?"

"He's waiting outside," Donna said, who was Tammy's matron of honor and led the way. "Let's go, sis. The music is playing."

Rose leaned in and gave Tammy a light kiss on the cheek before leaving the room. "I'm so proud of you. You look beautiful."

Tammy gave her a caring smile, "Thanks, mom."

Tammy listened to the music and then heard the familiar wedding tune of *Here Comes the Bride.*

Donna shook her hair and raked her fingers through it. "That's your cue, sis. It's your last chance to run," she laughed.

Tammy slapped her sister's arm. "You're terrible. I have no intention of running. Dwayne is the best thing that has happened to me."

"He sure is. We have both found our perfect men. I don't know what I'd do without Jason. He saved me." Donna played with Tammy's hair one last time. "We've come a long way, sis."

Tammy smiled. "We sure have."

"Okay, everyone is waiting to see the beautiful bride, including Dwayne, who is out there waiting for you. Now, go get him," Donna said, with a huge smile.

Tammy nodded, took a deep breath, and followed her sister out of the room. She smiled and struggled to hold back her tears when she saw her dad, looking sharp in a grey suit. His arm was bent at the elbow, ready for Tammy to take it.

"Hi, dad," she whispered.

"You look beautiful," her dad said with a smile.

Tammy hooked arms with her dad, and together they walked to the arbor where Dwayne was waiting. She nodded and smiled at all the familiar faces of friends and family that were there to share this special day. She couldn't help but feel like the luckiest woman in the world. Before Tammy stood, the man she had met and fallen in love with over seven years ago, and today he was to become her husband.

She admired how he stood tall and assertive with glassy eyes, dressed in a black tuxedo, a white shirt, and a black bow tie. It was the first time she had ever seen him in a suit of any kind, and he looked dashing and delicious. His long blonde hair cascaded over his shoulders and blew gently in the breeze. He turned to face her as she walked toward him. He winked and gave her one of his heart-warming smiles that melted her heart many years ago. Tammy smiled back and couldn't believe she was about to marry the gorgeous man that stood before her.

Standing next to Dwayne were their two sons, Matt and Justin, both also dressed in tuxedos. She smiled at the boys, looked down at Matt's hands, and saw he had the ring box.

By the time Tammy and her dad reached Dwayne, the music had stopped, and silence fell upon the crowd. Her dad looked so proud as he let go of Tammy's hand and gave her a light kiss on the cheek before taking his place next to Dwayne's brothers. Tammy took a deep breath, faced Dwayne, and took his extended hand.

Dwayne smiled and whispered, "Hi."

Tammy laughed. "Hi."

Their guests heard them, and soft laughter erupted amongst them.

The sun was high in the sky and radiated its intense heat as Dwayne and Tammy said their vows.

A few minutes later, the minister smiled. "I now pronounce you man and wife."

Dwayne and Tammy kissed passionately to the sounds of the loud cheers and whistles coming from their guest, and when the music played, they danced.

By the end of the ceremony, the temperatures were now soaring in the late nineties, and Tammy laughed when she saw Matt rip off his bow tie and undo some buttons. "Why don't you

and the other kids go in the pool? I told everyone to bring swimming trunks. Yours are in the house."

Matt's face lit up. "Can I?" he screamed, as he ran off to tell the
other kids.

Dwayne and Tammy celebrated with their family and friends
into the early evening. They still had to drive to San Diego for
what would be their short two-day honeymoon, which was all the
time they could take off because fishing wouldn't wait.

Tammy said goodbye to her dad, who would leave the next day.
"Thank you for coming, dad. It meant a lot." Tammy said from her
dad's arms. "I'll call you soon."

"You've found yourself a fine young man there, Tammy. I may
not say it often, but I'm proud of you."

Tammy closed her eyes and squeezed her father's waist.
"Thanks, dad."

Tammy turned to her sister. "No fighting with mom while I'm
gone," she joked. "I know how you guys can be. Dad is taking my
car home, so you, mom and Matt can ride with him."

"Donna took Tammy's hand. Thanks, sis. I'll be heading back
home in a couple of days. It's going to be fun hanging with mom
and Matt until then. We will be fine. I promise there will be no
fighting. I'm older now," she laughed.

Once in the truck, Tammy rolled down her window and waved
at her family and friends standing in the driveway. "I love you
guys!" she yelled. She turned to Dwayne and smiled. "I love you,
too."

Dwayne pulled her in close and kissed her hard on the lips. The
crowd screamed, "Get out of here and go get a room." Dwayne
laughed as he put the truck in reverse and backed out of the
driveway.

CHAPTER 17

Tammy leaned against the tall stack of traps in their backyard and wiped her brow. She was tired, but her spirits were high. Another lobster season was behind them, and after catching up with all their bills, she was pleased to see they still had money left in the bank.

"God, it's a warm one, and it's only March," Tammy said while trying to catch her breath after stacking the last trap. She pulled her aching body away from the traps and arched her back. "I need an ice-cold Pepsi and a cigarette."

"Sounds good," Dwayne hollered from the other side of the yard where he was coiling rope into a barrel.

Tammy returned a few minutes later with two sodas and took a seat at the patio table, anxious to light a cigarette. "Here you go."

"I'll be right there," Dwayne said, dropping the rope.

Tammy lifted her sore legs onto the nearby chair and released a heavy sigh. "God, I'm so tired." She took a hit from her cigarette and closed her eyes. A few minutes later she heard the phone ring from inside the house. "Damn it. Why does it always ring the minute I sit down?" She groaned in agony as she slowly returned her feet to the ground and pulled herself up from her comfy chair. "I'll be right back," she said as she entered the house.

After the fourth ring, she picked up the phone. "Hello." There was silence. Tammy repeated herself, "Hello?" Tammy thought she heard the faint sound of crying. Worried, she spoke with an edge and louder. "Hello! Who is this?"

"Tammy, It's Donna," she said between heavy sobs.

Tammy held the phone tight with both hands. "Donna, are you okay? Why are you crying?" Tammy waited anxiously for her to speak, but all she could hear were the increasing sounds of sobbing. Tammy felt the panic rise to her chest. "Donna, what's going on? Talk to me," she said, raising her voice and feeling scared.

"It's Jason." Donna cried into the phone.

Tammy's heart hammered beneath her chest. "What about Jason? Is he okay?"

Donna sucked back her tears. "I'm at the hospital. He had a seizure."

Tammy felt her knees turn weak and stumbled over to the couch. "What? Oh my god, is he going to be okay?"

"I don't know yet. They have to run all kinds of tests."

"When did this happen?" Tammy asked, as she clenched her still racing heart.

"About two hours ago. We were coming back from the movies, and he suddenly lost control of the truck. His eyes rolled to the back of his head, and his body jolted uncontrollably. It was horrible. I grabbed the wheel and steered the truck to the side of the road, where we ended up in a ditch. The car behind us stopped and made sure we were okay and then went to go find a phone to call 911." Donna took in a sharp breath. "Jason was unconscious by then. He had hit his head on the steering wheel. I thought he was dead."

"Oh my god, Donna. Do you want me to come out there?"

Donna's voice seemed a little calmer when she spoke again.

"No. No, you have Matt to take care of. You can't bring him here. I don't want him to see his uncle like this. His sister Terry moved out here last month; she is here with me."

Tammy released a sigh of relief. She was thankful Donna was not alone. "Oh, that's good to know. Is there anything I can do? I feel so helpless."

"No. I'm just sitting here with Terry waiting for the test results to come back, which might be hours."

Suddenly the familiar annoying phone booth recording came on. "Please deposit fifty more cents to continue with this call."

"Damn it! I ran out of change," Donna snapped down the phone.

Tammy spoke quickly. "I love you, sis. Hang in there. I'm sure he's going to be okay. He's young and healthy. Call me collect as soon as you have any news. I don't care what time it is."

"Okay, Tammy, I will. I love you too. Bye."

"Bye," Tammy replied in a somber tone.

Still shaken by the news, Tammy remained on the couch for a few minutes trying to process what her sister must be going through and how terrified she must be feeling. Tammy couldn't even imagine and wished she were at the hospital with her.

Dwayne immediately saw the sadness in her eyes and the look of worry she wore on her face when she returned outside. He stopped what he was doing and rushed over to her. "Hey, are you okay?" he said, while placing his hand on her shoulder.

Tammy looked at him with her glassy eyes, fell into his arms, and cradled her head against his chest.

Dwayne felt a rush of fear and wrapped his arms tight around her trembling body. "Hey, sweetheart. You're scaring me. Who was that on the phone?"

Tammy sniffed back her tears. "It was Donna."

Dwayne rubbed her back and kissed the top of her head. "Is she okay? What's going on?"

"It's Jason. He had a seizure, and he is in the hospital."

Dwayne pulled back, his jaw dropped, and he gasped. "Oh, no! Is he going to be alright?"

Tammy shook her head. "She doesn't know yet. She's at the hospital with him. They are running a bunch of tests. I told her to call me as soon as she knows anything."

Dwayne fell into one of the patio chairs and, like Tammy, the news stunned him. "But he's so healthy. He works outside all day, climbing and trimming trees. The last time we saw him, which I know was a while ago, he looked great. Are they sure it was a seizure?"

Tammy took a seat next to him. "That's what Donna told me. I guess we'll know more after they've run the tests," Tammy shook her head in despair. "God, poor Donna. She told me Jason's sister moved out there last month and is at the hospital with her. That makes me feel a little better; otherwise, I would have found a way to get out there. But she doesn't want Matt to see Jason the way he is."

Dwayne nodded. "That makes sense. Let's wait to hear from her, and then we'll decide what we're going to do."

Tammy gave him a loving smile. He always knew how to put things in perspective. It was one thing she loved about him. "You're right. I don't want to over-react. I must stay calm for Donna's sake, and I won't say anything to Matt until I know what's going on."

Worried about Jason, Tammy had a restless night and was concerned when she still hadn't heard from Donna by morning. She desperately wanted some answers and called Donna's house, but as she predicted, she got the answering machine. After the recorded message had played, Tammy spoke. "Donna, it's Tammy. I'm so worried about you guys. I couldn't sleep last night. Call me as soon as you can. Love you."

With her back to the kitchen doorway, she was startled when she heard Dwayne's voice behind her. She turned and saw him leaning against the doorjamb with a sadness lingering in his eyes and his arms folded.

"No news?" he asked.

Tammy shook her head and ran her hand through her hair. "No."

Dwayne took her in his arms, and Tammy wrapped her arms tightly around his waist and rested her head on his chest. For the next few minutes, they stood in silence and just held each other close.

"God, I hope Jason is going to be okay," Tammy said, feeling safe in Dwayne's firm grip.

"Me too. Why don't I make you some coffee while you wake Matt for school? I'm sure we'll know more later today."

For the rest of the morning, after Tammy returned from taking Matt to school, the mood in the house was somber. Everytime the phone rang, Tammy's heart skipped a beat, hoping it was Donna with some news, but sadly it wasn't.

"I need to keep busy," Tammy said, after spending the last hour cradled in Dwayne's arms on the couch.

"Do you want to go work on the crab gear? We need to get some traps in the water this weekend, and I promised Matt he could help us."

Tammy stood up from the couch. "Sure. That's a good idea. I'll bring the phone outside in case Donna calls."

Tammy struggled for the next hour, trying to stay focused on attaching the doors to some new traps, but she lost it when she poked her finger on a piece of wire. "God, I can't stand this! Why doesn't she call?" Tammy yelled, as she threw her pliers across the yard and licked on the blood trickling down her finger.

Her outburst startled Dwayne, who stood close by putting new zincs in the traps. He reached over and took her hand. "Hey, calm down. She will call us when she can. She's got a lot to deal with right now. Don't be upset with her. Put yourself in her shoes."

Tammy suddenly felt embarrassed by her selfish act. "You're right. God, I'm sorry. I'm just scared, that's all."

"I know you are. I am too, but Donna will call when she has news."

Suddenly the phone rang from the patio table where Tammy had set it. Tammy gasped and covered her heart with her hand. She looked at Dwayne with wide eyes and raced over to the table. Dwayne quickly followed and rested his hand on her shoulder as she picked up the phone.

"Hello," Tammy said, unable to hide the anxiety she was feeling.

"Tammy, it's Donna." Her voice was flat.

Tammy turned and took Dwayne's hand. "Hi, Donna. How is Jason?"

Donna's next words scared her. "Not good. He's in surgery."

Tammy squeezed Dwayne's hand and looked at him when she spoke into the phone. "Surgery? For what?"

Donna took in a deep breath. "They did a brain scan and found a tumor. It's pretty big, but they won't know if it's benign or cancer until after surgery."

Tammy held her hand up to her mouth and choked back her tears. "Oh my god, Donna. I'm so sorry. When will you know?"

"Sometime later today or tomorrow."

"Is Terry there with you?" Tammy asked.

"Yes. I've not slept in two days. We're going to stay here until he's out of surgery, and then I'm going home to take a shower and try to sleep for a few hours. I want to come back tonight. I need to be here." Donna cried.

Tammy squeezed Dwayne's hand hard, not believing what she was hearing. "Do you want me to come out there?"

"No, Terry is here. Let's see what the results are. I'm hoping it's just a fatty tumor, and he will be fine. I'll let you know as soon as the doctors tell me. I have to go. I love you, sis."

"I love you too, Donna."

"What's going on?" Dwayne asked after she had hung up the phone.

"They found a tumor on his brain. Donna says it's big, and he's in surgery right now."

"Oh my god. Is he going to be okay?"

"They won't know until after surgery. They need to find out if it's benign or not. God, this is horrible. What if it's cancer?"

"Let's not go there, okay. We have to think positive and hope for the best." Dwayne took her hand. "Come on. Let's forget about working on traps today. Let's go for a drive up the coast to Malibu for a little while and try to clear our heads. I'll buy you lunch. Donna won't be calling for a while. It will do us both good."

Tammy gave him a warm smile. Yet again, he knew how to make her feel better. "You're right. Let me change out of these dirty clothes. A drive to Malibu sounds good."

Donna called the following morning when Dwayne and Tammy were in the backyard loading crab traps into the truck to take to the boat.

Tammy threw off her gloves and raced to the phone that lay on the patio table. She took a seat with bated breath and answered the phone. "Donna, is that you?"

Donna's voice sounded flat, and from her sniffs, Tammy knew she had been crying. Tammy sensed the news wouldn't be good.

"Yes, it's me," Donna said, in a somber tone.

"So, what's going on? How's Jason?" Tammy asked, trying desperately to hide the fear in her voice.

Donna broke into heart-wrenching sobs the minute she spoke. "He has cancer, Tammy!" she cried.

Tammy's jaw dropped, and she put the phone on speaker so Dwayne could hear, who had joined her at the table and was holding her hand. Dwayne shook his head and raised his hand to his brow in disbelief.

"Oh my god. No!" Tammy shrieked.

Donna continued to cry, sucking in the air between her words. "They found a tumor the size of a goddamn lemon. How could that be? He's never felt a thing."

"Did he ever complain of headaches?" Tammy asked.

"Jason is hard-headed and had never complained about anything. He hates the doctors. If Jason had headaches, he never told me about them because he knew damn well I would have dragged his ass to the doctors."

"And they said for sure it's cancer?" Tammy asked in a soft voice.

"Yes. they told me it was a Global blastoma grade-four tumor."

Tammy glanced over at Dwayne and creased her brow. "What does it mean?"

Donna's crying intensified. "It means he only has about six months to live."

Tammy gasped, and Dwayne squeezed her hand tight. "What! Are they sure?"

"Yes, they are sure. They removed ninety-nine percent of the tumor, but they couldn't do a complete removal because of where it is on the brain, and that little piece will grow back and kill him."

Tammy was numb. She didn't know what to say. "But how can that be? He's so young. He's supposed to turn forty this year."

"I know." Donna cried. "I don't know if he will make it. Oh, Tammy, what am I going to do?"

Donna's tears tore at Tammy's heart, and she wished more than anything that she was close by and could hold her sister tight and give her the support she needed. Tammy didn't need to think about her next words or discuss them with Dwayne. "Donna, we're coming to see you," Tammy said, as she gave Dwayne a hard stare.

Dwayne nodded, and Tammy threw him a grateful smile.

Donna sounded not only surprised but also relieved. "You are?"

"Yes, we are. We'll drive there. Matt is out of school next week. I want him to come too. Jason is his uncle. Is that okay?"

"Of course. Yes, That's fine." She paused and whispered in a calmer tone. "Thank you."

"Hush. There is no need to thank me. You are family, and so is Jason. I just wished we weren't so far away and saw more of each other." Tammy released a heavy sigh and wiped away her tears. "Oh, Donna, I can't believe this is happening. Why Jason?"

"I swear I can't get a break in life," Donna said with a sharp tone. "I'm finally happy, and now I'm going to lose the guy that made it all happen."

Tammy had no words. There was nothing she could say that would ease the horrific pain her sister felt. And then it hit her. Donna would become a widow at the young age of thirty-six. How could life be so unfair? Tammy wondered. Donna had already had her share of trying times, and now this. Tammy tried to comfort her sister as best she could for the next few minutes until Donna told her the doctors were there to talk to her.

"Okay, Donna, I'll let you go. We'll be there next week, but call me when you can, okay?"

"I will. I love you, Tammy."

Tammy's voice was flat. "Love you too, sis."

After hanging up the phone, Tammy let her tears fall. It was the first time in her life that she had to deal with someone dying who she knew and cared about. She couldn't wrap her head around the thought that Jason would not be with them next year. How could such a healthy, young man be facing death in just six months? "What are the odds the doctors are wrong?" Tammy asked Dwayne, who was now standing behind her with his chin resting on her head as he embraced her from behind.

"I hate to say it, but pretty slim, I would imagine," he said as he buried his head in her hair as he tried to hold back his own tears.

"I'm sorry I told Donna we would go see them before talking to you first. I just need to support her somehow," Tammy confessed, still cradled in Dwayne's arms.

"It's fine. I would have suggested it anyway."

Tammy freed herself from Dwayne's hold and twisted her body until she met his eyes. "There's another reason I want to go."

"What's that?" Dwayne asked.

"If what the doctors are saying is true, then this trip will probably be the last time we will see Jason alive. It's kind of our last goodbyes."

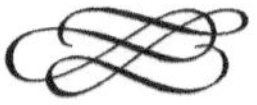

A week later, after driving for sixteen hours, they pulled into Jason and Donna's driveway. It was their first visit to Colorado, and Tammy wished it were under better circumstances.

Before their trip, Tammy and Dwayne sat Matt down and had a heart-to-heart talk with him about Jason and told him that soon he would fly with the angels and that they wanted to see him before he left. Tammy wasn't sure if Matt quite understood what they were trying to tell him, but the sadness she saw in his eyes told Tammy that he probably did, but she remained strong for her son and refrained from breaking down and sobbing in front of him.

Donna must have heard them pull into the driveway. Within minutes she stood at the side of the car before they stepped out. Immediately Tammy cried and quickly exited the car. "Donna," she sobbed as she ran into her sister's arms.

Tammy couldn't help noticing how fatigued her sister looked. Her skin was pale, and the sparkle had disappeared from her eyes. Her hair was uncombed and a tangled mess. The bathrobe looked too big for her frail skinny frame.

"Oh, Donna, I'm so sorry. I don't know what to say. I still can't believe it."

"I know, me neither. Jason is inside. I try not to cry in front of him. So, let's pull ourselves together before we go into the house," Donna said, showing more strength than Tammy had at that moment.

Tammy nodded and broke away from their embrace. "Okay. I didn't think he'd be home from the hospital yet."

"He just got home yesterday."

"How is he doing?" Dwayne asked who was standing next to a confused Matt as he had just watched his mom and auntie cry heavily in each other's arms.

Donna wiped her eyes with her hand. "As well as can be expected. He's frail, of course, and has constant headaches. He stutters, which is an aftereffect of the seizure, and he also has a hard time remembering anything. He has also lost a lot of weight, so don't be alarmed."

Feeling more composed, Tammy took Donna's hand. "Come on, let's go inside. Show me where the kettle is, and I'll make us some tea," Tammy said, with a subtle smile.

Donna followed suit and broke a small smile. "Sounds good. Thank you so much for coming out. Terry is staying here too. You'll get to meet her soon. She just ran to the store."

"Stop thanking us. We want to be here," Tammy told her, as she led them into the house.

Once they were inside, the first thing Tammy noticed was that all the curtains were drawn.

"Sorry it's so dark in here, but Jason can't stand the sunlight with his constant headaches," Donna told her.

Donna led them through the living room and into the kitchen where, to Tammy's surprise, Jason sat at the table drinking coffee. Tammy noticed straight away that Donna wasn't kidding about his weight loss. She hardly recognized him. She couldn't believe that the man before her used to be the meaty rugged guy that had the strength of a bull, and was now skin and bones with sunken shallow eyes, and half his head was shaved and partially covered with a bandage. He looked over at them, and through all his pain, he smiled. Tammy struggled to hold back the tears that were ready to burst and smiled back.

"Hi, Jason," she said, as she approached the table. She saw Jason was about to stand.

"Oh, please don't get up." She turned to Matt, who hadn't said a word since they arrived.

Jason saw the boy's uneasiness and raised his hand. "Give me five there, buddy," Jason said with a forced smile and a strained, cracked voice.

Matt smiled at his uncle, giving him a high five, and then took a seat next to him.

Dwayne was the last to reach the table and shook Jason's hand before taking a seat. The vibe was tense and uncomfortable. Tammy and Dwayne didn't know what to say to Jason. They were numb and still in shock by his appearance.

Jason was the first to speak. "Thanks for coming out, guys. I appreciate it." Jason said and then shook his head. "Can you believe this shit?"

Tammy continued to fight back her tears. "No, and it's not fair." Tammy hesitated before continuing, but needed to know. "Is there nothing they can do, Jason?"

Jason took Donna's hand, who stood beside him with her hand resting on his shoulder, and gave her a loving smile. "Oh, sure, they can feed my brain with radiation and my veins with Chemo to slow down the inevitable."

"Well, isn't that a good thing?" Tammy asked.

"Not really. It may give me an extra three months, but I'll be so sick from the treatment, what's the damn point?"

Tammy creased her brow. "So, what are you saying?" fearing she already knew the answer.

"I'm not doing any of the treatments." Jason raised his hand.

"Before you say anything or try to talk me out of it, Donna and I have discussed it. I don't want to prolong this any more than I have to and put Donna through any more suffering. I want to go out with some bit of dignity."

Tammy looked over at her sister, who gave her a slight nod. "I understand, Jason. In fact, I admire you," Tammy said in a soft voice.

Donna left Jason's side and went to the corner of the room, where she grabbed a cane. "Jason has to take a nap soon, but he likes to walk around the yard first." She looked over at Dwayne. "Why don't you and Matt go with him? Tammy and I will make some tea and sandwiches for everyone."

"Sound good," Dwayne said, as he took the cane from Donna.

Tammy watched with a torn heart as Jason stood slowly with the aid of Dwayne.

"God, Donna, I don't know how you are coping with this?" Tammy said, as she looked out the kitchen window at the three guys.

Donna stood next to her. "I have no choice. I have to be strong for Jason."

"I don't need to get too personal. But are you going to be okay once… well, you know?"

Donna gave Tammy a half-smile. "You can say it—once he dies."

Tammy shied away. "Yeah. Will you be okay, financially?"

"Yes, I will be for a while. This house is paid for thanks to some money Jason's dad left him. Jason has saved some too. I should be okay."

Tammy was relieved and rolled her eyes. "Oh, good. That makes me feel a little better."

A few minutes later, they heard the front door open and close. "Oh, that must be Terry back from the store. Thank god she is staying here too. She said she would stay as long as she needs to."

Terry entered the kitchen carrying a bag of groceries and set it down on the counter before introducing herself. "Hi, you must be Tammy; I'm Terry," she said with an extended hand.

Tammy ignored her hand and opened her arms and embraced her. "Hi, Terry. I'm so sorry about what is going on with your brother."

"Thanks. I still can't believe it. He's my only and baby brother. He's always been there for me and our sister, Carol."

"Oh, that's right, I forgot Jason had two sisters. Is she here?"

Terry shook her head. "No, she lives in California and has kids. She's going to be coming out next month sometime."

Tammy saw the resemblance between her and Jason. They both had the same high cheekbones and silvery grey eyes. Terry's hair was long and blonde, just like Donna's, and for a moment, Tammy thought they looked like sisters. She knew how close they had become since Donna had married Jason, and it showed. Tammy knew that when she and Dwayne returned home, Donna would be in excellent hands. Terry had promised to be there and guide her through the heartbreaking journey they were about to endure. For Tammy, it was a comforting thought.

Tammy and Dwayne stayed in Colorado for as long as possible, which ended up being almost two weeks. School break would soon be over, and if they didn't start fishing for crabs soon, they would have to dig into their small savings account to pay for the upcoming bills.

During their stay, they tried to help Donna in any way they could by cooking meals, going to the stores or cleaning the house. Whatever Donna needed, they tried to be there for her, along with Jason's sister, Terry.

Jason, Dwayne, and Matt bonded in a bittersweet way. Dwayne and Matt spent many hours with him out in the yard where Dwayne would fire up the barbecue some afternoons, and he would talk to Jason about guy stuff, fishing, hunting, cars and motorcycles. All of which were hobbies they both shared.

In Dwayne's earlier years before he met Tammy, he had spent most of his late teen years and early twenties on motorcycles. There were days when he and Jason would sit in the garage and admire Jason's polished shiny Harley Davidson Knucklehead, and

Dwayne listened intently as Jason talked with pride about the motorcycle he restored from the ground up.

Tammy and Donna had many tearful moments cradled in each other's arms in disbelief over what was happening. Tammy couldn't believe that Jason was dying a slow death, and there was nothing any one could do to save him. How could life be so cruel? Tammy kept asking herself, and why Jason? The man that took her broken sister in, loved her unconditionally and finally gave her the life she deserved. How was Donna ever going to recover from this? Tammy couldn't even imagine.

On the day they were leaving to return to California, the emotions were high for everyone. How do you say goodbye to someone when you know it would be for the last time and that you would never see him again? Tammy remembered her sister's words. *I have to be strong for Jason,* and Tammy knew she would have to be too.

Jason laid on the couch with two pillows supporting his head, and a light blanket covered his frail body. Tammy sat gently on the edge of the couch, being careful not to squish him while everyone else stood behind her. She took his hand and gave it a gentle kiss. Jason, whose eyes were half-closed, gave her a weak smile. It took all her willpower to hold back her tears as she spoke. "I'm so sorry we can't stay any longer. I really wish we could. I'll be calling Donna every day to see how you are doing okay?"

Jason nodded. "Thank you for everything. You take care of each other. You have a beautiful family, Tammy."

Tammy sniffed back her tears that were trying to escape. "I will. I love you, Jason."

Jason gave her hand a gentle squeeze. "I love you too, Tammy."

With ease, being careful not to disturb him, Tammy lifted herself off the couch and turned to Matt. "Why don't you give your uncle a kiss goodbye on the cheek, and after that we will wait outside for Dwayne with Auntie Donna."

Matt, who now understood that Jason was dying, sauntered

over to his uncle and laid his head gently on his chest. Tammy turned away and wiped her now moist eyes with her hand.

"I love you, Uncle Jason."

"I love you too, buddy," Jason said as he slowly lifted his arm and cradled his nephew.

"Okay, sweetheart, let's go wait outside Tammy said, once Matt stood away from the couch. "I'll see you outside," Tammy whispered to Dwayne. She gave Jason one last caring smile, left the room, and found Donna sitting on the front step smoking a cigarette.

"I didn't see you come outside," Tammy said before lighting a cigarette of her own.

"I snuck out while you were saying goodbye to Jason."

Tammy sat next to her sister, and once again, they cried in each other's arms. "Are you sure you're going to be okay?" Tammy asked. "I'm so worried about you."

Donna sniffed hard. "Yeah. Terry will be here. I don't know how but I'll get through this."

They remained on the steps embraced until Dwayne came out, and after one last emotional goodbye, they got in the truck. Donna stood on the steps and waved with tears gushing down her cheeks. Tammy was doing no better. She waved her hand high out of the window and screamed, "I love you, Donna!" as Dwayne backed the truck out of the driveway.

Tammy kept her promise and called Donna every day. On the days she was fishing Malibu, she'd call the minute she was home. Sometimes she had to leave a message because after eight, Donna turned off the phone so it wouldn't wake Jason.

By late July, Tammy and Dwayne had begun the grueling task of getting ready for lobster season. Rose, Tammy's mother, would arrive in September just like the previous years, to take care of

Matt while they fished the remote island. But this year, she was going to go to Colorado first before coming to California. Like Tammy, their mom and Donna had spoken often on the phone. Jason was now bedridden and on morphine for the pain. They all knew his time was near, and Rose insisted on being there for Donna when Jason was finally at peace.

Rose arrived in Colorado in the first week of August. Four days later, while Dwayne and Tammy worked on the gear in the back-yard, Donna called with the devastating news that they knew was inevitable.

"He's gone, Tammy. Jason is finally out of pain." Donna cried down the phone.

Tears flooded Tammy's eyes. "Oh my god, Donna, I'm so sorry. Where's mom?"

"She's right here next to me."

Tammy could hear her mom's sobs in the background. "Tell her I love her. She's too upset to talk, and so am I."

Donna told Tammy of Jason's passing—that he passed peacefully in his sleep after weeks of living in excruciating pain. After Tammy reluctantly hung up the phone, Dwayne pulled her into her arms, where she immediately buried her head in his chest and cried hard for the death of Jason, and her sister, who was now a widow.

Matt must have heard his mom's loud cries and came out of the house, strolling with his head hung low.

Dwayne suspected he knew and held out his arm. "Come here, buddy."

"Uncle Jason is dead, isn't he?" Matt said, tears pooling in his eyes.

Tammy raised her head and wiped her eyes before extending her arms. "Yes, he's gone, sweetheart. Come here."

Matt's lips quivered, and tears flowed down his cheeks as he ran into Dwayne and Tammy's arms for comfort and remained there for some time. It was the first time Tammy and her son had experienced the death of someone they loved. Tammy was numb, and it broke her heart. Jason's passing devastated her as well as seeing her son experience such raw emotions at such a young age. It was something she couldn't make better for her son, and that, too tore at her heart.

Honoring Jason's wishes, Donna had Jason's body flown out to California seven days later, where he was laid to rest next to his father, not too far from the house where Donna had lived with him before they left the state.

After the emotional services, Donna returned to Colorado with their mom and Terry. Rose insisted she'd stay with Donna until Tammy and Dwayne left for the island, which was only a few weeks away.

Haunted by images of Jason's slow death in the house they had lived in, Donna sold it within a year and bought a new one twelve-miles away. Terry kept her promise to her brother to take care of Donna and has been by her side ever since Jason's passing by moving into a house nearby. Slowly, with Terry's help, Donna tried to ease back into her life without Jason, but her wounds were raw—her heart shattered. As heart-wrenching as it was, Tammy called her often and listened as her sister poured her heart out. "I'm so lost, Tammy. I don't know if I can go on without him. He was my everything. He took care of me and loved me for who I am. He didn't care about my history. I'll never find another Jason."

Her sobs tore at Tammy's heart. She had no words to comfort her. Instead, she cried with her and let her speak about her pain.

"This hurts so much. Why does life have to be so cruel? Haven't I gone through enough? This isn't fair. I don't deserve this, and Jason didn't deserve to die. He was such a good man." Donna cried to Tammy.

For the first time, Jason's death made Tammy realize just how precious and short life was. Now, more than ever, she wanted to fulfill her mother's only wish of being reunited with her three daughters. Her mother wasn't getting any younger, and as much as Tammy hated to admit it, her mom was showing small signs of aging such as forgetfulness and confusion.

But three years after Jason's death, Tammy still had not accomplished it, and it haunted her daily. Matt was now fourteen, and like Tammy, he had caught on quickly to all the grueling chores that came with fishing lobsters. Alongside his parents, Matt worked every season getting the gear ready, and was often Dwayne's deckhand when they fished crabs in Malibu.

Tammy's mom continued to come out every year and watch Matt while they fished the island, and this year was no exception. She arrived just under a week ago, and Dwayne and Tammy were ready to embark on their tenth year of fishing together.

The first week of the season was always full of high expectations and hope. It was the week Dwayne and Tammy expected to make the most money during the entire season. The lobsters had not been fished in six months, so the season's first catch was usually the best.

Like every year, Dwayne and Tammy left the dock in debt, but amazingly, they always got caught up after their first trip. Tammy didn't mind that they weren't getting rich from fishing and weren't saving a lot of money. It's what they loved to do. Tammy got used to living on the edge with elevated nerves until they paid the bills. She conditioned herself over the years. It was all part of the fishing, and will always work itself out. And every year, it had. Fishing carried them through the year, provided a home for them, and allowed them to work together as a team and spend their days on the ocean. Tammy couldn't think of a better place to work.

They made the crossing in good time and pulled into the harbor just before the sun went down, connecting with the other boats via radio. They had seen a few of the captains over the previous weeks when they had dropped off their gear, but there were a few they had not seen or spoken to since the last season. For Tammy, it was always good to return to the fleet that felt like family over the years of fishing together.

The eve before baiting the traps always had an essence of excitement in the air. Every year was going to be the year that they would all have a record catch and fill their bank accounts.

Many of the crew members and captains did not sleep that night, including Dwayne and Tammy. There was always too much to do, and everyone was anxious for the sun to rise so they could begin baiting the traps because the sooner they baited, the sooner the traps would start to fish—tonight was no exception. Dwayne and Tammy worked hard into the morning hours, and only got two hours of sleep before leaving the harbor in the *Little Boat* to bait their traps.

They baited all 250 traps by nightfall on little sleep and aching bodies from prepping the night before. They pushed themselves through their pain and only stopped a few times for short, five minute breaks.

When they returned to the harbor, they spent the rest of the evening getting both boats ready for pulling the gear the next day. For the past few years, it had worked well with Tammy pulling traps on her own on the *Little Boat* in the morning, then meeting Dwayne in the harbor at noon so they could pull the rest of the gear together.

After another night of very little sleep, Dwayne and Tammy were eager to pull the first trap of the season and said their good-byes with a quick kiss before driving out of the harbor in separate boats.

Tired but excited about what the season may have in store, Tammy hummed a cheerful tune as she made her way over to the first set of traps.

Ten minutes later, she had the rope to the first trap of the season in the pulley, anxiously waiting for it to spring out of the water and land on the trap table, and, when it did, she was shocked by what she saw.

The trap was empty—not even a short lobster. In all the years they had fished the island, this had always been a good spot.

Tammy's jaw dropped. "What the hell?" she gasped. "Well, that's not a bloody good start." Being the first trap, Tammy tried her best not to feel discouraged, and after refreshing the bait, she quickly dropped it back into the water, eager to go on to the next one.

She wasted no time and sped off to the second trap and quickly pulled it out of the water. It was no better than the first one. "Frigging empty!" Tammy cussed. "God, we'd better have something in the third one. This is eerie," she said out loud, feeling somewhat worried.

After pulling five traps and only getting three short lobsters, she should have at least twenty keepers by now; Tammy was beyond worried. It scared her. "Where the hell are all the lobsters?" She said with her lips quivering. "I have to call Dwayne and see if it's any better at his end. God, I hope so."

Tammy put the boat in idle and pulled the microphone off its cradle. "Dwayne, you got me? Over."

It took Dwayne a few minutes to come back. "Yeah, I got you. Over."

Tammy noticed his flat tone and could tell he wasn't happy. "Are you catching anything? Over."

"I have two keepers out of ten traps. I hope it gets better than this. Not a good way to start the season. How about you? Over." Dwayne said, sounding somewhat discouraged.

"Well, you've done better than me. I've pulled five traps and gotten only three shorts." She raised her voice a notch. "What the hell is going on? Over."

"You're kidding! Well, shit, this isn't good. I'm going to give Mitch a shout and see if he's doing any better. If he is, he probably won't tell me, though. Fishermen never tell." Dwayne said, followed by a forced laugh. "I'll call you back in a few minutes. I'm out."

Tammy hung up the microphone and thought about all the money they had invested in getting to the island and how much they were in debt. "Shit. This isn't good," she whispered under her breath.

While she waited for Dwayne to get back to her, she pulled three more traps out of which she got one legal lobster and three more shorts, which had to be thrown back into the water. "Hurry and grow up, so I can keep you," she yelled at the small lobsters as she tossed them overboard.

The sound of Dwayne's voice over the radio startled her. "Hey Tammy, you got me? Over."

Tammy quickly reached up and grabbed the microphone. "Yes, I'm here. So, did he tell you?" she asked with bated breath.

"Yep. He's not catching any either. He said he has six lobsters out of twelve traps, and the other boats aren't doing that great either."

A rush of panic swept through Tammy. "Dwayne, this is not good. What are we going to do? Over."

"Maybe the lobsters don't know it's opening day. Over." he joked, trying to make light-heart of the situation that had him concerned, but he didn't want to worry Tammy. "We'll talk more back at the harbor. How many more traps do you have left to pull? Over," Dwayne asked.

"About twenty. Over."

"Okay, I'll see you back at the harbor when you are done. Call me when you are heading back in. I'm out."

After pulling the rest of the line, Tammy was even more discouraged. Before heading back to the harbor, she called Dwayne to let him know she was done. She returned with eight lobsters when normally she should have at least fifty to a hundred from the line she had just pulled.

The *Little Boat* was much faster than the *Baywitch II*, and Tammy reached the harbor before Dwayne. While she waited for him, she put her measly catch of lobsters into a receiver and restocked the bait. Fifteen minutes later, she heard the familiar sound of the *Baywitch II* and saw Dwayne heading her way.

When he was close enough, he waved, wearing a solemn look. "This doesn't look good," Tammy muttered under her breath.

For the first time, after a day's catch, Dwayne tossed her the line without smiling. Tammy didn't smile either as she tied off the boat.

Once the boats were secured and the motors shut off, they could talk. "So, how did it go?" Tammy asked, as she stepped on to the *Baywitch II*.

"Lousy," Dwayne replied, still wearing a frown. "I got fifteen lobsters."

"Well, that's better than my eight," Tammy said. "What the hell are we going to do?"

Dwayne put his lobsters in the receiver with the ones Tammy caught and rinsed his hands off in the ocean water. He turned to face Tammy, looking concerned. "I don't know . The day isn't over yet. Maybe the rest of the gear will be better."

"And if it's not?" Tammy said with her hands on her hips. "We are screwed. We owe so much money back home. And how are we supposed to come back out here if we don't have the money to buy more bait and fuel?" Tammy said with an edge to her voice.

Dwayne shook his head and brushed by her. "I don't know yet, Tammy. I don't have all the answers. You know as well as I do this is the worst opener we've ever had. Let's pull the rest of the gear and see what it's like before we fret over what we don't have."

"Easy for you to say. I'm scared, Dwayne."

Dwayne rubbed her shoulders and cracked a small smile. "It will be okay. Maybe the moon has something to do with it. I don't know, but I won't get discouraged so quickly. Now come on, the clock is ticking," he said as he jumped on the *Little Boat* and fired it up.

The rest of the day wasn't any better. Trap after trap, they pulled up empties or ones with shorts and very few keepers. As the day dragged on, the words between them became fewer and fewer. They were both on autopilot, doing the tasks together that they had done for years. But this year, there were no cheers or claps or joyful laughter—just frowns and many cuss words when another trap came up empty.

On their way back into the harbor, Tammy shouted above the loud noise of the motor. "Now, do you feel discouraged?" Tammy said with sarcasm. "And I'm also a little worried, I might add."

Dwayne ignored her question. "This is so frigging weird. I don't get it. And it's not just us. No one is catching any lobsters. Where the hell did the lobsters all go?" He slowed down the boat and headed to their mooring. A few of the other boats were back, including Mitch on the *Sea Life*.

"I'm going to swing by Mitch's boat and see what he thinks."

Tammy nodded and glanced over at the *Sea Life*. "He's on the deck waving at us. Maybe he has some good news."

A few minutes later, they pulled alongside Mitch's boat. Tammy threw him a line, and once they were tied off, Dwayne turned off the engine.

"Hey, guys. I hope you did better than I did today. It is the worst I've ever seen it out here," Mitch said, with his arms folded.

Dwayne shook his head. "I doubt it. We're going to be lucky if we have fifty lobsters. That won't even pay for fuel." Dwayne moaned.

Mitch nodded. "I hear ya. There's nothing out here. Kinda freaky, don't you think?"

"I'd say if this doesn't change in the next day or so, I don't know what we're going to do," Dwayne said. He turned and looked at Tammy, who was sitting on the edge of the boat. "Tammy is pretty worried. I can't say I blame her."

"You're damn right, I'm worried," Tammy snapped.

Dwayne forced Tammy a smile before speaking to Mitch again.

"Yeah, we need that kick start here, and it just ain't happening this year. You know how it is. You leave town owing everyone money and can't return until we can pay them," Dwayne laughed.

Mitch cracked a laugh. "Yeah, you got that right."

"I think we will stick it out another day and see what tomorrow is like before we make any hasty decisions," Dwayne said, seeking approval from Tammy.

Tammy nodded.

"Okay, man. Well, we're going to head back and get ready for tomorrow. Good luck out there."

"You too, man," Mitch said, as he untied their line and tossed it over to Tammy.

Tammy couldn't think it could get any worse, but the next day proved her wrong. By the end of the day, exhausted and emotionally drained from worry, Dwayne and Tammy were at a loss on what to do.

After returning to the harbor with their nerves on edge, they hosed and cleaned the *Little Boat* in silence. Once she finished, Tammy grabbed the straps to her slickers and spoke with a sharp tone. "So, what are we going to do? Am I cutting bait for tomorrow, or can I take these damn things off?"

"I don't know, Tammy. What do you want to do?" Dwayne said, matching her tone.

Tammy rolled her eyes. "You're the captain, you tell me."

"Don't pull that with me, Tammy. We are in this together," he snapped and shook his head before softening his voice. "Tell you what. Before we get into a fight, let's drop everything and have some hot chocolate. We'll calm down and discuss our options."

Tammy mellowed her tone, "Sounds like a good idea," she agreed as she peeled off her slickers and hung them on a hook behind her. "I'll have the drinks ready in a jiffy."

Ten minutes later, Tammy smacked her lips from the sweet taste of the chocolate sliding down her throat "Damn, that tastes good." She leaned back in the deck chair and closed her eyes. She loved these rare moments where she felt like she was being rocked gently to sleep by the swift motion of the boat swaying in the harbor.

Dwayne had taken a seat next to her, and he, too had his eyes closed as he thought deeply about what they were going to do.

"You know we don't have any choice but to stick it out here. We are committed to all the traps we have in the water, and all the bait will go bad if we don't use it," he said.

Tammy sighed, "I was afraid you were going to say that," as she sat up and took another sip of her drink. "But what if the rest of the week is just as bad? How are we going to pay all the bills we owe and have enough money to come back out?"

"I don't know yet, Tammy. We are going to have to wait and see where we stand by the end of the week."

"Well, from what I can see, it doesn't look very promising." She shook her head and sighed again. "Where the hell are all the bloody lobsters?"

"A few of the guys are saying it's because of El Nino."

Tammy creased her brow. "The what? What the hell is that?"

"It's when the surface waters are warmer than usual. When we have an El Nino, the lobsters don't crawl as much. Whether it's a myth, I don't know. But this is the year of the El Nino, and we don't have many lobsters. So, what does that tell you?"

Tammy shook her head and gulped down the rest of her drink before pulling herself up out of her chair. "All I know is if we don't start catching some lobsters pretty soon, we're going to be in deep shit. I guess I'll go cut some bait if we are going to stay here."

Tammy and Dwayne worked hard for the rest of the week, from sunrise to sunset. They spent hours moving gear in the hopes the new spots would bring them a good catch. They baited with extra bait and measured the smaller lobsters twice in case they were right on the brink of being legal. They couldn't afford to make any mistakes and throw away a keeper. Each day they became more discouraged as the catches became fewer and fewer. They were tired and sore. Their muscles ached, and their tempers grew short.

"Fuck! I'm sick of this!" Tammy screamed, after they had pulled another empty trap.

The tension on the boat was strong. Spirits were low, and Tammy was at her wit's end. Most days, they pulled the traps in silence, and each time another empty trap came up, Tammy held back her tears and yelled a few choice words to vent her frustrations.

Each night back in the harbor, Tammy yearned to go for a long walk to gather her thoughts. But there was nowhere to go. She was stuck bobbing around on a thirty-foot boat. For the first time in all her years fishing, she didn't want to be there. She had known from day one that every year was a gamble. They forked out thousands of dollars, hoping they would make ten times or more back. Their gambles had paid off until now, but this trip had Tammy afraid for their future. How would they ever climb out of the hole they had dug themselves into?

On their last day, any hopes they'd had of getting a good catch were gone. They just went through the motions of pulling their gear as quickly as they could. They wanted to pack up and head back to the mainland as fast as possible to sell what lobsters they had. Afterward, they would then try to figure out what the hell they were going to do.

Within twelve hours of returning to the mainland, feeling exhausted and with little enthusiasm for the rest of the season, Dwayne and Tammy sold their smallest catch ever from an opening season. They made just enough to catch up on their rent and pay a few of the other outstanding bills. The rest would have to wait until next month. Tammy just hoped their next catch would be better. "Hey, let's not say anything to my mom about how terrible fishing has been. I don't want her to worry," Tammy said on their way back from the store.

Dwayne nodded. "Sure."

Tammy was beyond distraught. For the first time since she had fished, she was scared and feared what the rest of the season might be like. She couldn't believe how drastically the catch had dropped, and it wasn't just them; all the boats at the island had one of their worst openings ever. She and Dwayne had worked so hard, and like every year, they were expecting a good payoff with extra money left in the bank. But so far, their goals were nowhere near being reached.

"What are we going to do?" Tammy said, "My mom will leave in three weeks. Fishing Malibu won't cut it."

Dwayne reached over and rubbed her thigh. "I know. There was a message from Stan, an old fishing buddy of mine I'm still in contact with. He is fishing off Dana Point. He wants me to call him. Maybe he has some ideas. I'm sure everyone has heard how bad it is out at the island by now. I'll call him as soon as we get home."

Tammy folded her arms and leaned back. "Isn't that north of San Diego?"

"Yes, it is," Dwayne replied.

"Okay, and remember, don't say anything to my mom."

When they arrived home, Tammy joined her mom and Matt in the backyard while Dwayne made his phone call. Matt was always super excited when they returned. He was always so eager to share with her his adventures with his nan, which is what he now called her. The worry that consumed her derailed her return home. Tammy forced her smiles as she tried to listen to Matt's recap of his week with nana. But she heard none of it. Her mind was distracted. Anxious to hear about Dwayne's phone call with Stan.

Dwayne told her he had set aside enough cash to buy more bait and fuel, but they would have nothing after that. They desperately needed a good catch on their next trip, but he feared it might be a repeat of the last one.

Tammy couldn't wait any longer. She was dying to know what Stan and Dwayne discussed and told Matt she'd be right back.

She walked into the living room just as Dwayne was hanging up the phone. Tammy stood in the doorway, leaning against the doorjamb with her arms folded. "So, what was all that about?" She said with a sense of urgency.

Dwayne, who was sitting on the couch, showed a slight smirk when he spoke. "Stan says they are slaying them down in Dana Point. Every day his traps have been plugged."

Tammy's jaw dropped. "What? How can that be?"

Dwayne shrugged his shoulders. I have no idea. I guess the El Nino is good for the coastal waters."

Tammy rolled her eyes. "Just our luck to be fishing in the wrong spot during an El Nino."

"Stan says we should move all our gear down there. He said we'd make a killing."

Tammy gasped, and her eyes grew wide. "You're kidding, right?"

Dwayne's smirk reappeared. "I'm not sure if I am. I would like to see for myself before committing."

"And how do you plan on doing that?" Tammy asked.

"Stan has offered to take me out on his boat early tomorrow morning so I can see his traps as he pulls them."

Tammy nodded. "That's not a bad idea. What time would you be leaving?"

"Well, it is a two to three-hour drive from here, and he leaves the dock at five, so I need to leave no later than two in the morning." Dwayne hesitated. "But I also want to take some of our gear down there in the truck."

Tammy shook her head and scrunched her brow. "What? But we have no gear here except for the sixty bare ones in the backyard, and they have no rope and aren't ready to fish yet."

"Those are the ones I'm talking about. Look, what if they are slaying them down there? Wouldn't it be a good idea to have some gear with me to dump in the water? Instead of racing back here."

Tammy ran his idea through her head. "Yeah, I guess," she mumbled, feeling defeated. She checked her watch. "It's already three o'clock. So, what are you saying? We need to hustle and get the gear in the yard ready?"

"Not necessarily all of them right now. I can probably fit only fifteen in my truck. Let's rig those up and load them in the truck. It will take a few hours, and then we can work on rigging up the rest. Whatever we don't get done, you can finish up while I'm with Stan."

Tammy walked across the room and took a seat next to Dwayne. "So I guess we're are not heading out to the island tomorrow?"

"I'm not too excited about that place after last week. I'd like to go check out Dana Point and decide what we are going to do when I get back."

Tammy patted his thigh. "Okay, Captain. You're the boss. Now I just gotta figure out what I'm going to tell my mom."

"Just tell her the truth. We're trying a new spot. No big deal."

"Yeah, you're right. I don't know why I'm afraid to tell her. It's not like she pays any attention or knows where we fish in the first place," Tammy laughed. She smacked Dwayne's leg before pulling herself off the couch. "Well, those traps aren't going to rig themselves. Let's do this," she said, as she motioned with her hand for Dwayne to get up. "I'll put Matt to work, too. He's a good helper."

For the rest of the afternoon and well into the night with the floodlights lit, they worked hard getting most of the traps rigged, and with Matt's help, they stacked fifteen of them in the bed of the truck.

When ten o'clock rolled around, Tammy insisted Dwayne stop working, take a shower and try to get at least a few hours of sleep.

"You can't go all night and then be out on a boat all day with no sleep," Tammy barked when Dwayne protested.

Dwayne knew better than to argue. He had lost this battle. "Fine. Are you going to be able to finish the last dozen traps?" Dwayne asked.

"Yeah, I got this." She turned and gave her son a loving smile. "You are done too, Matt. Why don't you go inside, wash up before Dwayne jumps in the shower, and watch some TV with nan? It's almost your bedtime."

Matt scrunched his face, "but mom."

"No buts, Matt. You've been a tremendous help, but it's getting late."

Matt folded his arms and let out a heavy sigh before heading into the house. "Fine."

Tammy shook her head and chuckled at his mannerism before heading back to work by herself with the floodlights illuminating the yard and the radio playing in the background. By midnight she had all the traps rigged and stacked by the back gate, ready to go if needed. She was filthy, her body was sore, and it exhausted her. She was too tired to take a bath and made a pot of coffee for Dwayne before crawling into bed next to him, and before she fell asleep, she woke him with a smooch and a cuddle.

Dwayne stirred and smiled when he felt Tammy's arms embrace his chest.

"Time to get up, sweetie," Tammy whispered in his ear, kissing him on the cheek before she closed her eyes.

"Hey, babe. How did it go?" Dwayne whispered in a sleepy voice. She didn't reply, and then he heard her faint breathing through her nose. He soon realized she was already asleep. He smiled at the thought and, with care, gently slid out of her arms and left the room.

ammy slept undisturbed for a good solid seven hours. She couldn't remember the last time she had gotten such a good night's rest. She was thankful for her mom being there to take care of Matt. Tammy had watched over the years, the close bond that had formed between Matt and her mom. They had something special that couldn't go unnoticed.

Tammy didn't like that she couldn't communicate with Dwayne while he was out on the boat with Stan. Her mind wouldn't rest. The anticipation of how they did was driving her crazy. If the catch was good, what will Dwayne's next move be? She didn't even want to think about what they would do if it were bad.

Her questions would soon be answered when she heard Dwayne's truck pull up in the alley and park in front of their garage. She was outside coiling rope with Matt while her mom sat at the patio table, reading a book and drinking hot tea.

Eager to hear his report of the day, Tammy dropped the half-coiled rope on the ground. "I'll be right back," she told Matt, as she raced through the back gate to join Dwayne.

When he exited the truck, Tammy was just walking around to

the driver's side. She paused; his beaming smile told her he had a good day.

"Tell me you have good news," Tammy said as she wrapped her arms around him and pulled him in close. "I've missed you."

He looked ragged and tired. His clothes smelt of bait, and his skin felt dry from the sun. He beamed her another smile, squeezed her tight, and gave her a long hard kiss. "It was better than good. It was unbelievable! I've never seen so many lobsters in one trap."

Tammy's eyes grew wide. "Really!" She wiped a fish scale off his cheek. She was worried about him. As much as she wanted to talk about what he wanted to do next, he needed to rest. "You look so tired. Why don't you take a shower and a nap? We can talk later about what you want to do."

Dwayne took both her hands and gave her a hard stare. He shook his head. "No, I want to take more traps down there while the fishing is good. No one knows how long it will last. If it sticks around, we can make up for the awful catch we had last week."

Tammy gasped and rolled her eyes. She placed her hands on her hips and gave him an icy stare. "Dwayne, you can't drive back down there. You need to get some rest."

Dwayne shook his head. "I'll be fine. We need to get the rest of the traps to the harbor and in the water. It's going to take three trips. Stan said he would take them out on his boat first thing in the morning if we have them stacked on his dock and ready to go."

Tammy used a sharper tone. She didn't like his plan, and she hated it when he acted so hard-headed. "I won't let you drive all that way with no sleep."

Dwayne cracked a sarcastic laugh. "You have no choice, Tammy. I'm not missing out on this opportunity. I'll be fine."

Tammy folded her arms. "Yes, I do have a choice, Dwayne. We both do. Especially for our safety, and it's not safe for you to drive. You've hardly slept in the last twenty-hours." She pondered for a minute and then smiled at him. "Tell you what. Help me stack the next load onto the truck, and I'll take them down."

Dwayne questioned her. His face was masked with surprise and uncertainty. "What? Are you sure?"

"Yes, I'm sure, and I won't let you talk me out of it. Write down the address and the boat slip number. We can relay. While I'm gone, you rest, and I'll do the same when you take the second load down."

Dwayne raised his hands in defeat and laughed. "Okay, you win. I know when I'm defeated. Matt can help too."

Tammy smiled. "Good idea. Hey Matt!" Tammy hollered.

It took them an hour to load the truck, and by four, Tammy was on the freeway driving to Dana Point. She hoped to be there in two hours, but an hour into her drive, the traffic was crawling at fifteen miles an hour. She spat out her words. "Shit, I forgot about rush hour." The traffic was going to cost her another hour.

By the time she reached the unfamiliar marina, the fishing boats were quiet, tied up to the docks with no one on board. She was the only one there. Tammy walked down the ramp onto the dock lined with lobster boats searching for Stan's vessel called *Fishing Fool*. She released a smile when she came upon it almost immediately. "Well, that's good it's close to the ramp," Tammy whispered and scanned the area around the boat in search of a good place to put the traps. She found the perfect spot on the other side of the boat and wasted no time in grabbing the first load.

Her first task was to climb on top of the stack of traps and untie the hand truck Dwayne had remembered to grab at the last minute. After struggling with the tight knots Dwayne had made, she used all her strength to lift the heavy metal hand truck over the top of the traps while keeping her balance as she lowered it to the ground. Her chest heaved, and she sucked in air as she slowly eased herself down the traps and off the truck. "Well, that was a chore," she gasped.

After she rested for a few minutes, she climbed the stack again to untie the top traps and then wondered how she would get them down by herself. She didn't want to overthink it and put on her gloves she had stuck in her back pocket and pulled a trap forward.

Tammy took in a deep breath, and with both hands, she grabbed the heavy trap and pulled it to the edge, where she balanced it as she climbed down and planted her feet firmly on the ground. She stood on her toes and stretched her body to the max and smiled when she discovered she could reach the trap. Slowly she inched the heavy trap more to the edge, praying it wouldn't come crashing down on top of her. When it was finally at a pivoting point, she pulled hard and took the full weight of the trap, guiding it to the ground as she let out a loud painful grunt. "Fuck, that's heavy!" she hollered. "Why do they always seem much heavier when they are out of the water?" Tammy repeated the maneuver two more times until she had three traps stacked on the hand truck. "God, this is going to take forever, and we have two more trips to do. This is bloody insane," Tammy complained, as she pushed the heavy load toward the ramp. When she reached the top of the ramp out of breath, she stopped and peered down the steep ramp. "Now, how the hell am I going to wheel this down there?" She feared it would gain speed and get away from her.

Again, Tammy took a deep breath and slowly pushed the hand truck to the crest of the ramp. "Well, here goes nothing." She planted her feet firmly on the wooden ramp as she inched the hand truck down the incline by taking baby steps. It took all her strength to hold it back from getting away from her, and as she neared the bottom, she felt she was losing it and ran the last four feet. "Fuck!" she yelled, as she finally touched the dock where she stood the hand truck upright, and leaned forward, gasping for air. Tammy keeled over and rested her hands on her knees as she sucked in oxygen. "Shit, I have to do that five more times. I'm going to bloody kill myself."

After catching her breath, she found the strength to push the heavy load of traps to the dock next to the boat. She rested again before stacking them. "This is bullshit. We better get some friggin lobsters after all this." Tammy cursed as she wheeled the empty hand-truck up the ramp to grab another load.

It took her just over an hour to take all the traps down to the dock. By the time she was finished, beads of sweat had poured from her brow. Her hair was drenched, and her soaked t-shirt stuck to her moist back. Tammy could hardly lift the hand truck into the bed of the truck and released a loud moan as she slid it up onto the tailgate and pushed it with a hard shove.

By eight-fifteen she was back on the freeway heading north. She was pleased to see rush hour was over and made it back to the house within two hours, even after stopping to get gas.

It surprised her to find Dwayne already awake and dressed, packing some last-minute items.

"Oh man, you look beat," Dwayne said, when she staggered into the house, holding her back. He walked across the kitchen and held out his arms.

Tammy welcomed his embrace and rested her head on his chest. "That was a lot of frigging work for one person. My back is killing me." She looked around the room. "Where's Matt and mom?"

"They are in Matt's room doing a jig-saw puzzle. Tell you what, I'll have Matt help me load the next stack. Why don't you go soak in the tub and get some rest?"

Tammy smiled and pulled herself out of his embrace while squeezing her side. "You don't have to ask me twice. There's gas in the truck. Wake me up when you get back; I'm going with you on the boat. I want to see the catch for myself."

Dwayne kissed her forehead. "You are such a trooper. It's one reason I love you. I'll see you in a few hours."

*D*wayne returned at two o'clock in the morning feeling and looking as tired as Tammy did when she had made her trip. He knew they would have to leave no later than three-thirty to make it to Stan's boat by six, and even that was cutting it close. But he had to get at least an hour of sleep before making the trip one more time. He set the alarm for three and let his clothes fall off his body onto the floor before quietly crawling into bed next to Tammy, who was sound asleep.

When the alarm went off, Dwayne turned, mumbled, and pulled the sheets over his head. Tammy stirred and was surprised to see Dwayne lying next to her. She gave his shoulder a gentle nudge. "Dwayne, wake up."

"Five more minutes," he whined from beneath the covers.

"What time did you get home?"

"About an hour ago," he groaned.

Tammy nudged him again. "I'm sorry, I know you're tired, but we have to get up. We can't be late. Stan may leave without us." She pulled the covers away from her body and stood to her feet. "I'm going to go make us some coffee. Come on, babe, wakey, wakey," she said, before giving him another nudge.

Dwayne rolled onto his back and pulled his head up out of the comfort of the covers. He rubbed his eyes and yawned. "Okay, I'm up."

Before leaving, Tammy snuck into Matt's room, where he was sleeping on the top bunk. She tip-toed across the room and kissed his hand softly that was hanging over the edge. "I'll see you tonight, buddy."

She left a note for her mom, thanking her for being there, and then quietly tip-toed out of the house.

With it being so early, there was no traffic, and they reached Stan's boat in record time with even thirty-minutes to spare, which gave them enough time to load the traps onto the boat.

"You made it," Stan said before taking a hit off his cigar and a swig of coffee, which he held in his other hand.

Dwayne shook his hand. "Yeah, neither one of us got much sleep last night. We took turns bringing the gear down while the other one slept."

Stan cracked a laugh. "The things we do to catch a lobster."

Dwayne nodded. "No, kidding."

Stan turned to Tammy and smiled. "So, you are the Mrs."

Tammy gave him a friendly smile and held out her hand. "I sure am. I've heard a lot about you."

Stan gave Dwayne a devious smile. "What have you been telling her?" he chuckled.

Even if Dwayne hadn't told her that Stan had been fishing for over twenty years, Tammy saw the signs. He was older than Dwayne. Probably in his late 50s. Like most fishermen that had spent their days being baked by the sun while on the ocean. His skin was dry and rough looking. His dark brown hair was mid-length and had no style. He wore a black t-shirt that showed off his buff, tanned arms. It was something Tammy had noticed on all the fishermen she had met—no matter how old they were, their arms were always muscular from hauling gear all day.

Tammy soon discovered that Stan ran a tight ship. Five minutes before the top of the hour, Stan fired up the boat while she and Dwayne finished loading the last five traps onto the deck. Stan checked his watch. "We'll be heading out in approximately five minutes. If there's anything you need from your truck, you'd better grab it now."

Dwayne glanced over at Tammy. "Need anything?" he asked.

Tammy shook her head. "No, I'm good. I already put the ice chest on the boat."

"Okay, then we're out of here," Stan yelled above the loud sound of the engine. "Dwayne, I'll let you untie the boat," he said from the helm.

Tammy jumped on the boat and stood out of the way so the two men could prepare to leave the dock.

It didn't take them long to reach their destination, and within a half-hour, Tammy was baiting the first of their traps to prepare for them being dropped in the spots Stan recommended.

"You could give these traps a few days' soaking if you wanted to. Nothing is going to eat the lobsters like at San Clemente." Stan told Dwayne as he pushed the first trap over the side and into the water.

"That's good to know," Dwayne hollered as he grabbed another baited trap.

It took them a couple of hours to get all the traps in the water, and then they headed over to Stan's gear and anxiously waited for him to pull up his first trap.

Tammy stood close to Dwayne and the trap table and peered into the water to watch the trap immerse.

When it landed on the table, Tammy gasped. The trap was plugged with lobsters. Most of them looked legal too. "Holy shit!" Tammy squealed. "It's loaded. And the lobsters are huge."

Dwayne beamed her a smile. "I told you."

Stan handed her a gauge. "Here, why don't you measure them, and I'll drive to the next trap."

"A lot of them don't need to be measured," Tammy laughed. "I can tell just by looking at them they are twice the legal size."

The number of lobsters that were in the trap stunned Tammy. By the time they had finished measuring the lobsters, Stan had thirty legal lobsters in the barrel. "Wow! That's incredible," Tammy said. She quickly baited the trap and tossed it over the side before they grabbed the next one close by.

They continued down the line, and each trap was just as good as the first one. Stan did not have one empty trap and very few shorts. By the end of the day, Tammy felt excited about the few traps she and Dwayne had in the water. Stan's catch that day was as good as a normal opener at the island.

"Is it always this good out here?" Tammy asked, as she jumped off the boat onto the dock and tied the line around a cleat.

"No. I've never seen it this good before. It's normally like Malibu, but this El Nino we have this year makes the lobsters crawl for some reason."

"Not at the island," Dwayne chuckled.

Stan shook his hand. "Well, I hope this turns it around for you. Let me know how it goes. Do you have any more gear you can put in the water?" he asked.

"Nah, it's all on the island."

"Well, you might want to think about bringing some down here."

"That's not a bad idea. I'll think about it." Dwayne shook his hand. "Thanks for everything. You've been a great help."

"My pleasure. Now I gotta tend to these lobsters. We'll talk soon, guys."

They left Stan to tend to his business, and once they were in the truck, Dwayne turned to Tammy and draped his arm over her shoulder. "What do you think about heading out to San Clemente and grabbing some more gear to fish here?"

Tammy creased her brow and gave Dwayne a sharp stare. "You're kidding, right?"

"No, I'm not. I'm serious. It's where the lobsters are, and we need more gear in the water if we are going to make any kind of real money."

Tammy leaned her head back and closed her eyes for a moment. She didn't like Dwayne's idea. "But it will take us a day to get there and then another day to get back here, and that doesn't count pulling the gear out of the water and stacking it on the boat." She shook her head. "And then we still have to bait and put them in the water here. When the hell would we sleep? I'm still exhausted from last night."

Dwayne rubbed her shoulder, "I know. I'm tired too. We could do it in shifts and drive through the night to the island. We could be on the *Baywitch II* by this evening. It has fuel, and we have bait in the freezer. What do you say? If we push ourselves, we could be at Dana Point with a boat full of traps by late tomorrow night. We could spend the night on the boat at a guest dock and dump them the next morning."

Tammy buried her head in her hands. "Oh, I don't know, Dwayne. I am so damn tired as it is."

"You can sleep in the truck on the way home. I'll drop you off at the house so you can rest some more while I get the boat ready and load up the bait."

Tammy shook her head. "No, that's not fair. I won't have you do all the work."

Dwayne gave her a loving smile. "Does that mean you'll do this with me?"

"Yes, I guess. We are in this together, after all."

Dwayne planted a big kiss on her lips. "Yes! Okay then, let's get going. I'm excited. Aren't you?"

Tammy laughed at his enthusiasm. "I'll start getting excited after I've gotten some rest—no need to drop me off at the house. I'll come down to the boat and help you load up the bait. We can go to the house together and pack some food and clean clothes. I hope Matt will still be awake. I miss him, and I want to say goodbye to him and see how mom is doing."

Tammy fell asleep as soon as they were on the road heading north. She slept soundly for the next two hours. It was only when the truck came to a full stop and woke her up. She looked out the window and saw they were in front of their house.

"Hey, we're here, sleepyhead," Dwayne said as he gently nudged her shoulder.

Tammy rubbed her eyes. It was still light out. "What time is it?" she asked.

"Almost seven. I want to be on the boat within the hour."

"Sure. I just need to clean up and grab a few things and pack our food."

Matt came out to greet them and asked with wide eyes about the fishing. Tammy couldn't hold the excitement in her voice and told him about the amazing catch Stan had, and that they were heading out to the island to grab more traps to take to Dana Point.

"Can I go?" Matt asked.

"No, you can't go. You have school."

Matt let out a loud moan of disapproval. "God, I hate school." He moped into the house.

Dwayne and Tammy made it to the boat in record time, and by eight-thirty they had everything loaded and were heading down the main channel for a long ten-hour crossing to the island.

Dwayne was at the wheel, but Tammy could see how tired he was. He kept rubbing his eyes, and she watched as they periodically closed for a few seconds. He was exhausted. Tammy approached him and took his hand. "Hey, why don't you go lie down for a bit and get some rest. You've not slept in almost thirty-six hours. I can drive for a while."

Dwayne smiled at her. "Are you sure? It's a clear night, and the stars are out. You shouldn't have any problems."

"Yes, I'm sure. Let me grab my jacket, and then I'll take the wheel."

He leaned in and gave her a soft kiss on the lips. "Thanks. A nap would be good."

Tammy drove for the next four hours while Dwayne slept with no interruptions. She wanted him to sleep as much as he could because she knew once they reached the island around six in the morning, there would be no time for rest. He emerged from the cabin with his hair uncombed and his clothes wrinkled, but what caught Tammy's attention was his large grin.

"Hey handsome, feeling better?"

Dwayne steadied himself as he climbed the last two steps onto the deck, looked out at the vast ocean, and saw Catalina behind them.

"Oh, wow, we're on the backside of Catalina Island."

"Yes, you slept for a good four hours." Tammy stood up from the Captain's chair. "Now it's my turn. Wake me up when we are almost there."

Before she left, Dwayne took her in his arms and gave her a long sensual kiss. "You're amazing."

Tammy tilted back her head and laughed and patted his chest. "You're not so bad yourself. I love you."

He squeezed her waist." I love you too. Now go on, get some sleep," he said, as he patted her behind.

As much as Tammy needed sleep, she never had slept well on a boat, especially moving at eight knots across the ocean. She had slept little over the past twenty-four hours, and as exhausted as she was, she couldn't fall asleep. For the next few hours, she laid wide awake, feeling frustrated, and finally gave up on sleep.

"What are you doing up?" Dwayne asked, looking surprised to see her.

"I can't sleep. And I got bored." She laughed and walked over to Dwayne's side, where he cradled her in his arm. Dwayne shook his head. "You're going to be sorry."

By the time they reached the harbor a little after six in the morning, Tammy felt the fatigue immensely and would have given anything to be curled up in her bed right about now instead of being on a cold, damp boat on a remote island. They were not surprised to see the harbor empty. It was light out, and the boats were probably out pulling their gear already. Dwayne didn't want to lose time calling them on the radio and wasted no time driving over to the first trap while Tammy balanced herself to put on her slickers, which was always a challenge on a moving boat.

For the next five hours, Dwayne and Tammy pulled fifty traps and stacked them on the boat. Tammy struggled with the last ten. Her back burned from the constant heavy lifting, and every time she grabbed a trap, she winced, as her body was in pain, she could barely coil her fingers around the wire to get a good grip on the trap. Each one seemed to weigh more than the previous one. Every time she dragged one off the trap table to stack it, she released a loud moan of agony.

"We better get some goddamn lobsters after this," Tammy hollered, as she steadied herself against a stack of traps while a large swell passed under the boat. When it had passed, and the intense rocking subsided, Tammy took her place with the gaff while Dwayne drove to the last trap.

It was almost eleven o'clock by the time they had fifty traps tied down on the *Baywitch II*.

"How are you holding up?" Dwayne asked, looking concerned. "I want you to go down below and get some rest. You've been going for over thirty hours and have only slept for a few hours in the truck."

Tammy was about to protest, but Dwayne raised his hand.

"And before you try to start an argument, I'm ordering you. I'm not asking you." He gave her a wink. "I'm using my captain's rank. okay?"

Tammy arched her back to pull out a few of the knots she was feeling. It didn't work. Her back was on fire. Her entire body ached as though she had never experienced it before, and she was on the verge of tears. It hurt to walk or raise her arms. Her legs felt like lead weights, and she dragged her feet as she made her way to the cabin. "No argument from me. I'm in so much pain right now." Tammy looked at the steps that descended into the cabin. She feared her legs would not carry her and inched her body lower to the ground until she was sitting on her behind.

Dwayne looked down from the helm, wearing a puzzled look. "What are you doing?"

"My legs are killing me. I'm afraid I'll fall if I try to walk down the steps, so I'm going to scooch down them on my butt."

Dwayne snickered. "Okay, and you can't come back until you've gotten some sleep. Captain's orders."

"Aye, Aye, Captain," Tammy said sarcastically.

I t surprised Tammy that she dozed off, but it didn't last long. The seas were growing, and the swells rocked the *Baywitch II* vigorously, and from inside the cabin, it was much more intense. Fearing she might be thrown from the bed by an angry wave, Tammy pulled herself to her feet and held onto the table for balance. Tammy peeked out of the cabin window and saw it was still light and suddenly jolted her head back when the ocean smacked the plexiglass of the cabin window. "What bloody time is it?" she whispered out loud, as she scanned the cabin. "Ten bloody years, and we still don't have a damn clock on this boat." Tammy pulled up her sleeve and squinted at her watch. It was two o'clock in the afternoon. She slept for roughly two hours.

"How are you doing up there?" Tammy hollered up to Dwayne. But he couldn't hear her over the loud engine. Tammy braced herself as another wave crashed against the hull before attempting to climb the steps up to the deck. She stopped midway and held on as the boat rocked heavily for a moment before climbing the last few steps.

When Tammy stepped out onto the deck, the sudden chill stung her face. Dwayne sat at the helm, bundled in a sweatshirt with the hood up. He hadn't seen her, and when Tammy rested her hand on his shoulder, he jumped.

"Damn, you scared me," he said, as he turned his upper body to face her.

"Sorry, I didn't mean to." Tammy was disturbed by how tired he looked. His eyes were dark and heavy, and his skin was pale. "Are you okay?"

"Yeah, hanging in there. You didn't sleep much."

"Nah. You know I have a hard time sleeping on the boat. I got a couple of hours in, though. I'm good."

Tammy watched Dwayne closely as he continued to drive and saw his eyes close for a few seconds before he'd shake his head and rub his eyes. She counted him doing it four times in five minutes and nudged his arm. "Why don't you let me drive. You're falling asleep."

"No, I'm not," Dwayne said defensively, as he held the rail for support.

Another wave hit the boat, and Tammy quickly took hold of the back of the captain's chair. "What's with this bloody ocean? I didn't hear of any weather coming."

"It just picked up a short while ago. I'm sure it will pass. Just some winds are making the swell increase," Dwayne said before giving his eyes another rub.

Tammy had seen enough. "Okay, that's it. Get up. I'm driving; lie down. You've been going since last night," Tammy said, using a stern voice.

Dwayne didn't argue and stood up from the captain's chair. "Okay, stay on that course," he said, pointing to the compass. "The autopilot is on, but we both know it goes off course a bit, so keep an eye on it. It's a new course. We're going to Dana Point, not the Marina."

"I know," Tammy said, as she took a seat, pushing Dwayne

towards the steps of the cabin. "Now go on, get out of here. I'm going to wake you when we are an hour out of port if you are still sleeping. I don't know the harbor. You will have to take us in."

Dwayne nodded and disappeared down into the cabin.

Tammy yanked her sweatshirt off the hook where it hung by the wheel, and while bracing herself with one hand, she slid it over her upper torso and welcomed the warmth before making herself comfortable in the Captain's chair. "Man, it's rough out here," she scowled while holding the wheel tight.

The waves continued to roar for the next hour, slamming the boat hard with bodies of water. The swells were not huge, but big enough where Tammy had to be constantly holding onto something for balance. "How the hell does Dwayne sleep in this shit?" Tammy called out, as the boat rocked hard from side to side. "I hope it's not going to be like this the whole way," she added, while looking out at the white-crested waves. "I don't know if my body can take eight more hours of abuse from the ocean," Tammy complained as another wave threw her off balance and into the wall of the helm. The side of her body hit the wall hard. "Ouch! That bloody hurt."

Finally, after two more hours of increased swells and wind, the weather calmed down, and Tammy eased her hold on the wheel and gave her cramped hands a rest. She checked her watch. They still had another four hours to go before they would be an hour out of Dana Point. Amazingly, Dwayne had slept through the rough seas and was still sound asleep when Tammy peeked her head through the doorway of the cabin. Tammy checked the skies and noticed clouds were rolling in and off to the distance, and saw where the clouds met the ocean. "Oh, wow! That looks like a fog bank." Very rarely had they hit fog, and when they did, Dwayne had always taken the wheel because it was so easy to get off course. Tammy had considered waking up Dwayne, but waited until they were closer. "I'll let him rest some more. I've got this."

Tammy kept her eyes peeled to the open waters ahead of her as the boat neared the thick fog bank that spanned for miles across the surface of the ocean. She wondered how thick it was and what her visibility would be like. But she wouldn't know until they were in the thick of it. Doubting herself and her inexperience, thoughts of waking Dwayne crossed her mind again, but this was an opportunity to gain the experience she lacked, and she chose to let him sleep. Her stomach churned with nerves as she grabbed the wheel and looked ahead at the eerie fog bank.

The clouds were getting denser and closer to the boat. Tammy checked her compass and saw the boat was still on course. She stuck her head out the side of the helm and felt the dewy mist in the air. In about an hour, the sun would go down. Tammy wondered if there would be enough time to pass through the fog before the skies turned dark?.

The tunnel of fog showed no mercy and engulfed the *Baywitch II* within minutes, leaving Tammy with a sense of isolation from the rest of the world. Tammy tightened her grip on the wheel. The thickness of the fog hindered her ability to see twenty feet in front of her. Regret and panic consumed her. "Fuck. I can't see a damn thing." Tammy expressed her fears out loud to herself. "I'm so friggin scared right now. What if there is another boat up head? I might hit it." Tammy's brow dripped with sweat, and her hands trembled around the cold metal wheel at the helm. Tammy released a huge sigh of relief after checking the radar and saw no flashing green dots, which meant there were no other boats in the area. "That's good there aren't any other boats near us." The compass told her they were still on course as she crawled along at a slow six knots.

Tammy scanned the entire perimeter of the boat and saw nothing but thick fog for what seemed miles. "Man, this is creepy." The fear of a drifting log or debris in their path prompted Tammy to slow down the boat even more. The last thing they needed was a hole in the boat. Still clutching the wheel, frozen with fear, Tammy's hands trembled. "God, what was I thinking? This is too bloody scary." Afraid to leave her station for even a second, she cried for help. "Dwayne!" But the loud noise of the engine blanketed her voice.

The minutes turned into what seemed hours. Her arms were tired from constantly steering, trying to stay on course. The aching she felt in her heavy, misty eyes caused the radar and compass to be a blur. Tammy gave her head a vigorous shake. When she did, the wet strands of her hair whipped her face. "Damn it! When is this going to end?"

When the skies darkened to the color of coal, Tammy searched hard for stars and saw none. They had been her savior many times in the past and had guided her home. Dwayne had told her one time when her eyes were tired from looking at the compass to pick a star and follow it. They never move, and it will lead you home. Since then, it had worked, and Tammy had preferred the navigation of a star over a compass. They were her angels in the sky and provided a sense of security. "I can't see one star. Where are you? My angels. I need you," Tammy cried.

From lack of sleep, Tammy strained to keep her eyes open or stay focused. The blanket of fog confused her bearings. There was no glimpse of a coastline. They were completely shielded from the rest of the world. Tammy tried to erase the horrific images that haunted her mind of them crashing on the shore, or even worse, slamming into another boat and possibly killing themselves or someone else. "God, I wish Dwayne would wake up. I have no idea if I am still on course." Angry with her stupidity, Tammy stomped her feet and screamed. "I don't want to do this anymore."

Tammy had lost all track of time and remained glued to the helm, desperately seeking for any signs that the fog may be lifting. After what seemed like an eternity, she believed it finally was. Suddenly she could see a few feet beyond the bow and then fifty feet more. She screamed with joy when she was able to see a hundred feet, "Oh my god, we are coming out of the fog bank." Tammy jumped up and down and cried happy tears. "We are going to make it. I did it." Tammy smiled and looked up to the skies. "Hello, stars. I've missed you." She suddenly jumped back when she felt something touch her shoulder.

"Hey, it's only me," Dwayne said, who stood behind her.

Tammy spun around and threw herself into his arms, "God, you scared me. I'm so happy you are awake. What a bloody ordeal I had."

Concerned, Dwayne broke free of their embrace. "What do you mean? What happened?"

"We hit a fog bank. It was bloody awful, and it lasted for hours."

Dwayne's jaw dropped, "You're kidding? Why didn't you wake me?"

"I was afraid to leave the wheel. I couldn't see shit. What if we hit a log of something for that few minutes I had left? I was so frigging scared. I never want to drive in the fog again."

Dwayne gave her a huge grin.

Tammy wasn't amused. "What are you smiling about? It wasn't funny, Dwayne."

"Don't you see what you did? And you did it all by yourself. I've always been afraid to let you drive in the fog because you can become so disoriented and get lost fast." He pulled her in his arms and kissed her hard on the lips. "But you didn't panic, you drove through it and kept your wits about you. Give yourself a big pat on the back, girl. I'm so proud of you."

Tammy rested her head on his chest. "I'm so tired. I think I will be able to sleep on the boat for once."

"Go on. Go down below and sleep the rest of the way. I've got this. I love you. Well done!"

She gave him a long, drawn-out kiss. "I love you too." And went down below.

The silence of the motors and the stillness of the boat woke Tammy from her well-needed sleep. She yawned and stretched, stopping mid-way when pain shot up her back. She winced. "Ouch!" Her back was on fire.

Dwayne must have heard her and peeked his head through the cabin doorway. "Are you okay?"

Tammy moved slowly, holding her side as she slid her aching body out of bed. "Yeah, my damn back is on fire. Are we here?"

"Yes, we are. Do you want to lie down some more?"

"No. I need to walk around." Tammy looked through the cabin window and saw it was dark outside. "What time is it?"

"Almost midnight."

Tammy used her hands and crawled out of the cabin to the deck, where Dwayne helped her to her feet. "Wow, it took us a long time to get here."

"Yea, the fog slowed us down. That was smart of you to slow down the boat."

"Yes. I slowed way down. I could have walked faster. It took forever."

Dwayne rubbed her shoulders, and Tammy hunched her back to reap the full benefits of his massaging hands. "God, that feels good. I'm so bloody tired." She pulled herself to a standing position and scanned their surroundings. There were six other boats tied in slips where they were docked. A few were sailboats and the rest commercial boats. "So, where are we?" Tammy asked.

"We're in Dana Point harbor."

"And what is the plan, Captain?" Tammy said with a hint of sarcasm.

"Well, I figured we could leave around five and bait these traps as we dump them, and then after, we can pull the traps that have been soaking for a few days. What do you think?"

"Okay, then. Let's go down below and grab some sleep. We only have a few hours."

T ammy had a restless night and got little sleep. She woke in a foul mood and to the sound of her stomach growling. Acid came roaring through her stomach with hunger pains. Living off granola bars and cans of tuna fish were not cutting it.

She didn't know what time it was and again wished they had a clock in the cabin. It was pitch black inside the boat, which told her it was still the wee hours of the morning, but she was too irritated and hungry to go back to sleep. Her hands searched for the flashlight stashed under the pillow in the dark. Once it was in her hands, Tammy held her breath and realized the boat was too quiet. The gentle snores from Dwayne couldn't be heard. She patted his pillow and discovered he was not lying next to her.

Puzzled, Tammy pulled herself out of bed and threw on a pair of jeans and a sweatshirt before heading up to the deck. She looked around the boat, and up and down the docks. Dwayne was nowhere to be found. "Where the hell is he?" Tammy whispered, checking her watch. It was nearing four, and they needed to leave in an hour. She scanned the docks for a guest bathroom, spotted it at the end, and then noticed Dwayne's exiting one, and stepped off the boat to meet him half-way.

"Hey, good morning, beautiful. Did you get some good sleep?" Dwayne asked, looking all perky and wide-eyed. Tammy didn't know how he did it.

Tammy frowned. "No. I didn't get hardly any, and I'm so bloody hungry."

"We'll grab a can of tuna and orange juice before we head out, okay."

"I'm sick of bloody tuna. I want a damn meal," Tammy snapped.

Dwayne gave her a smirk. "Well, look who got out of bed on the wrong side," he chuckled. "Tell you what, after we finish for the day, we'll dock the boat at the guest dock and go look for a restaurant, and I'll buy you a nice meal."

"I can't wait. I'll probably eat two meals. I'll meet you back at the boat. I'm going to use the restroom."

They left the dock at five and were eager to pull the few traps that had been soaking for the last few days, but they needed to unload the traps they had on the boat first.

Tammy struggled through the morning, getting each trap ready to dump while Dwayne drove the boat to the various spots. Over the past few days, her body had not recovered from the intense labor she was continually putting it through. She didn't know if she could make it to the end of the day. She was so tired that she was on the verge of tears. Any kind of body movement was followed by excruciating pain. Her back was on fire, her hands were swollen, and she could hardly move her fingers. Her legs were stiff, and she could barely feel her feet. Tammy was sure of it because of the way her boots felt, extra tight around her ankles. She struggled to keep her balance on the moving boat and many times stumbled back into the stack of traps, thankful Dwayne was facing the other way. She didn't want to do anything to prevent today's achievements from happening, and hid how much her body hurt from him. This season was already off to a terrible start, and if Dwayne knew the intense pain she was experiencing, he would insist they'd not work today. Tammy just wanted this to be over with. She wanted to go home and sleep in her warm bed after sitting down to a home-cooked meal and taking a hot bath with plenty of bubbles. Taking a day of rest would mean putting all those luxuries off for another day.

Tammy envied Dwayne's stamina, but it's what kept her going. He was definitely the backbone of their fishing business and kept their spirits high even through the low times. She loved how he always looked out for her and made no plans for their fishing adventures without talking them over with her first. He treated her as an equal partner, and she admired that about him.

After they dumped the last trap, Tammy wiped her brow and looked at the empty deck. It was a glorious sight.

Wearing a huge grin, Dwayne rubbed his hands together. His eyes were wide. "Are you ready to go pull some traps now and see how many lobsters we have?"

Tammy knew she should be excited, but for the first time, she wasn't feeling it. She just wanted to go home. "How do you do it? You just keep going."

Dwayne laughed. "Money, baby. It's all about the money. How are you holding up? Are you okay?"

Tammy lied. "Yeah, I'm fine. Just a little tired. I'll feel better once I see that first trap plugged with lobsters."

"That's my girl. Come here and kiss me."

It took them twenty minutes to get to the first trap that had been soaking since they left for the island over three days ago. Tammy finally felt the adrenaline rush she was used to each time they approached a trap. She was in position, holding the gaff ready to hook the line as Dwayne drove up to it.

"Got it!" she yelled in triumph.

Dwayne gave her a huge smile as he watched her wrap the line around the pulley. "Okay, here we go—trap number one. Bring me the money, baby!" he yelled.

Tammy laughed, and peered beneath the surface of the water as she anxiously waited for the trap to make an appearance through the murky water.

When it broke through the water and landed on the trap table, their hearts sank. The trap was empty.

"What the fuck?" Dwayne said in disbelief.

"Oh, come on! You're kidding me! Not again," Tammy snapped. "This is bullshit!" she yelled. "Now what?"

Dwayne tried to calm her down. "Maybe it's just this trap. Let's stack this one and move it to another spot and go to the next one."

"I'm sick of stacking and moving traps," Tammy screamed as she yanked the trap from the table and slid it to the back of the deck with force.

Dwayne waited until she was safely holding the rail before putting the boat in gear and heading to the next trap. The second trap wasn't any better. It had one legal lobster and two shorts.

"I don't understand. Where the hell did the lobsters go? Three days ago, Stan's traps were plugged," Dwayne said in despair.

"Are we fishing in the right spot?" Tammy asked.

"Yes, look out there. The guys are all fishing here. There are buoys everywhere. I don't get it."

"Just our fucking luck," Tammy said as she stacked another trap. "And where are we supposed to dump these traps? We've never fished here before. We have no idea what the hell we are doing, Dwayne."

For the first time, Dwayne came unleashed. "I don't freaking know, Tammy. Your guess is as good as mine. You're right! I don't know what the hell I'm doing. We both saw the lobsters in Stan's traps and took this chance. Well, it looks like it was a bad decision. I just hope it gets better."

Tammy softened her tone. Dwayne was right. It was both their choice to make a move; it was wrong of her to blame Dwayne. "Me too. Let's go."

After pulling ten more traps and only getting a few legal lobsters, Tammy broke down into tears. "I'm so sick of this, and I'm so bloody tired. Where the hell are the lobsters?" she cried.

Dwayne turned off the boat. He was just as upset and tired as Tammy, but he refused to give up hope. "Hey now. I'm sure it's going to get better. Hang in there, okay. Why don't you take some time out and chill for a bit?"

Tammy shook her head and snapped. "No! I've worked too damn hard. I want to be there when we finally catch some lobsters. I'll be fine. Come on, let's keep going."

Dwayne nodded. "Okay." He fired up the boat to head to the next trap.

By the end of their line, Tammy was mortified. They caught twelve lobsters. "What are we going to do, Dwayne? These lobsters won't even buy us groceries for a week. We are so screwed." Tammy stood next to Dwayne at the helm as he drove back to the guest dock. Neither one smiled. Dwayne turned to Tammy, his face long and his eyes distant. "I don't know. I'm going to call Stan over the VHF radio when we get back to the dock and see how he did. I hope he is still on the boat."

Tammy looked away and wiped a tear that had escaped. "I don't know how we are going to pay our bills. We owe two months' rent, slip fees, and two truck payments. And god knows what else."

Dwayne reached across and rested his hand on her shoulder. "Let me talk to Stan first before we fret about bills. He may have an answer. He's fished here for years."

"I hope so. How much longer do we have before we reach the dock?"

"About fifteen minutes," Dwayne replied.

"I'm going to go lie down. I'm so sore. My body is so damn battered. And for what? I'm so pissed off right now," Tammy snapped, as she headed down into the cabin.

As soon as he tied the boat up to the dock, Dwayne wasted no time trying to reach Stan on the radio.

"Hey, Stan. You got me? *Baywitch* here. Over."

There was silence.

Dwayne tried again. "Stan. Its Dwayne on the *Baywitch*. Have you got me?"

A few seconds later, Stan's voice came over the radio loud and clear. "Hey, Dwayne. I got you. Over."

Tammy had heard the conversation and crawled out of bed. She moaned with every move and crawled up to the deck, and remained quiet while the two men spoke.

"Hey, Stan. We just got in from pulling the traps we had soaking for a few days. Not many lobsters. Nothing like the pull you had the other day. I was wondering how you did today. Over."

"I hear ya on that, Dwayne. I had a lousy catch today, and from what I hear, none of the boats had a good catch. Over."

Dwayne's face turned pale, and the little smile he had soon disappeared.

Tammy's jaw dropped, and her eyes turned wide.

"Oh, wow, that's not good. So where do you think all the lobsters went? It's like they just disappeared. Over."

"I have no idea. Strangest thing I've ever seen. I'm going to give it another go tomorrow. If the traps are empty again, I hate to say it, but the mad crawl might be over. Which will really suck for you guys after all the traps you moved over here? But that's fishing; you just never know. Over."

Dwayne gave Tammy a worried look as he spoke over the radio. "Well, I hope that's not the case. Let me know when you get in tomorrow. Over."

"I sure will. Have a good night. I'm out."

Dwayne replaced the mic in its cradle. His eyes looked dazed.

"Are you okay?" Tammy asked.

"I'm just worried. It sounds like the lobsters are gone. No one had a good catch today."

"We're really screwed if that's true. We've invested so much bloody time and money. How the hell are we ever going to recover from this?"

"I don't know, Tammy. I'm not going to think about it until tomorrow. Let's hope the lobsters are back."

Tammy tugged at the straps of her slickers and yanked them down her arms. When her arms were free, she pulled the slickers down her legs as fast as she could and over her boots. Tears streamed down her face like a leaky faucet. The brokenness finally unleashed something inside of her. She picked up the slimy slickers and threw them hard at the stack of fifty traps on the deck of the Baywitch. "I am so frigging done with this shit," she yelled at the top of her lungs. She wanted to be heard above the roaring noise of the engine. She steadied herself as a wave passed under the boat. "I'm sick and tired of chasing god damn lobsters all over this fucking ocean. Look at me. I'm a bloody mess!"

Dwayne stood at the helm. "Look, I'm sorry, okay. But we both knew we were taking a chance by coming here. We'll take these traps we have on the boat to Malibu and just fish Malibu for the rest of the year."

Tammy raised her hands. "No, I'm done, Dwayne! I've had it. We won't make enough money to live and pay what we owe if we fish Malibu so early. I can't do this anymore. I'm sick and tired of being broke all the time and being away from Matt. These last few days have almost killed me, and for what? We're still no better off."

Dwayne's jaw dropped. "Are you saying you're done for the day? Do you want to take a break? What are you trying to tell me, Tammy?"

Tammy collapsed onto the deck of the boat and leaned against the traps. She brought her knees to her chin and buried her head in her hands. Her tears were heavy.

Dwayne took the boat out of gear and let it idle. They were in open waters on their way back to Marina del Rey with fifty traps, which they planned to drop off in Malibu the next day. He checked his surroundings; the boat was safe, and he then approached Tammy. He knelt at her side and rested his hand on her shoulder. "Tammy, talk to me. What's going on?"

Tammy lifted her head. Her face was drenched with tears. "I can't do this anymore, Dwayne. I'm so tired. My hands are wrecked." Tammy held them up. " Look at them. The cracks are so deep they are bleeding. I can barely move my fingers. And look, my fingers are so swollen that my wedding band is cutting into my flesh. My body is so sore that I can hardly move. I have never worked so goddamn hard in my life and have nothing to show for it."

Dwayne cradled her in his arms. "Come here. It's okay. We'll get through this."

Tammy pushed herself away and shook her head vigorously. "No, Dwayne! You don't understand I can't do this shit anymore. I'm packing it all in. I'm done. Every year is a gamble on whether or not we make money. Some years we barely make it, and this year did it for me. I can't live with the stress anymore. I want to get a regular job where I get a damn paycheck every week and not wonder where the next dollar is coming from."

Dwayne's face turned pale. His eyes were shallow. "You're serious, aren't you? This is it?"

Tammy nodded. "I'm afraid so. I'll still fish for fun with you. I love the ocean. I just can't work my ass off like this. I miss Matt. He is growing up so fast, and I'm missing out on so much. I want to be a mom to him before he gets too old to need me. I miss my friends." She released a slight chuckle. "Shit, I don't have any close friends. I'm gone too much to make any." She took Dwayne's hand and looked at him with sad eyes. "I just want to be homebound for a while."

"Wow. Well, if that's what you want. I'm not going to force you to fish. I'm behind you one hundred percent. I want you to be happy. But what will you do?"

Tammy leaned her head back against the traps. "I don't know. Maybe I'll start a boat wash-down and detailing business. I'll help you get these traps to Malibu and the ones left in Dana Point, but after that, I need to find something else to do."

Dwayne squeezed her hand. "Okay, but I'll miss you on the boat. I'll have to hire a deckhand."

"Matt can help you, and I can help you get the gear ready. I just don't want to travel miles across the ocean anymore."

"It's okay. You've been a trooper. Do what you have to do. I love you."

Tammy's body collapsed into his lap. "I love you too. Thank you. I'm so tired. I'm going to go lay down."

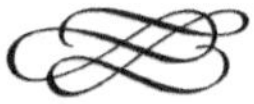

Tammy took both of Dwayne's hands and held them tight. "Are you sure this is what you want to do? Don't make any hasty decisions."

Dwayne shifted on the bench where they sat in the backyard of their home. "Yeah, I'm sure. Fishing is not like it used to be. I'm struggling just to pay the expenses. Fishing for spider crabs and you doing boat washdowns keeps us afloat. You quit three years ago, and it's not been the same since," he confessed. "I hate going to the island by myself and being away from you and Matt." He gave Tammy a serious stare. "I'm done. I want to do something else with my life."

"Well, what would you do? Work on boats all year? You'd hate that."

Their two dogs joined them, Sprity, a feisty Jack Russell, and Harley, a mix between an Australian Shepherd and a Hikitia Husky. When Tammy began spending more time at home, she had convinced Dwayne to get a couple of dogs. It made her feel safer when Dwayne was gone fishing for weeks at a time. Tammy smiled at her canine companions and gave them both a playful back rub. "Hey, guys." She said as she leaned down and allowed them to lick her face.

Dwayne shrugged his shoulders. "I don't know yet. Tell you what, let's go camping. We will be away from the boats and the marina and I'll give it some more thought. We'll spend some time with Matt and see what our options are."

Tammy gave him a large grin and patted him on the thigh." Yeah, Matt is seventeen now. I'm not sure how many more camping trips we have left with him before he decides it's not cool anymore to go camping with his parents. When do you want to leave?"

"How about in the morning?"

"Sounds good. I'll go tell Matt and start packing." Before she left, she nuzzled nose to nose with the dogs. "These guys would love to go camping, too, I bet."

"So, we've spent three days camping and still haven't decided on whether or not you want to quit fishing," Tammy said, as she threw two rolled-up sleeping bags into the back of the truck. She turned her head and saw Matt was busy taking down his tent, and the dogs were chasing ground squirrels down into their holes.

Dwayne used the tailgate of the truck for a table to pack up a lantern. "I don't know what to do. I'm burned out. I'm not getting any younger."

Tammy lifted a tote and slid it in the bed of the truck. "Well, whatever you decide, I'm behind you one hundred percent. We'll manage."

"Do you miss it?"

Tammy turned to face him. "Miss what?"

"Fishing."

Tammy propped herself up on the tailgated and used it for a seat. "Yeah, I miss it. I miss working with you and being on the ocean, but I don't miss not being home or being away from Matt and being dog ass tired all the time. Fishing for me now is a hobby and not a job, and I'm okay with that." She held up her hands. "And look, I have fingernails now too," she laughed.

Dwayne nodded. "Yeah, I've been around the ocean my entire life. I'll never be able to give it up completely."

Tammy rubbed his arm and gave him a loving smile. "And there's no reason you should. You'd still have the *Little Boat* if you quit, right? You wouldn't sell that, would you?"

"Oh, heck no. I have to have at least one boat."

"Well, then, the ocean would be at your disposal whenever we all need a fishing fix. That's what I do now. I jump on the *Little boat* with you and Matt for a fun fishing day on the ocean."

Dwayne paced around the truck and raked his fingers through his hair. "God, I don't know what to do."

"Hey, honey. No one is asking you to make a choice. When the time is right, you will know, and until then, don't stress over it, okay."

"Yeah, you're right. Come on, let's finish packing up and get on the road." He looked over at Matt, who was playing with the dogs. "Almost ready, Matt?" he hollered.

"Yeah, I'm coming. Just gotta grab these two chairs," Matt yelled.

"Hey, I have an idea," Dwayne said from inside the cab where he sat behind the wheel, waiting for Matt and the dogs to climb in the back seat.

"What's that?" Tammy asked.

"Instead of taking the regular route home, let's go the back way over to the five freeway. It's pretty country back there, and it would be nice to do some exploring on our way home."

Tammy beamed him a smile. "Good idea."

Dwayne fired up the truck and turned his head to look at Matt. "What do you think, Matt? Do you want to do some exploring? It will extend our camping trip for a few more hours."

"Sounds great!" Matt said with enthusiasm.

Tammy opened the glove compartment and pulled out a map. She opened it and studied it for a few minutes. "It looks like we take Maricopa highway, which is the thirty-three."

Dwayne nodded. "Yep, that's right. I used to ride my motorcycle through there. It's pretty. You'll love it."

Tammy's eyes sparkled. "Oh, I'm excited." She looked at the map again. "I guess we will have to turn onto Lockwood Valley Road, and that will take us to the five freeway."

Dwayne backed out of their campsite. "Let's go," he said, and gave Tammy a loving smile.

Tammy settled back in her seat and glanced out of the window as the truck drove to the exit. Soon they were the only vehicle driving on an endless two-lane highway with spectacular views of mountain ranges and pine trees that went on for miles.

Tammy sat up to take it all in. "God, it's just gorgeous out here. I've not seen another car since we left the campground." She reached over and placed her hand on Dwayne's thigh and gave it a gentle squeeze. "It's so peaceful, and it's only two hours away from home."

Dwayne scanned the views. "It sure is."

"We need to do this more often. I'm so relaxed right now," Tammy said, as she leaned back in her seat.

"It would be nice to move to the country and retire, don't you think?" Dwayne stated.

Tammy looked at Dwayne with a creased brow. "Retire? I'm only in my late thirties, and you are in your forties. Retirement won't be happening for a while, I'm afraid." She took in a deep breath. "But yeah, to retire to a place like this would be awesome. I grew up in the country in England, and I miss it. I miss the small, close-knit community. I get so tired of the city and the rat race sometimes. We're always on the go." She released a heavy sigh. "Ah, if only," she chuckled.

Dwayne squeezed her hand that was still resting on his thigh. 'Well, it's nice to dream."

"Look, I see houses," Tammy said, as they drove along Lockwood Valley Road. "What town is this?"

"I have no idea. I've made it out here."

"Wow, to live out here would be something. They have no neighbors. I wonder what people do for a living?"

"Who knows? Maybe they are retired or have a long commute."

Tammy sat up straight and took everything in. The little town mesmerized her and she kept her eyes glued for more houses peeking through the pine trees. "Look, there is a sign up ahead. It says Frazier Park, three miles.

"It must be another small town," Dwayne said.

"Oh, fun!" Tammy squealed.

Soon they were surrounded by more houses nestled amongst the pine tree. Tammy looked to her right. "Look, a pond and people are fishing in it. How cute is that, and look, there is a playground for the kids too?" Tammy said, her voice exploding with excitement.

"There's a baseball field too," Matt said from the backseat.

"You like this town, Matt?" Tammy asked.

"Yeah, it's pretty cool. It's so quiet. Not many cars and only a few stores."

Dwayne pulled up to a flashing red stop signal and looked to his left. "I wonder where that road goes?"

Tammy followed his stare. "Let's go take a look."

Dwayne made the left turn. They pulled up to another stop sign. "This must be the main road that goes through the town. Look, they have a few stores and some restaurants," Dwayne said, as he made a right.

Tammy looked across the valley and up at the tall mountain covered with pine trees. "And look at that view. This town is based at the bottom of that mountain."

"That must be Frazier Mountain. They have everything they need here, and I've not seen one traffic light."

Tammy beamed Dwayne a smile. "Let's come back next weekend and explore this place. I want to see more of it."

"I'm spending the night over at my buddy's house next weekend. We're going fishing, remember?" Matt butted in.

Tammy turned her head to look at him. "That's fine, me and Dwayne can come up. She rubbed Dwayne's leg and gave him a flirtatious smile. "What do you say?"

"Sounds like a plan to me."

"I've been thinking about this place all week," Tammy said as Dwayne took the Frazier Park exit off the freeway.

"Me too." He turned to Tammy and grinned. "We should see if there are any real estate offices and go check out some houses. What do you think?"

Tammy creased her brow. "You want to buy a house up here? What will you do for a living? I don't see an ocean nearby, or boats for that matter. You haven't officially quit fishing. And I do boat wash-downs for a living, don't forget."

"I know. I just want to look around. We're up here. We might as well."

Tammy shrugged her shoulders. "Okay. It won't hurt, I guess. Then we can try out that pizza place I saw last week."

Tammy and Dwayne scanned the signs over the buildings in search of a real estate office. A few minutes later, Tammy hollered. "There's one! Pull into that driveway."

Dwayne saw where she was pointing and parked in front of the building. "I wonder if they are open on Saturdays," Dwayne said.

"Well, the only way to find out is to try the door," Tammy said, wearing a sarcastic grin as she stepped out of the truck.

Dwayne reached the front door of the office before Tammy and pulled the handle. The door swung open in his direction. "They are open." He smiled.

A pretty, middle-aged woman sat behind a desk studying some papers. She looked up over glasses. "Hi. Can I help you?"

Dwayne approached her desk and extended his hand. She smiled and gave him a firm handshake. "Yeah. We're just checking out the town and we're wondering if there were any properties we could check out. This is my wife, Tammy, and I'm Dwayne."

She gave them a friendly smile. "I'm Kate. We have some listings," she said, turning to a file cabinet against the wall behind her.

"This is a charming town. We passed through it on our way back from camping last week and came and checked it out." Tammy said.

Kate spoke as she fumbled through the file cabinet. "I love it here. I've been here for over twenty years. The people are great, and we all know and watch out for each other." She pulled out a file. "Here you go. This is a list of all the houses for sale in Frazier Park and the surrounding towns. I'll give you a map and my business card. If you see anything and want to go inside, call me. I'd be happy to show you around."

Dwayne took the papers and browsed through them. "Wow! This is great thank you so much." He looked at the papers again and then at the map. "This one doesn't look like it's too far. It says it's on Lillie Lane."

"Yep. About five minutes away."

Tammy took the papers from Dwayne's hand and studied them. "Is that the right price?" Tammy asked.

"Yep. It's an old house. No one has lived there for over fifteen years. It's going to need a lot of work. You'll find the prices of the property up here pretty cheap."

"I'd say," Dwayne replied. "That's a fifth of what houses cost in the city." He turned to Tammy and took her hand. "So, do you want to go check it out?"

Tammy smiled. "I do."

Dwayne shook Kate's hand. "Thank you so much, Kate. We'll be in touch."

Kate smiled. "My pleasure. If you decide to move up here, you will love it."

Tammy studied the map while Dwayne put the truck in gear and headed into town. "Keep going straight up that hill," Tammy said and pointed up ahead.

A few minutes later, Dwayne spotted Lillie Lane. "There it is."

Dwayne turned the truck onto a dirt road and started checking the addresses. Halfway up the street, he spots it. "There it is on the left."

Tammy crouched her neck and looked through the window on Dwayne's side. "Oh, wow! She's not kidding. It needs a lot of work. It looks like something out of an old John Wayne movie," Tammy chuckled.

"Come on, let's go take a closer look," Dwayne said eagerly, and turned off the truck.

Tammy looked at the old wooden rickety fence surrounding the property. It had a good lean to it. "I wonder how old this fence is," she said, as she walked through the gate.

"Probably as old as the house," Dwayne chuckled.

Tammy took in a deep breath and filled her lungs with the fresh air. "God, the air up here is as good as the ocean, and look at that view. We can see the entire mountain from here."

"Yeah, we're pretty high up. The map says five thousand feet."

"They must get snow here. God, it's been ages since I've seen the snow." She grabbed Dwayne's hand. "Come on, let's look around."

"This is a big lot. Much bigger than we have at home, and look, there is an old garage, another building, and then some kind of covered area over to the left," Dwayne said excitedly.

Tammy pulled Dwayne toward the old cabin. "It's a cute place, but man, will it need some work. Not trusting the old wooden steps that led up to the house, she lightly placed her feet on each step, in fear they may cave beneath her."

"Careful," Dwayne said, who was close behind her. "This whole place may collapse."

Tammy laughed and peeked through the dusty front window on the porch. "It looks pretty big inside."

Dwayne stood next to her and admired the heavy wooden door. "I think this whole place needs to be torn down. There's no way we could bring it up to code. But man, the size of the property is great, and I love that view."

"Who would have thought such a place existed just a few hours out of the Marina. I could see us living here. The dogs would love it."

"You do?" Dwayne said. "What are you saying? You want to move here?"

Tammy skipped down the steps and spun around in a circle with her arms spread like an eagle. "Well, look at this place, Dwayne. We could make this a home. I could grow the garden I've always wanted. We'd have all this space. It's perfect. And look, since we've been here, not one car has gone by."

"I hear you. But what would we do for a living?"

"I have no idea," Tammy laughed. "Who says we have to move up here right away. We could come up on weekends and fix it up, and besides, Matt is still in school. He only has two years left. I wouldn't pull him out of school."

Dwayne gave Tammy a sweet smile and took her in his arms. He kissed her passionately on the lips and gazed into her eyes. "I like your way of thinking. I wouldn't mind changing our lives over a period of time. I guess you could call it a slow transition. I could still fish while we figure out what we want to do."

Tammy gave him a big grin. "Really! You like the idea of living up here too?"

"I do. Shall I call Kate, or do you want to look at some other places?"

"No. This is the one. It's screaming home to me, and I don't need to look anywhere else. Call Kate."

"Well, instead of trying to find a phone-booth, let's just go back to her office. I'm sure she's still there."

Tammy wrapped herself in Dwayne's arms and smiled. "Are we really going to buy this place?"

"I don't know, Tammy," Dwayne laughed. "We've never bought a house before, but the price sure is affordable. Just don't get your hopes up, okay."

"I won't. Come on, let's go. I don't want to miss Kate."

Tammy and Dwayne couldn't stop smiling when they left Kate's office over two hours later. Tammy leaped down the steps and did a sexy twirl at the bottom. "I can't believe we may be homeowners soon."

"Me neither. I didn't have any plans to put an offer on the house today, and not only that, it's the first and only house we've seen."

"I know me neither. I can't wait to tell Matt."

Tammy sat outside at the patio table with her morning coffee and admired the beautiful view of the mountain. She had done so for the past ten years since she and Dwayne had taken the plunge and brought their diamond in the rough piece of property. She inhaled deeply, her arms extended into a full stretch, and filled her lungs with the refreshing air. "God, I'll never get tired of this." Tammy enjoyed her morning ritual of having at least two cups of coffee while reading a couple of chapters from a good book. Afterward, she would be ready to feed their seventeen chickens and what she believed to be now over one hundred pigeons.

The chickens were among the first things they had bought when they finally moved full time to the mountains—two years after they had purchased the property.

Matt had graduated high school just shy of nine years ago and still lives in the city where he has been an electrician ever since. Dwayne's son Jason moved out of state and has his own family now. He keeps in touch and tries to visit a few times a year.

The marina's two-hour commute soon grew old, and they cut

ties with the marina completely. Dwayne quit fishing, sold both boats, and was able to fix up the guest house, which is where they have been living for the last eight years.

It had been a struggle in the beginning. While they worked on making the guest house livable, they lived in a tiny trailer left on the property when they bought it. Dwayne worked in construction for the first few years, and Tammy dove into the new internet technology and began an online sales business. She also helped Dwayne on some of his jobs and spent a lot of time working on their property. She especially loved the weekends because that was the time they spent working together building the guest house. She missed working with him.

Tammy had no regrets. She loved the slower pace of life, the sparsely populated town, and the friendly people that had welcomed them with home-baked apple pie and new friendships. Tammy planned on checking her vegetable garden after the birds had been fed and giving it a good soak before the scorching sun rose high in the sky. Tammy wasted no time starting the garden and looked forward every year to picking her fresh vegetables and bringing them to the table. It was a dream of hers to have a garden someday, but it had been impossible while fishing and gone for weeks at a time.

Tammy looked over at the main house and chuckled. It still looked exactly like it did when they first bought the place, except the master bedroom was now her office. Complete with a computer and everything she needed to run her online business. They hadn't planned to live in the guest house for over eight years, but their only free time was on weekends when they didn't have to work. The guest house, or as they liked to call it, the tiny house, was cozy and easy to maintain, but the downside was they had no room for guests, which both their parents had pointed out when they saw the place for the first time.

Even though Tammy no longer fished, her mom missed America and continued to visit every year. When they moved to the mountains, she would stay in the hotel just out-of-town by the freeway.

They had long talks over tea at the patio table outside the tiny house. "I can't wait to see the new house built, Tammy," her mom had said on many of her visits.

"Me neither," Tammy would laugh. "One day, it will be done, and you can stay in the tiny house. Our problem is, we only have weekends to work on it."

Tammy was pleased that her dad had made a quick visit when he was in the states on a book tour a few years ago, and since then, his first question had always been when he called, "How is the house coming?"

Tammy would try to talk to her dad at least once a week. Now that she had a computer, she helped him with book orders from his website. Stored at her house was an inventory of his books, and when orders were placed, Tammy shipped them out. A shipment was expected any day now with his latest book. Her dad had been calling every morning to see if they had arrived. Tammy hoped to see a UPS truck pull up in front of her gate this afternoon so she would have good news for her dad tomorrow.

Tammy looked up and smiled. Dwayne suddenly appeared at the doorway of the tiny house. He yawned and raked his hands through his uncombed hair. The sunlight glistened on his bare chest as he felt for his cigarettes in the shorts he wore, and joined Tammy at the table.

"Morning, beautiful," he said, as he took a seat and lit a smoke. "Want one?" he asked, holding out the pack.

Tammy reached over and took a cigarette. "Sure." She leaned back and took a deep drag. "Man, I love these mornings. What time do you have to leave?"

"As soon as I'm dressed and have loaded up the birds." He glanced at his cell phone he had just set down on the table. "In about half an hour, I guess."

Tammy took a sip of her coffee. "Did you ever think you'd get back into falconry?" Dwayne shook his head. "Nope. If it weren't for that falcon I heard a few years back, I'd still be doing construction."

Tammy chuckled at the memory. "Yep. That ignited the fire again, and within a few months, you had a falcon. Now, look at you. You quit construction, have six falcons, and do bird abatement for a living. You went from the ocean to the sky," Tammy laughed.

"Yeah. It was back in my teens when I started it. Way before I met you." he chuckled.

"I know. I remember you telling me. I would have loved to have known you back then," Tammy said, with a loving smile.

"So, what are your plans for today?"

Tammy released a heavy sigh. "Well, I'm hoping my dad's books arrive today so dad will get out of my hair and quit calling me all the time. I also have a ton of work to do in the office." She petted Harley, who rubbed his back against her legs. "And I'll take these two for a good hike," she said, as she gave Harley a mean back rub.

Dwayne leaned in and gave Tammy a peck on the cheek before standing to his feet. Okay, I have to get out of here. I love you. I'll see you tonight."

Tammy smiled. "Okay."

~

Tammy checked her cellphone. It was almost three o'clock. "Where the hell is the UPS guy? God, I hope those books come today." Tammy mumbled as she walked across the yard to the tiny house with Harley and Sprity following closely behind. She turned around and looked at them. "Yes, I know you want to go for a walk, but I can't leave yet. I'm afraid I'll miss the UPS truck." Tammy suddenly froze. "Shh, do you hear that?" Tammy asked her dogs as she raced to the front fence. "It sounds like a truck." She leaned over and looked down the street. "Yes! It's UPS."

She grinned. "Oh, please stop here," she begged out loud. A few minutes later, her wish came true.

Tammy beamed at Tom, the UPS driver, with a huge smile when he stepped out of the truck.

"Afternoon Tammy. I have a heavy package for you."

"Yes, they're my dad's books. He's been calling me all week about them. Can you set them on the front porch for me, please?" Tammy asked as she opened the gate.

"Sure, no problem."

After Tom had left, Tammy wasted no time calling her dad in Ireland. She hoped her Dad would answer the phone and not his new wife of three years, whom she had never met or knew. She still considered Joanne her other mom, even though she and John had divorced many years ago. Tammy still kept in touch with Joanne as often as she could. She might not be her father's wife anymore, but she would always be family to Tammy.

Tammy released a sigh of relief when she heard her dad's voice on the phone. "Hey, Dad, it's Tammy. Your books came."

"Well, about bloody time. I'm glad to hear it. I'm going to email you some addresses of readers that have ordered the book. Can you ship them out tomorrow? And Andrew will put the book up on the website, so you'll be in charge of the orders."

"Got it, dad."

"So, how's the house coming?" John asked.

Tammy rolled her eyes. He never failed to ask. She gave him her usual answer. "Fine, dad. Maybe it will be done by the time you visit again."

"That would be nice. Listen, I have to go. Thanks for letting me know the books have arrived."

"Sure, no problem. Love you, dad."

"Love you too."

Tammy ended the call and gave her two dogs, who sat at her feet, a huge smile. "Guess what, guys! We can go for a walk now. Come on, let's go."

Tammy spent the next morning loading up her car with books she had packed for shipping last night. Dwayne had left for work a few hours ago, and she wanted to get to the post office early so she would have the rest of the day to do other projects that she had planned. She stood back and looked at the pile of manila envelopes on her back seat from readers anxious to read her father's book. She was so proud of him and what he had accomplished. "What an amazing feeling it must be to have people order a book you wrote," Tammy mumbled to herself as she put the last few envelopes in her car. "I'm going to write a book someday," she confessed out loud. "And I know exactly what it's going to be about," she added with an attitude, before pushing the car door closed. "Now, where the hell did I put my keys?"

Tammy headed into the office to begin the dreaded search for her keys when the phone rang. She looked at the number on the caller ID and didn't recognize it. "Hello?" she asked with some uncertainty.

An unfamiliar male voice came on the line. "Hello, is this Tammy?"

"Yes, it is. Who is this?"

"I'm a friend of your dad. My name is Jeffery. I'm afraid I have some sad news."

Tammy heard him take a deep breath. It scared her. "What is it? Is my dad okay?"

"I'm so sorry, but your dad passed away early this morning."

Tammy screamed at the top of her voice. "Oh my god! No!" Her knees buckled, and she fell to the floor. Her sobs were fierce. "How can that be? I just spoke to him last night. He sounded fine. He was happy after I had told him the books had finally arrived."

"It was very sudden. He had a heart attack."

Tammy shook her head in disbelief and rocked herself. Tears pooled from her eyes. "I can't believe this—not dad. He was only sixty-nine. He was supposed to be around for another twenty years." Tammy's heart ached from the pain, knowing she would never see her father again or hear his voice. She couldn't hold back her tears long enough to talk. Her body trembled, and her hands shook. "I'm sorry, I have to go," she said, as she hung up the phone.

It was then that she let herself go and screamed, "No, dad! No! Oh my god, dad! Why you?" She brought her hand up to her mouth to muffle her pained cries and continued to rock back and forth with her knees tight up under her chin. "This can't be happening. Please tell me I'm in a bad dream. Come on, Tammy, wake up." But she didn't wake up. "I have to call Dwayne and my sisters. Oh my god and mom." Tammy had another round of hard tears. "It will devastate mom." She cried out. Her mom had told her once that she never stopped loving her father, and funnily enough, her dad had said the same thing about her mother. "God, they were just too stubborn to admit it to each other," Tammy yelled out loud. She thought of her sister, Donna, and Jenny and wondered how they would react. Things she had wished she had done raced through her mind. Shit, dad never saw his three daughters together again since he left home when I was twelve years old. That was thirty-two years ago.

Her mom's voice haunted her mind. *I only have one wish: to see all three of my girls in the same room. Is that too much to ask Tammy?* "No, it's not, mom," Tammy whispered. "I should have done something about it years ago," she said in an angered tone. Tammy spat out her next words. "I won't let you down, mom."

Tammy turned around and walked over to a photograph hanging on the wall. It was one of her and her dad at Disney World in Florida. She must have been about fourteen. It was shortly after her parents had divorced. Tammy spent the summer with her dad. She traced her dad's face with her finger. "Oh, dad. I'm going to miss you so much. Why is life so unfair?" Tammy took down the frame and kissed the picture. Tears streamed down her face. "I love you, dad." She sniffed hard to push back her tears. "I can't believe you are gone," and placed the picture on her desk where it would be close. "I need to call Dwayne."

He answered on the second ring, and Tammy's emotions took over. She cried hard into the phone, unable to speak.

"Tammy! Is that you?" Dwayne asked, in a panicked state. All he heard were her sobs. "Tammy, talk to me! Are you okay?"

"My dad is dead," Tammy said between her heavy tears.

"Our dog is dead? Oh, no! Which one?" Dwayne cried.

Tammy continued to cry and choked out her next words. "No, my Dad! My dad is dead."

"Oh my god! No! What happened?"

Tammy continued to choke on her words. "He had a heart attack. He's gone, Dwayne."

"Oh, sweetheart. I'm coming home. I'll be there in an hour. I love you."

"I love you too. I gotta go."

Tammy didn't remember the last few days. They were a blur. She walked around in a daze, numb, and feeling the saddest she had ever felt, unable to wrap her head around the fact that her father was gone. Tammy thought of his writing and how, just last month, they had a long conversation over the phone about his latest novel that he had been working on. He had so much more to write. And now that book will never get finished.

Tammy waited a day before calling her mom and sisters. As she had expected, her mom took it the hardest. "I need to see my girls, Tammy. This could be me tomorrow. I'm older than your dad by five years." Rose had cried into the phone.

"I know, mom. This is just as important to me as it is to you. Now, even more, since dad has passed." Tammy replied.

Tammy sat on the grass in a lounge chair wrapped in a blanket, chilled by the night air. Two days had passed since the devastating news of her father's death, and it was all she could think about. She looked up into the night skies and watched a shooting star, smiling for the first time in days. "Hi, dad, is that you?" It brought her comfort thinking it was. Tammy turned and looked at the old house that still needed to be built and whispered, "Dad will never get to see the new house." Thoughts of her dad's house in Ireland clouded her mind. It was a place she had never visited but had every intention to one day. It was a part of her dad unknown to her. She had no idea how her dad had lived or what his office looked like. Growing up, Tammy remembered her father always had a reading chair. Did he have one in his home in Ireland? Tammy sat up straight. She needed to know these things and connect with the last part of her father's life. And the only way she could do that was to go to Ireland.

Lost in her thoughts, Tammy didn't hear Dwayne open the gate to the grass. "Hey, are you okay? It's getting cold out here," he asked before taking the seat next to her.

Tammy nodded and smiled. "I'm going to Ireland."

Dwayne's jaw dropped. "What?"

"You heard me. I'm going to Ireland." Tammy rubbed his knee. "I need to do this. It just hit me. His funeral will be there, and I wasn't sure If I could go because I don't have a passport. But there's a way to get it expedited. But there's more to it. I need to connect with where dad lived before they sell the house. And not only that, Jenny and Donna can't afford to travel. One of us needs to be there for dad."

Dwayne nodded. "I get you, Tammy. Do whatever you must do. I'm behind you one hundred percent. You know I won't be able to go because of all the animals."

"Yeah, I know that, and thank you."

A week later, Tammy arrived in Dublin, Ireland. She had doubts she would make it in time for her father's funeral, which was to be held the next day. But the passport office came through and issued her an emergency passport two days ago. Tammy scanned the small airport in search of Elsa, her step-mother, who Tammy hardly knew. A woman resembling pictures Tammy had received stood away from the crowds waving her hands above her head. Tammy smiled, and waved back, then walked in her direction with her one suitcase in tow.

"Elsa?"

"Yes. Tammy, hi."

Tammy freed her hands from her luggage and embraced Elsa. Tears immediately flowed. "I can't believe dad has gone."

Elsa welcomed her embrace and held her tight. "I know me too. It's a shock to all of us."

Tammy pulled away and wiped her tears. "Were you there?"

Elsa shook her head. "No, I was at the store. I found him when I returned."

Tammy gasped. "Oh, I'm so sorry."

Elsa pulled out a tissue and dried her eyes. "It's okay. I'm just happy you are here. Andrew is flying in tomorrow morning and will stay in town with his wife."

"Oh, wow! I've not seen him in over twenty years."

"I've met him a few times," Elsa replied. "Come on, let's get on the road. We have a two-hour drive ahead of us."

Tammy didn't speak much in the car. This was her first time in Ireland, and she sat in silence, taking it all in. It was beautiful and reminded her so much of England with its luscious green rolling hills and damp, dewy weather. "I can see why dad moved here," Tammy whispered to herself.

Tammy immediately saw the big red barn that her father had bragged about many times when they pulled into her father's driveway. He hadn't been joking when he told her it was huge, and he had no idea what he was going to use it for. It had become a frequent joke during their phone conversations. Tammy looked around the few acres of land that surrounded the stone farmhouse and wept. This is what her dad always wanted—a house in the country where he could write his books.

Elsa opened her door. "Are you ready to go inside?"

Tammy shook her head. "No, I need a few minutes. I'll be there in a bit."

Elsa rested her hand on Tammy's shoulder. "Take your time. I know how difficult this must be."

Tammy waited until she was alone, and then the tears came heavy. Through her tears, she spotted her dad's red car parked in the barn and his Wellington boots sitting outside the house's back door. Tammy didn't know if she could go into the house without losing it, and screamed, "I can't do this, dad," as tears continued to gush down her face. "I want to see you." Tammy tilted her head back into the seat and let out a heart-wrenching cry. "This is so fucking hard," she sobbed and buried her head into her hands.

Tammy didn't know how long she cried for the loss of her dad. Elsa had come out once and asked if she was okay, and Tammy had nodded. Somehow, Tammy found the strength deep within to gain her composure and tried to focus on finding the door handle to the car through her swollen drenched eyes. The unbearable pounding headache that tortured her head was the worst she had ever experienced. Rubbing her temples didn't provide any relief.

The skies were now dark when she stepped out of the car. Tammy embraced herself to block out the night time chills and once again looked up to the stars. A bright star caught her attention, and she smiled. "Hi, dad. Do you see me? I'm sorry I never came to your house sooner. I would have loved for you to show me around and go into town for lunch with you." Tammy blew a kiss to the star. "I miss you," and turned to walk towards the house.

When her hand touched the doorknob, Tammy took a deep breath before turning the knob and then slowly entered her father's home, and found herself standing in the kitchen. Elsa must have heard the door and came from another room off to the left. Like Tammy's, her eyes had evidence of tears. She raced to Tammy and embraced her. "I miss your father," she cried.

"I know. I do too. I feel dad here. I'm so glad I came." Tammy glanced around the cozy country-style kitchen with its wooden cupboards and pine floors.

"Do you want a cup of tea?" Elsa asked.

Tammy took a seat at the large wooden planked table. "Sure, that would be great." and scanned the counters and saw many of her dad's favorites, Gingersnap cookies, Marmite, and treacle, and then she spotted his hat hanging on the back of the door. "Oh, dad," she whispered, before she left her seat and freed the hat from its hook. "I remember this hat. He's had this for ages," Tammy said, as she glided her fingers across the top of it.

Elsa glanced over her shoulder. "Yes, that was his favorite. Take it home if you'd like."

"Can I?"

Elsa nodded. "Of course."

Tammy didn't return to her seat. Instead, she walked over to one of many of her dad's bookshelves and began looking through his collection. Many she recognized from when she was a child. "Wow. I can't believe dad still has some of these."

"Yes, your dad rarely got rid of his books. Those books have moved everywhere with him," Elsa smiled.

"And still no TV, right?" Tammy joked.

"That's right. He's never owned one, as I'm sure you know."

Engrossed in getting to know about her father's last chapter of life, Tammy wasn't paying attention to where each doorway led and soon found herself in a living room. A cozy brick fireplace decorated with what she recognized as her grandparent's brass ornament collection was the room's focal point. "Wow! I remember these," Tammy whispered while carefully picking one up to inspect it. Memories of her grandparents flooded her mind and the house where they lived. Pictures of her and her sisters and one of a young man who had an uncanny resemblance to her dad adorned the mantel. "That must be Andrew. Damn, he looks like dad." To the left was another picture of three young men. All looked like dad. Tammy realized they were the other two half-brothers she had never met.

Through her tears, she glanced around the room and clutched her heart when she focused on the brown armchair with a pair of slippers next to it. Draped over the back was a wool blanket. "Oh, dad," Tammy cried as she slowly walked over to the chair and took a seat. Chilled by her emotions, she pulled the blanket from the back of the chair and buried her face into the soft wool. It had the scent of her dad's cologne—Old Spice. "God, I miss you so much, dad."

Tammy stayed in the chair for some time, afraid to leave the comfort that her father's scent brought her. That was, until she noticed another door off to the left.

Tammy had a feeling she knew where it led and dragged herself out of the chair and wrapped herself in her father's blanket. When she reached the door, she took in a deep breath and slowly turned the handle. Her intuition was right; it was her father's office. Frozen in the doorway, her body trembled, and her emotions were high from seeing her dad's office for the first time. Tammy gasped and bought her hand up to her mouth before releasing a heart-wrenching cry. "Oh, my god."

The room was wall-to-wall bookshelves, posters of his book covers, and many awards. In the middle of the room were two desks connected in an L shape; Tammy walked over to the desk and slid her hand over the mahogany wood, as she pictured her dad sitting in the leather chair creating his next novel. She took a seat, leaned back, and closed her eyes as tears streamed down her face. All of her dad's dedicated work over the past thirty years had come to an end. There would be no more stories. Tammy couldn't believe it. His sudden departure from the world numbed her to the core. When she opened her eyes and glanced over his desk, the memory of how organized he had always been popped into her head. Everything on the desk had a place. To the left was a yellow legal-size notepad. Tammy picked it up and recognized her dad's neat handwriting. There seemed to be notes for the book he had been working on. To the left, next to a container of pencils, Tammy saw a trinket she had sent him a few years ago for his birthday and smiled. It was a small statue that said *World's Greatest Dad.* She picked it up and studied it before holding it close to her chest. "He still has it."

As sad as the moment was, Tammy felt at peace sitting in her father's chair. She felt his presence and snuggled into the blanket still wrapped around her shoulders. The connection she yearned for had been made. Her trip to Ireland had filled in the blanks when it came to the last chapter of her dad's life. She had no more questions.

Tammy wanted to make her father proud, just like he had done her for all his life. She couldn't have asked for a better father and was who she was today because of him. Tomorrow was going to be the hardest day of her life when she would stand before family and friends to read the eulogy at the funeral. Tammy hadn't begun to write it; she couldn't. It was just too hard. But sitting in her dad's office had given her the strength she had been missing. Through her words, the world would know what a great man he was, and that he had left behind an amazing legacy. Tammy felt confident she could deliver the farewell he deserved.

On the day of the funeral, Tammy had no problem spotting her half-brother Andrew amongst the crowd of people gathered to say their final goodbyes to John. He was a younger version of their father, with short black hair, a chiseled chin identical to her dad's, and a tall body frame. She collapsed into his arms and let her tears fall. Andrew held her tight until Tammy was able to pull herself together. "The last time I saw you, you were just a toddler. I'm sure you don't remember me," Tammy said, with a half-smile. "I can't believe how much time has gone by. Dad's death has made me realize how short life really is."

"I've seen pictures of me sitting on your lap when you lived at dad's house in Lonesridge. Does that count?" Andrew laughed. "But we have the next two days to catch up and get to know each other."

Tammy gave him a caring smile and took his hand. "Yeah, I'm going to like that."

By the time Tammy headed home, her heart was filled with memories of her dad's home and the funeral. She felt she did her father proud, and hoped he was smiling down upon her from heaven as she read the eulogy. On the plane, heading back to America, Tammy reminisced on reconnecting with her half-brother Andrew, who reminded her so much of her dad. They compared their childhood days and laughed at how similar they were. Andrew talked of his two younger brothers, Conner and Bobby, who could not travel to Ireland. "I sure hope I get to meet them someday," Tammy said while listening to Andrew describe them. Together through tears and laughter, they toasted to the memory of their dad in the pubs, and when it was time to say goodbye, Tammy felt she had gained a lost brother.

On her long journey home with plenty of idle time to think, Tammy's thoughts turned to her mother and her one wish, to have all of her three daughters together. Guilt swept through Tammy. Her mother had dreamt about a reunion for years, but Tammy had always been too busy to give it much thought. Bust as she sat on the plane, alone and deep in thought, she realized her mother was right when she had said, "any one of us could die tomorrow." Tammy was done procrastinating and knew it was time to make it happen, but Donna struggled as a widow and didn't have the funds to travel. The only way Tammy could make it happen would be when her mom visited the states. Tammy was going to call Jenny in England and see if she could come with mom on her next trip.

Tammy smiled when she spotted Dwayne at the airport and raced into his arms. She kissed him hard and melted into his embrace. It felt good to be held by him. It's where she belonged.

Dwayne held her tight. "Oh, I've missed you so much, Tammy." He kissed her again and studied her eyes. "How are you doing? Are you holding up okay?"

Tammy nodded and rested her head on his shoulder. "Yeah, I'm okay. I'm so tired." She looked up and gave him a loving smile. "Even though it was one of the toughest things I've had to do, I'm glad I went. It gave me closure."

"I wish I could have been with you to support you," Dwayne said, with pity in his eyes.

Tammy patted his chest and pulled away. "It's okay. How could you with the farm we have back home," she chuckled.

Dwayne changed the subject. "Hey, if you feel up to it, Matt wants to meet us for dinner. He wants to hear all about your trip."

The thought made Tammy smile. "I would like that. I've not seen much of him since dad passed, and I have to remember he lost a grandpa too. I'll call him from the car and see where he wants to meet."

"Sound good," Dwayne said, as he grabbed Tammy's luggage.

They arrived at Coco's restaurant shortly after five. Tammy was exhausted, but she was excited to see Matt. Tammy figured she could sleep in the car on their drive home.

Anita, Matt's girlfriend of two years, also joined them. They had met at a party and were the same age.

Tammy beamed her a smile as she took a seat at the table across from them. "I didn't know you were going to be here."

Anita laughed. "Surprise."

"You look good." Tammy always loved it when Anita wore her thick, long black hair down. It was far too pretty to hide and tie back. "Your hair looks great."

Matt raised his hand and ran it across Anita's head, pulling her hair back away from her face. "You do have pretty hair." He turned and faced Tammy. "How are you doing, mom? Are you okay?"

"Yeah, I am. It was rough, but your grandfather is smiling down upon us. I'll miss him. But going to Ireland was a good decision. It filled in so many gaps with the relationship I had with him, and even though he is no longer with us, and as strange as it may sound, I feel closer to him."

Dwayne took Tammy's hand and kissed it. "It makes sense."

Matt turned to Anita and smiled, and she nodded. "Well, we were going to wait until after dinner to tell you, but I think you need cheering up," Matt said with a huge grin.

Tammy looked at him suspiciously, "tell me what?"

"Anita is pregnant."

Tammy gasped and raised her hands to her mouth. "What!" She turned to Dwayne, who looked as shocked as she felt. "Oh my god, I'm going to be a grandma."

Matt and Anita laughed together, "Yes, you are mom," Matt laughed.

"And you are going to be a daddy." She turned to Anita and took her hand. "And you will be a mommy." Tammy shook her head in disbelief, and dabbed her eyes with a nearby paper napkin. "I can't believe it. I'm going to be a grandma. My baby boy is going to be a dad."

Dwayne reached across the table and gave Matt a firm handshake. "Congratulations, son."

I guess that makes me a grandpa, right? Can I have that title?" Dwayne joked.

"You're damn right, you are," Matt laughed. But his laughter was cut short when he noticed Tammy looked sad and seemed to be deep in thought. "Mom, are you okay?"

"Yes. I was just thinking about how sad it is that your grandfather will not be here to meet his first great-grandson. It's strange how one great life has ended, and a new one is about to begin," Tammy said, as she wiped away a tear.

"Yeah, me too," Matt replied. "I know we are not married yet, but the baby will have grandpa's last name."

Tammy sucked in some air. "Oh, that's wonderful. Your grandpa would have been so proud of you." Tammy shook her head to keep back her tears. "I still can't believe he's gone. I've been thinking a lot lately about all the stuff I want to do in life. Life is so precious. None of us know how much time we have. Look at Donna's husband, Jason. He was so young when he died." She turned to Dwayne and squeezed his hand. "We have to get our house built. I want my mom and your parents to see it." Tammy thought of the other things she had been procrastinating on for years. "I want mom to see all of her girls together. Do you realize it's been over thirty-two years since we were all together?" She looked over at Matt. "Jenny has never met you, Matt."

"I know, and I've never met her kids either."

Tammy leaned back in the booth. "God, there's so much I want to do. I've had an idea for a book ever since I was with Steven. I'm going to think more seriously about that, too."

Dwayne sat up. A look of surprise blanketed his face. "A book? You never told me you wanted to write a book."

Tammy laughed. I haven't told anyone. It's just an idea I've carried with me all these years. I'm just going to give it some more thought—anyway, enough about me. Let's order our food. I'm not sure how much longer I'll be able to stay awake," she joked.

CHAPTER 31

Tammy woke the next morning anxious to call Jenny in England. She couldn't wait to tell her she was going to be a grandmother as well as her idea about Jenny coming to the States with their mom.

Tammy calculated in her head the years the twins had been separated and was stunned, "Wow! Thirty-five years." She glanced at the latest two pictures she had of them hanging on the wall. They no longer looked alike—Donna had long bleached blonde hair and wore a lot of make-up. Jenny was the opposite—little make-up and long dark brown hair. Tammy wondered if she would notice any physical similarities or habits in person. It was impossible to tell from a photograph.

After her usual three cups of morning coffee and seeing Dwayne off to work, Tammy settled into a patio chair outside the tiny house and dialed Jenny's number. She answered after three rings.

"Hello Jenny speaking."

"Hey Jenny, it's Tammy. I'm home now."

"Oh, hello Tammy," Jenny said in a thick English accent. "I was going to call you later today to see if you were home. How was it? I'm so sorry we couldn't make it to Ireland. We will miss Dad immensely."

"Yes, he will be missed. It was one of the hardest things I have ever done, but dad's at peace now. It was a beautiful service, and we made dad proud. Please don't feel bad about not being there. You are always there for mom when I can't be."

"Thank you, Tammy. I got the pictures you mailed from Ireland, and I'm glad you called. I wanted to talk to you about mom."

Tammy raised her tone a notch. "Is mom okay?"

"Well, I hope so. She's been acting differently lately."

Tammy creased her brow. "Different? How?"

"I'm sure it's nothing serious. She just seems to forget a lot lately, and she seems a little confused about some things."

"Like what?" Tammy asked.

"Well, the other day, she put her shoes on the wrong feet and never realized it until I said something to her. She laughed it off, but I found it strange."

"Wow, I can see why. Do you think it's just old age?"

"I don't know, Tammy. She's not that old, and her body is as fit as a fiddle. I just wanted to let you know mom has changed a bit, and I'll be visiting her more often so I can keep an eye on her."

"That's good to know, Jenny. Keep me posted on how she's doing."

"I will."

Tammy smiled when she spoke. "I do have some brighter news."

Jenny's tone switched to a lighter tone. "You do. What is it?"

"I'm going to be a grandma." Tammy squealed into the phone. "Matt and Anita are going to have a baby."

Jenny gasped. "Oh my goodness! I'm going to be an auntie. Oh, congratulations, Tammy. I'm so happy for you. It's such a shame dad will never get to meet his first great-grandchild."

"I know." Tammy hesitated for a moment and decided not to mention to Jenny her idea of coming over next year with their mom. She felt it wasn't the right time after what Jenny had told her about their mom's health.

After their conversation had ended, Tammy left to take a much-needed shower. She hadn't bathed since leaving Ireland. Standing naked, she checked the water with her hand before stepping into the shower stall, and closed her eyes as the water soothed her. "Man, that feels good," she whispered and reached for the soap. After a few minutes, she paused when she felt the lump again on the underside of her right breast. "Huh. It's still there." Tammy ran her hand around the area. She had discovered it a week before her trip to Ireland. It was still that same size. Tammy assumed it was a bug bite and thought nothing of it. But today, she became concerned. "Bug bites don't last two weeks." Tammy squeezed it. It was hard and about an inch in diameter close to the surface. "I wonder what it is?" Thoughts of cancer crossed her mind, but she quickly discarded the ridiculous notion with a vigorous shake of her head. "I'm only in my forties. I'm too young to have cancer." Tammy decided if the lump were still there next week, she'd make an appointment with the doctors. For now, her mind was made up not to say anything to Dwayne or Matt.

Tammy continued to check for the lump every night, and her anxieties increased when it was still there a week later. "Fuck. What the hell could it be?" she wondered after stepping out of the shower Friday evening.

Dwayne knew her well and noticed her sad look. "Hey, are you okay?"

Now dressed in her bathrobe, Tammy took a seat next to him on the small two-seater couch. "I hope so."

Dwayne sat up from his relaxed position. "What does that mean?"

"I'm not sure. It might be nothing, but I've had this lump on my breast for over three weeks, and it's not going away."

Dwayne rested his hand on Tammy's knee. "Don't you think you should go get it checked? I'm sure it's nothing serious."

Tammy nodded. "Yeah, It's probably a swollen gland or something. I'll call the doctors on Monday and make an appointment," she replied and gave Dwayne a reassuring pat on the thigh.

Tammy was relieved when Wednesday finally arrived. She had an appointment with her doctor in the afternoon and was looking forward to having any worries of cancer be erased.

"Do you want me to leave work early and go with you?" Dwayne had asked in the morning.

Tammy shook her head. "No, I'll be fine. I'll call you as soon as I'm done."

After the doctor had examined her, Tammy waited anxiously for his prognosis. "I won't know anything until I look at the mammogram. It will be in a couple of days."

Tammy rolled her eyes. "You mean I have to wait a few more days," she whined.

"I'm afraid so. You will need to come back on Friday for the results."

After making an appointment at the front desk, Tammy stormed out of the clinic feeling frustrated. She didn't want to worry anymore. This was clouding her mind every day, and she struggled daily to be productive. Before heading home, she called Dwayne from her car.

He answered on the first ring. "Tell me it's good news," he said, sounding anxious.

"I didn't find out anything. The doctor won't know until he looks at the mammogram. I have to go back Friday." Tammy scooted down in her seat and let out a big sigh. "This sucks."

"I know it does, hon," Dwayne said. "But at least you are getting checked. I'm sure it's nothing, and this will be all behind you next week."

"Yeah, I know. But all this waiting and not knowing is driving me nuts."

"Just hang in there, babe. It's just a few days."

"I will. I love you," Tammy said in a softer tone.

"I love you, too."

Friday couldn't come soon enough for Tammy. She'd had enough worrying and was ready for some answers, but the doctor had a different plan.

"What do you mean I need to see another doctor and have a biopsy?" Tammy shrieked.

"So we can take a sample and see what the lump is."

Tammy hesitated before she spoke. "Do you think it's cancer?"

"I'm not going to make any guesses, Tammy. The results from the biopsy will tell me. Until then, try not to think about it, and keep yourself busy by taking your mind off it."

"Easy for you to say," Tammy snapped.

Four days after she'd had the painful biopsy, Tammy and Dwayne were hiking with their dogs when Tammy's cell phone rang. She pulled it out of her back pocket, looked at the screen, and gasped. "It's my doctor's office."

"Then answer it," Dwayne said, while nudging her arm.

Tammy took a deep breath and took the call. "Hello."

She recognized the voice of the receptionist at the clinic. "Hi, is this Tammy Mellows?"

"Yes, it is," Tammy replied, unable to hide her nervousness.

"Hi. This is Sheila at doctor Shelton's office. We need to schedule an appointment for you to discuss your biopsy results with the doctor."

"Can't you just give them to me over the phone?" Tammy asked.

"No, I'm afraid not. It has to be done in person."

Tammy didn't want to wait any longer. "Can I come in today?"

"Let me put you on hold for a minute, and I'll check."

Tammy suddenly heard classical music playing in her ear.

"What is going on?" Dwayne whispered while petting Harley.

"They have the results of my test. She's checking to see if I can go in today to discuss them."

A few minutes later, Sheila came back on the line. "Can you come in at four?"

Tammy glanced at her watch. Even though her phone had a clock, she still liked to wear a watch. It was two-thirty. Yes, I'll be there."

"Great, we will see you then."

After ending the call, Dwayne took her hand. "Are you okay?"

"Yeah, just nervous. What if it's cancer? I never thought I'd be thinking of cancer at my age."

"Let's not think those thoughts. Let's wait to hear what the doctor has to say."

"It's all I've been thinking about. It's hard not to."

With his free arm, Dwayne wrapped his arm around her waist and pulled her in. "I'm sure you are fine. I want you to relax. Everything is going to be okay."

Tammy nodded and rested her head on his chest. "We should get back. I want to take a shower before we go."

CHAPTER 32

On the short drive to the doctor's office, Tammy and Dwayne were silent. Both deep in thought. Tammy rubbed her sweaty palms as she glanced out of the window, wondering how she would feel on their drive home. When they pulled into the parking lot, Tammy's anxieties peaked. From the car, she looked over at the double doors to the building entrance and was fearful of exiting the car. Was she about to begin the hardest battle of her life, or had life thrown her a curve-ball? Would she be able to continue living with no fears and put all of this behind her? She had so many unanswered questions, and they would be all answered on the other side of that door.

She felt safe in the car. Life was good, and she didn't want it to change.

Dwayne pulled her out of her concerning thoughts. He rested his hand on her knee. "Are you ready?"

"As ready as I'll ever be."

Dwayne stepped out of the car, walked around to the other side, and opened her door. Before Tammy took his extended hand, she rubbed her palms again and tried to stop her body from trembling but failed. She stood before Dwayne, where he clutched her waist. Her breathing was heavy, and her eyes looked down at the ground.

"Hey, it's going to be okay," Dwayne said in a soft voice, as he rubbed her shoulders. He kissed her lightly on the lips. "Relax, okay."

Tammy couldn't speak and nodded as she took his hand and held it tight. Her feet felt like cement as she took time walking to the clinic. Her brow dripped sweat, and she wanted to turn around and run back to the car. She didn't want to know her fate. Afraid, Tammy dug her nails deep into Dwayne's hand as they approached the door. Before they entered, Tammy looked at Dwayne, unable to hide her worry.

He gave her a loving smile. "You are going to be fine," he said, as he opened the door,

Tammy took a deep breath and entered the building. She scanned the waiting room, and it was quiet. After they had checked in, they took a seat and waited. Tammy didn't let go of Dwayne's hand as he held her in his arms and tried to soothe her trembling body. A few minutes later, a young blonde nurse appeared through the door that led to the examination rooms. She called Tammy's name. "Tammy Mellows," scanning the room.

Tammy slowly raised her hand. "Here."

The nurse nodded. "Follow me, please."

The nurse led them to a small room where they both took a seat next to each other. "The doctor will be right with you." She closed the door behind her.

Tammy tried to read her eyes for any clues of her fate. Did the nurse know? Tammy wondered. If she did, she wasn't giving away any clues. Were they trained to do that? Tammy thought. "Thank you," Tammy said, as she took Dwayne's hand again.

After the nurse had left the room, Tammy lowered her head

onto Dwayne's chest. "What if I have cancer? I can't stop thinking about it."

Dwayne tightened his hold on her and kissed the top of her head. "Let's just wait and see what the doctor says."

After what seemed like an eternity and reading every poster on the wall, they finally heard a knock on the door.

"Come in," Dwayne called.

Tammy pulled herself away from Dwayne's chest and tried to calm her nerves. She again tried to read the doctor's eyes for any clues on what he was about to tell them, but like the nurse, he wasn't giving anything away.

"Good afternoon, Tammy. How are you feeling?"

Tammy sat up straight. "That all depends on my test results," she said, with a hint of sarcasm.

Doctor Shelton took a seat across from them in front of a monitor and opened up her file. Tammy took a deep breath and waited. Dwayne squeezed her hand.

"Well, the tests came back positive, I'm afraid. You have breast cancer."

Tammy and Dwayne gasped at the same time. "No!" Tammy screamed in a panicked state. "I'm too young."

Dwayne pulled her in. "Shh, let doctor Shelton speak. What stage cancer does she have?" Dwayne asked.

"Tammy has an invasive Carcinoma, and from the mammogram images, the size looks to be between stage one and two." He released a subtle smile. "That is good. It looks like we caught it early, but we will know more after we have checked your lymphnodes for any spreading."

"Oh my god, I can't believe this is happening. I don't want to die."

Doctor Shelton tried to calm her. "Tammy, medicine for breast cancer has come a long away, and the survival rate is very high if it's caught early. But you will have to go through some rigorous treatment to ensure we remove the cancer and take preventive medicine to stop it from coming back."

"What kind of treatment?" Dwayne asked.

Tammy shook her head, sat up straight, and spoke with a stern voice. "Look, I can beat this crap. I honestly don't have time for this. Tell me what I have to do, and I'll do it."

Dwayne turned and looked at Tammy with wide eyes. Her sudden change of attitude surprised him.

"I like your attitude," Doctor Shelton said, with a smile. "Well, you have a few choices. All of which will be discussed in detail with your advice counselor. She will go over everything with you and will help you make the right decision for you. The two prescribed treatments are a lumpectomy, where we will remove a partial part of the breast where the cancer is, followed by radiation treatment."

"Radiation treatment," Tammy barked.

"Yes. It will destroy any lingering cells. Your other choice is a full removal of the breast or breasts, and no radiation would be required, and we would do reconstructive surgery."

Tammy lowered her head. "God, I feel like I'm in a nightmare."

Dwayne pulled Tammy into his space and cradled her in his arms. "Does she have to decide now?" he asked.

Doctor Shelton shook his head. "No. We will assign Tammy an advice counselor who will go over everything in detail with both of you, and she will make sure the right decision is made for Tammy."

Tammy's head was spinning with words she'd never heard before in her lifetime, survival, surgery, cancer, mastectomy. She was petrified. Everything she had experienced before in her life seemed so trivial compared to this. She thought back to the many battles she had conquered in the past, escaping Steven and his warped world of heroin addiction, becoming a commercial fisher-woman when many doubted she could—overcoming alcohol addiction. If she could beat those challenges, then she knew she could and would beat cancer.

"So, what happens now?" Tammy asked.

"Your advice counselor will call you in the next day or so to set up an appointment, and once a decision has been made on what treatment you want, we can set up a date for surgery as soon as possible." Doctor Shelton put Tammy's file on his desk and folded his arms. He gave her a caring smile. "Tammy, you will have a great team behind you at the CBCC clinic, where you will be treated."

Tammy nodded. "Thank you. I'm just really scared right now. You hear about others getting cancer, and you never think it's going to happen to you. I feel like I've just been thrown under a bus."

"I'll be here for you," Dwayne told her, as he stroked her hair. "We'll fight this together."

Tammy gave him a loving smile. "I know you will. I couldn't do this on my own."

Doctor Shelton extended his hand to Dwayne. "She's in good hands. Take as much time as you need in here. I'm going to call the advice counselor, and we will be in touch."

"Thank you, doctor," Dwayne said.

Tammy lifted her head and sat up straight. She folded her arms and leaned back against the wall. "Thank you, doctor."

After doctor Shelton had left, Tammy let out a heavy sigh. "Wow! I never in my wildest dreams would have thought I would get cancer. Especially at my age."

"I'm in shock," Dwayne replied. "But you're going to be fine. The doctor believes it's in the early stages. I'll be there all the way with you."

Tammy shook her head. "Surgery, radiation. Bloody hell. I wasn't expecting this."

Dwayne rubbed her knee. "Are you ready to go? We can talk more at home." He paused. "Are you going to call Matt?"

Tammy raised her hand to her brow and flipped back her head. "Oh god, I have to tell Matt. He has no idea about any of this. I didn't want to worry him and figured I'd only say something if the news were not good." She took in a deep breath. "Yes, I'll call him tonight. But I'm not telling anyone else. Definitely not my mom. She doesn't need to know. I'm not going to scare her."

"What about your sisters?" Dwayne asked.

Tammy gasped, and she raised her hand to her dropped jaw. "Yes! I need to tell them. My aunt on my dad's side died of breast cancer. It's in our genes. I don't even know if they've ever had a mammogram, but they need to get checked." Tammy raised her hand. "But that's it. I honestly don't want many people knowing. This is my battle, and once I know I'm in the clear, and I'll be okay, then I will tell others."

"I understand." He took her hand. "Come on, let's go home."

When they reached the car, the first thing Tammy saw was a pack of cigarettes sitting on the dash. She leaned forward in her seat, grabbed the pack, and crushed them in her hand before throwing them out of the car window.

"What are you doing?" Dwayne shrieked.

Tammy gave him a hard stare. "I'm done with cigarettes. I have cancer." She paused for a moment. "Wow. It feels weird saying that —no more smoking for me. And you know something? I'm okay with it. It's like a switch went on. When you face fighting cancer, quitting smoking doesn't seem so hard. Huh, I'll be damned. So many times I've tried to quit, but I know I will succeed. I have no desire to smoke any more." Her eyes grew wide. "I'd be afraid to."

Dwayne released a slight chuckle. "Okay, then. I guess we are quitting."

Tammy placed her hand on his shoulder. "You don't have to. You don't have cancer."

"I'm not going to smoke in front of you. I told you we are in this together." He leaned in closer to her. "No more cigarettes for both of us."

Tammy nodded with approval. "Okay, then. The next thing I have to do is call Matt, and then hopefully, my advice counselor will call tomorrow, and I can begin to kick cancer's ass."

Dwayne beamed a huge smile. "There you go. Keep that attitude."

Tammy wanted to wait a few hours before she called Matt. She was still in shock over the life-changing news that she had cancer. Dwayne joined her on the grass where she had sat since they arrived home. Their mood was somber. "Here, I made you a cup of tea."

Tammy turned her head and managed to give him a weak smile. "Thanks."

Dwayne sat in the chair next to her. "Are you okay?"

Tammy had her knees up under her chin as she cradled her body. She nodded. "Yea. I'm just stunned by all this. There's so much shit I want to do in life, and when you're told you have cancer, it puts it all into perspective." She turned to face Dwayne, "I mean, imagine if I just ignored the lump for a year. It might have been so far along that I'd be dead before the age of fifty. And even now, they don't know if it has spread to my lymph nodes. What if it has?"

Dwayne took her hand. "I know, hon. I still can't believe it myself. You are a healthy, kick-ass woman, and it's that quality about you that will help you beat this thing."

"Oh, I have every intention of beating it. I plan on being around to welcome my first grandchild, and my mom still needs to have all of her daughters together." She shook her head. "God, that's something I've been putting off for years, and I could really kick myself now. It's going to have to happen when mom comes out next year. Jenny is going to have to come too, and then we can do a road trip to Colorado."

Dwayne chuckled. "Slow down. We have no idea how you are going to be feeling next year. You will have just gone through cancer treatment. Let's take care of you first, and then think about the other stuff."

"I know, but Jenny says mom has been acting strange lately. I want to do this before it's too late. It's a promise I made to mom years ago."

Dwayne's voice became stern. He knew how stubborn Tammy could be. "And you will, once you are well enough to take on the task and travel."

Tammy rolled her eyes. She knew she wasn't going to win this debate. "Fine." She checked her watch. "I need to call Matt. Can you grab me the phone?"

"Sure, it's in the house. I'll be right back."

Tammy remembered her mom's favorite quote as she took a sip of tea for courage before calling Matt. *Never underestimate the power of a cup of tea.* Tammy took a huge sip and savored the hot liquid as it slid down her throat. "You're right, mom," Tammy said out loud, as she took another large gulp. The urge for a cigarette kicked in again for the numerous time since she had thrown her pack out of the car. Tammy did what seemed to work to overcome the craving. She took a deep breath and said out loud. "You have cancer. You can't smoke anymore." The simple reminder relaxed her need for a cigarette substantially. Feeling the cravings going away, she smiled and took in another deep breath.

Dwayne returned with the phone and handed it to her. "Here you go."

After three rings, her son Matt answered the phone. "Hey buddy, it's your mom."

"Hey mom, how's it going?"

Tammy took a deep breath. "Well, I've been better."

"What's going on?" Matt asked, sounding worried.

"Well, it seems I have breast cancer."

"What?" Matt gasped.

"Now, I don't want you to worry. The doctor believes it's in the early stages, and I should be able to beat this thing." Tammy was determined to hold it together, even though she was scared to death. She gripped the phone hard as she spoke and bit her lip to hold back her tears. "I'm going to be fine."

"You better be," Matt said, with a nervous laugh. "We'll come up this weekend."

"That would be great. I'll know more by then."

They talked for a few more minutes, and Tammy told Matt she would have surgery and radiation treatment, and Matt said he would be there for her.

"I love you, Matt. We'll see you this weekend."

"Love you too, mom."

After she had hung up the phone, Tammy broke down and cried for the first time since she had been told she had cancer. Telling her son made it seem all surreal. She had a lot to live for, including the birth of her first grandchild, and she'd be damned if she was going to let cancer take it all away from her. Dwayne scooched his chair closer to her and wrapped her in his arms. "We'll get through this. You've always been a fighter and a strong woman."

Tammy shook her head and straightened her back. She held her head high as she spoke. "You're damn right I'm a fighter. I've got this. Okay, enough of the sappiness. After calling my sisters, I want to have a nice quiet dinner and watch a movie. I need to take my mind off this crap."

"You got it," Dwayne said with a loving smile.

"I want to go with a lumpectomy." Tammy had told Wendy, her advice counselor, two days later. "A mastectomy and then reconstructive surgery scares the hell out of me," Tammy confessed.

Wendy sat across from her and nodded. "We have covered all the basics for each option, and I think you have made the right decision. You will have to go through seven weeks of radiation therapy and five years of taking the medication Tamoxifen, which is a hormone therapy drug and will help prevent the cancer from returning," she said before removing her glasses.

"I'm okay with that," Tammy replied.

Wendy put her glasses back on and looked down at her notes. "Okay then, I will schedule you for surgery next week, and a nurse will call you later today with all the instructions and more details," she told Tammy.

Since learning that she had cancer, Tammy's life had been a blur. Each day rolled into the next. Everything she had done revolved around her fight against the horrible disease. Tammy couldn't believe how her life had changed in just over a week. And now here she was lying in a hospital waiting to be taken into surgery.

Dwayne had just stepped out for a cigarette. He was finding it harder to quit, but then again, he hadn't been told he had cancer. He had cut down a lot, and refused to smoke in front of her. Tammy had faith he would eventually quit altogether. They had just finished making all the necessary phone calls to Matt and a few friends to let them know she was about to go in for surgery. Tammy was anxious to have it all behind her and be waking up in the recovery room. Surgery didn't scare her. Her worry was the outcome of her lymph nodes. Had the cancer spread? She feared it had.

Dwayne returned, looking more relaxed, but the worry in his eyes was still visible. "How are you doing, babe?" he asked, with a loving smile.

"I'm good. I wish they'd take me in. I hate laying here doing nothing."

Dwayne chuckled at her remark. She never was one to sit still. "Well, you'd better get used to it. You're going to be laid up for a while."

"Not if I have anything to do with it," Tammy barked. "I won't let this shit keep me down. I may rest for a day or so, but I gotta keep busy to keep my mind off this crap, otherwise, I'll go crazy."

"I hear you. And you will do whatever you want to do and not what the doctors tell you. I already know," he laughed.

A few minutes later, they were approached by a male nurse. "How are you feeling, Tammy?" he asked.

Dwayne stepped aside so the nurse could check Tammy's vitals.

"Good," Tammy replied.

"Well, I'm here to take you into surgery, and when you wake up, your husband will be in the recovery room waiting for you." He looked over at Dwayne and gave him a nod.

It suddenly felt so surreal for Tammy, and she choked back her tears. She wasn't going to cry.

Dwayne took her hand. "I'll be right here. I love you."

Tammy saw the tears pooling in his eyes, and felt tears trickle down her cheeks. "I love you, too."

Dwayne walked alongside the bed she was being pushed in, holding her hand tight until they came to the double doors where he wasn't allowed to enter. He kissed her hard on the lips. "You're going to be fine." She watched as the doors swung closed behind her. All he could do now was wait.

"Tammy, can you hear me? Tammy, it's Dwayne."

Tammy blinked a few times. She heard his voice, but her eyes felt so heavy. She strained to open them.

"Tammy? It's Dwayne. It's over. You're in the recovery room."

Tammy tried to open her eyes again and managed for a few seconds.

She felt him take her hand. "Hey sweetie, can you hear me?"

She remembered everything and opened her eyes once more. She had just had surgery. She looked up and saw Dwayne's beautiful blue eyes and his gorgeous smile looking down on her. "Hi," she whispered.

"Hey, beautiful. You're awake."

"Am I?" She was now semi-conscious, and scanned the room with just the movement of her eyes. "Where am I?"

"You're in the recovery room. They brought you here about an hour ago. The doctor will be here shortly."

Tammy closed her eyes for a second. The last thing she remembered was when she tried to count back from ten. She remembered only getting to seven. She suddenly remembered why she had surgery. The fear swept through her. "Did they say anything about the cancer? Did they get it all?"

"The doctor will tell us when he gets here."

Tammy tried to scooch herself up and felt the tight bandages around her chest. "Ouch. That wasn't a good idea."

"Easy. You have stitches. What are you trying to do?" Dwayne asked, surprised by her sudden movements.

"I want to sit up. My neck hurts."

"Oh, you're going to be a hard one to keep still. Come on, let me help you."

A few minutes after Dwayne had helped Tammy get comfortable, they were greeted by Tammy's surgeon. He extended his hand to Dwayne. "I'm doctor Peterson." He turned and smiled at Tammy. "How are you feeling, Tammy?"

"Sore and thirsty." Tammy didn't want any small talk. She wanted to hear about the cancer. "Did you get it all? How big was it, and how were my lymph-nodes?"

Dwayne took her hand and listened intently as the doctor spoke.

"The surgery went really well. We managed to get all the cancer, which was about the size of a grape, and I'm happy to say we removed nine lymph nodes, and they were all clean, which means it has not spread."

Tammy and Dwayne released a huge sigh of relief at the same time and smiled at each other with tears in their eyes. "Oh my god. That's so good to hear. Thank you, doctor." Dwayne said.

"It's all good news, Tammy. We caught the cancer early. You'll be following up with radiation therapy in a few months after you have healed." He smiled. "It looks like you are going to be fine."

Tammy rested her head back in the softness of the pillows and let her tears roll down her cheeks. She believed the worst was behind her. The cancer was gone. After radiation, she should be able to get her life back on track, but she knew the worry of it returning would haunt her for the rest of her life. She never believed she would ever get cancer and now her number one concern was, would it come back?

Not only had her life been transformed, but her outlook on life had changed. Death had come knocking at her door with a small warning and a reminder that she will not be on this earth forever, and she should make the most of it while she has the privilege of being here. Tammy thought about Jason, whose life was cut too short by cancer at the young age of thirty-nine, and her father's recent death. Once she was well, she would start doing the things she had been putting off for years.

She looked over at Dwayne and smiled. She was so lucky to have him by her side. They had built a life together, and now he was here for her when she had been knocked down. He leaned in and kissed her forehead while he held her hand. "How are you doing?"

"I'm good. When can I go home?"

Dwayne chuckled. "You just had surgery, woman. I'm sure it won't be for at least a few hours." He watched as Tammy strained to keep her eyes open, and within a few minutes, she was asleep. He gently brushed her bangs to the side and released his hold on her hand. "I'll be back in a few minutes. I'm going to go call Matt," he whispered.

CHAPTER 35

Tammy was making the hour drive from her radiation therapy to home. It was one of the days she made the trip alone. Dwayne went with her when he didn't have to work. Her treatments were going well, to her surprise, and she wasn't experiencing any side effects. She was in week five and had two more weeks to go. She couldn't wait until she didn't have to make the two-hour round trip five days a week at the crack of dawn to get her daily dose of radiation. What a way to start your day—she had said to her friend Mandy, who drove with her three times a week. They had become close since meeting at a neighbor's barbecue a few years ago and, like Dwayne, had been there for her during her fight with cancer. "Who needs coffee? Radiation will get you going," Tammy had laughed, while riding with Mandy one morning.

Along with the radiation treatment, Tammy took Tamoxifen and showed her displeasure when she was told that she would have to take it for the next five years.

Tammy was anxious to get home. After healing from her surgery and before the radiation treatments had begun, she and

Dwayne didn't want to put off building the house any longer and dove right in. They tore down the old house with the help of many friends and Matt. They drew plans up, and in their spare time, they began the build.

For Tammy, it couldn't come at a better time. It was excellent therapy for her. It helped take her mind off the brutal treatment she was still going through, and instead, dream about the future she and Dwayne would have in their new home. After she had attended to her work tasks, she planned to spend the rest of the day digging dirt for the foundation of the new house with some neighbors' help.

By week seven—her last week of radiation, Tammy was struggling. Her breast area where she was receiving the treatment was severely blistered, and the lotion that the doctors had prescribed wasn't helping. Fatigue was an issue every day, and her mind was a constant blur. She couldn't focus or think straight, and her entire body ached. There was no working on the house during the last week of treatment. She slept, and on her last day of radiation, it surprised her at how emotional she became. She hugged the technician, Brenda, who had become a familiar face every morning for the past seven weeks. "This may sound weird, but I'm going to miss you," Tammy cried.

"I'm going to miss you too, Tammy. You stay strong, okay."

Tammy nodded and gave her another hug. "I will."

Life returned to what Tammy now called her new normal, slowly. She no longer took life for granted. Those days of thinking she was immortal were long gone. Life was a precious gem, and she needed to make every day count. She and Dwayne continued to chip away at the new house. Her father, John, may never see the house built, but Dwayne and Tammy were determined that his parents, Cathy and Charlie, and her mother Rose would see it before their health declined. Sadly, Charlie had been diagnosed with early signs of Alzheimer's, which crushed them.

"God, I hope my dad gets to see the house built before he gets too sick," Dwayne said, when he first found out two months before Tammy was diagnosed with cancer. And Tammy had concerns about her mother's health, too.

Dwayne and Tammy took daily hikes with the dogs, which helped rebuild Tammy's strength after radiation, and three weeks after completing her radiation treatment, she was feeling pretty good. Her blisters had healed, and her skin had returned to its normal color. She was excited about the days ahead and getting her life back on track. But she became concerned when she suddenly had a shortness of breath on a hike she did daily with no issues. She stopped in the middle of the trail, bent over, and heaved her chest.

Dwayne stood beside with a look of worry. "Are you okay?"

Tammy continued to suck in oxygen. "I can't breathe," she gasped.

"Do you want to take a break?" Dwayne asked.

Tammy remained bent over at the waist. Her hands gripped her knees. "Just for a minute." She took a few more deep breaths before straightening her back. "Why am I out of breath? I hike this trail all the time."

Dwayne shrugged his shoulders. "Maybe you're just having an off day. We spent all day yesterday working on the house. You may have overdone it. You are supposed to be still taking it easy, and you worked your butt off yesterday. Do you want to keep going or turn around?"

Dwayne wasn't surprised by her reply. "No, I'm not quitting. Let's keep going." But fifty yards later, she had to stop again and catch her breath. "God, this sucks. I can't breathe," she said, as her heart raced beneath her chest. She raised her hands and turned around. "I'm done. Let's go back to the car," she said, as she leaned on Dwayne's arm for support.

"Are you sure you're okay?" Dwayne asked. "I can take you to the hospital if you'd like?"

"I'm not going to the hospital; I'm just out of breath. I'll be fine," Tammy snarled.

The next day Tammy had forgotten all about the incident until she went to a friend's house to water their house plants because they were out of town. She was surprised at how out of breath she was after climbing the flight of stairs. She sat at the top and gasped for air. "God. I have no energy," she panted. Tammy wondered if her body was still recuperating from radiation or if it was some of the side effects of the Tamoxifen.

At her appointment with her oncologist the next day, Tammy mentioned it to him.

"How are you feeling, Tammy? Any abnormalities or changes?" her doctor asked.

Tammy hesitated for a minute—wondering if she was overreacting. "Well, I've been out of breath a lot lately." Tammy tried to shake off her concerns with her hand. "But it's probably no big deal."

But it seemed Doctor Baton wasn't so sure. "Okay. Tell me more."

"Well, my husband and I went on a hike the other day, and I had to stop a few times to catch my breath. I've never had to do that before, and yesterday I barely made it up a flight of stairs."

"Tammy, I'm going to schedule you for an ultrasound. But I want it done today. Can you stick around while I get it set up? Obviously, something is going on, and I don't want you to have to come back. You live an hour away."

"Sure, that fine," Tammy said, puzzled by his urgency. "What do you think it is?"

"I can't say for sure until you have the ultrasound."

Tammy returned to the waiting room and called Dwayne. "Hey. I'm going to be here a little longer."

"Everything okay?"

"I hope so. I told Doctor Baton about my shortness of breath, and now he wants to do an ultrasound."

"Well, that's good, Tammy. At least he's not ignoring it. You're in good hands. I'm sure you're fine. He's being precautionary."

"Yeah, I guess you're right. He said I could go home after the ultrasound, and they will call me with the results as soon as they have them."

"Okay, sounds good. Call me when you are on your way home."

"I will. Love you."

"Love you too."

For the rest of the day, Tammy tried not to worry about the ultrasound. She believed Dwayne was right, that they were just cautious and that she had nothing to worry about, even though her shortness of breath was still present. She tried to keep her mind off of it by keeping busy with her work and doing projects in the new house. As more hours passed, she became more relaxed, and her fear that something could be wrong had subsided.

"Any news from the doctor?" Dwayne asked, before he headed off to work the next morning.

"No, nothing yet. I'll call you if I hear anything."

Dwayne smiled and gave her a light kiss on the cheek. "Sounds good. In the meantime, take it easy, and don't be doing too much."

Tammy laughed. She loved how he always watched out for her. "I have some work to do on the computer, and I want to do some yard work."

"Tammy, yard work is not taking it easy."

"I won't do too much. I promise."

Dwayne shook his head. "You're impossible," he joked.

Tammy was pleased when she had all of her work done for her online business completed by eleven. She could now catch up on some weeding that had been neglected because most of their spare time had been spent working on the house. It was a crisp May morning with scattered clouds in the sky, and a comfortable sixty-eight degrees. It was perfect weather for gardening and for the dogs to watch from under a shade tree.

Like always, when she was alone, her thoughts drifted to the day when she first learned she had cancer. She couldn't believe that was seven months ago. She remembered how scared she was when she first found out, and the fear was still present that it might return. Her doctors had told her that the first five years were the most critical. After that, the odds of the cancer returning, even though it would still be a concern, would drop substantially. It would require her to see her oncologists every three months for the first two years, then every six months after that.

The ringtone of her cell phone interrupted her thoughts. Tammy rose from her knees and raced to the phone, sitting on the bench. "Hello."

"Tammy, it's Doctor Baton. I have the results of your ultrasound."

Tammy felt a lump rise in her throat. "Is everything okay?"

There was an urgency to Doctor Baton's voice when he spoke. "Actually, no. I need you to listen to me carefully and do exactly what I ask."

Fear swept through Tammy, and her brow dripped with sweat. "Okay."

"I want you to stop whatever you are doing. Do not make any sudden movements and get yourself to the nearest emergency room as soon as you can. Do not drive yourself."

"Why? And if I go to the ER, they will have me wait for hours."

Doctor Baton raised his voice and spoke with a sharp tone. "Tammy, you have four blood clots on your lungs—also known as pulmonary embolisms. You have three on the right lung and one on the left. This is nothing to mess around with. If they travel to your brain, it could mean instant death."

"What?" Tammy shrieked. "I've never heard of this."

"It's pretty serious and explains your shortness of breath. Now listen to me. When you get to the ER, you tell them you have four PE's on your lungs, and trust me; they will take you right away."

Tammy was shocked. "Really? But I feel fine today."

Doctor Baton expressed his frustration with her questions.

"Tammy, don't put this off because you are feeling okay. Get yourself to the hospital now! The ER will contact me once they have admitted you."

Tammy cowered from his raised voice. "Okay, I will."

After ending the call, Tammy wasted no time calling Dwayne. "Hey, I just got off the phone with my doctor, and he told me to go to the emergency room. I could call Mandy to take me because he told me not to drive."

Dwayne sounded alarmed. "The emergency room? Why?"

"He says I have blood clots on my lungs."

Dwayne gasped. "Shit! I'm coming home. I'll be there within the hour. I'll take you to the hospital. Don't do anything until I get there. Go have a cup of tea or something," he said, unable to hide the panic in his voice.

Dwayne made it home in record time. He wasn't sure how many driving laws he broke, but he was thankful he didn't get caught. He found Tammy sitting on the grass, sipping hot tea with their two dogs at her feet. "Hey, how are you feeling?" he asked with a look of worry.

She turned and smiled. "I feel fine. I did, even before the doctor had called me. I'm not sure why I have to race to the emergency room?" she confessed.

"I know why. I called some friends on the way home and talked to them about pulmonary embolisms. They are serious and can be deadly."

"That's what my doctor told me. He told me not to make any sudden moves."

"A guy at work told me his wife had cancer like you and went through the same treatment. She had a blood clot, and she died in her sleep."

Tammy gasped. "What! Oh shit. Now I'm terrified. This is worse than the damn cancer."

Dwayne hated how badly it scared her, but she needed to

realize the urgency. "I'm just trying to put it in perspective for you. I'm not trying to scare you. Let me put the birds away, and then we are heading straight for the hospital."

Tammy nodded. "Okay. Do you want me to do anything?" she asked.

"Yes, sit still. I know it's hard," he chuckled.

Tammy stuck out her tongue. "Oh, stop. I listen when I want to."

"Exactly. Only if you want to," he laughed. "I'll be right back."

An hour and a half later, Dwayne hooked Tammy's arm with his and walked her slowly through the doors of the emergency entrance. Tammy scanned the waiting room. It was busy. "Wow, this place is packed. They won't see me right away. Look at that guy over there. The towel wrapped around his hand is covered in blood," she whispered. "He needs a doctor more than me."

Dwayne led her over to the receptionist. The middle-aged woman wearing glasses looked up from her computer monitor and gave him a half-smile. "Can I help you?" she asked.

Dwayne unhooked his arm from Tammy's and rested it on the counter. "Yes. My wife has four PE's on her lungs, and her doctor told her to come straight to emergency."

Tammy waved her hand and gave the nurse a faint smile.

The nurse looked surprised. "Okay, I'm going to call for a wheelchair for your wife and get her admitted to the trauma unit right away." The nurse said, as she quickly picked up a telephone and made a call.

"Wheelchair? Trauma unit?" Tammy said with a creased brow. "I can walk. I don't need a wheelchair."

The nurse hung up the phone and gave Tammy a stern look. "In your condition, anything can happen. The wheelchair will be here soon."

Tammy and Dwayne didn't have to wait too long. Within a minute, a hospital porter approached Tammy pushing a wheelchair. "I want you to ease down into the chair slowly," he instructed her.

Tammy did as she was told, and Dwayne followed close behind as they wheeled her into the trauma unit. She was greeted by three doctors who helped her up onto the bed, immediately hooked her up to an IV, and took her vitals. Fear swept through Tammy. This was serious, and she watched with concerns as she was being probed, poked, and pricked.

"We've talked to your oncologist, and he is sending your records over." A nurse told her, as she put yet another needle in her arm.

"What's that for?" Tammy asked.

"It is a blood thinner. You are a fortunate lady. It's bad enough to have one blood clot, but you have four. It only takes one of those to break loose and travel up to your brain."

"Is she going to be okay?" Dwayne asked.

"We are going to monitor her very closely and continue to give her the blood thinner through IV until she has another scan. More than likely, she will have scans done on her legs tomorrow, because that is where blood clots begin—especially behind the knee. So we will want to check for that."

"Tomorrow?" Dwayne questioned. "You mean she's being admitted?"

"Oh yes, she's not going anywhere until those clots have gone."

"How long will that take?" Tammy asked.

"It all depends on how your body reacts to the blood thinner. It may take anywhere from one to five days."

"Five days," Tammy hissed.

The nurse gave her a stern look, just like the nurse at the front desk. Tammy was getting used to them. "Now you just lay still. You don't need to be fidgeting around," the nurse told her.

"I can't stay here for five days," Tammy protested.

This time it was Dwayne that gave her a stern look.

"Oh, yes, you will," he barked. "Now I'm going to step outside and call Matt. I love you. I'll be back soon."

Tammy showed her bottom lip more than she needed to, "love you too."

After four hours of being monitored in the trauma unit, Tammy was relieved when they finally moved her to a different ward. Even though she wasn't allowed to get out of bed or walk around, she appreciated the window and a view of the outside world. The doctors had told her she would have a scan on her legs tomorrow to see if she had any more clots. Until then, she was to take it easy and only get up to use the bathroom, which she soon found out was a chore because she was still hooked up to an IV and had to drag the apparatus around with her.

"Hey, as much as I want to stay with you all night, I need to get home. I have to feed the falcons and the dogs," Dwayne said from her bedside, as the sun went down.

Tammy took his hand. "Yeah, I know. Call me in the morning, okay. And plan on going to work. There's nothing you can do here but sit around. Why lose money? I'm in good hands."

"Are you sure?" Dwayne asked, with a creased brow.

Tammy nodded. "Yes, I'm sure. Matt is coming up tomorrow for a while. I'll be fine. You bought me plenty of reading material and puzzle books."

Dwayne leaned over and kissed her softly on the lips. "I'll be here tomorrow afternoon. I'll feed all the animals before I leave."

"Okay, I'll see you then."

Tammy drifted off to sleep soon after Dwayne had left and didn't wake until she heard one of the nurses' voices.

"Rise and shine, Tammy. Breakfast will be here in a few minutes, and then I'm taking you down for your scans."

Tammy rubbed her eyes and turned her head away from the bright sun beaming through the window. "Can you close the blinds, please?" Tammy asked, as she pulled herself up to a sitting position. Tammy scanned the walls and saw no clock. "What time is it?"

"Almost seven," the nurse replied, as she placed a tray of food in front of her. "I'll be back in thirty minutes. Make sure you are finished with your breakfast by then."

By lunchtime, Tammy was back in her room after having the scans and was waiting for the doctor to tell her their findings. He showed up just before two.

"Hello, Tammy. How are you doing today?" he asked.

Tammy smiled. "Good, thanks."

"That's good. Well, we found three more clots behind your right knee."

Tammy was shocked. "Really? Why am I getting these clots? This is scary. Especially since I hear they can travel to your brain and kill you."

"Yes, they can, which is why we are keeping you here until all the clots have dissolved."

"But what if I get more after I leave? Do you know why I'm getting them?" she asked again.

"I believe it's because of the Tamoxifen you've been taking, and I don't want you to take them anymore."

"But that's for my cancer?" Tammy said, sounding concerned.

"It is. But I think you will be better off taking nothing at all. We will monitor you closely and have you come in more frequently over the next five years, which is the critical time frame when the cancer is at a high risk of returning."

Dwayne entered the room while they were talking. Tammy threw him a big smile. "Hey, I wasn't expecting to see you for a few more hours."

Dwayne shook the doctor's hand. "I left early so I could come here. So what's going on?" Dwayne asked, as he stood next to the bed and held Tammy's hand.

"I was just telling Tammy that we found three more clots

behind her knee and that it's probably a side effect from the Tamoxifen. It's rare, but it has been known to happen."

"Oh, no," Dwayne gasped.

"As long as we monitor her blood and keep her on blood thinners, she should be okay. For the first week after she goes home, Tammy will need to take Lovenox, which is injected into her abdomen twice a day."

Tammy's eyes turned wide. "Whoa. Wait a minute. I have to do it myself. Stick a needle in my stomach." Tammy shook her head. "Hell no. I can't do that."

"I'll do it," Dwayne called out with no hesitations.

"You will?" Tammy said, shocked by his words.

"Of course, I will," Dwayne said to the doctor. "Twice a day?"

"Yes, twice a day, and then she will be on Warfarin until her blood returns to normal and is not at a danger level of coagulating."

Tammy was confused. "How will you know? I'll be at home."

"You will have to come here once a week and have your blood checked."

"Once a week? For how long?" Tammy questioned.

"For as long as it takes to get your blood back to normal. Your blood will be checked, and your medicine doses adjusted accordingly."

Tammy laid back against the pillow and sighed. "I recently got done driving here every day for radiation, and now I have to come here every week for this. I used to be so damn healthy. What the hell happened?"

"And you will be again," Dwayne told her.

"So, how long will I be here?" Tammy asked.

"You should be able to go home tomorrow. The clots are shrinking. The nurses will go over everything in detail with you before we release you."

Tammy had been making the weekly two-hour round trips to have her blood checked for the last six months. She was hoping this would be her last time. Now that she had a three-month-old grandson, she was eager to put all of her health scares behind her and begin making memories with her grandson. She was thankful that her mother wanted to skip coming out this year and get well herself. It would give her and Dwayne a chance to finish the house and take care of her health. Her mom promised she would be there the following year.

The nurses had hinted that her blood was looking good, and if the results were good today, she wouldn't have to be checked anymore. But her emotions were split. Yes, she was excited to have the ball and chain, released and no longer have to make the long drive every week. But the visits put her mind at rest when she was told things looked good. The test told her she had no blood clots. If the visits stopped, she would no longer have that peace of mind. She would have to rely on signs from her body that something was wrong, just like when she was out of breath on a simple hike that she had done daily. But Tammy had also heard that people who had died from blood clots had no prior symptoms in many cases. The thought terrified her. Not only did she have to fear cancer returning, but also blood clots.

As she drove on the desolate five freeways surrounded by miles of farmland, she thought again how precious life was. She was still young and wanted to be around to see the house completed that she and Dwayne had been working so hard on. She thought again of her dad, who would never get to see it, and then her mother, who she feared would never see it either. Tammy still had not told her mom or her sisters about her health scare and probably wouldn't until they convinced Tammy she was out of danger. She didn't want anyone to worry. When her mother might visit in September, which was just five months away, Tammy thought that would be a good time to tell her.

Tammy thought of Dwayne's parents, Charlie and Cathy, who were now in their late seventies, and had moved into assisted living because of Charlie's Alzheimer's progress. It saddened Tammy and Dwayne that neither one of them would see their house finished either. If only they had started the house sooner, Dwayne and Tammy had often said.

With Matt's help on the weekends whenever he could and some good friends, they had made substantial progress on the house, but it would still be a year before they could even think about moving in.

Tammy wiped her sweaty palms on her jeans as she entered the blood and cancer clinic. A place she had gotten to know well since she had been diagnosed with cancer over a year ago. She received all of her radiation treatments here, and now she had her blood tested weekly. She knew the girls at the front desk on a first name basis, and always spent a few minutes having a friendly chat with them before heading to the blood clinic. Tammy was going to miss them if her results were good.

When she entered the blood clinic, Molly's friendly smile, the phlebotomist nurse who did the test every week, greeted her.

"Hey, Tammy. I'm all ready for you. Have a seat."

"Hi, Molly," Tammy said as she took her usual place and waited for Molly to prick her finger."

"So this might be the big day where I may tell you I don't want to see you anymore," Molly laughed.

"I know," Tammy said, with a nervous smile.

The test only took a few minutes, and Tammy waited anxiously for Molly to read the results.

Molly looked up and smiled. "They are good, Tammy. You don't need to come back, and you no longer need to take the blood thinners."

"Really? That's awesome," Tammy said, but she couldn't help feeling a little sad and concerned. "If I stop taking the blood thinners, isn't there a danger I may get the blood clots again?"

The nurse gave Tammy a reassuring smile. "The clots were caused by the drug Tamoxifen which you haven't taken in over six months. Your blood work has been good for the last month. You're as good as new, Tammy."

Tammy laughed. "Okay, then. I guess I'm a free woman."

After saying goodbye to the girls at the front desk and telling them the good news, Tammy pulled out of the parking lot and called Dwayne on her cell phone to tell him the good news. "I'm all done. No more blood work. They said my blood is fine, and I can stop taking the blood thinners." Tammy beamed.

"Yes! That's fantastic. I'm taking you out for dinner tonight to celebrate," Dwayne said, sounding elated.

"Sounds good. I am kind of worried, though, that my blood won't be getting checked every week. It gave me peace of mind knowing my blood was okay."

Dwayne tried to reassure her. "I'm sure they wouldn't tell you to stop coming or not take the meds if they weren't one hundred percent certain you would be okay. Now, stop worrying. You're healthy. Life is getting back to normal again. You're a grandmother, and we are building a house together."

Tammy smiled at his words. Like always, he knew just what to say. "You're right. I feel great. My strength is back, and I want to hustle on the house before mom gets here in September."

But their dreams were soon crushed when Tammy received a call from her sister Jenny, in England, a few months later.

She sounded somber when she spoke. "Hi, Tammy I'm calling about mom."

Tammy's heart sank, and she sat on the edge of the bed where she was folding laundry. "Is she okay?" Tammy asked, matching her sister's somber tone.

"Not really. She's been diagnosed with dementia. I'm afraid she won't be able to travel to America anymore."

Instantly tears pooled in Tammy's eyes. "Oh my god. How bad is she? Does she recognize you?" Tammy asked. The only thing she had heard about dementia was that the victims of the disease soon stop recognizing people—even their spouses and children. The thought terrified Tammy.

"Yes, she does, but we are not sure for how long. She is very confused. She hallucinates a lot. Just last week, she said there were thousands of ants crawling on her wall. Of course, there wasn't, but to her, it was real. She was petrified. I didn't know what to do. It was horrible to watch."

"Oh, Jenny, I'm so sorry I'm not there to help you. I feel awful."

"No, don't feel bad. You took care of dad's place when he passed. I can take care of our mom. But it's so heartbreaking, Tammy. The sparkle has gone from her eyes. She looks like a lost soul."

Tammy suddenly realized that it was now too late to fulfill her mother's one wish-*I just want to see my girls all in the same room one more time.* She had waited too long. Donna's status was still in limbo, she couldn't go to England, and now her mom would never set foot on American soil again. Tammy let the tears trickle down her cheeks. It crushed her to know she had let her mom down. She took a deep breath before she spoke. "Jenny, I'm going to talk to Dwayne. I think I'm going to come to England."

Tammy heard the surprise in her sister's voice. "You are?"

"Yes, and I'm not going to put this off like I've done with so many things in the past. I don't want to wait until mom no longer knows who I am. I couldn't bear the thought of being in the same room with her, and I am a stranger to her. A child she gave birth to and raised. I don't think I would be able to handle it."

"I understand, Tammy."

Tammy wasn't finished talking. "From what I understand, little by little, we will lose the mom we know until only an empty shell remains. I want to see her before that happens." Tammy paused, and choked back her tears. "I guess in my own way I'll be saying goodbye to mom while she still knows me. It might even be the last time I see her. If I go, it will be my first time there in over thirty years. I don't know if I'd be able to make it over again."

"I know, Tammy. We have missed out on so much as sisters—all three of us. I last saw you at my wedding, and as for Donna, I was fifteen when I last saw her. We are twins, and yet we don't know each other at all. It's unfortunate."

Tammy tried to hide her tears, but Jenny was crying too, which didn't help. "I'll call tomorrow after I've talked to Dwayne. But knowing Dwayne, he will probably tell me to go after I tell him about mom's declining health. He is going through the same sadness with his dad."

Tammy didn't waste any time talking to Dwayne. As soon as he walked through the door, she patted the empty cushion on the couch where she sat. "Hey, I want to talk to you. Have a seat."

"Am I in trouble?" Dwayne joked. He made himself comfortable next to her, and put his arm around her shoulder. "What's up?"

Tammy rubbed his knee as she spoke. "I talked to my sister Jenny today, and my mom is not doing good."

Dwayne pulled her in and hugged her. "I'm so sorry. Are you okay?"

"I am, but I think I should go to England while my mom will still be able to recognize me. She won't be coming to the states anymore."

Dwayne spoke in a somber tone. "None of our parents will see our house finished."

"I know. God, I wish we had started it sooner."

"Me too, but we didn't have the cash flow."

"Yeah, I know. And mom will never see her daughters together again. I feel like I let her down. My sisters and I should have done something." Tammy leaned back in the cushions of the couch and released a heavy sigh. "We've been so wrapped up in our own lives, and then Donna with her status in limbo. It just never happened, and now it never will."

"Hey, don't be so hard on yourself. You've had a lot to deal with over the past few years with your father's passing and then the cancer and the blood clots. We don't plan any of this shit, but yes, go to England. Be with your mom and Jenny. At least she will have two of you, which is more than she's had in a long time." Dwayne furrowed his brow. "How many years has it been?"

"Over thirty years," Tammy replied. "It will be so good to see Jenny again, too. Sisters should not go this long without seeing each other." Tammy raised her hands. "How did we become so estranged? God, we have years of catching up to do. So that's settled. I'm going to England?" She smiled.

Dwayne grinned. "Yes, you are going to England."

Tammy returned a huge smile. "I'll call Jenny in the morning." She tilted her head slightly, "Next week is not too soon, is it?" she asked.

Dwayne chuckled. "Didn't we just talk about how we procrastinated so much over the past few years? Next week is fine."

"Great, I'll book my ticket after I've talked to Jenny. Wow! I'm going to England. I wish you could go with me."

"I wish I could too, but who's going to watch all the birds and animals?"

"Yeah, I know. I'll miss you," Tammy said, as she folded into his arms.

Dwayne gave her a tight squeeze. "I'm going to miss you, too."

CHAPTER 38

For the first time in over thirty years, Tammy stepped onto British soil. It was going to be her home for the next two weeks. Memories of her teen years immediately flooded her mind. She stood in Heathrow Airport, waiting for her baggage. The last time she was here was with her father when she moved to America at seventeen. She was forty-eight, a wife, a mother, and now a grandmother or as she likes to call herself, Nana. She had spent two-thirds of her life in America, and yet she felt like she was returning home to tie up loose ends that had been haunting her for years.

After claiming her baggage and going through the customs' daunting task, she stepped outside of the airport and burst into laughter. "Oh my god, wouldn't you know it? It's bloody raining. Just like it was on my last night in England." She let go of the hold she had on the trolley that held her luggage and held her face up to the cloudy skies. She opened her mouth and allowed the raindrops to tickle her tongue. "Hello, England. I'm back," she said, and laughed again.

She looked across the road and saw the long line of bright red double-decker buses. "Gosh, I haven't seen one of those in years," she giggled. She then noticed everyone driving on the other side of the road. "And to think, at one time in my life that seemed normal. I'm glad I won't be driving over here." The rain came down heavier, and Tammy pulled her trolley under the airport's entranceway. She looked at her watch and saw she had four hours to kill before she was to take a two-hundred-mile coach ride up to Leeds, where Jenny would meet her at the bus station. The coach ride would take seven hours because of the many stops it would make, and she wouldn't arrive until two in the morning. Tammy was planning on sleeping most of the way. She had gained eight hours from the time difference and was already feeling the effects.

Tammy knew she had to call Dwayne and Jenny to let them know she had arrived. Tammy smiled—she couldn't wait to hear Dwayne's voice. She couldn't believe how much she was missing him already. He had been so worried at the airport, knowing that she would be six-thousand miles away in a strange country.

"It's my homeland. It's not strange to me," she laughed. I'll be with family," she reminded him.

"I'm still going to worry about you, just like I did when you went to Ireland."

Tammy soon found a phone booth. After spending a good five minutes figuring out how to make an international call with a credit card, she finally heard the familiar American ringtone. Dwayne answered the house phone on the second ring.

"Hey, babe. I made it," Tammy squealed into the phone.

"Tammy! I miss you," Dwayne hollered back.

"I miss you too. I miss my cell phone. It doesn't work here,' she laughed. "It feels so weird to be back here, but at the same time, it's bittersweet. I have so many memories. I wish you were here with me to share them."

"I do, too. We will go together someday. I promise."

Tammy thought of all the places she would like to show

Dwayne— where she grew up, her old school, and the Tridale moors. "I would like that."

Tammy filled him in on her flight and her upcoming scheduled coach ride to Leeds. "I'm nervous about seeing Jenny," she confessed. "Why is that?" she asked herself out loud. "She's my sister."

"Well, you haven't seen her in decades. This is huge, Tammy." Dwayne told her. "You can't just pick up where you left off. Of course, you are nervous. You have to get to know her all over again. And the same goes for her. I'm sure she is feeling the same way."

"I know. It just seems wrong to feel this way about a sister."

"It's not wrong, Tammy. If anything, it's sad that it's taken this long for you two to be together again. Make the most of it. Embrace and send me lots of pictures," he said with a laugh.

"Oh, I already have a bunch, and I'm still at the airport," she joked. "At least I can use my phone to take pictures."

"I can't wait to see them. I'll call Matt after we hang up and tell him you arrived safely."

"Thanks. I'll call him on my sister's or my mom's phone tomorrow. I'm going to call Jenny next."

They remained on the phone for a few more minutes, and after proclaiming their love for each other many times, Tammy finally hung up and called Jenny.

She heard the familiar thick accent of her sister. "Hello Jenny speaking."

"Hey, Jenny, it's Tammy. I'm here in bloody England," she laughed, with tears streaming down her face.

"Oh my gosh, I cannot believe it," Jenny cried. "Tommy and Kate can't wait to meet you."

"I can't wait to meet them either. How old are they now?" Tammy asked.

"Tommy is twenty-one, and Kate is twenty."

Tammy thought about all the time she had missed out on

getting to know her niece and nephew. "It's so sad that they are that old, and this is the first time I will meet them. It's the same with Matt. He is twenty-seven, and you've never met him."

Jenny released a heavy sigh. "I know. And he's a new daddy too. How is that little grandson of yours? I love the pictures you sent. He is adorable."

"Oh, Jenny, he stole my heart the day he was born, just like Matt did." Tammy released a heavy sigh. "It's so sad that mom will never get to meet her great-grandson."

"I know, and now Kate is pregnant. So Stuart and I are going to be grandparents. She's due at the end of the year."

Tammy gasped. "That's fantastic! You never told me."

"I was going to last week when I called you about mom, but when you told me you might come over, I figured I would wait to tell you then."

"I can't believe we are going to see each other in less than twelve hours," Tammy confessed. She sniffed back her tears.

"Me neither. We have so much catching up to do. Kate will give me a ride to the bus station, because Stuart has to leave for work at five."

"You never learned to drive then?" Tammy asked.

"No. We have great public transportation here in England. There's no need for a car like there is in America. And besides, Stuart drives. We don't need two cars."

"Makes sense to me. America is so spread out. You can't get anywhere without a car." Tammy changed the subject and realized she was paying for this call with her credit card. "Anyway, we have the next two weeks to chat. My coach gets in at two in the morning at Leeds bus station. If there are any delays, I will call you at one of the stops."

"We will be there. Can't wait to see you, sis."

"Me neither. Love you."

"I love you too, Tammy."

Tammy's hand trembled as she hung up the phone. She was

overcome with emotions. Tears streamed down her face. God, how she wished Donna was with her. The best she could do for her mom was to have two of her daughters together. Tammy checked her watch. She still had three hours before she needed to be at the bus terminal. She hadn't eaten since breakfast on the plane and went in search of a restaurant.

After a delicious fish, chips, and mushy peas lunch, Tammy was now convinced there was no comparison when it came to English fish and chips. They truly were the best. On her way to the bus terminal, she stopped at a shop inside the airport and loaded up on English candy she had not had in years for the coach ride. She suddenly felt like a little kid in a candy store. All her favorites from her childhood days were still around, Barratt fruit salad chews, Black Jacks, Cadbury's Flake Chocolate, Wine Gums, Crunchie, and Quality Street all-sorted chocolates. "God, I'm going to get sick." Tammy laughed to herself, as she stuffed the candy in her bag. But it was all so good, and she couldn't resist.

She arrived at the bus terminal thirty minutes early. Fatigue and jet lag were certainly beginning to kick in. Her eyes were heavy, and her body ached. Tammy was sure she'd be able to sleep most of the way.

After handing her luggage to the driver who stored it on the bus, Tammy found a seat near the back and was pleased when the bus left the station that her row remained empty. She had it all to herself. She spent the first hour looking out of the window, taking it all in and reading every road sign, admiring the small English shops and quaint English homes. The further they got out of London, the less traffic there was, and Tammy was in awe of the rich green rolling hills. Living in California, she'd forgotten how green England was. It was beautiful and lush. As the sun began to set and she strained to see anything in the evening shadows, Tammy nestled her body into a comfy position and soon drifted off to sleep.

She wasn't sure how long she had slept, but the slowing down of the bus woke her. Tammy looked out the window. It was pitch black, except for the lights of the station up ahead and a few surrounding buildings. She scanned the bus and saw there were a few new passengers. At the precise moment that Tammy wondered where they were, the bus driver announced it over the intercom. "We are now pulling into Wakefield," he repeated, for the second time. "All remaining passengers going to Leeds. This will be a fifteen-minute stop."

Tammy remembered Wakefield. They were about ten miles from Leeds. She couldn't believe that she would see Jenny in less than half an hour if the bus didn't make any more stops. Tammy left the bus stretching her legs, and took a much-needed bathroom break. She wasn't too keen on using the one on the bus.

"We'll be leaving in ten minutes," the bus driver hollered, as she stepped off the bus."

Tammy turned and smiled. "Thanks. Hey, is the next stop Leeds?" She asked.

"Yes, ma'am. Should be there in about twenty-five minutes."

Tammy nodded, and made a quick dash for the bathrooms.

When she returned to her seat, the bus pulled out of the station a few minutes later. Tammy rooted through her purse for her hairbrush and cosmetics and spent the last leg of the trip freshening up. Her nerves peaked, and beads of sweat surfaced on her palms. City lights outside the window caught her attention. The sight was familiar. They were driving through Leeds. A place she knew well and was the last place she'd lived in England. She scanned the old buildings and recognized them all. The Queens Hotel was still there. A place she had spent many nights drinking with co-workers. Across the road was the hotel she used to work at. Tammy saw that the bus driver had turned down the street where the train station was. It was still there, and a block further down, she saw the bus depot.

Her twenty-four-hour journey was ending. It was almost two o'clock in the morning, but she wasn't tired. She had slept for most of the bus ride. She was too excited to sleep. There were very few cars on the road, and the streets were practically empty. Tammy peered out of the window as they pulled into the bus depot, and saw Jenny immediately, standing inside, pointing at the bus she was on. Tammy gasped. "Oh my god, there she is, and that must be her daughter." They were the only ones inside. Tammy saw Jenny wipe a tear from her eye. She wasn't sure if she had spotted her on the bus.

When the bus came to a stop, Tammy took a deep breath and wiped away a few of her own tears. She couldn't believe she was finally going to be holding her sister after thirty-plus years.

Tammy was one of only three passengers left on the bus by the time they reached Leeds. It didn't take the bus driver long to get their luggage, and he had it lined up on the curb when Tammy stepped off the bus. She thanked the driver and turned to look at the window where Jenny was standing. Jenny smiled, waved, and raced towards the double exit doors with her daughter following closely behind. Tammy grabbed her luggage and walked as fast as she could to meet her, and within seconds she entered the building. She saw Jenny holding out her arms, racing towards her with tears gushing down her cheeks. Tammy let go of her luggage and ran over to her sister.

"Jenny! Oh my god. I can't believe I am here," Tammy squealed as she tried to see through her teary eyes. She wiped them with her sleeve and wrapped her arms around Jenny.

Jenny embraced Tammy and held her tight. "Oh, Tammy I've missed you so much."

Overcome with emotions, Tammy's body trembled to the core. She cupped Jenny's face in her palms and released a nervous laugh, "you still look like the Jenny I remember. You haven't changed a bit, and you look great." Her hair was longer and darker. It was now straight. Tammy remembered it being shorter and wavy when she was younger.

Jenny smiled through her tears and kissed Tammy on the cheek. "You still look the same too. Skinny as ever, I see. And you still have that red hair."

Tammy laughed and smiled at her pregnant niece. "This must be your daughter, Kate."

Jenny released her hold on Tammy and embraced her daughter. "Yes, it is."

Kate smiled and walked over to Tammy's open arms.

"It's great to finally meet you," Tammy said, tears still rolling down her cheeks. You are beautiful."

Kate blushed. "Thanks."

"Where is your son?" Tammy asked.

"He lives with his girlfriend. They will be popping in tomorrow," Jenny replied, and then took Tammy's hand. Well, come on then. Let's get home. You must be bloody knackered."

"I don't feel that bad. I slept on the bus for most of the way."

Jenny chuckled. "Well, I am. I don't remember the last time I stayed up until two o'clock in the morning." She hugged Tammy again. "Gosh, where has the time gone, Tammy. We have our whole lives to catch up on in just two weeks."

It was a short twenty-minute drive to Jenny's house. Tammy and Jenny had talked for the entire ride, but the mood had turned somber.

"So, how is mom doing? Tammy asked. "I missed her coming out last year."

Jenny turned to face her from the front passenger seat. "Not good. Don't be surprised when you see her tomorrow. She has aged a lot since you saw her last."

Tammy waved her hand. "Oh, come on. She can't have aged that much." Tammy said with a nervous chuckle.

"She's not the same mom, Tammy. I just want to warn you, so

you won't be too shocked when you see her. We are going over there tomorrow when Stuart gets home from work."

Tammy wondered if Jenny was exaggerating their mother's health, and if she wasn't, Tammy feared her reaction. She had to hold it together for her mother's sake.

When they pulled up in front of Jenny's house, Tammy stood outside in the fenced front yard and admired the surroundings. Her sister lived on a quiet cul-de-sac street in a semi-detached house. She thought back to the many times she had wondered what her sister's house looked like. It was quaint, and when they walked inside, it sparkled. The house was spotless from top to bottom, and everything had its place. Tammy trod lightly through the living room to look at a collage of pictures hanging on the wall. She whispered when she spoke carefully not to wake her husband, Stuart. She looked at the photos and saw it had her, Donna, mom and dad, and Jenny's two children. "I love this," Tammy said softly.

"It's a way to keep the family together," Jenny replied in a whisper. "Do you want some tea?" she asked.

Tammy shook her head. "No, I'd better not. I'm going to try and get some sleep. Otherwise, I'll be no good tomorrow."

Jenny approached her and hugged her. "I'm so happy you are here."

"Me too."

The next morning after her daughter and Stuart had left for work, Tammy and Jenny spent the morning having coffee and sharing stories of their separate lives over the past thirty years. Jenny pulled out tons of photo albums, and together, they sat on the couch, and Tammy listened as Jenny told her the stories behind the pictures. They laughed, they cried, and they embraced each other as the gaps were filled in about one another's lives.

"Oh, Jenny, you have a beautiful family, and it looks like you've had a wonderful life so far. I'm sorry I haven't been a part of it except for the occasional letter and picture."

Jenny took Tammy's hand. "I'm sorry too, now that the kids

have grown up, Stuart and I can do more." She gave Tammy a large grin. "In fact, I may have a little surprise for you before you leave. But I'm still talking to Stuart about it."

"Well, what is it? I hate surprises," Tammy laughed.

"I can't tell you yet."

Stuart arrived home shortly before three. Tammy remembered him well. When she had last seen him, his beard was black. Now it was a silvery grey. Tammy thought it looked better grey. After he had changed, they left to go to their mother's flat. Tammy knew the route well from her school days. Every landmark they passed sparked a memory waiting to be revisited. When they pulled into the grounds of where their mom now lived, Tammy scanned the neighborhood. "I know this area well. My old flat was just across the road." Tammy pointed with her hand in the direction of her old flat. "And down there is the pub I used to hang out at. I wonder if it's still there?"

"Yes, it is," Jenny replied.

"Wow. It's like time has stood still. I'm going to have to take a walk later and check out my old flat."

Jenny had told Tammy earlier in the year that their mother lived in assisted living. She still had her own one-bedroom flat, but there were trained caregivers on the premises around the clock. It had gotten to the point that Jenny and Stuart didn't feel comfortable leaving mom alone without any help if she needed it. Tammy agreed.

Tammy stepped out of the car and liked what she saw. Rose bushes and luscious green grass surrounded the grounds. It was quiet and had a peaceful atmosphere to it. You would never know behind the row of oak trees that there was a busy main road. "This is beautiful," Tammy said.

"The people here are very nice. Mom lives up there on the second floor flat."

Tammy looked to where she was pointing. "How many flats per building?"

"Four. Two upstairs and two downstairs."

Tammy saw they were about a dozen buildings. "They look to be a good size," Tammy said as she scanned the area.

"They are, and the staff checks on everyone every day. They serve meals or mum can cook; she has a kitchen. They have events like bingo, movie night and stuff."

"Bingo. I can't see mom playing bingo," Tammy laughed.

Jenny chuckled. "Believe it or not, mom loves bingo. I told you she has aged. Now prepare yourself."

Tammy took a deep breath. "Okay. Let's go. I'll follow you."

Jenny rummaged for her key to their mom's flat and finally retrieved it from the bottom of her purse. "Ahh, here it is. Are you ready?" she said, as she took Stuart's hand and led the way up the stairs.

Tammy followed closely behind, unsure of what to expect.

After unlocking the door to their mother's flat, Jenny stood at the bottom of the dark narrow stairs and hollered. "Mother, it's Jenny; someone is here to see you."

There was no answer. Stuart led the way up the stairs with Jenny close behind. "Hello, mom," Jenny called again.

Tammy suddenly heard the faint voice of her mom coming from upstairs. "Is that you, Jenny?"

"Yes, mom. We are coming up the stairs. There's someone here to see you."

"I'm in the kitchen," her mother called back.

Jenny turned and smiled at Tammy, and waited for her at the top of the steps with Stuart. "Are you okay?" Jenny asked Tammy.

Tammy nodded. "Yeah, I just can't believe I'm here in mom's flat."

"Me neither. Come on. Mom's going to be so shocked to see you. I had told her that you were coming, but I think she's forgotten already."

It alarmed Tammy that her mother would forget that her daughter would be visiting from America. "Is she that bad?" Tammy whispered.

"She's not the same, Tammy. I had warned you." Jenny took Tammy's hand and led her to the galley kitchen. They found their mother stooped over the counter, spooning sugar into a cup. Tammy's heart sank. It was worse than she had imagined. She didn't recognize the frail lady with grey hair and wearing a long nightie. Tammy watched as her mom put four teaspoons of sugar into her cup. Jenny walked over and took the spoon from her hand. "I think you have enough sugar, mom." She wrapped her arm over her shoulder and guided her to face Tammy. "Look who is here, mom."

Tammy looked into her mother's eyes and cried. Her mother's eyes that had always smiled back at her and believed in her were lifeless. Jenny was right; the sparkle had gone. Tammy knew the mother she once knew was slowly disappearing. "Hello, mom," Tammy said, as she sniffed back her tears.

Her mom gave her a sweet smile. "Tammy! Oh, my goodness. You came all the way from America to see me?"

Tammy approached her mom and embraced her. "I did, mom. I figured it was my turn to come to see you."

Rose looked over Tammy's shoulder. "Is Donna with you?"

Tammy felt a lump rise in her throat. Her mom was still clinging on to her one wish. "No, mom, I'm afraid not."

Her mom nodded. "Well, I have two daughters here. I never thought I'd see the day." She freed herself from Tammy's hold and gave her another smile. "Do you want some tea?"

"I would love that, mom. Thank you. I'll help you fix it." Tammy turned to Jenny and spoke in a soft voice. "She remembers that I live in America, but yet she forgot that I was coming over to visit?" she questioned.

Jenny nodded. "Yes, her long distance memory is sharp. She

remembers a lot. It's her short term memory that is bad. You can tell her something, and a minute later, she will have forgotten."

Tammy nodded. "Oh, I see."

Rose released a nervous giggle, which soon turned into tears. Jenny pulled her into her arms. "Mom, what's the matter?"

"I can't believe my Tammy is here from America in my flat, having tea."

Tammy's body shook. Her heart was heavy, and her hands trembled. "Oh, mom, don't cry. Come on, let's fix tea together. You can show me where everything is. Okay?"

Her mom nodded and wiped her tears. "The cups are in the top cupboard. Jenny, can you put the kettle on."

"Sure, mom. Then I'll go join Stuart on the sofa and let you two finish making the tea."

Tammy stayed in the kitchen with her mom, but remained quiet as she helped her. She was still trying to wrap her head around the vast changes in her mom. It was the first time she had ever seen her mom with uncombed grey hair, no make-up, or nail polish. Something her mother had always been adamant about.

Her mother snapped her out of her depressing thoughts. "Do you want some biscuits with your tea?" she asked.

Tammy had to think for a minute. Biscuits? And then she suddenly remembered biscuits were cookies in England. "Sure, mom, I'd love some. Where are they? I'll put some on a plate."

"I have your favorite. They are in the cupboard next to the cups. "Chocolate digestives. You used to love them when you were a kid. You would never save any for anyone else." Her mom laughed. "I always had to hide some, otherwise you'd eat them all."

"Ooh, yummy. I still love them. I've not had one in years."

"Come on, Tammy, I want to show you my flat," her mom said, after setting down the plate of cookies on the coffee table.

"But what about the tea, Mom?" Tammy said as she put the tray down.

Her mom took her hand. "In a minute," she said and led her to the other side of the room to a large picture window. Tammy looked out onto the grounds below. Green grass and rose bushes just like the ones in the front of the building adorned the grounds below. Tammy noticed a small wooden bench and horses in the field beyond. "You have a nice view, mom."

"I love sitting here and watching the horses. They come by every day and stand by the fence, wagging their tails. There are two of them. I think they come to see me."

"I'm sure they do, mom," Tammy replied and then noticed the shelf of photo frames. Tammy walked over to the shelf and picked one up. "It was a picture of Jenny and Stuart at their wedding. "You have a lot of pictures, mom."

"Well, I never see anyone, so these make me feel close to you all."

Tammy picked up a picture of her, Dwayne, and Matt on the *Baywitch II*. Tammy remembered sending her the picture many years ago. It looked like mom had not forgotten anyone. There were pictures of Donna, her dad, and even some old photo of mom from the sixties wearing miniskirts. "Look at you, mom," Tammy said, admiring how beautiful her mom looked in the picture.

"That's when I first met your dad. I used to be a knockout."

Tammy laughed. "Yes, you were."

Her mom's apartment was small, with one bedroom, a bathroom, kitchen, and living room. Her bedroom was decorated in her favorite color, purple, with more family pictures on the white dresser.

"We are going to the shops for you, mom. What do you need?" Jenny asked when they returned to the front room.

"Chocolate," Rose replied.

Jenny laughed. "You always say that. You have loads of chocolate, mom. I'll go take a look in the fridge and write a list."

"Are you ready?" Jenny asked Stuart, who was still sitting on the couch, letting the three women have their space.

"Yep. Let's go."

Tammy was surprised they were all leaving. "Is mom going to be okay by herself? Does she want to go with us?" Tammy asked.

Jenny shook her head. "No, she doesn't like crowds. She panics. She hasn't been to the store in months. Stuart and I go for her three times a week."

Tammy gasped. "You never told me that."

"Oh, Tammy. So much has changed. She feels the safest here in her flat. We come by four to five times a week, and there are plenty of people and staff that are constantly checking in on her." Jenny hooked arms with Tammy. "Come on, let's go. We'll talk more in the car and while we are shopping."

Tammy walked over to her mom, who was now sitting in a recliner, drinking her tea. "Do you want the TV on, mom? We'll be back in a bit."

"Oh yes, my favorite show is on." She looked over at Jenny. "What is it called?"

"East Eden, mom," Jenny replied.

Stuart used the remote on the coffee table and found her mom's show before heading over to the stairs to follow Jenny and Tammy out to the car.

Tammy sat in the back, and Jenny sat next to Stuart in the front while he drove. She turned her neck to talk to Tammy. "How are you doing, sis?" she asked.

"Okay, I guess. I just can't believe how much mom has changed. She's like a different person, and it's happened so fast. I can see why she can't come to America." Tammy let out a heavy sigh. "And she never will again." Tammy thought of all the things her mom would never see. The house they were working so hard to build, her son Matt, and her new great-grandchild.

Unless Donna made it to England, which Tammy doubted, her mom would never see her other daughter again. The thought horrified Tammy. There was so much she should have done sooner, but instead procrastinated. A quote popped into her head, *"Don't put off until tomorrow what you can do today."* A quote she had heard for years suddenly meant something to her, and made a lot of sense. Why hadn't she lived by that years ago? she wondered.

"No, I'm afraid she won't be able to travel anymore," Jenny said, pulling Tammy out of her upsetting thoughts. "In fact, Stuart and I are looking into putting her into a home. I'm not sure how much longer she will be able to live by herself. I worry about her constantly when I'm not with her." Jenny confessed. "I have to work."

"I can see why," Tammy replied. "I think you are doing the right thing." Tammy paused for a moment and chose her words carefully, not wanting to offend Jenny. "In fact, do you mind if I stay with mom while I'm here? I can sleep on her couch."

Jenny smiled, which put Tammy at ease. "Of course, I don't mind. Why would I?"

"Well, I've not seen you in ages either. But I'm not sure when or if I will ever see mom again. And if I do make it out here again, the odds are that she won't recognize me. I want to spend as much time as I can with her." Tears pooled in Tammy's eyes. "I guess, in a way, this is my goodbye to mom."

"Oh, Tammy. Make those memories with mom. Do what you have to do. I understand. We'll be by every day after work, and we'll spend some time together. In fact, Stuart and I have been talking, and we are thinking about going to America next year."

Tammy's eyes lit up. "You are? What about mom?"

"If we find her a good home, she will be taken care of. Stuart and I need to do things for us too. Our kids are adults now, and I don't want to wait another thirty years before seeing you again. I'll be dead," she laughed.

Tammy matched her laugh. "You have a point there."

"I hate to say this, Tammy, but since dad died and mom's health has taken a turn for the worst, you and Donna are all I have left. We have to stick together."

"You're right," Tammy said, as she looked at Jenny and gave her a big smile. "You know there is something I would like to do if you do come to America."

"What's that?" Jenny asked with a furrowed brow.

"I'd like to take a road trip in honor of mom to Colorado."

Jenny's eyes became bright. "You mean to Donna's?"

Tammy nodded. "Yes. You have not seen your twin since you were fifteen and mom's only wish was to have all her daughters in the same room. If the three of us are all we have, then we need to reunite our sisterhood and have a steak dinner together, where we will raise our glasses to mom."

"Oh, Tammy, I think that's a brilliant idea. I would love to see Donna. Gosh, I often wondered if we still look alike."

"Well, you know from the pictures she has sent you, you can see her hair is blonde, but put that aside, and yes, you guys still look alike. Not as much as you did when you were younger."

"Really?" Jenny questioned.

"Yes. I mean, you have both lived in different cultures, so of course, you aren't identical, but you both have the same smile. Your eyes are identical, and you both play with your hands too much," Tammy laughed.

Jenny looked down and saw she was rubbing her fingers into her palms and quickly stopped. "No, I do not," she protested and then laughed. "Oh, Tammy, I'm getting teary-eyed just thinking about it. Thirty-five years later, we are finally going to be together. What a reunion this is going to be."

CHAPTER 40

When they returned from the store, they found their mom still sitting in the chair glued to the TV. Tammy wanted to cook her mom a special meal and remembered her favorite was Shepherd's Pie.

"Hey, mom, Jenny and I are going to cook dinner. Do you want to help?" she asked. "It will be fun to all cook together. Don't you think?"

Stuart had finished putting the groceries away and took a seat on the couch. "Go on, Rose. When was the last time you cooked a meal with two of your daughters?"

Rose beamed a cute smile. "I would love that. What are we making?"

Tammy took her mom's hand and helped her out of the chair. "It's your favorite, Shepherd's Pie."

"Oh, I love Shepherd's Pie," Rose said, as she followed Tammy into the kitchen where Jenny was already peeling the potatoes.

She turned to her mom. "Do you want to help mom?" Jenny asked, and pulled a chair out from the small bistro table that sat in front of the window. "Why don't you sit here and break up the mincemeat into a bowl or, as Tammy calls it, the hamburger," she laughed.

For a brief moment, while she laughed, joked, and cooked dinner with her sister and mom, Tammy felt reconnected with her family. How she wished Donna could have been with them. So much time had been lost between all of them. A simple thing like cooking dinner that most families do every night and take for granted, was a memory Tammy would carry with her for the rest of her life. She knew it would never happen again once she returned to America. The thought that the three of them would not be in the same room also saddened her. And if it were to happen, Tammy knew her mother's health and declining memory would not allow her to realize it.

Tammy tried not to cry as her mom reminisced on the times she could remember. She talked a lot about their father, and Tammy wasn't sure if she remembered that he had passed away. She spoke as if he was still alive. "When was the last time you saw your dad?" she asked.

Tammy didn't know what would happen if she reminded her he was dead and instead gave a simple answer. "It's been a while, mom."

Over dinner, Tammy told her mom about the house she and Dwayne were building, and showed her some pictures she had brought with her, but her mother was confused. "You're building a house? Why?"

"So we can live it in, mom. We live in a tiny house right now. We want to live in a bigger house."

"But I thought you lived on a boat," she said.

"That was years ago, mom. I don't fish anymore. We moved to the mountains." She looked over at Jenny with a blank stare and then tried to jog her mom's memory some more. "You've been to the house, mom. You always stay in the hotel by the freeway because there is no room in the tiny house."

Tammy continued to tell her about her changed life, but as

Jenny had told her, any recent news she would forget about a few minutes later. Her mom still believed that Tammy was fishing and lived on a boat. For her, time had stood still.

After dinner, Jenny and Tammy did the dishes while Stuart kept Rose company in the living room. Before they left to go home, Jenny showed Tammy their mom's routine. "Here are her night pills," Jenny said, as she handed them to her. "When no one is here, a nurse comes every morning and around dinner time to give them to her. But I already called them and told them you would be staying here."

Tammy nodded and put the pills on the kitchen counter. "Can I take her for a walk in the morning? Do you think it would be okay?"

"Yes, she loves going for walks around the grounds; just don't take her to any crowded places."

"Where I used to live is just across the road. I would love to see it. Do you think she'd be okay walking over there?"

"Yes, as long as you hold her hand while walking across the main road." Jenny glanced around the clean kitchen. "Okay, then. Well, everything is put away in here. Mom will probably watch TV for another hour, and then she'll be ready for bed. Stuart and I will be here tomorrow afternoon, and we will bring your luggage."

Tammy smiled and hugged her sister. "It feels so good to be here. I guess I'm living in these clothes until I see you," she laughed.

Jenny walked to the stairs where Stuart was waiting. "Call me if you have any problems."

"Will do. Love you, sis."

"Love you too. We'll see you tomorrow."

An hour later, just like Jenny had said, her mom was ready for bed, and after tucking her in, Tammy kissed her good night and closed her bedroom door.

Still exhausted from her travels, Tammy called it an early night, made her bed on the couch, and soon drifted off to sleep. She wasn't sure how long she had been sleeping, but the sound of her mom talking from her bedroom woke her. Confused, Tammy sat up and pinned her ears.

"I will not leave. You leave," she heard her mother say.

Tammy knew there was no one in the room with her mom, but her mom was having a full-blown imaginary conversation with someone.

"You come here every night and tell me to leave. I won't. Do you hear me?" Her mom said in a louder and harsher tone.

Tammy wondered what she should do. Should she go in there? What if her mother has forgotten she was visiting, and she scares her? Suddenly she heard her mom scream.

"Get out!"

"Shit," Tammy whispered under her breath. "What the hell should I do?" Tammy tip-toed across the living room in the dark, feeling her way with her hands until she reached the opening of the kitchen doorway, where she turned on the light. Her mom shouted again.

"I told you to get out!"

Tammy looked at the clock hanging on the wall. It was two in the morning. "Shit, I can't call Jenny at this hour. She has to go to work in the morning."

Tammy left the lights off in the living room and tip-toed over to the door of her mother's room, using the glare from the kitchen lights to find her way. She pinned her ear to the door and held her breath. There was silence on the other side. Tammy remained quiet and continued to hold her breath as she listened hard for any sounds coming from the room. Her heart soon relaxed when she heard the faint snoring sound coming from the other side of the door. Tammy realized her mom was sleeping, and released a huge sigh of relief before quietly returning to the couch.

The sound of a kettle whistle from the kitchen woke Tammy. She stirred, wiped her eyes, and sat up. "Mom, is that you?"

Rose hollered from the kitchen. "Of course, it's me. Who else would it be?" she snapped.

"Sorry, mom. Just checking," Tammy replied, surprised by her mom's mean spirit. "Are you making coffee?" she asked, standing up from the couch.

"No. I'm pissing in the sink," her mother barked. "What's with all the stupid questions?"

Her mom's demeanor shocked Tammy. Last night she was sweet and loving, and together they shared so many fond memories, and this morning, she was acting like the wicked witch from the east.

Tammy walked to the doorway of the kitchen, where she found her mom pacing. She slammed the cupboard door shut after grabbing a cup and snarled at Tammy. "What are you looking at?"

"I wonder if you need any help."

"I don't need your help. Why are you here?"

"I'm here visiting with you. I want to spend some time with you," Tammy said, in a soft tone attempting to calm down her mom.

"I don't like visitors. I like to be alone. Why don't you go back to America and leave me alone?"

Her mom's words crushed Tammy. Surely she didn't mean what she had just said. Did her mother even know what she was saying? Tammy wondered. Tammy stared at the woman that she no longer knew. That was not her mother standing before her. Her mom would never talk to her in such a spiteful way, with words that were only meant to hurt. It was the disease talking, just like last night when she heard her in the bedroom. Tammy believed that subconsciously her mother was yelling at the disease to go away. Tammy folded her arms and sobbed as she watched the awful disease of dementia possess her mom. She wanted to hold her tight and protect her from the sickness that was invading her mind and stripping her of all the goodness she once owned.

Her mother stood in the kitchen and narrowed her eyes at her. "Why are you crying? Stop being a baby."

Tammy shook her head. She wasn't going to talk back and try to reason with her. She read about the mood swings of dementia and knew this would pass. She just didn't know how long it would last. "I'm going to take a bath. I'll make my coffee when I get out."

"Fine," her mom said, without looking at her.

When Tammy returned thirty minutes later, she knew her mom's mood had flipped. She was still in the kitchen, sitting at the table. She was looking out of the window and hadn't heard Tammy enter.

"Hi, Mom," Tammy whispered, unsure how her mother would react.

Her mom turned and beamed her big smile. "Tammy. You're awake. I made some coffee."

Tammy smiled back, feeling relieved, and poured herself a cup of coffee. She sat across from her mom and took her hand. "How are you feeling? Did you sleep okay?"

"I slept like a baby all night long," she replied with a smile.

Her answer told Tammy that her mom had no recollection of her screaming last night.

Tammy nodded. "I'm glad you slept well. I thought we'd go for a walk this morning. Would you like that?"

Her mother smiled again. "Yes, I would like that. But I don't want to go to any shops."

"Don't worry; we won't go to any shops. I used to have a flat close to here. I thought we'd take a walk over there and look at it."

"I remember that. Yes, you did."

"Okay, then. Let's get you dressed and find you a coat, and we'll take a nice morning stroll together."

When they stepped outside into the damp morning air, Tammy took a deep breath and filled her lungs. She'd forgotten how chilled the mornings were in England. She looked down the pathway and saw the haze. Dewdrops blanketed the grass, and the air smelt clean. She locked arms with her mom, and they walked. The first thing Tammy noticed was how slowly her mother walked. And it wasn't because of her age. It was because every few minutes, she had to stop and look at something and ask so many questions. She had stopped at the edge of the grass and stared down at it, "Why is grass green?" she asked.

Tammy didn't have an answer. "I don't know, mom."

Further down the path, her mom stopped again, picked up a twig, and then looked up at the surrounding trees. "I wonder which tree this fell off?"

Tammy waited patiently while her mom continued to investigate the twig. "I don't know, mom. There are lots of twigs on the ground. It could be from any of these trees."

Tammy watched as her mom bent down and picked up a leaf. "Do you think this twig and leaf fell off the same tree?"

Tammy shrugged her shoulders. "Maybe."

When they reached the main road, Tammy saw the fear in her mom's eyes. "I can't cross the road, Tammy. The cars are going too fast."

Tammy took her hand. "Mom. There is a crosswalk. The cars will stop for us."

Her mom took Tammy's hand and squeezed it tight. Tammy winced from the pain of her grip. "How do you know they will stop?" her mom asked with fear.

Tammy led her to the curb. "Because there is a traffic light and when it turns red, they have to stop. It's the law." Tammy pushed the button at the crosswalk. "Now, when our light turns green, it means we can walk."

Her mom looked at the crosswalk light. "It's red."

"It will change in a minute," Tammy replied. When the light turned green, and the cars had stopped, her mom stepped back from the curb. "I can't do this, Tammy."

"It's okay, mom. You're with me. I won't let anything happen to you," she said, as she squeezed her hand tighter.

Rose hesitated and then slowly took Tammy's lead. Tammy quickened her pace, fearing her mom may freak out in the middle of the road. But she did not. When they reached the other side, Tammy praised her like she would a child. "Good job, mom! You did it."

Tammy knew the area well. She spent her last few years in England in this neighborhood. She turned onto the familiar road, Manor Terrace, and immediately spotted her old flat. Emotions and memories raced through her. She stood in front of the red brick terrace house and looked at the door that was once her entranceway to the ground flat where she used to live. Ironically, it still looked the same except for the fresh white paint job on the window frames.

Her mom stood by her side. "Is that your old place?" she asked.

"Yep, it sure is." Tammy looked at the window off to the left of the door and remembered the room as if it were yesterday. It was the main room to the flat where she had her bed. She pictured the small kitchenette and chuckled when she remembered she shared the bathroom with her neighbors.

She thought back to her last night in England. She had gotten drunk at her surprise, leaving the party, and had come home and called her boyfriend, Ian, from this flat. For the first time, she had told him she was leaving him and going to live in America. Tammy realized how wrong that was of her leaving Ian in the dark until the night before she was to leave. She wondered where he was now. Did he ever marry or have kids? "So many memories," Tammy whispered to herself. She turned to her mom and saw she was shivering. "Come on, mom. Let's get you home. You're cold. I'll make you a nice hot cup of tea."

When Jenny and Stuart arrived later in the afternoon, Rose was taking a nap in her bedroom. Tammy had used the time to call Dwayne and Matt and give them the sad news about her mom's health. "Did you know mom has severe mood swings?" Tammy asked Jenny.

"Oh, yes. I should have told you about those. She can be quite nasty at times."

"I'll say," Tammy said. "This morning, she was awful. She told me to go back to America."

"Well, I see you didn't listen." Jenny laughed. "You're still here."

Tammy stuck out her tongue. "Ha. Ha. Very funny. I just ignored her and took a bath. By the time I got out, she was fine."

"Yep, that's all you can do. Don't argue with her. That will just make it worse and agitate her more."

"After I have gone for a walk with mom tomorrow, I think I'm going to jump on a bus and visit Tridale. I guess I want to take a trip down memory lane. This morning mom and I went and saw my old flat. It brought back so many memories. Now I want to see Tridale and see the house we grew up in. I also want to take a walk on the moors."

"That's a great idea, Tammy. Do as much as you can while you are here. It's only a twenty-minute bus ride. I'll be at Mom's place by noon tomorrow. So take as long as you need."

Tammy patted her knee. "Thanks."

CHAPTER 41

The next morning, Tammy was pleased to find her mom in a pleasant mood, and after going for their morning stroll, she left for her much-anticipated trip to Tridale. By ten, she was sitting on the upper level of a double-decker, traveling down the familiar roads that she had done so many times as a child. Every street held a memory. She recognized many of the old stone buildings, and even some familiar pubs were still around, which surprised her.

When she stepped off the bus in the heart of Tridale, it was pouring rain. She laughed. Memories of her last night in Leeds popped into her head again. She knew every part of the town, and it all came back to her as though she had never left. It seemed time had stood still in the quaint little town she once called home. She looked up to the sky and stuck out her tongue. She giggled when the cold raindrops splashed on her tongue. The rain was coming down hard, but Tammy didn't care. In fact, she loved it. The English rainfall felt good.

She looked up at the steep road that led to the moors and headed up that way first. Every step took her deeper into her memory vault. She had friends that used to live on this street. She stopped and looked at the house they used to live in and reminisced back to the days when they played outside in the yard. She could see as clear as day herself as a child playing, hopscotch with her schoolmate on the sidewalk.

When she reached the edge of the moors, the rain was beating hard against her face. She had no umbrella or hat, and her hair was drenched. Her sweater stuck to her arms, and the wool sagged around her wrist. Tammy squeezed them to wring out the excess water. Her jeans were tight against her skin from being soaked and squeaked against her thighs as she walked. But it didn't faze or upset Tammy. She was back on the moors after being away for so long, and it felt bloody fantastic.

She knew her way around the moors like the back of her hand; it was her after school playground as a child. She headed for the wading pool first, wondering if it was still there. She smiled when she saw it still was and was surprised to see it overflowing from the downpour of rain. She spent so many summer days at the pool with her sisters and friends from school. Her mom would bring them a packed lunch, and they would spend entire days there. When she grew older, Tammy ventured on her own with her sisters or school mates.

Tammy looked up into the distance and saw the trail that led to the tarn and walked that route next. On either side of the trail stood tall bracken and fenced yards to the houses that backed up to the edge of the moors. The trail still looked the same, and Tammy wondered how many times she had walked and ran up and down it in her younger years. She had spent most of her childhood years on the moors, hiding in the bracken, chasing foxes, and searching for hedgehogs.

It took her roughly ten minutes to reach the tarn. The rain continued to pour and splashed when it hit the surface of the water. Tammy stood before the tarn and smiled. She pictured herself as a much younger Tammy, wearing Wellington boots and wading in the water, looking for frogspawn and leaping through the water trying to catch tad-poles. Many times she'd trip, lose her balance, and fall in. But those were the times when she would laugh the hardest. Her times on the moors were happy times—filled with laughter that she shared with childhood friends and her sisters. Tammy wondered whatever became of those friends. When they had all left school, they went their separate ways and never kept in touch.

Tammy spent the next few hours on the moors hiking the familiar trails that she knew so well. She was revisiting her childhood and wasn't ready to leave. She wanted to ignite as many memories as she could—some that she had long forgotten. When she was ready to go, she was surprised the gate at the back of a hotel was still there and still unlocked. As a child, it had been her passage to the moors from the house she had grown up in when her family was still together.

Tammy pushed on the gate and walked down the long driveway that would take her to the narrow dirt path at the top of her old street. As she walked down the street, she took a minute to remember all the people who lived in each house when she was growing up. The houses hadn't changed much except for paint jobs, new windows, and spruced up yards. Tammy was surprised that she could remember most of the names of her old neighbors. Children she used to play with and their parents. The grumpy old guy Stan would yell at them for playing outside his house and making too much noise. And then she saw it.

Tammy gasped, and tears pooled in her eyes. There it was. Her old house. The house where she was once part of a family, where they all sat down and ate dinners. They played board games at night; it was a house with two parents and three children. Tammy cried when she looked up and saw her old bedroom window, and next to it was the window to her mom and dad's room. She cried harder when she saw the wooden gate across the driveway. It was now red. It used to be green. It warmed her heart to see it was still there because she had watched her father build it in the garage and had helped him hang it on the hinges. He was so proud when he had stood back and admired his work. "It's still here, dad," Tammy whispered through her tears.

Tammy stood there for some time. She was picturing the layout and every room in the house. But when the memory of her mom crying as she held her daughters and told them that their father had moved out crept into her head. Tammy knew it was time to leave, and she did.

After her emotions had subsided, Tammy walked through the town, and saw the grammar school was still there, and more fond memories of her school days returned. She stopped and had a scone and tea in a café, and afterward, she jumped on a bus back to her mom's flat—by which time the rain had stopped.

She found her mom and Jenny sitting outside on a wooden bench underneath a shade tree. Stuart was inside changing some burned-out light bulbs and doing some other small tasks.

"My God, look at your hair. Your clothes are soaked," Jenny said.

Tammy giggled. "Well, it rained most of the day for my walk through Tridale and the moors. Of course, it stopped when I got on the bus to come back here."

"Sounds like typical English weather," Jenny joked. "Hey, Stuart and I want to take you out for dinner tonight. Mom will be fine with the TV on."

"Sounds good. It would be nice to spend some time with you guys." Tammy looked down at her wardrobe. "I guess I should go take a bath and change."

Jenny nodded and laughed. "Good idea."

～

Tammy couldn't believe how fast her time in England went by. When it was time to leave two weeks later, she wasn't ready. She felt like she was finally getting to know her sister again, as well as her family. Her children were no longer just names in a letter and faces in a photo. They were real people she had grown to love.

The hardest part was saying goodbye to her mom. Tammy knew deep in her heart that this would be the last time she would look into her mother's eyes, and her mother would recognize her as her daughter. Tammy's heart was in pieces. She didn't want her mom to forget her, but she knew it was inevitable. For Tammy, this was a final goodbye, whether or not she made it back to England. Over time, Tammy would become a stranger to her mother. It had already begun. The handwritten letters that her mom used to write to her had stopped arriving a few months ago. There were no more phone calls, and soon her mother's lips would stop calling her name. Tammy couldn't wrap her head around the thought that there would come a day that her mom would forget she had three daughters. The pain was unbearable, and Tammy sobbed, as she held her mom for what might be the last time as mother and daughter, as Tammy knew it. This would be one of the last memories she would have of her mother, before dementia stripped her of her soul and mind. What a cruel disease, Tammy thought. "I'm going to miss you, mom," Tammy cried.

Her mom cried too. "Why do you have to go, Tammy?" she asked, between her tears.

"Because I live in America, mom. My home, my husband, and my son are there. And I have a grandson now, too." Tammy mentioned her grandson to her a few times during her visit, but her mother soon forgot an hour or so later.

"Can you come back tomorrow?" her mom asked.

Tammy shook her head and sniffed back her tears. "No, mom, I'm afraid I can't. I live too far away."

Her mother's mood suddenly changed. She glared at Tammy and narrowed her lips. "Fine then." She released herself from Tammy's embrace. "I'm going to go make some tea. I'll see you later."

Tammy watched with disbelief, as her mom marched off to the kitchen. She turned to Jenny, who was wiping the last of her tears away. "Now what? I just go?" Tammy whispered.

Jenny nodded. "I'm afraid so. She won't remember any of this by tonight."

It was hard not to feel hurt by her mother's actions, but Tammy had to remember her mother was not herself anymore. She picked up her flight bag, and Stuart grabbed her suitcase. "Okay, then. Bye, mom," Tammy called from the front room, and walked over to the doorway of the kitchen. Her mother had her back to her and was putting a tea-bag in a cup. She didn't turn to look at her and said, "bye."

"Oh, Jenny, I feel awful leaving you here to take care of mom. It won't be easy," Tammy said, from the back seat of the car.

"It's okay, Tammy. I'll manage, like I said before. You took care of dad and went to Ireland. It's my turn now. I'll keep you updated on what's going on."

Tammy reached over and squeezed Jenny's shoulder. "Thank you."

"You don't have to thank me. She's my mom, too. Stuart has been a lot of help. We'll get through it," Jenny said ,while giving Stuart a loving smile.

By the time they reached the airport, Tammy's tears were flowing again. "Oh, I hate all these goodbyes," she sobbed, after checking in her baggage, holding Jenny tight. She and Stuart could go no further with her at the airport. The departing gate that led to the flight's lounge was just a hundred yards away. It was time to say goodbye once more.

Jenny was also crying. "I know, me too."

"I'm so glad I came. I needed this. I need to reconnect with my roots, and you. I love you, sis," Tammy said, as she wiped her eyes.

"I love you, too. We will do our best to come to America next year. Let's see how mom does, and I'll let you know."

Tammy nodded, then hugged Stuart. "Thank you for taking care of Jenny. You are a good man."

Stuart smiled. "Thanks, she's my world."

Tammy took a deep breath and hugged her sister one more time. "Well, then, I guess this is it. Bye, sis."

"Bye, Tammy. We'll see you soon, I promise."

Tammy couldn't hold back the stream of tears that gushed down her cheeks, and cried hard as she spoke. "I know. I'll call you when I'm home. Bye." She stepped back, reluctantly walking toward the gates. Every few steps, she turned her head, and saw her sister and Stuart standing arm in arm, waving their arms high. Tammy waved back until she walked through the gates, and could no longer see them.

It was still daylight when the plane finally took off two hours later. Tammy had a window seat, and leaned as far forward as she could, watching her native land fade off into the distance as the plane climbed up into the skies. "Bye, England," Tammy whispered, then closed her eyes and dreamt of her mom when she was of mind and body.

When Jenny called a month later to tell Tammy they had booked their tickets for America; Tammy almost dropped the phone. "You're kidding. When will you be here?"

"September of next year," Jenny squealed into the phone.

Tammy counted the months in her head. "That's in just over a year. Wow! I can't believe it. You're coming to America. What about mom?" Tammy asked. "How is she doing?"

Jenny released a heavy sigh. "Oh, Tammy, she is much worse since you saw her. She forgets everything. She left the gas on the cooker once and the bathtub running. Thank god the nurses check on her regularly when I'm not there. But it's not safe to leave her alone. We've found her a nice home, and this weekend she moved in."

Tammy spoke with a somber tone. "You're doing the right thing, Jenny."

"Thanks. It's just hard. We'll go there every weekend to visit her, and whenever we can go after work. But at least we have peace of mind, and we know she will be safe." Jenny released another heavy sigh. "Just last week, one of the staff where she lives now found her walking at night in the pouring rain in her nightie and bathrobe. She had no idea where she was. It's time, Tammy."

"Oh, my goodness. That's terrible—poor mom. I agree, Jenny. It's time." After saying her goodbyes and hanging up the phone. Tammy raced out to the yard to find Dwayne. He was inside the new house taking measurements. She raced over to him, unable to hide her excitement. "Dwayne! Dwayne."

He looked up startled and stood up from his knees. "Hey, what's up? Are you okay?"

Tammy came to a sudden stop and heaved to catch her breath. "Jenny and Stuart are coming to America. They've booked their tickets."

Dwayne's eyes grew wide. "What? When?"

"Next September. In thirteen months."

Dwayne glanced around their unfinished house. The framework was completed. It had a roof and windows. The wiring and light needed to be installed, which Matt planned on doing with the company he worked for. The plumbing would be done in a month. Wow! We have just over a year to finish this house and be moved in so they can stay in the tiny house."

Tammy looked around the shell of the house. "Yep. Think we can do it?"

"I guess we will find out," Dwayne laughed. We have lots of work ahead of us. Cabinets have to be installed, as well as, drywall and installation. We need to install the floors and carpeting, and paint all the walls. Oh, and let's not forget all the tongue-and-groove for the high vaulted ceilings. The planks will have to be stained and nailed up by hand."

"We got this," Tammy said, with a ray of confidence." We are also going to have to fix up the tiny house. It's going to need a paint job and new carpeting, I'm sure."

· · ·

They worked hard over the next year in a race to move into the new house before Jenny and Stuart arrived. But they had another reason to expedite the completion of the house. Now that their grandson was older, Tammy was eager to have him spend weekends with them. There was no room in the tiny house.

They spent many late nights after working all day staining, painting, or installing cabinets. But the excitement of Jenny visiting and spending more time with their grandson kept them going, and they pushed through the fatigue and sore muscles. They got only a few hours of sleep every night, and a week before Jenny and Stuart's arrival, Tammy was sitting on the couch in their new home beaming a huge smile. "I can't believe we did it," she said to Dwayne, who was positioning the recliner beneath the window.

"Me neither. I've always said we make a great team."

"We still have a tiny house to do. It will need a good cleaning before pulling out the old carpet and putting in the new. And I want to paint the walls too."

"We have a week. I think we can do it," Dwayne said.

Tammy glanced around the house they built. It was beautiful with a rustic charm and lots of natural wood. A wood-burning stove sat in the corner of the main room, surrounded by slate tiles and a majestic log mantel made from a fallen tree off their mountain. Another log stood tall in the center of the room, also from the mountain. It supported the loft that looked down over where she sat on the couch. One day I will write my book up there, she thought to herself.

Tammy felt a twinge of sadness, knowing that none of their parents would see their labor of love. They would have been so proud of them both. How she wished they had started the house sooner, before their parents' health had failed them.

The week flew by, and Tammy raced to get the tiny house completed with Dwayne's aid when he wasn't working and her good friend Mandy. She couldn't believe with just a day to spare before she would have to pick up Jenny and Stuart from the airport, the tiny house was finished. She sat outside on the patio and wiped her brow. Dwayne handed her a tall glass of ice tea. "I can't believe we did it. Everything looks fantastic," Dwayne said with pride.

Tammy smiled. "It sure does. And I even planned a road trip. Everything is booked. We leave in four days."

"We need to find someone to watch the animals sometime so that I can go with you on one of these trips," Dwayne said in a somber tone.

"I know, but you can't just ask anyone to take care of the falcons. And you would worry the whole time we were gone. They need special handling. Very few people know how to take care of a falcon. Let alone six?"

"Yeah, I know, but I'm still going to figure something out eventually." Dwayne changed the subject. "Are you excited?" Dwayne asked.

"I am, but I'm also really nervous. The three of us have not been together in decades. It's going to be emotional, but also strange. I wonder how Jenny feels about it? She hasn't seen her twin since she was fifteen. I still can't believe it's been that long." Tammy leaned back and gave her head a shake. "God, where has the time gone?"

"Well, it's going to be a memorable trip, that's for sure."

"It is. We are going to stop in Vegas on the way and then the Grand Canyon on the way back. I also want to take them to Laughlin and the small town of Williams. We have missed out on so much that I want to make memories with my sisters again. It's what mom would have wanted. This road trip is not only for us, but for her too."

Dwayne took the day off from work the next day. He couldn't go to Colorado with Tammy, so he wanted to make sure he would be there with her at the airport to pick up Jenny and Stuart.

The flight arrived on time, and after waiting a few hours in the arrival terminal while they cleared customs, Tammy finally spotted them walking up the ramp. She waved her hands high above her head and screamed, "Jenny!"

Jenny heard her, and scanned the terminal until she spotted Tammy, and beamed at her with a huge smile. Stuart waved, and Dwayne waved back. "They're here," Tammy cried, as she leaned into Dwayne and hugged him.

"Yes, they are. I'm looking forward to meeting them both for the first time."

"I know you and Stuart will get along. You guys have a lot of the same interests."

"Oh, I plan on taking him shooting, fishing, and hunting when you guys get back from Colorado."

"He'll love it," Tammy laughed, while walking towards her sister. "There's not much of that in England."

Within minutes, Tammy was in the arms of Jenny, with her eyes full of tears. "Oh, I can't believe you're are here."

"Me neither. I shouldn't have waited so long." Jenny wiped her eyes and hugged Tammy again. "But we are here now, and it will be the first of many trips."

"Oh, I hope so. You are welcome anytime. You know that, right?"

Jenny laughed, and then smiled at Dwayne. "Hello, you must be Dwayne."

Tammy left her sister's arms, wrapped her arms around Dwayne, and gave him a loving smile. "Yes, this is my man."

Dwayne squeezed Tammy, then leaned in and gave her a lingering kiss before letting go to give Jenny a friendly hug.

Stuart approached him and smiled. "And I'm Stuart. Good to finally meet you, mate," he said, in a thick English accent.

"You too. Core blimey. I'll be talking like you English folks by the time you go home," Dwayne joked, while trying to imitate an English accent.

Stuart laughed. "I dunno about that. Might take a bit of work," he laughed.

Tammy and Jenny laughed out loud at their husbands making fun of each other. "Oh, this is going to be an interesting visit with these too, "Tammy laughed. She took Jenny's hand. "Come on, sis. Through those doors is America, and I want to show you a piece."

The sisters locked arms and together skipped out of the airport into the glorious California sunshine while the guys continued to make jokes, while lagging behind them.

"So does Donna know we are coming?" Jenny asked, from the back seat of the car. Dwayne was driving, and Tammy sat in the front passenger seat. Stuart sat next to Jenny.

Tammy turned her head to face her. "Yes, she knows. I called her a couple of months ago. I thought about surprising her, but what if she had plans or something? It would suck if we drove all the way out there, and she was out of town."

"So how did she seem? Is she excited?" Jenny asked.

Tammy nodded and then giggled. "Oh my god, yes. She's been asking all kinds of questions about you since I saw you last year. I sent her pictures, and she still can't believe that we will all be together in a few days," Tammy laughed again. "I can't either."

"When was the last time you saw her?" Jenny asked.

"Oh gosh, it's been a long time. It was when Jason died. God, that was so sad. He was way too young. It's a shame you never met him. He was a nice guy and did so much for Donna." Tammy paused. "She's remarried now. He sounds nice, and Donna seems happy, which is the most important part, but I think a piece of her heart will always be with Jason."

"Yeah, I know. I'm sorry I didn't either. Gosh Tammy, there's so much I wish I had done. We missed so much growing up."

"I know we did. I hope we can all make up for the lost time and make this the beginning of our newborn sisterhood. Not just for us, but for mom too."

Jenny smiled. "I agree. Before we left, I told her we were finally getting together, and about the road to Colorado, but there was no recognition from her. Just a blank stare. It's so heartbreaking."

"I know. I would like to think she knows, and somewhere inside of her, she is smiling with joy, knowing her three daughters will be together again. I was crushed when you called me a few months ago and told me she could no longer speak, and is now bedridden. Got what a horrible disease. It just strips the victim of everything."

"I won't lie, Tammy. It's been hard watching mom slowly disappear from us. I no longer know what she understands or even hears when I talk to her. I try not to cry when I visit her, and I talk to her just like I've always done. Like she understands everything I'm saying. What helps is having Stuart with me. He is with me every time."

Tammy looked over at Stuart, smiled at him, and then took her sister's hand and gave it a gentle squeeze. "Thank you for being there for mom."

Jenny shook her head to fight her tears. "Okay. I'm going to cry. Let's talk more about the trip. As much as I can't wait to see Donna, I'm also excited about going to Vegas. We are really going to Vegas?" Jenny squealed.

Tammy chuckled at her excitement. She wanted this trip to be memorable, and had planned their trip and booked the rooms in Vegas. They would stay at the Luxor on the strip, and she had booked two rooms at a hotel near Donna's house. She had left the return trip wide open, figuring they would find a hotel in Williams for the night after spending some time at the Grand Canyon and Monument Valley. Laughlin would be their last stop, and from there, they would head home. "Yes, we are going to Vegas. You will love it. We'll spend one night there. Play the slots and walk the strip, then head out in the morning."

Three days later, Stuart and Dwayne put the last of the luggage in the car, and Dwayne shook Stuart's hand. "Now, you take care of these two girls, okay, and I'll see you all when you get back."

"I won't let anything happen to them," Stuart replied with a nod.

Dwayne turned to Tammy, who was rooting through her purse next to the car for her keys. She smiled and pulled them out of her purse. "Found them," she yelled in triumph.

Dwayne pulled her into his arms and kissed her hard on the lips. "I'm going to miss you. Call me every chance you can, and be careful out there. I'm going to be worried about you."

Tammy patted him on his chest." I'll be fine. Don't worry, okay? I'm going to miss you, too. I wish you were going with us."

"I do too." He kissed her again. "Now go on, get in, and I'll get the gate."

"Bye. I love you," she said, before stepping into the car and starting the engine.

Dwayne watched from the driveway and waved as they descended down the road. Tammy looked in her rearview mirror until she could no longer see him and then looked at Jenny sitting in the back seat. "The road trip has begun. Fasten your seat belts; you are in for a long ride," she laughed.

Stuart, who was sitting in the front, laughed. "What have I gotten myself into—you three girls together. This is going to be interesting."

"My God, I've never seen anything like it," Jenny said, as they walked the Vegas strip later that evening. "It's after nine, and it's still bloody hot out," she laughed. "And with all these lights, you'd never know it was nighttime unless you looked up at the sky."

Tammy laughed at her sister, who looked like a kid at Disneyland. Her eyes were wide, and her smile was big. "And there are no clocks in Vegas," Tammy added.

Jenny creased her brow. "There aren't, why?"

"Because they want you to lose all track of time and just keep gambling."

"Really! Wow, those crafty buggers. Well, they are not getting any more of my money," Jenny announced. "I couldn't believe all those people sitting at the slot machines, and they just kept feeding the machines with money. How much were they spending?" Jenny asked.

"A lot," Tammy chuckled.

"Well, I spent $10.00. That's enough for me," Jenny said adamantly.

"Yes, and you won $10.00, so you broke even."

"Yes, I did," Jenny said with pride, as she continued to look in awe at all the bright lights and everything Vegas offered. "I can't believe all these people. It's crowded."

"Yep. It's the city that never sleeps." Tammy glanced at her watch, "but I'm ready to call it a night. I want to be on the road early tomorrow."

"Sounds good to me," Stuart said. "This place is wearing me out."

After a hearty breakfast and a few last plays on the slots, they were back on the road by seven but soon made a detour when they came upon the Valley of Fire National State Park. "Oh, I've always wanted to see that place." Tammy squealed as she hit the brakes and skidded off to the side of the road with a dust trail on her tail.

"Hey, steady on there lass," Stuart said from the back seat.

Tammy laughed. "Do you guys want to go check it out?"

"I'd love to," Jenny said.

"Great. This is what road trips are all about—exploring. This place is supposed to be amazing. We'll spend half a day here. What do you say?"

The detour was just what they needed after the hustle and bustle of Vegas. It was peaceful, refreshing, and beautiful. The views and rock formations were spectacular. "God, I'm so glad we stopped here," Tammy said, while taking one last look at the breathtaking views of the valley. "I want to bring Dwayne here. I don't think he's ever been here."

It was after ten in the evening when Tammy had to pull into a gas station to refuel. They were about two hours away from where Donna lived, and Tammy called her to give her an update. "Hey, Donna, we are almost there. But we took a detour and won't arrive until around midnight. So I figured we'd check into the hotel and come see you in the morning."

"Wow. You are almost here. Yes, that would be fine. I don't think I can stay awake for another two hours," she laughed. "Hey, Tammy, why am I so nervous about seeing you guys? I've been a nervous wreck all day."

"I think we all are. Jenny was saying the same thing. It's been over thirty-five years since we've all seen each other. God, I wish mom could have been with us."

Donna released a heavy sigh. "Me, too. It breaks my heart when I see the pictures Jenny sends me. She used to be so full of life. I miss her, Tammy."

"We all do, Donna. It's one of the reasons why we are doing this. For mom. Jenny is going to take home a picture of all three of us together and put it next to mom's bed."

"Okay, well, I'm about to cry now. I can't wait to see you and hug you both. I'll see you in the morning. Love you."

"Love you too. Bye."

Tammy hung up the phone and choked back her tears. In less than twenty-hours, she and her sisters would be reunited after thirty-five years. She couldn't wrap her head around it. For years she'd been thinking about this moment, and now it was finally about to happen. She smiled at the thought and returned to her car.

"So, are you ready?" Tammy asked Jenny over their breakfast in the hotel.

"As ready as I'll ever be," Jenny replied, before taking a sip of her coffee. "I can't believe I'm going to see her. I never thought I would," she said, as she tried to steady her trembling hand. "Look at me. I can't stop shaking."

Tammy rested her hand on Jenny's. "I know, me neither. I have butterflies in my stomach, and it's churning so much from my nerves. I feel like I'm going to throw up."

"Jenny had a hard time sleeping last night," Stuart said. "She worried that she and Donna wouldn't get along."

Tammy looked surprised. "Why would you think that?"

Jenny shrugged her shoulders. "I don't know. I guess I'm being silly. But remember how we always used to fight when we were kids?"

Tammy laughed. "Jenny, that was a long time ago, and like you just said, you were kids. You're a grown woman now. I don't think Donna is going to chase after you and pull out chunks of your hair like she used to."

Jenny laughed. "I guess you're right. But still, she's a stranger to me. I just hope I like her."

Tammy chugged down the last of her coffee. "Well, there's only one way to find out. Are you ready?"

Jenny and Stuart finished their drinks, while Tammy made a quick call to Donna. "Hey, Donna, we're on our way. We'll be there in ten minutes."

"Wow, I can't believe it. I'm so nervous."

"We all are. See you soon."

When Tammy turned onto Donna's street, she felt the tears pool in her eyes. She strained to see the road ahead. Her sweaty palms slipped on the steering wheel so much that she had to wipe them on her jeans. She took short, deep breaths to calm her racing heart that beat beneath her chest, but it was no use. She heard Jenny whisper to Stuart in the back seat where they sat together holding hands. "How do I look?" she asked him.

"You look beautiful," he replied.

Tammy took a deep breath and swallowed hard to remove the

lump wedged in her throat. "How are you doing, Jenny?" she asked, as she looked at her through the rearview mirror.

"I'm not sure. I'm shaking all over. I hope I can get out of the car."

Tammy had to search for Donna's house. She had moved since her last visit, when Jason was sick. She slowed down to read the numbers of the houses and soon spotted it on the left. Tears streamed down her face. She laid into the horn and wound down her window.

"What are you doing?" Jenny yelled, while covering her ears with her hands.

"I'm letting Donna know we are here. It's been a hell of a long time, and I want to make a bloody entrance," Tammy laughed, and hollered out the window and turned into her driveway. "Donna! Donna!" she screamed with tears gushing down her face.

Within seconds the front door opened, and Donna came running out with her husband that Tammy had yet to meet, following close behind. "Oh my god! I can't believe it! You are here!" She screamed, with her arms wide open, as she raced towards the car.

Tammy was the first to exit the car and raced over to Donna and hugged her hard. "We made it. I can't believe it either." She turned and looked towards the car and watched Jenny step out. "And look, here is Jenny."

Jenny wiped her eyes and laughed hard. "Hello, Donna."

Tammy stepped aside and watched as her two sisters raced into each other's arms and embraced. They wrapped their arms tight around each other with tears flowing down their cheeks. "Thirty-five frigging years. I can't believe you are here," Donna cried, and squeezed her tighter.

"Me neither. Oh, Donna, I've thought about this moment for so many years. Wondering if it would ever happen, Jenny said, between her many tears.

Tammy looked on and smiled, unable to keep up with the

continuous flood of her own tears. Finally, they were all together —the three sisters separated by divorce, and an ocean so many years ago. Tammy walked over to her sisters, and each one opened their arms to let the other one in. For the next few minutes, they held each other tight and cried, while the two husbands looked on with tears in their eyes, too. Together they whispered. "We did it, mom, we are together. Just like you had wished for."

After the emotional reunion, Donna led them into her home, and the first thing Jenny saw was a picture of mom sitting on the mantel. She walked over and picked it up. "I remember this day. It was Christmas dinner at my house about five years ago. Look how beautiful she looked."

Tammy and Donna approached her and stood on either side and stared at the picture of the mom they knew, and had now lost. "How I wished we had done this sooner," Tammy said in a somber voice.

"I would like to think mom knows we are together. I told her before we left, and when I go home, I'm going to share everything with her and show her the pictures."

"I believe she does," Tammy agreed.

"Me too," Donna said with a nod.

Tammy pulled away from her sisters. You know, all my life, I've procrastinated on stuff that I've regretted later, like Dwayne and I building our house. None of our parents got to see it. We finally reunited, but mom is not here to witness it. I waited to visit dad's house in Ireland until after his death. I'm done procrastinating. I've thought about writing a book for years, but I've been too afraid to start it because I don't think it will be good enough for the literary world. I have so much that I want to share. I want to give others hope, and I want to tell people to chase their dreams and never give up, and then there is the price to pay if you procrastinate.

Jenny and Donna looked on with wide eyes, as Tammy took a

stand and told them about a dream she'd had been keeping to herself.

"When I get home, I'm going to start writing it. There will be no more procrastinating in my life, and I'm going to call it Reckless Beginnings. And I will dedicate it to mom and dad."

ACKNOWLEDGMENTS

I couldn't have written these books without the continued support of my husband *Gordon Grant*. On the days I struggled, he showed me encouragement and with his words of wisdom pushed me through the difficult days. Thank you for believing in me. I love you xoxo

My dear friend *Joanie Barker* who has been waiting for these books for years. Our hours of discussions over coffee about the books has finally paid off. Your friendship is a treasure. Thank you for your amazing support.

Reviews help not only authors but readers too.

If you enjoyed this book please take a moment to leave a review. I will be forever grateful. Thank you.

When I first had the idea to write *Reckless Beginnings* over thirty years ago, I intended to write one book. I had a strong message of HOPE for others that might find themselves caught up in the web of an addict. As you can see, I had a lot more to say after *Reckless Beginnings* was published.

I also received many emails from readers asking what happened to Tammy after her life with Steven. Soon after, *Better Endings* was born, a story about chasing dreams and never giving up—another strong message. It was a fun story to write. It bought back some wonderful memories of my fishing days, and I am thrilled that it won the Readers' Favorite gold medal award for Best Fiction Adventure 2020.

Prior to these two books being published, a magical event happened in my life, which you read about in this book, *The Reunions*—my sisters and I were finally reunited after thirty-five years but not without sacrifices and regrets. The regrets of procrastination weigh heavily on me regarding this special reunion and many other things that I finally got around to doing, but waited too long to do.

Writing the final book in the series made me realize just how precious our lives are, and that we should make every day count. Live it to the fullest and enjoy every moment. Don't sweat about the small stuff, and be thankful for another glorious day.

I'm happy to announce that *The Reunions* won Reader's Favorite gold medal for best Fiction Adventure 2021

Where I am today:

I never in my wildest dreams would have thought that my debut novel Reckless Beginnings would take me on such an incredible journey. *The Reunions* will be my sixth book since *Reckless Beginnings* was launched in 2018. It's been an amazing ride, and I can't wait to bring you more stories.

The Reunions is the final book in the *Tammy Mellows Trilogy*, which, as many of you know, is based on my life. Maybe in another ten years, I will have a few more chapters to write. But in the meantime, I thought I would bring you up to date.

I'm happy to say I have been cancer-free for ten years and continue to get checked every year—(Ladies, get your mammograms). My husband and I still live in the mountains in the house we built from the ground up, and hubby is still a falconer. We are now proud grandparents of two wonderful grandsons. My son is still a fishing fool, and fishes every chance he gets.

Sadly, my mother passed away in October 2019 from dementia. She is at peace now, and I know she is watching over her daughters with pride.

To My Readers:

I would not be where I am today without my readers. It is because of you and your continued support that I enjoy creating stories. I get excited when I write them, and I'm anxious to bring them to you. You are an amazing group of people that makes this author feel good about her work. So thank you to those I am mentioning and the many others that have read my work. I'm sorry I couldn't mention all of you:

Pamela Grant Provence (the best sister-in-law), Jennifer Dobos-Bubno (my awesome niece) Pat Shupinski Fayo, Jennifer Bryan-Vawser, Pam Shear Vogt, Ruth Benson, Agnes Shapiro, Darlene Johnson, Gloria Marchegiano Seevers, Bambi Rathman, Janet Weisbred, Virgie Lane, Christina Mages, Cathy Friedland Yahiaoui, Lori Chasko, Bea Followhill, Gloria Youngbauer, Sylvia Dominick, Heather Oman, Rachel Blackburn, Susan Campton, Teresa Moyer, Laura Mclendon, Jazmine FA, Nancy Gorman Schadd, Dainelle Williams, Tammy Powell, Nancy Reed Legowsky, Donna Land Dobbs, Tina Myers, Christine Davis, Michele Ann Wate, Christine Close, Lecha Haney, Reena Agarwal Gilja, Dyana Hulgan, Debbie Felkner Carney, Barbara L. Waloven, Kay Enderline, Dana Duplantis, Amy Weaver, Lisa Murray, Denise Burt, Pauline Grime, Peggy Patterson, Karen Wright, Elaine Sapp, Sherry Brown.

The author and book community is an amazing group of people I am proud to be a part of. I am thankful for the great friendships I have with not only readers but also many authors. Many, I consider close friends. We support each other, and I think in a way, we all know that if need be, we will listen when times are hard or not going our way. They will encourage us, read our work, and give us valuable feedback. We are not in a competition; we are a family. Thank you for your friendship to those I have mentioned below and to all the others whose paths I have crossed. I highly suggest you check out these author's books:

Sharon Gloger Friedman, Erina Bridget Ring, C. M. Santoro, G.C Allen, Beth Worsdell, Carol Koris, Anne Perreault, Susan Schild, Annette Glahn, Maria Henriksen, Carmina Levergne, Barbara Josselsohn, Jill Hannah Anderson, Kerry Anne King, Marcie Keithley.

I hope you've enjoyed the final book in the *Tammy Mellows Trilogy*, and will continue to read my future books.

Until next time: happy reading.

Love ,

Tina

xoxo

ABOUT THE AUTHOR

ABOUT THE AUTHOR

Tina Hogan Grant loves to write stories with strong female characters that know what they want and aren't afraid to chase their dreams. She loves to write sexy and sometimes steamy romances with happy ever after endings.

She is living life to the fullest in a small mountain community in Southern California with her husband and two dogs. When she is not writing she is probably riding her ATV, kayaking or hiking with her best friend – her husband of twenty-five years.

www.tinahogangrant.com